GW01071992

Autumn Blockbuster 2020

Charlotte Phillips • Karin Baine
Laura Marie Altom • Barbara Wallace

MILLS & BOON

CONTENTS

Sleeping With The Soldier
Charlotte Phillips

ABOUT CHARLOTTE PHILLIPS

———

Charlotte Phillips has been reading romantic fiction since her teens, and she adores upbeat stories with happy endings. Writing them for Harlequin® is her dream job. She combines writing with looking after her fabulous husband, two teenagers, a four-year-old and a dachshund. When something has to give, it's usually housework. She lives in Wiltshire.

These and other titles by Charlotte Phillips are available in ebook format from millsandboon.com.au.

DEAR READER,

Well, here we are again—but this time I'm part of a team! This is the first book I've ever written in collaboration with other authors, and I hope you have as much fun reading it as I did planning and writing it.

Writing is usually very solitary—just me and my laptop— but with this book I've had three other fab authors to brainstorm and chat with. We shared photos and decor plans for the flat in Notting Hill, and bounced around ideas for the café where all the flatmates meet up.

The best bit has been seeing glimpses of Lara and Alex in the other books in The Flat in Notting Hill series. For once the road to happy-ever-after for my couple isn't the limit of their story, and I can see a bigger picture of their friendships and their lives together. Add to that the wonderful vibrancy of the Notting Hill setting and this story really leaped off the page for me. I hope it does for you, too!

Love

Charlotte x

For Sam, who keeps me smiling
when I think I'm rubbish. I am so proud of you.

CHAPTER ONE

LARA CONNOR WAS aiming to corner the rich Notting Hill market in boutique lingerie and she wasn't about to achieve that heady dream with French knickers that looked as if a club-fingered chimp had sewn them together.

She stared in disbelief at the mass of pale pink silk and delicate lace now rucked up in a tangle of mad stitches beneath the foot of her sewing machine and gritted her teeth hard enough to make her jaw ache. Above her head the banging started again with a new urgency that really brought out the hostility in her.

She liked to think she was a glass-half-full kind of person, laid-back, live and let live, default mood: happy. But the noise pollution emanating from the flat above all night, every night, had meant her sleep had been broken for weeks now. Tiredness had pushed her normally sunny attitude to the brink of her patience and, frankly, if it didn't stop now, murder might be on the cards.

She lifted the foot of the machine, disentangled the ball of expensive fabric from the needle and examined it. Beyond saving. She lobbed it across the room into the 'remnants' bin. The knickers weren't even salvageable enough to go into the 'seconds' bin. And having sunk every penny into this venture, she couldn't afford to keep slipping up like this. The 'remnants' bin was looking far too full for her liking, and it was all the fault of the Lothario upstairs, who apparently couldn't let a day pass by without getting laid.

The clanking and banging in the pipes had begun a few weeks ago, not long after Lara had moved in. The sudden increase in noise coincided with the return of the soldier brother of Poppy, who owned the flat upstairs. Lara had got to know Poppy quite well over the last four or five weeks, and her flatmate, Izzy. A brief hello on the stairs had quickly progressed to coffee and chat in the downstairs café. Both girls were excited to hear about Lara's lingerie designs. Izzy had even bought a couple of samples. On her own in a new place, Lara was especially pleased to have made friends. If only Poppy's brother could have a *smidge* of her consideration.

Sitting in Ignite, the ground-floor café, while Lara updated her blog courtesy of the free Wi-Fi, she'd picked up plenty of gossip from the other old-fire-station residents about Alex. He was rumoured to be some military hero, honourably discharged from the army after frontline action abroad. The building was also awash with gossip about his endless stream of women; the word was that he bedded a different one every night! And two or three times she'd actually seen said women, sporting that giveaway combination of evening clothes, bed hair and smug smile, making the walk of shame when she'd nipped down to the café for a takeaway coffee first thing in the morning. Lara had watched pityingly; she couldn't think of anything more pointless. With all this evidence taken as a whole, there was no real question as to the source of the noise pollution that was tiring her out, disrupting her work and thus costing her money, of which she had absolutely no more.

The first couple of times it might even have been funny. His bed must be shoved right up against the radiator, because the water pipes for the top flat were clearly shared by her own little studio flat below. At first she'd rolled her eyes in exasperation and—possibly—a hint of wistful envy. Not that it had anything to do with the military hero himself, of course; in her opinion he sounded far too attractive for his own good. But still, it had been a long time since she'd last seen any action in that department. That was what big aspirations did to your life. There had to be sacrifices; something had to give. Lara Connor had plans and ambitions, and she intended to keep her eye on the prize.

The next step on that journey to success was the small shop she'd managed to secure in Notting Hill for the next two months. Her own pop-up shop to showcase her own line of vintage-inspired lingerie. The rent on this little flat was extortionate and had eaten away at her savings, but it was worth it so she could live near the premises and she'd been working all the hours she could muster. Sewing was only a part of it—there was marketing to think of, the shop to fit and decorate. Night and day her mind was filled with nothing else. She was already exhausted, just with the workload she had to shoulder, but she cared about none of it because this was the next step in her game plan, from which she would not be distracted.

Certainly not by some inconsiderate love god living upstairs. The endless noise was beginning to jeopardise her carefully laid plans, and she quite simply was not going to stand for it any longer. Especially since it now seemed that all night was no longer adequate for his needs. This morning she'd heard the familiar slam of the door as his most recent conquest left the building. But this time it hadn't been followed by the welcome peace that she needed to produce the intricate lingerie she designed herself to the exacting standards she demanded. She worked with delicate, fine fabrics. Silks, lace, ribbons, velvet. The kind of garments she made took skill and close attention to detail. Absolute concentration was required.

Instead, what she'd had was half an hour of mad hammering. For the first few minutes she'd tried to ignore it, waiting to see if one of the other residents would intervene. Surely she couldn't be the only one driven mad by this? But as the minutes ticked by and the noise didn't abate she came to realise that clearly no one else *was* around to intervene. They'd all gone out to work, of course, while work for Lara took place right here. She needed to concentrate on her sewing. Everything was riding on this stock being perfect. Seconds were not an option.

As she pushed her chair back grimly and grabbed her door key from the table the bashing overhead began again in earnest, bringing a fresh wave of anger to bubble up inside her.

All night, every night was one thing. Was she now expected to put up with this racket all day too?

Enough was enough.

Shoulders squared, teeth gritted, she took the stairs up to the top floor grimly, ready to give Poppy's inconsiderate brother a piece of her sleep-deprived mind, and the planned outburst screeched to a halt on the tip of her tongue as she rounded the corner at the top of the stairs. The hinge on her jaw seemed to be suddenly loose.

Poppy's inconsiderate brother?

Correction: Poppy's all but naked, roped with muscle, fit and breathtakingly gorgeous soldier hero brother. His modesty was saved only by a very small white towel, which was held up on his muscular hips by a single fold. Hard muscle twined the tanned biceps and broad shoulders. His stomach was drum-tight and his short dark hair was damply tousled. Smoothly tanned skin gave away the fact he'd spent months abroad in action before coming here. By sheer will she fixed her eyes above his neck when all they wanted to do was dip lower and check out those perfect abs.

And OK, for a moment she *might* have been stunned into silence by the revelation that, actually, the rumours were true, Poppy's brother really *was* drop-dead gorgeous, and by the fact that his modesty was hidden by the tiniest of white towels, but then he'd gone on to ruin the effect by raising his clenched fist and hammering on the closed door of the flat, reproducing the sound that had driven her to the edge of her sanity for the past half an hour. Up close it was monstrously loud and her already aching head throbbed in protest.

'I think,' she snapped, in the coldest voice she could muster, 'we can safely assume that everyone who lives on the other side of that door is either out or deaf.'

Alex Spencer stopped, knuckles poised mid-hammer, and turned sideways to look at her. Her thick blond hair was piled up messily on her head with a pencil stuck through the middle of it, she had a full rosebud mouth, and wide china-blue eyes that would have been captivating if they hadn't got an expression in them that implied she'd quite like to see him decomposing in a ditch. She wore a pale pink cardigan with the top two buttons undone, revealing a silky smooth expanse of flawless porcelain décolletage, cropped jeans and bare feet. And even though he was so tired he could hardly see straight, and not only because he'd just spent a very active night in bed that involved anything but sleep, his pulse managed a jolt of interest.

'And you are…?' he said, raising sarcastic eyebrows as if she were the one who looked out of place and it were perfectly normal to be walking the corridors wearing a bath towel.

'The poor sap who lives downstairs,' she snapped. '*Directly* downstairs, to be specific. Right below *you*.'

He stared at her, his tired brain struggling to process what she was saying. It felt as if he were thinking through a very large wad of cotton wool. Technically, thanks to the way his sickening insomnia had progressed, night time for him had pretty much now turned into day and vice versa. Thus it was currently an hour or so past his bedtime and his patience was balanced on a knife edge.

'What are you talking about?'

The question opened the floodgates and he took a defensive step backwards.

'Your night-time action is ruining my *life*,' she wailed. 'All night, every night, crashing and clanking pipes while you get your rocks off with whatever girl you happen to have brought back. Your bed must be right up against the radiator or something. The noise travels down the pipes and echoes round my bedroom as if I'm in the bloody room with you. It's utter selfishness! I can hear *every move you make* and I can't take it anymore!' She raised her hands up and pressed them to the sides of her head as if she thought it might explode. 'I can't *have* this kind of distraction. I've only got a week or so left before the shop launches and I'm going to go crazy if I don't get some uninterrupted *sleep.*'

The blue eyes took on a hint of madness, and an unexpected twinge of sympathy twisted his stomach because restful sleep was currently an elusive thing for him too. It had been since he'd returned from his recent overseas tour via the hospital. He'd worked his way through convalescence at breakneck speed after the chest injuries he'd sustained in a roadside bomb, only to learn that he wouldn't be going back. Physical injury was one thing, an early end to his career was quite another. Discharge from the army had not been what he wanted, no matter that it was honourable. He had a lot on his mind, he kept telling himself—it was no wonder that he didn't sleep like a baby at night.

'The shop?' he said.

'I'm in the middle of launching a pop-up shop in Portobello Road. It's my first try at moving into proper retail instead of market stalls. I need it to be a success and *nothing's* going to stop me, including your libido!'

Her angry explanation of her business commitments brought a lurching reminder that currently his own life was cruising along rudderless. It wasn't as if he had a direction right now, or plans to consider. Lack of sleep had no consequence in *his* life, aside from the fact that his routine was getting a bit out of kilter, and who really cared about that? Since his social circle currently consisted of a group of girly flatmates, an old friend who was hardly ever there, and his kid sister, concern about his sleep pattern wasn't exactly a buzzing topic of conversation. And since his sleep problems were rooted in an unrelenting spate of cold-sweat nightmares that made staying awake through the dark hours extremely attractive, he'd quite like to keep it that way.

After operations to remove shrapnel and four months of medical care, his physical recovery was as complete as it was going to get. He'd worked hard to regain his fitness, thinking that would be an end to it, believing he'd got off lightly. He hadn't counted on the nightmares continuing. He hadn't told anyone about them, not even Poppy, vaguely thinking that verbalising their existence might somehow give them even more of a grip on him. Easier to just evade sleep and hope they would subside. To help things along, he filled his waking hours with distracting activity, taking full advantage of the sudden lack of discipline and routine in his life after years of moulding to the requirements first of boarding school and then the armed forces.

The sense of purpose and the camaraderie that he'd come to take for granted in the army left a gaping hole in his life now it was unexpectedly gone. Hence the appeal of filling his time with far less challenging distractions. For the first time in his life he'd thrown himself into having fun, losing all sense of his current pointless existence by bedding as many women as possible. It wasn't difficult. Women seemed to fall at his feet with minimal effort on his part, just the way they always had done.

Except, possibly, for this one.

'If this carries on I'll report you to the local council for noise pollution,' she was snarling. 'Can't you phone Poppy?'

He cast exasperated hands down at himself in the small towel.

'With what, exactly? Do I look like I've got a phone stashed on my person? If my sister would just haul herself out of her pit and *answer the bloody door*, I wouldn't *need* to be making any noise,' he yelled at the closed door, pressing his point by adding in another quick bash on it, which made the crazy neighbour from downstairs stiffen like a meerkat.

'Will you *stop* with the knocking?' she hollered. 'Is Poppy deaf?'

'Not as far as I'm aware.'

'Then she's not bloody *in there*, is she? You've been hammering on that door for half an hour and it's loud enough to wake the dead.' She threw her hands up in a gesture of exasperation. 'For Pete's sake, she must be at *work*. I saw her the other day and she mentioned she was on call this week.'

The implications of that information burst through his mind in a flurry of exasperation. Poppy could be gone for hours and he couldn't bring himself to interrupt her work as a medic for something as ludicrously embarrassing as locking himself out. Her flatmate, Izzy, had just moved out and the only other person with a key was his friend Isaac, who was supposedly crashing in the extra room but who actually spent more time away than he did at home. He was currently globetrotting between swanky new potential continental venues for his chain of cocktail bars.

He had to face facts. He could hang out in the hallway in a towel for a chunk of the day until Poppy got back. Or he could sweet-talk the interfering neighbour, who looked as if she'd be glad to see his head on a spike.

He stepped away from the door, anticipating that an apology might not have quite the clout it needed if he was still within hammering distance of it.

He spread his hands.

'Look, I'm sorry. What's your name?'

She narrowed suspicious eyes at his newly amenable tone.

'Lara Connor.'

'Lara. I'm Alex.'

She nodded at him, not a hint of a smile, so he tried a bit harder, attempting to mould his face into an apologetic expression.

'I'm sorry for the noise. The *disruption*. I had no idea I was bothering anyone. It's not as if anyone else has complained.'

Quite the opposite. The biggest problem he had was wriggling out of any follow-up dates. He had absolutely no desire to ruin what was a very nice distraction plan by bringing anything so emotionally demanding as a proper *relationship* into the situation.

As apologies went it was all a bit pants in Lara's opinion.

'Why *would* anyone else complain? No one else has a bed directly below yours,' she said. 'And I don't need an apology or a load of rubbish excuses. What I really want is some kind of assurance that you'll make an effort and stop the racket.'

'I'll move my bed away from the wall,' he conceded. His voice was clipped and very British. She noticed he didn't offer to interrupt the endless flow of women through his bedroom.

'Right,' she said. 'And what about now? You can't keep hammering on that door—my sanity is hanging by a thread. What are you going to do until Poppy gets back?'

She folded her arms and frowned at him.

He shrugged resignedly.

'I'll just have to wait it out. Unless you'd like to take pity on me.'

'I don't think so,' she said, smoothing her hair back from her face.

'It could be hours.' His expression took on a pitiful look. 'I don't even have a jacket.'

'Tough,' she said. 'It'll do you good to put up with a bit of discomfort for a change.' She made a move towards the stairs, wondering how far he might go with the grovelling, enjoying the upper hand. She'd let him suffer a bit longer and then offer to let him wait in her flat.

His grovelling had apparently reached its limit. Silence as she descended the top step and then a sudden flurry of bangs on the door started up again. She turned back to him incredulously.

He shrugged, his upraised knuckles poised at chest level.

'You know, I'm really not *convinced* Poppy isn't in there,' he said. 'Maybe if I knock long enough, she might show.'

He put enormous emphasis on the words 'long enough', making it crystal clear he was prepared to knock all day if necessary.

Anger bubbled hotly through her as she stared at him, seeing the challenge in his eyes and knowing that if she wanted to get any work done today at all she would have to give on this. It was all she could do to force herself to act rationally, when what she wanted to do was snarl at him like a fishwife. She would give on this because it was in her best interest, thereby retaining the upper hand rather than dragging herself down to his level, but he needn't think this was over. Not for *one moment*.

'Come on, then,' she said, turning back towards the wrought-iron staircase.

She glanced around to see him looking after her. The few paces extra distance would have given her an eye-wateringly fantastic full body view of him if she hadn't bitten her lip in her determination to keep her eyes fixed from the neck up.

'What?'

'I give in. You win. I've got more important things to do than stand here arguing with you. You can use my phone if you want to try and get hold of Poppy.' The words stuck in her craw because she really didn't *need* a half-naked ex-soldier blagging his way into her flat when she had a mountain of silk knickers with velvet ribbons and frills to sew on the back. 'I haven't got her work number, but you must know it, right? Or I think I've got Izzy's number somewhere. Maybe we can get her to drop by if she still has a key. You can wait in my flat if you like,' she added grudgingly.

She led the way down the wrought-iron stairs before he could say anything triumphant. If he did that she might be tempted to call the police.

CHAPTER TWO

ALEX FOLLOWED HER down the narrow stairwell and into her flat, and, if he'd thought a few bras hanging over the bathtub in Poppy's flat was a girly step too far, this was a whole new ballgame.

There was an enormous clothes rail directly opposite, stuffed to breaking point with clothes. And not just any clothes. Everything seemed to be made of silk, satin, lace and velvet. Subtle pinks and creams hung alongside vampy deep reds, peacock blues and purples. There were spools of silk and velvet ribbon in every colour imaginable. In one corner of the room was a headless mannequin wearing a black silky bra with tassels along the cups and matching knickers. He stared at it for an incredulous moment. Rolls of fabric were stacked against the wall and hung over the back of the sofa in the corner and the room was dominated by an enormous trestle table with two different kinds of sewing machine on it.

'Is it just you living here?' he asked as she crossed the cramped room to the kitchen area at the other end. He was used to Poppy's roomy flat. This was a shoebox in comparison.

She nodded.

'It's a one-bed studio. There isn't much space but it's in such a perfect location for my shop. The time I'm saving by living so close kind of makes the lack of space worth it.' She nodded towards the sofa. 'Have a seat. I'll make some tea.'

'And what exactly is it that you do?' he said, picking his way through the clutter to the overstuffed sofa. It was covered in a brightly coloured patchwork throw and he had to move a huge pile of silk and lace remnants before there was room to sit down.

She was clattering about in the tiny kitchen area in the corner. There was a doorway at the side of the room with a length of some filmy cream fabric hanging across it as a curtain. He narrowed his eyes, trying to get his bearings. Her bedroom must be down there on the right if it really was situated underneath his, as she claimed. He shook his head lightly because he had absolutely zero interest in how she spent her nights.

This was a means to an end, nothing more, a marginal step up from waiting it out in the hallway upstairs. He had no desire whatsoever to find out more about the infuriating woman from downstairs. He sank onto the sofa, shifted to one side uncomfortably and tugged out a pale pink feather boa from underneath him. For Pete's sake.

'I design and make my own line of boutique lingerie,' she said.

It was impossible to miss the faint trace of pride in her voice.

'Knickers, camisoles, nightgowns, slips, bustiers, basques. You name it.' She counted them off on her fingers. 'Vintage inspired, Hollywood glamour, that kind of thing. I like to make the most of the female figure.'

His mind reeled a little. She might as well have been speaking in some foreign language and he'd felt enough of a fish out of water already in the past couple of weeks, thank you very much. After living at close quarters with soldiers for the best part of the last few years, much of that time in the roughest of conditions, moving in with a group of girls was like living with a gaggle of aliens. Everything was scented. *Everything.* There was girly underwear hanging over the radiators. The fridge was full of hummus, low-fat yogurt and other hideous foodstuffs that filled him with distaste, the topics of conversation mysti-fied him and the bathroom was full of perfumed toiletries. He'd grabbed the opportunity when Poppy's friend Izzy had moved rooms a few weeks ago to draft in male back-up in the form of his old schoolfriend Isaac, but in reality it had made little difference because Isaac was hardly ever there. Alex was out of his depth as it was, and now he was catapulted into a room full of lingerie.

'I've been selling from market stalls for ages now, building up a customer base,' Lara was saying. 'And I have a blog—*"Boudoir Fashionista".*' She made a frame in the air with her hands as if imagining the title on a shop sign.

'A blog?' he repeated. The conversation was becoming more surreal by the minute. He leaned his head back against the sofa. His headache seemed to be intensifying.

'Mmm…' She continued to clatter about in the kitchen, not turning round. 'I showcase my lingerie, blog about fashion and beauty. I've been wanting to expand the business for a while, try my hand at retail, but it's such a gamble in terms of cost, you have no idea. And then I started looking into pop-up shops.'

He didn't answer. Her voice was sweet, melodic even, pleas-ant to listen to. He closed his heavy eyes to ease the thumping headache, a side effect of his crazy off-kilter sleep pattern that seemed to be becoming a regular thing.

'It's just a short-term thing, so less risk. There are places that advertise opportunities. You take on empty premises, some-times even just for a day. I couldn't believe it when I found the place on Portobello Road—it was like a dream. I've got it for the next couple of months. Perfect timing for me to take ad-vantage of the run up to Christmas and long enough to see if I can make it work.'

Lara gave the tea a final stir. Busying herself in the kitchen was an autopilot way of taking her mind off how much tinier the already minuscule flat suddenly felt with him in it. Small it might be but it had still been at the absolute limit of what she could afford. Desperate to give everything to the pop-up shop opportunity, she'd quickly realised that living nearby would be a huge advantage. Failure was absolutely *not* an option.

She'd give him the tea and then try to track down Izzy. The thought of having him here under her feet all day made her stomach feel squiggly. She had *tons* of work to do and she'd lost nearly an hour this morning already to first his noise and now the follow-up chaos. She didn't have *time* to step in as rescue party for neighbours. She turned back to cross the room to him. Three paces in and she came to a stop, smile fading from her face, mug of tea in each hand.

He was fast asleep.

He looked completely out of place among the frills, ribbons and lace that festooned the sofa. He had the most tightly honed muscular physique she'd ever seen outside a glossy fashion magazine, his shoulders were huge, his abs perfectly defined. One huge hand rested against his chiselled jaw as if he'd been propping his chin up when he nodded off.

She watched him for a moment. In sleep the defensive expression on his face when he'd given her his half-arsed apology for the noise was nowhere to be seen. The dark hair was dry now, the short cut totally in keeping with his military background; she could easily imagine him in uniform. The face below was classically handsome. His cheekbones were sharply defined, followed up with a firm jawline and strong mouth. Her eyes roamed lower and she caught her breath in surprise.

The upstairs landing was pretty shadowy and he'd been turned away from her for much of the time. Add in the fact that she'd been making a heroic effort to keep her eyes from wandering below his neckline and as a result she only now got a proper view of his body. A twist of sympathy surged through her.

The left-hand side of the tautly muscled chest was heavily puckered and ruched with a web of scar tissue. She pressed her lips together hard. Of course she'd heard from Poppy that Alex had been injured in action but, having heard and seen the evidence of his sexual prowess, she'd assumed whatever had happened to him must have been pretty minor.

Whatever had happened to cause that scarring could most certainly *not* be pretty minor.

She put the two mugs down on the edge of the sewing table and moved closer to him, hand outstretched towards his shoulder to shake him gently awake, and then her eyes stuttered over the shadows beneath the dark eyelashes. He looked exhausted, and no wonder. From what she knew of him, he barely ever slept. His breathing now was rested and even. She withdrew her hand. Why not let him sleep? Yes, she could try and contact Izzy or Poppy, but really she'd wasted enough time today already on this situation.

She tugged the multi-coloured patchwork throw from the side of the sofa. Her foster mother had made it for her and it was deliciously huge and comforting to snuggle into. She tucked it gently over him. He didn't even stir.

Five minutes later and she had her own mug of tea at her elbow as she got back to her sewing. She had the finishing touches to do on fifty-odd pairs of silk knickers. And that was just for starters.

It felt as if hours had passed when a moan of distress made her foot slip from the pedal of the sewing machine. She'd been so engrossed in her work that she'd almost forgotten she had a house guest. The room had grown dark now in the late afternoon; the small light from the sewing machine and the angled lamp above her workspace were the only sources of light. She stood up and looked curiously at Poppy's brother, sprawled in the shadows on the sofa. Deciding she must have imagined it, she moved to sit back down.

He twisted in his sleep.

She frowned. Abandoning her chair, she took a step towards him. His hands were twisting in the throw she'd draped over him and he let out another cry. Almost a shout this time, enough to make her jump. She watched his face as it contorted. Sympathy twisted in her stomach as she caught sight again of his scarred chest in the dim light. Where was he right now in his mind? In the middle of some hideous battle?

His body twisted sharply again and she couldn't stand it any longer. She reached out to shake him awake, to take him away from whatever horror he was reliving.

First there was the vague impression of something stroking his upper arm. Tentative, not rough. And then there was the scent, something clean and flowery, like roses. It reminded Alex vaguely of his mother's dressing room back at their country home, with its antique dressing table and ornate perfume bottles and he flinched at the thought. It had been years since he'd visited the family home and he had absolutely no plans to do so in the foreseeable future. Why would he? For a place filled on and off with so many people, so many offshoots of the family, it had been bloody lonely for a kid.

He opened his eyes, disorientation making his mind reel.

He struggled to place himself in a panic. Not his army quarters. And not his room in his sister's flat, with its calming military organisation. Instead he was in a room that could only really be described as a *boudoir*. And it was getting dark.

He struggled to his feet, his mind whirling. Of course, he'd been locked out of Poppy's flat and the downstairs neighbour had offered to make him tea. That was the last thing he remembered. He looked down at himself as the quilt covering him fell away and saw that the towel around his hips was hanging askew. He snatched it closed again. Horrified, he realised he'd been sleeping here in a stranger's flat with his scars on show for her to view at her leisure.

The blonde neighbour was standing a few feet away, an expression of concern on her pretty face. The sewing machine was lit up on the desk by a bright angled lamp. A neatly folded pile of pink silk lay further down the table. A tentative smile touched the corners of her rosebud mouth.

'Are you OK?' she asked. 'You were…' a light frown touched her eyebrows '…calling out in your sleep.'

The heat of humiliation began at his neck and climbed burningly upwards as he regained a grip on reality. He'd had a nightmare. In full view of her. Had he shouted? What had he said? How could he have been so stupid as to let himself fall asleep here?

'What time is it?' he managed, rubbing a hand through his hair as if it might somehow help to clear his foggy head.

'Nearly six,' she said. 'I was just about to wake you. Poppy's home, I think—I heard her go up the stairs to the flat. So you should be able to get back in now.'

Six?

He'd slept the entire day. He avoided her eyes. What must she *think* of him, just falling asleep like that? And then having a bad dream, like some kid. He couldn't quite believe that he could relax enough to fall asleep in a strange place with a strange person. His tiredness must be a lot more ingrained than he'd thought it was.

'I can't believe I fell asleep,' he blustered. 'You should have woken me.'

'I couldn't really believe it either,' she said. 'Of course *I* think my business plan is the most interesting topic of discussion on the planet.' She smiled. 'But it made you nod off in the space of about ten minutes.'

He shook his head. What the hell must she be thinking?

'I'm sorry.'

'It's a *joke*,' she said, making a where's-your-sense-of-humour? face. 'I'm joking?'

'Right,' he said. Awkwardness filled the room, making it feel heavy and tense. He had to get out of here.

'I *was* going to wake you,' she said, 'but I didn't have the heart.'

'Oh, really?' He zeroed in on that comment. Was this some kind of sympathy vote because she'd seen his awful scars? Or worse, because he'd cried out in his sleep? He didn't do sympathy. And he didn't do bursts of emotion either. Nearly thirty years in the stiff-upper-lip environment of his military-obsessed family did that for a person. Stoicism was essential. His father had made that pretty damn clear when Alex was just a kid, an attitude later reinforced at boarding school and then in the army. Emotion was something you stamped on, definitely not something to be expressed among strangers.

'You looked so peaceful,' she went on. 'And you've clearly been getting hardly any sleep if your noise pollution is anything to go by.'

There was an edge to her voice that told him she was still narked about that. He didn't let it penetrate, there was no need to, since he had absolutely no intention of running into her again after today.

'Cup of tea?' she asked him. 'Your last one got cold. Are you sure you're OK?'

He shook his head, automatically folding the enormous throw and placing it neatly at the side of the sofa. He had no idea how she could live in such a cluttered room without going mad. It jarred his military sense of order.

'I am perfectly fine,' he snapped. 'And I've taken up enough of your time. Now I know Poppy's back I'll get out of your way.'

He headed for the door as she watched him, a bemused expression on the pretty face.

'Bye, then,' he heard her call after him as he pulled the door shut.

A thank-you might have been nice.

Then again, she didn't have time for niceties. Neither did she give a stuff as long as Alex curbed the disruptive noise from upstairs.

Forty-eight hours had now passed with a definite reduction

in noise levels although she'd seen no corresponding drop in the stream of disposable girls visiting. That was the thing about working from home for all waking hours—the comings and goings of other residents in the building amounted to distractions, and she couldn't fail to notice them. He must have moved his bed away from the radiator because the endless clanking had ceased. Not, of course, that she was dwelling on Alex Spencer's bedroom activities.

What mattered was that normal sleep quality had been resumed and thank goodness, because the launch of the shop was only a week away now. Just time to fit in a quick shower this morning and then she would head over there to add a few more finishing touches to the décor before she began to move stock in. She'd managed to track down a beautiful French-style dressing screen, the kind you might find in a lady's bedroom, gorgeously romantic. No run-of-the-mill changing cubicles for her little shop. Still, she wanted to try it out in different positions until she found the perfect location for it.

She rubbed shampoo into her hair, closing her eyes against the soap bubbles and running through a mental list of the hundred-plus things she needed to get done today. A full-length gilt-framed mirror had been delivered the previous day; it would provide the perfect vintage centrepiece for the small shop floor, and she needed to decide where best to put that too. Then there were garlands of silk flowers to hang and some tiny white pin lights to add to the girly atmosphere she wanted to achieve.

The torrent of water rinsing through her hair seemed to be losing its force. She opened one eye and squinted through the bubbles up at the shower head. Yep. The usual nice flow was definitely diminishing. And without the sound of the running water she was suddenly able to hear a monstrous clanking noise coming from behind the wall and above her head.

'What the hell…?' she said aloud as the water reduced to little more than a trickle. The clanking built to a crescendo.

Oh, just bloody *perfect*. Naked, covered in bubbles and with her hair a bird's nest of shampoo, she climbed out of the shower unit and wrapped a towel around her. A quick twist of the sink tap gave a loud clanking spurt of water followed by nothing. She grabbed her kimono from the hook on the back of the bathroom door and shrugged it on as she took the few paces to the kitchen to check the water pressure there.

She didn't make it as far as the sink. Horrified shock stopped her in her tracks as she took in the torrent of water pouring down the wall of the living room, pooling into a flood and soaking merrily into a pile of silk camisoles she'd left in a stack on the floor.

'No-o-o!' she squawked, dashing across the floor, picking up armfuls of her lovingly made garments and moving them to safety on the other side of the room. She kicked the metal clothes rail out of the way as she passed it, the few garments hanging at one end already splashed by the ensuing torrent of water.

She rushed to the cabinet under the sink, found the stopcock and turned off the water supply as she tried madly to rationalise what could have happened, then she stood, hand plastered to her forehead as her mind worked through the implications of all this. Some of her garments had been soaked through—there went hours of work down the drain. The water continued to spread across the floor in a slow-moving pool. She knew instinctively from the clanking in the pipes that this wasn't going to be some five-minute do-it-yourself quick-fix job. The building was ancient. Behind the glossy makeover of the flat conversion was interlinked original pipework. That much was obvious from the racket they made when the love god upstairs was entertaining.

She had absolutely no money to spare for a plumber. She wondered if any of the rest of the building was affected. Surely it wasn't just her? In a panic she opened the flat door with the intention of knocking on the door opposite and instead ran smack into Poppy, who was on her way up to her own flat with a chocolate croissant in one hand and a takeaway coffee in the other. Poppy's mouth fell open at her insane appearance.

'What the hell happened to you?'

'My flat's flooded,' Lara gabbled. 'It's like the deck of the sodding *Titanic* in there. I've got a shedload of stock in the room, my shop launches next week and I've got no hot water.'

Poppy didn't so much as flinch. She exuded utter calm. Maybe it was a side-effect of medical training that you simply became good in any crisis. Lara shifted from one foot to the other while she leaned around her to see into the living room.

'Have you turned off the water?'

Lara nodded.

'It seems to have stopped it getting any worse. But just look at the mess.'

Poppy walked into the room and put her coffee down on the trestle table.

'I see what you mean,' she said, peering at the enormous spreading puddle on the floor and the piles of silk and velvet clothing now strewn haphazardly on the other side of the room.

'I need this room to work in and now I'll be behind with my stock levels,' Lara wailed.

The full implications of the situation began to sink in. She'd been running at her absolute limit to get the pop-up shop off the ground in so many ways, working all hours, hocked to the eyeballs financially, using her living accommodation as workspace. She had absolutely no back-up plan. Despair made her stomach churn sickly and she clutched at her hair in frustration. It felt matted and sticky from the puddle of shampoo she'd been unable to rinse out.

'Not to mention the lack of running water,' she added. 'I'll have to stick my head under the tap in the café toilets downstairs.'

'You rent, don't you?' Poppy said, unruffled, crossing the room to look at the huge dark patch on the wallpaper. 'Have you called the landlord?'

Lara sat down on the sofa and put her head in her hands. She'd been far too busy having a meltdown of major proportions to do anything as practical as that.

'Not yet.'

'It will be down to the landlord to get it sorted, not you. You don't need to stress about cost.'

That was lucky, because *cost* was one thing she really couldn't do any more of right now.

'It isn't just that,' Lara said, pressing a hand to her forehead and trying to think rationally. Already there was a musty smell drifting from the soaked wood floor and bubbling wallpaper. 'It stinks in here—it'll permeate my stock. I'm hardly going to dominate the market with seductive lingerie that smells like a damp garden shed, am I? Not exactly alluring and sensuous, is it? And even if I could leave it here, there'll be workmen traipsing through. I can't risk any further damage. My back's against the wall with the shop opening next week. And I can't stay here anyway if there's no running water.'

She could hear the upset nasal tone in her own voice and bit down hard on her lip to suppress it. She didn't do emotional outbursts. That kind of thing elicited sympathy and she was far too self-reliant to want or need any of that. But she'd given her everything to this shop project and now it felt as if all her hard work had hit standstill in the space of ten minutes.

Poppy, who clearly didn't know or care about the not-liking-sympathy thing, joined her on the sofa, put an arm around her shoulders and gave her an encouraging smile and a squeeze.

'Come and stay with us for a few days, then, until it's sorted out,' she said. 'The boxroom's free—you'd be welcome to it. It's pretty titchy, but at least it's dry. And even better…' she waited until Lara looked at her and threw her hands up triumphantly '…I have running water! Cheer up, it'll all seem better when your hair doesn't look like a ferret's nest.'

Lara felt her lip twitch.

Poppy's grin was warm and friendly. But still the shake of

the head came automatically to her, like a tic or an ingrained stock reaction. Lara Connor didn't take help or charity. She'd got where she was relying only on herself.

'I couldn't possibly impose on you like that,' she said. 'I'll be perfectly fine. I'll figure something out myself.'

Figuring something out herself had featured in a big way on her path in life. Taking offers of help didn't come easily to Lara. Relying on other people was a sure-fire route to finding yourself let down.

'You've got a headful of shampoo and no running water,' Poppy pointed out.

Lara touched her hair lightly with one hand. It was beginning to itch now, and seemed to be drying to a hideous crispy cotton-wool kind of texture. She hesitated. Her back really was against the wall over the shop. She groped for some kind of alternative solution that she could handle on her own but none presented itself. Even if she had enough room at the pop-up shop to store all her extra stock, she couldn't exactly move in and live there, could she? There was one tiny back room with a toilet, no furniture, no space, no chance.

'Stop being ridiculous,' Poppy said in a case-closed tone of voice. 'It really is *not* such a big deal. It makes perfect sense. I've got a spare room and you're stuck for a day or two. Where's the problem?'

'I don't like to impose,' Lara evaded.

Poppy made a dismissive chuffing noise.

'If you were imposing, I wouldn't ask you,' she said. 'Come on, it'll be a laugh. Things have been a bit quiet since Izzy moved in with Harry—it'll be nice to have someone else around for a bit.' She stood up. 'You can get straight in the shower and rinse that shampoo out, and then you can ring your landlord and sort out a plumber.' She made for the door as if the subject was closed.

Poppy made it all sound so straightforward. But then of course she had a proper family background, supportive childhood and, let's not forget, her big brother on the premises. She had no need to let coping with a crisis be complicated by things like pride and self-reliance and managing by yourself.

'Just a couple of days, though,' Lara qualified, finally giving in and following her. 'Just until the water's sorted out, and I'll pay rent, of course.'

With what exactly, she wasn't sure. But she would find a way. She always did. Being indebted to someone really wasn't her.

'It's only small, I know…' Poppy said apologetically.

'It's absolutely perfect,' Lara said, wondering vaguely how she could possibly fit all her stock in here. The room was tiny, the only furnishings a small dresser and lamp and the narrowest single bed Lara had ever seen. But in terms of living space, it was a gift. She supposed it might seem small to Poppy and her friends. Lara had heard them talk about boarding school and their families; spacious living was clearly the norm. Lara had had many bedrooms over the years. The dispensable bedroom was part of the package when you were working your way through the care system. She'd lived with a succession of foster families over the years and a room of your own still felt like something to be prized. And after the flood debacle, it really was. 'I can't thank you enough,' she said. 'All I need to do now is source some storage for the rest of my stock. Until the shop gets going I've got a bit of a stockpile. I'll have a look and see if there's somewhere locally that I can keep it cheaply.'

Poppy flapped a hand at her.

'There's no need for that. You don't want to be putting those gorgeous clothes in some hideous manky lockup. You can keep them in Alex's room—there's tons of space in there.' She led the way along the hall and opened the door on what was possibly the neatest room Lara had ever seen. The bed was made with symmetrical coin-bouncing perfection, the top sheet neatly folded back in a perfect white stripe across the top of the quilt. She narrowed her eyes as she took in the radiator, the ends of which were visible either side of the headboard. Goodness knew what acrobatics he'd been performing in this room to make the hideous racket she'd had to put up with.

After the cosy bohemian colour of the rest of the flat, the room was practically austere. Poppy moved to one side so Lara could see properly. Open shelving ran the length of the opposite wall, filled with perfectly folded rectangles of knitwear and T-shirts. Gleamingly polished shoes were lined up neatly in pairs along the lowest shelf. A shelf was devoted to books, their spines lined up in order of height. Not an item was out of place, not a speck of dust marred the clear floor space. A dark oak wardrobe stood at the side of the window. Lara imagined his shirts and jackets would be hung in colour co-ordinated perfection if she were to look inside.

'Wow,' she breathed.

'I know,' Poppy said, completely unfazed. 'He's a million times more tidy and organised than I am. That's what comes of being packed off to boarding school at the age of five and then later going into the military. He's the most organised, methodical person I know.'

A pang of sympathy twisted in Lara's chest at the thought of Alex as a five-year-old fending for himself when he had a family of his own back at home. She'd been forced into that situation by necessity; there simply hadn't been an alternative for her mother. She couldn't comprehend why anyone would want to send their child away when they didn't have to, and they probably paid a fortune for the privilege too.

'He does all his own washing and ironing,' Poppy was saying. 'He just needs a bit of, well, female influence in his life.'

Lara looked at her with raised eyebrows. Female influence? Poppy grinned at her.

'Maybe not *that* kind of female influence. I'm not sure he's short of that.'

He certainly wasn't, judging by the frequency of his overnight guests.

'He needs someone a bit more long-term in my opinion. He's spent far too long with only blokes for company. Who knows? Perhaps a roomful of lingerie might put him in touch with his feminine side a bit more.'

'Are you sure he won't mind having the clothes rails in here?' Lara said doubtfully. 'I mean, it's so *tidy*. I've got quite a lot of loose stuff too.'

Poppy shrugged.

'I'm doing him a favour here, letting him stay. It's my flat, after all.' She tossed her hair back. 'Do you want a hand moving in?'

CHAPTER THREE

HEADING TOWARDS MIDNIGHT, and the landing and stairs were customarily dark as Alex propelled his latest evening companion towards the top flat—Name: Susie; Age: Twenty-six; Occupation: Medical Secretary; Favourite Drink: Strawberry Daiquiri…whatever the hell that was. He'd need to ask Isaac—although he'd bought a few this evening.

He opened the front door and ushered Susie down the dimly lit hallway to his bedroom. The rest of the flat was quiet. Poppy could sleep for England and Isaac was still out of the country. This last week after his encounter with the quiet freak downstairs, Alex had found himself grudgingly attempting to keep the noise down and so he skipped his usual stop-off in the kitchen for a nightcap. Not that it had anything to do with any personal regard for Lara Connor, of course, although he had to admit to a nod of admiration for her business drive. It was more a desire to keep her off his back and live an easy life. And after the embarrassment of sleeping the day away in her flat, he'd done his best to avoid bumping into her again. To that end, he'd also shifted his bed away from the wall a little. Apparently it had worked, since he hadn't heard a word from her since.

As he opened his bedroom door it was the scent that hit him

first. It assaulted him even before he flipped the light switch and it put him immediately on edge. Sweet floral notes that took him right back to the rose garden at his family home in the country. The memory wasn't a particularly welcome one. Then again there were precious few childhood memories that were. Susie hung on to his arm and stifled a tipsy giggle, which trailed away as light flooded the room.

'*This* is your room?' Her voice registered shocked disgust, and the fun tone was completely gone, as if he'd lobbed a jug of cold water over her for perfect instant sobriety. She let go of his arm. 'Oh, my God, you *live with someone*,' she wailed. 'I knew it was too good to be true. Where is she—out somewhere? Working?'

The perfect order by which he'd lived his life since he was just a small kid at boarding school, reinforced first by the cadets and then by the army, had been completely in evidence when he'd left the flat some six hours ago for his usual Friday night out. A place for everything and everything squarely in its place. In his absence the room had been inexplicably turned into what looked like a bordello. Clothes racks full of silk and satin nightwear stood alongside the wall; the floor space to one side of the room was stacked with baskets of frilly knickers and lacy bras; there was an overflowing box full of bars of ladies' French soap from which the cloying girly smell was emanating and, most unbelievably, there was a padded clothes hanger over the door of his wardrobe on which hung a long and flowing peacock-blue silk dressing-gown thing trimmed with matching marabou feathers. He felt as if he'd stumbled into some insane dream world.

He suddenly remembered Susie standing next to him and shook his head lightly as if to clear it.

'I'm not with anyone,' he said. 'I'm single.'

Her tone now shifted to sickened.

'You mean this stuff is *yours*? I should have listened to my friends, all those warnings about one-night stands and weirdos. Where's my phone?' She opened her handbag and began to paw through it. 'What are you, some kind of cross-dresser?'

'Of course not,' he said, exasperated. 'For Pete's sake, do I *look* like I might enjoy wearing women's clothing?'

'They never do,' she said, pulling out her phone and scrolling through it. 'I've watched enough reality TV to know that the ones to watch out for are the masculine types. And they never choose the kind of clothes that blend in either, oh, no. It's always a bloody prom dress.' She pointed an emphatic finger at him. 'Or a silk negligee.'

The situation was careering way out of control. He held up placating hands.

'There's obviously been some kind of a mix-up,' he said.

'Too right there has.' She turned away from him. 'Taxi, please,' she snapped into the phone. 'I'll be waiting outside Ignite, Lancaster Road, Notting Hill.'

'It's probably something to do with my sister,' he called after her as she marched back down the hallway to the front door.

'Yeah, yeah. I bet that's what they all say!' she yelled back over her shoulder.

He heard her high-heeled shoes clattering down the stairs as she made a swift exit. He turned back to his room, took in the clutter of girly clothing and breathed in the head-reeling scent of roses.

He'd had enough trouble sleeping when the room was the epitome of calm and orderliness. How the hell was he meant to manage now?

Lara woke to the muffled banging of knuckles on a door and floundered for a moment to get her bearings in the dark. She felt vaguely closed in.

It came slowly back to her overtired brain.

Flooded studio. Damaged stock. Poppy's boxroom.

The knocking continued and she wondered vaguely if it was the front door. Sex-god Alex must have locked himself out again. There was a hint of self-righteous satisfaction in that thought, especially after what she'd learned this afternoon from the emergency plumber who'd investigated the root cause of her flooded flat. A ten-minute conversation had made it clear the flood problem went a lot deeper than a need for a new washer. The old fire station might have had a modern makeover when it was converted to flats but it turned out the glossy living space papered over some serious cracks in the original pipe network. It all made perfect sense now. The pipes servicing her flat were clearly linked to those above and below, hence the insane racket from Alex's bedroom activities travelling down so effectively to her bedroom underneath.

In fact, according to the plumber, the pipework showed signs of recent stress—clearly this was what had caused the plumbing to give up the ghost. So not only was her lack of sleep down to Poppy's sex-crazed brother, but now the flooding of her flat could be attributed to him too. He was fast becoming her least favourite person and therefore any initial guilt she might have felt about imposing on him by using his bedroom to store her stuff had been very easily suppressed.

The brief temptation to just let him knock all night was trumped by the desire to tell him exactly what she thought of his nocturnal activities, the damage of which had now surpassed simple noise pollution. She threw the covers back and grabbed her robe from the back of the door.

Turned out the knocking was coming from inside the flat. She'd been right about one thing though: it was Alex again.

'Is no disruption too inconsiderate for you?' she snapped. He jumped and turned to look at her. She had a mad sense of déjà vu at the sight of him with upraised knuckles hammering on Poppy's bedroom door. Except that this time he was fully dressed. The dark blue shirt made his eyes look almost slate in the dim hallway light and her stomach gave an unexpected flip.

* * *

The ability to speak momentarily disappeared because it felt as if his tongue was stuck to the roof of his mouth. Lara's soft blond hair lay in messy bed-head waves over her shoulders. She wore a pink silk dressing gown, with wide sleeves, that ended a good couple of inches above her knees. His eyes dipped to her legs before he could stop them. The slight sheen of the silk against her skin seemed to give it a porcelain quality and the pink colour of the gown picked out the soft fullness of her mouth. He floundered for speech as the unexplained transformation of his bedroom made sudden sense. Was she somehow *staying* here? Why the hell would she be doing that when she had her own perfectly good bedroom down one flight of stairs?

The door clicked open behind him and Poppy finally staggered out, yawning and squinting at the light.

'What the hell's all the noise about? I'm on duty in a few hours.'

He took his eyes off Lara, not without some difficulty, and rounded on his sister. She looked at him with one half-lidded eye.

'My bedroom looks like a tart's boudoir,' he snapped. 'What the hell is going on?'

'For Pete's sake, it's just a few pairs of knickers,' she protested, an incredulous tone to her voice as if his room didn't look like some vintage cathouse. 'There's been a flood in Lara's flat so I've invited her to stay in the boxroom. She needed to store some of her stock for a bit and since there's *masses* of spare space in your bedroom, I couldn't see the problem. Can't this wait until the morning?'

'No, it can't,' he snapped back. 'Have you seen it in there? You didn't even ask me. It's an invasion of my privacy and I'm not going to stand for it.'

He'd always known Poppy's patience was not at its best when she was tired and he braced himself for a sibling argument of monumental proportions.

She drew herself up to her full height.

'Don't, then. Find yourself another flat if you don't like it. Or you could go back home.'

A low blow, and he could tell by the way she shifted her eyes away from him that she knew it. The subject of their inheritance from their grandparents hung between them as strongly as if it had been a visible sack of cash in the corner of the hallway. After getting access to it at the age of twenty-one, Poppy had put hers away, stashed it sensibly for the future, and now she had this flat to show for it. Living for the moment, he'd frittered his away on swanky nights out with Isaac while at university and later while on leave from the army. Expensive holidays were the order of the day. When he had time to himself, he made that time count. One particular ill-judged week in Las Vegas with the lads had reduced the pot considerably. He hadn't given it a thought at the time, hadn't needed to, because he'd had a *career*. Now that career was cut short he found he didn't have the funds any longer for a house deposit, and he needed what was left to start over. Without Poppy's offer of a place to stay he really would be reduced to returning to the family home and the thought filled him with distaste. If it was a choice between that and living in a room full of knickers, he'd just have to put up.

Poppy cast exasperated hands up at the ceiling when he didn't respond.

'I can't *do* this. I am *not* discussing your sleeping arrangements at one in the morning when I've got to be at work in a few hours. The underwear stays. You either put up with it or you move out.' She turned away and stopped any further argument by shutting her bedroom door on him. He stared at the panelled wood, feeling Lara's eyes on his back.

'She loves me really,' he said.

'I'll be out of your hair as soon as the plumbing's fixed in my flat,' Lara said, and instead of what should surely be an apologetic tone he picked up an undeniable pointed edge to her voice.

'Plumbing?'

She leaned against the hallway wall and crossed her arms. His mind insisted on noticing how the silk of the gown lovingly clung to her perfect curves. By act of sheer will, he kept his eyes on her face.

'Yes, plumbing,' she said. 'Turns out your energetic nocturnal activities have put the pipe network under too much strain.'

He stared at her.

'What the hell are you talking about?'

'Half the plumbing in this place is years old—it dates back way before the flat conversion. They might have built things to last back then, but no one reckoned on your bed being shoved up against it. The pipe running down from your bedroom radiator finally gave up the ghost today. It dislodged and because my flat's directly below it caused a flood. I've got no running water down there and damaged stock, and if it wasn't for Poppy I haven't a clue what I'd do.'

'I moved the bed away from the radiator,' he protested.

'Too little too late,' she said, and as she spoke he noticed the dark smudges beneath the indignant eyes. A twist of guilt spiked in his stomach because he'd seen how completely immersed she was in her damned pop-up-shop project. In terms of actually living a productive life right now, he'd just slipped into negative territory. Living a quiet life and not hacking anyone off surely wasn't meant to be this hard. The feeling of uselessness and lack of direction that he'd been shoving away pretty much since he'd returned to London made a sudden gut-churning comeback.

She looked on as he passed a hand tiredly over his forehead. She could feel the climb down as he spread his hands.

'Look, I'm sorry about the flood. You're sure it was down to me?'

An apology? And a marginally more genuine one this time since he really didn't have anything to gain from it. He wasn't

shut out on the landing half naked now, was he? In acknowl-
edgement she curbed her angry tone a little.

'According to the emergency plumber, the problem origi-
nated in the area of pipework attached to your radiator, so that
would be a yes.'

He made a move towards the kitchen and she followed him
and watched from the doorway as he filled the kettle.

'Hot drink?' he said, eyebrows raised.

She shook her head and he took a single mug from the
drainer.

'Any idea on timescale?' he said. 'How long do I have to live
in a *frou-frou* bordello?'

'Do you mind? My stuff is classy, not tarty,' she snapped.

He sighed. 'Of course it is.'

'The plumber did that thing where they suck in their breath
and shake their head pityingly,' she said. 'I'm guessing at least
a few days. Plus you have to factor in the weekend. He's made it
safe but he's not going to actually *do* much else until Monday.'

He thrust an enormous heaped spoonful of instant coffee
into the mug and topped it up with hot water.

'You're really going to drink that now?' she said, eyeing it.
'You'll be buzzing.'

He glanced at her. She could see the dark circles beneath his
eyes even from here. Why would anyone who looked that tired
want a caffeine boost?

'Yup.'

He turned around to face her, leaning back against the worktop. Her heart rate upped its pace a notch at the intense look in
the grey eyes. The last time she'd been this close to him he'd
been asleep, his face relaxed. Now he looked drawn and tense.
He looked as if he needed a good night's sleep.

'You mentioned some stock was damaged,' he said.

She nodded and sighed.

'Some camisoles,' she said and, seeing his questioning frown, added, 'like vest tops, you know, with the string-type shoulder straps. Also some silk knickers.'

There was no denying it had been a setback. The water marks had ruined them.

He shifted awkwardly on his feet, clearly not massively comfortable with discussing women's underwear in the early hours of the morning.

'Look, I know I can't make up for the time you've lost but at least let me pay for the damage,' he said, his hand sliding around to the back pocket of his jeans. He produced a wallet and opened it.

She looked at him, surprised. An apology *and* an offer to make amends.

'It's fine,' she said, shaking her head. 'It's enough that Poppy's letting me stay here. That's a massive help. I hadn't a clue what I was going to do.'

'That doesn't help with your stock damage, though, does it?' Completely ignoring her, he pulled a wad of notes free. She stared at them, a hundred different things running through her mind that she could do if she had an extra cash injection. She rejected them all.

How easy it must be to just have access to that kind of money whenever you needed it, just paying off your problems when they arose. He probably had a massive trust fund at his disposal. She might have her back against the wall and no ready cash but what she had to show for it had never been handed to her on a plate. Everything she had was the result of hard graft. That was the way she wanted it. She didn't want to feel beholden to anyone else, that way she knew any success was hers alone and couldn't be snatched away. Yes, the pipes breaking might have been down to Alex but the whole pipe system was shot to hell as it was and there was no way she would be accepting his money. She would never have taken up Poppy's offer if she hadn't been desperate.

'I don't want your money,' she said, holding a hand up to stop his outstretched handful of notes.

He hesitated a moment, watching her face intently, and then put the money away.

'OK, then.' He took a sip of the coffee that was so black it looked like engine oil. 'But if there's anything I can do to help, let me know.'

Throwaway comment or genuine offer, she didn't know. At least he'd accepted responsibility. Her opinion of him stepped up the tiniest notch.

'I will,' she said, knowing she wouldn't. She turned for the door and headed back to bed, leaving him to sip his horrible drink and wondering what the hell problem he had with normal sleep patterns.

Sleeping in the daytime had a major drawback, Alex now found. Pitch darkness was almost impossible to achieve, background noise kept rousing him, and every time he came awake he was faced with the hideous violation of his ordered personal space. Staring at the four walls of his room in Poppy's flat was a great deal less palatable and restful now that they were festooned with women's underwear.

He eventually gave up at around three in the afternoon, showered, dressed and headed out for a head-clearing walk. The October Saturday afternoon was crisp and sunny as he turned onto Portobello Road with its buzz of shoppers. The colour and pace was rousing. He was almost past the shop before he realised it was Lara's, his overtired brain only processing the eye-catching pink and black sign when he'd taken half a dozen paces onwards.

He stopped in his tracks and backed up, looking up above the gleaming glass window, to where 'Boudoir Fashionista' was painted in a curly black handwritten font on a pink background. Another sign hung on the closed door. 'Opening Soon', it said.

Not that he hadn't had his absolute *fill* of frilly underwear back in his own home, but curiosity nonetheless meant he couldn't stop himself from just having a quick look to see what her big dream of a pop-up shop looked like inside. He moved to the glass and framed his hands around his eyes to see in.

Inside, with just a couple of overhead lights on, he could make out a counter at the back of the small shop floor, open shelving that was currently empty, some stacks of boxes, and, in the middle of it all, Lara, apparently trying to heft a package that was at least twice as big as she was across the floor. It teetered on one corner and looked momentarily as if it might topple through the plate-glass window taking her with it. What the hell was she thinking?

Before he knew what he was doing he was trying the door, and when it didn't open he knocked on it, hard. He watched as she heaved the package to lean against the wall and then practically saw her eyes roll as she clocked him watching her. She crossed to the door, undid a few bolts and opened it.

'What are you doing here?' she said. She certainly didn't sound pleased to see him.

'One wrong move and you'll be pinned under that thing for a week,' he said 'What the hell are you doing humping furniture like that around on your own?'

She glanced across at the six-foot-high package of tape and bubble wrap.

'It's a full-length mirror. I'm trying to decide where I want it.' She tilted her chin up indignantly. 'And I'm not an invalid. I'm perfectly capable of moving a few sticks of furniture around.'

Sticks of furniture? The mirror was enormous, a good couple of feet taller than she was and generously wide.

'Don't be ridiculous, you'll end up in traction. And then where will your damn pop-up shop be?' He walked straight past her into the shop and crossed to the packaged mirror. 'Where do you want it?'

* * *

For the umpteenth time he rested the mirror against the wall
of the shop and watched as Lara leaned back and surveyed the
floor as a whole. The shop door was closed again, but through
the plate-glass window he could see shoppers rubbernecking in
interest at them. She'd painted the walls the palest of rose pink.
The floor was polished wood and there was an original fireplace
to one side. Lara had made the most of the feature, stringing it
with pale pink silk flowers and white pin lights. In the centre
of the small floor space there was now a low oval French-style
table painted cream. The small counter at the back of the shop
had a tongue-and-groove effect in cream-painted wood and
there was a painted wooden dressing screen with scrolled edging that Lara kept moving around because she couldn't decide
where she wanted the changing-room area to be. The whole
effect was girly enough to have him feeling completely out of
his comfort zone.

'What about there?' he asked, without much hope. She'd had
him move the damn thing all over the place, trying out all four
walls and every corner.

She shook her head, one finger tapping at the side of her chin.

'No, I think I liked it best the way we had it first.'

He squashed his exasperation, not without some difficulty.
He could appreciate perfectionism as much as the next military man but this…

He caught her looking at him, an apologetic smile playing
at the corner of the lush mouth.

'I'm sorry. I'm a nightmare, I know. I just want so much for
it to be perfect.'

'No problem.'

He moved the mirror back to where it had started nearly an
hour ago. In the interim she'd got on with decorating the shop
around him, stopping every now and then to order him about.
There was a part of him that couldn't fail to be impressed by
her drive and determination. Not to mention the fact that her

dreams were mapped out. She had a game plan that she was clearly taking in stages. And no wonder he was intrigued by that in light of the fact that his life was currently cruising along with absolutely zero direction.

'So what's the big deal about refusing help?' he said, glancing at her as she watched him heft the mirror around. 'I mean, I did *offer* the other night. You could have just spoken up then that you needed some fittings moving around.'

'I didn't want to impose. I'm doing enough of that just by staying at the flat.'

He shrugged.

'It's no big deal. Poppy wouldn't have offered if it was. She'd do the same for any of her friends.'

His blasé tone made it clear he thought she was making a mountain out of nothing. Of course he would think that. The rich were surrounded by freeloaders, weren't they? Hangers-on probably came with the territory, and she couldn't bear the thought of being seen like that.

'I guess I'm just used to doing things by myself, that's all,' she said. 'Problems come up, I find my own way round them. I don't like to take anything or anyone for granted, so I get things done myself.'

She'd made that mistake far too often when she was a kid to make it again now.

'Even if it means getting trapped under something heavy?' he said. 'You can't shift furniture like this about yourself,' he added, his tone appalled. 'You really will injure yourself.'

'Of course I can,' she said indignantly. 'I put up the shelves myself. I painted the walls myself. I can hump and bump a bit of furniture around.'

Not that it hadn't been too heavy for her. He was right about that: it had been a struggle. Whereas he could clearly shift furniture around all day without breaking a sweat.

'Yeah, well,' he said gruffly. 'Any more of that needs doing and I want you to ask me.'

She opened her mouth to politely decline the offer and he held up a hand to stop her.

'As a favour,' he said. 'For Pete's sake, accept some help. I'm not asking you to sign your name in blood.'

His tone was final, subject closed and she found herself inclining her head in acknowledgement, not that she would stick at it if the situation arose. She couldn't deny it was nice to have the fittings finished in here and it would have taken her twice as long on her own, but she certainly didn't intend to make a habit of leaning on anyone else. Especially him.

'You're very driven,' he said, changing the subject.

She crossed to the wooden counter and pulled herself up so she was sitting on it.

'Yeah, well, it's been a dream for a long time. Finally trialling a shop is a really big deal for me. There's a lot riding on it.'

Her entire savings just for starters.

'How did you get into it?' he said. 'I mean, isn't it a pretty niche market, underwear?'

His tone was vaguely awkward and a smile rose on her lips at his obvious fish-out-of-waterness when it came to discussing lingerie. She imagined he would be the type of man she sometimes encountered on her market stall, obviously out of their depth as they chose underwear for a wife or girlfriend with no clue about bra size or colour choice.

'I've always been into sewing,' she said. 'It's grown from that really. Specialising in lingerie came later when I went to college. I'm inspired by vintage fashion, that Hollywood era where women were glossy, curvy, glamorous. When I designed my first collection I based my ideas on that.'

She watched him positioning the mirror, not looking at her, and her mind drifted back down the years. She hadn't been into much of anything really as a child, apart from keeping her head down. Until she'd been fostered by Bridget, that was. The last in a long line of foster homes where Lara had apparently not been a good fit. Being a *good fit* was a hideously elusive thing. She'd tried everything over the years to be that. Living with Bridget was the one and only time she'd come even close. She'd ended up staying there until she was old enough to go to college. Bridget had been a seamstress and had taught Lara everything she knew. And finding something she was not only good at but was also passionate about had been the biggest turning point in her life.

She'd realised while at college that she was talented at dressmaking. On the heels of that came the realisation that she could make a living at this if she wanted to. She could make her own stability, her own home life, without having to rely on anyone else. If she worked hard enough she'd never need to worry about being a good fit ever again. She'd have a life of her own.

'You decided against working for anyone else?' he said.

She shrugged.

'I started out that way, did some time for a high-street fashion line. But I'm a bit of a control freak. I like doing things my way. I like the idea of making my own success. I know I can rely on myself, you see. I won't be letting myself down.'

'And you learned to sew before college?'

The mirror was in place. He took a step back.

'That's perfect,' she said, jumping down from the counter. She crossed the shop to join him and began tugging the polystyrene corners and protective film off the mirror, revealing a gilt scrolled frame and flawless glass. He moved in to help her. 'I learned to sew when I was about fourteen.'

'Your mum taught you?'

She looked at him for a moment. He'd shifted a bit of furniture around. Was she really going to kid herself that he wanted to hear her life story? He was probably just being polite, filling the silences.

'Something like that,' she said.

She bundled the packaging up into a ball and shoved it into the corner next to a couple of bin bags, then turned back to survey her shop floor. It was exactly as she wanted it and excitement sparkled through her at how the project was coming together. Before she could stop herself she'd reached out to touch his arm. He looked down at her hand in surprise.

'Thanks for helping out,' she said. 'I owe you a favour.'

For the first time since she'd met him, she got a smile that didn't have an undertone of exasperation about it. It creased his grey eyes at the corner and lifted the strong mouth. He really was gorgeous and her stomach gave an unexpected flutter.

'I'll think of something,' he said.

CHAPTER FOUR

ALEX THREW HIMSELF bolt upright, panic racing through his veins, certain he'd just shouted out loud.

It had been the same as always. The windows bursting into cracks, held in place by their film covering. The feeling and sound of massive pressure beneath the vehicle as the explosion ripped through it. Smoke and dust filling the space around him, the air thick with it. He could taste the explosives in his mouth. Then the aftermath, the melting hot asphalt on the road beneath him and the disorientation as he staggered through smoke and wreckage to look for Sam and for the driver of the vehicle. Private Sam Walker had been accompanying him. One of his unit, one of his own.

He stared around him in panic, a twist of sheet clutched in one fist and the pillows damp against his back.

There was a book open to one side of the bed where he'd been trying to stave off sleep by reading. Late autumn's golden sunlight slanted through the gap in the curtains. And the bedroom was full of ladies' underwear.

His pulse slowly began to climb down towards normal, his breathing began to level. Somehow the festooning of his room with lingerie and nightwear put such a mad skew on his surroundings that it calmed him in a way his usual military-ordered bedroom didn't. This was reality. There was no way of confusing this room with his army existence. He was home. He was no longer part of the army. His responsibility was discharged.

He checked his watch. Late morning. He must have finally dropped off to sleep around five. It could be worse. Six hours' uninterrupted sleep wasn't a bad count by recent standards. And he couldn't have shouted aloud. Poppy and Lara were probably hanging around the flat; they would have heard, Poppy would have burst in here without a moment's thought. He swung his feet off the bed and headed for the shower, stood under the torrent of hot water. Maybe this was what counted for an improvement; maybe he would be able to get longer and longer stretches of sleep until he could find some level of normality. He would not succumb to these nightmares. He would get through this.

Strong coffee. That was what he needed now to get rid of the last grasping tendrils of the dream. Five minutes later and he was heading downstairs to the ground-floor café and its industrial-strength espresso.

Ignite channelled quirky but cosy with a nod to the history of the building from the original fireman's pole still in the middle of the shop. Framed black and white wall prints hung on the exposed brickwork of the walls, showing the building when it was a fire station instead of a block of flats. It ran a steady trade in Sunday brunch, the air was filled with the delicious smell of frying bacon and hot coffee and Lara was sitting at the corner table with a pot of tea, a laptop and an untouched blueberry muffin.

She didn't even glance up as he walked in, and he watched her at his leisure as he waited to pay for his coffee. Her blond hair was piled up on her head today, a pink fabric flower pinned at one side, and she was wearing a fitted floral blouse that showed off her curves to perfection. In terms of distraction she easily beat Marco, who stood behind the counter, and a surge of heated interest spiked through him—interest that hadn't really come to the fore when he'd had her pegged as annoying neighbour. There was no need to fudge the fact he was looking at her because her entire attention was focused on the open laptop screen. Did she never do downtime?

'It's Sunday,' he said, coming to a standstill, coffee in hand, next to her table.

She looked up at him, china-blue eyes wide.

'And your point?'

'You're working,' he said. 'Again. Do you never take a break?'

'I *am* taking a break,' she protested. 'I'm updating my blog and I'm checking over my launch fliers and thinking about where I can hand them out.' She pushed the opposite chair out with one of her ballet flats. 'Sit down—you can tell me what you think.'

'Not sure I like what it says about me, that you think my opinion on women's lingerie might have value,' he said. Then the immediate need for coffee won over and he sat down and took the pale pink piece of stiff card she held out.

'You'd be surprised how many of my customers are men,' she said. 'Hanging round the market stall looking awkward, usually on a quest for something red with peepholes. I soon put them straight. Women like classy and glamorous, not tarty.' She pointed at him with her pen. 'So, actually, I'd be interested in your feedback.'

He looked over the invitation with its loopy black handwriting and silhouette image of a curvy female form.

'You're having a launch party on Thursday night?' he said.

She nodded.

'I'm opening from six until eight. Late-night shopping with pink champagne and nibbles, that kind of thing. You'll come, won't you?' She swept on breezily before he could get in an immediate thanks-but-no-thanks. 'I've invited half the building to drop by. Poppy's coming, and Izzy and Tori. I just need to drum up as much interest as I can, need to think about where I can hand these out. Marco says I can put a stack of them on the counter in here.' She pressed a hand to her forehead. 'And I'm doing a big post about it on my blog, and then I need to keep building up the anticipation on the Facebook page. Not to mention tweeting about it…'

He held up a hand to stop the stream-of-consciousness torrent.

'You'll drive yourself into an early grave. When did you last take a break?'

She waved a hand at the untouched blueberry muffin and half-full teacup and raised her eyebrows.

'This is *not* a break,' he said, exasperated. 'You're putting yourself under far too much pressure. What you need is fresh air and exercise.' The words were out of his mouth before he registered what he was doing. 'Come for a run with me this afternoon.'

She stared at him as if he'd just suggested she jog naked down Portobello Road.

'Are you insane? I don't do running.'

'I know,' he said. 'I can tell by the way you're so manic. Physical fitness feeds the mind. You'll be able to work twice as efficiently afterwards.' He nodded at her muffin. 'Much better than the sugar rush you'll get from eating that stodge.'

She narrowed her eyes at him, as if trying to decide whether he was joking.

'Really?'

He nodded, taking a huge swig of his coffee.

'One hour. You can spare one hour. And you do owe me a favour. I'm fed up with running on my own.'

It was becoming clear that being alone with his thoughts might not be the best therapy for dwelling on the past. And testing though it might have been heaving furniture around her shop the previous day, it had also been the first hour in a while that he'd been engaged enough by something that the past hadn't encroached on his thoughts. The rest of the day yawned emptily ahead of him without his current distraction of choice—female company. And it occurred to him as she leaned forward to speak to him, giving him a fabulous view of her perfect creamy cleavage, that he was a fool. There was no sense in trawling bars and clubs on Sunday daytime when he had a perfectly good contender right here.

'I meant cooking you lunch or buying you a coffee,' she said. 'Not letting you distract me from my work to run round Notting Hill like a headless chicken.'

'My runs are structured, not some random dash,' he countered. 'You're so manic that you'll probably find it calming to do something physical for a change.'

She paused.

'And we can distribute some leaflets while we're out,' he said.

She tilted her chin upwards in a way that told him *that* was the real pull for her in this scenario. Everything she did seemed to be about furthering her damn business plan.

'Done,' she said. 'And I am *not* bloody manic.'

She slammed the downstairs door of the flats behind her and saw that he was already there. Ready and waiting for her in running gear that was worn in enough to show he took his fitness extremely seriously. She glanced longingly through the window of Ignite, where she could be sitting right now with her laptop and a doughnut. She forced a smile, turned to face him and clocked his bemused expression.

'What?' she said as he looked her up and down. 'I'm not some gym bunny, you know, with all the kit. I did the best I could in the time.' She looked down at herself. 'I borrowed the running shoes and shorts from Poppy. The T-shirt's my own. I embellished it myself.'

'You don't say,' Alex said, staring at the loose cotton T-shirt, the front of which was smothered in a sprinkling of pink sequins. Her hair was caught up in a ponytail and tied with a pink scarf and she was wearing pink lipstick. He wondered for a moment why the hell he had thought this would be a good idea.

She moved behind him and unzipped his backpack.

'What the hell are you doing now?'

A wave of her floral perfume as she leaned in close to him knocked his senses off-kilter. He craned around to see her stuff a wad of her pink leaflets into the bag.

'This is meant to be for an energy drink, or an iPod, or a mobile phone, not masses of stuff,' he grumbled.

'It's just a few leaflets,' she said, totally ignoring him and zipping it back up. 'No need to roll your eyes—you must be used to lugging ten-stone backpacks across deserts for days at a time. A few slips of paper are hardly going to weigh you down.'

He nodded down the street.

'Holland Park's in that direction. Brisk walk first,' he said as she began limbering up and jogging from foot to foot. 'You need to warm up properly, don't want to pull any muscles.'

She kept pace with him as he started down the road, and five minutes later they turned into the park. Holland Park was quiet and peaceful with lots of open green space, but also nature trails and walkways and a stunning Japanese garden. The ground was covered in temptingly kickable autumn leaves in red and gold and the air was crisp and clear. Trees filtered golden sunshine. The appeal of running, which had so far eluded her, kicked in. This place was a real haven from the buzz of the city.

There was something about his hugely muscled frame in its well-worn sportswear that made walking fast look cool as opposed to looking as if he were late for a bus or rushing for a toilet. She really wasn't sure she could pull cool off in Poppy's shorts, which were really on the small side for her curvy hips but gaped massively at her waist. She retied the drawstring grimly and tugged her T-shirt down as far as she could.

She must have been mad to agree to this. She could have been spending this time drafting the next couple of days' worth of Facebook posts, uploading the photos she'd taken of some of the new raspberry silk knickers she'd designed with the frills on the butt.

Alex made a valiant effort not to let his eyes slide continually down to her bare legs. This close it was impossible not to notice the smooth cream of her thighs, and there was a fragility to the porcelain skin and blond hair, blue eyes colouring that belied how strong-willed and driven she really was.

'Have you done any running before?' he asked.

She shrugged.

'I've been able to do it since I was a toddler.' She sighed as he pulled an unimpressed face. 'No, I haven't. Not proper running. Not since I was at school. I'm not some madly fit exercise freak—it has to fit around everything else in my life.'

'Any exercise at all?'

'I like swimming,' she said unexpectedly. 'I used to go a lot. No time for it since I came here though. I let everything slide really that isn't related to the business. It's only a couple of months. I wanted to throw everything I've got into it.'

A spike of envy at her sense of purpose jabbed him behind the ribs. He couldn't help admiring her focus and determination, that refusal to let anything divert her from her goal.

'We'll take it steady, then,' he said. 'One minute gentle jogging, then one minute walking. Ready?'

He broke into a slow jog and she followed suit next to him.

'What about relationships?' he said after a moment.

Just because he'd never seen her with a man, didn't mean there wasn't one.

She let out an amused noise alongside her speedy breathing.

'Some of us just don't have time for that stuff,' she panted.

He couldn't fail to miss the barb in that comment.

'Meaning that I do—right?' he said.

He glanced at his watch and slowed down into a walking session, keeping it brisk to maintain the heart rate. She kept pace next to him, clearly not as unfit as she'd made herself sound. Then again, he couldn't remember the last time he'd met anyone with so much energy. She was constantly on the go.

She took the bottle of water he passed to her and took a sip. He was aware of her watching him over the bottle.

'I suppose everyone's entitled to *some* time out,' she conceded. 'How long will you be staying with Poppy? She said something about an honourable discharge. Is that permanent? No going back to the army?' She handed the bottle back.

He gritted his teeth.

'I won't be going back. The discharge is an end to it. That chapter of my life is well and truly over.'

Saying it out loud made it no more palatable. It still felt vaguely unreal, even months later, with everything tied up.

'You don't sound so pleased about that.'

He shrugged.

'I'm not. I didn't want to be discharged—the army was my life.'

She didn't comment for a minute or two, but he could feel her eyes on him.

'I saw your scars,' she said at last. 'When you fell asleep in my flat.' Her voice was full of sympathy. 'I'm really sorry.'

He carried on walking in silence for a moment, noticing she didn't push for any more details. The gap sat there in the conversation, and she was leaving it to him to elaborate.

'There was an incident,' he said eventually. That word seemed so inadequate as a description. The relentless guilt churned sickly in his stomach as he recalled it. Guilt that he was walking through this glorious park while Sam, who he'd promised to look out for, had been gone in an instant on Alex's watch.

'A roadside bomb,' he clarified.

He indicated the left side of his chest lightly. 'This was down to shrapnel—it sliced below my shoulder blade and then settled in my chest muscle. The medics removed it but there wasn't much they could do about the scarring.'

The physical side of the injuries he could talk about. She certainly wasn't the first woman to ask about them. Coping with them and recovering at breakneck speed had been his way of proving his strength, to himself as much as anyone. He clenched his fists lightly. If only putting the experience out of his mind could be as straightforward. Nagging doubt about his mental strength continued to plague him. The sickening guilt that he'd failed Sam was never far away, seething beneath the surface of his mind. He had offered encouragement to that young soldier when he'd struggled at first with his posting. He had helped him get a handle on his fears. He had assured Sam he would look out for him and he'd let him down on an epic scale.

The frustration that he couldn't seem to just fast-track the recovery of his mind in the same way as his body was relentless, and worse was what that said about his strength or weakness as a soldier.

'You're lucky to have your family to support you through something like that,' she said.

The ludicrousness of that comment brought a laugh that he failed to suppress.

'Did I say something funny?'

He glanced sideways at her, saw her puzzled frown and shook his head.

'I'm not laughing at you. My family aren't really like that, except for Poppy. We're not close. Stiff upper lip and all that.'

He kept walking, wondering if she'd let the subject drop now.

'What are your plans now, then?' she said. 'If the army's out of the question.'

Apparently not. He shook his head.

'I haven't got a clue. I've known exactly how my life would play out since I was knee high. There was a long line of military family members to live up to when I was growing up, never any question that was the route I'd take. Tons of army anecdotes bandied around at family gatherings. I enrolled at Sandhurst when I finished university and then pushed myself up the ranks. My future was mapped out. To suddenly not have one is a bit of a curved ball, to be honest.'

Understatement of the year.

'OK, then, well, what was your Plan B? You have to have a back-up plan. Like me, for example, if this pop-up shop doesn't work out then I'll probably look into building up an online presence more, try pushing the internet shopping angle. You must have at least an idea of the direction you want to take, even if you haven't pinned it down to a specific career path.'

'I've never needed a Plan B. What would be the point? My Plan A spanned pretty much the whole of my life. I thought if I took a bit of time out and stayed with Poppy I could work out my next move.' He thought for a moment. 'It would have to be something active, I think. I'm not sure I'm suited to sitting behind a desk.'

She didn't answer and he checked his watch.

'Time's up, let's pick up the pace again,' he said.

Twenty minutes of alternating jogging and brisk walking and he had to admit she wasn't the ditsy glamour girl she seemed. Not entirely anyway. Although he could see from the flush high up on her cheekbones and the damp tendrils of blond hair escaping her ponytail that she'd pushed herself, she'd nonetheless kept pace with him for the full distance.

'You've done well,' he said. 'You sound like you have zero time for exercise but you must be doing something right.'

She shrugged and smiled, pushed a damp lock of hair out of her eyes.

'I'm always on the go. The business keeps me really busy, especially at the moment. I've thrown everything I've got at this pop-up shop. All my spare money's tied up in it. I've got no choice but to make it work.'

'Doesn't that worry you, having so much invested in it?'

She smiled.

'If I stopped to worry about everything that could go wrong, I'd never get anywhere. You can't get rid of any risk completely. I mean, I'd planned this move into retail within an inch of its life but I hadn't factored in the problem with the plumbing in my flat. If it hadn't been for Poppy offering me the boxroom I would have been in serious trouble there.' She shrugged. 'But you have to accept some risk if you're going to move forward. Sometimes you just have to put yourself out there to reach your goal.'

It was hard not to get swept along by her drive. That dogged refusal to contemplate failure. She made anything seem possible. Spending time with her was like having an injection of optimism and, goodness knew, he had been in dire need of some of that these past months.

He slowed to a standstill as they approached a fenced-off playground area and nodded at a park bench.

'Need to cool down now,' he said. 'Stretches. Last thing you need is to pull a muscle.'

She followed him reluctantly to the bench and gripped the back of it in the same way he was, self-consciousness kicking back in. A stone's throw away the sandy-floored playground was jam-packed with small children clambering over wooden equipment and rubbernecking Notting Hill mums. Alex Spencer, ex-army, with his honed body hot and sweaty in muscle-hugging sportswear, was clearly a big distraction to the female species at large.

'Now stand on one leg and hold the other leg behind you, hold your foot above the ankle,' he instructed, oblivious to the fluster he was causing in the playground.

Clearly her attempt at the exercise was inadequate because he was suddenly in her personal space, one hand pressed softly at her lower back, holding her steady and the other covering her hand as she gripped her own ankle, holding her foot high behind her. She felt envious eyes boring into her back from the direction of the playground.

'Feel that stretch?' he said.

Maybe she would do, if she weren't too busy feeling unexpectedly *melty* at the closeness of his muscular body and his huge hands on her. There really was no denying how breathtakingly gorgeous he was. There was also no way she was going to have a swooning moment over him. She had far too much on her plate to let *that* kind of distraction slip past her guard.

'Absolutely,' she said loudly.

Another half-dozen or so stretches out of the way and it occurred to Lara that she was missing a trick right there with Alex's captive audience. Unzipping his small rucksack, she removed a wad of leaflets and crossed to the playground while he leaned against the back of the bench and swigged from a bottle of water.

She walked into the playground and handed a leaflet to anyone who made eye contact.

'Lingerie?' A dark-haired woman with a designer pushchair took a leaflet and read it with interest.

'It's a pop-up shop,' Lara said, full of pride. 'In Portobello Road. Boutique lingerie and nightwear. Vintage inspired. I'm having a launch party on Thursday and I'll be there for the next couple of months. I'd love it if you'd drop in. And tell your friends.'

'Maybe that's the secret, then. I need to get me some boutique lingerie.'

She nodded in Alex's direction with a knowing wink.

Lara laughed out loud, glossing over a deep-down glimmer of pride that it clearly wasn't *that* outrageous a suggestion that she could be the other half of someone who looked like an Adonis.

'We're not together! He's just my...' she searched for the right description '...*running partner.*' As if she had time for daily jogs around parks and sets of stretches. 'Military-style personal training,' she added, purely off the top of her head.

She followed the gaze of the yummy-mummy contingent as Alex, seemingly oblivious to the attention, poured a few lugs of the water over his head and tousled it through his short hair.

The dark-haired woman leaned in towards her.

'Bloody hell, having him as a personal trainer would be way more motivating than the gym.'

'There you go, doesn't your head feel clearer for that?' he said as they headed back to the flat.

Well, she hadn't thought about the shop for half an hour or so, if that was what he meant. Not that it had anything to do with exercise, more about being fascinated by the reality of what she'd simply assumed was a privileged and fabulous up-bringing. Plus there was the physical diversion provided simply by looking at him. Of course, she hadn't been the only one seduced by that—he'd had half the playground drooling over him.

'That could be your Plan B, right there,' Lara said, nodding back towards the park as they walked away.

Alex looked sideways at her.

'What do you mean?'

'Personal training,' she said. 'You wouldn't be short of clients. I mean, just look at you. You're a bored lady-who-lunches' dream. You could be the new Zumba.'

'I'm not sure if that's a compliment or an insult,' he said. 'On the whole I'm leaning towards insult.'

'Who cares which it is if you can make money out of it?' she said, her eyes shining. He could almost see her mind ticking over as she thought through whatever insane idea it was she was trying to pitch. 'You could make a killing. Once I'd told them you were just taking me for a run and they got past the fact that we weren't an item I nearly got trampled in the rush. You did *say* you didn't fancy some desk job. You're bored with exercising on your own instead of bawling out squaddies on route marches or whatever, so take on a couple of clients and earn some cash while you're at it. At the very least it could be a stopgap until you decide what you really want to do.'

'I'm not sure,' he said doubtfully, struggling to keep up with the torrential pace of her mind. She totally ignored him.

'OK, then, maybe not *exactly* that, but what I'm saying is you need to put yourself out there, try out some ideas, maybe think outside the box and make your own opportunity. The perfect job isn't just going to materialise like magic and drop in your lap while you hibernate in your sister's flat and pop out every now and then to pull women. What about a fitness boot camp for kids? You've got that military presence thing going on—no one would dare backchat you. The country's full of overweight teenagers sitting playing Call of Duty or chatting on Facebook. You could be a one-man combat for the obesity crisis. I can see it now—*Rid Notting Hill of Couch Potatoes*.' She held her hands up as if imagining the slogan as a headline.

The first spark of positivity he'd had in weeks unexpectedly lifted his spirits. Insane though some of her stream-of-consciousness ideas were, it was hard not to get swept along by her enthusiasm. She made anything seem possible and she was becoming more distracting by the second.

'Oh, and you have to come to the launch now,' she said airily. 'A few of them asked for business cards and, of course, you don't have any, so I handed out my leaflets instead. You could literally *see* their ears prick up when I mentioned you'd be there.'

Oh, just bloody *great*.

As he followed her up the stairs to the flat the rest of the afternoon now seemed to lie empty ahead of him, especially as he was actually feeling positive for a change. Optimistic, even. A half-hour chat with Lara and her energy and enthusiasm was infectious. Already his mind was running with the idea of some kind of business centred around fitness; it could fit his skills set on so many levels.

He didn't want their encounter to be over. It wasn't just that she was so distracting, it was how cute she looked with her blond hair dishevelled for once instead of polished, the flush of her cheeks from the exercise, the smooth shapely legs in the shorts. It was how she made anything seem possible. He liked her. On every level. And since his own fitness level was way above a thirty-minute jog-walk session, he was now a mass of pent-up mental and physical energy. He was at a loose end until the end of the day. Taking all of this into account, the perfect afternoon scenario was obvious.

Prolonging the afternoon with her in his bed would be the perfect solution.

'Would you like to get a drink?' he said, thinking ahead. Drink, chat in the sitting room, ending up in his bedroom.

'Ooh, yes, that would be perfect,' she said. 'Could you make me a pint of lemon squash while I have a quick shower?'

Not exactly what he had in mind. He followed her past the kitchen and she turned back to him at the door of the boxroom, tugging the band out of her hair and ruffling it. Anticipatory sparks were simmering hotly in his stomach at the thought of where this could lead.

'Thanks for the run,' she said. 'I'm expecting my productivity to at least double this afternoon now, otherwise I'll be lodging an official complaint.' She was looking up at him, smile on her face, her eyes shining and cheeks pink from the fresh air and exercise. The relaxed look was such a contrast to her usual polished style and it suited her. She looked absolutely adorable and he reached a hand out to tuck a stray lock of hair behind her ear.

Her initial reaction was shocked surprise at the unexpected touch, and as a result sensibility took a few moments to kick in. A few moments in which he cradled the nape of her neck in one of his huge hands and executed the most deliciously bone-melting kiss she'd ever had. Her body clearly couldn't give a toss about sensibility and kicked straight in with a hike in her heart rate and a mass of hot fluttering in her stomach.

Her mind had been set so resolutely in work mode these last weeks that all thoughts of her personal life had been swept under the carpet. It simply hadn't entered her radar that there could be any more to this than…well, than a *run*. Also, he looked like a sportswear model and she was currently hot, sweaty and wearing a hideous ill-fitting shorts and T-shirt combo. All of which might not have mattered one bit if the fact that he usually picked his women up for one night only hadn't popped into her mind. That last thought brought common sense whizzing back and she disentangled herself from him just as he was sliding his free hand around her waist.

He was clearly at a loose end for the rest of the day and couldn't see the point in going out on the pull when he now had someone living in. Whereas she had three days and counting before the shop launch and a million and one things to do in that short space of time.

She'd had enough disposable people dip in and out of her life to add another one. Relationships in her opinion should be about stability, not about shallow motives, not something that could be picked up and put down on a whim. Not that she hadn't partaken in an occasional flurry of dating, always when she was between projects or had a bit of extra time on her hands, but so far none of those flurries had translated into anything that could survive being shoved aside by what was *really* important in her life: her work ambitions. That held true more than ever right now because things were at such a pivotal point. More than anything she needed to keep focus, keep her wits about her. No being distracted from her goals because she'd been propositioned by the fittest guy she'd come across in years.

She locked her knees before they could slide out from under her.

There was no denying her attraction to him. He could see it in the speed of her breathing and the hard peaks of her nipples through the thin sequinned T-shirt. Nonetheless, deny it she did.

'I'm sorry, Alex.' Just the way she said his name upped the heat in his stomach a notch. 'I've got too much to do to while away an afternoon in bed with you.'

'I wasn't thinking about being idle.'

He saw the blush that comment invoked and liked it.

'And attractive though a hot fling might be to some people, I'm not that kind of girl. And even if I was, I'm juggling
enough things as it is right now. I daren't add sex to the mix or
the whole lot could go tits up.'

He shrugged.

'There's no need for it to be complicated,' he said. The worst
thing he could have said, apparently, because she took an extra
pace back and gave him a my-mind-is-made-up smile.

'Why does that not surprise me?' she said. 'I know your routine better than you do. I've lived downstairs from it for weeks.
I'm not interested in being one of your disposable pickups,
making the walk of shame the morning after. I'm better than
that. I don't do one-night stands or shallow flings. If and when
I meet someone I intend it to have some meaning a bit deeper
than a quick tumble in your bed.' She shrugged. 'Plus I'd like
to be able to live in the same flat as you without things getting
awkward. I'd like to have coffee with you or go running with
you without any tension. I don't need any hassle in my life.'

Hassle? He stared after her as she headed for the bathroom.

'Where does that leave us, then?' he called, just before she
shut the door on him.

'Exactly where it did before,' she called back. '*Flatmates*,
Alex. I'm going to take a shower and get back to work.'

He hadn't expected a knockback. Mainly because they never
happened.

From his room he could hear the shower running, his mind
insisting on imagining her naked curves wet and covered in
soap bubbles, and then various doors opening and closing as
she returned to the boxroom, changed clothes and left the flat,
presumably on her way to the shop. He lay on his bed with his
hands clenched, his entire body a coiled spring of latent sexual tension. He could still feel the full softness of her top lip
between his own, could imagine the creamy silk of her bare

thighs beneath his hands. And kicking around the empty flat was making him feel worse by the second.

He left his room for the bathroom, showered, dressed and headed for the front door. What the hell? There were plenty of other single women out there who weren't workaholics.

CHAPTER FIVE

So much for fresh air and exercise aiding productivity. Lara had spent the past few hours shoving Alex Spencer and his delicious kiss firmly out of her mind only to find him right back there again five minutes later. Which only made her even more furious with herself when she eventually returned to the flat to discover the woody scent of his aftershave still lingering in the bathroom and no sign of him in the place. Based on what she knew of him, there was only one explanation: Her knockback a few hours earlier hadn't fazed him one tiny bit. He'd simply refocused his efforts in the usual direction. He'd clearly gone out on the pull.

Why did it bother her so much?

The churning deep in her stomach felt an awful lot like disappointment. Had she really been hoping that the interest he'd shown in her—moving fittings around for her in the shop, cajoling her into taking time out—might stem from genuine liking and concern? It was plain as day that what he really was hoping to gain from it was an easy lay. She should never have expected anything else and she didn't have time to spare to be sucked into this stupid debate with herself.

Poppy was making toast in the kitchen.

'No Alex?' she said, smiling as Lara walked in. 'You two seemed to be getting on like a house on fire.'

Lara shook her head and uttered a light laugh.

'No, he's just been giving me a hand shifting stock, that's all. I don't think he wants to get to know me beyond flatmate levels. Plus he seems to have a crazy social life and I'm up to my eyeballs in work.'

She could hear herself gabbling, protesting too much, and forced herself to stop before Poppy picked up on it. She had absolutely zero interest in how Alex Spencer was spending his evening. She crossed to the counter and concentrated on putting the kettle on.

Poppy sat down at the table.

'I'm not sure his social life is all it seems, to be honest,' she said, nodding her head as Lara held up a mug with a questioning expression. 'He's been through a lot these last few months.'

Lara busied herself, getting together instant coffee and milk from the fridge.

'You mean his injuries? He hasn't really mentioned them.'

Poppy shook her head.

'He wouldn't. He wouldn't let anyone fuss over him, even when he was in the hospital. He doesn't want sympathy, thinks that should all be directed at the soldier who lost his life. The lad was younger than Alex, such a waste.' She looked up at Lara. 'You have to understand his army mates were like family to him. I think that made it a lot harder. He feels responsible.'

Lara's mind reeled with the information. What exactly had Alex been through?

'It's not just the physical injuries. To him they're part of the job. He accepted that risk when he signed up. If anything, leaving the army seems to have been more of a wrench.'

Lara nodded.

'He did mention he was looking for a new direction. I tried to brainstorm a few work suggestions for him.'

Poppy stared at her in surprise.

'Did you? It's more than he's let any of us do.'

And what exactly did *that* mean? That he was interested in what she had to say? Her heart gave a tiny and poorly judged skip because it was a far more likely scenario that Lara was too pushy and hadn't let him get a word in.

'Just because we come from a big family doesn't necessarily mean there's a big support network going on there,' Poppy went on. 'And it's especially difficult for Alex when it comes to army stuff. My father's had an incredibly successful army career, really full-on stuff. He works for the United Nations as a military advisor and that's meant a lot of travel over the years, for him and for my mother. Alex and I had a nanny when we were very young, then boarding school when we were old enough. Alex went from school to university to Sandhurst then straight into the army. He had his whole life mapped out—right from the get-go he knew where he was heading and he seemed happy with that. He threw himself into army life, climbed the ranks at breakneck speed. It was like he was born to do it.' She gave Lara a rueful smile. 'In a way I suppose he was.'

Lara looked down at her coffee mug.

'He can be a bit gruff sometimes but don't be too hard on him. His whole life has changed, his whole future, and not through his choice. I'm not sure he's having an easy time coming to terms with that—that's partly why I offered him the room here. The last thing he needs is my father harping on about military careers when Alex has had to give his up.'

Fresh air and exercise had also failed epically at living up to the promised restful sleep. One ear cocked for the expected arrival of Alex with unnamed conquest, furious with herself for actually being *interested*, Lara finally dropped off somewhere in the small hours. And now her alarm was going off, it was still dark and it occurred to her as she stared one-eyed at her own haggard reflection in the bathroom mirror while she brushed her teeth that she'd been so preoccupied with Alex's behaviour the previous day that she'd forgotten today's plans involved moving her stock from the flat to the shop.

Stock that was currently being stored in his bedroom. Where he was, presumably, holed up with whatever conquest he'd managed to pull the previous night. She might not have heard him make it home but that didn't make her any less certain he was in there. And since he had the most erratic sleep routine of anyone she'd ever met, he could sleep in for *hours* yet.

She didn't have hours. Time was, as usual, of the essence. She couldn't just tiptoe around him; she had work commitments. That the thought of seeing him in bed with another woman made her feel icky had absolutely no place in the debate, and she crushed the unhappy churn in her stomach as she walked down the darkened hallway.

She paused outside his bedroom door. Should she knock? On one hand it would be the polite thing to do, but then again it was only just coming up to six o' clock in the morning. October mornings included pretty full-on darkness at this time. Surely it would be far easier and much quicker to just tiptoe into the room and start by taking the stock nearest the door, mainly stuff that was boxed. She could leave the big clothing rails and the boxes near the window until later, when hopefully he would be up and his bedroom companion had been dispatched.

She held her breath and pressed the door handle down, eased the door open a crack and crept into the room.

As sleepless nights went, it made a change to be kept awake by something other than nightmares or sex.

Alex had undertaken his usual strategy the evening before, and he'd had no trouble finding company in the bar he went to. He never did. Unfortunately the rest of the evening hadn't panned out in the usual way. Engaging in conversation was even more wearing than usual and, worse, he seemed to have no real interest in where the evening was heading. He felt antsier than ever and the company just wasn't cutting it. At a little past midnight he'd made his excuses and returned to the flat. Alone. And sleep had eluded him ever since.

That Lara had knocked him back needled at his pride, yes, but it wasn't just about the snub. Nor was it the physical pull of her. She was very pretty, of course, and the girly, glamorous clothes she chose with her curvy figure and creamy skin really did it for him. It was both those things but more than that too. He *liked* her. More than he was used to liking someone. She had a zest for life that was intoxicating to him in this limbo state he felt so trapped in. She had her own goals, her own standards, without reference to anyone else's. And she made him feel as if he could have that too.

Somewhere before dawn, as he was finally drifting towards dropping off through sheer exhaustion, he heard the bedroom door snick open.

The dim light from the hallway lit her up in silhouette and her light perfume drifted across the room, putting his senses right back on standby.

Lara was creeping into his room under cover of darkness and surely there could be only one explanation why she might do that. Perfectly understandably, she'd spent the rest of yesterday having second thoughts about knocking him back, probably followed by a sleepless night, and now she'd decided to take matters into her own hands.

He watched, his eyes completely accustomed to the darkness, since he'd been lying in it for the past five hours. She tiptoed to the side of the bed, and, really, was that her best attempt at stealth?

There was a clatter as she caught her foot on one of the wretched metal clothes rails and then a moment later a muffled yelp as she fell over a box. And then she picked herself up and paused, obviously gauging whether she'd woken him or not. He saw her head on one side in the semi darkness, as if she was listening closely.

In one swift movement, he leaned up from the bed, caught

her around the waist and pulled her into his lap. Waited for her to melt into his arms as he groped for her mouth with his, his whole body firing up with hot anticipation.

Instead of the anticipated breathy sigh she let out an anguished squawk that wouldn't have gone amiss on a throttled parrot and karate-chopped him in the neck.

Thirty seconds later and Lara had disengaged herself from him, scrambled across to the light switch and snapped it on, all the while hideous thoughts tumbling through her mind of three-somes and goodness knew what else. She stared across the room at him as he blinked in the bright light, sheets pooled around his waist, super-toned naked torso, short hair lightly dishevelled. And she couldn't stop herself exclaiming in surprise.

'You're on your own!' she said.

Alex, sitting at the scrubbed kitchen table in a T-shirt and shorts, held up two fingers as she spooned instant coffee into a mug for each of them and she rolled her eyes as she added a second spoonful for him.

'No wonder you're perpetually awake,' she remarked.

'Yeah, well.' He looked at her over the rim of his coffee mug as she handed it to him. 'My sleep pattern may have become a bit...' he paused '...off balance since I got back. And don't change the subject. What the hell were you doing sneaking around my bedroom in the small hours if you weren't planning on jumping my bones?'

Was there no end to his arrogance when it came to women?

'I can't believe you'd just assume that,' she said.

He continued to look at her, eyebrows raised, and she took a big sip of her coffee.

'I was coming in to get my stock,' she said. 'I want to start taking it over to the shop today. There's still so much to do to get the shop ready before Thursday and I've still got to organise food for the launch evening to hand round with the pink champagne but I haven't even looked at it yet.' She sighed. 'I'm sorry I woke you. I was trying to be as quiet as I could.'

A herd of elephants might have a better line in stealth than she did, in his opinion.

'You didn't wake me,' he said shortly. 'I couldn't sleep.'

'Even without a...' she paused to pull a disapproving face '...*companion*, you're still awake half the night? Don't you *ever* sleep?'

He had absolutely no desire to discuss his sleep patterns with her or anyone else.

'And there was no need to sound so damn shocked,' he carried on, ignoring the question. 'I don't bring women back every night.'

She was watching him steadily, eyes narrowed.

'And even if I did, I don't see that there's anything wrong with that. We're all consenting adults.'

She shrugged, not meeting his eyes, but her body language screamed disapproval.

'Whatever floats your boat, I suppose.'

'What's that supposed to mean?'

She tipped the rest of her coffee down the sink and put the mug in the dishwasher. He could literally see her disengaging from the conversation.

'Nothing. Just that having disposable people in my life isn't really my bag. To me it just seems like a horrendous waste of time. Time I haven't got to spare.'

'That's because you obviously haven't had a *disposable person* in your life who's any good,' he countered, holding her gaze until he saw the blush climb up her cheekbones. Nothing was easy with her. He couldn't remember coming across someone who felt so damned challenging and it was clear that talking the talk wasn't going to cut any ice when it came to impressing her. He'd have to try a more practical approach.

He stood up and walked round the table towards her and

rinsed his mug out at the sink. The heady floral scent of her French perfume made his senses reel.

'Come on, then,' he said, leading the way back to his room. 'If you need to get your damn stock.'

'Back to bed, is it, now?' she called after him.

'Well, I'm hardly going to get any sleep now with you clattering in and out, am I? Tell me what needs shifting and I'll give you a hand.'

His third navigation of the narrow stairwell and of all the bloody people to bump into when he was loaded down with boxes of knickers.

Isaac slung his duffel bag over his other shoulder and stared.

'You're back, then,' Alex said, stating the obvious.

'What the hell are those? And that?'

He pointed out the clear polythene clothes cover hanging over Alex's arm, through which peacock-blue satin and feathers were visible.

'It's a negligee,' Alex said. Since he'd moved in with a gang of women it felt as if a whole new world of vocabulary had opened up. 'And these are ladies' knickers.'

'*Seriously?*' Isaac pulled a shocked face. 'I leave the country for a couple of weeks and suddenly you're the authority on women's underwear. Is there something you're not telling me?'

For Pete's sake.

'I'm moving some stock for the girl who lives downstairs. *Lived* downstairs,' he corrected. 'She's taken Poppy's boxroom. Long story. She runs an underwear shop.'

Lara chose that moment to back out of the flat door behind him with an armful of lacy bras.

'Lara, this is Isaac.'

She nodded at him, squeezed past them on a cloud of delicious perfume and disappeared down the stairs. Isaac watched her go.

'I take it all back,' he said, clapping Alex on the shoulder. 'Nice work.'

'It's not like that,' he said. He was beginning to wonder what the hell it *was* like.

CHAPTER SIX

LARA HAD DECIDED on a pale pink fitted dress that she'd designed herself, hoping it would hit the right note of old-school
Hollywood glamour, and teamed it with heels that would kill her
feet after a couple of hours but which gave the perfect impression. Drinks and nibbles were laid out on a temporary table in
the middle of the shop, fairy lights were in place and switched
on, lending a soft girly note to the shop floor. Every item of
stock was lovingly hung or folded in exactly the right place.
Fliers had been distributed everywhere she could think of. All
that was left to do now was wait, and hope she would be buried in the rush of customers.

Her stomach was a knot of tension as she unlocked the shop
door and positioned the stand-up sign on the pavement outside.
The pink and black helium balloons fastened to it bobbed in
the evening breeze.

She leaned back against the counter. Nothing yet. Worry
began to gnaw at her insides that this had all been a crazy idea,
that she'd sunk her entire savings into a venture that would
never get off the ground, no matter how hard she worked. She
struggled to crush it back down as she stared at her perfect but
deserted shop floor and then Poppy and Alex were sweeping

into the shop, followed by a couple of other fire-station residents. Two minutes later and a group of women dressed for the office crowded in, clearly on their way home from work. She noticed Alex pouring champagne into glasses and managed a smile at last. Worry was gone, the shop was buzzing and she was on her way.

Poppy, standing in the middle of the shop, leaned around Alex and pinched a breadstick, dunked it in one of the bowls of dip and ate it. Next thing he knew she was standing still and staring at the table, which was covered in bite-size nibbles.

'You helped Lara with the food?'

She stared at him with an incredulous expression and he ran a defensive hand through his hair. Somewhere along the line, helping Lara shift a few boxes of stock had graduated today into collecting a case of sale or return champagne and helping her organise the food. After all, what else did he have to be doing? Lying in bed staring at four walls? Walking or running aimlessly around Notting Hill?

'No, not really,' he evaded.

'Don't deny it! That's your signature dip. The one with the secret recipe that you always said you'd take to the grave.' As if to confirm it to herself she fumbled another breadstick from the pot and used it to lever an enormous scoop of dip into her mouth.

He shrugged and grabbed a cheese tartlet so he wouldn't have to look at her knowing grin.

'What's the big deal?'

'No big deal. Just that the last time I clocked your views on Lara's lingerie business you weren't quite so enthusiastic.' She took a sip of her pink champagne. '*Tart's boudoir*, wasn't it?' she said.

He looked at her in exasperation and saw the smile on her face, knew she was teasing. She touched his arm and leaned in.

'She's lovely, Alex. Makes a nice change.'

'Yeah, well, it would do. Except it's not like that. We're friends.'

She waved across the shop floor at Izzy, who'd just arrived.

'God knows what you've been doing traipsing round half the bars in Notting Hill as if your life depended on it,' she said with ill-hidden disapproval, putting her empty glass down. 'Friends is a bloody good start.'

Question was, would friends be enough?

He had to hand it to Lara: she was good at what she did.

He'd watched her for the last half hour, moving effortlessly from customer to customer, greeting people with a smile as they entered the softly lit shop from the cold darkness of the street outside. Nothing was too much trouble. Determination to make the venture a success was obvious in her every move.

'So you can offer tailored running classes?' the dark-haired woman at his elbow said. 'Would that be as part of a group or is it on a one-to-one basis?'

He tore his eyes away from Lara, who was holding up a raspberry lace vest and smiling on the other side of the shop.

'Either,' he said distractedly.

Whatever Lara had said at the playground, she'd obviously given him a great sales pitch. He'd been inundated with thirty-something women asking him about personal training, certainly enough inquiries to demonstrate that he could have a viable business here, if he chose to pursue it.

It felt vaguely against the natural order of things to be handing out his phone number to women when he had no intention of going to bed with them. Exhausted with their questions, he glanced around for an escape route and realised Tori had entered the shop while he was preoccupied. Just what he needed. She couldn't have timed it better if she'd tried. He immediately excused himself from the crowd of women, and headed straight over to her via the counter, where he took a couple of fresh glasses of pink champagne.

She looked up at him as she flipped randomly through the clothes rail near the door.

'You look tired,' he said, handing her one of the glasses.

Truth be told he was quite taken aback by the change in her demeanour since he'd last seen her at Izzy's house party. That had been over a month ago now and she'd been full of enthusiasm about her fabulous new boyfriend.

'Just for future reference,' she said, taking an enormous slug of champagne, 'when you say "you look tired" to a woman, what she actually hears is "you look like crap".'

He laughed.

'You don't look like crap. You never have.'

She raised her glass in acknowledgement. She was the life and soul of every party she ever went to and yet here she was looking through the rails by herself in the corner. Even the stripes in her hair seemed less vibrant than usual. He'd known her long enough to pick up immediately that something wasn't right. Maybe there was trouble in paradise.

'You've got it bad,' Tori commented.

He stood back a little.

'Got what bad?'

She gave him an exasperated look.

'Lara,' she said, making his stomach do a crazy backflip. 'I've been watching you for the last five minutes. For Pete's sake, Alex, we've known each other since we were kids. I've got eyes. I can tell.'

'How can you tell?'

'You mean besides the fact you're actually *attending* a party in a ladies' knicker shop? Let me think...' She tapped one finger against her jaw in an exaggerated gesture of consideration. 'You can't take your eyes off her. And last time we met you tried to resurrect our friends-with-benefits agreement but you haven't so much as given me a second glance so far tonight. Don't suppose you want to revisit that conversation now?'

He had absolutely no inclination whatsoever to do that. And

having it pointed out to him brought any delusions about how much he liked Lara crashing down around his ears. He had zero interest in pursuing Tori, or anyone else for that matter. Tori was waiting for an answer, an expectant look on her face. *Awkward.* He spread his hands apologetically.

'Tori, I'd love to but—'

She punched the air in a gesture of triumph.

'There you go. I rest my case.'

For all the jokey posturing he still thought for a moment that there was a hint of disappointment in her smile, but of course he had to be mistaken. She'd made herself quite clear at Izzy's party. Mark was, for her, the real deal. The *benefits* part of their friendship was, for her, well and truly over with.

'It's not like that,' he protested. 'She thinks I'm only after one thing and, to be perfectly honest, I'm not sure I'm up to offering more than that right now.'

He could see from Tori's smile that he wasn't fooling either of them. They'd always had an easy confidence like this; he knew he could trust her.

'I'm damaged goods, Tori,' he said at last. 'I don't want to put that on her.'

He watched over Tori's shoulder as Lara crossed the shop towards them, smiling and chatting to customers, working the room like an expert. Tori moved a pace sideways to block his view and grab his full attention.

'That's such crap, Alex,' she said. 'Damaged goods? For Pete's sake, everyone has a past. We've all got baggage, and you've decided that she'd make a judgement call about yours without even *asking* her opinion. That's really not fair, is it?' She turned away from him and began flipping through a rail of pastel silk dressing gowns. He watched as she rejected each one. 'Take your time, get to know her properly and show her there can be more between the two of you than just sex,' she said. 'You're here, aren't you? Offering support, helping her out. I'd say that's a step in the right direction.'

Lara finally reached them and Tori dropped her voice quickly and held up a short pink silk nightie.

'Have you got anything…*edgier*?' Tori asked her.

After a while smiling made your cheeks ache, and it really should come a lot more naturally based on the fact the launch was turning out to be a fantastic success. The turnout was brilliant, the buzz around her stock delighted her, and she'd already made lots of sales.

Lara caught herself looking over at Alex yet again and dragged her eyes back to the counter, forced herself to focus on processing the sale and talking to the customer. He'd made a real effort on her behalf this last couple of days, while taking great care to keep things on a friendly level between them. No more flirting or invading her personal space. She'd begun to wonder if he was trying to impress her, somehow show that she meant more to him than his usual conquests, maybe even prove that his interest in her went beyond disposable fling. Helping her shift her stock, for example, even pitching in with the catering. She hadn't expected that, hadn't expected him to *cook*, for Pete's sake!

Now it seemed that all he'd been doing was passing the time because, let's face it, he had nothing better to do.

He'd spent the early part of the evening surrounded by prospective fitness clients; she'd picked up snippets of the conversation herself every time she walked past him and she was secretly delighted at his new positivity. He'd also turned out to be a brilliant side attraction to her designs. Note to self: keep a hot guy on the shop floor at all times to maximise female footfall. And then somewhere in the last twenty minutes or so, Tori had arrived, and suddenly networking for a prospective fitness business seemed to have gone out of the window. She could see them in her peripheral vision, talking quietly, in each other's personal space. They obviously knew each other *extremely* well.

And that was when the unhappy churning in Lara's stomach had kicked off.

Now Tori stood at the counter paying for a beautiful but undeniably racy basque and French knickers set in black silk, decorated with intricate lace and feathers, and some lace-topped silk stockings.

Poppy, looking on, sighed wistfully as Lara wrapped the delicate garments in pink tissue paper.

'It must be lovely to have someone in mind when you buy this kind of thing,' she said. 'They are *so* beautiful. Not that I need anything like that.' She nodded towards the nightwear rail on the other side of the shop. 'I'm going to buy a pair of those silk pyjamas.'

'They're so gorgeous, aren't they?' Tori said. 'Not that there's any point in me looking at them. Silk pyjamas would be a bit run of the mill for Mark's taste, no matter how lovely.' There was a resigned edge to her tone. 'In Mark's opinion, the saucier, the better.'

'All of this is for Mark's benefit, then?' Alex said, joining them.

Lara's stomach gave another twist at his obvious interest in Tori's relationship. First he'd spent ages talking quietly to her in the corner and now this. Try as she might to deny it, maybe dismiss it as first-night nerves, deep down she knew perfectly well what it was and she might as well face facts.

She was jealous.

'How are things with Mark?' Concern showed on Poppy's face. 'It feels like we've hardly seen you recently. Is everything OK?'

'Of course!'

Tori's smile was a little too broad, her tone a little too light-hearted to really sound genuine. Poppy was waiting for her to elaborate, as she always did. Instead she simply handed over her credit card to Lara. For the first time in history, it seemed, Tori was reluctant to talk about herself.

* * *

Lara's feet ached inside the skyscraper heels but she couldn't have cared less. Poppy had left a while ago with Izzy, each of them carrying a pink and black ribbon-tied carrier bag. Tori had disappeared back home to Mark. But even after all the potential fitness clients had gone, Alex had stayed. From beginning to end he'd been there for her shop launch, not giving it a miss or dropping in for a grudging half hour or so because she'd cajoled him into it. His support had gone above and beyond a favour. With the shop launch occupying every spare space in her mind, she hadn't allowed herself to consider what, if anything, *that* might mean. Maybe he was just being polite. Maybe he had nothing better to do.

It was full dark now outside and cold, a little past nine. She supposed he would go straight on to the pub now. Or the bar. Or wherever it was he disappeared to during his evenings out. The thought brought a twist of disappointment, which had no place amid her euphoria at the way the evening had gone.

She focused her mind on her work. All that was left to do now was tidy the shop and cash up. Alex carried the pavement sign in from the darkness of the street.

'Thanks for all your help today,' she said, crossing to the counter breezily to avoid looking at him. 'It's been a fantastic success. You can get off now. I'll just cash up and tidy round a bit.'

The shop floor seemed suddenly still and quiet after the buzz of the evening. His voice came from behind her.

'I'll stay while you lock up and then I'll walk you back.'

So she'd been wrong about him finishing the evening with his usual routine. Her stomach gave a slow and deliberate flip at that throwaway comment and what it might mean if she let it.

'There's no need.'

She heard his exasperated intake of breath.

'It's pitch dark out there and I assume you'll be carrying your takings? Don't argue.'

She moved around the shop, tidying up. Just turning the sign on the door around to read 'Closed' gave her a spark of happiness. This was *her* business, *her* shop. She'd worked so hard for this evening and it had gone well. She was acutely aware of him beside her as she cashed up and put the takings in her bag. He made her feel protected, cared about, and that touched her on a level she rarely allowed anyone to reach. She'd allowed that to happen, of course, accepting his help when she took help from no one. There was danger inherent in that, but she'd believed herself immune to it because she wasn't interested in the quick shallow flings he favoured. Now he'd moved the goalposts, his usual routine and line-up of conquests interrupted, and as a result her opinion of him was no longer such a great defence. Watching him with Tori had shown her she liked him a lot more than she admitted, to him and to herself.

Now that some of the stress of the project had been alleviated her consciousness of him seemed to have increased a hundredfold.

'It's been a huge success,' Lara said. Her eyes sparkled and she looked absolutely radiant in the soft pink lighting of the shop. Alex's heart turned over softly. He waited while she flicked the shop lights off and locked up and then she was next to him, walking the icy pavement in the clear night air.

'You seem to get on well with Tori,' she said after a moment.

His interest sharpened instantly that she'd even noticed.

'I've known her a long time,' he said. 'She used to come and stay with us in the school holidays when Poppy and I were kids.' He paused. 'We've dated on and off over the years. Actually, not even dated really, more ended up together when both of us happened to be free. Nothing heavy.'

She uttered a little laugh.

'Nothing ever *is* heavy with you, is it?'

He considered that for a moment, dug his hands deep in his pockets as they walked.

'You have to understand what my life was like, in the army. I was away so much, and I put so much of myself into it that there wasn't much left for anything or anyone else. And it's a very regimented way of living. For as long as I can remember I've had someone else to answer to—be it a housemaster at school or a senior officer. Suddenly having all this freedom was weird. I could do whatever I wanted, whenever I wanted. I'd had years of heavy. I decided to make up for lost time.'

Silence for a moment.

'So is that what you were doing? Tonight with Tori. Making up for lost time?'

His heart was picking up the pace tentatively.

'No, we were just catching up. That side of things was never such a big deal and it's in the past now. We're friends, nothing more.'

'Because she's with Mark?'

'Not just that, no. What's with all the questions?' He threw caution aside with a throwaway comment that he could pass off as a joke if he needed to. 'Jealous?'

'No!'

Her immediate sharp denial told him all he needed to know and tendrils of hope began to climb through him.

A pause.

'Just interested,' she qualified.

'It might have escaped your notice but I haven't been out with anyone recently, Tori included. It's kind of lost its charm.'

'Why's that?'

'Isn't it obvious?' he said, exasperated at last by the interrogation. 'Do you think I make a habit of hanging around ladies' clothes shops? Don't you think I'd rather be out at the pub right now, keeping it simple? I've spent my whole life answering to other people, living by the rules, and these last few weeks have been the first time in my life I've been free to live it up without regard for anyone else. And now I find I don't bloody *want* to. I'd rather be chatting to a gang of women and drinking pink champagne if it means being with you.' He stared up at the sky. 'What have you done to me?'

For a moment there was silence and he chanced a glance sideways. She wasn't looking troubled or as if she was gearing up to give another rendition of her rejection speech. She was smiling up at him and that was all the encouragement he needed. He stopped walking, tugged her into his arms and kissed her.

His room back at the flat was channelling its usual sparse military as Alex crossed the room to close the curtains. The soft glow from the bedside light highlighted the ordered shelves and perfectly made bed.

'This room is in dire need of soft furnishings…' Lara began as he moved back towards her, and then he stopped her mouth with a kiss and all thoughts of décor disappeared from her mind like smoke. He cradled her face in both hands, his thumbs stroking her jaw softly as he caught the curve of her lips in his, easing them apart and caressing her with his tongue. Sparks of heat spread slowly through her body to melt in her stomach and tingle between her legs. His shoulders were huge and broad, tightly muscled. She let her hands slide up his chest and around his neck, let her fingertips slip through his hair as he curled huge arms around her. Reservations about disposable relationships melted from her consciousness; they required presence of mind, and the all-encompassing force of her physical response to him had swept that away. Her past relationships had never stifled her ability to keep her head, not like this. What was it about him that made her rational mind switch off?

Her perfume filled his senses.

It was like unwrapping the most decadent of luxury gifts. Layer by gorgeous layer, velvet, lace, silk, crystals. He found the zip at the nape of her neck and slid it smoothly down to the base of her spine. The silk dress slipped easily from her shoulders and fell into a soft gleaming pool at her feet. Beneath it he found a slip so thin it was almost translucent. The soft glow of the lamp on his bedside table gave her skin a creamy sheen against its peach silk and he caught his breath. He was used to living in the roughest of conditions and everything about her exuded luxury, the decadent scent of her skin, the soft slinky fabrics unfamiliar beneath his fingers. There was a femininity about her that was so intoxicating it made his senses reel.

He slipped the thin straps of her slip off her shoulders, and followed his progress with soft kisses, tracing her collarbone, moving lower. Her skin was as smooth and flawless as the silk clothes she wore. Beneath the slip there was a delicate lace bra, and he moved his lips across its roughness to suck her nipples gently through the gossamer-thin fabric. She moaned softly and arched her back, and desire surged through his body at her reaction. He slipped the straps of her bra off her shoulders as her fingertips found the buttons of his shirt and pushed it from his shoulders, then she slid her hands lower to tug the button of his jeans, remove them and free his erection. Her fingertips played lightly over his length, making nerves flutter softly in his groin, and he caught her hand before he could lose control. Curling an arm around her waist, he lowered her to the bed, and there she lay before him in the soft lamplight, the beautifully cut bra and knickers highlighting her curves perfectly. Her underwear was made to be seen, and he found her self-confidence in her body intoxicating.

He let his hands play over her body, exploring, revelling in the hitch of her breath as his fingertips found the silky skin of her inner thighs, in the tensing of her body as he teased his fingers beneath the soft lace of her panties, stroking her apart and then sliding two fingers inside her. She gasped against his neck as he found the sensitive nub at the very core of her and circled it lightly with his thumb as his fingers picked up a deliberately slow rhythm. With his free hand he cupped her breast, pinching the hard point of a nipple lightly between his fingers, pushing her slowly higher until she tensed against him as she found her climax.

A moment passed as she lay curled against him, and then she tipped her head back and found his mouth with hers, her tongue slipping softly against his, firing him up even further. Then she leaned upwards, moving above him, her blonde hair silky against his cheek as her lips moved to his neck. Then lower still. He failed to stop himself tensing as her kisses strayed towards the ruined skin on the left-hand side of his chest, his fists clenching tightly at his sides. He hadn't given it a thought before, hadn't cared what any of his partners since the accident might think about him.

She mattered.

She was so beautiful, so perfect, and the thought that she might find him repellent filled him with sudden dread.

Her progress didn't falter. The line of kisses continued softly over his chest as if the twisted and puckered skin weren't even there. Relief washed over him, and with it desire for her that swept away all restraint. In one swift movement he turned her gently on her back, then leaned away briefly to find a condom in the drawer to one side of the bed.

Lara's heart thundered so fast and hard that she fancied he might hear it. As he slowly circled her slick entrance with his rigid erection she wanted him so much that she raised her hips from the bed, trying to take control and push him forward, yet he made her wait, teasing her until she thought she might cry out before he finally thrust forward, taking her in one deep fluid movement. His hands found hers on either side of her head, twining her fingers in his own as he found his rhythm, thrusting forward smoothly again and again, all the while holding her gaze with his own until she could hold back no longer and she cried her pleasure against his neck as he took her over that delicious edge. A moment later and his body tensed against her own as he followed her.

As her breathing evened she curled her body against him, tugging the blanket free of its perfect hospital corners and snuggling into him deliciously, already her thoughts breaking up into sleep.

Faint notes of her perfume still clung to her hair and Alex closed his eyes and breathed them in. Her fingers entwined in his, and he felt a sense of peace that had eluded him since he'd arrived home.

For the first time in weeks he didn't fight sleep when it came. Big mistake.

CHAPTER SEVEN

IT STARTED WITH a couple of shivers as he lay next to her. Not enough to drag her fully back to consciousness from the delicious deep, sated sleep, but just enough for awareness of his presence to seep in, for the deliciousness of the previous evening to surface in her mind and make her stomach flutter before she sank back down into slumber.

And then there it was again. Soft muttering. This time she opened her eyes and frowned in the dim light of the very early morning. She was curled snugly against Alex, his arm curled protectively around her, her head nestled comfortably in the hollow beneath his jaw. She inhaled the warm, musky scent of his body. The feeling of warmth and safety warmed her to her toes.

She moved up onto one elbow and screwed her eyes up, looking down at his face in the semi-darkness with its strong bone structure. No longer pinned down by her, he suddenly flailed his arms and shouted aloud, making her jump, and she scrambled into a sitting position. Her mind backtracked madly to the day they met—had it really only been a week or so ago? He'd fallen asleep in her flat while she worked. His sleep had been disturbed then too.

She leaned across and clicked on the lamp on the bedside table. Deep in sleep, he didn't wake. And little wonder—he was clearly so sleep-deprived that once sleep had him in its grasp it wouldn't let go easily. Worry twisted in her chest as she watched a frown cross his face. Beads of perspiration shone on his brow. Muttering kicked back in, louder this time. Vague, garbled words, none of it intelligible.

Unable to bear the anguished twisting of his body a moment longer, she reached a hand out to shake his shoulder, and when that didn't work she began patting his cheek lightly.

'Alex?' she ventured.

His arms flew back against the headboard and a strangled shout that was leaning towards a scream left his lips. In a panic, Lara did the only thing she could think of.

The dream had Alex right in its dark grasp, fear and despair pelting through his veins as he staggered through the smoke, tasting its acrid bite at the back of his throat as he tried to call out for Sam, desperately searching for him and for their driver.

And then a sudden flood of icy coldness dashed full-force into his face and he was scrambling to sit up, disorientated, water dripping from his face onto the sheets. He screwed his eyes up and tried to focus in the unexpected bright light.

'What the hell...?' he spluttered. The fragments of the dream were still whirling in his mind, his heart pounding thickly in his chest.

His eyes slowly began to adjust. Poppy's flat. His bedroom. Present day. Lara was sitting a few feet away from him on the bed, the sheet clutched against her chest, the empty glass from his bedside table in her hand and an apologetic look on her face that did nothing to mask the underlying fright.

'I tried shaking you,' she said apologetically. 'You were muttering in your sleep and thrashing about. Nothing worked. And then you really shouted and I kind of acted on reflex.'

Her voice trailed away. Her hair lay in loose waves over her bare shoulders and her china-blue eyes were wide with worry. She looked utterly beautiful and hideous shame boiled through his veins as he comprehended what had happened. Making love to her had lulled him into such a state of euphoric hope that he'd stupidly thought he might have beaten off some demons. What a fool he was for thinking he might have turned a corner with his nightmares just because Lara was in his bed. What the hell must she think of him, crying out in his sleep like a baby?

His flailing mind chose that moment to treat him to a hideous memory of his father, one of thousands of similar memories, berating him as a seven-year-old for crying as he was decamped back to school yet again. His face burned in spite of the cold water that still clung to his cheeks. Emotional displays were shameful, something to be avoided at all costs, and avoiding them had become second nature. When he was awake. Apparently his unconscious self still needed a few lessons in self-control.

He attempted to joke his way out of it.

'Your reflex reaction is a bit sledgehammer-to-crack-a-nut, isn't it? Remind me not to get on the wrong side of you.' His hair was damply sweaty as he ran a hand through it.

She didn't smile. Her pretty face was full of sympathy, fuelling the humiliation all the more. He couldn't bear to have her pity him.

'What's going on with you, Alex? Is this to do with your injuries? The roadside bomb? Poppy mentioned how difficult it's been.' She put her hand on his arm gently. 'You can talk to me, you know.'

'You've been discussing me with Poppy on the quiet?' Mortification kicked up another notch.

'Not in a negative way,' she said. 'She was concerned about you, that's all. She could see we were becoming friends.'

'It's nothing to do with Poppy or anyone else,' he snapped. 'There's nothing to talk about.' It came out more strongly than he'd meant it and he caught the tiny recoil on her face. She took her hand away and cut her eyes away from his. He forced his voice into a light tone. 'So I had a bit of a disturbed night—I probably drank too much at the launch. No big deal.'

He avoided her eyes, instead swinging his legs off the bed and putting on shorts. The silence in the room was heavy with tension. He needed to get out of here for a few minutes, calm down. Then when he came back the moment would be over with.

'I'll be right back,' he mumbled, heading out to the bathroom.

Lara watched the door close behind him and gritted her teeth against the wave of miserable disappointment churning in her stomach. Two words: *Unrealistic expectations*. Had she really thought that after his romantic declaration of feelings for her, followed by the most unbelievable stomach-melting night, things might actually be rainbows and butterflies from now on?

No. But it might have been nice if they could get past the morning after before her hopes were dashed. She of all people should know better than to expect more. This was *her* life after all. Rainbows and butterflies had never featured before—why the hell should they be putting in an appearance now?

Her mind was working overtime. There was more to this than a one-off or a glass too many of pink champagne. From what she'd seen and heard of him last night he certainly hadn't drunk that much. Her thoughts kept going back to the unsettled sleep he'd had back on the sofa in her flat. And now something else clicked into place in her mind. His major overuse of caffeine. The odd hours he kept—sleeping in the daytime, up and about half the night. Try to palm this off as a one-off or a phase, he might, but she knew better.

Whatever this was, he apparently didn't have enough regard for her to be straight with her about it. And really—was that such a big ask? She pushed her fingers back into her hair, trying to think clearly. The way he'd helped her with the launch, their growing friendship, the way he'd been with her last night. Had all that just been a stepping stone to bed after all? Had he just upped the ante after she'd knocked him back after their run, playing the game, pretending he wanted to get to know her until he got what he wanted? Anything deeper than that was apparently not on the agenda.

Self-preservation kicked sharply in and she threw the covers back from the bed. She padded quietly around the room, picking up her clothes, finding her shoes, all the while squashing the feeling of hurt stupidity for thinking there might be more to this than just sex.

In the bathroom Alex filled his palms with cold water and held them against his face, wondering how the hell to play this now. He could kick himself for falling asleep. So wrapped up in the deliciousness of having Lara cuddled up to him, he'd relaxed for once, not even sparing a thought for his nightmares. He was filled with hot shame at what he might have done or said in his sleep; it had certainly disturbed her enough that she'd lobbed water over him. In any other situation it might have been funny.

His immediate reaction was to back off. At speed. He'd intended to have fun for a while, not to get in so deep with a girl that he actually cared what they thought of him. In getting to know Lara he'd somehow lost sight of that objective. The sensible thing now would be to draw a line under the whole thing. Go back to being nothing more than neighbours who made small talk. Yet the thought of not seeing her again except in passing, of just being acquaintances, made his stomach lurch with disappointment.

He gripped the edges of the sink and looked down at his hands. He would have to find another way to deal with this instead of ending it. He just needed to put in a bit of distance. His best option was surely to fob her off, dismiss the nightmare as one of those things, and then find a way to make sure it didn't happen again.

He took a deep breath as he walked back down the hall and pushed open the bedroom door.

She was dressed. Or at least dressed enough to indicate the

night was well and truly over. She wore her pink frock from the launch party and the beautiful undergarments hung over one arm. Her shoes were in her other hand. Worse, her face was full of disappointment. Clearly in him. And who could blame her? Had he really assumed she would still be interested in him after this? Naturally being woken up to his girly screaming had put her off.

'You're leaving,' he said, stating the obvious. His stomach churned with despair at the realisation that he'd blown this.

'I should never have stayed,' she said. 'Last night was a mistake.'

'There's no need for you to go,' he said quickly. 'I'm sorry if I overreacted or scared you. It was just a dream, just one of those things. This doesn't normally happen.' OK, so that was stretching the truth more than a little but he'd worry about that later; if he had to stay awake twenty-four-seven from now on to hide his weakness from her then he would manage it somehow. He held a hand out to her. 'Come back to bed.'

She rolled her eyes at the ceiling.

'So you want to dumb down this whole thing between us until all it's about is sex,' she said. 'I don't know why I'm even *surprised*.' She took a step nearer the door, then turned back and flung a hand up in a gesture of exasperation. 'It's not the bloody *dream* that's the problem. It's your reaction. It's the way you've just fobbed me off and then suggested bed as if sex might just divert me from getting to know you on any deeper level than that. *A bit of a disturbed night?* It was way more than that. And you can try and pass it off as a blip or a one-off if you want, but I'm not an idiot. This isn't the first time it's happened, is it? What about when you fell asleep back in my flat—you had a nightmare then too, didn't you? And that's why you're always trying to stay awake. Why didn't you just say you're having trouble sleeping? Don't you think I *care* about that?'

He groped for an answer that wouldn't make him look a total arse. He'd thought he'd got away with the sleep disturbance in the flat that day. She'd never mentioned it since. It felt suddenly as if he were under the spotlight and defensiveness kicked in.

'What is this—twenty questions?'

Disappointment filled the blue eyes at his curt tone.

'No, this is me wondering why you're not being straight with me and realising I already know the answer. You said it yourself the other day. You've never been with a disposable person who's any good. That's how you see yourself, how you see this, isn't it? A quick fling. OK, you might have had to jump through a few extra hoops this time to get your way, but you got there in the end, didn't you? Like an idiot I thought there might be more to us than that.'

She headed for the door while he stared after her in horror, seeing how the conclusion she'd reached must look so obvious to her in the light of his previous behaviour, his string of one-night-only girlfriends.

'There *is* more to us than that,' he called after her.

She paused. Turned to look back at him from the open door-way.

'OK, then, prove it,' she said. 'Sit down with me now and be straight with me about what just happened.'

He stared at her, groping for something to say that would turn the situation around and failing. Because he knew exactly what she'd think of him if he sat down opposite her and told her all about his night terrors. About the bomb blast and his broken promise to look out for a nervous soldier who looked up to him. About his failure to be of any use whatsoever to those whose safety was ultimately his responsibility. The silence yawned between them until she shook her head.

'I've got work to do,' she snapped.

The door clicked shut behind her.

It didn't have the best flouncing-out value when you were only going feet away down the hall but she'd given it her all anyway, cutting her eyes sharply away from him and slamming the door behind her. At least the walk of shame was only a few paces. Bloody Alex. She should be euphoric after yesterday's success but instead she was filled with stomach-wrenching disappointment.

Back in the boxroom she sank onto the narrow bed and rubbed her scratchy eyes with her fingers. The clock on the dresser told her it was a little before six. Five minutes later and she was heading into the shower, mind forcibly refocused back where it should have been all along. Her work.

Coffee in Ignite accompanied by an enormous *pain au chocolat* that would undoubtedly go straight to her hips, then she would head in to open the shop. She ate it anyway, because the size of her hips was irrelevant now that she wasn't intending to get naked with a man again any time soon. Had to go and sleep with him, didn't she? She should have known better. She stared at her laptop screen and focused hard on updating her blog with photos from the launch. Anything to crush the feeling of stupidity, and the underlying prickle of concern for him that he really didn't deserve, because however hard he might try to brush it off those nightmares were no picnic.

Somehow the concern was worst of all because it told her she actually *cared* about him.

Try as she might to concentrate on writing a blog post, her eyes kept wandering to the door. Which of course was insane because he hadn't exactly beaten the boxroom door down upstairs to try and talk to her. She'd heard nothing from him from the moment she slammed his bedroom door. And why would she? It all fitted. He'd got what he wanted—why would he want anything more to do with her? The only difference between her and all his other walk-of-shame girls was that she'd slammed the door on the way out instead of kissing him goodbye.

As she polished off the last of the pastry, not really wanting it but grimly eating it out of principle, the door of the café opened and her stomach gave a disorienting flip. She bit her lip hard enough to hurt because her eyes might have been glued to the door but she hadn't for one moment thought he actually might walk through it. He crossed the room towards her via the counter, where she heard him put in his usual order of coffee strong enough to strip wallpaper. And then he came to a standstill next to her table, by which time her heart was thundering so loudly in her ears that it was a wonder she could hear him when he spoke.

'I'm sorry,' Alex said.

Her hair was loosely tied at one side, curling over her shoulder, and the porcelain cheekbones were without their usual touch of colour. She looked tired and fragile. *His fault.* A prickle of guilt spiked inside him and he wondered briefly if it would be better to just leave her be instead of subjecting her to his attempts to move on with his life. Then Tori's words from the previous evening flitted through his head. *We've all got baggage, and you've decided that she'd make a judgement call about yours without even* asking *her opinion. That's really not fair...*

Lara looked up at him, pen clenched in one hand, face carefully neutral. Her posture was stiff and guarded, giving nothing away.

'For what?'

'For everything. Can I sit down?'

A pause. And then she nodded at the opposite chair. He pulled it out and sat opposite her, looked down at the table for a moment, gathering his thoughts, then looked up and into her cautious blue gaze.

'I know how it looks, but you're wrong,' he said. 'This is not just about a one-night stand or a quick fling for me. I told you that last night and I meant it.'

She held his gaze levelly, giving nothing away.

'But that didn't make it any easier for me to tell you about my nightmares. What the hell would you have thought if I'd dropped in a quick warning before we went to sleep? If I'd told you that I might freak out somewhere in the small hours? You'd think I was a complete nutter.'

He looked back down at the table.

'Truth is, I'd had such a great time last night that for once I didn't stress about going to sleep. I didn't think I could have a nightmare when I was feeling so…well, so relaxed.'

He glanced up to see her expression soften a little. He tried hard not to see it as a sympathy look. If he did that, he might not be able to continue.

'I haven't told anyone about the dreams. Not even Poppy. I didn't want to worry her. It's my problem, no one else's and I'm dealing with it in my own way,' he said.

The counter girl chose that moment to walk past and place a supersized mug of black coffee in front of him. He nodded his thanks as he took a huge slug of it, relishing its strong bitter taste and waiting for the buzz to kick in and sharpen his senses.

She nodded at the mug, a cynical expression on her face.

'That's you dealing with it your own way, is it? Overdosing on caffeine and avoiding sleep.'

'Short-term management,' he said. 'In actual fact things have improved. Already the dreams are getting less frequent, I just need to give it more time.'

Not strictly true. They were less frequent because he *slept* less frequently. But he had no wish to undermine the improvement by analysing it too deeply. He was convinced he just needed to give it time. Surely the longer he spent out of the army, the less he would dwell on it, right?

'What are they like? The dreams?' she ventured. Her voice was tentative, as if she was worried he might snap at her.

His stomach churned a little at the question. Verbalising what happened hadn't really been on his agenda when he'd come to find her; he'd simply hoped to apologise and talk her round. But here it was, his chance to prove he was totally on top of this. Totally in control. He gripped the mug of coffee hard in one hand and curled the other into a fist, forced what he hoped was an I'm-in-total-control-of-this neutral expression onto his face.

'They're always the same,' he began, keeping it short. Keeping it *vague*. That was best. 'The explosion, the heat and the smoke. And then this awful sense of disorientation.' He dug his fingernails into his palm and glanced around the café. Chatting customers, background music, *reality*. 'And then I wake up.' He forced a grin. 'Or in this instance, I *get* woken up by being dunked in cold water.'

She smiled back, but the smile was a size too small.

'You scared me half to death,' she said.

'I'm sorry.'

She shook her head slowly.

'It must have been an awful time for you. I can't possibly imagine what it must be like to have that in your head. Have you had any counselling? Don't they offer that kind of thing?'

'I'm not some basket case,' he said defensively.

She rolled her eyes.

'I'm not suggesting you are. I want to help, that's all. I want to understand. I'm not passing judgement.'

He wasn't about to confide in her beyond the most basic level. Better by far to keep things simple between them, to keep it fun. For neither of them to get too attached. Wasn't her independence part of what was so attractive about her? She had her own life, her own agenda that had absolutely nothing to do with him. She was far too preoccupied with her own goals to really *need* him and he found that so appealing about her, that she demanded sole responsibility for her own life.

'I thought you of all people would understand that this is something I want to handle myself,' he said.

An indignant frown touched her eyebrows.

'What's that supposed to mean?'

'Miss I'll Shift My Own Furniture,' he said. 'Didn't you tell me you hated relying on anyone else's help?'

A grin twitched at the corner of her mouth and his spirits lifted. He pressed on.

'Is it so wrong to try and get through it myself first before I drag anyone else into it? It wasn't a personal judgement about you—I haven't told *anyone*.'

'No, it's not so wrong.'

He covered her hand with his, noticing she didn't pull her fingers away.

'Does that mean I'm forgiven?' he said.

She looked up at him through narrowed eyes.

'Depends.'

'On what?'

'That you don't try and hide it from me. Or anything else, for that matter. I need you to be straight with me. And you stop trying to stay awake twenty-four-seven.'

'Anything else?'

'You buy me another pastry.'

'Done.'

CHAPTER EIGHT

NORMAL COUPLE. HE could do that. In those early days when he'd left the army, keeping it casual had been the automatic choice. Freedom to go where he chose, when he chose, with whomever he chose had held a novelty value that was intoxicating after the years of rigid structure in his life. Yet throughout that time of shallow one-night stands and partying, he'd found no real sense of satisfaction. There had still been that uncomfortable sensation of being rootless, of having no direction.

Now he understood why. When it came down to it, he had missed it. The sense of *belonging* that school and the army had provided. He only truly realised that now he was beginning to regain it. He revelled in the sense of direction that the new business gave him, in the steadiness that living with Poppy offered, and now in the happiness that being with Lara brought. Casual really wasn't him. He had a sense of moving forward now instead of living a disposable, inconsequential, limbo life, and he wanted that feeling to stay. Letting his relationship with Lara become steadier was the inevitable next step.

Now that things were sorted between the two of them he felt more certain of that than ever, confident that he'd taken another step towards building a normal life outside the regimens of the army, putting the past further behind him. He'd been frank with

Lara, right? Just a couple of nightmares and he was handling them himself, no biggie. Surely it was only a matter of time now before they disappeared completely.

Girlfriend—*check*. New and promising fitness business—*check*. Place to live that had no bearing on his past—*check*.

A group of people were just drifting into Ignite for wine and tapas as Alex passed them and climbed the stairs to the flat. He'd just finished his very first personal training session—up until now it had all been about assessing fitness levels and planning exercise schedules and diets. Now he'd actually embarked on proper fitness sessions with a couple of clients. Things were moving forward. With every step he insisted to himself that life was back on the right track.

The laughter and chat could be heard as soon as he walked through the door and he followed it to the kitchen. Isaac was sitting at the table, leaning back in his chair with a grin on his face, Poppy was busy at the stove, whirling a huge wok around, and Lara was at the counter opening a bottle of wine.

'You're back again, then, mate,' he said to Isaac, crossing the kitchen and sweeping Lara's blond hair to one side so he could kiss her cheek.

Poppy made retching sounds from the other side of the kitchen.

'What are you, twelve?' he asked her. 'Just because you're perpetually single.'

She shot him a look and turned back to the stove. Lara held up a wine glass and raised her eyebrows but he shook his head and crossed to the fridge instead for an energy drink. Wine was not a good option if you wanted to disprove all suspicion of sleep deprivation. He'd end up falling asleep at the kitchen table.

'How did it go, then?' Lara said. 'Your first full-on personal training session.'

In his experience commanding soldiers was infinitely easier. For a start they didn't question his authority or answer back. Or stop to reapply lipstick. Yet at the same time he couldn't deny it was nice to actually have a sense of worth and purpose again. OK, so it might only be short term, he hadn't absolutely decided where he might go with it yet, but at least he was earning now. At least he could feel he was moving forward. And the more he thought about it, the idea of running some kind of boot-camp-style class was really appealing, dealing with groups of people at a time. Maybe he could try it out on adults first and if that worked think about pitching the idea to schools.

'Challenging,' he said. 'Having my orders questioned at every turn is a new and interesting experience, but yeah.' He shrugged. 'On the whole it went well.'

'I thought I'd cook,' Poppy said. 'Since you've got your first session to celebrate. And Isaac's back, of course,' she added as an afterthought, glancing at him. 'We haven't had a group meal since Izzy left. I'm doing Thai green curry, fragrant rice and a slaw. Lara's bought cakes from the café and Isaac…'

'I've got the drink angle covered,' Isaac said easily. 'Pull up a chair.'

Poppy dished the curry up into huge bowls and joined them around the table.

'How long you staying this time?' Alex asked Isaac, forking up some rice.

Lara noticed Poppy glance up sharply at him from her plate. She could see how it might be annoying that Isaac essentially treated Poppy's flat like a hotel. Things had changed quite a bit now from when Lara had first moved into her studio flat downstairs. Izzy had still been living with Poppy; Tori had been forever dropping in; there were constant parties and girly chats.

Isaac shrugged.

'Couple of days. Depends what comes up.' He winked at Lara. 'No two days are ever the same. I'm heading to Blue later. You should all come along.'

'Blue?' Lara said. What the hell was that?

'Isaac's bars have a colour theme,' Poppy supplied. 'Blue is in Islington.'

'How long have you all known each other?' Lara said. Isaac only seemed to stay over the odd night, despite the fact he was obviously stumping up for the rent. How lovely it must be not to have to think where every penny was coming from. It was clear he and Alex got on like a house on fire. Although, glancing at her, she didn't think Poppy looked quite as comfortable.

Isaac leaned back in his chair, swirling white wine around his glass.

'I've known Alex and Poppy for years,' he said. 'Alex and I were at school together. I used to crash at their place every school holidays. You've no idea the dirt I could dish on the pair of them.'

Out of the corner of her eye, she saw Poppy visibly tense at that comment. Next thing she was on her feet, heading to the fridge with her back to them. She returned to the table with a bottle of water.

'Dirt?' Lara said.

Isaac shrugged easily.

'Nights out, holidays, that kind of thing. Trip of a lifetime to Las Vegas.'

'Hah, you're so funny,' Alex said with tones of deepest sarcasm. She threw him a questioning look and he flung up a hand. 'I blew half my inheritance on an ill-judged week away with him and the guys. Let's just say Lady Luck wasn't in my corner in the casinos.' His tone was throwaway.

He might as well be speaking in some kind of foreign language. Lara had zero comprehension of a world where there was such a thing as an inheritance, let alone a swanky holiday to blow it on.

Isaac topped up their drinks, hovering the neck of the wine bottle briefly over Poppy's glass as she put her hand over it. The camaraderie between him and Alex meant the kitchen was full of laughter as they reminisced. By the time the meal was finished Lara had built up a picture in her mind of a rich childhood and adolescence, of an enormous country pile in the Cotswolds, of posh holidays and a friendship group, all of whom were too cool for school. With every anecdote she felt more and more like a fish out of water. At last Poppy stood up and began clearing plates from the table.

'Want some help?' Isaac offered.

'That's OK, I've got it,' Lara said quickly, getting up. Relief surged through her that the meal was over, closely followed by irritation at herself for being so bothered. This wasn't school. She wasn't the perpetual new girl anymore. Why should she even care whether she fitted in here or not? Living in Notting Hill was a strategic career move, not a popularity test. She opened the dishwasher and started stacking crockery.

'In that case—' Isaac looked at his watch '—I'm heading into the city. The night is young and all that. Anyone want to come along?'

Poppy shook her head immediately.

'I'm on duty in an hour,' she said. 'Night shift. I need to get moving.'

'You go,' Lara said. 'I'll finish clearing up.'

'Laters, then,' Isaac said, holding a hand up and heading out of the door. Moments later the front door of the flat slammed behind him. Poppy headed to her room to get ready to leave for work.

Alex cleared the glasses from the table as Lara wiped the surfaces.

'You were quiet,' he said.

'Was I?' She kept her back to him as she stood at the counter. Her life was a whole different ballgame from his. Apart from the fact they happened to have ended up in the same flat, they had absolutely nothing in common. Their lives were literally miles apart. How could she possibly expect to fit into his world once the first flush of novelty wore off? An unhappy prickle of doubt climbed her spine. How long could a relationship survive before those kinds of fundamental differences started to cause cracks?

'Yes, you were.' He moved across to her at the counter, and tugged her by the hand to sit down next to him. She could see the concerned expression on his face. 'What's up?'

She pitched her tone of voice at light, hoping to make it look as if it really weren't such a big deal. *That's it, Lara. Shrug it off.*

'Your upbringing was just so different from mine,' she said simply. 'Yours and Poppy's. Big family, loads of relatives, friends down for the holidays.' She paused. 'It was just interesting, listening to you all talking about it, reminiscing. I couldn't really relate to any of it.'

He shrugged.

'Yeah, well. It had its downside too,' he said shortly. 'What about you, then? You haven't told me much about your background. Except that your mother taught you how to sew, didn't she?'

'Not my mum. Not exactly,' she said.

She smiled cautiously back at him and took a sip of her wine.

'Foster mum,' she corrected.

'You were fostered?'

He sat up straight; she'd spiked his interest now. Her background had had the ability to do that when she was a kid too. In many a school playground she'd been a new and interesting life form. New starts were hard.

'My mum was very young when she had me.' She watched for his reaction. 'She was only fifteen, just a kid.'

To his credit he didn't flinch, so she carried on.

'She tried her best but she just couldn't look after me properly. It wasn't that she didn't want to, she just didn't have any support. Her own parents weren't much help.' She shrugged. 'Long story short, I ended up being taken into care.'

His face was full of concern and her stomach lurched a little despairingly. So far he'd only seen strong Lara, independent, driven Lara who made things happen for herself. She didn't want to be seen as weak or in need of sympathy.

'And then you were fostered?'

'I was.'

'What about your father?'

She shook her head. *Who?*

'I never knew him. I'm still in touch with my mother, we see each other now and then, but we're not close. We never really had a chance to be. I don't blame her. She had everything working against her and she wasn't much more than a child herself. I didn't have any brothers or sisters, like you have Poppy. It's always been just me.'

'What was your foster mother like?'

Which one? For Lara, there had only been one who mattered. The others didn't deserve a mention; they barely even registered for a thought.

When she thought of that time, the time when she'd at last felt settled, the smile came more easily. 'Her name is Bridget. I went to live with her and her husband and they were lovely. Warm and friendly. Bridget was the one who taught me how to sew—she'd worked for years as a seamstress and she was brilliant at it. She made all her own clothes, toys, soft furnishings, you name it. Up until then I'd drifted through life with no real direction and then suddenly I found something I was good at and someone who was actually interested in me.'

She thought back to the hours she'd spent learning how to shape seams, put in darts, sew button holes. Bridget's endless patience with her stream of questions. The enthusiasm for her new skill that almost bordered on greed in her eagerness to learn more, practise more. 'My whole business has stemmed from there. I did a costume design course at college, got some work experience, then started making my own stuff.'

'Are you still in touch? She must be really proud of you.'

She nodded.

'I see them when I can. Talk on the phone, and visit, that kind of thing. When I hit sixteen and went to college I moved out of their house and found a room to rent. I started building up my own life, looking out for myself, and I've been doing that ever since.'

Alex watched her as she swirled the wine slowly around her glass. Had he ever come across someone so independent, so determinedly self-reliant? It gave a very attractive sense of security to what was happening between them—he was comfortable in the knowledge there was no way her happiness and well-being could ever be totally dependent on *him*. No need for him to worry about things stepping up a notch between them because he knew she could manage perfectly well—and perfectly happily—without him.

'So you can see it was a bit like an alien world to me, listening to you and Poppy and Isaac chat through your childhood,' she said. 'I didn't really know how to engage with that. We're really very different, you and me.'

He could tell by the tone of her voice that she didn't consider that to be a good thing.

'Your childhood sounds idyllic,' she carried on. 'You were so lucky growing up, having this massive family, financial security, a big country home.'

He couldn't hold back a cynical laugh.

'Yeah, well, it might look Pollyanna from the outside, but it's really not.' He lobbed aside his reservations about alcohol and sleep and poured a splash of wine into an empty glass for himself. 'I don't think security and happiness is about having blood relations, not really. Poppy and I are up to our ears in relatives but scraping the bottom of the barrel when it comes to support and family love.' He smiled at her frown. 'Money helps, of course, but up until now I've never been brilliant with that. I got my inheritance at the same time as Poppy but it's mostly gone now. She was the sensible one, investing it in bricks and mortar. I never really thought ahead that far—my whole life revolved around the army. I never thought for a second I might need the money for a back-up plan. Instead I frittered it away on holidays with the lads, lost a whole load of it back there in Las Vegas—Isaac wasn't joking about that. All in the name of fun.'

He looked at her small, indignant face. She'd been up against so much as a kid and she'd triumphed in the face of it. He couldn't help but be impressed by that kind of tenacity. He'd had all the financial trappings and foot-in-the-door family reputation that anyone could want to get him ahead in life. Just look how far she'd got without any of that.

He reached out across the table top and took her hand in his.

'You've pushed yourself to get where you are and that's something to be proud of—you didn't get there on the strength of your family name or your father's reputation. When you look at your business and your shop, at everything you've achieved, you know that you've done all of that on your own. The credit's yours.' He paused. 'I wish I could say that.'

'You can. You were a captain in the army. They don't just hand things like that out on a plate.'

He shrugged cynically.

'I come from an old military family—we go way back. My father has contacts at the highest level. I'd be a fool to think my family's reputation hadn't helped me get where I am.' He paused and swallowed. 'Where I *was*. Unfortunately it doesn't count for much anymore. And since I left the army any interest I did have from my family has melted away. Do you know that since I left hospital my parents haven't visited even once?'

Was it worse, Lara wondered, having all that prospective love and support just sitting there but having it withheld? How was that better than not having it at all? At least she knew where she stood. There was no disappointment because she had no one to be disappointed *in*.

'I guess what I'm saying is that you and I are not so different,' he said. 'It might seem like that on the surface. I've got relatives coming out of my ears and you've got none to speak of, but mine are completely useless. They have nothing to do with my life, no interest in me. We might come at it from different directions, but basically both of us are on our own.'

He downed the glass of wine in one and stood up from the table, his face set. Saying it out loud dragged it out from the recesses of his mind and the familiar taste of bitter disappointment rose in his mouth. For the longest time he'd had institutions in his life to replace what his family lacked. First school, then university, then the army. A circle of long-term friends to give that feeling of belonging. The floundering feeling he'd experienced in those first weeks after discharge from the army, the rootless feeling that he was going it alone, made an unwanted comeback. He'd made inroads since then, settling into Notting Hill with Poppy, finding Lara, finding a new direction in his business plans. The last thing he needed was to revisit that pointlessness.

She looked up at him with a questioning expression and he leaned over to smooth her hair back from her forehead and kiss the creamy softness of her brow.

'I'm going to take a shower,' he said.

Lara's rose-tinted view of his perfect upper-class childhood felt suddenly skewed and her heart twisted a little for him as he left the room. She could tell he was unsettled. All those people in his life to support and love him were really people to live up to or to disappoint. She felt a new and unexpected affinity with Alex, a closeness that she hadn't realised was there. Maybe they weren't so far removed from each other after all. The thought of that brought a surge of heated desire for him deep inside her at a level beyond that provoked by his gorgeous face and his muscular body.

Without thinking what she was doing, she put the dish cloth down on the counter and left the kitchen to walk slowly down the hallway towards the bathroom. The strength of her need for him somehow transcended her usual presence of mind, breaking down her self-control. When had she ever let her guard down like this with a man, revelled in the physical deliciousness of being with someone unfettered by the endless thoughts of self-preservation by which she lived her life?

The thundering sound of water from the shower was audible from outside the door. She tried the door before knocking and it opened smoothly. With Isaac gone and Poppy at work until the morning, he clearly wasn't bothered about privacy. She was. The last thing she wanted was Isaac dropping back and bursting in unexpectedly. She closed the door behind her and twisted the spring lock.

The room was warm and the air heavy and damp with scented steam from the shower. It smelled fresh and spicy and made her heart skip into double time. The undeniably male shower gel, which he used as an antidote, he said, to all the pink and pretty girly toiletries that cluttered every surface in here.

Behind the steamed glass of the shower cubicle she could see the shadow of his huge shoulders tapering down to the tightly muscled torso. Heat began to course through her and pooled tinglingly between her legs. Slowly she stepped out of her clothes and padded barefoot across the cold tile of the floor to slide open the glass door.

She stepped into the shower unit beside Alex as if it were the most natural thing in the world and his initial surprise was quickly followed by a surge of arousal at her smooth nakedness. As the shower spray soaked her blond hair, darkening it, he slid his hands across her wet skin, circling her waist and pulling her tightly against him. He groped for her mouth with his, found it and crushed his lips against hers, hot need for her crashing through him. She knew exactly what she wanted from the moment and she took it on her terms. He found that completely mesmerising about her.

The masculine scent of his shower gel hung on the steamy air, citrus and bergamot filling her senses as she slid her hands over his soapy skin, feeling the rock-hard muscle beneath. He pushed her gently back against the wall, the smooth stone tile pressing cold against her shoulders and butt. His hands were everywhere now, exploring her, moving to cup her breasts, to hold them close together while he gently sucked their hard tips, sending dizzying sparks right through her to burn hotly between her legs.

Warm water sluiced over them as he moved slowly lower, taking his time, trailing a line of kisses softly down the hollow between her breasts, over her flat stomach and lower still. Kneeling before her now in the shower stall, he ran his hand down the length of her legs, and lifted one of her heels until her knee lay supported over his shoulder. Her legs were held firmly apart now, the better to expose her fully to his attention.

Lara leaned her head against the hard tile of the wall, the shower spray missing her face now, instead sluicing in a torrent down her body and over his. Nerve endings jumped and sparked between her legs as he kissed his way up her inner thighs, taking his time, making her wait. Then with one delicate stroke of his tongue he parted her swollen core and she heard her own sharp intake of breath as her head rolled deliciously back and her eyes fluttered shut. He found the sensitive nub and began to circle it softly with his tongue, one hand holding her against his mouth, the other first teasing lower and then sliding two fingers deep inside her in one smooth movement. He seemed attuned to her every response, moving his fingers in a slow and delicious rhythm, caressing her with his tongue until she felt herself climb towards that elusive height of sensation. Losing control, she curled her fingers into his dripping-wet hair and in response he increased his smooth pace until she cried her pleasure at the ceiling.

Before she could fold on her jellified knees into the bottom of the shower stall, waves of deliciousness still coursing through her, he'd slid the glass door of the stall open and grabbed a condom from the cupboard beside the sink. As the water thundered on in the empty stall behind them, he lifted her gently from the shower. Water splashed and pooled across the bathroom floor as he turned her to face the bathroom wall, clasping a firm hand around her waist, the other at her inner thigh. She felt the press of his rigid erection against her slick core and then he was inside her, filling her completely, taking her in long, slow strokes, his muscular torso firm against her back as he swept her wet hair aside and kissed the nape of her neck. The cold, smooth tile of the wall pressed against her hard nipples, her fingers traced marks in the condensation on either side of her face as she began to climb again. With him this time, feeling his breath quicken with every stroke he took. And as he finally tipped her back over that dizzying height of pleasure she felt him cry out his own ecstasy against her bare shoulder.

CHAPTER NINE

SHE LAY CURLED now into the crook of Alex's arm, in the soft pool of light from his beside lamp. His fingers entwined in hers, deliciously warm, sated and comfortable. Her things were starting to trickle into his room. Not much yet, just her robe and a few items of clothing. Funny how it felt like no big deal. Sleeping with Alex every night was spared full-on scary seriousness because she had her own room just down the hall and a separate shelf in the fridge. Not to mention a flat just downstairs that should be ready to move back into in a day or two. Outside the door the flat was quiet; there was no sign of Isaac returning. Then again, by the sound of it, when Isaac partied he didn't do it in small measures.

She frowned a little as she thought of Isaac, recalling Poppy's behaviour at dinner.

'Poppy seems a bit tense around Isaac,' she commented. 'Is there something going on between them?'

She felt him shake his head.

'She seemed OK to me,' he said. 'Fab scoff, as per. She's always been a great cook.'

'Typical brother, you are,' she said, exasperated. 'Completely oblivious. You could have put the atmosphere in that kitchen through a mincer. And Poppy couldn't get out of there fast enough. Honestly, men are so insensitive sometimes.'

He laughed softly into her hair.

'I can be sensitive when I want to be,' he said. She looked up into his grey eyes as he shifted in the bed, turning her gently and leaning up on one elbow to place an arm either side of her head. He tangled his fingers in her hair and kissed her so tenderly she thought her stomach might melt. She wrapped her limbs around his body, loving the fact that he was so tall and broad-shouldered, so heavily roped with muscle. She felt protected. Warm and safe. It wasn't just in the way he was with her in bed, it was in the little things he did, in not allowing her to walk a couple of streets home in the dark, in stepping in to move furniture around for her.

It was a sensation she wasn't used to experiencing, had in fact *avoided* feeling, instead substituting the need for it with her own drive and ambition. Letting herself relax into feeling safe had been something she'd learned to avoid growing up because it usually preceded the figurative rug being jerked out from underneath her. The feeling of contentment, of trusting someone else with her feelings, was something she'd learned to be wary of. She was older now, though, and wiser. She had her own life well and truly under control, providing for herself without the need for anyone else. She told herself this thing with Alex, whatever it was, didn't need to have any detrimental effect on that.

As sleep began to break her thoughts up she cuddled into him and let her guard slip a little. She could afford it.

Alex lay against her, breathing in the sweet scent of her hair in the darkness as she nestled her head beneath his chin, and stared at the ceiling. Through sheer will he held his eyes open, grimly refusing to let the comfort and warmth of his bed, of Lara curled against him, drag him into sleep. He wouldn't be making that mistake again. He listened as her breathing evened and gradually let the stroke of his fingers against the silky skin of her bare shoulder slow until it stilled. She didn't flinch. The room was silent.

Then he added on another twenty minutes just to be sure.

When he was certain she was fully asleep he shifted her gently from his chest and waited quietly while she snuggled into the pillows, then he moved across to the edge of the bed. Smooth, slow movements so as not to disturb her. There was no tripping over random items on the floor or bumping into furniture. When it came to moving in the darkness with stealth, Lara could learn a thing or two from him. He closed the bedroom door quietly behind him and headed to the kitchen, his laptop and a large mug of strong black coffee.

There was a surprising amount of admin and red tape associated with starting up a small business, even a fledgling one like his. At first the personal training thing really hadn't been much more than a way of buying some time, perhaps earning a bit of money while he decided on a proper new direction. Not to mention a way of keeping Lara and Poppy off his back with their seemingly endless career advice and suggestions of how he should be spending his time. Yet this last week, having taken his first couple of one-to-one clients out, talking through their hopes for weight loss and improved fitness and formulating a tailored fitness plan for each of them, he'd been surprised at how enthusiastic he was about the whole venture. Already he was planning to trial group running classes, and after that possibly week-long intensive boot-camp-style courses. The possibilities were endless.

Unfortunately there was more to it than spending all his time outdoors handling the practical one-to-one fitness stuff. There was advertising to think of, public liability insurance to consider; he needed to record his income and expenses. The list went on and on, and Lara had been impressed at his organisational skills, not knowing of course that he'd had hours to spare for designing a website, setting up accounting software, scouting around online for the best insurance deals.

When you slept less than four out of every twenty-four hours it was amazing how much you could get done.

Lara was so tired from her in-your-face working day that once asleep there was no waking her until her alarm went off at some godforsaken dark hour of the morning, and at which point she would leap out of bed and the whole damn work routine would start all over again. The last few nights he'd been able to slip back into bed shortly before her alarm, simply getting back up again for an early run as soon as she was up and about. He scheduled his fitness clients in the morning, usually after nine when the school run was out of the way, and before lunch. Then he would grab a few hours' sleep in the afternoon while Lara was occupied at the lingerie shop. By the time she was finished he was up and about and she was none the wiser. And that way, he could limit any sleep disturbance to when she wasn't there.

Lara would be able to move back into her own flat in days, now that the plumbing was fixed and the replastering of the water-damaged wall was under way. That would take the pressure off even further. After over a week of sharing each other's living space, that would be a step back. Staying together all night every night would likely become less of an automatic choice. Just a few more days of managing his routine and it would be easier.

In the meantime this was turning out to be the perfect solution to his nightmares. Squeeze them out. If he gave them as little opportunity as possible it stood to reason that they would happen less, that they would relinquish their grip on him. There had been no sleep disturbance at all for the last two days. And so the strategy, complicated though it was, appeared to be working. Until he could be sure he was rid of the nightmares, he intended to rigidly control his sleep pattern. Whatever it took to achieve surface normality, he was prepared to do it. Hope began to grow at last in his heart that the whole hellish experience might finally be behind him.

* * *

Isaac expertly popped the cork from the bottle of Perrier-Jouet to the background sound of cheers and claps filling the sitting room. Lara had never met anyone before so adept at producing like magic the perfect bottle to suit any occasion. She wondered if he kept a stack of bottles hidden away in his room, ready to whip out with a flourish when required. Relaxed shared flat-mates' dinner? Chilled bottle of Pinot Grigio. Announcement of former flatmate's whirlwind engagement? Top-notch champagne, nothing but the best would do.

He filled flutes one by one as Poppy held them out to him.

'I bloody well told you so!' Poppy said triumphantly, passing a flute first to Alex, then to Lara. 'Didn't I say that ring on Izzy's right hand was fooling nobody? Finally she puts me out of my misery and moves it to the correct finger.'

Lara could see excitement on Poppy's face mingling with a measure of relief that things had obviously worked out so wonderfully for Izzy. She looked blissfully happy with Harry's hand resting around her waist. Lara offered her own congratulations as she examined the swirl of silver on Izzy's left hand.

'It's beautiful, Izzy,' she said. 'Just so elegant.'

A pang of unexpected wistfulness surged through her stomach as she examined the ring, silver with a couple of diamonds, gorgeous in its simplicity. Not wistfulness for the ring, gorgeous though it was, but for how lovely it must be to have someone make that commitment to you, to be able to look forward to a shared future instead of a solitary one.

'Izzy and Harry,' Isaac said, raising his glass. They all followed suit.

'How's your father doing, Harry?' Alex asked.

Harry smile tightened almost imperceptibly.

'On the mend, thanks,' he said. 'Touch and go for a while back there but he's over the worst now. I guess we'll see when we go back in a few weeks for the wedding.'

There was an immediate shocked gasp from Poppy.

'*For the wedding?* You mean you're getting hitched in Australia, not here? You can't!'

'We're doing both,' Izzy said, smiling.

'Both? How's that going to work?'

'We're getting married in London first,' Harry said. 'Something more intimate, so Izzy can have all her friends and family there, and then we'll decamp to Australia afterwards for the full-on "official" take on it.'

'So chill out,' Izzy said, 'no one's going to miss out, you'll all be there. And actually, Lara, can I have a quick word?'

Izzy drew Lara quietly to one side as Isaac refilled glasses.

'I was wondering if you'd consider making my wedding dress?' she ventured.

A flush of genuine pleasure warmed Lara's cheeks. She was thrilled to be asked, to be trusted with such an important part of their day.

'Seriously?'

'Absolutely. Your lingerie is just gorgeous. And you do other clothes too, right, not just underwear? I'm right, aren't I? That dress you wore at the shop launch?'

Lara nodded.

'I make some of my own clothes, yes.' She clasped her hands together to contain her excitement. 'I'd *love* to do your wedding dress. It would be an absolute dream. What kind of thing did you have in mind?'

Lara sat down on the sofa and Izzy perched next to her, opening her tote bag and spreading a pile of wedding magazines out in front of her. As Izzy flipped through some cuttings Lara grabbed a pen and notepad and made notes furiously.

'I was hoping we could come up with a design that could double up for both weddings,' Izzy said. 'Nothing fussy, just simple lines.' She pointed to a magazine clipping of a full-length, elegant sheath dress, stunning in its simplicity. 'Kind of like this, but maybe with more of a drapey neckline.'

'Like this?' In a few strokes Lara sketched a draping column of a dress with a cowl neckline.

'Yes, exactly like that.' She clapped her hands together excitedly. 'I'm going to have an angora sweater for the service here—it'll be a very fine knit that I can wear over my dress. Hand-made. I've outsourced it to my mother!'

Lara smiled.

'And then the second wedding in Australia is going to be hot so I can just wear the dress without the sweater.'

'I'll put together some proper drawings for you and then we can fine-tune the design from there,' Lara said. 'I'll need to take full measurements from you. I'll need to know what shoes you're wearing, work out what lingerie will be best, that kind of thing. And we'll do fittings as we go along so we can make sure it's exactly what you want.'

'Perfect!'

Izzy's enthusiasm and excitement filled the room and another stab of envy poked Lara sharply behind the ribs. Izzy and Harry had been together for, what—a couple of months? And yet they were so utterly sure of each other that they were storming forward with wedding plans.

'It must be lovely to be so certain of something,' she said, before she could stop herself. 'Of *someone*.'

Izzy glanced up from the sketches and smiled.

'You're loved-up with Alex, aren't you?' she said.

'Of course.' Lara shrugged. 'But I haven't a clue really where we're headed. I've got so much on at the moment and the business always comes first. I don't have time to think about the future of any relationship. Not right now.'

Saying it out loud felt vaguely reassuring. There was a niggling sense of unease at her current situation that she'd tried hard to ignore. She hadn't counted on how happy it would make her feel, how secure, being with Alex. She looked across the sitting room to where he was joking around with Isaac, and her feelings for him bowled her over with their strong, confident depth. For the first time since her childhood she let her dogged tunnel vision slip and allowed herself to wonder if a solitary future really *was* the only option for her. There was no harm in dreaming, right? Maybe even in playing out the dream a little—why rule anything out? Surely Lara, with every aspect of her life under full control, could be open to seeing where this thing with Alex led without committing herself fully? In fact it would be odd if hopes and dreams *didn't* enter her mind right now—they were exactly what weddings were all about after all.

Mutual support. There was something deliciously couple-ish about it. Something that made Lara feel warm and happy deep inside, the unfamiliar sensation of being part of a team. Alex had been there for her at the shop launch, and now it was her turn to step up to the plate and return the favour.

Shame really that, in her case, mutual support had to include gruelling exercise. How much more palatable it would be if, for example, Alex ran a wine bar, like Isaac. She could quite happily envisage herself socialising, dressed in something sophisticated with a cocktail in her hand. She would be perfect for the role. Instead, here she was again, dressed in her mishmash of borrowed sportswear and bringing up the rear of a group of eight thirty-something women, all of whom looked a billion times more attractive than she did. Honestly, wasn't the whole *point* of needing to go to boot camp that you *didn't* already look your best?

This was Alex's attempt to diversify his test market from one-to-one personal training into fitness classes, leading a sample group of women on a cross-country run through the woodland of Holland Park. It had undoubtedly been preceded by one of his customary sessions of gruelling warm-up exercises and, possibly, instructions on how to keep up without turning into a sweating mess. Unfortunately she'd missed all that so she'd just have to wing it. She'd lost track of the time, sorting out loose ends at the shop instead of rushing here straight after closing.

Alex had timed the half-hour run carefully to make the most of the last hour or so of daylight.

The woman directly in front of her had chestnut-brown hair caught up in a perfect high ponytail and co-ordinating pink and black designer sportswear. As Alex led them uphill Lara was treated to an unwelcome view of her perfect pert bottom emphasised by skintight leggings. Insecurity stabbed her sharply in the stomach and she grimly did her best to ignore it and plod on through the mud and leaves. Since the night of the launch, nearly a week ago now, Alex had been there for her on every level. He'd given her no reason to think he'd be interested in anyone else, no matter how good they might look in Lycra.

She made a special effort to pull her posture together, hold her head high and present a bouncy jogging motion instead of her body's default attitude of staggering along. Unfortunately holding her head high meant she didn't spot a sudden hollow in the squelchy ground preceded by a protruding tree root. Didn't spot it, that was, until her foot had caught in it and she'd performed a dying-swan sort of movement that ended in a muddy splat as she fell flat on her face. Mercifully, being at the back of the group meant no one realised she was floundering on the ground behind them.

The running group jogged on ahead of her in perfect unison, manoeuvring through the trees with Alex's voice counting out the pace in loud shouts from the front. Lara scrambled back to her feet as quickly as she could, only to fold immediately back onto her knees the moment she attempted to put weight on her left ankle. The pain was horrible, making her head spin and sending stars across her field of vision. She watched the group putting more and more distance between them.

The main path was only a few hundred metres away, the end of the run a short distance along it. The choice was perfectly simple. Either she could draw attention to herself as the weakest link in the team, distract Alex from his very first test class, which up until now had clearly gone perfectly to plan, or she could do her best to limp to the end of the course.

No contest.

In her mind there wasn't even a decision to be made. She attempted gingerly to test her foot again and bit her lip. Painful, but manageable as long as she didn't keep her weight on it for too long. She pulled herself grimly into what could only be described as a limping jog, concentrating hard on not falling too far behind the group, and forced herself over the final leg of the run. By the time Alex brought the group to a standstill at the finishing point, she was reduced to lurching along like a total moron. Fortunately he was so engrossed in leading the cool-down exercises that he didn't notice her limping appearance at the back.

She leaned against a tree a short distance away and closed her eyes briefly. The cool-down exercises could go to hell. With no weight on it her ankle didn't feel too bad. Perhaps she just needed to give it a minute or two to recover. She waved at him from the sidelines as he caught her eye, and watched him talk to his adoring class. She could hear him bandying motivational phrases around. And then as the class finally dispersed he made his way over to her, an exhilarated grin lighting up his handsome face.

'You made it,' he said. 'I thought you'd got held up at the shop.' Then, eyes narrowing, 'Just how late were you? Did you do the warm up?'

'Just about caught it,' she lied, taking the bottle of water he offered and sipping it gratefully. 'I thought the class went brilliantly, didn't you? Just wait until the word gets around at the school gates—you'll be inundated.' She pasted on a beaming smile.

He turned back towards the path, zipping up his hoodie, ready to get back to the flat. Dusk was beginning to fall now and the street lamps were kicking in. Lara tried her weight on her ankle carefully and pressed her lips together. The pain was monstrous. She gritted her teeth and limped along anyway a foot or so behind him, which was fine for a few seconds until he turned back and put an arm around her shoulders. Oh, the bliss of having something to lean on. She shoved her arm around his waist and used him as a crutch. And just a couple of paces was enough.

'What the bloody hell is going on with your foot?' he said, stopping immediately. She could hear exasperation fighting with concern in his tone of voice.

She drew herself up to her full height. Not easy when only one of your ankles could bear your weight. She pasted a breezy smile on her face.

'I slipped a bit on the way round. It's nothing.'

Totally ignoring her, he was already on his knees in the mud, loosening the laces of her trainer. She couldn't stop a yelp as he eased it off.

'Lara, it's swollen. When did you fall?'

'Near the end,' she said. 'Just when we turned back onto the main path.'

'That was way back,' he said. 'Why the hell did you keep going? Why didn't you stop the class?'

And make a total fool of herself in front of Notting Hill's yummy-mummy set? Did he know *nothing* at all about female pride?

'There was no need,' she said. 'I wasn't about to make a fuss and put a stop to the class, not when it was going so well.'

He slid an arm gently around her waist and took her other arm over his shoulder.

'Let's get back to the flat. With any luck Poppy will be there and we can get her to look at it.'

'I don't need Poppy to look at it, I'm perfectly all right. Don't fuss.'

He stopped then and looked her in the eye. She saw with some surprise that he was fighting to control his temper. Just what the hell was the big deal?

'*Don't fuss?*' he snapped. 'You were part of my class and that makes you *my* responsibility.'

'And how exactly are *you* meant to be responsible when I didn't tell you what I'd done?' she said. 'Nothing would have made me pipe up in front of that gang of middle-class mums in their DKNY sportswear that I'd just slipped in the mud in my too big cast-off trainers. I'm over eighteen, Alex, I'm not made of *glass*, and I don't need Poppy looking at my foot.'

'However you try and dress it up, I'm accountable for this,' he said, as if he hadn't heard a word. 'For you *and* your foot. So for once in your damned independent life, accept some help. This isn't a laughing matter. If I'm going to be running these classes professionally then health and safety has to be paramount.' He shook his head and frowned. 'Maybe I should have done another risk assessment.'

Oh, for Pete's sake.

'Can you just stop with the health and safety?' she said, holding up a hand. 'A thank-you might have been nice instead of a dressing down. Perhaps you'd like me to get down in the mud and give you fifty press-ups? Do you really think I *wanted* to turn out in the freezing cold and schlep round Holland Park? I came because I wanted to give you some moral support.'

He stared at her.

'I appreciate that, but I can't have *my* responsibility compromised because *your* mind isn't on the class,' he said. 'If you've just come along for a jolly and you're not going to take it seriously then it's probably best you don't come at all.'

A *jolly*?

Despite the rapidly cooling air, a rush of boiling heat suffused her from the neck up.

She disentangled herself from his arm, elbowed him aside and limped ahead at speed. The pain in her foot was awful but the way she felt right now she'd rather walk fifty miles on it than spend one more minute leaning on him.

'Lara, stop,' he said, jogging alongside to keep up with her. 'Let me help you.'

She stopped next to him.

'There was nothing *jolly* about hauling myself around Holland Park in the freezing cold,' she said through gritted teeth. She shook him off as he tried to take her arm. 'I wanted to be there for you, the same way you were there for me when I was biting my nails to the quick over my shop launch. But now I know you don't want me to bother unless I've got some kind of *fitness* objective, I'll stay out of the way in future. Risk assess *that*!'

She stormed off again and this time he didn't follow her.

CHAPTER TEN

ALEX LET HIMSELF into the flat and found Lara in the kitchen with her foot up on one of the chairs and Poppy strapping the ankle up with elasticated bandage. Lara's arms were folded and she had a mulish expression on her face.

'What happened to not needing Poppy to look at it?' he said, exasperated. 'You were having none of it back at the park.'

'Oh, she tried her best to limp past me,' Poppy said, glancing up. 'Lucky for you it isn't broken,' she told Lara. 'Just a strain. Take it easy for a day or two and it will be fine.'

He knew just by the expression on Lara's face that hell would be freezing over before she took it easy. Poppy covered the whole thing with a tube bandage and stood up to pack away her first-aid kit.

He could feel the indignant vibes radiating from Lara. The instant Poppy left the room she put her foot on the floor.

Alex had begun the solo walk back to the fire station fired up with exasperation at Lara for not taking better care of herself and, worse, with fury at himself for not being in better control of the class. How the hell had he not noticed whether she was at the warm up or not? Irritation gave way to thinking through the situation. This had been a test class after all, a chance for him to fine-tune the running of things. Maybe Lara had done him a favour. Better that he picked up on any loopholes like this now, before a paying client had some kind of accident on his watch. He resolved to tighten up his protocol before going any further with the boot-camp model. But then calm thought returned, and with it came a stab of guilt at the way he'd gone off at her. Lara Connor with her single-minded attitude, determined to run her life on her own without letting anyone in, had turned out to support him in his new business venture, a business venture that by the way she'd been instrumental in setting up. When did Lara ever make time for anything except her own business plans? Yet she'd made time to come and support him.

'How is it?' he asked.

'It's perfectly fine,' she said in tones of pure frost.

He pulled out the chair opposite and sat down.

'I'm sorry,' he said. 'I didn't mean it to sound like I'm ungrateful for your support—'

'But you'd just rather take the *personal* out of personal training,' she cut in. She held her hands up. 'It's fine. I'm *more* than happy not to come to any more of your classes.'

'It wasn't about not wanting you at the class.'

She simply stared at him with a sceptical expression on her face. *Yeah, right,* it said. He ran a hand uncomfortably through his hair.

'It wasn't actually about *you* at all,' he said. 'It's about accountability. You have to understand I've spent years taking decisions that affect other people. The army was all about that for me—having people rely on me, following my orders without question or thought for the consequences. It was all about not letting people down, because when you stuff up with that kind of thing in an army situation people get hurt.'

He knew that better than anyone. His mind sideslipped madly back to that final tour before he could stop it. Private Sam Walker looking at him with that half grin on his face. *'I know you've got my back, sir. And I've got yours.'* He blinked hard and forced himself to refocus on the present, on Lara. Her expression softened a little, the cynical slant melting away.

'You're not in the forces anymore, Alex,' she said patiently. 'Lives aren't at stake. You don't have control of what other people do or say. You can do all you can to make sure things are safe, and you're doing that. You've covered the insurance angle, you're up together on warm-up exercises and risk assessments. But you can't control the fact that I turned up late and bent the rules, or that my heart wasn't in the run. You can't take the blame because I screwed up. You're not responsible for the rest of the world.'

'You're more than just the rest of the world,' he said. 'I care what happens to you.'

A warm and fuzzy stomach flip kicked right in and Lara pressed her hands over her tummy hard. He *cared*. She was used to taking care of herself on every level, taking responsibility for every aspect of her life herself; his downright refusal to let her go her own way without voicing his concern was completely new to her. The sensation of being looked after, of being *cared about*, was one that she'd denied herself for so long that she'd forgotten just how lovely it was.

Or how dangerous.

What exactly was she doing here, letting herself get so close to someone that being *cared about* came into the equation? It was the living-in thing, of course. That was why it had slipped past her guard. Circumstance and not conscious choice had meant they'd ended up sharing a flat. And maybe it was the Izzy-and-Harry thing a bit too. Being part of the whirlwind excitement of their fairy-tale happiness made anything seem possible. The warm and happy feeling was intoxicating. Would it really be so dangerous to just run with this and see where it led?

When he reached across the table and covered her hand with his, she didn't take it away.

* * *

Two hours later and if she had to put up with one more minute of sitting still in the flat with a constantly refilled cup of tea and a magazine, Lara thought she might scream. Not that she'd had any big plans for this evening except possibly to sort through some stock and then cook a meal, but now she was unable to do either of those things she felt hemmed in.

Still, when he appeared in the sitting room showered and changed she smiled at him through gritted, *bored* teeth because, actually, his concern was something she was liking very much. If only he could exhibit it in another way than ensuring her bladder stayed above the pint level with his endless cups of tea.

He smiled back, crossed the room towards her, and before she could make any comment he leaned down and picked her up from the sofa as if she weighed absolutely nothing. She was treated to a delicious wave of his aftershave, something woody and fresh, and she curled her arms around his neck immediately, her stomach beginning to fill with heat. Now *this* beat reading women's magazines.

'Where are you taking me?' she said in surprise as he failed to take the expected route to his bedroom. He kicked open the door of the flat and proceeded to carry her down the stairs.

'Ignite,' he said. 'I could see you were climbing the walls in there.'

'Could you?' she said, interested that he could be that perceptive.

'Yep. It was that tight voice you used when you thanked me for the tea.'

'I'm sorry,' she said, feeling guilty. 'It *was* the fourth cup in the space of an hour. I am grateful, really I am. I just don't *do* bed rest. It just isn't me.'

'You don't say,' he said, pausing in the stairwell to smile into her face. She smiled back and he planted a soft kiss at the corner of her mouth.

'I did think about Isaac's bar followed by dancing but I

thought that might finish you off,' he said, taking the stairs again. At the bottom he pushed open the door of Ignite with one foot and carried her across the restaurant to a corner table while the staff and customers looked at them with interest. He set her down gently.

'I can actually get around by limping, you know,' she protested. He raised sarcastic eyebrows at her and she backed down with a grin. 'But Ignite is perfect.' Just knowing her well enough to see that she'd been going stir crazy was enough to melt her heart. Dinner out was an unexpected bonus.

Ignite did a great line in wine and tapas when it wasn't being a coffee lounge and, tucking into a shared platter over glasses of chilled white wine, it was easy to let herself relax in Alex's company. She let her guard take the evening off, knowing normal self-reliance would be back in charge the moment she could put her weight back on her ankle. She didn't argue at his insistence throughout the evening that she keep her foot up on the opposite chair, or at his refusal to let her walk back up the stairs to the flat when the evening was over. Yes, there was a growing closeness between them, but she was fully conscious of it, that was the most important thing here. And she should be able to move back into her own flat at the end of this week. That would put a bit of distance right back into the situation. And so surely there was absolutely no harm in feeling a little bit cared about until then.

When sleep arrived later that evening, it was in his arms.

Lara stretched deliciously, blinked her eyes open, and tried to pull her scrambled sleep-fuzzy brain together. She felt well rested for once. None of the usual hankering from her body for more sleep, which she always steadfastly ignored. No disorientation about where she was—it seemed after years of sleeping, of doing everything alone, all it took was a few nights to get used to sharing her bed with someone else. *His* bed, if she wanted to split hairs. The golden autumn sunshine slanted through the curtains and into the military order, which was only tempered a tiny bit by the items of her own clothing slung randomly over the back of a chair. She turned her head to the left then and realised Alex wasn't there. His side of the bed had the covers thrown back.

Frowning, she leaned up on one elbow. The flat was quiet. None of the clattering from the kitchen that signified Alex making one of his endless cups of coffee. And it occurred to her that the room was unusually bright. She was used to scrambling around in the semi-darkness when she got up in the mornings. And then, as her mind began to focus properly, her stomach kicked in with a hideous lurching sensation. The kind of lurch that came when you overslept on the morning of an exam or missed a really important meeting. The kind of lurch that she never experienced because Lara Connor did not *do* lateness or poor organisational skills. Ever.

She was across the bed in one swift scrambling movement, grabbing at Alex's alarm clock with a flash of horror. Two facts careered madly through her brain: it was five minutes shy of ten o'clock and someone had switched the alarm off. Right about now she should be standing, perfectly groomed, behind the counter of her shop greeting the morning customers with a smile. Instead her hair was in its first-thing fright-wig mode, there was sleep in the corners of her eyes and her hard-won clientele would be greeted by a locked door and a 'Closed' sign.

She'd thrown herself out of the bed, plonked both feet to the floor and stood up before she remembered the previous day's injury. She yelped in pain and hopped back onto the bed, one hand clamped to her throbbing ankle, the other scraping through her hair as she put two and two together.

Alex had obviously, without so much as a whisper in her direction, taken a unilateral decision to let her have a lie-in, probably because of some personal-trainer opinion about resting injured limbs for *days*. Clearly it would be perfectly fine for him with the balance of his trust fund as a cushion to take a morning off work whenever he felt like it. She, on the other hand, had no back-up plan worth beans. Did he not understand she had a *business* to run?

Limping out to the kitchen, she found no trace of either him or Poppy, although his enormous coffee mug was upended in the sink.

She also found no trace of the keys to the shop despite turning the kitchen counter upside down. Her frantic call to his mobile phone went straight to voice mail and the only explanation was so unthinkable that she came to a shocked standstill in the middle of the room.

Alex wouldn't have opened the shop, would he?

The sign on the door read 'Open' and she could see through the glass door that Alex was standing behind the counter at the back of the shop.

'What the hell is going on?' She stormed through the door on the wave of anger and frustration that had built to a crest during the taxi ride. 'Who the hell do you think you are, opening my shop without even asking me? Taking my keys? Letting me oversleep?'

His welcoming smile disappeared like smoke.

'Thank you, Alex, for looking after the shop for me while I took a much-needed rest,' he said loudly. 'You twisted your ankle yesterday. That kind of injury needs to be rested, not squashed into a four-inch heel.'

He glanced downward at that moment to see she was wearing a pair of soft leather ballet flats and made a backtracking chuffing sound through his nose. 'Well, I see you've at least decided to be sensible about footwear,' he conceded.

She didn't bother to enlighten him that she'd tried half a dozen heeled pairs before admitting to herself that limping was a whole lot easier and less attention-grabbing in flat shoes. No way was she just passing across the upper hand. He was the one in the wrong here.

'But you should still be resting up,' he carried on. 'You never take a break. You're always on the go. And since I don't have any training sessions today, I thought I'd help you out. I've sold half a dozen pairs of those knickers that look like shorts and one of those sets of pyjamas.' He spoke with the triumphant air of someone who'd just discovered a natural flair for sales that would floor Alan Sugar.

'Without even *asking* me?' she snapped incredulously. 'Would it have *killed* you to ask me my opinion before you took over my business? You didn't even leave a note, for Pete's sake.'

'I was trying to do you a favour,' he said. He waved a hand around at the shop floor. 'The place didn't spontaneously combust just because you weren't at the helm for *one bloody hour*. I am not a total imbecile.'

His voice had suddenly taken on an icy cold and even more clipped tone than usual. She realised with a jolt of surprise how angry he actually was. It filtered through to her one-track work-obsessed mind that she might be overreacting here the teeniest bit, and she made a too-late effort to curb her tongue.

'It's my business, Alex,' she said, attempting to explain. 'It's all I've got.'

'So it's fine for me to take you out to dinner and pamper you a bit but when it comes to trusting me with something that actually *matters* to you, you revert to control freak,' he snapped, walking out from behind the counter and storming past her towards the door. 'Since this place is the only thing that's remotely important to you, I'll leave you to get the hell on with it.'

He was out of the shop before she had time to say anything else and slammed the door behind him so hard she was surprised the plate-glass window didn't shatter.

It took ten minutes to reorganise the counter back to her own liking instead of in his right-angles–lined-up obsessive military neatness. Ten minutes during which seething and self-righteousness gradually gave way to niggling doubt about who was in the wrong here and who exactly had overstepped the mark in terms of reasonable behaviour.

She couldn't fail to see that he'd made a careful list of the items he'd sold, and when she did a quick check of the till it balanced perfectly. He'd managed without a hitch. When you got right down to it, he was trying to do something nice for her, looking out for her. And of course he was confused as hell because last night she'd allowed that without complaint. But then it hadn't been about her beloved lingerie business, had it? Big difference between letting him spoil her with a meal and letting him take the reins of the most important thing in her life. The alarm bells that had started ringing yesterday when he'd helped her home after she'd twisted her ankle had gone into overdrive and she'd acted without thinking, concerned only with looking after the safe and secure little world she'd built for herself, believing that only *she* was capable of doing that.

She'd overreacted. He'd been spot on when he'd called her a control freak. And now she had to find a way of climbing down.

She managed until lunchtime. Her interim attempts to get hold of Alex went straight to voice mail and even a short rush of late-morning customers failed to stop the unhappy churning in her stomach. Her mind constantly picked at the situation, at her own behaviour. A bolt of ivory silk had been delivered for Izzy's wedding dress and she found herself staring at it miserably. Had she actually been daydreaming about having a future like that herself? Only now did she see how far beyond her that was, how unsuited she was with her present attitude to being part of a proper couple. If she couldn't relinquish control and put her trust in someone else, how could she ever hope to share her life with someone?

She ran her shop, her life, her world in her own way. The problem was, she wasn't really sure that was what she wanted, not anymore.

The first step towards change would be to apologise, of

course. If he would listen after the spoilt-brat way she'd behaved towards him. And unfortunately, it became slowly clear to her that the only way to climb down and convince him she wasn't just talking the talk but was actually serious would be to put her money where her mouth was. Or, more accurately, her shop.

If anything proved to her that she was in too deep here it was this one tiny action of turning the sign on the glass door of the shop to read 'Closed' when it was currently two o'clock in the afternoon. Three hours' business time left and she was sacrificing a chunk of it to sort out her personal life. She who didn't even *have* a personal life, let alone one whose importance interfered with shop opening hours. She did it anyway.

There was a moment where she faltered as she walked past the door of her own studio flat on the fire station stairs, a floor below Poppy's flat. A couple of weeks ago and everything had been so straightforward. The pop-up shop had consumed her every waking thought; she'd been utterly focused. She couldn't have imagined anything distracting her from that. And now look at her, back here when she could be working, because when it came right down to it she just couldn't let the situation lie.

Alex was in the kitchen at the flat, the open laptop on the table displaying some kind of fitness website. He glanced up at her in amazement.

'What are you doing back here?'

'We need to talk,' she said, putting her keys and bag down on the table and sitting down. His face was completely inscrutable, which didn't help at all. She had no clue if she was in with a chance of turning the situation around.

'You've shut the shop? In the middle of the day? Bloody hell, call CNN,' he said. She let that slide. She deserved it.

She looked down at her fingers.

'I may have overreacted,' she began. 'A little.'

His face didn't change in the slightest.

'What the hell happened to you that you can't even let someone lend you a hand for a morning?' he said. 'I've never known such a control freak.'

'It's not about being a control freak,' she protested. 'It's about being professional.'

'It's about having a chip on your shoulder about accepting help.'

She bit back the indignant denials that rose to her lips. She could deny it all she wanted but her behaviour today had spoken volumes. To herself as well as to him.

'I'm just not used to delegating and the shock of waking up and finding that you'd gone ahead and opened up without even asking what I thought—'

'What exactly are you trying to say?' he snapped, making it perfectly clear that edging around an apology simply wasn't going to cut the mustard.

'I'm trying to say I'm sorry,' she blurted out. 'I know you were trying to help. I'm just not used to people doing that.' She paused, and then corrected, 'I'm not used to *letting* people do that.'

'You don't say.'

She put her elbows on the table and pushed her hands into her hair, looking down at the scrubbed wood table top.

'Accepting help from people, handing over responsibility for things, that isn't something I do lightly,' she said. 'I promised myself a long time ago that I'd make my own success in life, that I'd get where I wanted to be on my own, without having to rely on anyone else's input.' She shrugged. 'I may have become a bit rabid about that.'

A smile twitched at the corner of his lips and her heart turned softly over.

'You think?'

She smiled back.

'I made the mistake too many times when I was growing up. Of trusting people, thinking I knew where I was and then having everything change again.'

'You mean your mother?' His gaze sharpened and he reached out and shut the lid of the laptop. 'I do get that, Lara. It must have been tough when you were small, but when you talked about it I kind of got the impression that things were much more settled after you were fostered.'

Of course he had. It was exactly the impression she'd intended to give. If only it had been that simple. Straight into care, touch base and straight out again to the perfect foster family. Accepted and loved. Integrated easily at school. Grew up well-adjusted with lasting supportive family ties. This was the real world though, and she'd quickly seen that life just wasn't that warm and fuzzy. Verbalising the reality didn't come easily but she forced herself.

'I gave you the airbrushed version,' she said. 'The bits I think are worth remembering.' She held a hand up in response to his questioning expression. 'You're not the only one with baggage, Alex. We've all got it. We all have to find our own way to deal with it. For me, it's about being in control, about making my own decisions and building a secure life. And for a long time that's been something that I've done on my own. I'm way past believing that anyone else is going to do it for me.'

She took a deep breath.

'I told you my mother couldn't look after me,' she said. 'I spent some time in a children's home and then I was fostered.' She paused. 'And then when that didn't work it was back into the care system until I was fostered again.' She managed a strangled laugh. 'And again. Unfortunately there must have been something about me that meant I didn't fit in. It takes time to settle in with new people and I'd just about start to get a handle on it, then it wouldn't work out and back I'd go. It was so unsettling. I was constantly changing schools, as fast as I made any friends it felt like I moved on again. Eventually I gave up trying.'

A surge of sympathy tugged at Alex's chest as he imagined her as a little kid being shifted from one household to the next. And something else, the oddest thing: the sensation of things falling into place, of *understanding*. Because once he'd been a kid of five arriving at boarding school loaded down with a trunk and a tuck box and rejection. That sense of not being wanted hollowed you out deep inside. He'd been able to fill the gap before long, with friends, with the teachers and pastoral assistants at school. Then later with his comrades in the army. He'd been lucky in that at least there had been continuity for him: he'd stayed at the same school throughout his childhood, had made lifelong enduring friends. Isaac was a case in point. For Alex, it had become his home and family. Lara hadn't even had that. Little wonder that she was so determined now to go it alone.

'It carried on until I hit my teens, backwards and forwards to this placement or that, and then one day I ended up with Bridget and her husband,' Lara said. He could hear the affection for these people in her voice. 'I stayed with them right up until I started college. That was the only place that lasted.' She gave him a rueful smile. 'By then I think the damage was done though. And there's still this niggling doubt that maybe I moved out before they could get fed up with me, and *that's* the real reason it worked with them and not the others.'

'Do you really believe that?'

She thought of Bridget's kindness, the time and effort she'd given to helping Lara settle in, and finding something she could focus on. She shook her head.

'No, I don't really believe that. It's just that for some reason the times I was sent back resonate more with me than the one time I got to stay. Like any criticism, I suppose. You always take more notice of the bad stuff—did you ever notice that?'

He stretched across the table and took her hand in his.

'By the time I went to live with Bridget I was only a couple of years away from college age. And when I found I had a flair for sewing and I could actually *make money* at it, well, that was like finding the perfect answer. If I took charge of my own life and made my own security, I'd never have to leave it. My mistake was looking for someone else to make that life for me. Thinking that I could somehow slot into someone else's perfect family. I decided I'd make my own future that no one could take away from me. There would be no more lurking fear that just as I got close to people I'd be moving on.'

'That's why you're so work-obsessed,' he said. It made perfect sense now.

'I don't see it as *obsessed*,' she said. 'I know I'm driven but it's not about making millions—it's just about making enough for me to put down some roots, so I can have some security.' She lifted her chin a little and gave him a look of triumph. 'Maybe buy a place and get settled. And it will be all the sweeter because I got there myself.'

'I get where you're coming from now,' he said. 'Your determination to do every minute little thing on your own, no matter what the cost. I can understand that. But you don't need to go it alone. Not anymore.'

She looked up at him and the expression on her face made his heart turn softly over.

'I'm sorry,' she said. 'I'm just not used to people being there for me.'

He stood up and rounded the table, pulled her to her feet and tugged her against him. She tucked her head beneath his chin as he wrapped his arms around her.

'Then get used to it,' he said.

CHAPTER ELEVEN

EVENINGS OUT ON the town were a thing of the past. His growing business brought with it a new routine. Clients in the morning and boot-camp groups a couple of afternoons a week. Lara had got the go-ahead to move back into the studio flat and now they split their time between his place and hers. Normal couple. Normal *life*. October was almost at an end now, soon winter would be kicking in, but Poppy had told him she was happy for him to stay put in the flat as long as he wanted. The sense of belonging somewhere again, of having a purpose, felt like finding his way home after being cast adrift and floundering for months.

And tonight, Lara was home first. He'd had a late training session and so she'd decided to treat him to a home-cooked dinner in his own flat. He was greeted by the delicious aroma of salmon with ginger, lime and coriander. There was a green salad and chilled white wine.

'The personal training sessions are really taking off,' he said as she sat down opposite him. He poured them each a glass of wine. 'Offering a taster session for free is really working out well. I picked up another new client today, word of mouth.'

'That's great,' she said.

There was a troubled undertone to her voice that belied the

breezy smile. In fact now he came to think about it, she'd been a bit detached and quiet this last couple of days. He'd assumed it was just that she was tired.

'What's up?' he said. 'Everything all right at the shop?'

Asking him about future plans made a cold little pebble of dread land in Lara's chest and she forced herself to carry on regardless. These last few weeks had been so great, for the first time in years she'd actually begun to let someone else's presence slip into her life. The temptation to just let it carry on, not questioning what it was or where it might lead, was overwhelming. Because that way she wouldn't have to run the risk of an answer she didn't want to hear.

Unfortunately the situation wouldn't allow for them to just drift along much further with no direction. The lease would be up before she knew it on the pop-up shop. Already she was halfway through. She needed to consider what her next steps should be with the business. And it wasn't just that—there was the flat to consider. She'd only intended on renting it for the duration of the shop lease and that had been done on the strength of her savings. There was no way she could afford to keep renting in Notting Hill in the long term.

'I've been thinking about the future,' she said, not looking at him. 'The pop-up shop is a really short-term lease, remember. Just until the end of November and then I'll have to ship out. Someone else will move into the premises, probably some Christmas shop or other.'

He frowned a little as he forked up some of his fish.

'OK, so what are you thinking of doing after that? Knowing you, you've probably got the next ten years mapped out.'

She took a deep breath and kept a neutral expression on her face.

OK, so he hadn't immediately leapt in with an enthusiastic torrent of suggestions of how they might proceed from here— *together*. She bit the inside of her cheek to distract herself from the surge of disappointment that brought. Just because she was making a conscious effort to take a step back from control freak didn't mean she had to flip to the other end of the scale and start working needy. He probably wasn't thinking beyond the next week or so, but his lack of future plans didn't necessarily have to have anything to do with his regard for her, right?

'That's the thing,' she said. 'I need to start thinking about where I'm going with it next.'

He tucked into the salad.

'The shop's doing well, isn't it?'

She nodded and took a sip of her wine.

'It's done really well, but it was only ever really an experiment. I need to start planning where I'm going with it next, whether I run with the retail thing and look for another shop or maybe trial internet sales on a wider scale.'

'Why not put some figures together for the different options and then we can talk it through?' he said. 'Weigh up the pros and cons.'

The long-ingrained urge to politely decline any offer of help rose to her lips just as it always did. This time she swallowed it. He was in her corner. In time sharing things with him would surely become less conscious and more natural.

'Great,' she said. And it was great. She felt more settled than she had in years, secure and happy.

As they finished the meal she stood up to make coffee and he joined her, curling his arms around her waist, kissing her neck from behind, making her so deliciously hot. She turned in his arms and he tilted her face up gently to meet his. Not fast or furious this time, no rushing. His mouth found hers and she melted against him. He picked her up and carried her down the hall to his room as if she weighed nothing at all.

Undressing her was an indulgent pleasure and Alex lingered over it, revelled in it, kissing her skin inch by silken inch until she was squirming with desire. Then he lay above her, feeling the soft curl of her arms and legs around him, binding him to her. Her soft cry of pleasure at his first thrust deep inside her thrilled him on a visceral level that drove his own arousal to an ever higher level. He plunged both hands into her hair and cradled her face as he took her, in long, slow, delicious strokes. Her china-blue eyes were wide as he looked down at her, holding his own gaze steadily, sharing every sensation with him. Feeling her writhe in ecstasy beneath him sent him careering beside her towards that shared height of pleasure.

Crazy, hot, short-term sex, this wasn't. This sex had strings. This was making love, savouring every touch, every inch of her skin. Wanting to please her more than himself. This was what it was like to let someone in.

The joy in that sensation was tinged with a gnawing edge of danger that he tried hard to ignore. Afterwards they lay sated in each other's arms and he felt her urgent grip on his shoulders slowly relax.

'I think I could get used to this,' she whispered against his hair as his breathing began to level. He could feel her own breath warm against his skin.

She settled lower, curling up into the crook of his arm, and he felt her smile against his shoulder as she twined his fingers into her own.

'These past few weeks have been great,' she said. 'I've been on my own for so long that I'd got used to managing everything. I actually thought I liked living that way. I used to tell myself that was the best way to be—no one to answer to but myself, no one to let me down. I never thought I could have this sense of belonging—I thought it was beyond me. It's so lovely, feeling protected and looked after by you, knowing it's not just me against the world for a change.'

She leaned up on one elbow and smiled into his eyes.

'I love knowing you've got my back,' she said. 'And you know I've got yours.'

She pulled away a little so she could find his mouth and kiss him. As the words registered in his mind a hideous black sense of déjà vu stormed through his veins like ice water, picking up speed as it reached his heart.

What the hell had he been thinking?

You've got my back...and I've got yours.

The words filled him with fear as he recalled the last time he'd heard them. Private Sam Walker, now deceased. He'd been unable to save him, unable even to *find* him in the aftermath of the bomb. He'd failed to look out for him after all.

She'd come to rely on him.

Lara Connor, who relied on no one, who did everything for herself, who decided what she wanted from life and found a way to take it without enlisting anyone else's help. And in a flash of unsettling clarity it came to him. That was what he'd found most alluring about her all along. Lara was someone who could manage perfectly well without him. She didn't need him to protect her or look out for her. He had to force her to accept help, such was her level of perfect control freak. As such, the prospect of letting her down or failing her hadn't come into play. And in encouraging her to change, in pushing her to lean on him and let him look out for her, he'd ruled himself completely out of the game.

He lay rigid in the bed next to her long after she'd fallen asleep, curled up in a warm ball against his chest, wanting the façade he'd created. Desperately wanting to be that man with that perfect life—beautiful girlfriend, fledgling new business, new life all mapped out just there for the taking. Knowing he couldn't be, knowing it was all for show and that underneath the exterior he'd created so carefully that he'd actually begun to believe in it himself, he wasn't that man at all.

The revelation that now she *needed* him, that she felt protected, that she was revelling in having someone looking out for her for once, that she saw a future with him, made tendrils of cold dread begin to curl through him. He wasn't up to that challenge. The last person he'd encouraged to depend on him had died on his watch. Just what the hell had he been thinking?

There was no struggle to stay awake tonight while he waited for her to fall asleep. He lay next to her in the bed, tense with shock at his own arrogant stupidity. So determined to channel normality that he'd actually begun to *believe* in his own fiction.

Her talk this evening over dinner about the next move for her business came back to him. Her lease would be up in a matter of weeks. Was that why he'd let this get so far when he really should have known better? Because, subconsciously, he'd always seen an end point in sight to this? He'd known from their first meeting that she was here for a couple of months, no more. She'd told him, that day he'd fallen asleep in her flat, that she'd sunk her savings into this couple of months. *Couple of months.* Deep down had he believed this to be temporary? Just another longer version of his flings, commitment free? And therefore safe.

As her breathing evened, he eased his way out of the bed and moved to the kitchen, the same way he had for the past few nights.

The old single bed in Poppy's boxroom was so narrow that Lara hadn't been able to turn over without bashing herself on the wall of the boxroom. Sharing Alex's big double bed after that was pure luxury and as she surfaced from sleep somewhere in the small hours she stretched deliciously to her toes before turning over to snuggle back up to him.

His side of the bed was empty.

For a disoriented moment she wondered if she'd overslept again and he'd got up to open the shop without asking her, like some crazy Groundhog Day rerun of the other morning. But no, the other morning the room had been light with sunshine, not pitch dark as it was now. She came awake more fully and pulled herself up onto her elbow, screwing her eyes up to read the digital clock on Alex's bedside table. A little past three in the morning. She lay for a few minutes, assuming he must be in the bathroom, or maybe getting a drink from the kitchen, but nothing. The minutes stretched ahead and she was wide awake now. Maybe he was ill.

That thought galvanised her into action and she threw the covers back and grabbed her robe from where it lay over a chair. The hallway was as dark as the bedroom. Poppy's bedroom door was closed and the bathroom was empty and silent. She padded down to the kitchen and immediately saw the slice of light cutting out beneath the closed door. She opened it and went into the room.

Alex visibly jumped as she came in. He was sitting at the table behind his laptop, a mug of coffee the size of a small bucket next to his hand, and a look on his face of pure guilt. *I'm caught,* it said. The guilt thing was so obvious that it shut out all other details as her mind searched madly for a simple explanation. What reason could a man have for sitting at his laptop in the middle of the night, sporting a guilty expression, except possibly for porn?

The instant that thought hit her brain, she marched across the room and took in his laptop screen. Not porn but the website for his new business. There was a notepad next to his hand and he was clearly working. Maybe he just couldn't sleep.

That thought in itself tripped some kind of alarm in her mind.

'What are you doing up?' she asked. 'I was worried. I thought you might be ill.'

He smiled at her.

'I just couldn't sleep. Thought I might as well get up and do something else.'

He pushed up from the table and attempted to sweep her into a hug. She batted his hands aside. Her mind was working overtime now.

She noticed with new clarity the dark shadows under his eyes as he failed to meet her gaze, shadows she'd noticed back in her flat when they first met, and like a bucket of cold water being sloshed over her she realised that those dark shadows had never really gone away. Her mind picked up other telltale details. The enormous coffee mug by his hand. The documents that strewed the table. His amazing ability to start up a business and cope with all the associated admin when she'd always felt as if she never had enough hours in the day.

'I couldn't sleep either,' she said. 'But I do what most normal people who can't sleep do at three in the morning. Warm milk and counting sheep. Whereas you've launched yourself into the working day.'

She waved a hand at the table, covered in papers, lists of figures, business card and poster samples. Her sleep-addled brain continued to make connections.

'I woke up three nights ago and you weren't there,' she said. 'It was some godforsaken small hour of the morning. I assumed you'd gone to the bathroom so I just turned over but you weren't there, were you? You were in here. Working. And your coffee addiction. On the whole, it's worse. I've never known anyone guzzle so much caffeine.'

She paused.

'This is about your nightmares, isn't it?' she said simply.

The words made Alex's stomach begin to churn.

'I'm dealing with it,' he said, clenching his hands.

'You told me you were dealing with it weeks ago,' she said. 'But staying awake isn't the answer. You're burying your head in the sand. That is *not* dealing with it.'

He sat down at the table and she tugged her silk dressing gown tighter around her and sank into the chair next to him, reached out to touch his wrist. He stared down at her hand, intended to comfort him, and shame began to climb burningly upward from his neck.

'You can't keep denying you have a problem,' she said firmly. 'I let you fob me off last time because I thought things were getting better but by the look of it they're worse than ever.' Her smile was supportive. 'You don't need to worry,' she said. 'I'm here for you. We'll get you all the help you need.'

On the back of his fears about being able to take care of her now came this. He was a total basket case. He needed *help*. In her offer to get him support, she'd just inadvertently confirmed his failure. He was a failure as a soldier, as a comrade and friend. And if he stayed in her life, he would fail her too. She deserved better than that after the constant let-downs she'd already endured throughout her childhood. He gritted his teeth hard and forged ahead with his only option.

'This isn't going to work between us,' he said.

She was close enough for him to hear her catch her breath.

'What?' she whispered.

He pulled his arm away from her hand, stood up and backed away to lean against the kitchen counter, wanting to put distance between them now, steeling himself to go through with this, knowing it was for the best.

'I've been pretending that it could. Playing at normality,' he said. 'Kidding myself that I could work a normal relationship. Dating, supporting each other, sitting round the table eating dinner while we talk about our day. Sleeping together. All those things that *normal* people do. But all the time I've just been using it to hide reality.'

'From me?'

He shook his head and ran a hand briefly through his hair.

'Worse than that. From *me*. I've been kidding myself that I can be the man you deserve, that I can look after you in the way you need. I'm not up to that, Lara. I'll let you down—it's inevitable. Just a matter of time.'

'You're *dumping* me?' she said, her tone incredulous.

'A clean break is best,' he said. 'I'm not good for you, Lara. I'm not what you need.'

She held up a hand at that and he saw anger rush to her face.

'Don't you dare!' she snapped. 'Don't you *dare* spin me that it's-not-you-it's-me line. I should have listened to my instincts when I twisted my ankle. You let me think I could *count* on you. Have you any idea how hard it was for me to accept that? And now you're just saying you didn't mean it after all? I should never have let this get off the ground. I mean, have I not learned *anything*?' She tipped her head back and laughed sarcastically at the ceiling.

'It's not a line.'

'How can this *possibly* be about you?' she asked him then. She waved a hand at him. 'I mean, look at you—you've got half of Notting Hill's women salivating after you. You're smart, brave, funny, gorgeous.'

He was shaking his head.

'It *is* about me. I can't be the person you need me to be.' He lifted his hands in an all-encompassing gesture. 'None of this is real,' he said. 'This thing we have. Relationship. Whatever you want to call it. I thought I was doing such a great job. I thought that by going through the motions I could actually *be* normal, but it doesn't work. It's all a façade. I'm not the person you think I am and I'm not right for you.'

The words fell on Lara like stones. In other words, she didn't fit with him. And as a knock-on effect, she supposed, with his sister or his friends. And he clearly thought he could spare her a rundown of her personal failings to live up by blaming himself.

She bit the inside of her cheek to stop the burning sensation at the back of her throat from turning into anything more obvious. Funny how the age-old survival techniques kicked right back in. It felt as if she were twelve again, another foster home not working out, holding her head up high as she packed her things up, all ready to move on and insisting to herself that she didn't care; *she didn't care.* It wasn't about *her,* oh, no, it was about finding the right situation, the right family setting for her needs, the right *fit*.

When it came right down to it, none of his excuses really mattered. At best, even if she accepted what he was saying, it meant he'd never been straight with her. If manufacturing some ludicrous normality and hiding his sleep loss was preferable to just being honest with her, then he had a very different view of how important this relationship was. Whatever the reasons were, she wasn't right for him. She didn't want or need to hear any more excuses, in the same way as she hadn't wanted or needed to hear the explanations throughout her childhood. She wasn't a good fit, either now or back then, and she never should have kidded herself that she could be.

She stood up from the table and pushed the chair carefully back into place.

'I'm not bothered, Alex,' she said. She didn't raise her voice. She dug deep for all the dignity she could muster. 'I don't *need* to talk about this. I don't need any of your excuses. It was good while it lasted but my work has always come first. No big deal.'

She backed away from the table and out of the door and then he heard her practically sprint downstairs to her own flat. He was on his feet before he'd given it a moment's thought, ready to run after her. He hadn't reckoned on this. Hadn't thought for a second she would make it about *her*. This was *his* screw-up. How could she possibly believe this could be due to some failing of hers?

Then instinct was pushed away by reason. This was for the best; he was letting her off the hook, doing her a favour. Clean break, as he'd said to her. He could go down that hallway, bang on her door and talk with her all night, but the conclusion would be the same. This couldn't continue. He'd been a fool to let it go on as long as it had. He simply couldn't have people relying on him and she really was better off without him. The only way forward now was on his own. He really should have known that from the start.

CHAPTER TWELVE

'How are you holding up?'

Lara could feel Izzy's eyes looking down on her from where she stood on one of the old second-hand dining chairs in the middle of her studio flat. Putting her heart and soul into making a wedding dress, the epitome of a happy-ever-after, wasn't the automatic choice of therapy for a broken heart, but she was fine. She could do this. She was a *professional*. Faking a breezy 'I'm over him' wasn't that much of a challenge, she found. But then again she was a past master of toughing things out with a brave face.

'I'm absolutely fine,' she said, around a mouthful of pins. 'It's for the best. I'm not cut out to be one of a couple. I never have been.'

Perhaps if she said that often enough to herself and everyone else, it might actually start to make her feel better. Some time this century might be nice.

Wedding-dress fittings from now would take place in her own little flat, a venue change from that first talk she'd had with Izzy about dress styles, up in Poppy's living room, champagne in hand, surrounded by her new friends. Lara hadn't set foot in the flat upstairs since things had ended with Alex. No matter that he was away somewhere right now, accompanying Isaac at the last minute on one of his endless bar scouting trips, running away from his problems. Apparently a flight of stairs wasn't enough distance for him; he'd decided to leave the country rather than run the gauntlet of bumping into her in the hallway. Her stomach gave its now familiar miserable churn as she failed yet again to squash him from her mind. Somehow that was the worst part of all, the lingering concern for him, reminding her just how far she'd fallen for him, just how much she cared.

Poppy's flat and the friends who shared it were as much a part of what was lost to her as he was. Her stupidity in thinking that misfit Lara Connor could fit in here, in rich Notting Hill, now amazed her. She should have known better. All that was left now was to see out the lease on the pop-up shop and this flat, and to finish Izzy's dress, of course.

She'd had to bring the big guns back into play. The old tactics she'd learned as a kid, shunted back and forth, never feeling settled or wanted. Withdrawal into her own company and refocusing on the one thing that had brought her answers: work. She'd committed to making Izzy's dress, and although she longed to run for the hills she was also a professional who took pride in her work. She wouldn't let Izzy down. Shame she wouldn't see the wedding itself though; she'd be long gone by then.

She took a step back, hands on hips, and surveyed the gown, currently pinned and tacked together so that she could easily adjust seams. Even half finished, it looked great.

'Oh, Iz.' Poppy sighed from the sofa. 'It's just gorgeous.'

Glamour. Excitement. Freedom. Full-on whirlwind distraction from the real world. When you got down to it, that was what Isaac's chain of bars was all about, providing his clientele with the ultimate distraction through sophisticated entertainment and leisure. *That* was what Alex needed. That was what he should have been aiming for all along. No ties. No responsibilities. For the first few days away, living it up in Isaac's world, the relief at relinquishing accountability for anyone else was overwhelming. No need to worry about letting Lara down, or anyone else for that matter.

She was better off without him.

For the first few days, he'd been convinced that he'd done the right thing by walking away. He'd thrown himself with abandon into a few all-nighters at the clubs, surrounded by pretty girls. Had told himself that he was having a *great time*.

Unfortunately there was only one direction to go when you were at the pinnacle of *great time*.

Without his carefully honed sleep pattern, the nightmares began to creep back in. Last night had been the most gut-wrenching, hideous one yet, leaving him cold and shaking in his hotel room. It seemed there was no end to it, no way of putting the past behind him.

Lara had made him feel as if he could conquer anything.

He kept coming across that thought unexpectedly, popping up from nowhere, despite his efforts to keep her out of his mind. The thought of her made his stomach clench with misery. Before he'd met her he'd been stuck in limbo, no clue how to move forward, his mind constantly occupied by his past. Her reassurance and help had got his business off the ground, had given his life some focus again. His nightmares might still have plagued him, but they'd felt somehow more manageable because he'd had a new life to anchor himself to.

Lara had had confidence in him when he'd had none left in himself, and without her encouragement, her endless optimism, he was utterly lost. He'd tagged along on this trip with Isaac at the last minute, anything to get away and maybe get some perspective. He'd called his fitness clients and told them he'd be gone for a few weeks. Yet living it up and playing the field wasn't the answer and he had absolutely no idea what was. And finally black despair surged through him as he fumbled his wallet from his pocket.

He sat on the edge of his bed in the nondescript hotel room

and flipped through until he found the card. Just to look at it, not necessarily to *call* the number on it. A military charity, offering help for soldiers under stress. He'd taken the number out of politeness when he'd left hospital months ago, brushing off the slightest mention of PTSD, never intending to call it, never believing he would need to. To call that number would be to admit defeat, to acknowledge that he couldn't do this on his own.

He picked up his phone.

He'd flown back to London alone, declining Isaac's offer to accompany him on the second leg of the trip. The flat was exactly as he'd left it, his room tidy to military standards of precision. The comfort that had once given him seemed to have diminished a little now. Lara had come with endless *stuff* that began to seep into his room. Clothes left hanging over chairs, cosmetics on the dresser. He'd had to fight the urge to tidy up after her, but now he kind of missed the mess.

He dumped his bag and headed straight to Portobello Road, determined to give this his best shot. He knew now that honesty was the only path open to him. By the time he'd finished she might be congratulating herself on her lucky escape. He came to a standstill outside the little shop with the pink and black sign, composing himself. Well, here went everything. Hadn't that been one of the most attractive things about Lara? That her reactions were never predictable? And she was used to being on her own, that much he knew. None of it gave him much confidence in the outcome. But damn it, he had to *try*.

He pushed open the door of the shop and went in. The usual floral scent of the French soaps and perfumes she stocked smacked him immediately between the eyes, the way it always did. Lara was at the back of the shop behind the little counter, gift-wrapping something pink and silky for a middle-aged woman, who glanced his way with interest. He saw Lara stiffen almost imperceptibly as she saw him, her blue eyes widening, and then her inscrutable expression locked into place. Not a single clue as to what his reception might be. As he approached she handed over one of her signature pink and black bags with the black silk ribbon handles to her customer and turned to him.

'Yes, sir?' She gave him a breezy smile. 'How can I help you? Looking for something for a girlfriend? You look like the quick throwaway-fling type. Let me guess—something red with peepholes.' Her just-served customer was looking on with interest and Lara swept past Alex to the front of the shop to hold the door open for her. 'I'm sorry but I don't think I'll be able to help,' she called back to him over her shoulder. 'I'm not sure what you were expecting but that kind of thing *really isn't me.*'

The emphasis on those last few words made it crystal clear that if he'd thought talking her round was going to be a piece of cake, he was sadly mistaken. She closed the door behind her customer, turned the sign around to read 'Closed', and turned back to him.

'Make it quick,' she said. 'Say what you've got to say. Time is money. Every minute I close the shop I'm losing sales.'

'I came to say I'm sorry,' he said.

He saw her press her lips together.

'For what?' she said. 'For letting me think we actually had some kind of relationship there, letting me buy into all of that, when it was all for show?'

He closed his eyes briefly.

'It wasn't all for show. The way I feel about you was and is not just for show. I'm sorry for hiding my problems from you but I truly thought I could deal with them on my own. And you have to understand that, in my family, throughout my life, that's the way it's been done. As far back as I can remember, emotional outbursts have been a sign of weakness. By the time I was seven years old I'd worked out that crying only made my father angry—it certainly didn't elicit any sympathy or affection. Soldiers don't cry. They don't show emotion.'

She was watching him steadily. He had no idea if any of this was counting for anything at all with her. He crossed the shop towards the counter, took a breath and turned back to her. She was watching him steadily.

'I thought I could put the past behind me and have this fantastic life with you,' he said. '*That* was the problem. I was kidding myself that I could actually do that. On my own, without help from anyone else. I thought if I lived a normal life with you, starting a new business, moving on, pretty soon it would become exactly that.'

'Pretending things are normal won't make them normal,' she said, her voice carefully neutral. She walked slowly across the shop towards him, her arms folded defensively across her body. 'You can't just gloss over the bad stuff and expect it to go away.'

'I know that now,' he said. 'It was partly my pride. I just couldn't bear your suggestion that I get help. You have to understand that was the last thing I wanted to hear. I'd spent so long denying I had a problem that agreeing to get help was unthinkable. I thought I'd rather manage on my own than admit that. I decided to throw myself into partying with Isaac and I lasted less than a week. I don't want that life. But if I'm ever going to have more than that I have to face up to my past. I realise that now.'

He held her gaze carefully and a tug of sympathy pulled at Lara's heart. Yet still she steeled herself.

'Have you any idea what a big deal it was to let you into my life?' she asked him quietly. 'How much that cost me? I've never been able to take my eye off the ball and relax with someone, not since I was a kid. I'd had too many times, you see, where I'd done that, where I'd put my trust in someone, when I thought I could put down roots and be part of a family. And then the whole thing would come tumbling down around me.

'That's why I don't like to rely on other people. I've never *had* anyone to rely on. Whenever I thought I was settling in somewhere, or I got used to a new school or made a friend, before I knew it I'd be swept back into care and the whole damn thing would start all over again with another family. I just…

wasn't a good fit.' She held her head high and carried on boldly, 'I made up my mind a long time ago that I'd make my own life, that I'd work hard and get my own security without having to look to anyone else's help to get me there. I knew I wouldn't let myself down. And then you came along and made me rethink all of that. And for you to just walk away from it as if it meant nothing…' she caught her breath '…that was the worst thing that could happen to me.'

She sank into the chair next to the dressing screen. Just what did he expect from her? How could he expect her to give this another try when he'd messed with her trust, that thing that was so difficult for her to give?

'There were three of us in the vehicle,' he said then, and her fingers clenched on the arms of the chair. She turned slowly to look up at him in stunned surprise, understanding what he was about to tell her.

She could pick up the tiniest falter in his clipped deep voice and her heart turned over in spite of the way she was trying to steel it against him.

'Alex, you don't need to put yourself through this,' she said. 'I don't need to hear this stuff. It's not relevant anymore.'

'I want you to understand,' he said, his expression steady. 'I don't want any more secrets. There were three of us. Driver, another soldier, and me. Same kind of journey taken countless times, no big difference about that day, nothing that made it stand out.' He shrugged. 'My memories of the bomb are sketchy. I remember a sense of building pressure, as if I could feel the explosion coming from beneath us before it really hit. I remember the smoke, the smell of explosives burning at the back of my throat. My eyes stung. And the disorientation, that was the most hideous part. I couldn't find the others. I couldn't see. I was staggering around. It was chaos.'

'It must have been terrifying.'

'It was. But at the same time it was no more than I'd signed up for. I knew the risks. We all did. I went into it with my eyes open. And I wasn't about to have some kind of meltdown after the event. Not when I still had *my* life, that would have been a mockery of the soldier who lost his.'

He looked down at the floor.

'Private Sam Walker, his name was. The soldier who was killed.'

There was a long pause before he said any more and when he did she could hear the strain in his voice.

'It was his first tour and sometimes it takes time to adjust. Suddenly it isn't a training exercise anymore, it's the real thing and people…well, some people struggle, that's all. If I became aware of that I always tried to step in where I could, give some kind of encouragement. He'd…well, he'd had some problems and I told him I'd look out for him. That I had his back.'

He drew in a rasping breath and at last he looked up at her. His grey eyes held a tortured expression that made her heart ache for him.

'When you said that to me the other night, about having my back, it brought it all rushing back. I panicked. That's why I backed away so quickly, why I wouldn't discuss it with you or listen to reason. That's what I meant when I said it was about me not being what you need. I was determined to get well in record time after the bomb. I pushed myself like crazy in rehab. I told you I was handling it myself, that I had it under control, that it was improving, and I meant all of those things when I said them.' He shrugged. 'I think maybe I was trying to convince myself as much as you. And I know I should have got some help but I was ashamed.'

She shook her head, but he talked over her, as though if he stopped talking now he might never revisit this.

'I felt so *weak*,' he groaned, his head tilting up at the ceiling as he ran a shaky hand through his hair. 'I was an exemplary soldier, Lara. I was determined to better my father and I'd pushed myself up the ranks with sheer hard graft, I wanted to prove that I wasn't just there because of the family name. Without all of that I had no idea who the hell I was anymore, and I certainly didn't feel like I was good enough for someone as lovely as you. I got off lightly, Lara. The driver suffered terrible injuries and Sam was killed. I was the most senior person in that vehicle and there was nothing I could do for either of them.'

He was shaking all over now, both his hands clutched at the sides of his head. She was up from the chair before she knew what she was doing, pulling him tightly against her. She felt him grip her tightly, his breath heaving.

'How could I possibly trust myself to look after you when I'd failed so hideously?' His broken whisper was hot against her neck.

'You didn't fail,' she said, holding him tight. 'You didn't plant that bomb. None of what happened was your fault.'

She continued to hold him, feeling the tension in his shoulders slowly relax.

'I can't sort this out on my own,' he said after a minute, his voice muffled. 'And I know I threw your offer of support back in your face but I'm asking you to reconsider.'

She disengaged herself from his embrace and took a careful step back.

'What's changed?' she said. She searched his face. 'Why should I believe this isn't just you talking the talk and then necking off to swig espresso and pop caffeine pills?'

'Because I've got help this time,' he said. He looked away from her while he tugged a wad of paperwork from the pocket of his jacket and handed it to her. She took it and scanned it.

'A military charity?' she said.

'They run a helpline. Support for ex-servicemen who are suffering from stress. The dreams, the anxiety, they're common PTSD symptoms. I'm going to take counselling, whatever they can offer me to deal with it. No more pretending I'm improving by avoiding sleep. I know it's not going to be easy, and I'm not asking you to give me an answer right away. I just couldn't bear to have you thinking this was somehow down to some shortfall of *yours*. I'm the one with the problem here, not you.' He reached across and took her hand in his. 'I want to be with you. But I still don't feel like I'm good enough for that.'

Accepting you had a problem, wasn't that the first step to recovery?

She looked at him.

'I don't need rescuing, or looking after, Alex, so you can quit thinking I have any need for you to do that. I've done perfectly well by myself all this time. If we're going to be together then what I want is to be part of a team for once. To not be on my own. But that means we give it our best shot, the bad stuff and the good stuff included, not some stupid idea of what you think it should be like where I'm wrapped in cotton wool and you hide anything from me that you think I won't like.'

'Is that a yes?'

A tentative grin touched his lips.

'It's not as simple as that.' She'd had a good dose of reality these last few days since he'd gone. It had made her refocus on her business plans and ambitions. 'Even if it was a yes, I'll be moving out in a few weeks. I've no idea what my plans are next. I need to give that some serious thought.'

'Move in with me at the flat,' he said immediately, grabbing both her hands in his. 'At least for now. Poppy won't mind—I know she won't. She's loved having you around. I know it all sounds like our plans are short term but that's just logistics. I'm in this for the long haul if you are. If you can give me a second chance. No secrets.'

That he'd been open with her about his past touched her deeply. That couldn't have been easy after denying it so vehemently to everyone including himself. And it still wasn't going to be rainbows and butterflies, at least for the time being. But, hell, when had her life ever been that?

She squeezed his hands. Maybe in each other they could finally find the security they both needed.

'OK,' she said at last, and then she was pulled into his arms. Her stomach melted as he kissed and kissed her.

'With one condition,' she said, coming up for air. 'No boot camp for me. Ever.'

He smiled down at her.

'Done.'

* * * * *

French Fling To Forever
Karin Baine

French Fling to Forever
is Karin Baine's debut title
for Harlequin Medical Romance!

Dear Reader,

I can't believe my dream of becoming a Harlequin author has finally come true! Thank you for buying my debut novel and being part of it.

French Fling to Forever sprang to life from one small item—a pink stethoscope. I wanted my heroine to be a real girlie girl, but one so emotionally scarred she can't see her own beauty. Bullying has become such a serious issue I thought it was important to highlight the long-term damage it can cause. Although I was lucky enough never to endure the cruelty Lola endured as a teenager, I definitely share some of her insecurities.

This is the story of her strength, and the fight back against her childhood tormentors.

Of course a hot Medical Romance wouldn't be complete without a sexy doctor, and a brooding French registrar is the perfect man to help Lola move on from the past. I hope you'll love Henri as much as I do… *Swoon!*

If you would like to get in touch you can reach me on Twitter, @karinbaine1, or on Facebook.com/KarinBaineAuthor.

Enjoy!

Karin

For Mum and Granny Meta.
I miss you both every day. xx

This book would never have happened without the
love and support of my husband, George,
and our boys. A mention also to the rest
of the family, who have put up with
my writer/hermit craziness for years!

I would need another book
to list all those who helped me on this journey,
but know I appreciate each and every one of you.
Especially Michelle Handyside, who
has answered my endless medical questions,
and Julia Broadbooks, who has talked me down
from the ledge on many, many occasions.

CHAPTER ONE

LOLA TOOK A sip of sweet tea and did her best to blank out the anxieties vying for space in her head. *Am I up to the job? Can I cope with making life-or-death decisions? Where are the toilets?*

Over the rim of her cup she watched a sea of blue scrubs fill up the hospital canteen. The laughter and general chatter of her new colleagues did little to comfort her. They were so at ease, confident in their surroundings. She was sure she was the only first-year doctor here with knots in her stomach. Despite her promise to herself that her placement here in the Belfast Community Hospital would be another step towards independence, she was tempted to run.

Until recently she'd always had her brothers close by, to reassure her and take her by the hand when she needed it. It had been her idea to leave home once she'd graduated from medical school, although she wasn't sure if moving across the city to flat-share with her best friend counted as a particularly bold move.

Right now she needed one of those warm bear hugs only big brothers could give. This sense of isolation wasn't alien to her, but it was still as daunting as it had been at fifteen, when her whole world had fallen apart. Even now, almost ten years later,

Lola couldn't shake off the paranoia that everyone was watching her and judging her and that at some point she'd be made to pay for being different.

She jumped as the first dramatic chords of her mobile phone's ringtone blared from her pocket and jolted her back from her nightmarish thoughts. It wouldn't do for her to get lost in those dark thoughts of pain and humiliation when she was due for her induction into the emergency department in fifteen minutes.

She was sure every pair of eyes in the room swivelled towards her as her clammy hands fumbled to retrieve the phone.

'Hello, sis.'

Instead of turning it off, she'd managed to accept a call from the eldest of her three big brothers. That protective older sibling intuition was uncanny.

'Er…hi, Jake.'

She would have given a sigh of relief if it hadn't have been for the 'No Mobile Phones' signs screaming at her from the walls. If she didn't take the call now the rest of the family would surely hound her all day, since it was they who'd insisted she carry this blasted thing. Tea abandoned, she hurried out into the corridor to avoid further disapproving stares.

'How's it going?' Jake unknowingly provided the virtual arm around her shoulders that told her she wasn't on her own.

'I haven't started yet. I'll phone you when I get home.' Tears pricked Lola's eyes that her siblings knew her well enough to pre-empt her anxiety in an unfamiliar environment. Despite their sometimes overzealous interest in her personal life, she didn't know what she would do without them.

'I'm in the car park. I've got something for you.'

Jake sounded so pleased with himself Lola didn't have the heart to snub him. Besides, an *actual* hug would surely set her up for the rest of the day.

'In that case I'll see you in a couple of minutes.'

This time she did hang up, and then raced through the gleaming white corridors to meet him, the flat rubber soles of her shoes squeaking on the polished hospital floors.

Jake stood waiting for her in the ambulance bay, his striking features attracting the attention of every passing female. All three of her brothers resembled their father with their swarthy appearance, whilst she was the image of her blonde-haired, green-eyed mother. Sometimes she believed that was the reason her father had distanced himself from her. She was a painful reminder of the woman who'd walked out on him and left him to raise four children alone.

'I came to wish you good luck.'

Jake pulled her into his arms, only releasing her when she was sure she could hear ribs cracking.

He thrust a crumpled parcel into her hands. 'And I got you this.'

'Thank you.'

She ripped off the tatty wrapping to reveal a shiny new stethoscope. The thoughtfulness couldn't fail to make her smile. Although she didn't receive much support from either of her parents, with her mother AWOL and her father more concerned about himself, her brothers more than made up for it.

'We made sure we got you a pink one—just in case.' Jake grinned at the family joke.

In order to keep her brothers from pinching her stuff when they were growing up, Lola had learned at an early age to mark her belongings in boy-proof colours.

'Thank you. It's lovely, Jake. But I really have to run. I don't want to stuff things up on the first day.' She gave him a peck on the cheek and slung the gift around her neck.

'No problem. You've got this.'

Another lung-squeezing embrace emphasised his complete support, but Lola was forced to wriggle away as time marched on. She said her goodbyes and waved him off, waiting until he was out of sight before she started running again.

Out of breath, she slid to a halt behind the group already assembled in A&E.

'How nice of you to join us.'

The cutting French accent of her new superior called to her above the heads of her colleagues. She'd heard tales of all the newbies falling for the Gallic registrar and she could see why. Henri Benoit was the stereotypical tall, dark and handsome dreamboat. It was as well Lola had sworn off men prettier than her, or she'd be devastated on a personal level as well as a professional one at starting off on the wrong foot with him.

'Sorry. My brother wanted to wish me good luck.'

Even to herself she sounded like a five-year-old on her first day at big school. Lola whipped the stethoscope from around her neck and wrung it between her hands. The shine of her gift had been dulled under the scorn of her superior.

'Well, Dr—' he scanned her staff pass '—Dr Roberts. In future could you leave your personal life outside the hospital doors?'

'It won't happen again.' Marking a target on her forehead was the last thing a self-confessed wallflower wanted.

'*Bien*. Now that we're all here I will show you where everything is before we let you loose into the big wide world.'

The use of Benoit's mother tongue didn't make him any less intimidating to Lola, but she could almost see the cartoon love hearts in the eyes of the other new female recruit standing next to her. Even the distinctly masculine members of the group were hanging on to his every word.

In different circumstances Lola too might have sighed at the sexy sound of a real live Frenchman instead of the usual Belfast brogue, but as far as she was concerned a scolding couldn't be considered romantic in any language.

Thankfully the heat was off Lola as the registrar took the lead on a whistlestop tour of the department, with most of his eager new staff members nipping at his heels. All except one thoroughly chastened recruit, who hung back and did her best to fade into obscurity.

'This is the resus room and monitoring station. These are the rooms for the walk-in patients...'

Lola did her best to absorb all the information he shot at them. He didn't seem the type to repeat himself, and she wouldn't draw any further attention to herself by asking questions. The cursed gift she had for bringing out the worst in attractive men always resulted in the highlighting of her own inadequacies.

One of these days she would coast through life like everyone else apparently did, without worrying about how she looked to those around her. But for now those cruel voices still whispered in her ear, sneering at her appearance, telling her she wasn't good enough to be here.

Lost in her own thoughts, she drifted into the hub of A&E behind her colleagues. As they attended the bedside of an elderly man Lola suddenly became all too aware that everyone was watching her with expectation. This time she definitely wasn't imagining it. Henri Benoit folded his arms across his chest and raised an eyebrow, clearly waiting for something from her.

Breath caught in Lola's throat and she stared back blankly, wondering what it was she'd done wrong this time.

'*Excusez moi* for interrupting your daydream, Doctor. This patient needs bloods to be taken and I was asking if you would kindly oblige.'

This second dressing down from him was well deserved. She'd let her mind drift from the present into the all-consuming memories of the past.

There was no way she'd ever make a success of her medical career if she couldn't get a handle on her personal issues. Something told her Dr Benoit wouldn't wait around for her to get with the programme, and she owed it to the patients to focus on their problems instead of her own.

With sweaty palms and jelly legs, Lola stepped out of her corner. 'Sir, I'm just going to take some blood.'

Following procedure, she kept the patient informed of her intentions as she approached the bed, trying to keep the tremor in her voice at bay. There was no place for uncertainty in the frantic pace of Accident and Emergency, and she would need an air of authority if she hoped to gain any respect around here. Any wavering in her confidence would only serve to alarm those under her care.

Unfortunately, nerves appeared to have completely got the better of her.

'Sorry, I can't seem to find a suitable vein…' A warm flush infused her whole body as she tapped the patient's arm and attempted to insert the needle a second and a third time.

'One of the key things to remember in these early days is to ask for help when it's needed and not let a patient suffer for the sake of your ego. I'll take over from here.'

Every one of Lola's fears were realised as the registrar used her as an example to the rest of the group of how *not* to be a doctor. The nodding dogs were probably grateful they weren't the ones under the microscope.

Henri Benoit's hand brushed hers when he took the needle from her and the rolling in Lola's stomach reached a crescendo. She backed away for some breathing space, praying she wouldn't embarrass herself any more than she already had by throwing up on his shiny black shoes.

'All done.'

With an ease that Lola envied he finished the job and bagged up the vials for the lab. Once he'd settled the patient again he returned his attention to the group. Although she got the distinct impression he was mainly addressing her.

'The best way to learn is on the job. So get acquainted with the Duty Nurse and assign the patients between you. I'll be around if you need me.'

Lola's shoulders sagged with relief when he left her and her fellow rookies to go it alone.

Naturally, as soon as Dr Suave was out of the picture, she

functioned as well as any other member of staff. All further procedures undertaken after that debacle in the morning went as smoothly as they had done in her training. And in any areas where she *did* need some assistance she turned to the nurses for guidance. They were more than helpful, given that she showed respect for their position and experience—which she suspected some new doctors failed to recognise as an asset.

However, she couldn't seem to shake off her disappointment in herself, replaying that monumental cock-up in front of her boss over and over again. At periods during the day she found herself frowning and wincing, which probably looked strange to people not privy to the abject humiliation going on her head.

The end of the day couldn't come quickly enough, and when her shift was over Lola changed into civilian clothes and headed straight for the exit. Her face turned up to the heavens, she let the rain fall and cleanse her weary skin, as though it would somehow wash away everything that had happened back inside those doors.

The umbrella she was eventually forced to put up proved scant protection from the elements. It blew inside out several times as she joined the throng of people heading towards the city centre. She'd agreed to meet Jules, her flatmate, for a night out, and after today she'd earned it.

Most evenings she preferred to study, but Jules had insisted on helping her celebrate her first shift. As an F2, a Foundation Doctor in her second and final year of the training programme between medical school and specialist training, she'd taken it upon herself to instruct Lola in the ways of hospital life inside and outside of the wards.

'We're going to a new place tonight that all the girls in work are talking about. Somewhere you can really let your hair down,' Jules had told her when she'd given her the address of the venue.

For Lola, that was even more terrifying than facing another shift with her French Fancy.

* * *

'In burlesque, the emphasis is on the tease rather than the strip.'

Miss Angelique's delicate accent filtered across the dimly lit room to reach the ears of her most reluctant pupil.

In Lola's imagination the exotic sight and sound of the instructor should have transported her to a fabulous Parisian nightclub, where glamour and sophistication went hand in hand. Unfortunately the rumbling sound of buses outside and the accompanying smell of diesel through the open window were a constant reminder that she was stuck in a dingy dancehall in Belfast's city centre.

'When did Northern Ireland become a hotspot for the French populace?' she muttered to Jules, who she now held entirely responsible for her bad mood. Prancing around as some trussed-up, half-dressed version of herself with one of Benoit's countrymen bossing her around wasn't exactly the perfect remedy for all that ailed her. 'Tell me again—why am I doing this?'

'To prevent you from ending up as some sad sack with only her books for company,' Jules said, before her attention wandered back to the stage, where Miss Angelique moved seductively to a teasing big band soundtrack.

'Maybe I like the sound of that.' Lola pouted, and watched enviously as the instructor demonstrated a dance with oversized fluttering fans, never giving away more than a glimpse of the ivory silk corset she wore.

The stunning Frenchwoman projected a confidence in her body she could only dream of. Oh, how she longed to experience that freedom of movement, absent of any self-conscious thought, even for a short while. But owning her own sexuality, regardless of other people's perceptions, was a skill Lola doubted even the fabulous Miss Angelique could teach her.

A pack of savage teenage boys had robbed her of *ever* having any confidence in her own skin. Their laughter still rang in her ears, and she could still see their sneering faces looming above her as they'd held her down and stripped her of her dignity.

She'd been a late bloomer—not helped by the fact that she'd had to wear her brother's secondhand clothes and had sported the same short hairstyle her father gave all his offspring. But it hadn't given anyone the right to call her names, to question her femininity, or demand proof that it existed.

She hated them for the pain they'd caused her—hated the school for not putting an end to the bullying before it had got that far. Most of all she hated herself for letting it happen. A stronger person would have fought them off before they'd exposed and humiliated her. A more attractive girl wouldn't have had to. In the end she'd let herself down, and she was still fighting to make amends.

'Now, ladies, we've already assigned your stage names for this evening, and we need to bring your alter egos to life. Help yourself to props.'

Angelique clapped her hands to assemble everyone at the front of the stage. The group dived in, and amongst a chorus of whoops and excited chatter they emerged sporting a selection of wigs, top hats and satin gloves.

Lola shuddered. Playing dress-up really wasn't for her.

'I have the perfect accessory for *you*, Luscious Lola.' Jules approached, sequinned nipple tassels stuck on the outside of her top, and proceeded to hook a shocking pink feather boa around Lola's neck.

'Why, thank you, Juicy Jules.' Lola addressed her friend by her burlesque name, too, and tickled her nose with the end of the fetching neckwear.

As much as she'd prefer to throw on an overcoat and hide from view, she couldn't flat-out refuse to participate and let her friend down. However, the first sign that she was expected to start stripping and she was out of there. It was one thing pratting around with props, but a whole different trauma if it involved taking her clothes off.

Next time Jules suggested a night out Lola would opt for somewhere dark and quiet—like the cinema.

Angelique glided around the dance floor to round up her protégées like glamorous sheep. 'I will show you some basics to get started. First we have the milkshake.'

She shimmied her ample cleavage and encouraged them to do the same.

'I don't have much to shake,' Lola grumbled looking down at her chest. This was *so* not helping her overcome her body issues. Although she didn't look like a flat-chested ten-year-old boy any more, she definitely couldn't pull off *that* move.

'Flaunt what God gave you.' Angelique lifted Lola's arms and shook it for her.

Lola smiled painfully on the outside even as her innards shrivelled up and died of shame. This was her worst nightmare come true. Quite possibly even beating the one about turning up to work naked. At least in that one no one expected her to *pay* for being publicly disgraced. She closed her eyes and prayed for it to stop.

'Good.' The Frenchwoman let her go with a wink. 'Now, we need to get that booty popping, too. Jiggle that *derrière!*'

Lola swore revenge on Jules for making her twerk outside the sanctity of her own home. She gritted her teeth and pretended that shaking her ass was a way she *liked* to pass the time, in case the tactile tutor felt the need to touch her again.

The only thing that stopped her from walking out was the fact that this was an all-female ensemble and not in the least sexually threatening. These women were here for a laugh, and at some point she might actually see the humour, too. Probably when she was at home, safely hidden from grabby French hands.

Interspersed between the tapping of stilettos as the group practised their steps, the scrape of chairs sounded across the wooden floor to put Lola's teeth even more on edge.

'Now take a seat,' Angelique invited them, and tutted when they did. 'Not like that. Like *this*.'

She slid a chair through her legs, seat first, in one fluid movement, and sat astride it.

'With our backsides flush against the back of the chair, we want to pop our legs over the top and lie back, grabbing on to the chair legs. It's all about balance.'

Lola *knew* she should have worn trousers.

Angelique demonstrated a variety of provocative grinding moves until she had her followers riding the furniture like dirty cowgirls. Once Lola's initial discomfort had passed, and she saw that the others were too preoccupied to watch what she was doing, she started to relax into it. This was supposed to be fun—a way to free herself from the tensions of the day, not add to them.

She emptied her mind from all negative thoughts and concentrated on being a good student. After all, this was only a chair, and she was fully dressed. If she stood any chance of moving on from the past she had to stop sweating the small stuff.

Surprisingly, once she let go she found herself enjoying the predatory nature of chair-dancing and the aggressive power it gave her—over the object, over her body. For once she had nothing to prove to anyone, and without the pressure she revelled in her sensuality.

In total abandon, she threw her head back and gave herself over to it—only to lock on to a familiar pair of male chocolate-caramel eyes staring down at her.

'Well, hello, down there...' The masculine French accent mocked her.

From her upside down view it seemed a long way up to find the voice. A pair of muscular jean-clad thighs filled her direct line of sight, but as she glanced up along the slim-fitting blue checked shirt emphasising a solid torso, she met the last face on earth she'd wanted to see smirking back at her.

'Dr Benoit.' Surprise at seeing the head of her department coupled with her awkward position in the chair turned Lola's voice into a husky rasp. Clearly there was a two-for-one deal on nightmares coming true that she hadn't been aware of.

'Dr Roberts.' He gave a slight nod of his head, that lopsided grin never leaving him.

Shame flushed through Lola's system, bringing tension to every muscle as she withdrew into herself. With as much dignity as was available to her in the circumstances, she unhooked her legs and swivelled around to sit in a more civilised pose.

Without the cover of her fellow juniors she had an unimpeded view of her uninvited guest's handsome looks. There was no denying that the strong smooth jaw and the slightly too-long black hair curling around his ears, along with that accent, gave him all the ingredients for the ultimate heartthrob. But not for her. In her experience good looks tended to hide cruel hearts, and thus far he'd proved no exception.

This little performance simply provided him with more ammo against her. As if it was needed.

'So this is how you spend your time off?' he asked.

Lola got the impression that he thought she would be better employed brushing up on her medical know-how.

The injustice of being caught out on her one night of respite and the sticky heat of embarrassment at her compromising situation crept along her body and made her snap. 'It is no one's business but mine what I do outside hospital hours. So if you'll excuse me...?'

She thought her heart would pound out of her chest as she retaliated. Normally she wouldn't dream of speaking to her superior in such a fashion, but she felt trapped, vulnerable beneath his stare, and she'd learned to fight back whenever she was placed in that situation. She pulled off the suffocating feather boa and made to get up from her chair.

Angelique appeared at her side and placed a restraining hand on her shoulder. 'Stay where you are. Henri's just leaving—aren't you, dear?'

She batted her false lashes and shooed him away—much to Lola's relief.

* * *

Henri slunk to the back of the room to take a seat, shaking his head in bewilderment. The familiar scene that had met him behind the studio doors—cackling females sticking their asses out—usually didn't impress him at all. But tonight, seeing one of his staff in Ange's ragtag bunch, had caught him totally off guard.

Lola—that was her name. It really didn't suit her. 'Lola' conjured up images of a showgirl, confident and sure of her every move. The opposite of what she'd shown today. As her supervisor, it now fell to him to draw those qualities from her. One more responsibility to add to his load, and certainly one he could do without.

She obviously had the book smarts to have got this far in her career, but as first appearances went…he was not impressed. He didn't tolerate slacking in his department. Not when he'd already stood by and watched his sister let her medical career slip away without a fight.

Even now Lola appeared to have separated herself from the rest of the group, hiding away in the corner. Although the assertive nature he'd witnessed when he'd walked in and her feisty tone when she'd put him in his place was a complete departure from the hesitant junior doctor he'd encountered earlier.

Relegated to the role of peeping Tom, watching her from the shadows, he was mesmerised by her body-rolls. Every move of her hips showed off the lace-topped stockings under that minuscule skirt and called to his basest needs. Clearly it had been too long since his last hook-up with the opposite sex if the sultry fashion in which Lola straddled the chair seat was making him envy the damn thing!

It wasn't a good idea to be thinking about his new recruit with her bouncy little blonde ponytail and ridiculous pink stethoscope this way. She'd already distracted him from the small matter of his niece's apparent truancy, which he'd come to discuss with Angelique.

Ange stalked over to his corner to wag a finger at him. 'I can't afford to have you scaring off my customers, Henri.'

His older sister gave him that withering look guaranteed to make him regress back into the role of reprimanded teenager. Given the years he'd spent under her wing, he'd had many a rap on the knuckles from her—but he still respected her, and would never purposely do anything to make her regret the sacrifices she had made for him.

'I only said hello,' he muttered, still unable to take his eyes off the performance behind her.

'Well, you shouldn't be in here anyway,' she huffed.

Angelique saved him the trouble of leaving by turning her back on him and ending the session with a round of applause for her trainee dancers.

'*Très bien*. Great stuff, guys. I'm afraid that's all we have time for tonight. I hope you've had fun.'

The flushed, smiling faces staring back at her said it all. Never one to miss an opportunity, she left him to go and hand out her business cards.

'I know this lesson was probably intended as a one-off, but if you want to join us I run classes most evenings. It's a great way to stay in shape and keep the man in your life *very* happy.'

The girls tittered. Henri groaned. He still couldn't quite come to terms with her line of work. Especially when it was his fault she'd traded in a proper career to earn money dancing half naked. If their parents hadn't been killed in that car crash, if Angelique hadn't had to raise a teenage boy on her own, she might have been a respected medical professional by now.

All her studying had gone to waste, her bright future gone in a puff of smoke, in order for her to put food on the table for her little brother. They'd both been handed a life sentence that cold winter's day which had robbed them of their mother and father. And where Angelique seemed to have made peace with the outcome, Henri knew *he* never would. He'd only managed to follow his dreams at the price of his sister's.

The one consolation was that Ange's audience these days mainly consisted of fun-loving females who wanted to learn burlesque, rather than inebriated leering men. If it hadn't been for one of those men in particular, neither Henri nor Angelique would ever have left Paris for the rain-soaked streets of Northern Ireland. Then again, without the beau who'd enticed his sister to Belfast they wouldn't have Gabrielle and Bastien in their lives—and that was unthinkable, even on the most trying of days.

Henri was forced to wait until Angelique's students had heaped their praises and thanks upon her before he could get a word in.

His patience was wearing thin. They had much more important things to be doing—like trying to figure out why Gabrielle had decided to start skipping school. With Angelique's ex-husband out of the picture, Henri felt even more obligated to his sibling. So much so that he'd undertaken a lot of parental responsibility for the children whose father had long since abandoned them. They needed to get to the bottom of Gabrielle's recent behaviour, but it wasn't a conversation he wished to have with an audience.

'Can we go now? I'm not comfortable as the only eligible male in the company of so many desperate women.'

Angelique turned to him, and only then did Henri realise she wasn't alone. The highlight of his evening stood open-mouthed behind her, emerald eyes now glittering with contempt.

Hands on hips, Lola took a step forward. 'Funny—I didn't get the memo that said we "desperate women" were dancing for anyone else's benefit other than our own.'

Henri cursed himself for the overheard harsh words that had caused Lola's soft pink lips to draw into a tight line.

Her features only softened when she addressed her instructor again. 'Thanks for an enjoyable night and it was lovely to meet you.'

Lola tossed her golden mane of hair over her shoulder and,

with self-righteous grace, made her exit, Henri put firmly in his place. The woman definitely had bite, and that had succeeded in piquing his interest. If only he could get her to show that passion and spirit in the workplace...

'*Idiot!*'

Ange brought him back into the room. With half their lives having been spent living and working in Northern Ireland their native tongue had almost been rendered a distant memory, but her accent increased when she was angry—and, boy, was she angry.

'I'm sorry. I didn't mean anything by it. I was just—'

'I know you don't like what I do, Henri, but this is how I make my living and you can't be rude to my customers. Maybe it's better if you stay away from now on.'

Ange didn't give him a chance to explain his irritability as she threw props back into the box with a ferocity Henri knew she wanted to direct at him.

'I won't say another word. Promise. I'll help you get locked up and then I'll take you home.'

Where they could both confront his niece about what was going on. The only reason he hadn't said anything to Gabrielle himself since the phone call from her headmistress was because he didn't want to step on Angelique's toes. It was *her* daughter they were dealing with, after all.

'Thanks, but I'll walk.' She pulled on a mac over her scant outfit and flicked off the lights.

'You can't go out there like that!'

Henri forgot himself and once again voiced his concern about her fashion sense, regardless that she'd reminded him time and time again that he wasn't her father. He couldn't help himself. It didn't bear thinking about that something should happen to the only important woman in his life and he hadn't attempted to prevent it.

'I'm an adult, Henri. I can look after myself, and sooner or later you're going to have to realise that.'

She all but shoved him out through the door, and Henri was given the brush-off by a second woman in as many minutes.

Lola kept her back ramrod-straight until she reached her car and crumpled into the front seat. She had taken the opportunity to have a private word with Angelique when Jules and the others had gone on to the pub, toying with the idea of continuing the lessons in an effort to kick-start her self-esteem.

Textbooks were great for swotting up, but they didn't help her deal with people face-to-face—and, for her, that remained the most daunting element of her job. For every model citizen she encountered, there were going to be times when she was alone with aggressive patients, or cocky men who couldn't keep their hands to themselves. She knew that, and accepted it, but she also knew she needed to get into the right frame of mind to deal with it effectively.

The protocol for those situations probably *wasn't* to burst into tears and curl into a ball. It would take even more bravery than she'd mustered to leave home and go through medical school, to tell potential troublemakers to back off with any authority.

Until this evening she hadn't realised how much inner strength she possessed. Dancing had helped her explore a side of herself she hadn't known existed, and she would embrace all the help available to embark on this new phase of her life and overcome her fears. It was too bad that Mr Ego of the Year had taken that sliver of newfound confidence and crushed it underfoot.

Lola groaned, predicting that the repercussions of tonight's ill-tempered exchange would surely be felt at work.

She couldn't remember the last time she'd spoken to anyone like that—never mind a man with the power to make or break her career. But the fault totally lay at Henri Benoit's feet. He had no business crossing paths with her outside the hospital and insulting her when she'd been so exposed. For an unguarded moment she'd let light break through the darkness, only for him to cast her back in shadow. The problem was she had no way of explaining that—or her defensive reaction to it—if he decided to haul her over the coals tomorrow.

'I won't cry,' she said out loud, determined not to let another arrogant male reduce her to a gibbering wreck.

Engine started, she threw her Mini into Reverse and put her foot on the accelerator.

A loud bang and the jolt of the car caused her to slam on the brakes.

She didn't dare look.

Whatever she'd hit, she couldn't afford it.

Outside, she heard a car door open and close, heavy footsteps coming towards her. She switched off the ignition and braced herself, but the footsteps had stopped—no doubt to survey the damage.

'Mon Dieu!'

The foreign curse instantly gave away the identity of her victim.

Lola closed her eyes. *Oh, please. Not him!*

She slowly unclipped her seat belt and got out of the car to enter into the fearful realm of the Frenchman's ire.

'I'm sorry,' she said, knowing she didn't sound a fraction apologetic.

He bent down to inspect the cracked registration plate of his red sports car. *Typical.* She couldn't have hit a clapped-out rust heap—it would *have* to be this shiny status symbol.

'Is this payback for what I said in there?'

The patronising tone he used grated on Lola's already sensitive last nerve.

'I'm not that petty. Besides, it's only the number plate that looks damaged.' It wasn't as though she'd written off his boy toy altogether.

'Does your clown car not come with mirrors fitted?'

He looked down his high-bridged nose at her with a smug expression she wanted to slap off his face. The car she drove was a luxury, allowed her by the generosity of her brothers, who'd painstakingly restored it from its rusty former self and made it hers with a bubblegum-pink respray. Not everyone was afforded the life of privilege she imagined he'd led, and any snooty slight against her family was the one thing guaranteed to make her blood boil.

'I would have thought your ego was big enough to use as a force field and deflect the Pink Peril.'

With three elder brothers, exchanging childish insults came as naturally as breathing for Lola. She already had a black mark against her for squaring up to him, so she might as well make it count. Besides, *he'd* gone down the snarky route first.

'The *Pink Peril*?' he echoed incredulously and the grin grew into a full-on beaming smile.

He was treading on dangerous ground now.

'My brothers named it,' she huffed, and told her easily pleased inner schoolgirl, which was squealing with hormonal appreciation at the appearance of man dimples, to shut up. It was surely another sign of trauma manifesting itself that she found a man insulting her attractive.

'Do I take it that's a reference to your driving skills?' His eyes shone with suppressed laughter, the skin creasing at the corners to elevate his hunk status.

'I have *excellent* driving skills,' she protested.

'So I see.' He lifted a thick dark brow as he glanced back at the damage.

'Look, I've apologised. I'll pay for repairs. So, if we're done here…?'

It was time she left—before she completely shot down her career. This man seemingly brought out the worst in her, and that wasn't conducive to a happy six weeks under his tutelage.

Far from helping her get over the day's trials and tribulations, this whole evening had simply heaped more stress upon her. At least with this latest disaster she knew she could count on her brothers to make any necessary repairs with the minimum of fuss. If only they could come to work with her tomorrow and clear up the mess she'd made there, too, she might have a chance of clawing back some respect.

'I think I have an apology of my own to make. I didn't mean to insult you in there.'

Henri ignored her need to end the conversation and perched his butt on the bonnet of his precious car.

'And yet you did.' She folded her arms across her chest as he brought up the subject of his slur against her character once more. He couldn't know the throwaway insult had hit her on such a personal level, but that didn't give him the right to end up the good guy here.

'The problem is between Angelique and myself. I shouldn't have taken it out on you. It's fair to say I don't exactly approve of the work she does.' A shake of his head emphasised his dismay.

'She seems like a woman who knows her own mind.' Lola didn't imagine a free spirit such as Angelique needed his permission to do something she obviously loved.

'Ah, but Ange doesn't always know what's *best* for her.'

The sincerity Henri expressed brought goosebumps along Lola's skin. Even though he might not agree with his other half's lifestyle choice, his devotion was beyond doubt. The only unconditional love Lola had ever had was from her brothers. The tragic tale of her failed past relationships was entirely to do with her reluctance to let anyone else get close. She considered Angelique a very lucky woman.

'It's chilly out here, so if we could get back to rectifying this mess I would like to get home. I really think your licence plate took the full impact, and I can get my brother to order you a new one. I hardly think it warrants involving insurance companies.'

What went on behind the doors of *chez* Benoit was none of her business—she certainly didn't want to warm towards the man responsible for ruining her entire day. All she wanted to do now was call it quits and start afresh tomorrow.

'In that case we can sort the details out at work. I can see you're in a hurry.'

He finally took the hint and Lola dashed back to her car to wait for him to move.

As she sat with her arms locked out straight, holding on to the steering wheel for dear life, she exhaled slowly. Everything seemed to hit her at once, and her heart started drumming so hard she thought she might just pass out.

One night of escapism, thinking she could be 'normal', and she'd played stripper, crashed her car and had another run-in with her boss—embarrassing herself at every step. It was more excitement in her life than she cared for.

The next six weeks working under Henri Benoit stretched before her like a prison sentence. One with absolutely no chance of getting time off for good behaviour.

CHAPTER TWO

BUILT TO SERVE the influx of inhabitants to the rejuvenated city, the predominantly glass and marble structure of the Belfast Community Hospital was bright and modern. Even now she was in the bustling corridors, under the glare of fluorescent light, Lola thought it a beautiful building.

These last few shifts had shown her that any chance for silent contemplation ended on the far side of the double doors, and Lola braced herself for the madness of A&E on a Friday night as she pushed them open.

'Nurse! Nurse!'

The loud, slurred speech of a waiting patient greeted her. A hand shot out and clamped around her wrist, immediately regressing her to that time in her life when she hadn't had the strength to fight back.

She screwed her eyes tightly shut, in an attempt to fend off the memories assaulting her, but it only succeeded in leaving her alone in the dark with them.

The busy reception area faded away, and the walls closed in until she was back in that small room crammed full of grinning faces. Her limbs were immobile, pinned down by unseen forces, leaving her completely at the mercy of her attackers. They were too strong for her, their hands tugging at her clothes until she was naked and shivering beneath them.

The actual assault had lasted only minutes—long enough to satisfy their cruel need to break her spirit. Once her humiliation was complete, the matter of her sexuality no longer an issue, they'd thrown her clothes at her and walked away. In hindsight, her ordeal could have been much worse, even though it hadn't felt like that at the time.

A shudder racked through Lola's body as she contemplated the alternative. It had taken her years even to let another man touch her after that betrayal, and she doubted she would ever have recovered if that band of delinquents had decided to take things any further.

The intervening years had been tough for her as she'd tried to come to terms with what her bullies had probably deemed no more than a prank. For her, the experience had left her wanting to run from the room screaming if a man so much as put his hands on her uninvited. Only her desire to practice medicine on the general public had put her on the road to recovery and stopped her freaking out completely at times like this.

The pressure eased from around her forearm, immediately releasing her from her torment. She blinked her eyes open to see a man she guessed to be in his sixties slumped in a plastic chair beside her. After a deep breath she extricated his fingers from her person and reminded herself that she wasn't a helpless teen any more.

'I'm Dr Roberts. I'm sure one of the nurses will be along shortly to assess your condition, sir.'

He had a small gash on his right cheek, which was letting a small trickle of blood further colour his already ruddy features, but she suspected from the stench of alcohol closing in around her that alcohol was the main reason behind his hospital visit.

'Am I dying, Doctor?' Red-rimmed eyes tried to focus on her, and it soon became obvious he was more of a danger to himself than anyone else.

It buoyed her confidence to know she was the one in control of the situation here, and she was able to reassure him with a pat on the hand. 'I'm pretty sure you're not dying, but I'll send someone over to see you as soon as possible.'

'Good.' He sank back into the chair, placated for now, and the sound of tuneless singing followed her on her way.

With the patient's concerns passed on to one of the nurses, with the advice that it might be wise to have him seen to and discharged before he settled down for the night, Lola lifted a file from the stack on the desk.

Her first patient was an elderly woman experiencing dizziness and fatigue. Possible dehydration, since the notes indicated an increased thirst and decreased skin turgor. No doubt this lady had been specifically left for Lola to deal with because of the apparently straightforward nature of the ailment, but she didn't mind. The role of general dogsbody gave her inner wallflower a chance to disappear under paperwork and the smaller jobs more experienced doctors deemed too trivial to waste their talents on. These small steps into the medical field would carry her through until it was her moment to shine. At which point she might need some anti-anxiety pills to hand.

With her bits and pieces gathered together from the storeroom, she made her way to the cubicle. The sight of the elderly lady waiting for her behind the curtain immediately put her at ease.

'Now, then, Mrs Jackson. I'm just going to take a wee blood sample from you, if that's all right?' A UE blood test would tell if the electrolytes and sodium were off—a further indication of dehydration.

The old woman smiled, the skin at the corners of her pale blue eyes creasing with laughter. 'Sure, I'm like a pin cushion these days anyway.'

Lola noted how sunken her eyes looked, and the dryness of her lips when she smiled. The dry mucus membranes were another sure sign her diagnosis was correct.

'So I don't need to worry about you passing out when you see this needle?' If only all her patients were this co-operative it would make her job a whole lot easier.

'No, dear. You do what you have to.' Like a professional blood donor, Mrs Jackson held out her arm and tapped on a raised blue vein. 'That's where they usually go for.'

The translucent skin was already punctuated with fading bruises from similar procedures. Lola cleansed the area with a wipe, grateful that she wouldn't have to put this lovely lady through the ordeal of chasing a suitable site to insert the needle.

'I think you could get yourself a job here,' Lola said as she tightened the tourniquet around the upper arm.

'Ach, away with you. I could never put in the hours you youngsters do. Sure, when would you ever find time to catch yourself a husband? Unless you're waiting for one of those handsome male doctors to sweep you off your feet?'

The inquisitive patient brought an uninvited picture of the suave Henri Benoit into Lola's head. Even there he looked smug that she was thinking about him.

'If you could just make a fist for me that would be great. Now, you'll feel a little scratch,' Lola said as she inserted the needle and let the woman's last question fall without an answer.

Thankfully she had managed to avoid said handsome doctor and the embarrassment of that evening thus far. So why did her senses conspire and refuse to let her forget him? The sound of his accent, the smell of his aftershave and the memory of his rarely seen smile wouldn't leave her. It was a godsend that their hands had only touched briefly or she would surely have ended up a victim of sensory overload.

She tried desperately hard not to think about taste.

Since that final humiliation at the club, he was the last person she would turn to for help. She wouldn't give him the satisfaction of seeing her inadequacy in action. Regardless of how many times she carried out standard procedures confidently and correctly, she couldn't shake off that look of disappointment he'd given her. Her fender bender in the car park had been the only time she'd witnessed the scowl slip from the registrar's face and the smile had somehow been worse. It had made him human, showed a softer side to him, and it had made her want to impress him so she could see it again.

'Could you hold that cotton wool for me there, Mrs Jackson?' Lola withdrew the needle and the helpful patient dabbed the spot of blood left behind. 'Now, you rest until we find a bed for you on the ward, and I'll get these sent off.'

'Thank you, dear.' The previously animated pensioner lay back, flattening her head of white curls into the pillows, and showed the first signs of fatigue.

Lola vowed to take all the necessary steps to get Mrs Jackson rehydrated and back on her feet as she returned to the nurses' station—and walked into a flurry of activity.

'What's going on?' she asked Jules, who was passing by in the herd of medics apparently gearing up for something more serious than an old dear having a turn.

'Emergency call. Ambulance is on the way with a patient in cardiac arrest.'

As Jules chewed on her pen Lola could see her body thrumming with anticipation for the arrival. Maybe it was the extra year's experience Jules had over her, but Lola hadn't quite reached that stage of life-or-death excitement.

'Would you care to join us, Dr Roberts?'

Apparently it took the invitation to be issued in a French accent to get her pulse racing.

'Pardon?' She turned to face Dr Benoit, incredulous that he had asked her to participate as if he was issuing an invitation to dinner.

'I'm sure they can spare you from treating minor cases for a while, and I think the experience will be good for you.'

He barely glanced in her direction and carried on flicking

through his notes. A prod of disappointment poked Lola in the abdomen as he dropped back into aloof doctor mode. A far cry from her sparring partner in the car park, but at least she knew where she stood with this version of Henri Benoit—and she wouldn't let him get the better of her.

Lola lifted her chin to meet the challenge. 'I would love to join the team.'

Equipment gathered in preparation, the assembled medical staff waited for the starting pistol, ready to get off the blocks, whilst Lola willed her limbs to stop shaking. The paramedics slammed through the door and galvanised everyone else into action.

Here we go.

'On the count of three.' Henri took charge as they surrounded the trolley. 'One, two, three.'

Between the paramedics and the doctors the seemingly lifeless body of an overweight middle-aged man was transferred from the stretcher onto the bed and hooked up to a bank of monitors.

'Get a line in, please, Lola,' Henri instructed.

With a very small chance of bringing the patient back, there was no room for her to freeze or panic.

'Starting CPR,' Henri announced, starting chest compressions.

Lola's scrubs clung to her suddenly clammy skin as she fought to insert the cannula. They needed it to inject adrenaline and try to restart the heart, and he had tasked *her* with the important job. Thankfully, with Henri pumping the chest to get blood and oxygen flowing around the body again, he made it possible for her to find a vein.

'I'm in.' She managed to keep the relief from her voice in a room full of people who did this every day of the week.

'Get the paddles on. Do we have a shockable rhythm?'

Henri's voice carried above all other noise and she focused on it alone to guide her through what was happening.

'Everyone stand back. Shock delivered. One milligram of adrenaline in. Stop for rhythm, please.'

They paused and listened for signs of life. Nothing. More chest pumps, more adrenaline and more shocks were delivered by the defibrillator to kick-start the heart—until he uttered the words she longed to hear.

'He's back.'

Lola stood back in awe as Henri's cool command brought a dead man back to life, indicated by the steady blip of his pulse on the screen.

Once the patient was stabilised Henri addressed the team. 'Good job, everyone. Lola, you too. You can go back to what you were doing.'

That commanding tone had turned softer, something she was unaccustomed to, and it was a wonder she heard it above the pounding of blood in her ear as the last minutes caught up with her.

Unable to speak, she flashed him a grateful smile and made her way out of the resuscitation room. The less frantic corridor outside was a welcome respite from the drama, and Lola took a minute to catch her breath. Only now did the reality hit her that she had played a part in saving a man's life. With no time to worry over who was watching as she administered the adrenaline, she had acted on pure instinct and skill.

A hand rested on her shoulder and forced Lola to concentrate on not collapsing onto the polished floor.

'Are you okay?'

Henri's brown eyes bored into hers until she felt her feet gradually slipping from under her.

He directed her to a seat. 'Here, sit down.'

'I'm fine. Really,' she insisted, wanting him to disappear as quickly as he'd arrived and leave her to stew in her own embarrassment.

'It is okay to have a little wobble.'

His pronunciation of that last word sounded so ridiculous for the sophisticated doctor she felt better already.

'These things—they are intense and difficult to handle at the beginning, but you did your job. You were part of the team that brought him back and you should be proud of yourself, Lola. Now, take five minutes and get yourself a cup of tea whilst it's quiet.'

As he left her Lola couldn't be sure if it was the first sign of compassion from him or his continued use of her first name that had sent another bolt of adrenaline to bring her own body back to life.

On doctor's orders she soon found herself in the canteen, paying for a cure-all cuppa. Her first time as part of the resus team had left her a little shaky on her feet, so she couldn't wait to sit down and take a time-out.

A *'Bonjour!'* much too cheery for it to have come from her superior greeted her in the seating area. The familiar figure of her burlesque instructor waved her over to a table in the corner.

'Come and join us. I didn't know you worked here. I take it you and Henri know each other?'

Angelique, dressed more conservatively than the last time Lola had seen her, directed her to a seat. She was accompanied by a teenage girl who bore an uncanny resemblance to Henri and his other half. It was unfair that one family had hogged all the would-look-good-in-a-bin-bag genes.

Naturally any child with that combination of DNA in her genetic make-up was bound to be a beauty, but she'd clearly been in the wars. Her otherwise clear skin was marred by a series of angry red abrasions across her cheek, whilst the beginnings of a purple bruise ringed her right eye.

'You could say that. I've just started my placement in A&E.

I'm Lola, by the way.' She introduced herself to the Benoit mini-me as she sat down with her tea.

'Gabrielle,' the girl mumbled, in that barely comprehensible manner all teenagers used in the presence of strangers.

'Are you here to see Henri?'

'Yes, but they told us he's busy with a patient. We'll just have to wait until he comes home to speak to him.' Angelique shifted restlessly in her seat, clearly more bothered about not seeing him than she was willing to let on.

'We were dealing with an emergency admission downstairs, but I'm sure he'll be free soon. Is there anything I can help you with in the meantime? If you want I can take you down after this and take a look at those cuts on your face?'

Lola turned her attention to the young girl, with her head bowed as she played with the food on her plate, a curtain of raven hair now falling over her face to hide the marks from view.

'That won't be necessary, thanks. The school nurse cleaned Gabrielle up before they phoned me to collect her. It's nothing serious, but they don't take any chances these days.'

Angelique's fidgety hands on the table gave away her real concern, and Lola thought perhaps she was simply being polite and didn't want to bother her.

'It's no trouble. As you say, it's better to be safe than sorry.' Besides, she was sure Henri wouldn't take too kindly to finding out his daughter had been sent away without some sort of examination.

'I'm fine. I tripped and fell in the playground—it's not a big deal.' The surly teen rested back on her chair, arms folded across her chest, practically daring Lola to disagree.

'Honestly, that's not even why we're here. We have a cake emergency that requires immediate attention. So, unless you know someone who can whip up a dinosaur-themed birthday cake in twenty-four hours, I'm afraid you can't help.'

A diplomatic Angelique stepped in to change the subject to one even closer to Lola's heart than her job.

'Whose birthday is it?'

'My son's. Bastien will be six tomorrow, and he's decided at the last minute that the only thing he wants is a dinosaur cake. I can't find one in the supermarkets, and bakeries need more notice than I can give. I was hoping to brainstorm with Henri— or get him to take a crash course in baking.'

The stressed mother let out a sigh as she planted an image in Lola's brain of the usually suave doctor up to his elbows in flour.

'I've been known to do a bit of baking myself.'

That was like saying Beyoncé did a bit of singing. The kitchen was Lola's natural habitat, and where she went to unwind at the end of the day. She didn't usually do commissions, but she'd made all manner of themed cakes for her brothers over the years. Where money had been scarce, imagination had been plentiful. A dinosaur might be fun.

'Are you saying you could do it?' This time Gabrielle appeared to be totally enamoured by her new acquaintance, her dark eyes shining with excitement.

Lola understood the love a sister had for a brother, and the need to see him happy even when he could be a royal pain in the butt at times.

'Maybe… I mean, I'm no expert or anything…' She knew she was capable of doing it, but those doubts crept in that her standards mightn't be good enough for a third party.

'I don't care if it's nothing more than a blob with eyes and scales, as long as I have something to give him. You're a lifesaver. Now, if you could have it ready by tonight, I can send Henri to get it. How much do you need for supplies, et cetera?'

Angelique began to rifle in her handbag, immediately dampening Lola's spirit. She baked out of love—not for financial gain.

'Whoa! I haven't agreed to do it yet. What if Henri doesn't want me involved? He sees enough of me here.'

There was also the matter of Lola not being thrilled with the idea of crossing paths with him again outside of work. She'd only just sorted out the last mess she'd made—with Jake's help. He'd stepped in and dealt with the aftermath of the fender bender so she didn't have to.

'It's not Henri's call.'

Lola didn't want to end up in the middle of a domestic dispute, especially when she really didn't know these people.

She drained her cup and stood to leave, hoping they would follow suit. 'Why don't we check with him anyway, before we make any definite plans?'

Henri probably wouldn't deny the child his birthday wish, but Lola couldn't afford to stuff things up again. As far as she was concerned this was *his* call.

Henri might have broken his vow to keep his distance from the pink princess after his lapse at the club, but it was worth it if his interference today had boosted her confidence even a fraction.

He knew Lola's capabilities were there, if she could just stop overthinking her every move. Whilst her job meant being able to assess a situation, it also meant being decisive. Aside from her fine display of booty-shaking, today was the first time he had seen her act without second-guessing herself. If a push out of her comfort zone was what it took to make a doctor out of her, then as her superior he felt obliged to continue. It was absolutely nothing to do with him getting a kick out of seeing her fired up.

Once Henri had made sure his coronary patient was stable he went to his office to strip off his scrub top. He could shower at home, but for now a clean shirt would help peel away the layers of stress from the day.

I know there's one in here somewhere.

He pulled open drawer after drawer, until a light tap on the office door interrupted his shirt search.

'Come in.'

'Dr Benoit...' Lola's voice trailed off as she caught him half-naked. Her wide eyes registered his state of undress, then shot towards the floor, the ceiling—anywhere but his bare chest.

'What is it?' he snapped, miffed by her visual dismissal. A white T-shirt rolled up at the back of his bottom drawer saved him from self-doubt and he pulled it on over his head.

'Angelique and Gabrielle are here. I…er…thought you would want to know.'

She scuttled away but Henri caught up and grabbed her arm.

'Where are they? Is something wrong?'

Lola let out a yelp and wrestled out of his grasp. 'They're outside. Gabrielle has taken a tumble at school, but insists she's fine, and Angelique wants to talk to you about Bastien's birthday. I'm just making sure you aren't too busy to see them.'

Lola backed away, rubbing the skin on her arm where he'd grabbed her.

Henri immediately regretted being so rough. He hadn't meant to scare her, but the thought of the girls in trouble had made him act without thinking.

'I always have time for my family.'

'In that case I'll show them in.' Lola frowned at him, making no attempt to hide her displeasure at his behaviour, and rightly so.

'Thank you, and…er…sorry about—' He gestured towards her arm when he realised *Sorry for manhandling you* would sound totally inappropriate.

'It's okay.' She managed a half smile before she opened the door to let Angelique in.

Gabrielle followed her mother inside and Henri spotted the red marks crisscrossing her pale skin. Emotion overwhelmed him once again. 'What the hell happened?'

'It's just superficial,' the rational voice of his junior assured him, even though he could see that for himself.

It didn't stop him from worrying.

'Gabrielle? How did this happen to you?'

His niece gave an exaggerated *tut*. 'I keep telling everyone it's no big deal. I fell over. End of story.'

Henri knew he wasn't getting the whole picture when she turned her face towards the wall and refused to look at him.

Out of the corner of his eye he could see Angelique's shake of the head, meant only for him—an indication that he wasn't to pursue the matter any further. It wasn't in his nature to stand idly by and pretend things was okay when they blatantly weren't, but in parental matters he had to defer to his sister.

'At least get a cold compress for that eye to stop the swelling.'

'I'll do it when I get home.' An eye roll accompanied the insinuation that he was being a fusspot.

'I actually wanted to talk to you about Bastien's birthday. He's changed his mind about a pirate party and decided he wants a dinosaur cake instead.'

The uncle/niece stand-off ended with Angelique's intervention and a completely different tangent in the conversation.

Now Henri was the one rolling his eyes. His young nephew changed his mind more often than Angelique changed costumes. The never-ending parade of after-school activities as he bored easily with one and moved on to the next attested to that. There wasn't time for a dull moment with him around, and Henri's life was the better for it. Without his sister and the kids to occupy his thoughts he'd probably be just another self-absorbed playboy, like so many he'd met in the profession.

'Surely that's an easy fix and not one that warrants Dr Roberts's time?' Lord knew what Lola must think, being called away from her patients to deal with trivial family matters. Especially when he'd called her out on her first day of placement for doing exactly the same thing.

'Not as straightforward as you might think at such short notice, and Lola has offered to help out. She thought we should get *your* approval before moonlighting as our personal cake decorator.'

There was definitely more than a hint of sarcasm there as

his big sister was forced to change the dynamics of their relationship by asking his permission to do anything. Lola stood quietly waiting for his approval and he got the impression she'd been strong-armed into helping.

'You dance *and* bake?'

He was learning something new about her every day. Probably more than he should. Events seemed to be conspiring against him—and his rule about not fraternising with his A&E colleagues outside of work. He had doctor friends, of course, but he preferred not to muddy the waters between himself and the junior staff.

Apart from friendships becoming strained when he had to exert his authority at work, there was also the temporary nature of their position here. There was little point in forging new relationships which detracted from his family responsibilities only for them to move on to their next placement. Not that he was anticipating spending any more time with Lola than was normal—she just seemed to *be* there, everywhere he turned.

'I do one much better than the other.'

The woman in question flushed pink as she underplayed her talents, but Henri had seen her in action.

'Well, I *know* you can dance…' He watched the bloom rise in her cheeks at the reminder that he'd seen her moves in all their glory.

Until that moment when he'd witnessed Lola giving herself over to the music he'd never seen the beauty of burlesque. Thus far it had represented everything he hated about life after his parents' deaths—the financial struggle and the guilt he harboured for being Angelique's responsibility when she was nothing more than a kid herself. That perception had altered when he'd watched burlesque empower a shy doctor before his eyes. It had brought Henri some understanding of his sister's insistence that she danced for no one but herself.

If it hadn't been for Angelique coughing, Henri might have forgotten he and Lola weren't alone in the room.

'So, Lola can make the cake and you will pick it up from her house tonight, Henri—yes?'

'Wait…what?'

'Great. You two can sort out the details and Gabrielle and I will go and buy the rest of the party supplies. Thanks again for offering to help out.'

Angelique swallowed Lola into her embrace in that gregarious manner which made it impossible to say no to the woman. The mere mention of culinary skills and Henri's unassuming colleague would have been a lamb to the slaughter in her presence. And even he now found himself roped into paying Lola an out-of-hours visit when it was the last thing he wanted to do.

Still, it wouldn't do to make a scene and have her think there was an issue. It was simply a matter of keeping his nephew happy. He'd have a discreet word with his sister later, about not putting him into compromising positions with his staff in future.

Lola watched open-mouthed as the French tornado blasted back out through the door, taking her offspring with her and leaving a trail of destruction in her wake. Henri was frozen to the spot, probably wondering what the hell he'd agreed to. Somehow Lola's offer to bake a cake had led to an appointment with Henri at her apartment. Her safe haven was about to be breached by the one man who could bring her temper to a boil with one flick of a switch.

Without Angelique's huge personality to fill the room Lola found herself alone with Henri in his tight white T-shirt. Although she was off men for the foreseeable future, it didn't mean she was immune to fine man candy. She could still picture his half-naked body when she'd walked in earlier—the speed bump abs and the trail of dark hair dipping from his navel into the waistband of his trousers, reminding her that he had the body to match the hint of sexy in his eyes.

It was enough to give her the vapours, trying to match the creases in his shirt with the defined muscles she'd only caught a glimpse of.

An awkward silence ticked between them as Lola played a game of hide and seek with his abs. At some point she was either going to have to make conversation or ask him for a quick flash to get reacquainted with his six-pack. She chose the option less likely to start a cat fight with his significant other.

'If you have a pen and paper to hand, I'll write my address down for you.'

'Of course.' Henri, too, snapped back to life and scrabbled on his desk for the requested stationery. 'I'm sorry if you've been inconvenienced. Angelique takes no prisoners, I'm afraid.'

'It's all right. What kind of person would I be to leave the birthday boy without a dinosaur cake? Anyway, I should think this makes us even now. I hit your car—I bake you a cake. Debt repaid.'

After this there was no reason for either of them to venture into each other's social territory, or for her to ogle her registrar again. The image of him stripped to the waist was imprinted on her brain for ever anyway.

She handed him the piece of paper with her hastily scribbled address. 'I'll need a couple of hours after work to get it done. Shall we say eight o'clock?'

Her steady voice belied her insides as they danced a jig at the thought of him waiting on her doorstep. She wasn't particularly relishing explaining it all to Jules, either.

'Eight's fine by me. Whatever it takes to have at least *one* happy child to go home to.'

The way Henri raked his hand through his hair told of his anxiety over one young person in particular.

'Gabrielle?'

He nodded. 'The bruises, the truancy…there's clearly something going on, but she refuses to tell us what.'

Lola knew he had to be confiding in her out of desperation—by all accounts he was usually a private man. She wasn't an authority on the subject of raising children, but she had been a teenage girl with bruises and excuses to avoid school.

'I hate to say this, but do you think there could be anything going on at school?'

Henri fixed her with an unwavering stare until she found it difficult to breathe, fearing she'd overstepped the mark. After a few heart-stopping seconds he let out a long sigh and brought her some much needed relief.

'She says not—goes mad at the suggestion I pay her teachers a visit—but it's getting to the stage where I might have to.'

Lola could imagine him going in, that feisty French temper at full blast, making things much worse for the young girl. Her brothers hadn't improved matters for *her* when they'd gone storming in with their fists flying.

'I'm sure she'll confide in you when the time's right for her. It's not easy for teenage girls to talk to anyone—especially their daddy.'

There'd been absolutely no point in Lola going to *her* daddy at the height of the bullying—he wouldn't have coped when he'd barely been able to hold himself together. Lola's relationship with her father now was somehow more distant than the one with her estranged mother. He was still around, but he'd never been the parent she'd needed. If Lola ever had children of her own she hoped they'd have a man like Henri in their lives to genuinely care for them.

Just as she was getting carried away by the *aww* factor of Henri looking out for his baby girl, she caught sight of his raised eyebrow and lopsided smile.

'What? I'm forbidden to voice an opinion? Trust me—you'll do her no favours by storming in and ignoring her wishes. Be there for her…let her know she can come to you when the time is right.'

Her speech had been a long time coming, and it was one meant for her own family, but it was as relevant to this situation as it had been then. Henri and Angelique needed to open the lines of communication with their daughter before things got any worse.

The adrenaline rush of speaking out left Lola dizzy and a little breathless.

Henri tilted his head to the side and gave her a grin that sent shivers through her very core. 'You think I'm Gabrielle's *father*?'

She didn't want to say yes and compound her mistake, since he was making it very apparent he wasn't. 'Father, stepfather, whatever… You're still her guardian.'

'I'm her uncle.'

'Oh. *Oh.*' The implications of that new information slowly filtered through to Lola's brain. If she was his niece, that meant—

'Angelique is my sister.'

He put an end to her struggle to put the pieces together and garnered another performance of her goldfish impression.

'I just assumed… You're clearly a very close family.'

She must have been blinded by their combined beauty not to notice the now obvious resemblance between them. Beautiful people always gravitated towards each other, so Lola had never imagined either one of the Benoits as singletons. If they were. For all she knew there could be more Model Trons stashed away—robots disguised as physically perfect humans whose mission on Earth was to make everyone who wasn't a perfect ten seem like a frump in comparison.

'Are you telling me you thought Angelique and I were a *couple*?'

A deep, rumbling laugh reverberated around the room and reduced Lola back to that bumbling rookie who knew nothing.

'I put two and two together—' She shrugged her shoulders as she chalked up another nomination for the Idiot of the Month award.

'And you came up with five. I guess we *are* closer than most since our parents died. When Angelique left Paris to be with the kids' father I decided to come and do my studies here and keep what was left of the family together.'

A sadness settled over Henri, stealing the twinkle from his smile as he spoke of his loss. It explained the close bond he had with his sister and her children. Hadn't Lola clung to her brothers, too, when their parents had bailed?

'And Angelique's partner is no longer on the scene?' It wasn't really any of her business, but if he was in a sharing mood it was better to find out the exact circumstances before she put her foot in it again.

Henri shook his head. 'Sean's been in and out of her life, but I think she's better off without him.'

'At least she has you to help out with the children and broker her cake deals.'

It was Lola's turn to have some fun and lighten the atmosphere before she was expected to reveal personal information in return. Although she no longer saw him as her arch nemesis, neither was he a friend. At least not one whom she was ready to trust with her deepest, darkest secrets.

'There is that.'

Henri's frown evened out into another smile and Lola was able to appreciate the beauty of it guilt-free now she knew he and Angelique weren't romantically involved.

'Well, I guess I'll see you at eight o'clock, then.' Lola cleared her throat and brought an abrupt end to the conversation. Today had been full of revelations, and she saw no need to explore any more. Henri was attractive and single. No big deal.

'I'll be there at eight to pick up the cake. You know—the one for *my sister*?' He teased her one last time before she left the office.

With the door firmly closed behind her, Lola rested her head against it and tried to regulate her heartbeat. There was bound to be a logical explanation for the flutter of her pulse every time Henri reminded her that he was unattached, and as a qualified doctor she was determined to find a cure.

CHAPTER THREE

HENRI TOOK THE slip road off the motorway and followed the now familiar route to Lola's apartment block in the Titanic Quarter. Next to Belfast Lough, and just a stone's throw away from where the *Titanic* had cast off her moorings, this area was highly sought after. He'd been surprised, after he'd followed the sat-nav here previously to collect the cake, to find a junior doctor could afford such luxury.

'We're here,' he announced, pulling on the car's handbrake.

Gabrielle remained slumped in the passenger seat next to him, staring out through the rain-splattered window.

'What about my chicken?' a small voice piped up from the back seat.

Henri saw Bastien in the rearview mirror with his arms folded and lips pursed, ready for a full-on tantrum.

'Don't worry. We're just here to thank the lady for making your cake and drop off her dish—then we'll get a bucket of secret chicken as soon as we're finished.'

Their 'secret' chicken had nothing to do with a recipe and everything to do with not telling Angelique. She would kill him if she found out he was filling her children with fast food, but he didn't want to deal with dinnertime dramatics tonight. Not when he was under strict instructions to make amends for not inviting Lola to Bastien's party.

If he hadn't spent most of the day before the party wrapped up in department meetings he might have saved himself the trouble of a house call now, but he hadn't seen her since taking delivery of the fabulous cake-osaurus.

'Can we get ice-cream, too?' The six-year-old bounced in and out of view.

'We'll see.'

Henri didn't give a definitive answer, but these kids knew how to wrap their uncle round their little fingers. If only Gabrielle would show similar signs of enthusiasm. She was quiet and withdrawn, and it scared the hell out of him.

Angelique had tried talking to her before work, but other than another 'I'm fine', there had been no progress. Henri hated watching his niece's pain from the sidelines when it was his job to help others, his duty to care for his family. But all he could do for now was heed Lola's advice and stay by her side.

Gabrielle unclipped her seat belt and exited the car without the usual coaxing it took to get her out in public. The eager exit boded well. Perhaps Lola's company would be enough to put a smile on her face.

Henri knew he should have phoned ahead when Lola answered the door wearing a pig-patterned fleecy all-in-one.

'Dr Benoit!' Her cheeks turned the same shade of cute pink as her nightwear. 'I...er...wasn't expecting visitors tonight.' She dropped her eyes to her matching pig-shaped slippers.

'So I see.'

The endearing sight turned his frown into a smile. He hadn't realised how much he had looked forward to seeing her until she'd opened the door in that ridiculous outfit and immediately lifted his mood.

'I wanted to give you your platter back and thank you again for helping us out. I'm in the doghouse for not inviting you to the party, but I really didn't think a room full of children on a sugar high would be your scene. Anyway, Bastien loved the cake.'

He ruffled his nephew's hair and hoped the cuteness factor would get him off the hook.

Lola took the plate from him with a smile. 'There's no need to worry. As long as the birthday boy was happy, that's all that matters.'

'I *loved* it!' Bastien piped up to give his expert opinion.

'There you go—you'll not get a better recommendation than that.'

There hadn't been much left to clean off the plate. The sumptuous chocolate sponge decorated with colourful sugar dinosaur figures had been delicious as well as a visual feast. Henri had enjoyed two slices and an orange brontosaurus in between games of pass the parcel and musical chairs.

'Did you really make it all yourself?'

Gabrielle hovered beside him, apparently as enthralled by Lola's talents as he was.

'I really did. It's not that hard. All you need is time and patience.'

'Not for me, then?' He didn't have the time to spare on hobbies and had absolutely no patience for sitting still, and he made no apologies for it. His no-nonsense approach to life had got him to the top of his field after all. But it didn't mean he couldn't appreciate a creative spirit such as Lola, whose imagination and eye for detail had put a smile on so many faces.

'Probably not.' Lola peered out at him from beneath lowered lashes, failing to hide her amusement at the very idea.

There was something very endearing about her standing there in her PJs, scrubbed clean of make-up and giving him that shy Princess Diana look. She was the typical girl next door—sweet and innocent, and completely in contrast with the sexy siren he'd seen writhing in that chair at the club. Against his better judgement, he was becoming more and more intrigued by his new member of staff.

'I'd love to try some time.' Gabrielle scuffed her boots on the floor and avoided eye contact with anyone as she voiced her interest.

Unfortunately Henri knew nothing about baking and even less about sugarcraft to be of any use to her. Still, if there was a chance this could improve her mood he'd find a way to make it happen.

'You're welcome to come over any time and I can show you the basics. If that's okay with Henri and your mum?'

Regardless that Lola was saving his bacon for a second time, she was obviously waiting for him to confirm this as a good idea. In terms of avoiding further entanglement with a colleague it was probably the worst thing he could do, but Gabrielle's welfare took priority. What harm could there be in letting her ice a few cakes if it took her mind off whatever ailed her for a few hours?

He held his hand up in surrender, refusing to be an obstacle to his niece's wishes—as per Lola's advice. 'Hey, it's fine by me. I'll run it by Angelique later, but I don't see a problem if it means there's one member of the family who can at least turn the oven on.'

That earned him a chorus of giggles from both children, and he could have hugged Lola for giving Gabrielle something to look forward to. However, throwing his arms around her when she was in her nightwear could be viewed as a tad inappropriate, so he settled for a subtle nod of the head in gratitude instead.

She nodded back. They understood each other. This was for Gabrielle's sake.

'I'm hungry. Have you got any ice cream?' Apparently the moment was lost on Bastien, whose impatience had sent him walking on in to the apartment.

'I'm not sure…' Lola watched, bemused, as he barged past her.

'Sorry about this.' Henri made a grab for his wayward nephew.

'No problem. It's too cold to keep you standing out there

anyway. Come in and we can sort out a time for Gabrielle to start her baking masterclass. I'll just put this plate away, then go get changed into something more…mature.'

Lola opened the door wide for him and Gabrielle to enter. If she was inconvenienced by their sudden invasion, good manners covered her tracks. He didn't think *he'd* be so accommodating if she turned up at *his* door with two inquisitive children when he was ready for bed. Although since he slept in the nude that could prove even more awkward.

'Not on my account,' he murmured, quite enjoying this injection of humour into his evening.

It brought another flush of pink to her cheeks before she scurried out of sight.

By the time Henri reached the living room Bastien had already discovered the games console and was busy setting up his favourite racing game.

'Look what she's got, Uncle Henri!' The child's face lit up as he expertly flicked through the set-up screen.

'Her name is Dr Roberts, Bastien, and it's very rude of you to come charging into a lady's house uninvited.'

'But she *did* 'vite us in.'

'Only after you'd made yourself at home. Oh, never mind. Just don't do it again.' Children were exhausting. It was as well he'd decided a long time ago not to have any of his own. Angelique's were a full-time commitment.

Henri took a seat on the leather settee next to Gabrielle, who sat on the edge with her arms wrapped around her knees. He wished he could wave a magic wand and make her worries disappear.

Lola returned wearing conservative jeans and a fitted floral blouse. Her hair remained the same, though: loose, wavy and free of its ponytail restraint.

'Right. Now that I'm dressed for company, can I get you guys anything to drink?'

'Can I have cola?' Bastien pushed his junk food limits even further.

'You know you're not allowed that. You can have water.' Henri had discovered the after-effects of giving his nephew fizzy drinks before bedtime to his cost. That had been one long night.

'We have fruit juice, too. Gabrielle, would you like some?' Lola came up with a timely alternative, which kept Bastien from further whining.

'Yes, please.'

'Let me give you a hand with the drinks.'

He followed Lola into the kitchen. Whatever spell she'd cast on Gabrielle, he thought they might be able to capitalise on it. If a friendship developed between the pair, there was a chance she might trust Lola with her secrets. All he had to do was convince her to relay any information back to him.

'The glasses are in the top cupboard,' she told him as she yanked the fridge door open.

'Tell me, Dr Roberts, are you moonlighting as an exotic dancer? Don't get me wrong, I'm sure you're worth every penny, but you know the rules about taking paid employment outside of the hospital.'

'Ouch!' Lola banged her head on the top shelf of the fridge. 'Pardon me?'

She lifted out the carton of pure orange juice which had been pushed to the back in favour of Jules's bottle of Pinot and closed the door.

'I just assumed you must be making extra money somewhere to pay for all this.' He motioned towards all the mod cons Lola took for granted now she wasn't tied to the family's kitchen sink.

'This is Jules's place. I pay rent.'

It seemed she would never be allowed to forget that one night of abandoned dancing at Angelique's burlesque class.

'Ah…'

The devastatingly handsome grin made Lola rue the less-than-flattering bed wear she'd been sporting on his arrival even more. Some people effortlessly exuded sex appeal in their nightwear, while others had all the sophistication of a cartoon pig.

In hindsight, perhaps she should have taken heed of Jules's countless attempts to persuade her to swap her jammies for something more enticing to the opposite sex. She'd resisted those little silk numbers that clung to every curve in favour of shapeless comfort in the belief that no man would ever get close enough for it to matter.

Since Henri had shown up uninvited, and practically stared through her fleecy protective layer, she might have to change her view. Especially when that appreciative gaze had warmed her insides rather than freaked her out.

Lola shooed away the mental image of standing before him in one of those provocative outfits that mocked her every time she walked through the lingerie department on her way to Matching Separates. She didn't want to associate him with a need to feel attractive. He was her boss, Gabrielle's uncle, and a man in whom she couldn't afford to invest any feelings.

Perhaps all this confidence-building was starting to pay off and she was beginning to function as a warm-blooded human, no longer tied to her *victim* roots. She hoped so. Not because she had any intention of fostering an attraction to her boss, but because she wanted to feel like any other twenty-five-year-old single woman, who could engage with a good-looking man without having a meltdown.

'Okay, so there's no more confusion, I can categorically state I'm *not* a stripper.'

'And I'm not father to a teenage girl—or anyone else for that matter. What age did you think I was anyway?'

Henri let his ego peek out at the idea that he could be perceived as anything other than a young, eligible bachelor. It was an invitation for Lola to get her own back.

She screwed her face up, as though she was really struggling with the idea that he wasn't an old fogey. 'Umm…eighty-five? Eighty-six?'

'Very funny.'

'Seriously, though, you have such a good way with the children, I'm sure I'm not the only one to have made that mistake. Obviously, it would've made you a teenage dad…'

'Obviously.'

Lola poured juice into the tumblers lined up on the marble work surface and slid one over to him. 'How are things with Gabrielle at the minute, Doctor?'

'Henri.'

'Pardon?'

'I've gatecrashed your quiet night in, and my nephew is probably destroying your living room as we speak, so I think you could drop the formalities and call me Henri.'

'Okay, *Henri*.' It sounded weird to say his Christian name out loud, as though they had some sort of personal relationship going on. Which they didn't, of course, outside of concern for his niece's welfare.

Henri cleared his throat and watched his juice as he swirled it in the glass. 'I'd be lying if I said I wasn't concerned about her.'

'No progress, then?' It was worrying when a girl that age shut herself off. Lola knew how quickly loneliness and despair spiralled into something more sinister. At least Gabrielle had a mother and a father figure to support her through whatever was going on. All it would take was a little trust for her to open up to them.

'She locks herself in her room all night and barely eats. I was surprised when she agreed to come with me tonight, but she seems genuinely interested in this new hobby. Thanks for offering your services—it's very much appreciated. I have another big favour to ask you, though. If she tells you anything that could help us get to the bottom of this, will you please pass it on?'

The impassioned plea was difficult to ignore when there was a pair of big brown eyes accompanying it. Gabrielle's behaviour didn't sound any different from that of a certain junior doctor, and Lola was starting to see why her brothers were on her case so much. It came from a place of love. Both she and Gabrielle were lucky to have such caring families, even if they were too close to see it for themselves.

'It's down to Gabrielle if she wants to talk about it. I'm certainly not going to push the subject and make her think we're somehow tricking her. But be assured I want to help wherever I can.'

Lola understood Henri's desire to find out the truth at all costs, but she also needed Gabrielle to feel safe here. For her, baking was a way to escape everything negative in her life, and she wanted it to be the same for her new protégée.

Although his frown was ploughing grooves into his forehead, Henri didn't argue with her.

'I'm hungry.' The young boy, whose strong Belfast accent differed so greatly from his uncle's, appeared at the kitchen door. 'You got somethin' to eat?'

He did, however, have the Frenchman's directness.

'We'll go soon, Bastien. Sorry—I promised to take them for fried chicken.' Henri grimaced and set down his glass.

'And ice cream?' Bastien reminded him.

'*And* ice cream.'

Henri winked, and Lola marvelled at his relaxed relationship with the child. If anything, he was a push-over with these kids, and this visit showed he would do anything for them— including sacrifice his pride to ask her for help. Despite her initial impression, Henri was a nice guy after all.

Bastien clapped his hands and reminded her that he was present—and hungry. An idea formed in her head to accommodate his needs *and* those of his sister.

'Fried chicken and ice cream sounds yummy. You know *I* haven't had any dinner yet, either.'

Henri picked up the ball and ran with it. 'Would you like to join us?'

'I would *love* to. Why don't you and Bastien go and fetch the food whilst Gabrielle and I set the table?'

Bastien ran off to share the news with his sister.

'It will give me a chance to talk to her,' she explained somewhat unnecessarily to Henri.

At least this way any prying now wouldn't sully their baking time in the future.

'I know. *Merci beaucoup.*'

Henri kissed her on the cheek, and just like that the touch of his surprisingly soft lips on her skin short-circuited all her anti-hunk defence systems.

Once Henri and Bastien had left, there was an air of expectancy between the girls for the conversation they needed to have. But Lola wanted to ask questions in a way that wouldn't frighten her off. She held the cutlery out to Gabrielle, as if she was trying to coax a skittish animal out of hiding with some food.

'How's the eye?' She carried on arranging the placemats on the table to prevent her concern from seeming like a big deal.

'Fine.' As before, Gabrielle kept her head down so her hair fell across her face.

Lola knew that trick. She'd used it countless times to hide from her brothers' prying eyes.

'You know you can talk to me if there's anything bothering you? Sometimes it's easier to tell a friend your problems than family. They're not as emotionally involved, and therefore tend not to rant as much.'

'Thanks.' The young girl lifted her head to afford her a half smile but her eyes were glassy with tears. Whatever her burden, she had clearly found no relief since their meeting at the hospital.

'I had a few "accidents" in high school myself—falling over people's feet and into their fists. It's all I can do these days not to slap those who tell you that your schooldays are the best days of your life.'

'Ha!'

The teenager's vocal outburst echoed Lola's thoughts on the subject.

'Exactly. I couldn't wait to leave. If I'd believed that was as good as my life would get I'd never have made it out.'

She'd had more than her inner turmoil to escape in high school, but it was important that Gabrielle knew there was light at the end of the tunnel if she was experiencing the same problems.

'And things *did* get better?'

Her interest sparked, Gabrielle halted her arrangement of the knives and forks. It gave Lola more than a hint that she'd touched on the right nerve.

'They did. I'm happy now.' Although she still bore the mental scars, if not the physical ones.

Gabrielle's sigh didn't sound as though she was convinced.

'I know things may seem insurmountable now, but in the grand scheme of things I'm sure they're not as bad as you imagine.' Lola had gone through some horrific times—to the point where she hadn't wanted to wake up in the mornings. But she'd fought through and come out the other side a better person than those who'd tormented her.

'Right now they're pretty bad.'

The soft voice made more impact on Lola than tears ever could. It was the sound of someone who'd already accepted defeat.

Lola could play twenty questions again, and get no further, or go with her gut feeling about the matter. Gabrielle was a beautiful girl with an exotic mother. People had a tendency to find fault with anything out of the norm, and Henri's niece was sensitive enough to take criticism to heart. Teenage girls—and boys—could be unforgivably cruel.

'Is there someone in school giving you a hard time?'

It would explain the truancy, as well as the mood. Lola had skipped her fair share of classes to avoid those making her life a misery. She'd had to put in a hell of a lot of hard work at home, to catch up on the lessons she'd missed, but it had been easier than listening to cruel taunts and mocking laughter.

Gabrielle's silence was deafening.

'In another few years those people and their opinions won't matter. You'll probably never see or think about them again.'

The white lie was for the girl's benefit. Lola doubted there was any point in telling her she spent a good chunk of her life reliving the nightmare over again. Gabrielle came across as a stronger personality than the young Lola had ever been, and there was every possibility she would find it easier to move on after high school if they could resolve the issue quickly.

'You have a bright future ahead of you. Don't let small-minded bullies prevent you from reaching your potential. The more school you miss, the harder it will be to catch up. And I'm speaking from experience.'

She'd be a lot further along in her career by now if she'd lived by her own words. Those years she'd wasted living in perpetual fear would never be recovered, no matter how hard she tried.

'You probably think I'm being stupid, but I just can't face it any more. They tell everyone who'll listen that my mum's a stripper, and that I must be adopted because I'm so ugly. Even if I don't see them in school they send me text messages and say horrible things over the internet.'

Gabrielle's shoulders sagged under the weight of the abuse, and her eyes brimmed with sorrow.

Lola swallowed the lump in her throat and tried to retain her composure. It wouldn't do to swamp the girl in an over-emotional hug.

She wasn't sure knowing the truth made the situation any easier. It was no wonder Gabrielle couldn't confide in her family. Angelique would be horrified to find out *she* was the cause of her daughter's suffering, and Henri might well use the information to stop his sister doing what she loved. Knowledge could be a dangerous weapon, and Lola had managed to land herself with a ticking time bomb.

Gabrielle sniffed, and reminded Lola that her welfare was the most important part of the equation. 'I would urge you to speak to your mum or your uncle—they're really worried about you. You should really let the school know what's happening, too, so they can put a stop to it.'

It was easier said than done, of course. In Lola's case teachers and family had only made matters worse and marked her as a target. She didn't even know how she could aid Gabrielle, short of being a shoulder to lean on.

Gabrielle shook her head violently. 'It'll only make things worse. You don't understand...'

'I've been there, sweetheart. I was a bit of a tomboy when I was young. Not really by choice. My dad raised me the same way he raised my brothers. I may as well have been his fourth son—it was no wonder I attracted negative attention. If these people are allowed to get away with picking on you, things will never get better for you.'

Sharing the horrors of her childhood had never been therapeutic for Lola—it simply reawakened that demon of dread in the pit of her stomach. She'd only opened up for Gabrielle's sake, so she knew there was someone who understood.

'It shouldn't matter where you come from, who you are or what you look like. People should be free to be whoever they are.' Gabrielle folded her arms across her chest and mirrored her feisty mother.

'I agree. Unfortunately there will always be those who revel in making other people's lives hell.'

'What did they do to you?'

Given her lineage, Gabrielle's directness shouldn't have come as a shock.

For her own sake—and Gabrielle's—Lola filtered out the most appalling aspects of her teen years. 'They teased me that they weren't sure if I was a boy or a girl.'

Any attack on a girl's appearance at such a vulnerable age would dent anyone's confidence. Especially at a time when popularity and boyfriends had seemed the most important things in the world and her friends had been pairing off to leave her as the odd one out. Placing value on those things had cost her so much.

'But you're *beautiful.*'

The compliment thrown Lola's way was appreciated, but she would never get used to receiving praise without thinking there was an ulterior motive. Her trust had been smashed to smithereens in one summer afternoon, never again to be given freely.

'And if I told you *you're* beautiful would you believe me?' Lola turned the tables back, doing her best to illustrate how skewed self-esteem became in these situations.

'No.' She glaned up at Lola from beneath lowered lids, every bit as cynical as she.

'For the record, you are *gorgeous.*' Lola cupped Gabrielle's face in her hands and tilted her head up. She wanted to look her in the eye as she said it, willing her to believe. 'But it's more to do with how you feel about yourself, isn't it?'

Gabrielle bit her lip to stop it from wobbling.

'I know it's difficult, but don't give those cowards power over you. Be strong.' Lola's words caught in her throat. She could easily have been talking to her younger self. In reality, it had taken years for her to heed that advice.

'I'm fed up with being strong. I just want to forget about everything.' Stress furrowed her youthful brow.

Lola recognised the destructive nature of those locked-in

emotions. The spectre of suicide had haunted the deprived council estate where she had grown up. Teenagers ravaged by the effects of drugs and alcohol, or those who just hadn't seen a way out of poverty, had taken their own lives on a shockingly regular basis. It was only seeing the devastation of the families left in the aftermath which had prevented Lola from seeking the same escape when her life had become unbearable.

Even though some of those issues plagued her still, Lola was glad she'd fought for the life she had today, and she would do everything to ensure someone in similar circumstances would get that second chance, too.

'There's nothing that can take your mind off your troubles better than a homemade cake.'

She'd done as Henri had asked and knew when to back off. At least they'd made a start on talks, even if they had yet to come up with an effective solution to Gabrielle's problems. It was clear that what this child needed was some fun to take her mind off everything—and that she could definitely help with.

'I can't wait.' Thankfully Gabrielle had now swapped her despair for a grin.

'We will bake up a storm in here as soon your mum gives the go-ahead. Who knows? Maybe we can get her involved, too?'

As keen as she was to have a cake buddy, she didn't want to interfere in what should be a mother/daughter bonding exercise.

The doorbell rang and sent Gabrielle scurrying back into her shell. 'Promise you won't say anything to Uncle Henri?'

She was putting Lola in a very tricky position. Henri was her superior, and he would be actively looking for answers regarding his niece's welfare. However, facing his temper against the consequences of betraying Gabrielle was the lesser of two evils. The child needed someone to confide in, someone to trust. As did Lola.

'I promise. When you're ready you can tell him yourself.'

The buzzer went again, and again, until she was forced to answer the door in case the neighbours complained about the noise.

'I'll bet you anything that's Bastien.' Gabrielle finished setting the table and carefully arranged her emotions back in order.

No good could ever come to someone afraid to express their feelings. At some point that bottled-up anger and sorrow would erupt into an almighty mess. It made Lola's decision to stay loyal to Gabrielle that much easier.

'Bastien, take your finger off the doorbell, please.' An unamused Henri sounded on the other side of the door.

She found him juggling takeaway bags and a mischievous child.

'Someone's impatient.' Lola took one of the bags off his hands as Bastien dashed inside.

'Sorry.' Henri shrugged as he lost control of his nephew again. 'I guess nothing stands in the way of a boy and his fast food.'

'I guess not.' Lola wished some of that devil-may-care attitude would rub off on his sister.

Henri walked back into the apartment as though this was an everyday occurrence for him. In fact this whole thing was surreal. He never imagined he'd find himself asking anyone for help regarding his family. Especially someone he hardly knew. Someone he wasn't even sure was up to the job. Yet here he was, eating takeaway with her and praying she could fix his niece.

'Did she tell you anything?' he asked Lola as they unpacked the cartons in the kitchen.

'She didn't go into details, but I think we're making progress.' Lola kept her back to him as she plated the food.

'So she told you *something*?' He didn't want Lola holding all the cards. This wasn't *her* family. All that was required from her was to pass on the information and let him deal with it.

'I swore to keep everything confidential, Henri. I'm sorry.' Lola tried to bustle past him.

As if he would be willing to leave it there. He sidestepped to block her path and forced her to look at him.

'Don't do this to me, Lola. I feel helpless enough without you holding back on me, too.' He kept his voice low, imploring her to see things from his point of view.

'I'm sorry. I promised.'

'At least tell me if I have anything to be worried about.' He couldn't help but wonder if she enjoyed having this power over him. After all, he was now at her mercy.

Lola raised her eyes to the ceiling and sighed. 'If at any time I don't think I can deal with this on my own I will let you know. For now, I think it's better Gabrielle works through this the way she wants.'

'She's my niece—my responsibility. She shouldn't be going through this on her own.'

If he had his own way he would wrap her up in cotton wool and protect her from everything negative in the world. He was the only consistent male role model in her life. And what use was he if he couldn't help her in her hour of need?

'The food's going cold.' Lola pursed her lips. She could be stubborn when the mood took her.

'I don't give a damn about the food. I want to talk about *this*.'

'What you want isn't always the most important thing in the world. The sooner you learn that the better.'

With a burst of bravado, Lola pushed past him and carried the dinner into the living room.

When he did finally take his seat at the table he was forced to turn his frown upside down. Bastien was revelling in eating his chicken with his fingers, leaving grease and breadcrumbs everywhere. Gabrielle's laughter at her little brother's caveman manners was a glorious sound.

Lola was right. It was progress. He was going to have to defer to her on the subject of his niece. However much it galled him.

CHAPTER FOUR

As LOLA MADE her way to the hospital the next morning her mind was less preoccupied with work than with her personal issues. There was no doubt that sharing her experiences with Gabrielle had been the key to getting the teenager to open up, but it had cost her a night without sleep. Nightmares and tears over those dark days, and worry over keeping Gabrielle's secrets from Henri, had kept her awake. Yet it would all be worth it to prevent Gabrielle any further pain.

If she didn't want the school or her mother involved, then all Lola could do was offer her friendship. Perhaps if *she'd* had someone to turn to, life mightn't have seemed so bleak to her back then.

Lola went about her rounds, treating fractures and poorly patients without incident, the distraction of work good for settling her nerves.

As she power-walked down the corridor, she encountered Henri for the first time since their impromptu dinner. A meal which had come to a surly end after she'd refused to divulge any information about his niece. Poor Bastien had been forced to eat his ice cream much more quickly than he would have liked.

As they marched towards each other she braced herself for

another attempt to break her loyalty. She nodded an acknowl-edgement and Henri grunted something unintelligible as he strode past. Whilst she didn't want another guilt trip about keep-ing him out of the loop, this was plain childishness.

She pivoted around. 'I appreciate how frustrating it is for you, under the circumstances, but I'm sure Gabrielle will come to you when she's ready. Snubbing me at work, however, is ri-diculous. Surely we're adult enough to separate our personal issues from our professional lives?'

When she said 'we', she meant *you*. He needed to realise that she wasn't required to jump at every click of his fingers. No doubt his control freakery was part of the reason Gabrielle didn't want him involved. One whiff of the goings-on and he would be at the school, sandblasting everyone he came into con-tact with. In Lola's opinion the matter needed handling with kid gloves—not a sledgehammer.

He did a heart-stoppingly slow U-turn to face her. 'I am try-ing to keep the matter private. That is why I hadn't intended discussing it in the middle of the corridor. I'm grateful for your help with my niece, but do not use that as an excuse to under-mine my authority at work.'

Another one-hundred-and-eighty-degree turn and he took off, leaving Lola with her mouth hanging open wide enough to fit both feet in. When would she ever learn that she and good-looking men simply didn't mix?

'Can you take this one for me? I'm run off my feet.' Jules offloaded a file into her hands as soon as she walked into the department.

'Sure.' Lola's heart sank as she scanned the case notes, but she didn't have the option of saying no. This was her job, and she was going to have to treat all patients equally—regardless of age or gender.

She paused outside the cubicle and took a deep breath. The way her heart seemed to be lurching into her throat one might have been forgiven for thinking she'd never been alone with a man before. It was the actions of a few who'd caused her to distrust the rest.

'Okay, Mr... Smith. I see you've been in the wars today.'

A man in his mid-twenties was lying bare-chested, his face and jeans covered in blood and dirt. With his once blond hair matted red, and the area around his right eye a beautiful shade of violet, he was a painfully colourful sight.

'I walked into a door,' he said with a smirk.

He'd clearly been on the receiving end of someone's fist, but Lola didn't argue. All she had to do was patch him up and get him out. She leaned in to clean away the blood and find the source. The smell of stale cigarettes and beer assaulted her, taking her back to another time and place.

Think of somewhere safe...someone safe.

As she dabbed at the cuts on his scalp and face with cotton wool she imagined Henri beside her, despite their recent difference of opinion. She could almost smell his clean fragrance, so reassuring and familiar. It gave her the push to carry on.

'I think you need a couple of stitches. Nothing serious.'

Once she'd cleaned the wound in order to start suturing, she became aware of her patient's eyes almost burning into her.

'Do I know you from somewhere?'

'I don't think so.'

She withdrew her hand as it began to shake. It wouldn't do to send a patient out with crooked stitches.

'I'm sure I've seen your face before.'

He propped himself up on his elbows to peer at her, crossing so far into her personal space his breath prickled her skin.

'I get that a lot.'

A step back to deposit the soiled cotton balls in the wastebin meant she could breathe again.

'I *know* you.'

He was up off the bed before she could react, pinning her into the corner of the tiny cubicle. 'We went to the same high school.'

Lola gasped for air as her throat closed over. This was her

worst nightmare come true—being confronted with her past with no obvious means of escape.

'You're mistaken. Now, if you'll climb back onto the bed, we'll get those stitches finished so you can go on your way.'

'I remember you. Lola Roberts.'

His revolting sneer confirmed that he'd witnessed the horrendous incident in her teens, maybe even been part of it.

He moved closer. She stepped back until she hit herself against the trolley.

'Please...'

It was a plea for him to stop. The same pathetic voice she'd used ten years ago. It hadn't worked then, either.

He ran a hand along her arm and her goose-pimpled flesh reacted violently against it, despite the barrier of her white coat.

'You're *definitely* all woman now, Lola.'

In her mind's eye she could envisage that sea of faces staring at her, feel the hands holding her down, hear their drunken jeers ringing in her ears as she sobbed. This time she would scream for all she was worth if it came to it. She'd worked hard to overcome that paralysing fear—this was her chance to finally lay some demons to rest.

'You can either sit back down and let me finish your treatment, Mr *Smith*, or I can call Security.'

A strategic crossing of her arms shrugged him off and hid her shaking limbs at the same time.

He narrowed his eyes at her. 'Don't get all uppity, now, Doctor. You're no better than me. I can still picture you, with your DIY haircut and secondhand clothes. If I remember well, you weren't so high and mighty when you were lying on the floor with your underwear pulled down.'

Lola's eyes burned with tears and memories, but she wouldn't let those bullies continue to have power over her.

'You were there that night? Perhaps I can pass on your details to the police. They're still looking for witnesses and accomplices to the sexual assault of a minor.'

It was a lie, of course. The incident had gone unreported
since her brothers had taken the law into their own hands and
risked being arrested themselves. The handsome rugby captain
who'd lured her into the trap had taken quite a few weeks to
heal after the beating he'd taken, and Lola had left the school
soon after that fateful night.

However, the threat of police involvement was enough to
make her patient turn pale and get him to back off. The sense
of power and relief at finding her voice again made her question why she didn't start *every* day by kicking some arrogant
male ass.

That immediately brought a certain frosty registrar to mind.
Henri was the perfect sparring partner—strong enough to boost
her ego when she got a verbal win against him, intimidating
without ever being a threat. A lot of her anxieties about him
had been laid to rest since seeing the way he was with his niece
and nephew. Behind the grouchy outer shell there was a loving
man with a heart of gold.

She ignored the thought about kicking his ass. It wouldn't do
to linger on how cute it was when she was seeing more of him
than her own family at the minute.

Unfortunately her lapse in concentration was an open invitation for a predator like Smith. He clamped his hand around her
elbow and jolted her back into the present danger.

'If you know what's good for you, you'll keep me out of it.
Right?'

She refused to let the mask slip and tried not to react to the
fingers digging into her skin—or the inner voice telling her
to knee him where it hurt and run. A big part of this job was
keeping calm in the face of adversity, and it didn't come more
adversarial than physical assault.

'Take. Your. Hands. Off. Me.'

She maintained eye contact, kept her voice steady, even
though every part of her was screaming either to karate chop
him away or crumple to the floor. If she ever wanted to succeed

and shake off the demons of her past she would have to front this out. This was a test of her courage and an indicator of how far she'd come in the past couple of years. One immature thug wasn't going to break her now.

'You're needed at Reception, Dr Roberts. I can deal with this.'

Henri barged in and the grip on her arm immediately relaxed. Mr Smith was decidedly less intimidating with someone bigger and stronger on the scene.

Although Henri's presence had changed the oppressive atmosphere in the cubicle, Lola wasn't thrilled at his interference. If she wanted Gabrielle to stand strong it was important that she lead by example and not rely on someone else coming to her rescue.

'I'm almost done here.'

'They need you *now*. I'm sure your patient won't mind if I take over.' He didn't give either of them a choice, bustling in to prep for suturing.

The story didn't quite add up. Why would anyone be so desperate for a first year's expertise over a registrar's? No doubt he thought she'd been taking too long with what was a minor injury. If he'd bothered to give her a chance to explain the delay in private he would have realised seeing this through to the end was more important to her than waiting times.

'If you insist.'

Not so long ago she'd have gladly deferred to her superior, but Mr Stompy-Boots had marched over her progress a second time. It was like taking one step forward and getting rugby tackled to the ground before ever reaching the touchline. For Henri's sake, this had better not be about his personal issues with her. Now that her inner badass was getting airtime, if he wasn't careful he'd find himself next on the list for a piece of her mind.

Her body shook with suppressed rage and residual fear. She didn't know which of the two men had done her more damage in the past few minutes. It was only the fact that she was physically and emotionally exhausted that put an end to her fight.

* * *

Henri waited until Lola had left and he knew she was safe before turning on the lowlife who'd had his paws all over her.
She'd held her ground, but he'd seen the terror in her eyes as
someone nearly twice her size had her cornered with no obvious means of escape.

He'd only come down to apologise for the way he'd spoken
to her earlier. After he'd had time to dwell on his behaviour
he'd realised he should be working to keep her onside for the
sake of his niece. As he'd waited outside the cubicle, trying to
form adequate words to express his regret, he'd heard part of
the conversation going on inside. Enough to prompt him to get
her the hell out of there.

Sexual assault of a minor?

It didn't bear thinking about that she'd been a victim of such
a serious crime, and thus it came as no wonder that she had a
tendency to be wary of others. Someone had stolen her trust,
her innocence, and here she was working to help others.

Lola was braver than he'd given her credit for. He'd burdened
her with his personal problems without a thought for her own,
even though since day one he'd pegged her as the weak link in
an otherwise dynamic group of ambitious new doctors. Now
not only was she his student, she was his family counsellor—
someone he'd come to count on as his friend.

It tore him apart that he hadn't been able to prevent her from
being hurt. Since no one had apparently been charged there
seemed little he could do now except be there for her and play
the role of protector that he'd perfected over the years.

As he approached the patient he was duty-bound to treat,
Henri's hands weren't as steady as they should have been with
the needle. In his opinion Mr Smith didn't deserve any compassion, and he'd be lucky if he didn't leave with more injuries than
he'd arrived with. But despite his personal feelings Henri knew
his career depended upon him being a professional at all times.

'Oww!'

A professional whose bedside manner had a tendency to slip now and again.

He closed the wound efficiently and without finesse. 'You'll need to come back in a few days to have the stitches removed.'

Henri leaned in until he was nose to nose with Lola's patient, taking some delight in turning the tables as the other man backed up against the pillows.

'Make sure you ask for me. There's no need for you to disturb Dr Roberts again. Do you understand?'

If people insisted on labelling him as intimidating, he'd use it to his advantage when called for.

There was no response.

'Perhaps we should involve the police after all. We both know your injuries weren't sustained by accident. I suspect men like you have a habit of getting on the wrong side of people. I can make the call now, if you'd like?' Henri stuffed his hand in the pocket of his trousers to retrieve his phone.

Smith scrambled to his feet and whipped the curtain back, showing more fear than Lola ever had. 'It's no skin off my nose. She's still a freak.'

Bare-chested, he crawled back to whatever hole he'd slunk out of. It wouldn't end there, as far as Henri was concerned. Even with only partial knowledge of what had happened before he'd arrived on the scene, he wouldn't rest until he knew the full story and found out what he could do to help Lola.

'You had no right to do that.'

Lola ambushed him the minute he set foot back in his office. Henri should have known she wouldn't take kindly to being sent on a wild goose chase to some non-existent emergency. But one look at her arms wrapped around her waist in a self-conscious hug and he knew he'd made the right call.

'I want to know what happened, Lola. I'm as responsible for my junior doctors as I am for my patients. You don't have to put up with anyone trying to make you uncomfortable when you're trying to do your job.'

His interference was a common source of discontent amongst all the womenfolk in his life. But after what he'd overheard he deemed it justifiable on this occasion.

'*Trying* to do my job? Admit it—this is about your lack of belief in my abilities as a doctor. You don't think I have what it takes, but I *will* prove you wrong. Difficult situations are part of the learning process, and I won't get anywhere if you keep jumping in to bail me out.'

She made no reference to the deeply personal aspect of the confrontation, but he could see the trauma of it reflected in those expressive sea-green eyes. If this was only about her journey into the world of medicine he would agree—the best thing for him to do *would* be to back off. After all, getting her to step up to the plate was what he'd wanted from the start. But this was about keeping her safe.

He toyed with the idea of dropping the subject altogether, to save her from further discomfort, but she was the one who'd made the passionate plea about Gabrielle needing someone to talk to about her problems. And Henri hadn't got his reputation from tiptoeing around people's feelings.

'I heard what you said. About the police.'

'It's not your concern.'

She stood firm, as obstinate as his sister and niece. Such independent spirit made it difficult for a man to be gallant without being accused of tyranny.

'When one of my staff is accosted in my department it becomes very much my concern, *chérie*. Were you hurt?' He balled his fists as his protective streak reared its ugly head.

'I told you—I was handling it.'

'I mean before. The assault.'

Even saying it left a bad taste in his mouth. He couldn't begin to imagine how it made Lola feel. She flinched, and he hated himself for making her relive it.

'No. I wasn't physically harmed, but I was humiliated… I really don't want to discuss this with anyone.' Lola shook her head and the tears sitting like dew on her eyelashes spilled down her face.

It came naturally for Henri to go and put an arm around her shoulders. Despite his outward appearance, he was still a tactile Frenchman at heart.

'If you need closure you can still press charges. I'll support you.'

Lola made a hiccupping sound as she swallowed a sob. 'I don't need your pity. Yes, things happened, and I had a hard time moving past them for a while, but that has no bearing on my training. If anything, I've become a stronger person for it. Not that it is any of your business.'

'As my niece is none of *yours*. Yet I understand your involvement is best for her welfare.'

He wanted her to take her own advice and let someone in. Despite the mention of her older brothers, he got the impression Lola was someone who preferred to work through her problems herself. He could empathise with that. Not once had he confided in anyone about the burden of guilt he carried over Angelique's failed medical career. It didn't mean it was healthy.

'The difference is that you came to me for help with Gabrielle. I, on the other hand, can fight my own battles.'

She was so determined to prove her strength she didn't even wipe away her tears. As though denying their existence would render them invisible.

He brushed the two telltale signs of her distress away with the pads of his thumbs. Although he couldn't say it without sounding like a patronising ass, he was proud of her.

'I have no doubt about that. I just want you to know that I care about you.'

At this moment in time someone needed to tell her that, show her that, and remind her she wasn't alone.

He'd only intended to give her a friendly peck on the lips—

not too far removed from the double cheek-kiss greeting he exchanged with his sister or his fellow countrymen. Except kissing Lola definitely wasn't the platonic gesture he'd imagined.

Her mouth was soft and yielding beneath his, and he couldn't resist dipping inside to taste her sweetness. She met him with a tentative nudge of her tongue and Henri was lost. With her head cradled in his hands, he deepened the kiss, every primitive urge he had rising above his good intentions.

Only when she stiffened against him did common sense prevail. He sprang away from her, eager for her to put back those barriers that he'd so stupidly breached.

'I'm so sorry, Lola.'

He raked his hands through his hair, repenting his sins immediately. All he'd done was compound her fears that no man could be trusted. Kissing her when she was vulnerable and frightened made him no better than the sleaze who'd accosted her in the first place.

It was no wonder she was frozen to the spot, those big green eyes wide and alert. He'd broken her trust in a moment of madness, with no rhyme or reason behind his actions except for pure, unadulterated lust. Inexcusable behaviour—and, apart from every other personal violation against Lola, most definitely a sackable offence. He'd screwed up big time and all he could do was beg for her forgiveness.

'This is entirely on me. I got carried away. You know I would never do anything to hurt you.'

He cringed at the words—probably used the world over to excuse a multitude of sins against women. In this case he meant them with every fibre of his being.

The only thing that unnerved him more than his loss of control was Lola's silence. It was no surprise that she'd shut herself off, since he'd heaped one violation on top of another. He was her superior, supposedly her friend, and he had no business laying a finger on her no matter what the circumstances.

'Lola, talk to me—hit me. Do something so I know you're okay.'

If it wouldn't have compounded the offence he would have shaken her. She was scaring the hell out of him. Had he pushed her over the edge into some sort of delayed shock? Post-traumatic stress wouldn't be unusual in such cases. He desperately needed her to come back into the room and leave wherever it was she'd gone in her head.

'I have to go.'

Those four little words as she blinked back at him and slowly returned to her body were enough for Henri to breathe a sigh of relief. Yet they weren't enough to stop him worrying as she left in a trance-like state. He wouldn't go after her—he'd done enough damage—but he would make sure to send someone to check on her.

Other than Lola, the only person who could possibly hate him more than he hated himself right now would be Gabrielle. With one selfish move he'd destroyed not one but two budding relationships.

CHAPTER FIVE

'I'M REALLY SORRY. Gabrielle was so looking forward to seeing you, and Angelique is at Bastien's parent/teacher evening at the school. I couldn't get hold of you to check this was still okay.'

Henri hovered on Lola's doorstep, almost using Gabrielle as a shield in front of him. Of *course* he hadn't been able to get her permission for a visit, since she'd avoided all forms of attempted communication from him. There were dozens of unread texts on her phone, and calls that she hadn't been able to bring herself to answer. She knew beyond all doubt how sorry he was about kissing her. The trouble was she couldn't fully fathom how *she* felt about it.

'You said you'd show me the basics…'

Gabrielle fidgeted with her braid and guilt-tripped Lola over her reluctance to let Henri get close stand in the way of her promise.

In truth, it was her own actions she was worried about—not his. He'd surprised her with that kiss. She'd had no idea he'd ever looked at her as anything other than a pain in his backside. Perhaps he'd simply felt sorry for her? Whatever the cause, it had made her question how she saw *him*. There was definitely an attraction there. An unwanted one.

'Maybe we should leave. If you'd prefer, you and Gabrielle can make arrangements for another time and her mother will accompany her in future?'

Now Henri was being the reasonable one. And she couldn't avoid him for ever when they worked at the same hospital—in the same department, for goodness' sake. Besides, what had gone on between them wasn't Gabrielle's fault, and she shouldn't be punished for it.

'Not at all. Come in.'

This evening was about having fun with Gabrielle. Everything else could wait.

'Phone me when you want me to pick her up.'

With his head down and shoulders slumped, Henri turned to leave.

Gabrielle faltered once she saw he was leaving. 'Aren't you coming in, too, Uncle Henri?'

Although she hadn't wanted to discuss anything in front of him, it was only natural she should want him nearby. Lola didn't want to upset her by sending him away and leaving Gabrielle with someone who was pretty much a stranger to her.

Henri halted, waiting for instruction. It put Lola's mind at ease that he wouldn't push her into anything she didn't feel equipped to deal with right now. If he could sit in a corner somewhere, without uttering one word in that accent that should come with a health warning, they might make it through the evening without any more drama.

'You're very welcome to stay, Henri,' she said, her breath hitching even as she invited him in.

This was a different kind of fear than she'd ever known before—an excitement about the unknown rather than the paralysing wait at another's mercy.

His face relaxed into a smile and he mouthed 'Thank you' as he brushed past her. Even that small contact sent a surge of electricity zapping across her skin. Evidently that one kiss had stirred a passion she hadn't even known was still there after everything she'd been through.

The timing couldn't have been worse. After all her hard work to get where she was today, she didn't want to jeopardise it by falling for her boss. It was only asking for trouble with a man like Henri.

She closed the door behind her visitors and took a deep breath. It was time to act her age and not be some shy teenage version of herself.

'I was hoping we could start with cupcakes?'

Gabrielle bit her lip, as if she was worried she was making an outrageous demand.

'With the fuss you were making about coming over here I thought we were dealing with an emergency,' Henri said dryly.

Lola got the impression there'd been quite a discussion between uncle and niece before they'd rocked up at her apartment. No doubt Henri had tried to talk Gabrielle out of going ahead with this, in order to avoid the woman he'd kissed without permission, and it would have taken a great deal on the young girl's part to stand up for what she wanted.

Lola didn't want either of them to regret the decision they'd made in the end.

'It's no problem, Henri. I offered to show her. Besides, the need for cake is most *definitely* an emergency.'

It was cool. They'd managed to be in the same room for five minutes already without anyone getting kissed or being over-emotional. She would take Gabrielle into the kitchen and disappear behind a cloud of flour and icing sugar.

'If you're sure…?'

'I am. Now, you make yourself at home and Gabrielle and I will go bake up a storm.'

She met his eyes, assuring him that events hadn't changed her desire to befriend his niece. Other more delicate matters could be worked out at a later date. When she understood herself how to resolve them.

Once Gabrielle was kitted out in an apron, to protect her de-signer hoodie from the ravages of margarine and eggs, Lola set her to work fetching basic ingredients.

'So, it's cupcakes you want?'

At least this was one area she was confident in. Those years of trying to feed four hungry men on a tiny budget hadn't been wasted—she could turn her hand to most things in the kitchen.

'Can we try chocolate ones? Uncle Henri always buys them for us as a special treat, but I'd love to learn how to make them myself. Any that Mum makes are usually either burnt or chewy.' Gabrielle screwed up her nose in disgust as she bore witness to her mother's crimes against baked goods.

So Henri had a sweet tooth? She'd had him down as more of a savoury type of guy. With any luck she could feed him cake until he was too full to move or even speak for the rest of the night.

'Chocolate cupcakes it is, then. I'll get the paper cases and you can make a start on weighing everything out.'

It was probably the easiest recipe for Gabrielle to follow herself, and any boost to her confidence, no matter how small, was a bonus.

'How are things at school?'

Lola had shown her how to mix the batter and waited until she was distracted before unleashing the question. Gabrielle had made the point that she simply wanted to hang out tonight, but it wouldn't hurt to find out how the ground lay.

'Okay…'

She was concentrating so hard on creaming the fat and sugar together she didn't seem spooked at the question.

Lola pushed her a tad further. 'Okay, good, or okay, the same?'

Gabrielle shrugged. 'The same. Do I add the eggs and flour now?'

'Yes. Fold them in gently with the cocoa powder, and when you have a nice smooth batter you can spoon it into the cases.'

Lola knew the change of subject was the equivalent of Gabrielle hiding behind her hair, so she tried a different tactic.

'I had an interesting time at work the other day. I had to treat one of the guys who made my life hell in school.'

Cake mixture dripped from the spoon as Gabrielle stood transfixed by the story. 'What happened?'

Lola put herself under pressure not to reveal the terror she'd still felt after all these years. This had to be a story about overcoming those fears and giving Gabrielle hope.

'Well, even though he tried to make me feel small, I dug deep and found the courage to stand up to him. That's the thing, Gabrielle—these people will always be immature and short-sighted, while we grow and develop.'

She omitted the part about Henri interrupting her breakthrough moment, since it spoiled the whole moral of her story. She didn't have to take abuse from anybody at any age.

'Wow. How did it feel?'

Gabrielle's eyes had nearly popped out of her head, she was so enthralled with the idea of giving those bullies a taste of their own medicine. Lola had to admit her reaction gave her a warm fuzzy feeling inside. It confirmed her view that she was becoming the confident professional she was supposed to be and not the simpering helpless damsel Henri seemed to think she was.

'Bloody brilliant. I thoroughly recommend it.'

She revelled in the picture of Smith stumbling when she'd mentioned the police and dismissed everything involving Henri after that point. The important part of the tale was told.

'And how did he react?'

'Honestly, I think he was scared. He backed off straight away. People like that are so used to putting others down to make themselves feel good they don't know how to react when they fight back.'

If Henri had only given her a few minutes more to shut Smith down completely she mightn't feel a little short-changed now. He'd denied her closure at the last minute.

Gabrielle was all picture no sound as she placed the tray of cakes in the oven. Lola prayed she was imagining shooting down her own tormentors in similar fashion. It would do her good to let rip and tell them—tell anyone—how she felt.

'Okay, cupcakes are in the oven, cooling rack is ready—all we need now is the frosting.'

Lola yanked open the cupboard doors, searching for the crucial ingredients.

'Shoot! We're all out of icing sugar. I must've used the last of it on Bastien's cake.'

She'd gone through a truckload of supplies since starting at the hospital, self-medicating after run-ins with infuriating registrars and difficult patients.

'I can go get some.'

Gabrielle yanked off her apron and ran out through the kitchen door before Lola could stop her.

'Uncle Henri, I'm just popping across the road to get some icing sugar. I won't be long.'

Lola wasn't sure which of the two adults was more horrified by that suggestion—although probably for different reasons.

'I'll go. I don't want you crossing that busy road on your own.'

Henri sprang up from the sofa with the same eagerness as Gabrielle. People were so desperate to get away from Lola she was in danger of developing a complex.

Gabrielle rolled her eyes. 'I know how to cross a road. I'm not *five*.'

'All she has to do is cross at the lights.'

As much as Lola didn't want to be left with Henri and be forced to have the talk she'd steered well away from for days, it was important Gabrielle was afforded some independence.

'Make sure you do,' he told his niece as he bowed to the pressure and handed her some money from his wallet.

'I'll be back in a minute.'

Gabrielle almost skipped out of the apartment, drunk on her

new freedom. It was amazing how much a small concession had changed her mood. Step by step they were gradually building her up. The ultimate goal was to give her enough confidence and self-belief that her detractors' cruel words would no longer hold any power over her.

'Be careful!' Henri and Lola shouted at the same time to the slamming door.

They exchanged the awkward smiles of two people unwittingly set up on a date. Except for the fact that it was her own fault they were out of supplies, Lola might have questioned Gabrielle's motives for volunteering.

'She's growing up fast.' Henri sighed staring longingly at the back of the door.

'Yes—and you have to let her. Trust me. I've been there with my brothers. I can only advise you from my point of view, as someone who's been there and is still wearing the "Wrapped in Cotton Wool" T-shirt, but you can't stop her from living her life and she'll only resent it if you do.'

Henri scrubbed his hands through his hair, mussing the once sleek locks as if he was battling the idea of letting go. 'Something's been bothering me since, you know… Well, a lot's bothering me…'

'Spit it out, Henri. It's not like you to be lost for words.'

They might as well get this sorted now, so she could stop swerving out of his path at work and get on with her job. He'd kissed her—he regretted it. There was little to get het up about as far as she could see. She kept telling herself that every time she replayed the moment in slow motion.

'What happened to you…it's not what Gabrielle's going through, is it? I mean, I've tried to convince myself that if things were that bad you'd tell me. I'd kill anyone who laid a finger on her.'

He was so agitated Lola knew she would have to put him out of his misery before he decided to lock Gabrielle in a tower somewhere for the rest of her life.

'No. Nothing like that. She has a low self-esteem issue—but, hey, who hasn't? Present company excluded...' Lola attempted to bring some levity back into the situation before he tried to shake the information out of her.

He closed his eyes and let a hissing breath out through clenched teeth. 'Thank goodness. I couldn't imagine having to go through that. *Je suis désolé*. That sounds so insensitive. How are you...after everything?'

Lola tried not to feel like an afterthought. It was perfectly normal that his main concern should be for his niece.

'Honestly? I was ticked off at you for taking over the care of my patient. It doesn't reflect well on me as a doctor if I'm not trusted to even suture a minor cut on my own.'

'That's not what it was about and you know it, Lola. The guy had his hands all over you—not to mention whatever went on between you in the past. I acted the way I would for any of my friends and family and I made sure that you were out of danger, first and foremost.'

Deep down, she knew that, but ingrained paranoia wouldn't let her believe that a man would get involved in her problems for purely altruistic motives. Except for her brothers, who wanted to keep her under lock and key, and she certainly didn't want another prison guard keeping tabs on her every move.

'I appreciate your concern, but for the record it's not necessary. I'm not going to get anywhere if I don't learn to stand on my own two feet.'

'Message received and understood. Now can we talk about the *other* elephant in the room?'

Now would be a good time for Gabrielle to return, so Lola could slink back to her safe place.

'I really don't think that's necessary.'

'No? Then why have you been avoiding me? All I wanted to do was apologise to you. It should never have happened. I just... I don't know... You were upset... I wanted to comfort you.

That's how it started, at least. But I had no right to kiss you. I don't blame you for hating me for betraying your trust like that.'

He loosened his tie and opened the top button of his shirt as he confronted his actions. And hers.

'I don't hate you. For that you would've had to have done something wrong.'

Her cheeks burned as she made her admission. She'd enjoyed having his lips on hers, but he shouldn't read any more into it than the fact that she'd gone too long without physical contact.

He tilted his head to one side and gave her his confused puppy face. He was really going to make her spell it out.

'I didn't entirely *hate* the kiss. Okay?'

Heat enveloped her whole body. With any luck it would burn a hole in the floor for her to disappear into.

'Now that we've got that out of the way I…er…should go check on the cupcakes.'

And stick her head in the oven while she was at it.

'Pardon?'

For an intelligent, worldly man, he was very slow on the up-take. The mystery of his single status was solved if he took *this* long to realise when a woman was telling him she liked him.

'For goodness' sake. Henri.' Lola threw her hands up in the air and walked towards the kitchen.

Gabrielle would be back soon, so there was no point getting into this now. He was off the hook, and she'd made a prat of herself for nothing.

She donned her oven gloves and waited for cake therapy to take effect. Unfortunately Henri was standing between her and her salvation.

'How can I believe you wanted that kiss when you were so tense in my arms?'

'I was confused. It had been a stressful day, if you remember? Now, I'm not going to stroke your ego any more. If you'll move out of the way, I'll get back to what tonight's supposed to be about. Gabrielle and cake. Nothing more.'

He folded his arms and leaned against the worktop, clearly with no intention of moving out of her way.

'If that was you enjoying yourself, I'm starting to feel a little hard done by.'

'Too bad.'

Her heart did that same stupid jig when he'd made a move on her the last time—and he wasn't even touching her. Yet.

'Why don't we try it again? Only this time going into it with our eyes open. Figuratively speaking, of course.'

He pushed himself off the counter and took a step towards her. Lola bit back a squeal but stayed firm, slowly nodding her response. What harm could one more kiss do now? It wasn't as if they were going to embark on some red-hot affair and blur that line between work and play even more. This was about satisfying her curiosity and salving Henri's bruised male ego. A Frenchman believing he'd failed as a Lothario must be devastating.

He came at her with such force he nearly knocked her off her feet. She clung to him, her stupid oven gloves around his neck, struggling to stay upright as he claimed her mouth. This time his lips were hard and demanding, yet every bit as passionate. She melted into him like chocolate in the sun and forgot all about her golden rule about keeping work and play strictly separate. And he was definitely prettier than her.

Perhaps it was that comforting smell wafting from the oven, or the knowledge that she definitely wanted this, but kissing Lola tasted even sweeter than he remembered. She was moulded to him, every one of her curves pressed against him, and preventing all logic from getting to his brain.

It didn't matter that they were colleagues or that he couldn't commit to someone with more baggage than he when she was teasing his tongue with the tip of hers.

He let his hands slide over the curve of her hips and down to the swell of her buttocks. She moaned when he pulled her flush against him, and there was a real danger that there was more than the cupcakes getting burned here. There was a fire blazing inside him for Lola, and only one possible way of extinguishing it. A kiss was one thing. Taking it any further would complicate all aspects of his life.

With great reluctance he loosened his hold and gave her one last soft kiss. 'This is probably a really bad idea.'

'Yeah. Probably.'

She looked up at him with desire-darkened eyes which didn't reflect what she was saying. Her lips were parted, swollen from his tending and inviting more.

In the scheme of things, he didn't see how much damage one last kiss could do. He moved in again, fastening his mouth on hers and warming himself in the last of their passion before the cold wind of reality blew out the flames.

A cacophony of noise rang out around them as if they'd triggered a *What the hell are you thinking?* alarm. The ear-splitting beep from the oven timer had gone off at the same time as Gabrielle sounded the doorbell.

Henri sprang away from Lola like a horny teenager busted by his parents while making out with his girl.

'I'll get that.'

'I'll get these.'

Lola scuttled away to rescue her and Gabrielle's cooking efforts, letting her hair fall across her face so Henri couldn't read her properly. She was as bad as his introverted niece at times—so careful not to let him know how she was feeling at any given moment.

Was he really so scary that no one could relax around him and say what was on their mind?

The irritating drone of the bell carried on until he was forced to leave Lola and their moment in the kitchen to answer the door.

'I thought you'd got lost,' he said, opening the door once he'd straightened his clothes.

'I was only gone for, like, five minutes.'

Another roll of exasperated teenager eyes and Gabrielle took herself and her purchases to the hub of the apartment. Everything important tonight was going on in that kitchen.

Henri checked his watch and confirmed the time. Five minutes was all it had taken for his world to be completely turned upside down. With anyone else a kiss wouldn't be such a big deal. Hell, he'd done more than that with women he barely knew. It held so much more meaning with someone like Lola, who was slowly easing her way into his life.

He couldn't promise her anything when he had so many commitments elsewhere. Yet he didn't think he was capable of resuming a strictly professional relationship now that he'd had a sample of what he might be missing. That side of her he'd seen in Angelique's class hadn't been a fluke. Behind that shy interior there was most definitely a passionate showgirl waiting to be coaxed into the spotlight. Lord help him, but *he* wanted to be the one to help her shine.

Henri flopped down onto the sofa, content to leave Lola and Gabrielle to bond over their baking whilst he was left alone with his thoughts. It didn't happen very often without someone requiring his assistance.

He'd only just relaxed back into the seat when Gabrielle screamed, and he was back on his feet and running in no time.

'What is it? What's happened?' His doctor instinct kicked in and he burst through the door to assess the scene and see what he could do to help.

He slid on the sticky red trail splattered across the kitchen floor. The carnage was worse than he'd feared. Gabrielle shrieked again as Lola attacked.

'What the hell…?'

'We got a bit carried away…sorry.' Lola grinned at him, chocolate frosting dripping from her chin, her hair white and caked in flour.

'So I see.' Henri surveyed the kitchen, in the aftermath of an apparent food fight.

'She started it!' Gabrielle squealed from behind a fetching buttercream beard.

'Well, I'm finishing it. Your mother will have both our lives if you go home like that.' It was true, Angelique would not be happy, but it was good to see his niece having fun for a change.

'Spoilsport!'

He turned at Lola's insult—only to meet a blob of chocolate cream flying through the air at him. Gabrielle was doubled over laughing as he scraped away the brown dollop and flung it back at Lola.

'Oh, you think that's *funny*, do you?'

He helped himself to the bowl of ready-made icing and prowled towards the giggling teenager. She ducked behind Lola, unable to hide the wide smile spreading across her face. Henri couldn't remember the last time they'd laughed together like this, and it was all down to Lola.

'Run, Gabrielle! Save yourself! I'll cover you.'

Lola blocked him at every turn, protecting her charge until she could make a run for it. Gabrielle sprinted out through the door and down the hall, and the sound of the lock turning on the bathroom door told them she'd made a successful escape.

'Very brave, Miss Lola. Unfortunately you've put yourself directly in the line of fire...'

He scooped out a handful of sweet goo and spread it over her face. Not to be outmanoeuvred, Lola returned the favour, until they stood facing each other as painted warriors.

'You don't scare me,' she said through short breaths.

'No?' He watched her chest rise and fall more quickly with every step closer he took.

'Maybe a little.'

'You *are* very pale.'

He caught a blob of icing on her lip with his finger, but before he could wipe it away Lola caught it with her tongue. Every part of Henri stood to attention when she drew his fingertip into her mouth and sucked it clean. Her mischievous grin said she knew exactly what she was doing to him—and where.

'Is it safe to come out yet?' Gabrielle yelled from the bathroom, and the guilty pair separated to a respectable distance.

'Yes, we've called a truce. Now get your butt out here and help clean up.'

Henri didn't want her to catch them in the act. There was no way of knowing how she'd react to her uncle and her friend getting it on. Even if she didn't mind, there was no point in getting her hopes up that this was some epic love affair when he didn't know what he was doing. If he started something with Lola and regretted it later there was every chance he could break more than one heart along the way.

A clean version of his previously flour-dusted niece appeared, shaking her head when she saw the iced faces before her.

'You two are such dorks.'

'You love us, really. Come here and give us a big hug.'

Henri and Lola flanked Gabrielle and moved in for a two-pronged attack, wrapping her in a group hug to smoosh their faces against hers.

Gabrielle's laugh reached deep inside to touch Henri's heart. Moments like this were few and far between when he and Angelique were so caught up in work. He made a mental note to set more time aside in future to have fun with the kids and remember that there was more to being a replacement father than rules and school pickups.

'Okay, guys, I think playtime is over. We'd better get this mess cleared up before Jules gets home or we're all in trouble.'

Lola was the first one to break the huddle and Henri reluctantly followed her instructions. In that happy kitchen all the stresses in his life had ebbed away and he'd acted without worrying about the consequences. Now he'd have to return to being the responsible adult who so many counted on.

After cleaning up, they sampled the fruits of the girls' labour until all three of them were in danger of going into a sugar coma.

'You can take the rest back for your mum and Bastien.' Lola boxed up the remainder of the cupcakes for Gabrielle, effectively ending the evening.

'Thanks for tonight.' Gabrielle reached up to give Lola a peck on the cheek as they left.

'Yes, thanks for everything,' Henri said as he, too, planted a kiss on her cheek.

If Gabrielle hadn't been there he might well have asked Lola for more. More than either of them were ready for. Perhaps this was one time when his responsibility to his family had saved him from making a huge mistake.

CHAPTER SIX

'OKAY, MR RUTHERFORD, the X-ray confirms there is a fracture in your shoulder, but the bone hasn't moved so we don't have to operate.'

Lola's burly rugby-playing patient was visibly relieved at the news. She'd warned him they might have to pin the shoulder, since the fracture was so close to the joint, but he was safe for now.

'Thanks, Doctor.' The shaven-headed, mud-splattered muscleman might look intimidating on the outside, but he'd been a model patient since his admittance and very respectful to Lola as she'd assessed him.

She'd have to stop being so judgemental about people's appearances when she knew how it felt to be on the receiving end of such shallow prejudice. If she hadn't spent so much time with Henri she'd still think of him as an arrogant Frenchman who cared for nothing except himself. It was their secret that he was a loving, caring family man whose kisses were more addictive than a tray of chocolate-chip cookies.

Lola got her mind back on the job and went to work fitting a sling around her patient to keep his arm immobile. There was still some residual panic at being on her own with a member of the opposite sex who could clearly overpower her if he chose to. Perhaps that fear would never entirely leave. But she was working through it. She also had the safety net of knowing one shout would bring Henri to her aid, and that notion of support without being suffocated was a novelty for her.

With each patient she treated successfully Lola was growing stronger. It was a shame Henri hadn't been there to witness her progression. She hadn't seen him since that night in her apartment, and old insecurities made her question his absence.

It was unfair of him to kiss her and leave her in limbo about what happened next. For her, responding to their attraction had added a new dimension to her life. Since leaving high school her main goal had been survival. So far she'd put herself through medical school, moved out of home, and now was starting a new career. There was some semblance of a normal human being emerging, but there was one aspect of adult life she'd thus far avoided.

Her track record with men was short and traumatic, and not something she'd seen the need to explore further. Until Henri had kissed her.

That desire, the tenderness in his every touch, was something she hadn't experienced in a long time, and she hadn't realised how much she was missing it. If there was a way to capture that passion and romance without handing over control of her life she might be tempted into *more* French kissing.

Now that she was inextricably linked to his family she didn't think Henri would intentionally hurt her and face the wrath of his sister and niece. Nor did she expect him to want to enter into any sort of long-lasting affair when he had so many other commitments. That suited her fine. She was only here for another month, and a fun, flirty fling might be just the thing to help her finally move on.

All she had to do now was get Henri on board before he had time to regret ever laying his lips on her.

'Hello, sis.' The sound of her brother's voice automatically shut out all thoughts of romance.

'Jake? What's wrong?'

Lola did a quick assessment to see what injury he might have been admitted with, but since he was standing upright, with no visible signs of blood, it didn't appear too serious.

'Nothing. I thought I'd pop in and see how you were since we haven't heard from you in days. Kyle and Matt are busy at the garage, otherwise they would've come, too.'

He'd find himself in Admissions very shortly, with the mobile phone he was waving in her face shoved somewhere the sun didn't shine for turning up here unannounced.

'You can't "pop in" whenever you feel like it, Jake. This is a busy hospital and you'll get me in trouble. Please feel free to pass that on to the other two.' She hooked her arm through Jake's and escorted him out of the department and back towards Reception.

Naturally this was the very moment she should cross paths with the elusive Henri.

He did a double-take as he passed them in the corridor. 'Is everything all right here?'

It was on the tip of Lola's tongue to explain the situation, but then she'd run the risk of another lecture about getting her priorities right. It wouldn't go down well for him to find out she was dealing with family matters when there was a queue of patients waiting to see a doctor.

'All under control, thank you, Dr Benoit.' She tugged at Jake's arm, determined to ditch him as soon as possible.

'The level of personal attention you give your patients is very admirable, but I think you might be needed back on duty.'

Henri was letting her know this was another black mark against her—and she'd been doing so well.

'Of course. I'm heading straight back after this.'

As soon as her toe had connected with her brother's rear end.

Far from impressing Henri with her feminine wiles, all she'd succeeded in was annoying him again. She dug her nails into Jake's arm.

'Ouch! What was *that* for?' he grumbled when Henri was out of earshot.

'I *told* you I'd get in trouble.'

Now she had *two* areas to work on with Henri before she'd get anywhere.

'Who's that? A foreign exchange student? Can I put in a request for a hot blonde next time?'

Jake wasn't being serious. Lola knew he didn't have a preference when it came to a woman's hair colour. Blondes, brunettes, redheads—they'd all claimed space in his bed over the years. He was an equal opportunities Casanova, who'd probably think all his Christmases had come at once if he had any inkling there was a burlesque-dancing Frenchwoman in town.

'That was my boss—so I *really* need to get back before I get the sack.'

She led him to the exit and all but pushed him out through the door. He really wasn't making this independence thing easy for her.

'Well, boss or not, he has no right to speak to you that way. Do you want me to have a word?'

Jake rolled up his sleeves, ready for his own brand of talking. If it hadn't been for everything Lola had endured, and the reasons behind her brothers' fierce need to protect her, she might have found it sweet.

As it was, their concern was holding her back from enjoying her new life to the full. 'No, Jake. I'm twenty-five years old. I can fight my own battles when I need to.' She kissed him on the cheek. 'I'll make sure to check in with everybody when I get some free time.'

'Okay...'

If he was unhappy with that arrangement he was smart enough not to say it. Small steps.

Lola waved him off, even though her legs were itching to run.

She had to catch up on her workload and somehow get back into Henri's good books before they completely lost momentum.

Jealousy was an alien concept to Henri but there it was, snaking through his veins and poisoning his whole system until he couldn't breathe. He shouldn't have looked back. Then he wouldn't have seen her kiss the handsome stranger on the cheek, sending a dagger straight to his heart. Only a matter of days ago she'd had her arms around *his* neck, her lips pressed to his and her body language telling him she wanted more.

He turned away in disgust and kept walking, every stride longer and quicker as he fought to leave the scene. This was *his* fault. He'd been too slow to acknowledge how much Lola meant to him and now someone else had swept in and turned her head.

Why would a beautiful, intelligent woman such as Lola sit around waiting for a few scraps of encouragement from a guy too wrapped up in his own world to appreciate her? Only an idiot would let her slip through his fingers, and since he'd never followed up on that kiss in her apartment Henri *was* that idiot.

All he'd had to do was take Gabrielle home and go back to Lola. Hell, he could even have phoned her and arranged a proper date—anything to show her he was interested. Instead he'd walked away and left her vulnerable to every predatory male who happened by. With her history she deserved better than that.

Lola had shared something painful with him when she'd told him about her past, and it gave them a deeper connection than he imagined she had with this fly-by-night Lothario. It was possible Henri had been overly cautious about getting involved with her, partly because of everything she'd gone through, but she needed someone who understood and respected her. Someone who would never hurt her.

If she was ready to move on, Henri intended to be that someone. He only prayed it wasn't too late.

With his thoughts occupied elsewhere, he completed his
rounds on autopilot. He said and did all the right things, giving credit to the staff where it was due and pointing out gaps
in their knowledge that needed improvement. All the time he
was trying to come to terms with the carnage a couple of kisses
and a dinosaur cake had caused.

Now questions were rumbling in his head about how he actually *felt* about Lola and what, if anything, he could do about
it. In the past his relationships with the opposite sex had been
separated into two categories—friends and lovers, with never
the twain to meet. It kept things simple when everyone knew
where they stood, with no expectations placed on either party.

Lola was different. Everything he wanted wrapped up in one
sexy package. It was a pity he'd woken up to that fact too late.

He dropped his stack of patient files with a thud, earning a
scowl from the senior nurse he'd disturbed at the other end of
the desk. Whoever this new guy was on the scene, he couldn't
have got much of a lead over Henri. This was the first time he'd
seen him with Lola, and she'd kissed him on the cheek—not
the mouth. Perhaps it was early days for the couple and Henri
still had time to make his move.

Then what? He couldn't offer her any more than an affair,
and that mightn't sound as appealing to Lola as it did to him.

Right now he couldn't see beyond his own desires, which
consisted of being with Lola and getting this other potential
suitor out of the equation. It would require some cunning on
his part, and the assistance of two irresistible children to make
it happen.

It was late afternoon when Lola had to track Henri down for
help with a case involving an elderly man with breathing difficulties. Despite the patient's insistence that he felt well enough
to go home after Lola had administered some oxygen, she
thought the wheezing in his chest was still cause for concern.
A chest X-ray had shown signs of infection, but she wanted

confirmation from a senior that it was necessary to admit him overnight for further treatment.

'Good call,' Henri said, stringing his stethoscope back around his neck after sounding the patient's chest and taking a look at the X-rays. 'We'll put in a request to get him moved to a ward, and start intravenous antibiotics as soon as possible to get the infection cleared.'

Although he'd concurred with her diagnosis, Lola wished she'd been confident enough to give the final say on the admission. 'I know I'm second-guessing myself, but I want to be certain I'm making the right judgement call.'

'I don't think we're ever really one hundred per cent sure on any case—we're not invincible—and you're right to check rather than take a gamble. But at some point you're going to have to show confidence in yourself and your diagnosis. How else will a patient feel safe in your hands?'

Once again Henri prompted her to consider how she could improve her standing here. Without the eyes of the other first-year doctors watching the exchange Lola didn't have the same inclination to want to cry. She took the comments in the manner with which they were made—as advice from a superior who wanted her to be the best doctor she could be.

At the minute it was the more personal aspect of her relationship with Henri which was bothering her. One word was probably all it would take for her to fall back into his arms. A braver soul would have asked him outright what those kisses had meant—if anything. Had it been it a heat-of-the-moment reaction to the smell of home baking, or did he genuinely have feelings for her?

She should be bold and ask him outright if she meant to reinvent herself as the sort of woman who could embark on a fling without a second thought.

'I'm working on it.'

She hovered by the desk, waiting for some acknowledgement that their friendship had progressed to something more.

But instead of a smile, a blush, or an action replay, Henri simply buried his head back in his paperwork. She took a seat in the empty chair next to him, close enough that she could read the handwriting on his reports. Flirting was a distant memory for her, but she was pretty sure it shouldn't result in the other person pedalling away on a swivel chair.

'Is there something else I can help you with?'

He was flicking through his personal diary at a rate of knots, oblivious to her attempt to rekindle the romance between them. Lola's bravado left her instantly.

Someone like Henri wouldn't have lost any sleep over a couple of snatched kisses with an easily impressed new intern. It hadn't been as much of a life-changing moment for him or an affirmation of his sexuality as it had for her. The idea that a sexy French doctor found her attractive in the first place should have been enough of a confidence boost without the expectation of more.

'I can see you're busy. It can wait.'

Next time she'd wait for the other party to make a move and save herself from the crippling embarrassment of rejection or, worse still, this apparent apathy towards her.

She slid her chair away, prepared to freewheel the whole way down the corridor before she would stand up and walk away under a cloud of shame.

'Don't go.'

Henri shot his hand out to stop her, catching her above the knee, his fingers branding the skin. She wouldn't let herself get carried away with the idea that this was in any way a demonstration of his devotion—more likely he wanted to discuss her patient's aftercare.

'Did I forget something?'

She'd already made arrangements for the patient's transfer onto a main ward and informed him and his wife of their plans. There was nothing else she could have done as far as she was aware.

'No. You were great. Nothing to worry about on that score.'

He was distracted again, pulling up the rota on the computer screen and cross-referencing it with his planner. This was doing nothing to put Lola's mind at ease.

She sat with her hands in her lap, doing her best not to rub at the spot where his hand had rested and give him any indication that she was affected by his touch.

'Is there something I *should* be concerned about?'

Henri slammed his diary shut and swivelled around to face her. 'I might need your help with something. Angelique has been offered a fantastic opportunity to take part in a burlesque event in Paris as a last-minute replacement for another dancer. The childminder is away on holiday, and I'm supposed to be at a conference this weekend. I wouldn't ask, but—'

'You want me to babysit?' Lola's once soaring heart plummeted into her shoes.

He was only keeping her sweet so there was someone on call to share the substitute parenting load. If she didn't enjoy Gabrielle's company so much, or believe that this would help their bond, she would politely decline.

'No. Yes. Sort of. I thought perhaps the kids could come with me to the conference hotel. There's a pool and a tennis court. I'm sure there's plenty for them to do whilst I'm in lectures.'

Henri fidgeted with the clasp on his diary, leaving the story half told. What was it he was expecting from her? She wasn't sure she was committed enough to go back and forth to God knew where in order to entertain his niece and nephew, regardless of their cuteness. For all he knew she could actually have a life outside of the hospital and his family.

'I'm sure a mini-break would do Gabrielle the world of good, but I'm not sure where I fit into your plans. I don't think I can commit myself to driving backwards and forwards every day to wherever it is you're staying.'

'I want you to come with us.'

'Pardon?'

Only the fact that he'd said 'us' and not 'me' stopped Lola from sliding off the chair and across the polished floor. This was moving faster than she'd anticipated even in her wildest, most erotic dreams.

'I know it's a lot to ask of you, but I don't want to let Angelique down when this means so much to her. The children are very fond of you, and I would prefer to leave them with you than to put them in some over-subscribed kids' club. I'll pay for everything—separate rooms, of course.'

There was no indication that he harboured any ulterior motive in getting her to the hotel other than babysitting. For 'separate rooms' she read, *Don't get any ideas*, and disappointment doused the flames of her ardour.

'I'd be glad to help out—and it will give Gabrielle and I more time to talk.'

Perhaps it wasn't such a bad thing that he wasn't planning a dirty weekend for the two of them. It took the pressure off having to reinvent herself as the sort of woman who jumped into bed with men on a whim.

Henri had picked up on that after one quick snog. There was no chance she would have carried that off if they'd ever made it to the bedroom. Her lights-off-and-duck-under-the-covers-before-anyone-can-see-me-naked approach to lovemaking wasn't conducive to the sizzling sex life the French were so famous for.

Getting involved with Henri would only serve as a reminder of how inadequate she still was as a woman. To date, her love life was a short and unsatisfactory tale for the few involved. The reality of sex had never quite lived up to the hype, and there was no reason to think even Henri could remedy that. Especially if the fault lay entirely at her feet and in her head.

There was little chance of her ever enjoying the physical side of a relationship when she wasn't comfortable with her body, never mind sharing it with someone else. This stint as his babysitter would put her firmly back into place as Henri's charge and nothing more.

The most she could hope to gain from the weekend was a chance to spend some alone time with Henri and the kids to help them bond, and at the very least she was getting an all-expenses-paid weekend away. All she had to lose was her heart. To the entire Benoit family.

With the conference being held in Donegal, crossing the border into Southern Ireland and changing their currency into euros had really given this work function more of a holiday vibe. Especially since he had a beautiful travelling companion seated next to him and a bouncy Bastien in the back seat.

'Uncle Henri says there's a pool and a park and *everything*!' His nose was pressed against the window as they pulled up outside the majestic five-star hotel.

'It's amazing!' Lola leaned forward in the passenger seat as the castle-like building came into view.

It was perched high up on the hill, surrounded by a golf course and overlooking the sea. The isolation of the Donegal coast was the perfect destination for busy medical practitioners eager to escape the stresses and frantic pace of their profession. Only time would tell how suited it was to angsty teenagers and inquisitive six-year-olds. Not to mention the possibility of a romance.

'Glad you approve.'

Henri really wanted them both to relax over these next couple of days, so they could actually get to know each other. As much as was humanly possible whilst they were wrangling his niece and nephew.

He wasn't in the habit of employing family members to help him seduce women, but having Lola as their chaperon seemed a less salacious proposition than asking her to spend the weekend in a hotel alone with him. It mightn't be the most sophisticated or well thought out plan, but it was the best he could come up with at short notice—and better than sitting back and watching her being wooed by the competition.

All he wanted was the opportunity to explore this thing happening between them. There were so many sides to Lola she could never be simply another warm body for his bed when he needed it. But if he threw himself into a relationship with her there was the concern that it would detract his time and energy away from his other commitments. A couple of days and nights holed up here would tell him everything there was to know about the implications of getting involved with someone as kind and unselfish as Lola.

It hadn't been difficult to get Angelique on board since she'd pitched the idea of working in Paris weeks ago. She had been offered a spot at her old haunt, that much was true, even if it wasn't as last-minute as he'd suggested to Lola. His sudden change of heart on the matter had raised Angelique's suspicions, but she'd jumped at the chance to have one last dance in Paris. After she'd phoned Lola to confirm she was voluntarily giving up her time to help out and not being held against her will, of course.

They were all exactly where they needed to be, and hopefully somewhere along the line he'd figure out the next stage of his plan.

Once they'd checked into the hotel, Henri insisted on carrying his and Lola's bags to their rooms. Angelique had packed the kids' things into rucksacks they were able to carry on their backs, much to Bastien's annoyance.

'This is so heavy I'm going to be too tired to play,' he said, collapsing onto the floor outside the bedroom door and showing his mother's flair for drama.

'Good. Maybe I'll get some peace.' Gabrielle stepped over him and let herself in with the key card.

'I hope you know what you're in for.'

Henri was talking to himself as much as his travelling companion. In the midst of his great idea he'd forgotten to factor in the time he'd spend refereeing between these two. He doubted the warring factions would call a truce long enough for any budding romance to fully bloom. They'd all be lucky if Lola didn't call it quits before the end of the night.

With the prospect of the bum-numbing talks he'd have to endure, and the sound of squabbling siblings, she was the one saving grace about this weekend.

'You mean this isn't all spa days and fine dining? How disappointing.'

Lola's eyes were bright with suppressed laughter, and Henri let go of the notion that he'd have to bribe his charges to behave. Unlike most single career women who crossed his path, Lola understood what these children meant to him and embraced everything that came with them. He didn't have to make apologies for who he was when he was with Lola.

'I know. I got you here under false pretences. Really you're in for forty-eight hours of tears, tantrums, and cries of "I'm bored!". And that's just me.'

'Well, you know where I am if you want me. I mean…just knock me up when you're ready. I mean…'

Lola slapped her forehead as she stumbled into one innuendo after another and Henri did his best not to burst out laughing. It gave him renewed hope to find he wasn't the only one preoccupied with thoughts of the bedroom.

'Lola Roberts, you have a one-track mind. I'm shocked. *Shocked*, I tell you.' He set her bag down at her feet and turned back to the room next door.

'Why is your face all red, Lola?' Bastien squinted up from his death throes on the floor.

Henri decided to save her any more blushes and lifted Bastien up by the rucksack so his legs and arms were dangling in the air.

'What I was trying to say was that I can take the kids as soon as you're ready.'

Lola had composed herself again, but Henri preferred her first offer. The one that didn't include a reference to anybody's offspring.

'I don't have any lectures to attend until the morning, so we could all go down together for dinner if you'd like?'

Although Henri had imagined a much more informal arrangement that would include drinks after the gruesome two-some had gone to bed.

Bastien's limbs windmilled in Henri's grip, wriggling like an insect picked up off the ground. 'I think I can walk now, Uncle Henri. Could you put me down, please?'

'Your uncle is an amazing doctor if he can cure broken legs with one hand.' Lola arched a cynical eyebrow at them both as the newly liberated Bastien bug ran into the room, laughing.

'I didn't get to be registrar for nothing,' Henri answered with a grin. 'Now, enough about my many, many, talents—tell me you'll join us for dinner?'

'Sure. I'll freshen up and meet you down in the restaurant in, say, an hour?'

They synchronised watches, then retreated to their separate rooms. Henri already knew the time he would spend with Lola would be the highlight of this entire weekend.

Henri's breath stuck in his throat as Lola walked into the restaurant. She'd swapped her casual travelling clothes for a floral baby doll dress that stopped just above her knees to show off her slim legs. Her hair was swept up into a messy bun, leaving her neck bare and begging for attention. Hers was a level of natural beauty that could never be achieved with an army of experts, and she had no idea how smitten half the room were with her as she wound through the tables.

Henri nearly spilled the jug of water over the table in his

hurry to get to his feet and call her over. 'There's a seat here for you, Lola.'

'Hi, guys.'

She took the empty seat beside Henri and covered her knees with a napkin. Gabrielle cast a brief glance up from her games console, smiled, and resumed play. Bastien stopped playing the drums on the table with his spoon for long enough to say hello.

'You look beautiful.' With three little words Henri managed to turn Lola's cheeks the same pale pink as her dress.

'Thank you.'

She ducked away from the compliment when she should have held her head high. No matter how hard he tried, Henri couldn't marry the two sides of her personality—that fearless siren he'd seen gyrating in Angelique's class, and the shy, insecure wallflower who hated any form of attention. Those low lifes must have really done a number on her if she couldn't see what he saw before him.

There was a great deal of whispering and elbowing going on from the opposite side of the table, and then Bastien threw his cutlery on the table and slumped into his chair. 'Uncle Henri, I don't feel very well.'

'Since when?' Not ten minutes ago Bastien had been using Henri's bed as a trampoline.

'Since now.' Bastien sighed, doing his best floppy ragdoll impression.

Henri left his seat and dropped to his knees in front of his nephew. He put a hand on his forehead. He wasn't running a temperature. 'You're not hot. Are you sore anywhere?'

Bastien shook his head.

'Maybe he's homesick.' Gabrielle added her diagnosis and cuddled her brother tight.

Bastien nodded his head—much too eagerly for someone supposedly ill. Gabrielle glared at him until he resumed his sad clown face. It was all highly suspicious.

'Is that right? And how do you propose we cure him, Dr Gabs?'

Henri didn't know what they were up to, but he was sure it had nothing to do with missing home. According to Angelique they'd been so excited to find out about their surprise getaway they'd barely slept last night.

'We could go back to the room and watch cartoons?'

He should have known they'd get bored sitting in a fancy restaurant when they were used to dinner on their laps with the TV on in the background. Henri tossed his napkin on the table. They didn't have to get the bill, since they hadn't had a chance even to order before the conspiring duo had concocted their own agenda for tonight.

'Cartoons it is, then. I'm sorry about dinner, Lola.'

'That's okay—the children are more important.'

Her resigned shrug and Lola's acceptance of his priorities should have warmed Henri, not left him cold. There was nothing he wanted more than to be with her, and he wished there was some way to convey that to her. So far this plan had backfired spectacularly. Rather than bringing he and Lola closer together, having the children here was pushing them further apart.

'No!'

Gabrielle's outburst made them all jump.

'I mean…that's not necessary. You two should stay and enjoy your dinner. I can take Bastien up to the room if you give me the key.'

'What about your dinner?' Sick or not, he didn't imagine that Bastien, away from the watchful eyes of his mother, would miss the chance to fill up on desserts without a good reason.

'We can order Room Service if Bastien starts to feel better.'

Gabrielle had it all worked out, and Henri wasn't sure what was behind it except for a chance to ditch the adults.

It was tempting to give in and finally have some quality time with Lola, but doubts still lingered. He glared at them, waiting for one of them to break and tell him what they were up to, but they simply batted their eyelashes and straightened their crooked halos.

Despite his reservations about leaving them to run riot through the hotel, he remembered Lola's words about giving Gabrielle more freedom. She was old enough to babysit her brother in a safe environment for an hour without getting into too much trouble.

He handed the key over with a word of warning. 'One dinner and one dessert only and I'll be up to check on you shortly.'

'Yes, Uncle Henri,' they chorused, and scampered out of the restaurant with the smiles of well-practised conmen.

Lola waited until they were out of sight before erupting into sweet laughter. 'They have you wrapped around their little fingers!'

'Ever get the feeling you've been had?'

Henri moved across to take the seat Gabrielle had vacated, so they were sitting face on, instead of side by side, with him trying to sneak a peek at her when he thought she wasn't looking.

'Definitely—but they're good kids. I don't think we need to worry about them ending up on the wrong side of the law just yet.'

'Perhaps not, but there's every possibility they'll have drowned in ice cream by the time I go up.' Unsupervised Room Service was probably an accident waiting to happen, but he was doing his best to adopt this new laid-back approach to substitute parenting Lola had advocated.

With the table now a child-free zone, Henri ordered some wine to accompany their preferences from the menu. It was beginning to feel more like a date—exactly what he'd hoped for—and yet a little Dutch courage wouldn't go amiss. There was every chance Lola could reject his idea of a fling, in which case he'd screwed *everything* up.

They waited in silence as the wine was poured, and Henri could see Lola's hands tremble as she lifted the glass to her

274 FRENCH FLING TO FOREVER

lips. There would be no need for nerves if she saw him as only a friend.

He sawed into his steak with renewed gusto, fortifying himself for the moment when he'd have to disclose his real motive for bringing her here.

Lola forced down every mouthful of dinner, even though her appetite had vanished along with the children. Without the accompaniment of minors she was simply a single woman being wined and dined by a handsome man. Something which her permanent state of spinsterhood didn't allow to happen very often. And it was being made especially difficult for her not to get carried away in the moment when neither one of them had any intention of going home at the end of the night.

She washed the growing anticipation down with a sip of wine, unwilling to get her hopes up that something could happen between them when Henri was here for work reasons, not her pleasure.

'Thanks for bringing me along this weekend. It's nice to get away for a few days.'

Although she'd had to bend the truth of her whereabouts to keep certain busybodies from interfering in proceedings. As long as her flatmate and her brothers didn't confer, she could come away from this without causing a scandal. There was no point in causing uproar over a potentially ruined reputation when any inappropriate behaviour was probably entirely in her head.

'It was for totally selfish reasons, I assure you. I didn't even ask if you had other plans.'

'Nope. I'm all yours.'

She took another gulp of wine after her clumsy attempt at flirting. There was no way she could bring herself to say what it was she wanted to come from their time together in case she'd got it completely wrong. She was trusting in Henri to read the signals and make the move. If he wanted to.

'What about the man you were with the other day? Are you sure *he* wasn't expecting your company tonight?'

Henri seemed to be toying with the food on his plate with the same enthusiasm Lola had for her own meal. When he gazed up at her, all that familiar bravado hidden beneath a furrowed brow, there was a genuine expression of worry that she'd rather be somewhere else.

Nothing could be further from the truth.

Lola blinked back at him mid-chew and swallowed the ball of anxiety in her throat. It was no doubt a difficult concept for Henri to grasp that she preferred some distance from her family. 'Jake? No, I told him I was busy. I'll catch up with him another time. And don't worry—he's been warned to stay away from the hospital in future.'

Henri placed his cutlery neatly in the centre of his plate with slow, deliberate movements. 'Whatever his name is, I hope he treats you right.'

'He's a pain in the backside, but he means well. It's just as well the other two are so busy with work at the minute or I'd have all *three* of them breathing down my neck.'

'All three of whom?' He was leaning across the table, eyebrows knitted together and staring at her as though she'd just landed on the planet.

'My brothers. Who did you *think* I meant?'

'I thought you'd traded me in for a triple threat.'

It took Lola a minute to comprehend the accusation of being a serial cheat. Once she'd stopped laughing she would put him right. Clearly her seduction technique needed work if he thought she was interested in anyone other than him. The thought of one romantic liaison brought her out in a cold sweat—any more than that would turn her into a complete basket case. She didn't know whether to be flattered or offended that he thought her capable of taking on three lovers.

I thought you'd traded me in...

Henri's words echoed in her head to remind her that he'd included himself in the list of her conquests and set her pulse fluttering once more. 'Are you saying you were jealous?'

'*Oui.* I don't want to think of you kissing anyone else the way you kissed me.'

Henri finally uttered the words guaranteed to make any woman swoon. But Lola's first instinct was to question his motives.

'Why not?'

This had to be about more than his ego being bruised or she'd inevitably end up getting hurt. It was important that he wanted *her* and not just a victory over some imagined foe. A one-sided love affair would never end well.

'I know we haven't talked about what happened between us, and that's entirely my fault. It was only seeing the possibility that I could lose you to someone else that made me face up to how much you mean to me.'

He reached across the table and took her hand, his touch reassuring her that this was frighteningly real and no longer a fantasy. However, she was realistic enough to understand that this couldn't be more than a fling. In a few weeks she'd be moving on to another department and Henri wouldn't give her another thought. If he wanted to be with her until then, it would be on her terms. At least that way she might be able to maintain some control over her emotions.

'I don't want anything serious, Henri. There's too much other stuff cluttering up my life to worry about being perfect girlfriend material. Got it?'

'I think I've got it. You want us to be lovers?'

The French accent was made to say that word. *Lovers.* It purred from his tongue, a deliciously exciting take on her blueprint for their future. The scandalous idea of using Henri only for sex was definitely a step forward in the adventures of New Lola. That way she'd get to have all the fun without any of the drama. *If* she was brave enough to agree to further involvement with a red-hot Frenchman with her limited experience. After all, Frenchmen were renowned for more than their egos and their cuisine.

'Yes.' She blurted it out before her insecurities caught up with her and convinced her that she wouldn't be enough for Henri—even as a lover. 'When my placement at the hospital is over, so are we. Both of us can move on with a clear conscience and our curiosity satisfied.'

That day in his office had given Lola a tantalising peek at what lay underneath his clothes. Now her body was on high alert at the promise of more. Goosebumps formed on the exposed skin of her arms and her nipples puckered against the thin fabric of her dress as arousal flooded through her, washing away any lingering doubts that she wanted this.

'*D'accord*. That's settled, then.' Henri tossed back the rest of his wine with the nonchalance of a Lothario who made indecent proposals every day of the week—when *she* could have done with a paper bag to breathe into.

Lola regretted not telling Jules about this weekend. She desperately needed her 'shut up and do it' brand of advice. Even though they were best friends, she hadn't shared with her any of the details about her involvement with the Benoits. Jules would undoubtedly have rejoiced at the idea of her roommate embarking on a torrid affair, but Lola wouldn't have been able to go to work every day imagining people sniggering behind her back. She'd had enough of that to last several lifetimes. But, paranoia aside, Lola was so far out of her comfort zone she needed one of Jules's motivational speeches to get her to the next level.

'The desserts look heavenly. Are you having one?'

Lola snatched the menu from the table even though her stomach was doing a double somersault. Another course would delay

the moment when she would have to act on her side of this new
verbal contract.

'No, I thought we could go back to the room. Unless *you*
want one, of course?' Henri was antsy already, checking his
watch and looking for the waiter.

Lola's once floaty chiffon dress was now clinging to the light
perspiration on her skin. Her head was spinning as she fell into
the fast-moving current of passion. She reached out and grabbed
for her one lifeline before she was swept away with no chance
of rescue. *My terms.*

'I don't want dessert, but I'm not sure I'm ready to simply
jump into bed, either. I don't normally do this sort of thing.
Could you give me a moment to get used to the idea first?'

Henri leaned across the table, forcing her to do the same so
she could hear him. They were as close as they could be without touching, his breath caressing her lips in an almost kiss.

'I'm not an animal, *chérie*. As much as I want to be with
you, I'm not going to drag you to bed before dinner even has a
chance to settle. I just wanted to go and check on *les enfants*.'

He withdrew again, leaving Lola wanting to face-plant into
the table. Who was the sex fiend now? All the while she'd been
thinking Henri was desperate to ravage her and he only had the
welfare of his sister's children on his mind. She'd have thought
less of him in the long run if he'd abandoned their care in favour
of his own selfish needs. Obviously the heat of the moment had
warped her own sense of priority, since she'd completely forgotten she was there with anyone other than Henri.

'Of course we should make sure they're okay.'

Then she could go and hide under the duvet in her own room
and spend the night revisiting her epic mistake in her head.

Once Henri had paid their bill they headed back to their
rooms. The atmosphere during their journey in the elevator to
the fourth floor was so charged Lola kept imagining he would
make a move on her. *Hoping.* She couldn't remember the last

time this level of anticipation hadn't had negative connotations. Medical school and work had all had her on tenterhooks in their own way, each forming that same weight of dread in her stomach as she waited for the sucker punch. This time, though, she was like a kid on Christmas Eve, impatient to get to the goodies.

Whilst she wasn't quite ready to consummate their new romance, there was no reason she couldn't have a little sample to tide her over. Her lips tingled with the memories of his, and she was tempted to take the initiative herself. If only it didn't seem so inappropriate now they were returning to their two mini-sized responsibilities on the other side of those metal doors.

The *ding* as they reached their floor signalled the end of their night, although Lola followed Henri to make sure the children were safe and sound.

Henri opened the door with the caution of a well-seasoned parent afraid to waken potentially sleeping little ones. He tiptoed inside and peered around the corner.

'Are they all right?' Lola whispered. Judging by Henri's muted reaction to the scene, they hadn't held any illegal raves in the hour they'd been left alone.

He backed out through the door again with his finger on his lips. 'They're asleep. Fully clothed and surrounded by dirty dishes, but asleep nonetheless.'

For a minute Lola could see his potential as a father. His loyalty to his sister was without question but there was more than a sense of him doing his duty where the children were concerned. From everything Lola had seen he was firm with them, and set boundaries where they were needed, but he was also very loving. He would make a great husband and father some day.

'I should get some sleep myself. Tomorrow is going to be a busy day.'

There was no formal itinerary planned, but she imagined a full twenty-four hours with Bastien would be an endurance test. She'd be sure to make full use of all the hotel amenities to fill the time for Bastien and Gabrielle in between Henri's appointments.

'Let me see you to your door—make sure you get home safely.' He closed the door and walked the two steps to her room.

'Well, goodnight. I'll see you in the morning.'

She went to unlock the door, but Henri settled his hand on top of hers to stop her.

'What? No goodnight kiss?'

His words warmed the back of her neck and turned her insides to liquid. One last smooch could be exactly what she needed to settle those bunched-up nerves and help her to sleep.

She turned slowly into his embrace, her breath hiccupping in her throat when he dipped his head to make good on his promise. Her eyes fluttered shut as he pressed his lips to hers, their gentle pressure soon building to the passionate exchange she'd been waiting for. Each time she was in his arms like this, being kissed in a way she'd only dreamed of, Henri chased away one of her bad memories to replace it with a happier, sexier one.

He cupped the curve of her backside and pulled her closer, fitting their bodies perfectly together. Lola heard herself moan and felt her hand slide from the door handle, all thoughts of leaving this corridor vanishing by the second. She was the filling in the sandwich between Henri's hard chest and the wooden door and she relished it. Pinned in place by his hands and lips, she'd never felt so wanted, so safe.

Lola all but slid to the floor when he let go of her.

'For the record, when we're both ready to take the next step you will have my *full* attention.'

His husky-voiced promise sent those goosebumps popping over Lola's skin once more and made the hairs on the back of her neck stand upright. If this was Henri when he was distracted, Lola wasn't sure she would survive him at full strength. Although she'd be happy to die trying.

On that thought, Henri took her hand and kissed it like a true gentleman. Only the wink as he left her gave away that devilish side she knew lurked within.

Lola sighed as she let herself into the bedroom, thoroughly dazed and now with absolutely no chance of a peaceful night's sleep.

CHAPTER SEVEN

HENRI WAS COUNTING down the time until he could join Lola
and the children again. He'd talked about and listened to ad-
vances in emergency medicine enough for one day.

It wasn't that he thought he knew everything there was to
know on the subject, but he could do with some light relief after
talks on such topics as evaluating paediatric trauma and medical legal caveats. He always welcomed new techniques and important literature which would improve everyday patient care
in the department, but he had a folder bulging with notes and
leaflets still to digest before tomorrow's workshops.

At any other conference he would've stayed for the after-
dinner drinks and the table quiz, where the competitive nature of those in the medical profession came to the fore, but
he could think of better ways to wind down. He'd checked in
with Lola on his mobile during the coffee breaks to find they'd
all enjoyed a full sports programme while he'd spent the day
sitting on his behind. Tennis, pitch and putt on the golf green
and swimming were just a few of the activities Lola had listed
when he'd asked what they were up to. Now, feeling guilty and
sluggish, Henri was hoping for a quick dip in the pool before
it closed for the night.

He hadn't expected to find anyone else splashing about in the water. Especially not his niece and nephew, who really should have been getting ready for bed.

The urge to tell them off faded once he saw Lola in there with them. Engrossed in the sight of her frolicking without a care in the world, he paused to watch her from the changing-room door. Although she was wearing a conservative navy one-piece, it clung to all her curves and made Henri glad he'd chosen shorts over unforgiving Speedos. The clothes Lola usually wore, although unmistakably feminine, did not do her body justice. She was beautiful—inside and out.

This was as close to naked as he'd seen her and, coupled with his memory of last night's doorstep clinch, it was pure torture. As soon as this weekend was over and he could hand over parental responsibility to Angelique he was going all out to seduce her.

Lola had been half right when she'd accused him of wanting to drag her straight to bed. That was exactly what he'd wanted to do. But he'd used the kids as a barrier to protect her *and* himself from his libido. She deserved more than a quick release for his frustrations.

'Uncle Henri!'

Bastien's squeal echoed around the pool and immediately sent Lola ducking for cover. She dipped below the water so only her head was clearly visible and Henri was able to walk closer without fear of embarrassing himself.

'I thought you'd be safely tucked up in bed by now.' He climbed down the steps and launched into a front crawl towards the trio bobbing about in the far corner. The water was warm enough to soothe his tired limbs, but refreshing at the same time.

'We were having so much fun we must've lost track of time.'

Lola's smile vanished beneath the surface as Henri drew closer. The last thing he wanted to do was upset her and yet she didn't appear remotely pleased to see him. This wasn't the happy reunion he'd dreamt of during those never-ending lectures.

'Lola taught me how to swim. Wanna see?'

Bastien doggy-paddled over, a bright sight to behold in his orange swim cap, armbands and goggles. His face was a picture of pride as he puffed and splashed his way towards Henri.

'Well done, you—and well done, Lola.'

He caught Bastien up in his arms and planted a kiss on his head. It was a miracle she'd even got him near the water when bathtime was a battle of wills to get him to take his clothes off.

'Gabrielle's an amazing swimmer, too. I told her she should think about joining a local club.' Lola deflected his praise back to the teenager currently torpedoing the length of the pool.

'That's a good idea. If she's interested we can check it out at the local leisure centre.'

Henri had known Gabrielle could swim, but the speed with which she was moving was an eye-opener for him. This was the sort of skill he and Angelique should be encouraging, instead of leaving her to wallow in her teen angst. They hadn't worried too much about her lack of friends outside school, but a swimming club would be a great way for her to meet people her own age and get her out of the house on a regular basis.

Lola beamed as he promised to follow up on her suggestion. She was investing a lot of her time and effort into these two, and he was lucky to have found someone who didn't feel threatened by his role as their guardian. Part of the reason he didn't do long-term relationships was that most women invariably ended up resenting either him or the children for their drain on their time together.

Gabrielle made her way back in record time, breathless and smiling. 'Hey, Uncle Henri. How was your day?'

'Not nearly as much fun as yours, I suspect. I'm exhausted just watching you.'

Even Bastien was now starting to show signs of fatigue, simply floating on his back and staring at the ceiling.

'After the tennis and the golf I *am* starting to get tired. And thirsty.' Gabrielle hitched herself up onto the side of the pool and squeezed the water from her braid.

'Give me five minutes to get a couple of lengths in and we can all go up and have hot chocolate in the room before bed.'

Henri took over from his niece, slicing through the water, in a hurry to join the happy band of spectators before the end of the night. He pushed himself until his lungs were threatening to burst, gulping down a breath with each turn of his head as he made the return journey. Before he'd come to a full stop Lola was already out of the pool, chivvying the others towards the changing rooms.

'Lola—wait.' Henri hoisted himself up the steps, eager to catch her for a moment alone.

He was sure she'd heard him. Her steps had faltered for a second before she carried on running towards the door.

'Lola!' He made certain she heard him this time, his voice booming around the four walls.

She paused, her back still to him, forcing Henri to run a couple of steps ahead so he could face her.

'Didn't you hear me call you? I just wanted to say thanks for taking care of everything today.'

'No problem. I just want to get changed and then we can talk.'

She was acting very strangely, with her hands held up to her chin, her arms covering her chest. It wasn't as if he hadn't seen a woman in a swimsuit before, and, frankly, he hoped to see her in a lot less very soon.

'Is everything okay?' It was in his tactile nature to reach out to her, so he was taken aback to see her withdraw into herself so much she hunched over.

'Fine.'

Her teeth were chattering, even though the place was hotter than a sauna. Something was definitely amiss, but Henri didn't want to make her any more uncomfortable than she obviously was. He didn't know what had happened since last night to cause her to retreat again. Perhaps a day with two active children was more of a passion killer than he'd anticipated.

'I hope you're still going to join us for supper?' He wasn't averse to bribing Lola with chocolate to get a few more precious minutes with her.

'I will. As soon as I get changed.'

She was off again, the patter of her bare feet across the wet tiles marking her escape from whatever it was that had spooked her.

Since the others were in the ladies' changing room, Henri had time for a quick, uninterrupted shower.

Although he was always on hand to help out with the children, both he and Angelique had drawn the line at him moving in. He had even more respect for his sister coping so well without a partner since he was relying so heavily on Lola. Twenty-four hours with an inquisitive six-year-old had only reinforced how difficult it was for his sister to have some time on her own—or privacy, for that matter.

At least Henri wasn't shy about his body or it would have been awkward for him when Bastien had walked in on him this morning. *Oh, God!* If he'd bombarded Lola with the same questions about 'down there' it was no wonder she'd been anxious to cover up. And now he'd left her to wrangle Bastien on her own.

He jumped out of the shower and gave himself a quick towel-dry. His clothes stuck to the layer of moisture left on his skin, but it was a small price to pay to save Lola from having to explain to Bastien why she didn't have a winkie.

The three water nymphs were sitting, waiting for him on the couch outside the gym, all fully dressed and yawning. If Lola was traumatised by Bastien's quest to know everything about everything before he was seven, she hid it well by letting the nuisance in question curl up on her lap.

'I'll carry the Tasmanian Devil if you can manage the gym bags?' Henri handed his wet swimming stuff over and scooped

Bastien up into his arms, not letting go until they were all safely inside the hotel room.

Bastien was still fast asleep when Henri put him to bed. He knew from experience that trying to get the child into his pyjamas now would be as easy as wrestling socks onto an octopus.

'Angelique will kill me if she finds out he's slept in his clothes two nights running.'

'I won't tell if you don't,' Lola whispered as she pulled the bedcovers around the sleeping babe. 'But it'll cost you that hot chocolate you promised me.'

Henri boiled the kettle and set three cups out, but Gabrielle shook her head. 'None for me, thanks. I'm cream-crackered. I just want to go to sleep. Why don't you and Lola take your hot chocolate into her room, so you can chat without worrying about keeping us awake?'

He applauded Gabrielle's attempt at matchmaking, even though it wasn't necessary. Lola's natural beauty and kind heart had captured his attention from the first moment she'd run into his A&E department.

'That's okay. I'm sure Henri wouldn't want to leave you alone. We can do it some other time.'

Lola was making more excuses not to be alone with him, but she'd underestimated the Benoit stubborn streak.

'You need some adult company. Now, stop talking and let me get to sleep.' Gabrielle climbed into bed and ended the subject.

'There's no point in it going to waste.'

He held out a cup and Lola took it with a sigh, surrendering to the tag-team guilt trip. If nothing else was to come of being invited into her room, he was determined to discover what was behind the look of fear when he'd grabbed her arm earlier.

Lola's hands were shaking as she unlocked the door. It was little comfort knowing Henri's hands were occupied with steaming mugs of chocolate when his sheer presence in her room would be overwhelming. They'd agreed not to embark on anything out of her comfort zone until they'd handed Gabrielle and Bastien back to their mother, but things were progressing between them with each passing moment. Although there were some areas she clearly needed to work on...

Henri rounded on her as soon as they were inside and he'd set the cups aside. 'Do you want to tell me what that was all about down by the pool? Did Bastien do anything to upset you?'

'No. Not at all. It was just me being silly.'

She didn't want anyone to take the blame for her hypersensitivity except the men who'd caused it in the first place. Not that there was a chance in hell of *that* happening. They were free to carry on with their lives, never looking back, while she couldn't seem to move on—no matter how hard she tried.

'It wasn't silly. I could see the terror in your eyes when I reached for you. Is it to do with what happened to you before?'

Henri kept his distance, as though he was afraid to touch her now, her skittishness having scared him off. The bullies had chalked up another victory.

She nodded, choking back her fear and determined to fight back. Henri deserved to know why she was still acting like a scared virgin when he'd done everything to make things easier for her. Perhaps if she actually gave that young, naïve Lola a voice she would regain some power over what had happened to her.

Henri stood silently, no longer cajoling and begging her to confide in him but waiting until she was ready.

Lola took a deep breath, in and out, exhaling all the anxiety that went with sharing the memory. 'I was a flat-chested, short-haired tomboy in my brothers' hand-me-down clothes. It was no wonder I was a target of ridicule. But that didn't mean I didn't have the same feelings as every other teenage girl, and I was flattered when the handsome rugby captain took a shine to me.'

She wanted to close her eyes and avoid that look of pity in Henri's eyes, but that would only make it easier for those hideous images to play back behind her lids.

'To cut a long story short—it was a prank. He got me to his house, his mates were there, and they held me down and stripped me to make sure I was a girl underneath the masculine clothes.'

Humiliation still burned all these years later. Her tears and screams had been drowned out in the cacophony of laughter and jeers.

'Bâtard!'

Lola's French was limited, but Henri's growl was enough to know he'd have dished out the same punishment as her brothers had.

'Needless to say, I have a few hang-ups about my body.'

'But you've had relationships since?'

It was so simple to someone so confident in themselves. Henri had probably never thought twice about anything that had happened to him in *his* teenage years.

Lola sat down on the edge of the bed, preparing herself to carry on with her sorry story. 'In hindsight, I should have gone to the police…had therapy. But I didn't have anyone to turn to for advice except three bloodthirsty brothers. I jumped from one disaster to another until I realised I'd be better off on my own.'

Her voice trailed off as she relived those moments of defeat when boyfriends had grown tired of dealing with her intimacy issues.

This time Henri came to her and knelt on the floor before her. 'They weren't worthy of you, Lola. Don't think for one moment you are any less of a woman because of what those scumbags did to you. You are beautiful. Never be ashamed of who you are.'

She stroked his cheek and felt his jaw tense beneath her palm. 'If only it was that easy.'

'Do you trust me, Lola?' He took her hands in his and leaned in, capturing her in his intense gaze.

'Yes.'

She said it more confidently than she'd expected. There'd been moments when she'd questioned his motives, but she'd never been physically afraid of Henri.

He got to his feet, gently coaxing her off the bed to stand with him. 'Will you let me undress you?'

'No.'

She attempted to sit down again. He'd overstepped the mark. There was no way she was stripping here in front of him when she was at her most vulnerable. Hell, she hadn't even been able to let him see her in her swimsuit without trying to hide her meagre assets.

He caught her by the wrist and pulled her up to face him again. 'Do you trust me?'

'Yes, but which part about me being afraid don't you get? I've spilled my guts about what happened to me and all you can think about is getting me naked!'

She'd clearly underestimated who she was dealing with if Henri was nothing more than just another sex-obsessed male, pretending to care so he could get her into bed. He might as well have ripped her heart out there and then.

'I only want to help you, Lola. This is why I'm asking for your permission to see you naked.'

The husky tone was back in his voice, making Lola's lady parts tingle despite her best efforts to remain immune to his request.

'Henri—' She didn't know where this was going, and that terrified her more than getting naked.

He let go of her hands, taking away her support. 'The next move is yours, *chérie.*'

'Only if you strip, too.' It didn't seem fair that she was the only one expected to be open to scrutiny. This wasn't a peep show.

'I will if you insist, but this isn't about me. How can we take the next step if you're not even comfortable in your own skin?'

Henri brushed his hand along her arm, electrifying all the little hairs he came into contact with and charging Lola with renewed sexual energy.

He was right. They were supposed to be embarking on a

scorching, rip-each-other's-clothes-off sex-fest. Not a chaste game of peekaboo or a therapy session. She wanted this, she wanted Henri and she was simply going to have to be bold about it to make this work.

With trembling fingers she unzipped her dress. Unless he turned on the main light she'd remain in relative shadow anyway. She peeled down the top half and shimmied out of the rest until she remained in only her underwear and heels.

Henri moved behind her and bent down to whisper in her ear. 'All of your clothes.'

'I… I…' She shivered, frozen to the spot by his words.

'Would you like me to help you?'

She bit her lip and nodded, her quota of bravado all used up in one act.

Henri didn't give her time to change her mind. His hands were warm on her skin as he opened the clasp on her bra and let it fall to expose her breasts to the cool air. Lola automatically tried to cover herself again, but Henri laced his fingers through hers and pulled her hands away. Her shallow breaths grew louder in the darkened room as he whipped her panties down her legs. She was completely naked, in a hotel room, with her fully dressed work colleague.

'Open your eyes and look in the mirror.'

She hadn't realised how tightly shut they were until Henri made her face the dressing table mirror. It took everything for her not to look away again. She was so pale, so exposed against Henri's form it was hard to watch.

He traced his hand along the curve of her breast. '*Belle*. You are beautiful, Lola.'

She quivered as he kissed the back of her neck, brushing the sensitive spot which was apparently connected to her knees because they threatened to give way. The mirror played an erotic dream sequence before her eyes as Henri cupped her breasts in his large palms and rolled her nipples to hard points between his fingers. Another wave of arousal flashed through her, pooling at the apex of her thighs and completely disregarding any argument against this.

Henri carried on mapping her body with his slow caress, tracing over the indent at her waist and sweeping over her midriff. Lola felt her inner muscles contract as he dipped lower, anticipating his final destination. She held her breath and closed her eyes, waiting for him to claim her.

'Don't you want to watch?'

There was an agonising pause as he coaxed her back to face the couple reflected in the glass. When she saw the image of her pale, aroused body enveloped in the safe arms of a hunky male, Lola realised that was exactly what she wanted to do. She was ready to witness her own sexual awakening.

The pale figure in the mirror guided her lover's hand between her legs, throwing her head back in ecstasy as he pressed into her.

Henri slid a finger inside Lola, ignoring his own desires to see her needs put first. She might never have justice for what those bastards had done to her, but she deserved to live her life like any other woman. Without fear, and accepting of her own sexuality.

It was promising to find she was guiding him where she wanted him to be, taking control back. He pushed deeper, stroking her until her legs were trembling and her moans were driving him crazy.

'Do you want to lie on the bed?' he asked, whispering directly into her ear, causing another shudder to ripple through her limbs.

'Yes...'

Her breathy response did nothing to abate the tightening of his trousers.

She was slumped against him, her head resting against his shoulder and one hand reaching up to anchor around his neck. It was down to Henri to get her where he wanted her.

As easily as he'd carried Bastien, Henri scooped her up into his arms. Lola clung to him as he carried her to the bed, her hooded eyes watching him carefully but not expressing that fear he'd seen once too often. She trusted him, and he knew how much effort that must have taken.

He laid her down on the covers so her legs were dangling over the edge of the bed, opening her fully to him. Her chest rose and fell with every sharp breath she took and she chewed her bottom lip as he stood over her. It would take a little more to get her as relaxed as possible, but Henri was confident he was the one to help her.

With one hand either side of her head, he braced himself on the bed to kiss her without lowering his full weight on top of her. He gently drew her bottom lip into his mouth and slipped his tongue in to tangle with hers. It didn't take long before she went limp beneath him, lost in the kiss and almost persuading Henri to draft a new plan. His erection strained painfully between them, but he was willing to suffer some personal discomfort in order to give Lola what she needed.

'Is this okay?' He was trailing kisses down her throat and over her collarbone, but he wanted to make sure she was with him every step of the way.

'Mmm…hmm…' Lola sucked in a breath through her teeth as he latched on to her nipple and made no attempt to stop him. With every lick and suck of that hardening peak she writhed beneath him, her shyness forgotten as she rubbed her body against his.

With deft fingers, he plucked the other pink tip to a bullet point, and Lola arched off the bed in response. She grazed her soft mound into his ever-increasing hardness until Henri was forced to take a time out, waiting for the fireworks going off behind his eyelids to cease so he could focus back on Lola.

When the tremors subsided, Henri moved farther down her torso, pressing soft kisses against her chlorine and soap-scented skin until he was kneeling at her feet.

'If you tell me to stop, I will.'

He wanted her to know that even now, lying naked and exposed, she had the right to say no and have it heard. Although there was a catch in her breath, Lola nodded and gave him the green light.

Henri danced the tip of his tongue over her stomach, feeling her muscles tightening as he dared to go ever lower. With his hands lifting her legs apart he buried himself between her thighs and lapped at her entrance. Lola's gasp spurred him on, and he plunged in to taste her arousal. Her legs were draped over his shoulders, her buttocks cupped in his hands, as he drove inside her and showed her how sex could be. Loving, enjoyable and totally freaking hot.

She was tugging his hair, scratching his neck with her nails, but never once did she ask him to stop. If the purring noises she was making were any indication, she had no intention of doing so. Henri circled that sweet bud, flicking and licking until Lola tensed around him. Even then he didn't stop. Through every contraction and release of her inner muscles he sought her out, unrelenting, until she almost bucked off the bed and cried out her release. Only when every last aftershock had left her body did Henri finally withdraw.

Lola lay panting on the bed, thoroughly ravished and gorgeous. Her mussed hair was a crooked golden halo around her head, her lips were swollen from his kisses and her legs were still parted and inviting. It would be so easy for Henri to take what he needed too, but that would make him no better than the other men she'd encountered. He wouldn't take advantage of her so callously.

Instead, he pulled the covers back on to the bed and helped her in.

'Thank you.'

From the glassy sheen of her tears, glinting in the darkness, he didn't think Lola was referring to him tucking her in. But sex wasn't something a beautiful woman should ever have to be grateful for. *Any* man should thank his lucky stars if he got close to Lola—he knew he did.

'My pleasure.' He kissed her on the forehead and received a lazy smile in return.

Something told Henri their idea of fun had just skipped to the next stage.

CHAPTER EIGHT

EVERY TIME LOLA cast her mind back to last night her body
tingled with awareness and a smile crept across her face. She
couldn't stop thinking about Henri and what he'd done to her—
for her. More than the mind-blowing orgasm he'd given her,
he'd literally made her face her fears.

Her tormentors' hold on her was gradually weakening under
Henri's careful guidance. He was providing her with a special
brand of therapy, ensuring she was at peace with her own body.
It was easier to achieve when Henri had left her in no doubt
about his attraction to her. In his company she was definitely
all woman. There was no room for ambiguity any more.

'*Lo*-la!' Bastien cried out as the tennis ball whizzed by her
head.

'Sorry!'

Despite her best attempts, the children hadn't had her full attention this morning. Since they'd all overslept, and with Henri
having a lecture first thing, breakfast had been a rushed affair.
It made her antsy. They hadn't even had a chance to talk in private, never mind embark on a follow-up to last night's events.
Exhausted by her exertions, and released from her inner turmoil, she'd slept soundly, thanks to Henri.

At the age of twenty-five, Lola was looking forward to her first adult relationship built on mutual trust and respect.

'I think you need a few more lessons.'

The mere sound of Henri's voice sent Lola into raptures. He caught the ball mid-flight in one hand and carried it over to her. The sun cast its favourable glow through his white shirt, highlighting the impressive muscles hidden under the 'sensible doctor' wear. Her body responded as if he'd stripped her naked again, her nipples beading under her T-shirt and that ache in her loins growing by the minute. There was every chance she would spontaneously combust if she was subjected to any more of his hotness without an outlet for her admiration.

'Are you offering?'

Her bravado was in direct correlation with her libido today. That moment she'd been avoiding couldn't come quickly enough now she'd had a taste of what Henri had to offer. His hands-on skills weren't limited to the workplace.

'Any time.'

The knowing wink he gave her was the stuff of erotic dreams—slightly ruined by Gabrielle's exaggerated cough and the reminder that there were children present.

'I thought you'd be caught up for at least another few hours?' She'd anticipated another day of outdoor pursuits to work through her Henri-less disappointment.

'I have all the notes I need, so I thought I'd ditch the workshop and get back to the fun stuff.'

Henri was addressing the kids, but Lola imagined he was talking to her. There was nothing she'd like better than to have more *fun* with him.

'Can we go home and see if Mum is back?' Bastien cast his racquet aside, clearly already taken with the notion.

'Is that what you want?' Henri asked, unable to hide the surprise and delight on his face. He checked his watch. 'I think Angelique's flight arrives in about two hours. If we're quick we could get to the airport in time to meet her. Everyone in favour of going home raise their hand.'

The unanimous decision was made as four hands shot up into the air. Although the hotel was fabulous, Lola couldn't wait to get back home and pick up with Henri where they'd left off.

'That's settled, then. As soon as we are ready we'll hit the road.'

Henri glanced over the heads of the bouncing children at Lola. The unspoken message was there that tonight was the night they'd finally leave all their baggage outside the bedroom door and focus on each other.

Lola had her bag packed in record time.

They collected Angelique from the airport and the children lit on her with fervent hugs and kisses. Lola didn't imagine they were parted very often, and it was sweet to see how much they'd missed each other. Even Henri wrapped his sister in a bear hug once Gabrielle and Bastien had let go of her.

The bond between the family wasn't unlike the one she shared with her brothers, and though Lola hated to admit it she was starting to miss them. So much had happened since her graduation, and there was no reason they couldn't share in the good times with her as well as the bad. If things went well between her and Henri she might even think about introducing him.

Once they were all delivered back to Angelique's house, with their assorted luggage, Angelique took Lola to one side.

'Thank you for everything. I haven't had a chance to say that, with all that's been going on, but I really appreciate your help. Between coming to the rescue with Bastien's cake, teaching Gabrielle how to bake and now babysitting, I don't know how I'll ever repay you.'

'It's no trouble at all—but I *was* going to ask about taking more of your classes.' The Benoits were certainly helping her to flourish, and Lola wanted to make the most of her newfound sensuality while the impetus was there.

'Say no more. The door's open for you any time. Anyone who can put a smile on my brother's face is worth their weight in gold.'

Angelique gave the same cheeky wink her sibling used to great effect. She was such a glamorous woman of the world… Lola imagined her tales of Parisian nights and Moulin Rouge-inspired experiences would put her own exploits with Henri to shame.

'Did you have a good time?' Lola didn't want to discuss her love life with her lover's sister. At least not until they'd fully established one.

'It was am-*a*-zing. I'm too old to make it as a chorus girl, but now I have that experience to cherish for ever. And, as glamorous and bohemian as that life is, I wouldn't want to give up what I have here. I'm a different person now.'

Angelique was beautiful now, in her mid-thirties, but she must have been a real stunner in her heyday. Given Gabrielle's age, her dancing career must have come to an abrupt end when they'd left France for Irish soil. Lola couldn't help but wonder if watching his sister's marriage crumble when she'd given up so much for love was part of the reason Henri wasn't interested in anything long term.

'Aren't we all?'

If these past weeks had proved anything, it was that people were evolving all the time—mostly for the better. The ones who stayed the same—well, they were losing out on all life had to offer.

'What's this? A girlie gossip?'

Henri slid his hands around Lola's waist, and the public display of affection in front of his sister was a milestone as far as Lola could see. Angelique was too important to him to let her in on their secret if it didn't mean anything to him.

'Were your ears burning, little bro? I was just telling Lola I can take it from here if you two have some…er…*catching up* to do.'

Angelique and Henri exchanged cheesy grins while Lola wanted to hide. This forthright French attitude to sex took some getting used to.

'You know I love Gabs and Bastien…but, yeah, I'm officially handing them back to their mother. I have a life of my own to get back to.'

He nuzzled Lola's neck, and it was all she could do not to throw herself at him in the middle of the hallway.

'I *was* starting to wonder. Please, Lola, take him away and spoil him. It's about time he had someone to take care of him for a change.'

She shooed them out the door, not giving them time to say goodbye to the kids. As well behaved as they were, Lola was glad of some respite and fully intended to heed Angelique's advice. Henri was so busy looking out for other people, he put his own needs last. A matter Lola would rectify as soon as possible.

The atmosphere inside the car was completely different without the excitable children in the back. Now there were only two super-charged adults, eager to get to their destination. It was a short drive across the city to Henri's bachelor pad—made even shorter as he put his foot down on the accelerator. He barely abided by the speed limits as the sexual tension inside the sports car fuelled their journey.

It was something of a relief when they pulled up outside the modern, detached villa that reflected his outward personality to a T.

'Sorry, I should've asked if you wanted to go home first.'

Henri pulled on the handbrake and gave her one last chance to change her mind. She didn't want to alter her path now, when this was the first step to her new beginning. Making love with Henri would change how she viewed herself and men for ever. It wasn't a view she would share, in case putting that much pressure on him ended in disaster.

'Jules isn't expecting me home until late. I don't need or want to be anywhere else.'

Lola's heart was in her mouth as she laid herself bare before him. One wrong move now and she could end up back at square one, crushed by the disappointment of her own inadequacy.

Henri was silent, the rustle as he removed his seat belt the only clue that he'd heard her request to stay. Lola unclipped hers too, making that commitment a firm reality. She reached for the door handle, deciding to take the initiative to go inside or else they'd end up sitting out here until it was time for her to go home. Now Henri knew exactly what he was taking on in this neurotic, damaged rookie doctor, Lola hoped he wasn't having second thoughts.

When the door didn't open, Henri reached over to do it for her. 'Child locks.'

They were chest to chest as he stretched across her, too close to ignore the magnetic force between them.

Their first hungry kiss was full of the pent-up lust and frustration built up over the last eighteen hours. Tongues vied for position and lips crashed together as the chemistry between them finally exploded.

The leather seat squeaked with every shift of their bodies, playing an unfortunate soundtrack against their passion.

'Shall. We. Take. This. Inside?' Henri asked between kisses.

Lola nodded, but it took several more smooches before they finally broke apart. They abandoned their bags in the car in their haste to get indoors, lighting on each other as soon as the door closed behind them.

Lola had done enough talking, had her fair share of soul searching, and now all she wanted was to *feel*.

She plucked the buttons on Henri's shirt open, eagerly ripping off the wrapper from her present. His chest was smooth and taut and his firm abs rippled beneath her fingers. This was the body of a man—not some spotty teenager who thought he was God's gift, with free rein to treat people however badly he wanted.

They stripped each other on their way to the bedroom, leaving a trail of clothes and underwear in their wake.

With Henri naked beside her, this time Lola didn't shy away from his gaze. She stood firm as he swept his eyes over her body, regardless that she was quivering inside. Although she was still being judged, she knew it came from a place of appreciation. Henri definitely liked what he saw. And Lola temporarily forgot her own state of undress to marvel at his. His erection stood proud and unrelenting, a confirmation of his desire for her.

The moment her nerves started to creep back she clung to Henri, and every kiss and caress kept them at bay. He backed her onto the bed, his hard body covering the full length of hers. Once upon a time she would have found that intimidating, claustrophobic, knowing he could trap her beneath him with minimal effort. But this was Henri—not the ghost of boyfriends past. Everything he did was out of desire. Something she'd spent too long running from.

Already primed since last night, and with Henri's hardness pressing into her flesh, Lola knew she was ready. She lifted her hips to make full contact, rubbing against him so his shaft parted her entrance.

'Lola—' Henri groaned into her neck and a jolt shot south through her, turning her breath to a gasp.

Her body thrummed at the first touch of him, waiting for more. Another tilt of her pelvis drew him farther in, forced another ragged moan from his lips. He wanted this as much as she did, and she saw no point in their torturing each other any longer.

'I want you…' she breathed into his ear, knowing he couldn't hold out for ever.

A lifesaver, a guardian and a therapist he might be, but beneath it all he was primarily a man. She traced the outline of his ear with her tongue and sucked his lobe into her mouth.

His first blunt entry made her cry out—not through pain,

but surprise. He filled her so completely it took a few moments for her to adjust to the new invasion.

'Are you okay?' Henri locked his arms out straight and levered himself off her.

Lola could feel him trembling from the restraint while he waited for reassurance that she was happy to continue.

'I'm fine.'

She took a few deep breaths, her inner muscles gradually easing to let him move freely again. He took his time at first, until she got used to taking all of him inside. The steady rhythm became familiar, relaxed her with every thrust, but the new Lola wanted more. She knew he was holding back—always thinking of her and what he thought she needed.

Lola ground against him, reached down to dig her nails into his buttocks and drive him on. Henri responded by withdrawing fully and then plunging straight back into her, their bodies slapping together with the force. With each new penetration Lola was drifting further from her body. The frequency and intensity increased in time with Henri's shallow breaths and Lola could hear herself moaning in response. She was climbing higher and higher. And then Henri pressed his thumb into her sex and the added pressure toppled her over the edge.

She clutched at his shoulders as she rode out her climax, releasing all her demons in one long cry. He chased his own satisfaction, pumping into her until he found it with a roar. When he'd given her everything he had, he fell onto the bed next to her.

They lay panting and smiling at each other, like two lovestruck teenagers experimenting with each other's bodies for the first time. In some ways she *was* that inexperienced young girl, finally discovering what all the fuss was about. It had probably always been this way for Henri, but she knew for sure that she wanted to discover if it would be as good between them every time.

There was only one way to find out, and as soon as they got their breath back she wanted to test the theory. If nothing else was to come of their time together other than making her feel good, she could live with it. As long as he didn't break her heart when he tired of being her mentor.

For now she was content to lie in his arms and pretend this feeling of complete and utter bliss was for keeps.

CHAPTER NINE

HENRI DIDN'T THINK he'd ever tire of kissing Lola. Almost a month into their fling, the flames of passion were burning so bright he was in danger of getting burned. It was a shame they'd wasted time avoiding their attraction—now they only had days left before it all ended. Suddenly time was moving way too fast. They needed to make every moment count.

He pressed his lips against hers once more, trying to coax her awake. These mornings waking up with a naked Lola curled up around him were the best way to start the day. He wasn't looking forward to starting night shifts, or to the day when she wouldn't be in his bed at all. Despite their agreement that this was a temporary arrangement, Lola had become part of his life—part of him. He was falling for her—hard—and he didn't know what to do about it.

Having already fallen into a pattern of going to work together when they could, and spending the nights in his bed, they were living as a couple. Even if they hadn't admitted that to anyone— including themselves. He'd never been in love before. He'd seen the havoc it had wreaked in Angelique's life and had always had that in mind when his relationships threatened to get serious. He couldn't afford to be weakened by such a destructive force when the whole family was still dealing with the fallout from the last attack.

Now he was starting to wonder if this was it, and love had sneaked in wearing a pink stethoscope around its neck. This terror taking hold of his heart at the thought of Lola walking away and him never seeing her again was new to him, but he wasn't convinced it could be any worse than the pain when everything crashed and burned. He had no future to offer her. He was tied to helping Angelique raise the children, and Lola would eventually realise she deserved more than last place in the pecking order.

And if Henri was tempted to give in to the whimsy he only had to think of his sister, who'd given herself completely to another, followed him to another country, borne him children and still been left in pieces. Love was messy and complicated and he'd do better without it.

'Hmm...?' Lola's moan in his ear meant they were both stirring.

'Morning.' He turned onto his side so he could stop overthinking this and get lost in the beauty of her yawning smile and still sleepy eyes.

'What am I going to tell Jules this time?'

Lola stretched out her limbs, then cuddled back into Henri's side. A far cry from that first night when she'd stayed over and then panicked about getting home before her absence was noticed—and another indication that they were becoming way too comfortable with the situation.

'You were abducted by aliens and spent the night on board the mother ship?'

'I think I used that one on Tuesday. And if I say I was with my folks again she'll wonder why I ever bothered moving out.'

'You don't think she's the tiniest bit suspicious that something's going on?'

A change in behaviour was always going to draw attention from those who knew them best. Henri had been dodging questions himself about the nature of their relationship—from his sister. But if they admitted they were involved it made it real—and why cause a fuss when it was all but over?

'I think she's too caught up in her own misadventures to notice anything. Besides, Jules isn't the type to hold back. If she thought I was getting it on with a colleague she'd be knocking on the door right now, waiting to hear all the juicy details.'

Lola slid her hand over Henri's chest, apparently ready to give her flatmate something to gossip about. He wasn't complaining. If Lola wasn't in a hurry to bring this out into the open, either, then he was worrying over nothing. After all, she hadn't expressed any desire to extend the parameters of their contract. For now it was only *his* heart at stake.

'You're not in any rush to leave, then?'

'None whatsoever.'

The wicked glint in Lola's eye as she hooked her bare leg around his waist ensured Henri was wide awake and ready to play. Her newfound confidence in the bedroom was a gift to them both and not one to be wasted.

Everything outside of the bedroom door could wait until he was forced to confront it.

'We have an unidentified male in his twenties. Witnesses said he was standing at a bus stop talking on his phone when an assailant punched him in the face and stole it from him. He was knocked unconscious and fell back, cracking his head on the pavement. He hasn't regained consciousness and has been vomiting.'

The paramedic went on to rhyme off his stats and observations while the resus team went to work, trying to get the patient stabilised.

It was Lola's job to suction away the vomit and clear his airways. It was a task she frequently carried out without a second thought, but at present one which she was finding difficult not to balk at. She put it down to the nerves bubbling inside her, knowing that today was the day she had to have a talk with Henri about their future. One in which, whether he liked it or not, they were now inextricably linked.

Her stomach heaved again. She'd been so incredibly stupid, and there were not enough tears or worry in the world to fix it.

'We're going to need a CT scan and possibly a chest X-ray. I don't think we should try and wake him up, given the possible neurological problems. I'll put in a call to the neuro surgeon and we'll get him moved as soon as we can.'

As ever, Henri was doing everything he could to prevent the worst possible outcome. He could always be counted on to do the right thing. That thought was the only thing getting her through the day without having a nervous breakdown. Henri would know what to do.

Lola just couldn't bear to see the disappointment back in his eyes when she told him what had happened.

A baby. All her hard work to get here and she'd ruined her career in a moment of madness. She was supposed to be leaving the department in a matter of days—the whole point of placements was to learn and move on. How could she do that now with a permanent reminder of her time in A&E and no chance of completing her training?

It must have happened that first night at Henri's. It was the only time they hadn't used protection, and she'd been so carried away by the idea of their fling she hadn't considered the consequences. Brief encounters weren't supposed to end in creating new life. She couldn't even do *that* right.

This was going to change everything—and, from where she was standing, not for the better. When Jules had offered her a room in her apartment neither of them had expected to be sharing with the screaming, pooping product of Lola's illicit affair with their registrar. She was going to have to move out, for a start. And go where? Back home?

If she was worried about Henri's reaction to the news it would be nothing compared to the outrage of her brothers. But what choice would she have as a newly qualified doctor on maternity leave?

Getting knocked up by her superior on her first placement hadn't been part of her life plan. There was no question that she'd wanted something with Henri that lasted beyond her six weeks on his department, but not like this. A pregnancy should evolve from a loving, lasting relationship. Not be an accident which was going to force them to be together.

She wouldn't blame him if he ended up hating her—he hadn't signed on for this, either. But the deed was done and there was a baby on the way. If nothing else he had the right to know he was going to be a father. Now it was all about finding the right place and time to break the news to him gently.

Lola set aside her personal issues to accompany Henri and their patient to the CT scan, waiting silently by his side as images appeared on the screen.

'That's a nasty injury. There are major frontal contusions and serious swelling.' Henri tapped his pen on the screen to point them out, but they were plain to see.

'So they'll operate to relieve the pressure on the brain?'

Perhaps the mothering instinct was kicking in already, but Lola could feel tears welling in her eyes as she stared at the screen. An unnecessary, needless act of violence could end this young man's life before it had barely begun, and *she* was stressing about entering into the next phase of hers.

'He's going to Theatre now, so the neuro surgeons can work on him. They might need to remove part of his skull, and there's a chance of permanent damage, but we've done all we can for now.'

Henri was preparing for the worst, but Lola was still praying he'd pull through.

'Did we find out who he is yet?' she asked, once they'd

left the claustrophobic scanning area. He was someone's son…
possibly someone's brother.

'The police are still on it.'

'I hope they track down his family. He shouldn't be on his
own.'

It could have been one of *her* brothers lying there. Moments
like this illustrated how important loved ones were. When she
was old and grey and on her deathbed, she imagined an even
bigger family around her. One of her own. One which included
Henri.

'They will. There are officers here, going through his belongings—it won't be long before they find a contact.'

Henri dropped an unexpected kiss on her head. It wasn't like
him to show her any affection at work, when they'd been so
careful to keep their affair a secret. An ember of hope flickered
to life inside Lola. If he wasn't ready to let her go they might
actually be able to salvage something from this mess.

'Fingers crossed. I'm sure they would want to be here with
him.'

'*Ma chérie*…always thinking of others.'

Henri stroked her hair back from her face, tucking the wayward strands from her ponytail behind her ear. Lola turned her
cheek into his palm and closed her eyes. Nothing else seemed
to matter when she was wrapped up in his warmth, and she
wished this feeling could last.

The words she needed to say hovered on the tip of her tongue.
But the swish of the double doors opening brought the tender
moment to an end and forced her to swallow her confession
back down.

She backed away, maintaining the illusion of platonic friendship for anyone who passed by. At least by the time her pregnancy started to show she'd be long gone from the department,
taking the scandal and her last connection to Henri with her.

That first day seemed a lifetime ago. In a lot of ways it was.
Lola wasn't that same timid girl who'd desperately tried to hide

from the registrar's view. Now she was a practising doctor, a lover and soon-to-be mother. Neither role was she ready to give up.

Whilst she was coming to terms with the idea of having this baby, she didn't want it to be at the expense of her career, or her relationship with Henri. She wished there was some way she could have it all.

The sadness which had been stalking her since she'd stared at those two blue lines on the pregnancy test finally caught up with her and escaped on a cry.

Henri pulled her into an empty side room and closed the door, obviously still able to compartmentalise all the areas of his life when everything in hers had merged into one.

'Hey, now... I know what you're thinking, but it's not one of your brothers lying there. We've done everything we can and his family will get here—don't worry.'

'It's all so *unfair*.' She hiccupped on another sob, her misery compounded by the fact that Henri assumed her tears were solely for the young man battling for survival. Although hers wasn't a life-or-death situation, everything was hanging in the balance for her, too.

She had to tell him. It was time for her to be brave and face up to whatever fate had in store for her next.

'I know, *chérie*, but I do have some good news for you. Gabrielle came to us last night and told us everything that's been going on with her at school. We've arranged a meeting with her teachers and the parents of the girls involved. It's all very civilised—no shouting, no angry mob with pitchforks—you'd be very proud.'

The worry lines that had accompanied every conversation Henri had had with her about his niece since they'd met had finally evened out. She hated to be the one to put them back.

'I'm so glad for all of you.' There *was* some relief to discover that Gabrielle had finally reached the stage when she was able to confide her troubles in someone other than Lola. Now not only could the school take some action against the bullying, but it also cut the number of secrets Lola was keeping from Henri to one.

'I'm not happy about what she's suffered, but at least we can start to do something about it now. You were right—I don't mind admitting it. There were no dramatics, maybe a few tears, and it all came out on Gabrielle's terms when she was ready. Thanks in no small part to you, she's really started to come out of her shell recently.'

'I don't know... I think her mum and her very understanding uncle had a lot to do with it, too.'

It was a weight off Lola's mind to know that the girl would finally get the help she needed, no matter how it came about. Henri was doing a good job keeping on top of his emotions, too, since no bullies had so far been harmed in the wake of Gabrielle's disclosure. It boded well for the next round of *Did You Know?* that they were yet to play.

'This parenting stuff is stressful. I admire anyone who can juggle it and a career at the same time.'

Henri was giving her the perfect opening. She knew he had respect for his sister, who managed to do both. And it wasn't as if she was asking him to pick one over the other. At this moment she wasn't expecting anything from him except to hear her out.

'It's all good experience for when you have children of your own. You'll take teenage angst and junk-food-obsessed six-year-olds in your stride by then.'

Lola attempted to steer him towards the role he'd have in another eight months. He'd had plenty of parenting practice over the years, and although it would be a shock, he'd shown himself to be decent father material. It was an attractive quality—even to a non-pregnant bystander.

Unfortunately the snort of derision he gave rendered it a moot point. 'One family is *more* than enough for me.'

'Are you saying you don't want kids of your own some day?'

Lola's heart splintered into a few more pieces. Despite all

the impracticalities they would have to overcome, she'd been clinging to the smallest hope that they could somehow make a future together. Now he'd ruled himself out of the loving family she'd imagined around her in that deathbed scene.

'Although my parents didn't intentionally leave us, I feel the same sense of abandonment as Gabrielle and Bastien. I have no intention of extending the legacy. How could I ever be an attentive father to anyone when every minute of my time is accounted for elsewhere? I have a responsibility to Angelique and the children, and I *won't* be another one to walk out on them.'

It was an admirable speech, with Henri making it clear there was no room in his life for anyone else—including Lola. She wanted everything he was telling her he couldn't give her. The fairy tale was coming to an end—without the happy-ever-after she'd longed for.

'I'm sure Angelique wouldn't want you to sacrifice your own happiness on her account.'

Lola couldn't decide if Henri was being completely altruistic or incredibly selfish in his loyalties. She'd endured the crummy childhood and fractured relationships, too, and it had only served to make her desire to create a loving environment for this baby even stronger. Saying he was committed elsewhere was an easy way to avoid admitting he had feelings for anyone other than his family.

Tough. She was going to make him tell her once and for all what she meant to him, and if he wasn't interested she would do this on her own. Lord knew she'd overcome worse problems than having a helpless baby depend on her.

'No, but like my sister, I know my own mind—and nothing is going to change it. Now, enough of the serious stuff. Let's talk cake. Gabrielle's signed up for the local swim team, so she can't make tonight's home baking session.'

Lola's head was spinning and her thoughts were jumbled, piling on top of one another until she was sure her skull would explode with the pressure building up inside. She needed him to shut up so she could think straight.

'I'm pregnant, Henri.'

Suddenly the room was too quiet.

Henri must have misheard. He'd thought she'd said she was pregnant.

'I said I'm pregnant.'

There it was again. The pair of watery green eyes staring at him held no trace of humour.

The bottom of Henri's world plummeted through the floor.

He loosened his tie and gulped in some much needed oxygen. *A baby?* He was always so careful, so responsible, so terrified of this ever happening.

'How? When?'

Lola's tears dried up with her frown. 'I hope you don't expect me to draw you a diagram of how it happened—I'm pretty sure you were there at the time. As for the when…it must've been that first time…you know…we were kind of in a hurry.'

He cast his mind back to that day, when they'd practically thrown Angelique and the kids from the moving car in their haste to get back to his house and consummate their relationship. They hadn't used a condom, but since Lola had never voiced any concern, he'd assumed she was protected.

'Aren't you on the pill?'

'No. Don't start blaming me, Henri. We both messed up.'

'If you'd told me we could have prevented this whole sorry mess with one little pill the next morning.'

Now everything was ruined. Never mind the professional disgrace of getting one of his junior staff pregnant, there was the impact it was going to have on the rest of his family. He'd spent the last ten minutes telling Lola exactly why he didn't want children of his own. For him to turn his back on Angelique and the children now, to support a family he didn't want, simply wouldn't be fair. Fate was playing a desperately cruel joke.

'Do you think I planned this? I'm only weeks into a career I've been studying for years to make a success, living off the goodwill of my flatmate and pregnant by a man who only wanted me in his life for six weeks. It's not the stuff of fairy tales, is it?'

Lola put up a very good argument, but she would have support from her brothers and her friends to get through this. She could go back to work after the baby was born and he would make sure she was financially secure in the meantime. Whereas Henri was the one people turned to in their hour of need—he had no one to do the same for him.

'Who can fathom what goes on in that head of yours? Perhaps you saw me as a safe option? You knew I would never shirk my responsibilities for a child, and I earn enough money to support a woman who can't handle the career she's chosen. I'm the one man you knew wouldn't hurt you.'

'In which case I was sadly mistaken. I'm not asking you for anything, Henri. I simply thought you should know what's happened. Now, if you'll excuse me, I have to at least keep up the pretence that I can do my job until my baby daddy buys me out of it.'

Although Lola's voice had lowered to a gravelly whisper, it was more powerful than if she'd punched him in the place where all this trouble had stemmed from.

Damn it! Deep down Henri knew this wasn't her fault, but the outcome was the same whether she'd planned his downfall or not. He was trapped by circumstance and stupidity with absolutely no chance of escape. This fun, no-strings, short-term thing had suddenly become a lifelong commitment.

He opened his top button, whipped the tie from around his neck. *Breathe in. Breathe out.*

This was the only time he'd actually sympathised with his ex-brother-in-law and understood a fraction of the reason he'd run away. This overwhelming, suffocating sense of responsibility was as close to a panic attack as he'd ever wish to get.

His lungs were heaving with every shallow breath, his heart was racing and sweat was breaking over his skin. If he didn't get this under control he'd pass out.

Although unconsciousness was preferable to his current mental state. A few minutes of complete oblivion might be nice, until he got used to the idea that he was going to be a father.

It would be easy to shake everything off and disappear—pretend Lola had never happened. But the difference between Henri and Sean was that *he* was an adult—not a man-child who'd happily let the woman in his life struggle on without any help. Henri had stepped up to the plate when he'd been able to, supporting Angelique financially and emotionally as she'd done for him. Now he'd ruined another woman's life.

He girded his shoulders for another load of guilt to be added to his burden. Although he'd do what he could, he'd let both Lola and Angelique down. Even if he couldn't give either the commitment they deserved, he'd die trying to help.

CHAPTER TEN

LOLA BARELY MADE it through the rest of her shift without emotionally imploding. The one saving grace of the day was hearing that after six hours in surgery the young male with the head injury had pulled through. His family were at his bedside, waiting for him to come round. There was a long road ahead of him but he'd made it this far against the odds.

Only the fear that she'd never stop crying if she started, and the determination to prove she could do anything she put her mind to, had stemmed the flood of tears and prevented her from drowning. Of course the news of impending parenthood was always going to come as a surprise to Henri, but she hadn't expected the slap in the face of his denial. The lovely, caring, child-friendly registrar she'd fallen for had turned out to be just another man capable of inflicting pain.

She'd had more time to get used to the idea—a whole extra twenty-four hours—but at no stage had she pointed the finger of blame. It didn't achieve anything except perhaps shifting responsibility entirely onto her. There was a baby on the way and it would be wanted and loved by at least one parent.

Lola rubbed her still flat belly and imagined the tiny person growing inside who'd caused all the trouble. This mightn't have been the introduction to motherhood she'd planned but, ready or not, it was happening. In a matter of months she'd have a little bundle of her and Henri's genes in her arms. One more to add to clan Roberts.

It was still early days, and there was no need for her pregnancy to disrupt the status quo just yet. She'd tell everyone when she was in the safe zone. Preferably when she was in labour and too high on gas and air to care what they said. For now it was best simply to carry on as normal, with a broken heart and a baby from a relationship no one knew about.

She turned the key in the lock slowly, trying to sneak into the apartment without Jules hearing her. In the privacy of her own room she'd be free to cry and wallow as much as she wanted, without fear of judgement or ridicule. Jules had warned her about the devastating effect the handsome French registrar had on newbies, and now she was paying the ultimate price. She couldn't face *I told you so* on top of everything else.

'Lola—is that you?'

She'd only made it as far as the hall before Jules sprang her.

'Yeah…'

'Well, hello, stranger. What brings you home?'

'I'm not feeling too well. I think I'll have an early night.' Lola hustled towards the bedroom—only to find a Jules-shaped obstacle in her path.

'Don't tell me your secret lover is otherwise engaged tonight? I thought you two were joined at the hip.'

'Wh—what?' Lola stuttered, racking her brain for a better cover story. Apparently she wasn't the expert at keeping secrets she'd thought she was.

'You didn't *really* expect me to buy that rubbish about staying with the family when you were so desperate to get away from them in the first place? Besides, you've been wearing that cat-got-the-cream smile that only comes from great sex. *I* should know. It's been killing me, waiting until you were ready to tell me. Patience never was my strongpoint, and since I have no gossip of my own it's only fair I get to hear yours.'

Jules widened her stance and folded her arms, trapping Lola in the small corridor so she couldn't outrun her lies. This was the same kind of pressure *she'd* put on Gabrielle when she'd been tasked with extracting her troubles. She'd forgotten that finally voicing your worries also released the emotions bottled up alongside them. The final barrier gave way and a torrent of sorrow began to pour down Lola's face before she even got to confirm Jules's suspicion.

'Oh, my God, Lola—what's wrong?' Jules immediately wrapped her arms around her and let her cry her heart out.

Lola was sure that was literally what she'd done. All that was left when she stopped was an empty space in her chest where Henri had once resided.

It only hurt because she cared for him so much. Regardless of all the warnings her heart and head had given out, she'd fallen for him during those glorious hours in his bed, discovering everything about him, and herself.

'I...' She choked, unable to find the beginning of her sorry tale. So much good had come from her tryst with Henri it seemed a shame to erase it and focus on the bitter ending.

'Come and sit down and I'll get you a glass of water. Do we need cookies, too?'

Jules manoeuvred her towards the kitchen and into a chair. However, no amount of cupcakes or cookies could fix this one. Although she'd usually eat her feelings away, her appetite had vanished along with her periods.

After a lot of banging about, Jules returned with two glasses and a bottle of wine. 'I thought this might require something stronger.'

Lola considered drinking herself into a stupor for a split second—before her subconscious piped up to remind her that her body was no longer hers alone. She promptly erupted into another bout of weeping.

The glasses clinked beside her as Jules set them down to comfort her again. 'You're scaring me now. All I did was offer you a drink—'

Lola gave her non-existent bump a fleeting glance, but it was enough to make her friend gasp in horror.

'You're not…?'

What could she do but nod her head? 'I'm pregnant.'

Jules collapsed into the chair beside her and grabbed her hand. 'Oh, sweetheart. Who's the father? Scrub that. It doesn't matter. I take it he's not interested, or you wouldn't be in such a state. Don't you worry. We'll get through this together.'

'Thanks…' Lola mumbled into her BFF's cleavage as she was swamped in another hug.

This was the reaction she'd wanted from Henri—a promise that everything would be all right, not resentment and blame. Losing Henri was the most upsetting aspect of all this for her— not the prospect of having his baby. She'd wanted him to love her as much as she loved him.

'What do you want me to do? Run you a bath? Make you a cuppa? Tell me what I can do to make this better for you? Give me the word and I'll hunt down the scumbag who's done this to you and make sure he's not capable of doing it again.'

The idea of Jules turning up on Henri's doorstep brandishing her stilettos as lethal weapons appealed to Lola's warped sense of humour. He deserved to feel as frightened as she was, but there was no need to burn all her bridges. When the dust settled they would have to have some sort of grown-up conversation about their child and Henri's involvement in its life—if any.

'Thanks for the offer. I might take you up on it some time. To be honest, I think I need to clear my head. I could do with some fresh air.'

'Whatever you need.'

What she needed was for Henri to be the one to put his arms around her and tell her everything was okay. Instead she set off outside into the night with no clue where she was going. She didn't know how or why, but she found herself walking into Angelique's burlesque class. Perhaps it was because it was the one place she'd ever really been free to be herself before Henri came along.

'Lola! I'm so glad you came.' Angelique, dressed in nothing but feathers and sequins, greeted her with a double cheek-kiss.

'I haven't booked or anything. If there's no space I can come back another time.' Lola could see there were already a few excitable women present, including a lively hen party. She'd made a mistake in coming here on her own, without Jules to chivvy her along.

'Not at all. We'd love another body—wouldn't we girls?'

Angelique took over the pushy-friend role, ensuring she joined the whooping women and became part of their strange dancing troupe.

'Now, I thought we'd do something special for the occasion. Most of you have been here before and learnt the basics. So why don't we put it into practice on the stage…for your stags?'

Angelique clapped and a small band of jeering men walked out onto the dance floor. The women were equally raucous at seeing their counterparts, and Lola imagined they'd stopped off in a few pubs before they'd brought the party here.

Lola held up her hand. 'That's me out.'

Dancing on stage for the entertainment of a group of inebriated letches wouldn't help her mood one iota. Besides, they wouldn't miss an ugly duckling like her slinking away, when there were so many bright and beautiful birds willing to shake their tail feathers.

'Where do you think *you're* going?' Hands on hips, Angelique did the best impression of a strict school headmistress she could manage in her frou-frou outfit.

'It's a step too far for me I'm afraid. Thanks, Angelique, but I think I'll head home.'

All she'd wanted was space to forget—not to have another

bunch of men wheeled in to heap more humiliation on her and add to this day from hell.

'Hey, I get that this is a big step, but if it's confidence you're working on then this is exactly what you need. Do you think *I* wasn't nervous about sharing the stage with girls half my age in Paris? You bet your ass I was. But I did it, and it was the best thing I've ever done. I didn't care who was looking at me—it was enough to know I was there, dancing for myself and no one else. Tonight was the bridesmaids' idea, and these guys are all taken. I'll keep them in line, so you'll have no worries on that score. My advice is to get up and do this for yourself.'

Angelique delivered her motivational speech and walked away, leaving Lola to make her own decision on the subject.

She looked again at the crowd behind her. Certainly the stags and hens had paired off, with eyes only for each other. A couple of other unattached ladies chatted excitedly, apparently none of them experiencing the same level of anxiety she had as she anticipated dancing up there.

She moved quietly towards the stage without anyone taking any notice. There was nothing special about the area itself—no spotlights or dazzling effects to make it any more remarkable than a raised platform. Lola supposed it was more about what it represented that frightened her. This was where they were supposed to show off, and she'd gained a lot more than dancing skills since attending the class.

In another few months her body would change beyond all recognition. This could be her last chance to do this. Especially when the news broke about her pregnancy and her friendship with Angelique changed irrevocably.

The only other time she'd been on show for a baying crowd had changed her life for ever. Maybe this time she could make it for the better. The prospect of being a single parent left no room for insecurities. She would have to lead by example if she was going to raise her child to be a warrior rather than a victim.

Although if she did this it would be her choice—and she most certainly wouldn't be naked.

'Do you have any costumes?'

Angelique clapped her hands together and gave a squeal. 'Do *I* have *costumes*? That's akin to asking the Queen if she has any hats.'

The Queen of the dance hall wheeled out a rainbow of sparkling corsets and accessories, and soon Lola was marvelling at the exquisite embroidery and daring styles on the rail.

'These are beautiful.'

'Does this mean you've turned to the dark side?' Angelique held an electric blue silk ensemble in front of Lola.

'I'm not sure it's my colour...' But Lola thought it might be worthwhile trying it on anyway.

Most of the girls went for the more risqué options—cleavage-enhancing, thigh-exposing outfits guaranteed to make an impression on the now seated audience. Lola on the other hand, chose a more modest pearly pink corset with matching frilly skirt. The girly princess style was more her than the vampy red and black siren suits, but it didn't stop her shaking with nerves, knowing that her lady bits were covered only with layers of chiffon and silk.

From the wings, wrapped in the stage curtain, Lola watched as the others took to the stage one by one. The response so far had been very positive, with dancers and spectators alike smiling and enjoying themselves. A few girls had even stripped off their stockings and gloves to throw to their admirers. There were no rules—no right and wrong ways to dance. It was all about letting go and celebrating their bodies.

For Lola, it was also about embracing her pregnancy and moving into the next chapter of her life.

Suddenly Lola was the last showgirl standing. Shaking. Panicking. And liable to vomit all over her bespoke 'coming out' frock.

'Lola?' Angelique gently rested her hand on Lola's shoulder. 'Do you still want to do this?'

'No.' It was an honest answer, but as she saw Angelique head for the stage herself Lola unwrapped herself from the curtain and stopped her. 'But I *need* to do this.'

For the first few bars of the song Lola couldn't move. She closed her eyes, let the sultry music wash over her and stepped out of her hiding place. The audience was a blur at the corner of her eye as she wiggled her way across the stage. She didn't dare look directly at them in case her wobbly legs gave way altogether. Then she really would make a spectacle of herself—and flash parts of her she was determined to keep secret in public.

There were a few wolf whistles as she stroked the full length of her black silk gloves, a chorus of cheers as she moved her hands down her body to rest them on her lap. Once she realised she wasn't going to be booed off she started to relax. She dipped to her knees and swivelled around, giving her booty a pop as she straightened again. With one foot crossed in front of the other, she sashayed to the back of the stage. She raised her arms above her head with a flourish, and slowly slid them back down to stroke her face in profile.

A salsa move forwards and back, combined with a turn, brought her to face her nightmare. There was no one laughing behind their hand at her attempts to dance, so she took that as a positive and carried on. It was all about revelling in her own body, touching every part of her as only a lover could. She stroked her fingers across her chest, dipped her hand between her legs and parted her thighs in a quick flash. It was empowering to say *You can look but not touch* as she bounced back up into a body roll.

Angelique had called it. This was more about knowing she *could* do it if she chose and nothing to do with content. Perhaps she could get the hospital trust to introduce corset and stockings as the new uniform as she was now so comfortable in it?

She kicked her leg out to the side and slowly teased her hand to the top of her stocking, her head thrown back in mock ec-stasy. It only worked for real when there was a Frenchman inch-ing along her thigh.

The faces of those pimply teens who'd made her ashamed of her own body faded with every body-pop and wiggle of her hips, until she was drained of all her energy. She'd done what she'd come up here to do and she wanted to finish on a high. With a sidestep, she bent over at the waist and gave a shimmy.

Lola Roberts was finally flaunting what God gave her.

She finished to a round of applause and a surge of adrenaline shooting through her body. For a fleeting moment she thought she saw Henri through her teary eyes. Real or imaginary, he was the one person in the room who *hadn't* enjoyed her performance.

Henri wished he'd never come. The sight of Lola performing up there only added a sense of urgency to the problem he'd come to discuss with his sister. He'd come for advice—not a reminder of what he'd thrown away.

Lola was blossoming before his very eyes. He only had to see her peacocking in one of Angelique's outfits to know how far she'd come from the girl who'd hated anyone looking at her. More than that, her confidence in her own abilities at work was growing every day, too. She'd jumped in today to help with that trauma patient without any coaxing from him.

It wasn't jealousy that consumed Henri as he watched her strut fearlessly in her costume, it was pride. At a time when she should be devastated about stalling her career she was owning this new side of her—living up to her showgirl namesake. The sparkle was back in her eyes as she mingled on the dance floor with the others, her head held high with every step she took in her stripper heels.

He walked away, realising he was superfluous to her require-ments. While she'd left her baggage up on that stage, Henri was still trailing his behind him.

Today had made him question every aspect of his connection

with Lola. He'd been unforgivably selfish and stupid for lashing out at her when it was himself he was angry at. It wasn't *her* fault he'd done the unthinkable and fallen in love with her. He'd already been afraid to tell her how much she meant to him when he was juggling his guilt and his responsibilities to Angelique. The revelation that there was a baby on the way had forced him to face those feelings and he'd reacted like a caged animal—attacking first before he got hurt.

They hadn't ever discussed carrying on their fling after Lola's placement ended. For all he knew she resented him for getting her pregnant, ruining her career and tying her to him for the rest of her days. But he loved Lola, and he'd nearly destroyed her because of it.

He sat in the front seat of his car, trying to make sense of the chaos he'd created. It wasn't fair to judge his relationship with Lola on the basis of the debt he owed to his sister. If he took Angelique and the children out of the equation, what was he left with? A woman he loved and wanted to be with and a baby borne of that union. It seemed so simple when he stripped away the layers of guilt and pig-headedness.

Above all, he wanted to be with her. Everything else would simply have to fit in around that. As long as she wanted him, too.

CHAPTER ELEVEN

LOLA DIDN'T KNOW how she was managing to function at work, but she wouldn't give Henri the satisfaction and phone in sick just so she wouldn't have to face him. To say she was devastated at his rejection was an understatement. Her tear-drenched pillow and the stockpile of brownies in the kitchen would attest to that. Perhaps she'd had a lucky escape from someone who would accuse her of getting pregnant to keep him, but it would take some time to see it that way. For now she was still pretty bruised.

She stepped into the cubicle to check on her next patient, an eighty-year-old woman who'd been admitted with breathing difficulties.

'Hello, Vera. Can you tell me where the pain is?'

The nursing staff had already made her as comfortable as possible, sitting her up to aid her breathing and attaching an oxygen mask.

'It's in my back.'

'And can you tell me—is it the pain or the breathing which is worse?' Lola could see from her notes that she'd fallen, and there could be confusion between her internal and external injuries.

'The breathing…' Vera stuttered out from behind the mask.

'I'm just going to listen to your chest, okay?'

Lola unhooked her stethoscope from around her neck and pressed it against the old lady's skin. She could hear the bubbling sound of fluid in the air sacs of the lungs—a definite sign of something more serious than a chest infection. Lola tapped on her chest and the dull thud replacing what should have been a hollow, drum-like sound also indicated that fluid could be collecting in between the layers of the lung membrane.

Chest X-rays and blood tests confirmed Lola's suspicion that she was battling pneumonia and that there was fluid there along with infection in the lungs. The poor woman was struggling to breathe, and with her medical history Lola didn't think the prognosis was good. She needed advice from someone who had more experience in this area, but she was appalled to find Henri was today's leading clinician.

Only the welfare of her elderly patient persuaded her to approach him.

'Lola! I'm so glad you—'

'If you have a minute, I'd like a second opinion on one of my patients.' She spread the notes out on the desk in front of him, trying not to brush against him or make eye contact if she could help it.

'Certainly. What have we got?'

He was much too cheery for a man who'd broken her heart only yesterday. If he didn't know the accepted etiquette after breaking up with a pregnant girlfriend was to appear shamefaced and grovelling for forgiveness she might have to remind him with a swift kick. *After* they'd treated the patient.

'An eighty-year-old female with pneumonia. Her breathing is laboured, but she has chronic heart and lung disease. I don't want to put her on a ventilator yet, in case we have difficulty getting her off it again.'

There was a danger she would become too reliant on it and would never manage to breathe on her own again.

'You're right. Continue with the oxygen and antibiotics for

now. Her next twenty-four hours will be crucial, but we'll do what we can to help her fight. Try to keep her as calm as possible, because anxiety will only affect her breathing more. Are her family here?'

Henri gathered the notes back into a neat pile and handed them back to Lola. She hated her body for betraying her as his fingers brushed hers. He had no right to still make her tremble with one touch after what he'd done.

'They're on their way.'

'I'll pop over with you and say hello.'

She didn't want to spend any more time with him than was strictly required. These last days were going to drag on if he insisted on torturing her by being near.

'That's really not necessary. I'm sure you have other stuff to do. All I wanted was some advice—and, trust me, if there was anyone else I could've turned to I would have.'

She turned on her heel before he could see how much she'd let him get to her.

'I need to apologise—'

'Yes, you do—but this isn't the time or the place.'

She didn't want to hear a half-hearted explanation of his behaviour dropped into conversation between patients. The least she deserved was a proper discussion about what they were going to do next. In the meantime she had people relying on her, and everything except Vera would have to wait.

'Hi, Vera. We've decided to keep topping up the antibiotics, and as soon as you're feeling a bit better we can move you up on to the ward. Okay?'

It was all about keeping her calm, giving her hope.

Vera nodded, although her eyes were wide with panic. Lola was concerned she was accepting defeat and giving up the fight.

'*Bonjour.* My name is Henri and I'm the registrar here. I wanted to come and see how you are.'

Lola rolled her eyes as he appeared—in full French mode. She was sure he exaggerated that accent for the effect it had on the ladies. It wouldn't surprise Lola if he actually had a broader Belfast brogue than her and this whole charade was solely to pick up women. Even Vera sat up straighter upon hearing it.

'We're just getting Mrs McConville comfortable until we can move her on to the general ward.' *I've got this.*

'*Très bon.* I've been in touch with your son and daughter and they want to come and see how you're doing.'

He was very calm, and Lola could see he was trying not to spook Vera by telling her of their arrival. It could be overwhelming—frightening, even—when families turned up en masse, weeping and wailing at the bedside.

'Can I get you a wee drink, Vera? Your lips are very dry…' Lola held a cup to her mouth so she could take a sip.

'What do you say I take you for a proper cuppa and some cake when you're feeling better?' Henri asked, and managed to bring a smile to the thin cracked lips behind the oxygen mask.

He did have a way with women of all ages, and it simply didn't fit with the cruelty he'd inflicted on Lola yesterday.

'Now, *that's* an offer and a half, Vera, isn't it? We'll have to get you fighting fit and get that date nailed down.' Lola carried on with the teasing since it was taking the woman's mind off her immediate problem. She was already starting to relax, and her breathing was a lot steadier than when she'd first arrived.

Henri must have noticed, too, and he began to remove Vera's mask. 'I'm just going to take you off the oxygen for a bit. I think the antibiotics are beginning to take effect and I want to see how you do on your own for a while. If you're in pain or struggling let me know and we'll put it back on again. Okay?'

Vera rubbed at her skin, where the straps had left marks, and sighed. 'It's my own fault for going out without a coat or brolly. I wouldn't be here if I hadn't got caught in that rain.'

'We all make mistakes. The important thing is what we do to fix them.'

Henri stared meaningfully at Lola, and it was all she could do not to reach across the bed and slap him. Was he really suggesting they should 'fix' her pregnancy? He sank even lower in her estimation.

'These things happen, but we can't beat ourselves up over them, Vera. Sometimes we've just got to man up and deal with it. We've got to have faith that everything will come good in the end.' Lola smiled brightly at Vera and hooked her chart over the end of the bed. All the while shooting invisible daggers in Henri's direction.

'And sometimes we overreact when we realise we've screwed up. Mistakes can turn out to be the best thing that's ever happened to us, only we're too stupid to see it at first.'

He deflected Lola's imaginary flying weapons with a smouldering look she didn't think was meant for their pensioner. Lola tried to ignore her overexcited internal organs as they went into overdrive. Although this had the markings of an apology, there was no guarantee anything would change between them. He was probably just trying to save face in front of Vera.

The woman lying between them turned her head, following their conversation back and forth as though she was at a tennis match. 'Have you two had a falling out?'

'No.'

'Yes.'

Henri apparently thought it was safer to have this out in front of an audience. But if this was his way of getting around her without a fight it wasn't going to work.

'Oh, dear. Has he been playing away, love? They're famous for that, the French, aren't they?'

Vera settled herself down for a good gossip and it might have been comical if this wasn't Lola's *life* playing out in the middle of the emergency department.

'Not that I know of.'

'No, but I did do something else unforgivable.'

Henri immediately allayed the fear that there might be another reason he didn't want to commit before it had a chance to form fully in Lola's worry bank.

'Has he apologised?' Vera's arms were folded, and her lips pursed as she planted herself firmly in Lola's camp.

'Sort of.'

Henri cleared his throat. 'That's what I'm trying to do now.'

Vera narrowed her eyes at him. 'You're not doing a very good job of it. You should be down on bended knee, begging for her forgiveness. I thought you lot were supposed to be experts at sweeping women off their feet? Make him *work* for it, Doctor.'

It wasn't often Henri who was the one taking orders rather than giving them, and Lola enjoyed watching him squirm at the bedside, trying to decide if he should actually get down on the floor.

'That's really not necessary, Mrs McConville. I wouldn't expect Dr Benoit to make such a gesture in public. I'm his dirty little secret.'

Lola left with a wink, trusting her new best friend to give Henri the pasting he deserved for treating her so appallingly while she organised a porter to move her patient to the general ward.

Lola didn't want to be part of a pantomime played out so Henri could salve his conscience. Even if he'd finally decided he would play a part in the baby's life it would never be enough. There was a 'buy one get one free' deal going here, and despite everything she still wanted him to take up the offer.

Otherwise it was going to kill her, being so close to the man she loved every day and getting nothing in return. She was thinking seriously about asking for a transfer before the end of her placement.

'Give me a break, Vera. I tried.'

Henri was still getting the stink-eye from Lola's bed-bound cheerleader. This wasn't easy for him. He could count on one hand the number of times he'd had to apologise in his life and for it to carry so much importance. Every time the words formed in his head he looked at Lola and nothing seemed adequate to portray the depth of his emotions for her.

He would have crawled on his hands and knees if he'd thought it would make any difference, but he could sense those walls already forming around Lola again—and he'd been the architect.

'If you love her you'll do more than try, you eejit.'

This indomitable spirit would serve the old lady well. Hopefully she would be back on her feet once the infection had cleared. Lola had made a difficult decision in keeping her off the ventilator at the first sign of her breathing difficulties, but it had worked out in the end. With the amount of problems Vera had going on already it would have been too easy for her body to give up altogether. This way she at least had a fighting chance.

'Let's get you sorted out first.'

He made way for the porter at the bedside, making sure Vera was comfortable before they moved her.

'I'm going, I'm going,' he said, in response to another glower.

Vera lifted her hand to wave at him as she was wheeled out of the department. She was a fighter, putting cowardly men who gave up at the first hint of trouble to shame. It was time he took a stand for something he wanted, *needed* from life.

He'd never known how to live for himself without always being mindful of how it would impact on his family. It was an exciting, if daunting prospect. Made worse with the knowledge that he'd given up a future with Lola when no one had asked him to. He'd jumped ahead, skipping the part where they could have had something meaningful, anticipating the reasons why it would never work.

He chased Lola down through the corridors. 'I'm an eejit, according to Vera.'

Her footsteps faltered and she spoke without turning to look at him. 'Yes. What's your point?'

'I thought I would be doing wrong by my family in spending more time with you. You don't understand... Angelique gave up everything to raise me after our parents died. How do you ever repay *that*? Well, I thought it was my duty to be there for her and the kids—make the same sacrifice she had made for me. She walked away from the very thing she loved to make sure I had a better life. I thought I had to do the same.'

The time, money and the other relationships he'd given up to atone were small gestures compared to the great loss he'd suffered at his own hand. Couldn't she see that?

'I don't think I would've wanted a three-way relationship anyway. What woman wants to be in competition with a man's *sister* for his affections? Badly done or not, this is for the best.'

She took another step forwards.

'But that's it. I was wrong. Angelique is perfectly capable of managing on her own—she doesn't need me. No one needs me. But I need *you*. I love you, Lola.'

His voice cracked as he said it and the implications of the words hit him. He'd never said that to anyone—not even his beloved sister. When he'd lost his parents he'd stopped believing love had any purpose other than bringing pain to those involved. That was still true now. But above all else Lola had to know that someone cared about her. Even if he was a complete imbecile who wasn't worthy of her.

'Maybe that's not enough. *I love you* is right up there with *I didn't mean to hurt you*. It's meaningless without the actions to back it up.'

Lola had put him in the same category as every other man who'd used and abused her on a whim. Unfortunately that didn't leave any room for him to make amends.

He stood helpless as Lola denied him redemption and disappeared through the door, but he didn't believe there wasn't still a flicker of hope. Those tears she was trying to hide were too real, too raw for her to be pretending she didn't care about him. It was down to him to give it one last shot and try to make it up to her.

If Lola needed a grand gesture to prove his love to her, she was going to get it.

* * *

Lola had no real desire to have another heart-to-heart with Jules about her predicament. She'd had enough of those for one day and had accomplished nothing.

Even hearing Henri say those three little words hadn't had the effect she'd imagined. There had been no choir of angels heralding the hallelujah moment when everything fell into place, because he hadn't yet told her this was for keeps. She'd been bitten twice now, so it was hardly surprising she was reluctant to take another man at face value. Especially since he'd proved he wasn't the man she'd thought he was.

Another temporary placement in his bed wasn't enough any more. She wanted a partner and a father for her baby. There was more than *her* future at stake here.

As she opened the apartment door it struck her that she was becoming very demanding of late, and unwilling to settle for anything less than she deserved. It was ironic that she was finally becoming an independent woman when everything was falling apart. But from now on she would put all her efforts into raising this child and leave all thought of romance where it belonged—in books.

The living room was in darkness, so she assumed Jules wasn't home yet—until she saw candles burning around the room. She dropped her bag on the sofa, to make sure she didn't stumble over it in the dark.

'Did we have a power cut, Jules?'

A shadow rose from the chair opposite and moved into the flickering candlelight. 'No power cut. No Jules. Just me.'

Lola swallowed her drool as Henri made his presence known—all six-foot-whatever dressed in a tux. The soft sound of blues music played in the background, and as her eyes adjusted to the darkness she could see rose petals strewn around the floor. She'd walked into her pre-pregnancy fantasy.

'How did you get in?'

'Jules very kindly lent me her key.'

'You told her about us?'

'I think she figured it out when I begged her to help me woo you.'

'*Woo* me?'

'*Oui.* Woo you.'

That accent slayed her every time.

He took a step closer and Lola resisted the urge to move back to a place of safety. There was no more running away from this for either of them.

'How do you propose to do that? Did Vera give you some more advice when I wasn't looking?'

Lola wasn't impressed with his track record so far. The last time he'd attempted to seduce her he'd combined it with baby-sitting duties and a work conference. He wasn't as smooth as his reputation led a girl to believe.

'I decided against grovelling on the hospital floor in favour of a more traditional approach. You danced for me last night, and I thought you might appreciate a partner this time.'

He slipped one hand around her waist and laced the fingers of the other hand with hers, leading her in a gentle waltz to the middle of the living room.

'You *saw* me last night?'

She'd thought she'd imagined him—*and* that look of disgust as he walked away. She stumbled over her feet, but Henri pulled her tight against him and carried on dancing.

'You were beautiful—so confident and sexy and carrying *my* baby. I was so proud, watching you up there.'

'Really? I thought you were ashamed of me.' Lola tried her best not to get carried away by the praise and Henri's acknowl-edgement of the child they'd created together. There was no point in getting her hopes up that they could be a family when her time here was almost up.

'Never. You're part of me, Lola, and I don't want to be with-out you ever again. Either of you. Will you marry me?'

He rested his hand on her belly, on their future, and Lola really wanted to believe it was possible to have everything she'd ever dreamed of.

'Not so long ago you were blaming me for getting pregnant and extending the time limit on our *arrangement*. I don't want you to propose because you think it's the right thing to do. What's happened to change the way you feel about me, us?' This wasn't going to work if he'd somehow been strong-armed into romancing her. Jules could be lurking in the shadows some-where pulling the strings and making him dance.

'Nothing has changed my feelings for you. I've been in love with you from the moment I saw you dancing upside down in that chair. I've simply been too afraid to admit it.' Big brave Henri confessing the slightest hint of fear was confirmation enough that this was the real deal.

Lola cast her mind back to that night in the hotel when he'd taken his time with her, understanding exactly what she'd needed. She pictured him today, with her pneumonia patient, going beyond the call of duty to make sure Vera was at ease. Instinct told her that Henri was everything he was selling him-self as with this stunt.

'Ask me again.' This time she wanted the moment free from doubts and suspicion.

'Lola Roberts, will you do me the honour of marrying me?'

Her battered heart finally waved the white flag. 'Yes, Henri. I will marry you.'

It seemed she wasn't done with testing her bravery just yet.

EPILOGUE

'I HOPE YOU'RE ready for this…' Henri whispered into Lola's ear and stood every hair on the back of her neck to attention. Family get-togethers were all well and good unless you were forced to keep your hands off your sexy fiancé—in which case they were damn frustrating.

'It can't be *that* bad.' Lola carried on setting the table for Sunday lunch, looking forward to an afternoon with Angelique and the children.

'My sister isn't renowned for her cooking—as you well know.' Henri gave a shudder and took his seat at the head of the table.

'I heard that!' Angelique carried in dishes of mashed potato and veg, while Gabrielle proudly followed with a platter of roast beef. 'I just wanted to do something to celebrate your engagement. Besides, Gabs did most of the cooking. All I did was boil the kettle to make the gravy.'

'*You* did this, Gabrielle? That's *amazing*. Well done.'

Lola hadn't seen much of the blushing teenager since she'd taken on a lot of after-school activities—including dance lessons with her mother. There hadn't been any more mention of problems at school, and Lola hoped life was starting to improve for her.

'Thank goodness we have one member of the family who can cook. I haven't had a decent home-made meal in about twenty years.'

Henri took a healthy scoop from each of the dishes as he sat down, and dodged the Yorkshire pudding Angelique threw at his head. It was the sort of camaraderie Lola had missed with her brothers.

'I should probably look into organising a family dinner at my dad's, too. God knows the last time they ate anything other than takeout, and it's about time I introduced you to them, Henri.'

She casually threw that at him, without referencing the inquisition he'd inevitably endure at the hands of her siblings. For safety's sake she might suggest he wear body armour for the occasion once they found out about her pregnancy.

Henri stopped wolfing down his dinner for long enough to stare. 'You want me to meet your family?'

'It's going to become obvious pretty quickly that something's up, and if I don't tell them about you they'll go into full stalker mode.'

Lola patted the soft swell of her belly under the table. They'd delayed sharing their news until they'd had the three-month scan, to make sure everything was progressing as it should, but she wouldn't be able to hide it much longer. No more secrets, no more lies. She couldn't wait for everyone to share in the good news.

'Wait…have you guys got something to tell us?' Gabrielle's cutlery clattered onto her plate at this revelation.

'Er…' Lola waited for Henri to drop the bombshell. He'd become quite the proud father already, poring over the scan pictures and trying to teach the baby French via her belly button.

'We're going to have a baby.'

He was positively beaming as he extended the Benoit family by another two. Telling them they intended to get married soon, so the baby would naturally take his surname—as would Lola.

There were gasps and happy whoops around the table—except from Bastien, who made an *'Eww!'* sound instead.

'I'm so happy for you both.' Angelique was on her feet at once to hug them, giving Henri an extra squeeze.

There was nothing but love in her embrace, and Lola hoped she and Henri could stop worrying that this would somehow have a negative impact on the family dynamic.

'I'm going to have a cousin!' Gabrielle rushed to kiss Lola, too, and immediately offered her babysitting services for when the time came.

Far from pouting about the prospect of being left out once the new addition arrived, everyone was as excited as the parents-to-be. Lola was lucky to be part of two loving families. She was sure her brothers would be putty in her baby's squidgy little hands, too, once they got used to the idea of their wee sister being pregnant.

'That means *you'll* have someone to boss about, too, Bastien.' Henri extracted a worrying grin from his otherwise unimpressed nephew.

'We have some news of our own to share.' Angelique diverted everyone's attention as she and the children shared knowing looks. 'I'm taking the kids to Paris over the holidays, to show them our old stomping ground and see the sights. It's about time they embraced their French culture, don't you think, Henri?'

'You're going on your own?' He tensed beside Lola, and she could see this would be a real test for him. But he had to let go if they were to stand any chance of making it as a family in their own right.

'Yes, Henri. I'm taking my kids on holiday to spend some quality time with them. Do you have a problem with that?' Her eyes glittered, daring him to challenge her, and there was a heavy air of expectation as they waited for his response.

Henri took a sip of water, rolled his napkin into a ball and rose from his seat. Lola tensed, afraid that everything they'd worked for was about to unravel before her eyes. He'd spent his entire adulthood caring for his sister and her brood, and this was the first time as far as Lola knew that they were striking out on their own. It was a lot for him to get used to.

Henri reached down and kissed Angelique on the cheek. 'I'm sure you'll have a lovely time. Make sure you take plenty of photographs, so I can see what the old place looks like now.'

'I will—but there's nothing to stop you two going to visit yourselves some time. There's nothing like a dirty weekend in Paris...'

Angelique trailed off, as if she was remembering one. It seemed she had some secrets of her own.

'How about it?' Henri asked when they were washing up in the kitchen.

'Hmm?' Lola was distracted by his thick forearms, dipping into the soapy bubbles, clearly visible now he'd rolled his sleeves up.

'I'm talking about Angelique's suggestion of a dirty weekend in Paris. It's the perfect place for a honeymoon.'

Henri encircled her waist with his wet hands and pulled her close. She couldn't remember one good reason why she would want to be anywhere else other than here in his arms.

'Why wait for a honeymoon when our place is only a short drive away?'

Paris could wait. Lola couldn't. She shrieked as Henri took her legs from beneath her and swept her into his arms.

'We have to go, Angelique. There's an emergency. I'll speak to you tomorrow. Maybe...' Henri yelled his goodbyes and carried Lola out to the car with the urgency of a man on a mission.

This time there was no question over his priorities, and Lola couldn't wait to reap the benefits. She was determined to show Henri exactly how much she loved him. Every single day.

* * * * *

The SEAL's Baby
Laura Marie Altom

ABOUT THE AUTHOR

After college (Go, Hogs!), bestselling, award-winning author Laura Marie Altom did a brief stint as an interior designer before becoming a stay-at-home mom to boy-girl twins and a bonus son. Always an avid romance reader, she knew it was time to try her hand at writing when she found herself replotting the afternoon soaps.

When not immersed in her next story, Laura teaches art at a local middle school. In her free time, she beats her kids at video games, tackles Mount Laundry and, of course, reads romance!

Laura loves hearing from readers at either P.O. Box 2074, Tulsa, OK 74101, or by email, balipalm@aol.com.

Love winning fun stuff? Check out www.lauramariealtom.com.

Books by Laura Marie Altom

Harlequin Western Romance
1086—SAVING JOE*
1099—MARRYING THE MARSHAL*
1110—HIS BABY BONUS*
1123—TO CATCH A HUSBAND*
1132—DADDY DAYCARE
1147—HER MILITARY MAN
1160—THE RIGHT TWIN
1165—SUMMER LOVIN'
     "A Baby on the Way"
1178—DANCING WITH DALTON
1211—THREE BOYS AND A BABY
1233—A DADDY FOR CHRISTMAS
1257—THE MARINE'S BABIES
1276—A WEDDING FOR BABY**
1299—THE BABY BATTLE**
1305—THE BABY TWINS**
1336—THE BULL RIDER'S CHRISTMAS BABY***
1342—THE RANCHER'S TWIN TROUBLES***
1359—A COWGIRL'S SECRET***
1383—A BABY IN HIS STOCKING***
1415—A SEAL'S SECRET BABY‡
1430—THE SEAL'S STOLEN CHILD‡
1435—THE SEAL'S VALENTINE‡
1466—A NAVY SEAL'S SURPRISE BABY‡
1480—THE SEAL'S CHRISTMAS TWINS‡

*U.S. Marshals
**Baby Boom
***The Buckhorn Ranch
‡Operation: Family

Dear Reader,

Have you ever been at a party where you didn't know anyone? Or maybe you did know people, but didn't really feel you belonged? That sensation is the *worst!*

Sometimes when I'm at a big writers' conference, I find myself lost in a sea of strangers. It makes me feel lonely and a little scared. I know I should use the opportunity to make new friends, but that's not always easy. Every once in a while, a kind soul wanders up to spark a conversation, and that lone sweet gesture changes everything.

When this story opens, Libby Dewitt's lost in not just a crowd, but seemingly, the whole world. She's *very* pregnant, estranged from her baby's father and even her parents. When her car, finances and health also let her down, she's forced to rely on the kindness of strangers, and she finds herself immersed in the kind of wondrous family she'd never dreamed possible.

Trouble is, her new life is an illusion. And her inevitable leaving will open old wounds. Making matters worse is the man whose mere presence gives her glimpses into the life she's always wanted, but fears may never be.

Will Libby make Heath Stone believe in second chances? Or is she destined to raise her baby alone? I'll never tell! Lol!

Happy reading!

Laura Marie

For my dear old friend and talented author, Amy Lillard.

Have I mentioned lately how blessed I feel to have you back in my life?!

CHAPTER ONE

"SAM? WHERE THE hell are you?" Southern Oregon's dense coastal fog absorbed Heath Stone's words, rendering his words useless in the search for his dog, who lately felt like his only friend.

Heath had let him out the previous night at 2200 for his usual evening constitutional, but the dog had caught the scent of something, and a chase ensued through the forest thick with sitka spruce, western hemlock and red cedar. Heath had spent the entire night searching the pungent woods, his footfalls silent on winding pine needle-strewn paths, all the while fighting the urge to panic.

Now, in dawn's fragile light, with his heart empty from mourning Patricia and the pain still too raw, he couldn't even consider suffering another loss. "Come on, Sam! Quit fooling around!"

Heath clapped, then whistled, hoping the shrill sound carried. It did not.

Thirty minutes later, he'd wound his way back to the one-bedroom log cabin that for the past year he'd called home. After relieving himself, he washed his hands and splashed cold water on his face.

He took an energy bar from the cabinet alongside the propane stove and a bottled water from the fridge. Stopping only long enough to retrieve his wallet and keys from the metal bucket he stored them in beside the door, he soon sat behind the wheel of the 1960 Ford pickup that his grandpa had bought new.

The trek down the cabin's single-lane drive proved daunting, with visibility being a few feet at best. After rolling down both windows, he called periodically out either side.

By the time he reached the main road, the fog had thinned to the point he could at least make out the double yellow lines on the pavement. Usually, at this time of the morning, he and Sam set out to fish on the Umpqua River. Most weekdays, the road was deserted. Hell, most weekends—unless his hometown of Bent Road was hosting a holiday festival or fishing tourney. Most tourists traveling north from Coos Bay on Oregon Coast Highway 101 blew right by the lonely road leading to the largely forgotten town. With no trendy B and Bs or campgrounds, visitors had no reason beyond curiosity to ever stop by. A fact that suited Heath just fine.

"Sam! You out there, boy?" Crawling along at the harrowing rate of fifteen miles per hour, Heath continued calling, intermittently scanning the faded blacktop for the potentially gut-wrenching sight of his wounded—or even dead—dog.

"What the—" He'd driven maybe five miles before pumping his brakes, having damn near hit not his dog, but a woman—a *very* pregnant woman—standing in the road's center, waving her arms. "What's the matter with you?" he hollered, easing the truck onto the weed-choked shoulder. "Got some kind of death wish?"

Upon killing the engine, he hopped out and slammed the door shut behind him. The dense fog stole the thunder of a gratifying bang, leaving him with a less satisfactory thud.

"Th-thank you so much for stopping." The ethereal blonde staggered his direction. Was she drunk? "M-my car broke down yesterday. I tried walking, but—"

"It's a good thirty miles to town."

She placed her hands protectively over her bulging belly. "If you could just take me to a phone, I'd…" Before finishing her halting sentence, she crumpled before him like a building that had suddenly lost its foundation.

He rushed to her, checking her pulse and finding it strong.

Abandoning his worries for Sam, he hefted the woman's deadweight into his arms and then onto his truck's passenger seat.

He then retrieved her giant purse from the road.

"W-what happened?" she asked, stirring when he buckled her in and set her purse beside her.

"You fainted. How long has it been since you've had a decent meal?"

"I—I don't know. I'm saving my cash for gas."

The fog had lifted enough to reveal a VW Bug as old as his truck. The backseat was crammed so tightly with the woman's belongings, daylight couldn't even be seen through the front window.

"I'll run you to my cabin—get you fed and call for a tow."

"Thank you—but I don't have the money for a tow or mechanic."

He closed her door. "You prefer I leave you out here for the crows?"

Groaning, she pressed her fingertips to her forehead. "What I'd prefer is to have never wound up in this position."

All too well, he knew the feeling.

Libby Dewitt struggled to stay awake while the stranger drove. Exhaustion—physical and emotional—weighed down her shoulders, making even turning her head an effort.

"Stay with me…" the man urged. "Sure I shouldn't take you straight to a doc?"

"I'm fine," she assured. It took much of her remaining energy to meet his curiously hollow stare. "Just tired and hungry."

"I can help with both of those issues. And since you're low

on cash, I'll see what I can do with your car. But fair warning, I'm good with a lot of things, but engine repair has never been one of them."

From somewhere inside she managed a laugh. "At this point, a cracker and glass of water would be downright gourmet. To expect more would be greedy."

His sideways glance spoke volumes, but at the same time, nothing at all. Again, she had the sense that part of him was emotionally missing. What had he been through?

He turned the truck onto a dirt lane so narrow the weeds grew between twin tire ruts.

Woods, dark and brooding, surrounded them, yet over a small hill, sunbeams punched through the fog, the soft light promising to end the day's gloom.

Over the next hill stood the sweetest log cabin—sun- and weather-faded with rich green moss growing between the logs' seams. Two smallish paned windows flanked a wooden front door. A wide, covered porch held two rockers and a pair of dead hanging ferns. The Pacific glistened in teasing strips just beyond massive pines.

"I-it's beautiful," she said, not trying to disguise her awe. "How lucky you are."

Parking the truck, he shrugged. "It's okay."

Okay? To be jaded about such a view implied he wasn't really alive at all. Despite the lousy circumstances she found herself in, Libby hoped she'd never lose her ability to be wowed by Mother Nature showing off.

"You able to walk under your own steam?"

"I—I think so…" To prove it she opened the door with an echoing creak, then placed her feet firmly on the ground. Her legs wobbled a little at first, but then held strong as the stranger set his arm about her shoulders, assisting her into his home. In another world she may have appraised his warm, strong touch, but for now she was merely grateful for the help. "By the way, I'm Libby."

"Nice to meet you. I'm Heath."

Inside, it took her eyes a moment to adjust to the dimness.

"Sorry about the mess." After leading her to a dilapidated yet comfy brown plaid sofa, he plucked a couple dirty shirts from the back of a wood rocker and a ladder-back kitchen chair. "It's just me around here, and, well..." He shoved his hands in his pockets. "There's not much need to clean."

She waved off his concern. "Considering I've spent the past two years in a tent, the fact that you have an actual roof ranks this place right up there with the Taj Mahal."

"A tent, huh?" He'd ducked in the fridge and emerged with milk, cheese and a carton of eggs. "Sounds like a good story." He set his finds on the butcher-block counter lining the cabin's front wall, then took an energy bar from a cabinet and tossed it to her. "Eat this, then tell me more about how a woman willingly spends two years sleeping under the stars."

Three bites later she'd devoured her snack and drank half the bottled water he'd also given her. "Thank you. That was delicious." She finished off the water, then patted her hands to her bulging belly. "Long story short, the father of this little gal considered himself a free spirit. He believed houses were the equivalent of cells, and marriage a life sentence."

Beating eggs, her savior asked, "You're talking about this guy in the past tense. Is he...dead?"

"Gosh, no." Though too many times than she'd liked, she could've cheerfully clubbed him. "Liam left me for a woman who makes fresh flower headbands. We all traveled together in an unofficial craft show circuit. I'm a potter."

"No kidding?" She didn't miss his raised eyebrows when he shot her a glance. Used to be, that kind of look by so-called acceptable society sent her dashing off for a discreet cry, but no more. She was done apologizing for the life she loved. "You make bowls and vases and stuff?"

"Uh huh."

"Eat up." He handed her a plate filled with eggs scrambled with cheese and two slices of whole wheat toast with butter.

"Oh, wow. This looks delicious. Thanks."

"No problem." After handing her another bottled water, he spun a kitchen chair around and straddled it, resting his forearms on the back. "Should've asked sooner, but want me to call anyone for you? There's gotta be someone you know who'd want to help."

She shook her head. "It's complicated."

"Yeah, well…" He looked to the door. "Make yourself at home, and I'll see what I can do with your car."

"I should probably tag along." She reached beside her for the oversize hobo bag serving as her purse.

"Don't sweat it. I've got this."

"You sure?"

"Yeah. But I'll need your keys." His half grin did funny things to her insides—or maybe it was just the satisfaction of for once having a full stomach. Regardless, she took her first in-depth look at her new friend and was duly impressed. Dark, slightly overgrown buzz cut and the most amazing pale green eyes. He wore desert camo fatigues, boots and a sand-colored T-shirt that hugged his pecs in a way a woman in her condition shouldn't notice.

Distracting herself from the unexpectedly hot view, she fished for her keys and handed them over.

"Thanks," he said. "Be back soon, okay?"

She nodded, and then just as abruptly as he'd entered her life, he was gone.

Hugging her tummy, she said, "Baby, if your daddy was as nice as our new friend, we might not be in such a pickle."

Tilting her head back, Libby groaned.

Despite this temporary respite, she could hardly bear thinking of the hours, let alone days and weeks, to come. She'd thought the journey home would be relatively simple, but it was proving tougher than she'd ever imagined.

* * *

"Sam!" During the short return trek to Libby's car, Heath squashed his many questions about the woman by continuing his search for his dog. "You out there, boy?"

The fog had burned off, making for an annoyingly hot and sunny day. No doubt everyone else in town was thrilled, but sun reminded him of days spent on the beach with Patricia and all of the perfect days they'd spent planning out the rest of their perfect lives.

On the main road, again looking to the shoulders for Sam, Heath's stomach knotted in disgust for the guy who'd left Libby on her own while carrying his child. Who did that? Here he'd have selfishly given anything for Patricia to have been with him long enough for them to have a kid, so he'd at least have something tangible beyond pictures to remember her by, yet that lucky asshole was about to have a son or daughter and didn't even care.

Within minutes he made it to Libby's Bug.

He veered his truck around to try giving her vehicle a jump, but the engine wouldn't turn over. The car was an older model he'd only seen while on missions with his navy SEAL unit in developing countries, meaning it didn't even have a gas gauge. Back under the hood he checked the fuel level the way he'd check the oil on any normal car. The stick read nearly a quarter-tank. Which meant he'd reached the end of his personal bag of tricks.

Good thing his cell got better reception on the side of the road than at his cabin.

Thirty minutes later, Hal Kramer arrived with his tow truck.

"Haven't seen one of these in a while," he said, backing out the driver's side door to climb down from his truck. He sauntered over to where Heath stood, wiping sweat from his forehead with a red shop rag. While appraising the situation, he twirled the left side of his handlebar mustache. "Girl I used to date up in Portland drove one of these. Whenever she drank too much wine, I drove. My legs were so long I usually ended up turning off the engine switch with my knee."

"Good times…" Heath said with a faint smile.

The burly town mechanic walked to the vehicle's rear, then lifted the engine cover. "You happen to check the gas and battery?"

"Yep." Hands in his pockets, Heath tried not to remember how frightened he'd been when Libby collapsed at his feet. He'd done his best to hide his fear from her, but inside, he'd been a wreck. Sam's disappearing act already had Heath on edge. The reminder of how frail Patricia had been at the end finished the job of making a normally unflappable guy a nervous wreck.

"All right, old girl." Hal crouched in front of the engine. "Let's take a peek under your knickers…."

While his longtime friend tinkered at the rear of the car, Heath looked inside. A pottery wheel occupied the passenger seat and an assortment of suitcases and boxes had been crammed into the back. When Libby told him she was a potter, he'd honestly thought she'd been joking, but maybe not. Did that mean she'd also been telling the truth about spending two years in a tent?

Oddly enough, if he counted the total time he'd spent on missions, he'd probably slept under the stars more than her, but that was different. Given a choice between a bed and dirt, the bed would always win.

"Try starting it!" Hal called.

Heath gave the engine another try. "Nothing!"

A few curses later, Hal appeared, wiping his hands on his rag. "Thought there might be a quick fix—loose hose or something—but I'm guessing this is electrical. Let me run it into my shop and I'll see what I can find."

"Sounds good." Heath would take Libby to town, where she'd be someone else's problem—not that he'd minded helping, just that with her gone, he could focus on finding his dog. "Have any idea how long it'll take?"

Hal shrugged. "Ten minutes. Ten days. If I need parts, depends on where they are and if the owner has the Ben Franklins to buy 'em."

Heath released a long, slow exhale. "Yeah… What if the owner's short on cash?"

"Is he from around here?"

"Nah. Belongs to a woman—she's passing through. The reason I ask is she's very pregnant, broke and must weigh less than a soaked kitten."

Scratching his head, Hal said, "Sorry to hear it. I'll certainly do what I can to keep costs down, but with vintage models like this I can't make any promises."

"I understand. I'll bring her round a little later. You two can sort out an arrangement."

"Sounds good."

Heath shook his old friend's hand, then helped him load Libby's car. With any luck the repair would be fast and cheap, getting her back on the road to wherever she'd been going.

And if the fix wasn't fast and proved expensive?

He closed his eyes, pinching the bridge of his nose. He hated being an ass, but if Libby had to stick around, he'd just have to make sure she stayed away from him.

CHAPTER TWO

LIBBY WOKE FROM a nap to the sound of someone splitting logs with an ax. Having spent many nights warmed by a campfire, she'd grown familiar with the rhythmic thwack and thump.

She'd curled into a ball on the sofa. A glance down showed she'd thoughtfully been covered by a soft, mossy-green blanket that'd even been tucked around her perpetually cold toes.

Rising and keeping the blanket around her like a shawl, she went in search of her host, assuming he was the one outside chopping.

She found him wearing no shirt and wielding an ax. His chest was broad enough to have earned its own zip code. No way was she even allowing her glance to settle long enough on his honed abs and pecs to give them a formal appraisal. Suffice it to say, he was built better than any man she'd seen outside of a movie.

Considering the cooler air and how low on the horizon the sun had dipped, she called, "Have I been asleep as long as I'm afraid I have?"

He cast a wary glance in her direction. "Yep. You snoozed right through lunch. There's a sandwich for you in the fridge. If you're still hungry, I can heat up some soup."

"I'm sure a sandwich will be fine. Thanks."

"No problem." He brought the ax down hard on his latest log. "After you eat, I'll run you into town. You were out cold when I got back from looking at your car, but I couldn't fix the problem. It ended up having to be towed."

"Oh." Stomach knotted with dread over what the repair may cost, she forced her breathing to slow. As much as she hated the thought, was now the time to officially cry uncle by asking for help? *No.* When she met with her parents, it'd be on her own terms. She'd gotten herself into this mess, and she'd get herself out of it. If her father had believed her a dismal failure before, he was in for quite a shock to see her life had only grown that much more pathetic.

"The town mechanic—Hal—does great work. He's honest and does whatever it takes to keep costs low."

"Good. I can't thank you enough for…everything." If he hadn't come along when he did, there's no telling what may have happened. As tightly as she clung to the stubborn streak and refusing to admit further failure to her parents, she'd finally reached the point where if it came down to protecting her baby's health, she'd have no other choice. A sobering fact she preferred dealing with later.

"Go ahead and eat your sandwich." He reached for another log. "I'll be done in a few."

"O-okay…" Was he dismissing her? Though his words were polite, she couldn't escape the feeling that his failure to make small talk or eye contact signaled he'd rather she be on her way.

Not surprising. If she were fortunate enough for this to be her home, she supposed she wouldn't want a stranger hanging around.

Running her fingertips along the rough-hewn porch rail, she—more than anything—couldn't wait to one day experience what it would feel like to truly belong. To have found her own special niche in the world where she was accepted and appreciated for who she was.

When she'd bolted from the home she'd been raised in, her

grand plan had been becoming part of an artistic community, but dreams have a funny way of dissolving when exposed to reality's ugly light.

"Go ahead and start eating," her host nudged. "Last thing I need is for you to suffer another fainting spell."

She cast him a slight smile. "Sure. Sorry. I tend to daydream."

His only response was a nod before reaching for his next log. His actions were needlessly, almost recklessly fast, as if driven by an invisible demon. Though curiosity burned to know more—anything—about this kind man who'd done more for her in an afternoon than anyone else in recent memory, Libby held tight to her questions instead, turning her back on him to enter the cabin.

With any luck she'd soon be on her way and this day and all of the rocky ones before it would fade into a mental collage featuring only happy times and none of the bad.

An hour later, Libby found herself once again alongside Heath in his truck, heading down the main street of the sleepy town of Bent Road. The rich smell of vintage leather seats mixed with his own masculine flavor of wood and sweat. During the whole trip he didn't say a word, other than a brief inquiry as to whether or not she was cold. At first she'd found the silence awkward, but then it brought her an unexpected peace.

With Liam, she'd felt pressured to always be talking. His constant need to be entertained had been exhausting.

The town sat in the midst of dense forest—a sun-dazzled glade forgotten by time. Historic, redbrick buildings held an assortment of businesses from drug and hardware stores to a lawyer's office and dentist. Window boxes and clay pots cele-brated summer with eye-popping color. Purple lobelia and red geraniums. Yellow and orange marigolds, mixed with pink and white petunias.

The floral kaleidoscope spoke to her on a long-forgotten level. Along with her dreams of simply having a home, she'd always wished for a garden. Not only would she grow flowers, but tomatoes and green beans and lettuce.

Thick ferns hung from every lamppost, and the sidewalks were made of weathered brick.

With the truck's windows down, she closed her eyes and breathed deeply. The briny Pacific blended with the sweet flowers, creating a heady fragrance she wouldn't soon forget.

Around the next bend stood an old-style strip-and-cabin motel. A sign built in the shape of a smiling, gingham-clad couple with rosy cheeks proclaimed in red neon that the place was named the Yodel Hoo Inn. Swiss chalet-styled, the dark log structure's every paned window were framed by sunny, yellow shutters. The paint was cracked and a little faded, but that didn't stop it from being fun. Towering pines embraced it and the attached diner. Thriving hanging flower baskets added still more pops of color.

"Everything's so pretty," Libby said more to herself than Heath.

He grunted. "Fourth of July fishing tourney, art festival and carnival's only a little over a week away. Whole damn town goes overboard with decorating. Lucky for you, you won't be around when the eight-hundred miles of red, white and blue bunting rolls out."

"Sounds amazing."

"Sure—as long as you don't get roped into helping take it all down."

He slowed the truck then turned into a gas station that had two pumps and a four-stall garage, each humming with activity. Her Bug sat midway up a hydraulic lift. The engine cover was open and three men stood around it in animated discussion, staring and pointing.

"That can't be good," she noted while Heath parked next to a tow truck with Hal's Garage emblazoned across the door.

"What?"

"All those guys debating over my car. In my perfect fantasy

world, I'd hoped it was already fixed, and the mechanic wouldn't have minded trading his services for one of my best clay pots."

"Uh, yeah. I don't think Hal does pots." Eyes narrowed, his befuddled look was one to which she'd sadly grown accustomed to seeing in others. Instead of viewing a glass as half-full, she saw it as bubbling over with a splash of orange and a maraschino cherry. Liam had constantly harped at her to be more realistic, but why? What did it hurt to be happy? Or at least, try?

After turning off the engine, Heath looked to her bulging belly, then asked, "Need help getting out?"

"No, thanks." She cast him a smile. "I think I've got it."

But then she creaked open her door, only to get her purse hooked around the seat belt, which left her hanging at a steep angle.

As was starting to be the norm, her rescuer anticipated her needs and was there to help before she could even ask.

"Sure you're ready for motherhood?" he teased, untangling her purse strap.

"Ha-ha…" She should probably be offended by his question, but little did he know, she'd wondered the same since learning she carried Liam's baby.

"How about trying this again, only with me here to catch you." He grazed his hand to her outer thigh, helping her swing her legs around. His touch proved electric, which was surprising, given her condition. Then he took her hands, guiding her the rest of the way down. Even though she'd set her sandal-clad feet to solid ground, her legs felt shaky beneath her. She needn't have worried, though, as Heath stepped in again, cupping his hand around her elbow to help keep her steady.

"Thanks." She tried acting normal, even though her runaway pulse was anything but!

"No problem." Easing his arm around her waist, he asked, "Wanna just wait in the truck, and I'll give you a report on what Hal found?"

"That's sweet of you to offer, but you've already done enough. I wish I had some way to repay you."

He waved off her gratitude. "Anyone in my position would do the same."

No, they wouldn't. Her ex was proof.

"Those guys standing around your car?"

"Yes?" She waddled around the garage's south side.

"The big one with the 'stache is Hal. The other two are his twin sons—Darryl and Terryl. They're identical, save for one's a crazy Dodgers fan, and the other's crazy about the Mariners. You may want to avoid them when the two teams play—not a good time."

She laughed. "I appreciate the advice. Hopefully, your friend Hal will get me back on my way in the next hour or so."

Famous last words.

After introductions—Libby hid her smile upon noticing the twins wearing hats from their respective baseball teams—Hal shook his head and frowned.

"Wish I had better news for you." He tucked a shop rag in his shirt pocket. "Electrical system's shot. Fried like Sunday-supper chicken."

Libby's stomach knotted so hard it startled the baby. She rubbed the tender spot where she'd kicked. "But you can fix it, right?"

"Well, sure. Me and my boys can fix damn near anything—pardon my French."

"You're pardoned. Just please tell me you've got the parts and I'll be on my way before sunset."

Darryl laughed. Or, it might've been Terryl. She'd forgotten which team each preferred.

The one wearing a Dodgers cap said, "Ma'am, finding all these parts is gonna take me hours—maybe days—on the internet. You'll be lucky if you're out of here in a month."

"You hush." Hal elbowed his son. Turning to Libby, he said, "You have my solemn word that I'll get your ride fixed as soon as possible. But I'm afraid my boy's right—it ain't gonna be fast, easy or cheap."

"Oh?" Stress knotted her throat. Was this really happening? She barely had enough cash for the gas she'd need for the rest of her drive to Seattle. There was no way she'd have enough for repairs and staying over however long it took to get the work done.

Swallow your pride and ask Mom and Dad for help.

Libby raised her chin. No way would she surrender just yet. "You don't really think it'll take a month to find parts, do you?"

Hal shrugged. "No telling till we get started."

Hugging herself, she nodded.

Heath didn't do tears, so when he noted Libby's eyes filling, he slipped back into take-charge mode. "Hal, do what you can, and since Libby doesn't have a cell, keep me posted."

"Will do."

To Libby, Heath said, "Let's see what we can do about finding you a cheap place to stay."

"I—I'll figure it out," she assured him. "I'm grateful for all you've done, but I can take it from here."

"Motel's just down the road a piece." Hal barked at his sons to quit lollygagging and get back to work. "Tell Gretta I sent you and she'll discount your rate."

"I think I have more pull with her than you," Heath said, already guiding Libby back to his truck.

"Wouldn't be so sure about that. She told me you missed Sunday supper yet again."

Heath ignored Hal's comment. He had his reasons for missing most every Stone gathering, and his mother damn well knew it.

It took all of three minutes to reach the inn that had been in his family since the 1940s, when Bent Road had been a weekend fishing mecca for Portland, Seattle and even San Francisco's wealthy vacationers. In the 1930s, the CCC or Civilian Conservation Corp, had provided badly needed infrastructure to the area to allow for its growth. But when a 1942 wildfire destroyed the row of vacation homes that had lined the coastal bluffs, the town's soul suffered a direct blow. The motel was lucky to have survived the fire.

Decades later, Bent Road's tourism consisted of Heath's family's place, and a few fishing lodges specializing in charter trips on the Umpqua River.

"This Gretta we're meeting is your mom?"

"Yeah." Heath had been so lost in thought, he'd momentarily forgotten Libby was with him.

"Do you two not get along?"

"We're good. It's complicated."

Her laugh struck him as sad. "I can relate."

When he pulled onto the inn's blacktop drive, she gasped. "This adorable place belongs to you?"

"Not me, but my mom. My dad died a long time ago."

"I'm sorry."

He shrugged, then parked the truck and killed the engine.

"Sit tight till I get around to help you climb out. We don't need you getting tangled again."

Heath hated the heaviness in his chest at Libby's continued intrusion upon his life, but he hadn't been raised to turn away someone in need. His time in the navy had only reinforced that tradition. Still, he needed to get back to his cabin. Resume his search for Sam, then get back to his new normal—a life he wasn't proud of, but at the moment, it was the best he had to give.

After helping Libby safely to her feet, he hovered alongside her, unable to shake the feeling of her being precious cargo. His mom never turned away a stray, and hopefully, she'd view Libby in the same light.

Just then his mom rounded the corner of the front office with her watering can in hand. "Hey, stranger." Gretta believed customers appreciated employees wearing gingham getups that matched the inn's sign, so in addition to her salt-and-pepper hair being braided, she wore a checkered red dress with matching red sneakers.

Her hug made him feel like the world's worst son for not having been by to see her sooner.

"Hi, I'm Gretta Stone." She extended her free hand to Libby. "Looks like you swallowed a watermelon seed."

Heath died a little inside. *Really, Mom?*

Fortunately, Libby laughed. "Yes, ma'am, I did. Hope the baby doesn't come out red-and-green." Her smile was accompanied by a wink. Meeting his mom's outstretched hand, she said, "I'm Libby Dewitt. Nice to meet you."

"Likewise." To her son, she asked, "To what do I owe this pleasure? I know you didn't stop by just to see me."

He'd wondered how long it would take her to get a dig in about his lack of recent visits. "Actually, I was out looking for Sam this morning and stumbled across Libby instead. Her car broke down, and—"

"Wait." His mom held up her hand, stopping him midsentence. "Libby, I want to hear all about your poor car, but Sam is my son's dog. Sounds like we need to launch a search party."

"For sure," Libby said. She turned to Heath. "Why didn't you say something when I first got here? Your dog is way more important than my busted ride."

Uncomfortable with having his problems on public display, Heath rammed his hands in his pockets. "I'll find him."

"Of course you will. With my help. And Libby, would I be right in assuming you're needing a temporary place to stay?"

"Yes, ma'am."

"Great." Gretta watered the plant nearest her. "Let me get you set up in a room, then—"

"Sorry for interrupting," Libby said, "but I'm strapped for cash. Think we could work out some sort of trade for a room?"

"What'd you have in mind?"

Never had Heath wished more to be a dishonorable man. All he wanted to do was get back to his cabin and resume his search for Sam—alone. He didn't want his well-meaning mom involved, and he sure didn't need the added concern of worrying whether or not Libby was on the verge of going into labor.

"I might not look like it," Libby said, "but I'm a hard worker. I could waitress at the diner. Clean rooms for you or do laundry. Run your front desk—pretty much any odd job you need done. I'm a potter by trade, so I can also make any sort of custom piece you might like."

Was it wrong of Heath that this was one time he wished his mom would turn away a stray? He had nothing against Libby. She seemed like a great gal. That didn't change the fact that in her condition, she needed to find a home base—fast. And Bent Road wasn't it.

Come on, Mom. Just say no.

Gretta once again extended her hand for Libby to shake. "You have a deal. I just happen to have a vacancy, as well as a family reunion fishing group who are really going through the towels. I've had the washer and dryer going practically 24/7, and could sure use help."

Libby's shoulders sagged. Relieved? "Thank you, ma'am. I promise I won't be any trouble, and just as soon as my car's ready, I'll be on my way."

Heath tried not to scowl. Libby was now officially his mother's concern, so why didn't he feel better? Maybe because her pretty, misty-eyed smile tugged at his long-frozen heart?

CHAPTER THREE

LIBBY SAT ON the foot of her new bed—the first true bed she'd slept on in two years, and could hardly believe her good fortune. Her constantly aching back practically sang! Beneath his curmudgeonly exterior, Heath was a sweetheart. After meeting his mom, Libby knew why.

Her new boss had given her fifteen minutes to "freshen up," then asked her to man the inn's front office desk while she traipsed around the woods for her son's dog. They'd both agreed night hiking probably wasn't a good idea for a woman in Libby's condition.

After splashing cold water on her face and running a brush through her hair, Libby still couldn't get over the wonder of her situation. She'd grown to appreciate the unique flavor of her rustic life, but a part of her had always wished Liam wanted more. Not just for them to share an apartment or house, but a commitment. She'd assumed he'd one day see the light—her light, their shared light—but she couldn't have been more wrong.

Hugging the baby, she said, "I'm sorry in advance for the mess you'll be born into. Once our car's fixed, there's no telling how my folks are going to take the news about you. In a perfect world, they'll love you like I already do, but..."

She shut up in favor of grabbing a tissue to blot her teary

eyes and blow her suddenly runny nose. What happened to her usually sunny disposition?

Instead of looking for possible trouble somewhere down the road, she needed to count her current blessings. Starting by meeting Gretta in the inn's cozy lobby.

The early evening had turned crisp and she found the conifer-laced air invigorating.

Up close, the inn was even more charming than she'd seen from the road. Steam rose from a small pool in a glade near the office, around which sat a group of six guys, laughing over beers. A gazebo, wreathed in ivy, ferns and thriving impatiens graced the grounds' far end. A glider swing and hammock stood amongst still more gardens that faced the row of rooms and a few cabins. Hydrangeas dazzled in shades of blue ranging between cobalt and sky.

The only thing missing from the idyllic scene was Heath's truck. A fact which she shouldn't have even noticed, let alone found the tiniest bit disappointing. He'd already done more than most anyone else would've given the circumstances. So why did she still want more? Oh, she didn't want things from him like food or transportation, but rather she had a sudden craving for his company.

"There you are." Gretta stepped out of the office. "I was just coming to find you."

"Here I am," Libby said with a nervous laugh, still not quite believing her luck over having stepped into such a perfect situation. "Reporting for duty."

"Good, good…" She held open the plate glass door, ushering Libby inside. "Is your room okay? Find everything you need?"

"It's beautiful—and so homey. The gingham curtains and vintage logging pics make it feel like a place you'd want to stay a nice long while."

Heath's mom beamed. "I'm so glad you like it. My son thought I was off my rocker for spending so much on redecorating last year, but my business has more than doubled, so he can keep any further advice to himself."

Laughing, Libby said, "Hands-down, the room you've loaned me is way more inviting than his cabin—not that I wasn't thankful he found me, but—" Libby felt horrible that her statement made it sound as though she was dissing the man who'd done so much "I'm sorry, that came out wrong. Heath's cabin is perfect. I just meant that you'd win should the two of you be in a decorating contest."

"I get it," Gretta said with another warm smile. "And I thank you. Though, in Heath's defense, home decor was never really his cup of tea. Now, his wife, Patricia, on the other hand..." A cloud passed over Gretta's once sunny expression. "Well, she was a pro."

"Was?" Libby asked.

"Poor girl died of cancer. For a while there we all thought Heath might go with her. It's been nearly fourteen months, but nobody seems able to reach him."

"I—I'm sorry." What Libby went through in having Liam leave her was bad enough; she couldn't even imagine the pain of losing a spouse.

Gretta shrugged. "By the time you get to be my age, you realize death's an inevitable side effect of life. But it's never easy seeing a young person go. Feels unnatural."

Not sure what else to do or say, Libby nodded.

"Anyway..." Gretta took a deep breath, only to let the air rush out. "Since my rooms are all full, you shouldn't have to do a thing, other than grab a few towels or ring up snacks, but I always like someone to be up here—just in case. If you run into any trouble, here's my cell." She jotted the number on a Post-it, then stuck it on a computer screen. She did a quick run-through on the register, then showed Libby what was available in terms of food and sundries in the lobby's small gift section. "Think you can manage?"

"Easy peasy," Libby said, despite this being her first real job in a while, outside of selling her art.

"Good." Heath's mom took her purse from beneath the front desk and headed for the door. "Oh—and thanks again for filling in. I'm not sure my son could handle losing his wife and his dog."

Heath cupped his hands to his mouth. "Sam! Come on, boy!"

Where the hell could he be?

The deeper Heath trudged into the forest, the madder he got—not just at his mutt, who knew better than to run off, but at the world in general.

As relieved as he'd been to escape Libby's perma-smile and adorably huge belly, he was also resentful of the man who'd turned his back on her. Since losing his wife, Heath had no tolerance for men who willingly shirked their responsibilities in regard to their women. He hadn't noticed a ring on Libby's left hand, which led him to assume the baby's father hadn't even married her to give his future child a name. Who did that?

"Sam!" he bellowed. "Get your ass home!"

A good half mile off, car headlights shone in the direction of Heath's cabin.

His mom, arriving to save the day?

He loved her. He honestly didn't mean for them to always be at odds, but for as long as he could remember, she'd had the need to save every broken animal and person in her world. What she couldn't seem to grasp was the fact that he was beyond saving. He had, for all practical purposes, died with Patricia—even his CO had said as much when he'd sent him packing. Being put on indefinite leave for failure to perform his duties had been one of Heath's greatest shames, but what was done was done.

No going back now.

"Heath?" His mom's voice carried through the ever-darkening gloom. "Where are you, hon?"

He groaned. Why couldn't she just go away?

If, God forbid, the worst had happened to Sam, the last thing Heath wanted was an audience when he broke down.

"Heath?" She sounded closer—a lot closer, when she rounded the trail's nearest bend. "There you are."

"God, Mom, I told you I've got this handled."

She shined a high-beam flashlight in his eyes. "Have you found him yet?"

"No."

"Then you obviously haven't handled squat."

"You look like you're about to pop," said one of the inn's fishermen to Libby after placing a bag of pretzels and a Snickers bar on the chest-high counter. The guy's thick, red curls stuck out the bottom of a hat covered in fishing lures. "When're you due?"

"Third week in July." Libby knew she should have looked forward to her child's entry into the world, but with her life so uncertain, the only thing the date brought was dread.

He whistled. "My wife just had our fifth, and I thought you look awfully close to the big day. Know what you're having?"

"A girl." Libby forced her usual smile. "I'm excited to finally meet her, but also a little scared."

"You'll be fine," the kindly man said with a wink. "Although, my wife would smack me if I went so far as calling labor easy."

Laughing, Libby said, "Honestly? That's the least of my worries. It's what happens once I take my baby home that has me spooked."

Even thirty minutes after the man left, Libby couldn't resume her interest in the romantic comedy she'd borrowed from Gretta's extensive library.

Libby's perch on the desk stool unfortunately afforded an excellent view of the landline phone.

It stared at her, taunted her, made her feel like a fool for not having long since dialed her parents' familiar number.

She'd always heard about the evils of pride, but lately, she felt at constant war with the emotion. Was it pride keeping her from crawling back to her folks in her current defeated state? Or self-preservation? With a baby on the way, did she even have the right to put her own desires ahead of her child's basic needs and protection?

Pressing the heels of her hands to her forehead, she willed an answer to come, when clearly this wasn't a simple black-and-white decision, but one shaded with a myriad of grays.

At her high school graduation dinner, when her parents told her that to pursue a career in art was ridiculous, that after college she was destined to spend a few years in a low-profile advertising position, then settle into a life as a society wife and mom—just like her own mother—Libby had initially rebelled by running with a bad crowd.

That summer, a protest rally gone horribly wrong had landed her in jail for vandalism. Her father had bailed her out, but basically handed her the edict that from here on out, it was either his way or she needed to hit the highway. She'd chosen the highway, and with him calling her a disappointment and loser on her way out his front door, she'd never looked back.

In the five years since leaving her prestigious Seattle address, she'd spoken only to her mother, and only on Christmas. Each time, her mother had begged her to come home. When Libby asked if her father's opinion of her lifestyle had changed, and her mother reported it had not, Libby politely ended their conversations and prayed that by the next year, her father would come around.

The fact that she was now broke, knocked up by a man who'd left her and she didn't even own a running car proved that everything her father had said about her being a loser was true. Was she destined to become a bad mom, as well?

"I don't feel comfortable leaving you."

"Go. I'm fine." Heath crossed his arms in a defensive posture. For the past two hours, he and his mom had crisscrossed the family land, looking for his dog. When they had no luck, she'd turned chatty, which only pushed him deeper inside his own tortured thoughts. Was Sam dead? Lying hurt somewhere?

Images of the dog led Heath's mind's eye to Patricia's dark last days. She'd been in such pain and he'd been powerless to do anything to help, other than demand more meds. To feel such helplessness for a woman he'd loved so insanely, deeply, completely had been far worse on him than any physical pain he might one day endure.

Having loved the deepest, and now hurt the deepest, what else was left?

"Great," his mom said. "You're *fine*—again. Only, clearly you're not, so whether you like it or not, I'll get Uncle Morris to look after the motel tomorrow, then I'll be out to help search for Sam."

"For the last time…" Heath cocked his head back, staring up at the stars. Common sense told him he needed all the help he could get in looking for Sam, but a sick foreboding got in the way. If the worst had happened, Heath would somehow have to deal with it in his own private way. "Thanks, but no thanks. I just want to be left alone."

"Duly noted." She took her keys from her jeans front pocket, then kissed his cheek. "See you first thing in the morning."

"Run into any trouble?" Gretta asked Libby the next morning from behind the wheel of her forest-green Ford Explorer. The fog had been as thick as it was the day before, but by nine, warm sun had rapidly burned it off.

"Nope. Everything was quiet, just like you'd expected." It'd been late when Gretta returned from Heath's, so they hadn't had much time to talk. It had been a long day, and Libby had struggled to keep her eyes open.

In her cozy room, she'd changed into pajamas and reveled in the luxury of indoor plumbing. When she'd slipped between cool sheets and eased her head onto not one, but two downy pillows, for the first time in months, she'd happily sighed with contentment.

Cupping her hands to her belly, she'd closed her eyes and smiled. But then her eyes popped open. All she could think of while drifting off to sleep was Heath.

The kind of warmhearted, honorable man she'd always secretly yearned for, but knew a broken mess like her would never deserve.

"Thanks for riding out here with me." Gretta turned onto the desolate road leading to Heath's dirt lane. "I'll have to introduce you to my brother when we get back. Morris has been married four—maybe five times?" She scratched her head. "After three I lost count. He's a hopeless romantic. He retired from the navy, made a fortune in the private sector and now I swear his only goal in life is making me crazy, asking for love advice." She paused for air. "He is a doll about helping out with the motel, though. He loves to cook, so the diner's his baby. The motel and restaurant have been in our family for generations. The two of us grew up in the little house behind it. After Heath's dad died, I moved back."

"It's good you and Morris are close." Libby angled on the seat as best she could to face Heath's mom. "I'm an only child, but always wanted a brother or sister."

Gretta snorted. "Be careful what you wish for. Having a sibling hasn't been all sunshine and roses. Morris and my husband—God rest his soul—used to get into horrible rows."

"Oh?" Libby didn't bother asking why, since she assumed chatty Gretta would soon enough fill her in with the details.

"My Vinnie—Heath's father—was a no-nonsense man. I guess twenty years in the military will do that to a person. Not long after he took retirement, we moved back here to take over the motel from my parents. Heath was such a moody teen in those days. He's named after Heathcliff from *Wuthering Heights*. Never did I think he'd turn out to have the character's same brooding disposition. Did I curse my own son?"

"I'm sure not." Although Libby had been curious about Vinnie and Morris's feud, anything about the elusive Heath was infinitely more entertaining. "Has he always been quiet and gloomy?"

"Not at all. In high school he was homecoming king, and made quite a splash on the basketball team. Everyone loved him—but he had his occasional spells when he enjoyed going off in the woods for fishing and hunting. In the navy—did you know he was a SEAL? He was all the time earning medals. But when he lost Patricia, he just gave up. Breaks my heart. Really does."

"I'm sure."

"Another thing that gets my goat is…"

Libby politely acknowledged Gretta's latest monologue, regarding her neighbor's refusal to plant an appropriate amount of potted flowers for the upcoming Independence Day festivities. But mostly, she stared out at the wall of green on either side of the road, wondering at the vast, remote stretch of land and the odds of Heath ever finding his dog.

Funny, a day earlier, though Libby always viewed her cup as half-full, lately, she'd begun doubting this practice. Beyond her healthy pregnancy, pretty much nothing before meeting the Stones had gone right. Now that she'd heard even part of Heath's tragic story, she was embarrassed for believing she had problems at all. No one had died—well, unless she counted the small piece of herself she'd have to abandon upon returning to her parents' home. She didn't doubt for a moment they'd take her and her baby in, but with the expectation she play by their rules, tossing aside her own hopes and dreams.

After a fitful night's sleep, Heath woke at dawn to resume his search for Sam.

He'd been out a few hours, then returned to the cabin to grab energy bars and more water.

The previous night, when his mom told him she'd be back, he'd hoped Uncle Morris was so busy with the diner that he wouldn't be able to help with the motel—in fact, he'd have rather she sent her brother as her proxy. Heath's easygoing uncle wasn't constantly nagging with questions, and he sure as hell would never be so insensitive as to suggest he "climb back on his horse" to find a new love as Gretta occasionally liked to do.

What kind of Happy Land planet was his mom living on that she believed for one second he'd ever be able to replace Patricia? The very idea was insulting.

After downing a piece of white bread smeared with peanut butter, he was loading bottled water into his knapsack when a car roared down his road.

While his initial thought was to punch a hole through the nearest wall, he soon enough realized that since his home was built of logs, that might not be such a great idea for his fist.

A minute later he glanced out the open front door to see his mom's perpetual smile. Making matters worse was the fact that she'd dragged Libby along with her.

Hands in his pockets, he did the right thing by heading out to the SUV to greet them, though he wanted nothing to do with either of their cheery smiles.

"Any luck?" his mom asked, first out of the car.

"Nope."

Libby had opened her door, but clearly needed help getting out. On autopilot, he went to her, steeling himself to ignore her pretty floral smell and the way her petite frame made him feel oversized and all thumbs. "Here we go again...."

"This does feel familiar." Her friendly grin did uncomfortable things to his gut. Made him wistful for days when he used to have an easy smile. Now nothing was easy—especially being around this very pregnant woman who reminded him all too much of what he'd always dreamed his life would be.

"Libby," his mom said, "I didn't even think to ask, but did you have breakfast?"

"No, ma'am."

Gretta conked her forehead. "I'm the worst hostess ever." She turned toward the cabin. "Let me whip up grub for us all, then we'll start our search. Heath, how about showing Libby the bench Grandpa made for your grandmother."

Lips pressed tight, Heath looked to the sky, willing patience for his mom to rain down on him.

"She's a pistol," Libby noted.

"That's one way of putting it." He gestured toward the pine needle–strewn trail leading to the property's bluff. "Feel up to a short walk?"

"Sure, though I'm not exactly steady."

"Let me take your arm—just in case. Last thing I need on top of my missing dog is a busted-up pregnant lady."

Laughing, she shook her head. "Thanks. I think?"

He shot her a sideways glance and came damn close to cracking his own grin while taking hold of her arm. It couldn't have been over fifty yards to the bluff, but worry over his guest's well-being had Heath working up a sweat.

Finally, they made it. Heath tried corralling Libby onto the bench his grandfather made as a romantic gift decades earlier, but she wasn't having it.

"Look at this view...." The awe he used to feel for the land rang through in her breathy tone. "It's amazing. The sun looks like diamonds on the water. Don't you feel like you can see all the way to Japan?"

"Don't get too close to the edge." She stood only a foot away from the two-hundred-foot drop.

"I'm fine," she assured him. "I've always had a great sense of—" In turning to face him, she wobbled.

Heath ran to her, tugging her into the safety of his arms. "Why can't you listen?"

With her baby bump pressed against areas it had no business

being, he set her a safe distance back while trying to figure out why just touching her produced such visceral results.

"I told you I was fine," she snapped. "Stop being such a worrywart."

Arms folded, he said, "My apologies for yet again charging to your rescue."

She held her arms defensively crossed over her chest, as well. "Did it ever occur to you that I don't need saving? That I'm doing fine all on my own?"

"Which is why you're living on charity until your car gets fixed? Even then, how are you planning to reimburse Hal?" The moment the acidic questions left Heath's mouth, he regretted them. He especially regretted the telltale signs of tears shimmering in Libby's sky-blue eyes. "I'm sorry."

He approached her, held out his hands to maybe touch her, but then thought better and backed away.

"Doesn't matter," she said with a shrug. "What would an apology help when what you said is true?"

"Yeah, but…" She'd returned to the ledge, which made his pulse race uncomfortably. Why the hell couldn't she just behave?

"Stop. I'm sorry your mom dragged me out here. After we eat, I'll ask her to take me back to the motel, and with any luck, you'll never see me again."

"Libby…" He rammed his hands into his pockets. In an odd way, even saying her name felt uncomfortably intimate.

"No, really, just hush. You're not the only one with troubles, you know? Maybe I didn't lose a spouse, but—"

"Mom told you about Patricia?"

Hand over her mouth, she nodded.

Was nothing sacred?

"I'm sorry for your loss, but that doesn't give you the right to take your pain out on others—especially your sweet mom."

No longer in the mood for sightseeing, Heath turned his back on the pint-size pain in his ass by heading back down the trail.

"What?" she called after him. "You got your feelings hurt, so you're just going to leave?"

Had she been a dude, he'd have flipped her a backhanded bird.

"Fine! Be that way!" she hollered after him. "Being sad won't fix anything, you know! Just makes you more sad, and—"

When she punctuated her sentence with a yelp, despite his frustration, he turned and ran in her direction. What the hell kind of trouble had she gotten herself into this time?

Only once he reached her, he found her yards down the bluff, pointing to a limp ball of fur, far down on the rocks below. Heath's mouth went dry, and his stomach roiled.

"I-is that your dog?"

CHAPTER FOUR

CARING LITTLE ABOUT his own personal safety, Heath sprinted a few hundred more yards down the bluff's edge until he reached the only somewhat sane route to the crashing surf.

After losing Patricia, he'd sworn to never pray again, and he held that promise even now. The concrete hardening his emotions told him this mission was all about recovery rather than rescue. As much as he'd loved that dog, no way would Heath leave Sam's body exposed to be pecked off bit by bit by scavengers.

The ground constantly gave way beneath him, as the rocks clattered in what had become a dangerous slide. Had he the slightest lick of good sense, he would have gone farther down the bluff to the established trail he usually used to access the beach, but in this case, urgency won over practicality.

Upon finally reaching the rocky shore, he ran until his lungs ached.

There was no hurry. No way even a tough guy like Sam could've possibly survived that fall, so why couldn't Heath stop running to get to him? Why couldn't he shake the feeling that just as it had on that sunny day when Patricia had slipped from him, his life was spinning out of control.

Sure, Sam was just a dog, but most days that mutt felt like

the only thing keeping Heath sane. Sam gave him a reason to get up every morning. Beyond the necessities of keeping him fed and watered and letting him in and out, Heath had found solace in watching his dog's tail wag the whole ride to their favorite fishing hole, or hearing him bark when the mutt chased after his ratty old tennis ball.

Twenty yards out, Heath hunched over, bracing his hands on his knees. He couldn't bear going farther.

Eyes squeezed shut, all he saw was the hospice nurse dragging that damned yellow sheet over Patricia's dear, faint smile. Ever since, he'd hated the color almost as much as he hated life.

"What're you doing?" a faint, wind-tossed voice called from above. "Hurry, Heath! We need to get him to a vet."

What was wrong with her?

Couldn't she see he was in pain? Why was she even there, when all he wanted was to be left alone?

"Run!" she hollered.

In a mental fog, Heath raised his gaze to Libby, only to find her animated and waving toward poor Sam's lifeless body. What was wrong with her that at a time like this, she refused to give him space?

"Heath, look at him! He's trying to wag his tail! Don't you know he's alive?"

Alive?

She might as well have been speaking Latin for all the sense the word made in Heath's grief-stricken mind. Hope had long since left his vocabulary.

But then a strange thing happened....

Seagulls rioted near Sam's body, and Sam gave a short *woof,* sending the birds flying.

Charging to action, Heath made it to Sam's side in well under a minute. He kneeled to scoop Sam into his arms, and instead of the cold, salt water–matted fur he'd expected, he was met with solid warmth, a whimper, a feeble tail wag.

Was he dreaming? Had he really been given this second chance?

A quick inspection of his dog showed why Sam hadn't come home. His feet were covered in purple sea urchin spikes. The urchins weren't poisonous, but clearly painful and if it hadn't already, infection was likely to set in.

Shooting to action, uncaring of his own comfort, Heath knelt in the rising surf. Cold water soaked his legs, but he ignored any physical pain to gingerly pluck spike after spike from the swollen and clearly tender pads of Sam's paws.

"Hang in there," Heath soothed, 100 percent focused on the task at hand. "We'll get all of these things out, then run you to the vet. In a few days, you'll be good as new."

Once again having purpose drove Heath to work even more efficiently. Guilt for not having thought to look for Sam on the beach much sooner caused acid to rise from his stomach and high into his throat until bile flavored his tongue.

"I'm sorry," Heath said, stroking behind the dog's silky ears.

Sam whined, lurching forward when Heath tugged at a particularly large and deep spike.

"Be gentle," a soft voice said behind him. Libby had somehow waddled her way to the beach and lowered herself onto a sun-bleached driftwood log.

"You shouldn't be down here." Though he couldn't have begun to explain why, Heath resented her presence. As a man who'd spent years in the business of saving others, it was a rush to once again be on the job. The purpose and drive felt damn good. The knowledge that for once in a very long time he was making a positive difference—if only to his dog—deeply mattered.

"I thought you might need help. What happened? How did he even get down here?"

"How do you think?" he growled. One glance at her crestfallen expression left Heath ashamed of his sharp words. "Sorry.

I've got enough on my plate in carrying Sam safely up the bluff. I don't want to have to worry about you, too."

"Who said you had to?"

Having removed all the spikes, Heath wedged his hands under the dog's fragile frame. Due to his negligence in not having remembered how much Sam enjoyed barking at the occasional sea lions who hung out on the point, the dog had been a while without food or water.

Crashing surf must've muted his bark.

"Drop it," Heath said, already heading for the trail.

"Why are you acting like this?" She chased after him, which only made him feel worse, but no way was he slowing. "You should be thrilled Sam's going to be okay."

"I am."

"So would it be too much of a strain to smile?"

"Shouldn't you worry more about keeping your footing on these rocks?" He kept his gaze focused on the winding dirt trail leading up the bluff.

Sam whined.

"Just a few more minutes, boy…" Heath had never wished more he'd kept up with his physical training. Were he in top form, scaling the hill would've been no big deal—not that it was difficult now, he just lacked the speed he'd once had.

"If you'd slow down just a little," Libby yapped, dogging his heels, "I could help soothe him."

"I've got this," he insisted. "*Please*—back the hell off."

She held up her hands, stepping away per his request, but her glistening tears left him feeling dirty inside. What kind of man yelled at a pregnant woman? What had happened to his honor?

Ha! He and honor and giving a damn about anything parted ways around about the same time the love of his life died in his arms.

"Would it kill you to let me in?" The woman might've temporarily let him be, but there she was, right back in his business. "I just want to help you—you know, like you helped me."

"I don't need help." Jaw clenched, Heath kept his gaze focused on the trail, mentally blocking Sam's heartbreaking whimpers.

By the time Heath reached the trailhead at the top of the bluff, the dog's ninety pounds had his untrained muscles screaming. How had he allowed himself to get so out of shape? Was he really so pathetic?

"You found him!" his mother cried as he approached. "Is he all right?"

"Find my keys!" he shouted back.

From behind him, the sounds of Libby's labored breathing did little to improve his mood.

"Would you like me to drive or hold poor Sam on the way to the vet?" Libby asked.

"You have no lap," he managed from between clenched teeth. His thigh muscles screamed from mounting the steep grade. Back when he'd been on the job, a trek like this would've been a cakewalk. Now, when his dog needed him, his body wasn't delivering as it should. And that further pissed him off. But the anger was good. It gave him much-needed energy to fuel the rest of his way to the truck.

"There are very few people I've disliked over the years," she said, "but you, Heath Stone, are definitely one of them. You're thickheaded and stubborn and obstinate."

"Aren't those all basically the same?"

"Well…" His mind's eye pictured her heart-shaped face all flushed and scrunched from concentration. And that image did nothing to improve his already dour mood. Because for the briefest flash of an instant, the thought of her coaxed his smile out of hiding. "They might be the same, but that's okay, because I wanted to emphasize how truly awful you are. When you first rescued me, I thought you were the kindest soul I'd ever encountered, but—"

"Do you ever shut up?"

"No! And for you to suggest it just makes me loathe you that much more."

At the top of the bluff, with both of them breathing heavy, Heath might have found the energy to laugh at her crazy-ass statement if he hadn't been carrying his injured dog. As if he cared if she *loathed* him.

But then, when the trail widened, she passed him, and all those blond curls bounced with her every snappy step. For a woman in her condition, she sure could move. Though from behind, she didn't even look pregnant. In fact, the way the morning sun shone through the flimsy fabric of her dress, not a whole lot of her was left to his imagination. His body's involuntary—and swift—reaction to the sight of her soft curves soured his mood all the more.

"I can't believe he's all right." His mom charged down the trail to meet them. "I set bowls of food and water in the truck."

"Thanks."

She reached to pet Sam, but Heath didn't want to slow his momentum.

"Why're you so prickly?" she asked when he sidestepped her. "Sam's safe. You should be overjoyed."

"I am. But he's not out of the woods yet." *Plus, I just had my first erection caused by a woman other than my wife....*

"He's going to be fine, you know?" While driving Heath's truck, for a split second, Libby took her eyes from the deserted highway to glance toward him and his dog. Sam had long since finished off his water and now started in on his food. His eyes had already brightened, and she found herself liking him much better than his doggy *dad.* "It's okay for you to relax."

"Could you please just focus on the road?"

Gretta followed behind them in her SUV.

Heath sat all stiff and straight and his handsome features were marred by the oddest expression. Was the big, strong guy trying not to cry? She'd been touched by seeing how much Sam meant to Heath. Was there a significance beyond any normal dog bond? Had he shared Sam with his wife?

Though it was none of her business, Libby couldn't help but ask, "Did you and your wife get Sam together?"

For the longest time, Heath remained silent. The way a muscle ticked in his hardened jaw set her on edge. Had she picked at a wound still too tender for casual conversation?

"I'm sorry." She steered the truck around a small branch that had fallen onto the road. "Please, forget I even asked."

"Yeah…" When he finally did speak, his tone was raspy. He stroked one of Sam's ears. "A friend told us his Lab-collie mix was having a litter, and we picked this guy out as a puppy. He had five littermates, but we could tell right away he was the one. He had spunk. He was always into everything. A little too curious for his own good—which I guess is how he landed in this predicament."

"Poor guy." She patted the dog's head.

A glance at Heath had her thinking he might say something more, but much to her disappointment, he did not. Which made no sense—not so much the lack of conversation, but why his sudden silence bothered her.

The relief shimmering through him after Sam's positive health report left Heath a little punch-drunk. He'd dodged a bullet with that one. Everyone from his mom and uncle to his old SEAL gang kept telling him it was time to move on. He needed to get on with things. Get back to work. There was always lots of *getting* in their well-meaning speeches, but none of their words amounted to squat when it came to making him feel even a fraction better about having lost his wife.

If he'd then lost her dog, too…

Well, he was just damned lucky it hadn't come to that.

The fact that he ultimately had Libby to thank for spotting Sam didn't escape him. As soon as the dog was doing better, maybe he'd take her to a formal thank-you lunch.

While you're feeling generous, think you owe her an apology for being such an ass on the beach?

Heath folded his arms, focusing on his dog rather than his pansy conscience, which had apparently gone as soft as his out-of-shape body.

"You're one lucky fella," said Cassidy Mitchell, the town veterinarian, while applying the last of Sam's bandages. She'd given him pain meds and antibiotics, and at the moment, with his giant pink tongue lolling and tail lightly thumping the metal exam table, the dog looked about as happy as could be expected. To Heath, the vet said, "Since you live a ways out, I'll send you home with supplies to clean and change these bandages. Once he starts feeling better, he's gonna want to go straight back to his normally wild ways, but just to be safe, I'd keep him inside and resting as much as he'll let you."

"Will do," he said, scooping Sam into his arms.

Gretta had left right after hearing Sam was okay. The commode in room ten had overflowed, and she'd had to meet the plumber. Heath would have called her, but he'd left his cell back at the cabin.

"Think you can handle carrying Sam's supplies?" the vet asked Libby.

Libby nodded, taking the multiple packages Cassidy's assistant had assembled.

"Sure you're okay?" the vet asked Libby. Heath had made brief introductions upon their arrival. "You've paled about ten shades since you first got here."

"I'm fine," Libby said, but having witnessed her previous faint, and seeing her expression look similar now, Heath wasn't so sure.

"Just in case…" The vet's teen assistant trailed them outside. "Let me take Sam's bandages and meds, and then you just open the truck door."

"You're both being silly." Libby made the trade-off, then opened the door. "I'm abso-lute-lee…"

Fine? Heath finished her sentence just as her legs buckled from beneath her.

CHAPTER FIVE

WITH SAM CENTERED on the truck's bench seat, Heath shot into action, now hefting Libby up next to the dog.

"She okay?" The pimple-faced teen assistant couldn't have been over sixteen. He'd paled as much as Libby.

"Hope so." Heath took Sam's supplies. "I'll run her to the clinic, though, to make sure."

Just as she had during her previous fainting spell, Libby woke within a few seconds. At which point, Heath, for the second time that morning, felt crazy-relieved. And guilty. If she hadn't followed him to the beach to get Sam, would she have passed out?

"Whoa…" She'd rested her head against the seat back, and now pressed her fingertips to her forehead. "What happened?"

"You fainted again."

She groaned. "That's not good."

"Nope. Which is why I'm running you to the doc."

"I'm all right. Please—" she stroked Sam's sleepy face "—take me to my room at the motel. I just need a nap."

"Probably, but I don't want it on my already full plate if it turns out there's something more wrong."

"Look…" Sighing, she hugged her belly. "The truth is, I can't afford to pay a doctor. I'm good. I *have* to be, because really, I don't have another choice."

"There's always a choice—this time, it's doing the responsible thing for your baby by letting me pay for your treatment."

"That's not necessary. I'm already feeling better."

"Perfect. Then you won't mind me wasting my own money to prove it."

Other than her pressing her lips together a bit tighter, Libby showed no other emotion. He was glad, because the day had been draining enough without her launching another fight.

He pulled to a stop at the red light on Archer.

With the Fourth of July so close, carnies were hard at work assembling rides on the elementary school's soccer field. The Tilt-a-Whirl resembled a praying mantis with its legs still folded on the flatbed trailer where it lived when it wasn't at play.

Back when he'd been a kid visiting his grandparents over the holiday while his dad was on leave, the annual carnival that started on the first was everything. Corn dogs and funnel cakes. Losing a month's allowance worth of quarters on the Coin Dozer game. Best of all, spending time with his family, back when they really had been a family.

The light changed and he made a left, heading toward the clinic.

With Sam peacefully napping and a warm summer breeze riffling his hair through the open windows, Heath could've almost been at peace if it weren't for the faint sniffles of Libby crying.

In no way prepared to deal with drama in the form of female tears—especially the pregnancy tears his married friends warned him were particularly potent—he tightened his grip on the wheel.

A few minutes later, past the fire station and library and the retirement home where, on a trip home for Easter, he and Patricia had teased each other about moving into when they both grew old, Heath pulled into the clinic's freshly blacktopped parking lot. The asphalt sounded sticky beneath the truck's tires and the pungent smell had Libby crinkling her nose.

"This is an all-around bad idea. I feel great. And what're we going to do with Sam?"

Heath drove to the far side of the lot, parking beneath a row of Douglas firs on a section of pavement still old and sun-faded.

Sam was fast asleep, and judging by his snores, would be for a while. The day was fine. The temperature was in the mid-seventies. With the windows down, he'd be equally as content in the truck as he would've been on the living room couch.

"He's gonna nap, just like the vet wanted."

One hand on her belly, the other on her door, Libby still looked unsure. In that instant, she looked so alone and afraid, something in his long-frozen heart gave way.

He wasn't a monster; he was just a man who'd essentially given up on his own life, but that didn't mean he had the right to inflict his messed-up shit on this lost soul.

He tentatively reached out for her, for an endless few seconds, hovering his hand in the neutral zone over Sam before reaching the rest of the way to Libby's forearm. Upon making contact, her vulnerability made him want to be strong. Not for himself, but for this fragile woman with an innocent child growing inside.

After giving her a gentle and what he hoped was a reassuring squeeze, they made eye contact for only an instant. He couldn't have stood more, so he looked away, swallowing hard, wishing his pulse to slow. He was afraid, so very afraid, but of what he couldn't comprehend. "Let's, ah, head inside. Get you checked out."

Her eyes shone, and she also shifted her gaze, sniffling before opening her door.

Heath hustled to her side of the vehicle in order to help her down.

It had been years since he'd been to Doc Meadows, but everyone in town knew appointments were welcome, but if you had something come up, the doctor and his nurse would stay as late as necessary to ensure everyone with a need was seen.

"Sure is pretty for a clinic…." Libby said, peering up at the three-story Victorian.

"Used to belong to one of the summer people."

"Summer people?"

"Rich folks from Portland, even San Francisco, who used to come here to spend their summers on the shore. After the 1942 fire, hardly any homes were left. This one was owned by a bank president whose wife fancied herself to be a *shade tree* architect." Heath was glad for the story. It distracted him from Libby's slow pace—more guilt stemming from the realization that he should have driven her to the door. What kind of idiot was he to have made her walk? "Want me to go get the truck?"

"For what?" She pressed her hands to the small of her back.

"So you don't have to exert yourself."

She waved off his concern. "You worry too much. And what's up with this new, polite travelogue version of your formerly crotchety self?"

"I'm not crotchety—reserved, maybe. Definitely not crotchety."

"If you say so…" He wasn't sure how she managed, but after casting him an exaggerated wink and grin, she sashayed right past him and mounted the stairs.

"You shouldn't be taking off like that," he urged, staying behind her in case she fell—at least that's the line he fed himself in order to not feel like a creeper for having accidentally caught himself yet again checking out her behind. "Last thing I need is for you to pull another fainting spell."

"I won't," she said from the top of the stairs, even though her exaggerated breathing told him she was winded.

He opened the door for her, ushering her inside the waiting room that his mom told him used to be the front parlor where Ingrid Mortimer—the former lady of the house—served formal tea every summer Sunday afternoon. He was just debating on whether or not to share the information with Libby, when the doctor's receptionist, Eloise Hunter, shot out from behind her desk to usher Libby into a wheelchair.

"You poor thing," Eloise clucked. The woman not only stood six feet tall—not counting her big red hair bun—but she was big around, too. And mean. But then his senior year in high school, she had caught him cutting all the roses from her garden for his latest crush. "Doc Mitchell's office called and said you'd be coming. We've got a room all ready for you." She glared at Heath, then said, "Your mother told me you dragged this poor girl all the way down Poplar's Bluff to get Sam. What's the matter with you?"

Seriously? "I didn't—"

"Don't blame him," Libby said to Eloise with one of her big grins. "I made it to the beach all on my own. I'm probably just a little tired."

Eloise didn't look so sure. "Just to be safe, let's let the doc have a look at you. Can't be too cautious when there's a little one involved." After another pursed-lip glare in Heath's direction, the receptionist ordered Heath to stay in the empty waiting area while she wheeled Libby off to an exam room.

For the longest time, Heath just sat there, staring at the overly fussy floral wallpaper.

He picked up a tattered copy of *People*. But the last thing he was interested in was some starlet's issues with drugs.

A good ten minutes later, Eloise returned. "Libby sure is a pretty little thing. Seems like she has a real sweet spirit."

"Yeah." He feigned renewed interest in his magazine.

Ten more minutes passed, then thirty.

He checked on Sam. Found the temperature in the truck still pleasant and the dog lightly snoring.

Back in the waiting area, Heath wasn't sure what to do with his arms and legs. He felt all squirmy—like a little kid forced to sit too long on a church pew.

What was going on back in that exam room? Was Libby all

right? Had she really hurt herself and the baby? If so, was it his fault? He should've insisted she stay up at the cabin with his mom. But then hadn't he told her to go back, and she'd ignored him?

Leaning forward, he rested his forearms on his thighs.

Honest to God, back when he'd been working, he'd waited out terrorists without feeling this tense. Even in the short time he'd known her, Libby had gotten under his skin. She had an energy about her—a spark, for lack of a better word—that struck him as pure radiance. For someone who had lived the past year and more in total emotional darkness, he was not only unaccustomed to being in the presence of light, but being around her physically hurt. It reminded him how much fun he and Patricia used to have, and how quickly that joy had been snatched away.

"You're sure you haven't had any spotting?" Kindly Doc Meadows asked the question while still making notes in Libby's newly made chart.

"No, sir. Other than being tired—and my back always hurting—I feel great."

"Hmm…" He removed his glasses, staring out the window at the clinic's parklike grounds. Not only was there a thick lawn, but there was also a garden blooming with riotous color and a meandering brick path that led to a gazebo. "Your blood pressure's slightly elevated, but the baby's heartbeat's nice and strong. We'll have to wait for your blood work and urinalysis to come back from the lab to have any definitive answers as to why you're fainting, but honestly, I think you're just plum worn-out. Do you have family you can stay with for the last few weeks of your pregnancy?"

Libby shook her head, though inwardly groaned. What should she say? Of course, she *had* family, but she wasn't ready to face them—not yet.

You make me ashamed to call you my daughter! Her father's

anger still raged in her head. *Go on, get the hell out of here and don't* ever *come back!*

The doctor sighed. "Pending no further immediate trouble, what I want you to do is get plenty of rest—and by plenty, I mean unless you're up for a shower or to tinkle, I want you off your feet. I hear you're staying with Gretta, and I know she'll take real good care of you."

"Thank you."

"You bet. But call if you experience anything out of the ordinary. Then we'll want to run you up to Coos Bay for an ultrasound and further testing."

"Sounds like a plan." A plan Libby had no intention of letting come to fruition. She couldn't imagine what that would cost, and she was already so deeply in debt to Heath and his mom that Libby wasn't sure how she'd ever see her way out.

"She still back there?"

Heath had been blessedly close to drifting off, when his meddling mother appeared in the clinic waiting room.

"Gretta Stone! Aren't you a sight for sore eyes." Eloise lumbered around the side of her desk to give Heath's mom a warm hug. Heath, on the other hand, got another squinty-eyed glare. "It's been forever since I've seen you."

"I know, I know," his mother said. "What with the motel's business picking up and getting ready for the Fourth, I feel like I don't have time to think, let alone breathe or play Friday night poker with my girlfriends."

"Well, just as soon as you steal the time, we'd love having you back. Clara Foster made the most incredible artichoke dip last week. You know how I've been going to the Weight Watchers meetings over in Coos Bay? Well, let's just say her dip ruined my whole week's points."

After both women laughed, then shared another hug, Heath had reached the end of his proverbial rope when it came to female small talk. "Eloise, don't you think you should check on Libby?"

"Heath!" Now, his mom was the one casting daggers. "Mind your manners."

Mind my manners? What was he, like, twelve? "All I want to know is if Libby's all right. She's been back there for over an hour. I've got Sam in the truck, and if it's going to be much longer, I need to—"

"You run on home, and get poor Sam settled." After patting his back, Gretta made a few motherly clucking sounds. "I'll take care of our little Libby."

Our Libby? When had that happened? They'd only known the woman barely over a day.

"Go on," Eloise urged, making sweeping gestures to send him on his way. "Your mom and I have this handled. Besides, I wanna hear firsthand what's going on with Hal."

Heath's eyes narrowed. "What do you mean? He has to find parts."

Eloise cast what he could only guess was a conspiratorial grin and wink in his mother's direction. "Oh—Gretta knows full well I'm not talking about car parts."

Both women found this hilarious.

Heath ignored them.

His mom's offer to deal with Libby's situation presented quite a dilemma. On the one hand, he'd like nothing more than to return to his cabin and stay there a month until he ran out of supplies. On the other, what kind of man had he become to abandon a pregnant woman? Especially since she might not have pushed herself hard enough to have landed up here if he hadn't been so short with her. Still, hadn't he done his part by delivering her to the doctor? What else could he actually do?

The decent thing—his conscience provided. *Like staying here long enough to ensure she's all right.*

Had he been on his own, he'd have growled.

* * *

"Oh, good." Lacy Claussen, the nurse driving Libby's wheelchair, parked her in the reception room. "Looks like you have a couple options for getting back to the motel."

"Thanks," Libby said, pushing herself up, only to have the nurse give her a gentle nudge back down.

"You heard what the doctor advised. You get to be pampered. Let me wheel you to your ride."

"All of this really isn't necessary," Libby complained, but she was thoroughly weary. She suspected her forced smile failed to reach her eyes and even though she discreetly covered a yawn, exhaustion sagged her shoulders.

"Nonsense." Gretta slapped the magazine she'd been reading on a side table. "Let's get you home and in bed, and then I'll fix you a nice, hearty stew. You do like stew, don't you?"

Tears welling in her eyes, Libby nodded.

What was she thinking? Allowing this dear woman to continue caring for her when she had a perfectly good family a mere phone call away? Did that make her essentially guilty of duping these lovely people?

No. Eyes stinging from the effort of holding back tears, Libby promised herself that just as soon as she felt better, she'd work hard to repay every penny these nice people had spent.

"Aw, there's no crying in this clinic…." Eloise knelt, wrapping her arm around Libby's shoulders, giving her a squeeze. "After a few days' rest, you'll feel so much better."

Libby nodded, but she wished she could be sure.

And then there was Heath, standing away from her and Gretta and Eloise and Lacy. He'd crossed his arms and backed against the wall. As usual, his expression was grim, but if she was reading him right, not in an angry way. If anything, she would've sworn he seemed…concerned?

"Let's get going." Gretta thanked Eloise, and Lacy wheeled Libby out of the clinic and into bright sun.

Heath trailed behind.

She wanted to thank him again for bringing her to the clinic, but while the nurse helped her into Gretta's SUV, he spoke a moment with his mom and then, shoulders hunched and hands crammed into his jeans pockets, he crossed the parking lot to his truck.

What was it about him that spoke to her? Was it the fact that they were both avoiding the past? Sure, she might accomplish this goal by forcing a bright smile through every rough patch, while he glowered his way through, but on some level they were kindred spirits in that they'd both essentially suffered a loss. He'd lost his wife. She'd first lost her parents, then boyfriend, then spirit—which was why she'd been driving home. To wag her proverbial white flag in her father's condemning face.

"Comfortable?" Gretta asked, jolting Libby from her thoughts.

"Yes. Thank you."

"Everything okay? You're missing your usual smile."

Libby flashed her new friend a half version. "Sorry, guess it's just been a long day."

"That it has." Gretta started the vehicle, placed it in Drive, then veered across the mostly empty lot toward the street.

It took every shred of Libby's willpower not to look back. At Heath. At Sam. At the strange connection she already missed.

CHAPTER SIX

LIBBY WAS STARTING to feel like a broken record about telling Gretta and her brother, Morris, that their help wasn't necessary, but when it came to moving her few belongings from her motel room into the guest room in Gretta's personal home, they weren't paying her much attention.

"I think we got everything," Gretta said to Libby, whom she'd ordered onto a living room recliner.

Fred, Gretta's smelly bassett hound, wandered up to Libby, rubbing his snout under her draping hand.

"Where do you want this?" Morris stood at the front door with Libby's most prized possession—her potter's wheel.

Before Libby could even ask who'd brought it over from her car, Gretta directed her brother to the screened back porch. "Once Libby's feeling better, Heath thought she might want to wow us with her skills."

Heath had been the one thoughtful enough to bring her supplies? The notion that he'd cared warmed her through and through.

She hadn't done anything to deserve these strangers' kindness, but she sure appreciated it. "Gretta, I can't even begin to figure out how to thank you. Not many people would be so kind as to welcome a stranger, quite literally off the road, into their home."

"I'll let you in on a secret...." Gretta hefted Fred to a mound of quilts and chew toys in the corner, then collapsed onto the recliner opposite Libby. "Nothing makes me happier than rescuing a sweet stray from the side of the road. I found old Fred baying outside the elementary school. Somewhere around here are a pair of cats I found as kittens, hiding under a bush in front of the hardware store. When you first got here, though my heart couldn't help but reach out to you, I'm not naive to some of the ugliness that's out there in the world. I did a quick internet search on you—you know, just to make sure you didn't have an obvious criminal record—only to get a shock to find not only had you been arrested, but you also have a perfectly good family up in Seattle."

While Libby's heart raced, she could have sworn she actually felt the color drain from her face.

"You can stop looking so worried." Gretta flashed her usual kind smile.

Fred had left his appointed corner and now begged for Gretta to heft him onto her lap—which she did.

"I just, well..." Libby honestly wasn't sure what to say. She hadn't exactly lied to Gretta, but she certainly hadn't been a fountain of information.

"It's okay. As for your arrest, I abhor animal testing, and back in my youth, might've done the same thing. Now, in some cases, I suppose it's a necessary evil, but it still breaks my heart. As for the matter of why you haven't called your parents for help, I suppose that's for only you to know."

Libby sighed, covering her face with her hands. "The vandalism charge happened a long time ago. I got in with the wrong crowd, and thought we were just going to a peaceful protest rally. One thing led to another and one of the guys tossed a Molotov cocktail into a courtyard. Everyone was running and screaming and a few people were hurt. Police charged and dispensed tear gas. It was awful."

"I'll bet."

"As for my parents… Where do I even begin? Back then, my dad was mayor. Every time his reelection came around, he expected Mom and I to be part of his campaign. I was arrested during Dad's bid for a third term in office. His opponent used my actions against him, blasting the area with a smear campaign. You know the kind, 'If the mayor can't control his own daughter, how can we trust him to run our city?' The night of the election, after my dad's concession speech, the dark look he gave me…" She shivered. "In that moment, I believe he truly hated me. Mom, too."

"I doubt they *hated* you—at least from what little I know about you, you seem pleasant enough."

"*Pleasant* isn't exactly what they were going for in their offspring—at least my father sure wasn't."

"Got any peanut butter?" Gretta's brother popped his head through the kitchen pass-through.

"In the cabinet. But I'm making a double batch of stew, so don't eat three sandwiches."

"Yes, ma'am." The burly man with a thick head of salt-and-pepper hair saluted his sister using a couple slices of wheat bread, then ducked back into the kitchen.

"Sorry about that." Gretta stroked Fred's ears. "Where were we?"

"Nowhere. I shouldn't have said anything."

"You didn't." Heath's mom winked. "I did. And I'm happy to let you hide out here for however long it takes you to get your car fixed, but after that you should go see your folks—not only for the baby's sake, but yours. I don't know the entirety of what happened between you, but maybe it wasn't as bad as you remember?"

Sitting at the kitchen table with her feet up on a neighboring chair, chopping carrots for Gretta's stew, Libby couldn't get the older woman's words from her mind. Could she have misread her father's harsh words and tone? No. But every year on Christmas, when she spoke to her mom, a piece of her shattered upon hearing the crack in her mother's voice. Libby missed her mom something fierce, but how did she just forget the horrible things her dad had said? Especially when every word had been true.

Mark my words. If you don't go to college, you'll end up pregnant, destitute and alone.

As if her father's words had been prophetic, Libby had become a knocked-up loser.

Gretta's house phone rang.

When she answered, Libby didn't mean to eavesdrop, but it was kind of hard not to when she sat five feet away.

"But Heath…" Gretta sighed. "You're being silly…. Of course Sam's important, but I think he'll be fine long enough for you to pop over here to share a meal." She winced as she tried to unscrew the Bloody Mary mixer she told Libby she used as her top secret base for her beef stew. "All right, but don't blame me if both of you starve to death."

Upon disconnecting, Gretta tossed her phone to the counter. "That son of mine makes me crazy. I can't imagine what's gotten into him to make him even more antisocial than usual."

Libby feigned intense focus on chopping her remaining carrots, but during Gretta's conversation, an idea had crept into her head that now refused to let go. Was it possible Heath wouldn't come to dinner because of her?

The next morning, Heath awoke to a hard rain and Sam licking the underside of his palm.

Groaning, he eyed the dog. "Need to go out?"

A thumping tail told him his answer.

His grandfather had built the cabin with generous eaves intended to keep the woodpile dry, but they also worked as a dry spot for Sam to do his business.

The dog's hobble was slow, but his eyes had brightened and

other than not being able to move as fast as he liked, he looked none the worse for his adventure.

When Sam finished, Heath ushered him back inside, changed his bandages and fed him, then helped him onto the sofa.

When the dog cocked his head and looked longingly outside, Heath gave him a rawhide chew he hoped would keep him happy for at least a portion of the morning.

It was only seven, meaning he had way too much time between now and bedtime.

He wouldn't have minded going fishing, but with Sam out of commission, that idea was nixed.

Heath tried reading but couldn't get into the three-inch tome on Afghanistan history.

A shower took five minutes. Dressing and brushing his teeth another five. Downing an energy bar and sports drink killed another three minutes, according to the glowing nightstand alarm clock.

Frowning, he grabbed his iPad, intent on at least catching up on national news, but the rain screwed with his already sketchy wireless signal.

He picked up his phone to see if it worked any better, only to see he had a message—no doubt from his mom. He was in the process of auto-deleting it when he noticed the number wasn't familiar.

Playing it on speaker, he got a jolt to hear the familiar voice of his old navy SEAL buddy Mason, aka Snowman—because he was from Alaska. "Yo, Hopper, did you fall off the earth? Nice job of keeping in touch, loser. Anyway, I've got vacation time coming, and Hattie's wanting to get out of town. Sorry for the short notice, but wanna hook me and my fam up for a few days' lodging over the Fourth? Assuming you're alive—call me."

Heath played the message again, just to be sure he hadn't dreamed his old friend's voice. Talk about a blast from the past. An unwelcome blast. Still, considering how many times Mason had saved his ass out in the field, the least Heath could do was give him a place to stay.

Sighing, he dialed his friend's number, made requisite small talk, arranged for Mason, Hattie and their three kids to stay at his cabin for the dates they would be in town, and in general tried to sound normal even though nothing could be further from the truth.

He was happy for his friend's newfound familial bliss. He really was. But that didn't make the cold edge of jealousy slicing his gut any easier to bear. Back when his fellow SEAL team members called him Hopper because of his knack for jumping objects while in a full-on run, Heath had believed he had his whole life mapped out. If only he'd known back then what a joke that would turn out to be.

Upon hanging up, he spent the next couple hours cleaning, welcoming the distraction from his thoughts.

But then, as he took a break to down a sports drink, another thought struck.

If Mason, Hattie and crew were at his cabin, where did that leave him? It'd be no big deal to bunk with his mom.

What *would* be a big deal?

Bunking with his mom *and* Libby.

"This is such a fun surprise." Two days later, Heath realized he hadn't seen his mother so smiley since her pickled eggs had won first place at the county fair. She held open her front door for him, stepping aside as he entered. "I'd give you a room at the motel, but with the holiday, I'm booked. Since Libby's in the guest room, that leaves you on the sofa—but you've always said it's comfortable, right?"

"Thanks." Had she been anyone but his mother, Heath would've snarled.

"Hey!" Libby called from the screened back porch that ran the length of the two-bedroom house. She sat in a low folding chair, legs spread wide with her pottery wheel between them.

Her hands and forearms were coated with red clay, and she'd piled her pale curls into a messy, lopsided pile atop her head. Streaks of clay lined her cheeks and dots decorated her forehead and nose. Though outside rain continued to fall, her smile radiated light throughout the otherwise gray space. "How's Sam?"

"Conked out in the truck. I'll grab him once this rain lets up."

"Are you hungry?" his mom asked. "There's leftover stew. Plus, I made a nice chicken-and-rice casserole. Pineapple upside-down cake for dessert."

He couldn't help but groan with pleasure. As much as his mom drove him crazy, her cooking made everything better—if only for the short time it took to share the meal.

"I'm starving," he said, not sure what to do around Libby. She made him uncomfortable. She was too pregnant. Too smiley. And far too pretty for her own good—or, would that be his good?

"Sit with Libby." His mom pointed him to a lawn chair. "You two have a nice chat while I make you a plate."

Fred, never one to miss a suspected handout, stood and stretched from where he'd been napping alongside Libby's right foot to lumber after Gretta into the kitchen.

For a few awkward seconds, Heath wasn't sure what to say, but considering he still owed her for having found Sam, he cleared his throat, then noted, "Thought you were supposed to be resting?"

"This is restful for me. Nothing makes me happier than working with my clay. Thank you for retrieving it all from my car."

"Sure. It wasn't a big deal." He wanted to say more—*should* say more—but the honest to God truth was that the sight of Libby working her hands up and down the water-slick clay had pretty much left him speechless.

"I'm feeling so much better," she rattled on, "that I've made quite a few pieces, and your mom arranged for me to have a small booth at the holiday art fair."

"You feel up to that? It draws quite a crowd."

"I feel amazing." He believed it. Her skin glowed a healthy peach and her blue eyes shone brighter than they had in the short time he'd known her. "Maybe I'll even earn enough from sales to pay back you and your mom, plus have enough left to fix my car and be on my way. Because, even as sweet as your mom has been, the last thing I want is to be an imposition."

He liked the way she single-handedly carried the conversation. Took the pressure off of him. "Don't sweat it. I imagine Mom enjoys the company."

"Hope so." She went at it again with her clay. As much as Heath wanted to deny it, he found her actions erotic as hell—like a scene straight from the classic Demi Moore and Patrick Swayze movie, *Ghost*. He'd never admit to watching it, but as it was one of Patricia's all-time favorite movies, she'd watched it once a week near the end. It had brought her comfort—believing her soul lived on. Heath wanted desperately to believe, but the truth was, he couldn't get past his anger over her having been taken from him before their lives together had barely begun.

"Here you go." His mother presented him with a plate heaped with casserole—not that he was complaining. For the first time in…he couldn't remember when, he was starving.

"Thanks." He dug right in.

"When will Mason and Hattie be here?"

"They fly in on the red-eye tonight, stay in Portland, then drive down some time tomorrow."

"I'm excited to see those twins. And the baby must be walking by now."

"I suppose." What didn't she get about the fact that even if his old friends' kids were pole-vaulting, he didn't want to hear about it? Witnessing other people being happy in their marriages and lives only reminded him how meaningless his life had become.

A glance at Libby didn't help his worsening mood. Couldn't she *craft* like a normal person? Did she have to draw in her bottom lip every time she stroked the clay upward, then exhale on the downward strokes? She made pot-making look downright obscene.

Sure that's not your own mind lowering her perfectly normal activity to the gutter?

He scowled all the harder.

"It's good you're here." Gretta plucked dead leaves from the fern alongside her chair. "I was just thinking how Libby's going to need some sort of booth arrangement for the craft fair."

"Gretta…" Libby's nostrils lightly flared as she curved her delicate fingers around the top of whatever she was making. "You're sweet for even thinking of it, but I told you, I can make do with the folding table that's in the backseat of my car."

"Why make do, when we have a big, strapping man at our disposal?"

"Mom…" Heath had finished his food and now took his plate to the kitchen.

"What?" Unfortunately for him, Gretta followed. "I was thinking we could use that old picnic tent I've got in the shed to keep Libby in the shade, then you could come up with some sort of shelving system with some of your father's lumber scraps he left piled up in the shed. I've got plenty of tables from the motel's banquet hall, but you'll need to run by Hal's to get the rest of the finished goods Libby has in her car—speaking of which, has Hal called you with any reports on the repairs?"

"Stop," he said under his breath. "I see what you're trying to do, and it's not going to work—no, more than that, it's ridiculous and downright embarrassing."

"What're you talking about?" She put foil over the casserole pan.

Still whispering, he snapped, "Whatever matchmaking thing you're doing with Libby. Give it a rest."

"Why would you ever think I'd want the two of you together? She's way too nice to be stuck with grumpy old you." After kissing his cheek, she popped the casserole in the fridge. "Since the rain's let up, why don't you bring in Sam, then see about that tent. It's been years since I've had it out, so it might need a good washing. I've got a few minutes so I think I'll just pop over to Hal's for Libby's things."

"Aye, aye, Cap'n."

His mother didn't look amused by his mocking salute.

Feeling like a fool for bringing up his matchmaking suspicions, Heath figured that ratty old tent wasn't the only thing needing a good hosing down. Had he imagined the fix-up vibe his mom had going? Why else would she be so consumed with helping Libby?

Is it such a stretch to believe Gretta actually cares about her?

No. But there was caring on a basic level, and then there was this whole scene his mother had set up where Libby was magically part of the family. When he'd plucked her from the middle of the road, he'd assumed she'd be in their lives for maybe a day—tops. Now, here it was Day 5, and she needed to go.

Why? Why did it even matter if his mother had made a new friend? Had he really become so selfish he begrudged his mother's happiness?

Heath groaned, covering his face with his hands.

Honestly, it wasn't his mother's happiness that was the problem, but the way being around Libby made *him* feel. He felt alive. And for a man who hadn't seen life in anything for a very long time, the sensation was akin to falling. And he needed it to stop.

CHAPTER SEVEN

LIBBY WOKE JUST past 3:00 a.m. with raging indigestion and an aching lower back. It felt strange helping herself to milk from Gretta's fridge.

Despite Gretta's kind, reassuring words, Libby couldn't shake her wish that she'd met the woman under different circumstances. Circumstances that didn't leave Libby feeling deeply beholden, with no immediate way to repay Gretta's many kindnesses. The same sentiment applied to Heath. Actually, everyone in town from Hal to Eloise to Nurse Lacy and Doc Meadows had been kind. How was it that these relative strangers treated her with far more understanding and compassion than her actual family—or even, her baby's father—ever had?

Eyes stinging with pending tears, Libby filled her glass, then returned the milk to the fridge.

Fully awake and miserable from head to toe, she shuffled to the screened back porch, breathing deeply of the cool night air. The grass must have been recently mowed as the sweet scent laced every inhalation. Crickets chirped, reminding her of the many nights she'd spent with Liam in their tent.

Looking at the past two years of her life, she couldn't begin to process where things had gone so horribly wrong. At the time, immersed in the happy glow of what she'd thought had been forever-love with Liam, sleeping outdoors had seemed perfectly normal. Now, as if viewing her recent past from afar, she realized how dysfunctional her relationship had been all along.

Sighing, she eased onto a patio rocker and managed to raise her swollen feet onto the ottoman.

The four vases she'd thrown after convincing Gretta she was healthy enough to do light work stood in a neat row along Libby's portable drying rack, barely visible by the light of the crescent moon. Alongside that, her portable kiln was all plugged in and ready to go.

She was pushing her luck to think her pieces would dry in time for the art show, but it felt good at least trying. Even after drying, they'd still have to be bisque fired and glazed, before firing them again. But considering her pieces sold for over a hundred each, if they did finish in time, and the show pulled a nice crowd, she'd be well on her way to repaying the many debts she owed all over town.

A faint jingling, and then footsteps on the brick walk, alerted Libby to the fact that someone approached.

Heart racing, she gripped the armrests, praying whoever—whatever—headed her way, was just passing through.

When the shadowy figure of a man paused in front of the screen door, her mouth went dry as she fought the urge to panic from fear of an intruder.

From outside she heard, "Damn it, Sam, calm down before you hurt yourself even worse. Fred, you need to hurry."

Moments earlier, adrenaline had surged through her. Now she felt flooded by calm and the curious sense of awareness that hummed whenever she and Heath shared the same space.

"Need help?" Now that she knew who stood outside, it was easy enough to guess Sam's condition had improved enough that he'd gotten tangled in his leash.

"Libby?" Heath opened the creaky screen door for Sam to bound through. Fred begrudgingly followed, only to collapse in a weary heap on the doormat. "What're you doing up?"

"Hey, cutie," she said to Sam, returning his enthusiastic welcome with plenty of petting and a hug. "I'm so glad you're feeling better." To Heath, she said, "I'm up because I feel like crap. What's your excuse?"

He actually chuckled. The sound not only surprised her, but warmed her. "Honestly, pretty much the same reason, but a different cause. You're probably blaming the baby, but I'm holding Mom's sofa responsible for my aching back."

"I'm sorry. Her guest room should be yours."

He shrugged, taking the seat next to her. "It's no big deal. The walk already worked out the kinks. How about you?"

Laughing, she said, "I have a feeling it's going to be a while before my back sees improvement—no matter where I sleep."

"Hang tight for a sec...." As abruptly as he'd appeared, Heath vanished inside the dark house, leaving her on her own with Sam and a now-snoring Fred.

"Where do you think he's going?" she asked panting Sam.

All she got for an answer was a wagging tail.

From the kitchen came a series of beeps, then the microwave's hum. What in the world was Heath doing?

She tried shifting in her chair, but no position felt comfy.

A few minutes later, Heath reappeared. "Lean forward."

"W-what?" He held something about the size of a package of Oreos, but she couldn't be sure. Maybe she just had a wicked craving for cookies?

"Humor me, and just this once do as I ask."

She did. And when he stood alongside her, she was surprised to find his masculine scent already familiar. He smelled outdoorsy, like the pines surrounding his cabin and briny sea spray drifting off the Pacific. His nearness made her hyperaware—even more off balance than usual. The flirty young woman trapped inside her wanted to giggle. The soon-to-be mother told her to keep herself in check. Nothing about her situation gave her a logical reason to crave anything more from this man than casual conversation.

"Let me know if it's too hot," he said, pressing something deliciously warm against her back. Instant pain relief brought on chills, then gratitude so complete as to knot her throat. Whatever he'd done, she was grateful.

"What did you put back there?" She touched the soft warmth, but still couldn't tell what it was.

"You'd laugh if I told you." His white-toothed grin shone in the faint moonlight. The baby lightly kicked, or maybe it was the sight of him that somersaulted her tummy? He was just so darn handsome.

"Promise, I won't."

"Okay, so back when I was a Boy Scout, we used to volunteer down at the old folks' home. Lots of them complained about aches and pains, but they couldn't use heating pads in their wheelchairs because they had to be plugged in. So Mom helped us make corn bags."

"Wait—this is corn on my back?"

There he went again with his supercute grin. "Told you you'd laugh. But yeah, it works great on back pain. My old roomies gave me crap about mine, but I was always catching them using it."

"I don't blame them. This feels so good I could purr."

"I'm glad."

She was, too. Since they'd first met, Heath had sent mixed signals. Always helpful, but also standoffish. Maybe for the rest of her time in Bent Road they could now at least be friends?

"All right, well…" He stood, crossing his arms, noticeably slipping back into his former distant self. "I'm gonna try getting back to sleep. You probably should, too."

"Yes, Dad." She winked, but he'd already left her.

Which made her sad.

Sam had stayed behind, though, and he wandered up, nudging his snout under her palm.

"That man's a tough nut to crack, you know?"

The dog wagged his tail.

Libby took that as a sign that when it came to her assessment of Heath, the dog agreed.

Fred, however, kept snoring.

Late the next afternoon, Libby wandered out to the yard to check on Heath, only to get a cold reception.

"Thought you're supposed to be resting?"

"I am." Libby ignored the perma-scowl that'd taken up residence on Heath's handsome features, culminating in a furrow between his brows. "But I made a few more vases I needed to set on the drying rack. Since I'm up, I figured I'd see if you need anything. Water? A snack?"

"Thanks, but I'm good." He'd been outside most of the day, jury-rigging the picnic tent that'd been in worse shape than his mother had anticipated. "And you need to sit. Last thing I need is for you to topple over again."

"Are you this bossy with everyone, or just me?"

He sighed. "Really?"

"It's a legit question, Heath. I'm sorry if this project is an imposition. If you didn't want to do it, why didn't you just tell your mom 'no'?"

After setting down the hammer he'd used to drive two hollow aluminum posts together, he rolled his shoulders, looking anywhere but at her.

Sam, not fazed by his owner's gloomy demeanor, rolled onto his back, wagging his tail while partying in the grass.

Fred observed his hyper doggie companion with great disdain.

"Look—" Heath got back to work "—I don't have a problem building you a tent. I'm glad to do it. I just have a lot on my mind, all right?"

"Like what?"

"You asked me if I was bossy with everyone, well turnabout's fair play. Are you this nosy with everyone?"

She couldn't help but laugh. "Actually, yes. Now, is there anything I can do to help?"

"Can you hand sew?"

Nodding, she said, "Nothing fancy, but I know the basics."

"Great. If you'll sit, I'll bring you a project. Deal?"

"You don't have to talk down to me as if I'm a child."

He clamped his hand over his mouth as if he wanted to say something, but held himself in check. He even went so far as to turn away from her, but then he turned back. "From the day I first saw you, even you have to admit, you've been a straight-up mess. So can you cut me some slack for wanting to keep you in one piece until your baby pops out?"

"*Pops out?* Could you be any more insensitive?"

"Lady, you'd be amazed by what I can do." Though she was 100 percent sure he hadn't intended any naughty connotations, the part of her that hadn't had a decent kiss in months zoned in on the double entendre behind his words.

Face flushed, she looked away.

"You know what I mean."

Yes, unfortunately, she did. But her apparently filthy mind preferred her own special interpretation of his words!

But wait a minute… If he'd asked the question, didn't that imply he'd thought the same dirty thing as her?

"What bee crawled in your bonnet?"

"Huh?" Ten minutes later, finally Libby-free in his mom's shed, Heath looked up to find his uncle. Could this day get any worse?

"You're banging around in here loud enough that I heard you all the way up at the diner."

"Sorry. Guess I'm in a mood."

"Wouldn't have anything to do with a pregnant little blonde, would it?"

Heath groaned. Was he that transparent?

"Your mom says you've been an ass ever since Libby came

to town. And don't you have old friends staying at your cabin? Why aren't you visiting with them?"

"Mason and Hattie aren't due for another couple hours. They're stopping by for the cabin key."

"Good. Should we whip up a barbecue? I'm sure they won't feel like cooking after their drive."

"They won't be hungry." Heath screwed the side board into the base of the shelf he was making out of the scrap wood left from over half a century of motel and home repair projects. It'd be ugly, but maybe he could work magic with the gallons of leftover paint?

"How could you know something like that?" Uncle Morris grabbed a baby food jar his father had long ago filled with screws. "I'm in the food business, and everyone's hungry before, during and after travel."

"Is that a fact?"

"Proven. I see it every day at the diner." Right about now, Heath wished he'd told Mason he couldn't use his cabin. "And speaking of cooking, your mom said Libby's quite the baker. Did you know she made the apple pie we had for lunch?"

"Thought she wasn't supposed to be on her feet."

"Oh—she wasn't. Your mom made real sure Libby did everything from her seat at the kitchen table. What's her story, do you know?"

"Nope." And he didn't want to know any more than he already did. The fact that she was alone and pregnant was just plain wrong. What kind of man abandoned a woman he'd knocked up? Let alone his own child?

"Your mom told me Libby comes from Seattle blue bloods."

"Oh?" She never mentioned that.

"Makes me wonder what could've happened with her family that in her condition she'd rather bunk with Gretta and you than in some big mansion."

No kidding.

"All I'm saying is that there's more to her than meets the eye.

You might want to ask her about it. It's been my experience that women like that sort of thing—talking about themselves."

"Yeah?" Heath let his uncle's advice flow in one ear and right out the other. Why Libby apparently wanted nothing to do with her family was none of his business. Although, he did wonder if, like her ex, they'd somehow hurt her, too. If so, why? Sure, she was stubborn as hell, but in some ways that could be seen as an asset.

"But back to our barbecue, what do you think? Ribs? Chicken? Burgers and dogs?"

"I'm not hungry." Come to think of it, every once in a while he had caught Libby with a sad expression. He'd chalked it up to indigestion or lingering bad blood between her and her ex. It had never occurred to him she had trouble with her family. As much as his mom and uncle drove him nuts, he also knew they were unconditionally there for him if ever he needed their help or advice. How alone must she feel, with no one on her side? "Did Libby say anything else about her family?"

His uncle feigned interest in another baby food jar, this one filled with tacks. "Thought you weren't interested."

"I'm not," Heath said. Only for some inexplicable reason, he very much was.

Beneath a sky streaked in orange, pink, violet and blue, Libby stood on the fringe of the impromptu pool party and barbecue, intrigued by the discovery of yet another new side of Heath. While Heath's friend Hattie and Gretta played in the water with Hattie and Mason's three-year-old twins, Vivian and Vanessa, Heath tended ribs on the grill, catching up with Mason, who held the couple's one-year-old son.

Heath's whole demeanor had changed. He stood taller, spoke louder and seemed to possess a confidence she hadn't before seen. Was he putting on a show for his friend? Or was he really all of the sudden this self-assured?

Sam and Fred stood alongside the grill, both on alert in the event a rib accidentally fell into their waiting mouths.

"Libby!" Gretta called from the pool. The water was heated and steam rose, making an eerie scene with the glowing lights. "Join us! The water's bathtub warm!"

"I would," Libby lied, "but I don't have a suit." She was already self-conscious enough about her huge belly, no way did she plan on baring more than an inch of unnecessary skin. "I'll go help Morris in the kitchen."

"No, you won't! You're supposed to be resting. At least come dip your feet in the water."

Knowing Gretta wouldn't easily give up, Libby made her way to the pool stairs. She wore a maternity sundress, at least sparing her the embarrassment of needing help to roll up pant legs. After slipping off her flip-flops and keeping a tight grip on the shallow-end handrail, Libby managed to lower herself onto the still-warm pool deck while immersing her feet in sinfully warm water.

Eyes closed, she happily sighed. "That *does* feel good."

"Told you," Gretta said.

"As usual," Libby admitted, "you were right."

"Of course I was."

Like human atoms, the twins rocketed from the pool to chase each other and a barking Sam.

Fred wasn't budging from the grill.

Hal, holding a can of beer in his hand, hopped in the deep end where Gretta bobbed in her cute one-piece. The way they suddenly had their heads together, laughing, as if sharing a juicy secret, left Libby wondering if the two of them might be more than *just* friends.

The twins squealed their way onto the swing.

Sam leaped up to join them.

"They're a handful." Hattie grimaced.

"They're also adorable," Libby said. "I see the resemblance."

Hattie's smile faded. "Actually, they're not mine, but my sister's. She died shortly after they were born."

Hands to her mouth, Libby said, "I'm so sorry. I had no idea."

"It's okay," Hattie assured. "I mean, not that it's an ideal situation—obviously, I wish my sister were still with them, but Mason and I love them like they're our own."

"But the baby is yours?"

"Charlie?" She grinned. "Yep, I gave birth to all nine pounds of the little chubster. I feel for you being this close to delivering. Do you already have your delivery plan in place?"

"Not really." That fact brought her indigestion raging back. "With any luck, my car should be fixed long before July 23, which is my due date."

"Oh, sure," Hattie said. "I can't imagine it taking that long for a simple car repair. You'll want to be with your family by then."

Gretta and Hal swam to the stairs. "We're going to check on Morris. He's supposed to be making potato salad, but he's been gone long enough to grow the potatoes."

"That's a man for you," Hattie teased, giving Hal a playful wink. When Hal and Gretta were out of earshot, Hattie said, "Where were we? Oh—you were telling me about your family."

Once Gretta left, Libby wasn't sure what to say. She didn't want to be disrespectful to Heath's friend, but she also didn't want to launch into her depressing life story.

After a few awkward minutes, Hattie asked, "Did I just stick my foot in my mouth? It's kind of a specialty of mine, so if I did—sorry."

"It's okay." Rubbing her belly, Libby said, "I do need a plan for delivery, but until my car's fixed I'm kind of in limbo."

"Sure. I understand. Lucky for you, your car couldn't have broken down in a better place. The first time Mason brought me and the girls out here was not too long after Patricia's funeral. You do know about him losing his wife?"

Libby nodded.

"Well, it was a really horrible time. Heath was in his own

THE SEAL'S BABY

death spiral and no one could snap him out of it. When his commanding officer gave him the boot, and Heath came out here, about a month later, Mason and I flew out to check on him. Once we saw how pretty and peaceful Bent Road is, we understood why this was the best place for Heath to heal. Patricia was an interior designer. She carried herself with this sort of Grace Kelly elegance I always envied. Everything about her was perfect. Clothes, hair, makeup, body, complexion—flawless. And the worst thing was that she was also really—I mean, *really*—sweet, so you couldn't hate her."

Libby's gaze strayed to Heath. *So that's the kind of woman you loved. No wonder you want nothing to do with a stray like me.*

"When she died, our circle was seriously scared for Heath. He retreated further and further inside himself, until he couldn't even properly do his job. The day his CO handed him his walking papers was hard on the whole team. They all tried getting his mind off of his loss, but nothing worked. We SEAL wives are pretty close, and I suppose the real kicker to all of this is that we're a tough bunch, constantly forced to deal with the reality that one day any of our husbands could leave for work, only to never come home. All the guys have plans in place— you know, in case the worst ever happens. No one in a million years could've predicted Patricia would be first to go."

"That's so sad…." As if he'd somehow known they were talking about him, for a split second, Heath met Libby's stare before she sharply looked away.

"What's even worse is what's become of him since. Obviously, he'll never find anyone as perfect for him as Patricia, but surely there's a nice woman out there somewhere who would not only take care of him, but convince him he's too young to just give up."

"Yeah…that would be amazing." How many times had she wished for the same—to be with a man who loved her and cared for her as much as she did him—only to have ended up with a cheating creep like Liam?

"Gosh—" Hattie smacked her forehead "—how inconsiderate am I? Going on about poor Heath when I didn't even think to ask about why you're pregnant and on your own. Do you have a handsome sweetie worried about where you are?"

Unable to speak past the knot in her throat, Libby shook her head, then stood, making a mad dash for the house. Or, more specifically, the privacy of her room. Hattie seemed like a genuinely nice person who, in another life, Libby may have welcomed as a friend. But right now?

She couldn't bear revealing to one more person just what a mess her life actually was.

CHAPTER EIGHT

"Where'd Libby run off to?" Heath asked Hattie while Mason took the ribs from the grill.

"Not sure. She dashed out of here the way I used to when I was carrying this guy and needed a restroom." She gave baby Charlie a jiggle.

"Mom-ma!" the kid said with a smile that made Heath's heart ache. Is this the stage of life he and Patricia would've been at?

"I know," she said in a playful tone to Charlie, who'd fisted a wad of her long hair. "Momma's hair's exciting, isn't it? But please don't pull so hard."

"That's my boy." Mason gave his son a quick peck on his chubby cheek. "Already SEAL strong. But do take it easy on your gorgeous mother."

"Aw..." With their son squeezed between them and daughters chasing poor Sam all around the yard, Hattie and Mason kissed, in the process displaying far too much tongue for Heath's liking.

"Geez, guys, get a room."

"Don't be a hater," Mason said with a wag of the meat tongs. "Where should I put the ribs while I'm grilling the sausage?"

"Set 'em in there." Heath pointed toward what his mom called an "event hall" in her motel brochures, but was essentially a big room with lots of tables and chairs, a kitchenette, restroom and karaoke machine.

"Will do."

With his friend out of earshot, Heath asked Hattie, "Think you could maybe check on Libby?" he suggested, not wanting to seem as if he cared about her welfare, because he didn't—at least not in any way that mattered. Of course, he wished her healthy, but that was the extent of his concern.

"Why don't you?" Hattie was back to jiggling the baby. "I'd feel awkward—especially since now that I think about it, I'm afraid it was something I said that might've made her bolt."

"Hattie..." Weren't women supposed to know better than to run around upsetting pregnant women? Like, wasn't there a secret code about that sort of thing?

She winced. "It just slipped out, but I did ask her for the whereabouts of her baby daddy."

"Why? It's none of your business."

"Lighten up. It was an innocent enough question. And anyway, what does it matter to you? She's just staying over a couple days till she gets her car fixed. You'll never see her again."

"You're a mom. Since when did you become so insensitive?" He couldn't fathom why, but Heath found the notion of Libby leaving deeply troubling. Granted, she was too bright a light to be in his life, but to every so often have a fleeting taste of life's potential might not be all bad.

"You're a SEAL. Since when do you give two shits about anything remotely touchy-feely?" Only just realizing she'd cursed in front of the baby, she covered his little ears. "Earmuffs, sweetie. Momma didn't mean the bad word, but she spends too much time around sailors and she forgot how Uncle Heath sometimes makes her crazy."

"Whatever." After squeezing Charlie's sneaker-clad foot, Heath said, "Don't you believe a word of what she says, little man. Your mom's the true nutcase." To Hattie, he said, "Guess I'd better do damage control."

Heath wound his way through the ever-increasing crowd—a few of his mom's motel guests and Friday night poker group had joined the party, as well as Eloise, Doc Meadows, and even Hal and his two sons, who'd no doubt smelled the ribs' sweet sauce all the way from the garage.

Just past the pool deck, Heath did a double take.

Hal was slow dancing with Heath's mom to the country music playing over Gretta's newly installed outdoor sound system. Wait—*slow dancing?* The thought of his mom and Hal together, as in a couple, was too much for him to add to his already full plate. Surely he'd misread the situation, and they were just friends?

"How's Libby's car coming?" he asked Terryl on his way past, just to be polite, not to mention get his mind off the possibility of their respective parents hooking up.

"Not so good. Every part we need's out of stock. Thought we found one in Italy, of all places, but turned out it was the wrong year."

"Sorry to hear it." Heath was already heading for the house, antsy to make sure Libby was okay. "Help yourself to food and beer. We've got plenty of both."

To avoid meeting anyone else, Heath ducked between two cabins, then stuck to the tree line for the rest of the short trek to his mom's house.

His pulse raced from worry. How could Hattie have been so rude? No—downright cruel. Why would she have brought up such an obviously sore subject?

Slow down there, man. First, how could she even know it was a taboo topic? And second, aren't you taking this a bit too personally?

Yes, but it was important for the baby that Libby remain calm. Hattie had no business messing up Libby's happy vibe.

Finally in the house, he'd expected to find Morris in the kitchen, but his uncle had apparently finished, meaning he and Libby were alone.

He found the guest room door closed, so he knocked, then shoved his hands in his pockets, suddenly not so sure this was a good idea. After all, if he wanted to stay emotionally detached from the woman, shouldn't he have hung out with the rest of the group?

"Y-yes?" Libby's muffled voice sounded raspy. Was she crying? Why hadn't Hattie kept her big mouth shut?

"Hey, it's um, me—Heath." He pressed his palm to the door. "We're probably gonna eat soon, and I, well, just wanted to make sure you get to the table. You know, in case you're hungry."

"Thanks."

"Sure. So can I help?" *Because if you're crying, you might need someone to talk to.* Not that he was any kind of expert on hurting. But then, wait a minute, yes, he damn well was. When it came to missing someone, he could have written the proverbial book.

"Y-you mean help me find food?"

"Well, that…and, you know, anything else you might need help with." He'd pressed his ear to the door and heard rustling. What was she doing? Was she on the bed? Was her back hurting again? If so, he'd be happy to warm the corn bag.

Shut up! Could you be any more pathetic? She apparently doesn't need help. Leave her alone. The sooner he ate his own supper, the sooner he and Sam could head back to the cabin.

Only too bad for him, Heath remembered his cabin was temporarily no longer his.

Sighing, he decided to switch courses. Instead of being vague, he'd be honest. "Look, Hattie told me she brought up your ex and you seemed upset. I'm really here to make sure you're all right—you know? Like, in your head?"

He might've heard her sniffle but couldn't be sure.

But then there was shuffling, and maybe footsteps.

And then he felt like the world's biggest creeper when she

opened the door and he damn near fell into her room from having been caught off guard while leaning on her door.

"Sorry." She swiped fresh tears from her cheeks. "I didn't
realize you were there."

"It's okay," he muttered, feigning interest in the door frame.
"I was, ah, just checking to make sure you were alive."

"Sure. Well…" She gestured for him to follow her into the
room. She sat on the foot of the bed. "I'm fine."

"Good. I know it's hard—talking about your past relationships with outsiders. It's bad enough talking about my wife
with my mom or uncle. But strangers…" He shook his head,
wishing he possessed more innate eloquence but hoping she'd
managed to at least get the gist of his meaning. That he cared.

Never a fan of the dainty rocker that was the room's only
chair, he sat next to Libby on the foot of the bed.

She looked as though she was about to say something, but
then launched into full-on tears.

At first he wondered if it would be best if he left, but then
his heart went out to her, and he slid closer, pulling her into
a hug. "It's gonna be okay," he said, too late realizing he was
lying through his teeth. For him, even well over a year later,
he still mourned his old life. Nothing would ever be the same.
But maybe for Libby, since she'd at least have her baby to keep
her company, things might be different? Better?

"I—I'm sorry for flipping out on you l-like this," she finally managed. "B-but when Hattie kept rambling on about
how amazing your Patricia was—beautiful and kind and smart
and talented and gorgeous—well, I got to thinking about how
I wasn't any of those things. And h-here I am, carrying Liam's
baby and even he doesn't find me d-desirable, then I guess I'm
d-destined to spend the rest of my life a-alone and m-misera-
ble…." Upon making that realization, she sobbed all the harder.

"Libby, no." Heath hugged her for all he was worth. "That's
not true at all. You're crazy talented. I've never been much of a
pottery guy, but your vases and bowls are pretty cool. Anyone

could tell it takes a lot of skill to make them. And as for Liam not finding you desirable, well…" Gripping her shoulders, he nudged her back just far enough to meet his gaze. "He's a fool, because I think you're adorable."

"Y-you do?" She sniffled, then peered up at him with her pretty blue eyes looming impossibly large on her heart-shaped face.

"Of course. How could any man not find you attractive? You're sweet and funny and thoughtful. Any guy in his right mind would think you're a serious catch."

"R-really?" She was still staring, and the intensity in her eyes caused him to forget to breathe.

Since he couldn't speak, either, he just nodded. For some reason he was fascinated by her sweet smell—watermelon and strawberries and snapdragons and summer-night air all rolled into one intoxicating fragrance he couldn't get enough of.

"B-because I think you'd be a good catch, too. N-not for me because I'm carrying another guy's baby. But if you ever thought you might…"

He couldn't fully focus on her words because as she spoke, she drifted closer and closer until her warm breath tickled his lips. His lonely lips. Lips that'd been so long without comfort or warmth they'd forgotten the simple, heady pleasure of pressing against…

She leaned closer.

As did he.

Closer.

Closer…

And then he wasn't sure how, but they were kissing, and he closed his eyes and groaned, slipping his hand under the curtain of her riotous hair. She tasted even better—sweeter—than she smelled, and he couldn't get enough, as if she was some kind of forbidden nectar.

She fisted the front of his shirt, making sexy mewing noises that made him instantly rock hard.

All thought gave way to raw sensation and pleasure and the certain knowledge that he was falling, falling and he didn't care. The only thing that mattered was making this pleasure last forever....

"Heath? Libby? Are you two in here? Supper's ready!"

As if slowly waking from a dream, Heath opened his eyes to find himself staring into Libby's dazed expression. Her cheeks were still tearstained. Her lips now kiss-swollen.

"Heath, hon?"

Libby jolted back, eyes wide, pressing her hands to her lips. "I'm so sorry. I didn't—"

"Lord, me, too. I—"

"It was a mistake," she said.

"Yes. A mistake. These things just happen, right?" Which was why his heart uncomfortably raced and his stomach knotted. Because he needed a logical reason for having not only done the unthinkable—*unforgivable*—when there was none.

After a series of hitched breaths, she managed a nod.

"There you are," his mother said, entering the room. "What're you doing? Why aren't you at the party?"

"I—I wasn't feeling well...." Libby's curls were a mess. Had he done that? If so, he couldn't remember. In fact, much of the past few minutes were a blur, save for the humming awareness of her still lingering on his lips. And the shame.

Patricia, I'm sorry. It won't happen again. I promise.

"S-so I came back here for a rest. But then Heath stopped by for a visit and..."

"My Heath? *Visiting?*" Laughing, his mom stepped closer, making a production out of checking him for a fever. "Ouch! He's burning up. Chatty Heath is a sure sign to call an ambulance."

Lips pressed tight, Heath willed his pulse to slow.

The kiss had been just one of those things that didn't mean anything. That's all.

"Well, you both look healthy enough to me." His mom

grabbed them both by their wrists. "Come on. Let's get back to the party before Hal, Terryl and Darryl eat us out of house and home. You know how much Hal loves a nice, hearty plate of ribs."

No, actually, he didn't. Their dance flashed into his mind's eye. "Is something going on between you and Hal that you're not telling me?"

"Don't be silly. We're old friends." She dropped his hand to help Libby onto her feet. "You're all flushed. Sure you feel up to walking? Heath could make you a plate and bring it back here…?"

"I feel fine." She forced a smile. "Let's eat."

Heath said, "You two go ahead. I'll be right there."

"Why can't you walk with us?" his mother pressed.

"I need to make a call."

Hands on her hips, Gretta asked, "Who would you be calling? Everyone you know is here."

"Mom…" He hoped his back-off look conveyed the full extent of how much he needed a few minutes alone.

"Okay, okay… I can take a hint. Come on," she urged Libby. "For whatever reason, let's give him a few minutes alone. Men. As long as I live, I'll never figure any of you out." After a dramatic eye roll, she was finally gone, blessedly taking Libby along with her.

Since the entire room smelled of Libby's sweetness, reminding him of her light, and the way she'd made him not only forget his pain but once again feel whole, if only for an instant, Heath retreated to the back porch to be alone.

But there he was accosted by her pottery wheel and kiln. And the memory of her clay-slick fingers working the wet, raw material.

Only when he was outside did he feel capable of drawing a full breath.

And only when he was a half mile down the well-worn trail

his mother and Fred used for their morning walks did he feel even remotely back to his normal gloomy self.

Leaning against the trunk of a massive Douglas fir, he closed his eyes, willing Patricia's image to come. He needed to recall *her* smell, *her* taste. But when he needed her most, he found that no matter how hard he tried, his memories of her had faded.

The notion enraged him. So much so that he lashed out at the tree until his fists were a bloody mess and tears of long-held grief finally escaped him.

Libby tried acting normal at the party, but how could she when her every thought centered around Heath's kiss?

How had it happened? Why? What had possessed her to press her lips to his? Or had it been the other way around and he'd kissed her? How was she supposed to remember when every nerve in her body still felt hyperaware of the moment they'd finally touched.

"Want more potato salad?" Darryl asked. Or was it Terryl? Even under normal circumstances, she could never keep them straight.

"That's plenty, thanks."

"Want a brownie?"

She shook her head. "You're a doll to offer, but I'm not that hungry."

Hattie and Mason and their three adorable kids shared a table with Morris and the redheaded fisherman she'd met in the motel lobby her first night in town.

"You should be starving," Darryl rambled on. At least she assumed it was Darryl due to the Dodgers cap. "When my cousin was in your condition, she ate anything that wasn't nailed down—that is, assuming it was salty or sweet. She hates vegetables. Dad brought a couple dozen doughnuts for the shop right before her baby was due, and I swear she ate darn near the whole box—cardboard included."

"That's a lot of doughnuts," Libby said with a half smile.

Heath, where are you? Why do I get the feeling you're avoiding me like Darryl's cousin avoids broccoli?

"Yeah, she did that with our Halloween candy, too."

When Darryl launched into a new story, she politely commented here and there, but couldn't entirely focus. She needed to find Heath, talk over what had happened and reassure him nothing like that would ever happen again.

Are you sure that's what you want?

The voice came from out of nowhere and rocked her to her core. *Of course,* that's what she wanted. She was weeks away from becoming a single mother. The only thing she needed to focus on was her baby and earning enough money to fix her car. After that, she'd eventually need to reconcile with her parents. Nowhere in any of that did canoodling with a brooding widower have a place.

Then why are your lips still tingling?

CHAPTER NINE

By the morning of the fifty-second annual Bent Road Craft Fair, Heath's fists had healed from his stupid fight with a tree, and he'd turned avoiding Libby and his mom into an art form.

He'd been up early each day, either fishing the Umpqua with Sam or working in the shed on her display shelves. Each night, he headed back to the cabin to share dinner with Mason, Hattie and their kids.

As much as it hurt being around them, and seeing them reminded him of the double dates they'd all once shared when he'd been with Patricia, it hurt far less than dwelling on the guilt he felt about that kiss. But he also found himself more often than he'd like revisiting Libby's sweet smell and taste.

While ground-hugging fog still cloaked his mother's backyard, he skipped the formal breakfast Morris had served in favor of loading Libby's tent and shelving in the back of his truck. Then he took extra care to wrap her creations with bubble wrap before packing them in sturdy boxes.

By the time everything was good to go, he hoped breakfast was long over and his mom and Libby would be getting ready for the fair.

He couldn't have been more wrong.

Morris, his mom and Libby all still occupied the kitchen table and his mother was in the midst of one of her stories about him that made him look like a doofus.

"—so there we were at the San Diego Zoo when Heath decided he wanted to hug the bears. I nearly died, I was so scared. Back then, the enclosures weren't nearly as safe, and at four, Heath was a pistol. When he got it in his mind he wanted to do something, there was no stopping him. Well, he made it within five feet of the grizzly before a zookeeper could grab him, but the bear let out such a loud roar that Heath messed his pants!"

While everyone shared a nice, long laugh at his expense, Heath cleared his throat. "I've got everything loaded, so I'm heading to the park."

"Do you know my site assignment?" Libby asked.

"No, but it won't be hard to find someone who does." He grabbed a cinnamon roll and waved on his way out the door.

"Heath, wait!" his mom called. "Actually, you need to hold back a little because Libby's going to need a ride. You might as well go together so she can direct you on how to best set up all of her things. Oh—and I want you to take one of the back porch chairs and an ottoman, so she'll get plenty of rest in between sales."

Libby interjected, "Gretta, that's really not—"

"I'll grab the chair," Heath said, "but I'm sure she'd be more comfortable riding with you than in my truck. Besides— What the—"

Fred helped himself to the cinnamon roll Heath had held in his right hand.

While his mom and uncle exchanged belly laughs as the hound slinked off to his smelly bed to devour his stolen treasure, Heath could've sworn he felt the heat from Libby's stare, but he didn't want to risk looking that direction. As far as he was concerned, the less contact they shared, the better.

"Damn dog…" he mumbled.

"Watch your mouth," his mother reminded. "And you should know better than to leave food lying around."

It was on the tip of his tongue to argue that the roll had been in his hand, but he didn't want to lower himself to petty arguing over semantics regarding a dog. If anything, the incident just made him all the more ready for Mason and Hattie and their brood to head back to Virginia Beach, so he could get back to the solitude of his cabin.

"Okay, so back to our logistics issue," Gretta said, "I've got a few quick cabin turnarounds I forgot about this morning, so I won't be able to get to the fair until my guests are ready. Since Morris is needed at the diner, Heath, that leaves you to take Libby to set up her booth."

Swell.

"Sorry to be such a bother," Libby said.

"It's not a problem," he said, even though being trapped next to her in the close confines of his truck very much was!

By the time Heath drove past the fire station, Libby had had just about all she could stand of his silent treatment. "It was just a kiss," she said in her most matter-of-fact tone. "It'll never happen again, so you don't have to keep avoiding me."

"I'm not avoiding you. Why would I do that?"

"Seriously?"

When he managed a sideways stare, she stuck out her tongue at him.

When he couldn't help but laugh, she asked, "See? Was it so hard to share a civil moment?"

"No, but for real, that kiss was a straight-up mistake. I'm not sure what happened—don't wanna know. No offense, but for all practical purposes, I might as well still be married, and you're carrying another guy's baby. He could show up anytime and realize he made a mistake. You two could get married and live happily ever after."

Libby folded her arms.

"What? It could happen."

"And this truck could grow wings and a beak. Trust me, Liam's long gone. Besides, even if he could find me, why would he want me?"

"You need to stop with the whole self-pity routine." He pulled the truck to a four-way stop a block from the park where the arts and craft fair was being held. "The kiss was a mistake, but I meant what I said about you being talented and attractive. Hell, if circumstances were different, back in the day I'd have for sure made a play for you."

"Well, thanks, but while your flattery is appreciated, it isn't necessary. I'm secure in the fact that I'm a talented artist, but the whole pending single-parent thing has me spooked. I know Gretta told you some of why I left Seattle, but once I get back, for the baby's sake, I'm going to have to eat a buffet's worth of crow to get back in my parents' good graces.

"As for my eight-thousand-pound outward appearance, I doubt I'll win any pageants soon."

"Stop. That's what I'm talking about. You may not realize it, but you're beautiful—and I mean that in a strictly platonic way. You have this inner glow about you that's extraordinary—*really*."

Her cheeks reddened from the intensity behind his stare. Had his eyes always been so green? His jawline so chiseled? He sported a couple days' stubble which made him look even more manly and rugged.

The driver in the minivan behind them honked.

Heath drove on, but not without shocking her by grabbing her hand and giving it a gentle squeeze. "I mean it. You're special."

"Thanks." She looked down, then back to him. Fragile morning sun tried breaking through the fog but ended up diffused and hazy, wreathing him in backlit perfection. At that moment she wished she was the kind of artist who captured scenes like this in watercolor or oils. That way she could keep him with her forever. Patricia might've died young, but she'd been lucky

THE SEAL'S BABY

to have shared even a portion of her life with a man like Heath. Libby hoped she realized that while she was still alive. "I think you're pretty special, too."

He shrugged off her comment but couldn't hide the faint smile tugging at the corners of his highly kissable lips.

By the time Heath set up Libby's tent and she'd unwrapped and placed all of her pieces, he had to admit the setup didn't look half-bad. "We make a good team."

"Yes, we do. Thanks again for all your help. I can't believe how you managed to salvage this wreck of a tent—and the shelves are perfect. Nice and wide and stable. And I love what you did with the paint." He'd taken at least five different shades of yellow that the motel's shutters had been painted with over the years and colored each row a corresponding shade. When viewed from afar, it looked festive, yet in a classy, organized way—especially with the green canvas tent. Because of what he'd gone through with Patricia, he'd never consider yellow a favorite color, but making Libby smile almost had him forgetting the memories the color dredged up.

"It was my pleasure. Need anything before the crowd gets thick?" The fair, which would kick off the first day of the town's Fourth of July festivities, didn't officially open for thirty minutes, but there were already quite a few lookers passing by.

"I hate to be a pain, but a lemonade from the snack wagon would be delicious. And if a funnel cake happened to fall on what's left of my lap, that'd be okay, too."

He shook his head, but wore just enough of a grin that she knew he didn't mind too much indulging her cravings.

It'd been a month since her last show—a summer festival held north of San Francisco. At the time, she'd suspected Liam had been fooling around, and right before making a big sale, her suspicions had been confirmed when she'd slipped behind their tent for packing materials only to catch him making out with Rachel—a supposed friend who made fresh flower head wreaths. Though her creations were lovely with curled ribbons streaming down the back, Libby had found the woman's actions abhorrent. Everyone in their circle knew Libby carried Liam's child. How could Rachel be so cruel? As for Liam? His behavior was repulsive—especially so when he outright admitted to having been unfaithful more than once, then blamed it on her for gaining baby weight!

Libby had felt not only stupid for being the last one to realize everyone had known what was going on, but embarrassed and hurt and disillusioned by having thought herself in love with a man capable of such despicable actions.

It wasn't fair.

But then neither was the way her own father had treated her. Though he'd never been unfaithful to Libby's mom, his actions in expecting both of the women in his life to always accommodate his needs were no less cruel.

The fact that her most important relationships had ended disastrously didn't give much hope for her romantic future.

"Here you go, your highness." She glanced up to find Heath presenting her snacks with a silly flourish that was so unlike him she laughed.

"Thank you, kind sir. Would you like to share?"

"As a matter of fact—yes. I still can't believe Fred stole my cinnamon roll right out of my hand." He sat alongside her in the second chair Gretta had insisted he cart along.

"That dog eats like a pregnant woman."

"True."

They chewed in companionable silence, hands brushing while tearing off chunks of the sugary, fried cake. Every time they touched, Libby tried ignoring the achy awareness just being near Heath evoked. When he drank from her lemonade, she especially fought the memory of his lips pressed to hers.

For an instant their gazes met and locked before he hastily looked away. Had he felt it, too? The attraction that had no business being there, but was growing ever harder to ignore?

"Great day, huh?" After taking their trash to a nearby bin, he'd reclaimed his chair, stretching out his long legs, tilting his head back to catch the warmth of midmorning sun.

"Beautiful. Couldn't be more perfect. You wouldn't believe how many of these things I attend that get rained out."

"Oh—I remember a couple of years when this show has been chilly. We for sure got lucky."

She liked that. The fact that he'd used *we* in regard to the day. It implied he had an investment in the outcome. Maybe not so much monetarily—although, she'd certainly offer to reimburse him for expenses he'd incurred—but emotionally. Even though he'd avoided her ever since that kiss, apparently he hadn't been as detached from her as his actions had implied.

When the crowd grew thick and Libby actually made a few sales, Heath was on hand to help her wrap and pack customer purchases. He was there again with a turkey sandwich for lunch and more lemonade before she'd even realized she was thirsty.

As the sun rose higher, so did the temperature, and thankfully the tent Heath had refurbished kept Libby cool in the shade. That said, the longer she sat next to Heath, sharing casual conversation on topics ranging from her favorite foods to movies, the warmer her feelings for him became. Which didn't even make sense because the longer they were together, the more she realized how adept he was at carefully steering talk away from himself. Was it his company she was enjoying, or the novelty of someone actually caring about what she said?

She was on the verge of calling him out when Mason and Hattie arrived with their considerable brood in tow.

"This is stunning!" Hattie gravitated toward one of Libby's favorite vases. It was squat and chubby in shape, but the iridescent glaze lent it a whimsical flair. Hattie manned the twins' stroller, while Mason held squirmy Charlie. "Look, hon, wouldn't this be pretty on that little side table next to the entry hall bench?"

Mason wrinkled his nose. "Huh?"

"Ignore him," Hattie said. "I'll take it. And could you please pack it extra sturdy so it survives our trip home?"

"Will do." Heath handled the packing, while Libby handled the cash.

"You two make a good team," Hattie noted.

Heath grunted. "I'm only here because I have nowhere else to go since you guys invaded my cabin."

Though she was sure he'd meant his lighthearted statement as a joke, Libby feared there was a grain of truth to Heath's sentiment. Was he only here out of a sense of duty? To make sure she didn't overdo it?

If so, that not only hurt, but tainted the pleasure she'd found in the day.

When Heath handed Hattie her sturdy package, the women exchanged hugs and the guys shook hands.

Once again on their own, Libby was just about to voice her laundry list of concerns when a woman who'd looked over her wares at least four times finally stopped.

"Sorry to interrupt, but my name's Zoe." She handed Libby her card. "I run a gallery in Coos Bay, and if you have time, I'd love to talk with you about carrying your work. It's quite lovely. I've never seen glazing with such a luminescent quality. How long have you worked in the medium?"

"About four years." Was this a dream? Libby struggled to maintain her composure.

"Well, I've been in the art world forever, and trust me, there are potters who've been at this decades who haven't got anywhere near your skill. Please call me."

"Thank you. I will."

"Good. In the meantime, I have to have this for my own collection." She'd selected a tall narrow vase made of three intertwining, vinelike structures meant to hold a trio of blooms. The primary glazing was yellow, but had a dreamy depth it'd taken Libby days to achieve.

While Libby worked in perfect union with Heath to complete

the gallery owner's purchase and packaging, Zoe asked, "You two must be excited. When's your baby due?"

"Oh—" Libby reddened. "He's not the father. Just a friend."

"I'm sorry. Please don't—"

"It's okay," Heath said. "Honest mistake."

"Well, still…" She accepted her package with a nervous twitter. "Please don't let my awkward assumption prevent you from giving me a call."

"I won't," Libby assured.

"How great is that?" Heath asked once Zoe was out of earshot.

"Pretty stinkin' great." Head spinning—for once in a good way, as opposed to feeling faint—Libby sat down before she fell down from excitement. "I've never had validation like this— from anyone—let alone an industry professional." Cupping her hands to her tummy, she turned introspective. "My dad told me art was a waste of time. Liam said pottery was a dying art—if I really wanted to make something of myself, try water color or quilting."

"But what did our Libby do?" *Our* Libby? Heath shocked her by reaching out, softly stroking her hair. His smile was equally as attractive as it was unreadable. Which only made her crave learning what made him tick all the more. "Exactly what you wanted, and look how it turned out. I'm happy for you. Mom and Uncle Morris—hell, damn near half the town will be, too."

"I couldn't have had such a successful day without your help."

He waved off her compliment. "All I did was wield bubble wrap and packing tape. You're the artist."

She still wanted to drill him on so many things, but now hardly seemed right. Not when for the first time in she couldn't remember when, she actually had something to celebrate.

"I hear congratulations are in order!" The moment Heath ushered Libby through his mother's back door, Gretta rushed from the kitchen to the screened porch to wrap her in a warm hug. "I'm so proud of you!"

"Thank you. It really was an amazing day. I made a little over fifteen hundred dollars, which means I can repay you for room and board and Heath for gas money and medical bills and all the supplies he bought for my booth, and hopefully still have enough left to fix my car."

"I can't speak for my son," Gretta said, "but as much as I appreciate your offer, I refuse to take one cent of your hard-earned money. Save it for getting home. I'm sure your parents will be thrilled to see you."

Libby paled. "I wish. Anyway, let me at least treat everyone to pizza."

"Too late." Morris held a pot in the crook of one arm, and nudged the porch's screen door open with his other. "To celebrate Libby's big day, I made spaghetti."

Long after their delicious meal and Heath had helped his uncle clean the kitchen and Gretta had gone to bed, Heath walked the dogs with Morris and helped him close up the diner.

Back at his mom's, he'd selfishly hoped Libby would have also called it a night, but she sat on the back porch, reading.

The dogs were ecstatic to see her, but then he supposed he'd be excited, too, if she rubbed his belly and lavished him with praise.

"Those two worship you," he said. "They're going to miss you when your car finally gets fixed."

"I'll miss them." Was that a wistful note in her voice?

She winced when she leaned back in her chair.

"You okay?" he asked.

Nodding, she pressed her fingertips to her temples. "It's just been a long day—wonderful—but long. My body's one giant ache."

"Sounds like you need a good soak in a tub."

"Ha! As heavenly as that sounds, even if I fit, I'd never be able to get out."

An idea popped into his head. "While I was waiting for these mutts to do their business, I noticed steam rising off the pool. It's bathtub warm. Wanna soak in there?"

"I couldn't..."

"Why not?"

"For one, I don't have a suit. And two, what if someone saw me?" The way she looked down made him wonder if she was specifically concerned about him seeing her. Why? He'd always found pregnant women beautiful. She was no different.

"Sounds like a lot of lame excuses to me. We'll turn off the lights. If we're quiet, there's no way anyone would see us."

"I couldn't..."

"Chicken? Haven't you ever skinny-dipped?"

"Heath!" She pressed her palms to her cheeks, but even in the dim light he'd have sworn he saw her blush.

"What? It's fun. Come on..." He held out his hand. "I dare you."

CHAPTER TEN

"DON'T LOOK!" Libby whispered, praying none of the motel guests were up. Though it was nearly midnight, there was the odd chance someone could still be about. "I can't believe I let you talk me into this."

"Best as I can recall," he said from the deep end, "it wasn't too hard. How was I supposed to know you've never turned down a dare?"

"Lucky guess?" It was no easy feat removing her panties. Her bra proved even worse. It was the anticipation of escaping the awful pressure of the baby's weight, if only for a little while, that drove her toward the pool even more than Heath's challenge.

The cloudy night provided the perfect cover, and soon enough, she'd immersed herself in liquid bliss. Her formerly pendulous breasts floated high and she barely felt the weight of her belly. Pleasurable relief washed through her in waves. Was this how good she'd feel upon finally giving birth? No— even better, since her daughter would finally be in her arms.

"How is it?" Heath asked from barely five feet away.

"Better than sex," she said without thinking, immediately regretting her choice of words.

He laughed. "Damn, if it's that good, maybe you haven't been doing it right?"

"You're awful!" She splashed water his way.

"Me? You're the one who first mentioned the *S* word."

"Whatever." Eyes closed, she leaned backward into a float, relishing the night's inky cloak. The dark lent her a freedom she hadn't found in a long time, and she was determined to steal every trace of contentment.

The water's warm hold made her eyelids heavy, and before too long, she couldn't be sure if the heady experience was merely a dream.

Cool breeze licked her hypersensitive nipples, bringing on a yearning for the kind of man's touch that had landed her in this position.

"You really are beautiful."

"Oh—sorry. I didn't know you were there." Startled to find she'd unwittingly floated alongside Heath, she tried standing, but the water was too deep.

For a moment she floundered, but as always seemed to be the case, he was right there at the rescue. Only when her baby bump brushed against his bare six-pack, all manner of havoc coursed through her.

"Oh, my God…" he murmured, still holding her unnecessarily close, but she wasn't complaining. If she'd thought merely floating had felt good, being held by Heath proved a decadence beyond measure. She didn't dare breath for fear of him letting her go. "You feel so good."

He held her tighter still, nuzzling her neck, burying his face in her wet hair as if he were breathing her in.

His erection was no secret.

The humming awareness between her legs was most unexpected, and yet suddenly all-consuming.

In the water's warm, dark cocoon, they could've been anywhere in time or space, and when their lips met, it was by some unspoken yet mutual admission that whatever happened next, they were both adults and more than okay with it.

He kissed her like a man starved, and she answered his

tongue's bold sweep, seeking to fill hungers all her own. For far too long she'd needed to be wanted, desired, and he made her feel all of that and more.

When she wrapped her legs around him and he entered her, it seemed like the most natural thing in the world. It'd been so long for both that neither lasted long, but long enough for mutual satisfaction to soon be found.

Finished, she sighed against him, resting her cheek on his strong shoulder.

"I'm sorry," he said, completely spoiling the moment. "I had no intention of doing that. It just happened."

"I know," she said, more for his benefit than her own. He was feeling guilty again. And she…well, she wasn't sure what she felt, other than regret that he was once again apologizing when what they'd shared had been special—at least for her.

Tears stung her eyes and as they drifted apart, she felt safe silently shedding them from a distance where he wouldn't be able to see. But then what would it matter if he did?

Obviously, what they'd shared had been nothing more than satisfying urges.

But if that were entirely so, why did her tears feel as if they might never stop?

"I'll grab a few towels," he said, already leaving the pool.

It was on the tip of her tongue to tell him not to bother, but what would that accomplish, other than ensuring a cold, soggy walk to the house? "Thanks."

"I am sorry," he said upon his return from the utility room.

"Stop. Don't you have any idea how horrible that makes me feel? I mean, I know we don't share any real connection, but I'd like to think we're at least friends."

"We are," he said, holding out a towel for her to step into, while politely looking away.

"And you don't have to act as if the sight of a naked woman will turn you to stone, Heath—especially considering what just happened."

"Forgive me for trying to be a gentleman."

She snorted. "I think you've already missed the mark on that."

"So you're saying you didn't want to be with me?"

Sighing, she wrapped the oversize towel sarong-style around her. "That's not what I said at all. If you were truly concerned about coming across as a gentleman, you'd still be holding me in the pool."

"I can't. You know that. I'm—"

"No—don't you dare say you're still with Patricia, because point of fact, like it or not, she's dead. No matter how hard you brood or pout or wish for her return, it's not going to happen, Heath. Meanwhile, here you are, very much alive, obviously with just as many needs as the rest of us mere mortals, yet there you go, running off to pretend what we shared didn't happen. Well—newsflash—it did! And having you inside me felt wonderful and life affirming and I'm not sorry!" The moment the words left her lips, Libby regretted them.

Even more so when Heath pitched his load of towels to the pool deck, then yanked on his jeans, T-shirt and leather sandals before storming away. He didn't even walk toward the house, but headed to the road.

"Heath? I'm sorry!" she shouted after him. "I don't mean to sound cruel, but you can't go on living this way, pining for your dead wife. It's not really living at all."

He kept walking. He didn't so much as turn around to acknowledge her words.

Hugging herself, once again feeling gravity's crushing weight upon her pregnant body, Libby felt terrible about the hurt her words had inflicted on Heath.

Of course, he rationally understood Patricia was never coming back. But in his heart? She feared that may be an entirely different matter.

Heath ran all the way to the crashing shore. His lungs and thighs burned, but he didn't care. Nothing mattered except running from the pain caused by not only Libby's harsh words, but his own outrageous actions.

What had he been thinking?

Obviously, he hadn't been thinking.

But what was he supposed to do about it now? An act like this couldn't be undone. There'd be repercussions.

Even worse, he didn't get his cabin back until Mason and crew left on the fifth to visit family in Alaska, meaning Heath had three more days trapped in the same house as Libby. Or did he?

Sure, it was the height of summer tourism season, but that didn't mean he couldn't just pop a tent somewhere—any-where—if it meant avoiding her.

Sure it's her you're avoiding, buddy? Or the way she makes you feel—not just alive, but good. Happy. Not remotely de-pressed. Even worse, when you're with Libby, you stop dwell-ing on the past.

Heath picked up a rock and hurled it with a mighty roar at the angry Pacific.

When would he stop feeling this way? When would he be able to forgive Patricia for leaving him and himself for not being able to keep his promise to her to never be with another woman?

The really ironic part about his situation was that Patricia never wanted this limbo for him. She'd made deathbed pleas for him to not only find someone else to love, but to live a life full enough for the both of them. She'd made him promise to follow through on all of their shared dreams—have kids and a great house. Take family vacations and grow old with someone while their children grew into adults and had children of their own.

Patricia had dearly wanted all of that for him, but in those agonizing moments when he'd watched life drain from her body, he'd wanted nothing more than to keep her with him always.

In those moments, he'd made his own promise.

I'll love you forever, he'd cried, holding her to him, refusing to let go until a nurse gently intervened. *I promise to never love any woman the way I love you.*

Sitting hard on the rocky shore, he planted his hands behind him for support and crossed his legs at the ankles.

Tipping his head back, he looked to the sky for answers, but heavy cloud cover only made him feel more alone.

"You slept late this morning," Gretta said when Libby wandered her way from the bedroom to the kitchen. "Feel better?"

I wish. "Great. Thanks."

"I was thinking, since yesterday was such a busy day, you should probably use today to rest. So how about a nice beach picnic? Morris loves cooking over a campfire, and we could wrangle a few harrowing SEAL stories out of Heath."

Oh, have I got a story for you! "Um, that sounds nice, but let's play it by ear. I'm really not feeling up to much."

"Of course. I'm sorry. Here I am planning out your afternoon when you haven't even had breakfast. Would you like eggs or oatmeal?"

"I can get it. Please, go on with whatever you were doing. I'm pregnant—not an invalid." Libby didn't mean to be short with Gretta, but she just wasn't in the mood for hovering. Come to think of it, she wasn't in the mood for much of anything other than hiding under the covers until her baby girl decided she was ready to enter the world. "I'm sorry. Guess after all of yesterday's excitement, I'm feeling kind of blah."

"That's understandable," Gretta said, ushering her to a kitchen table chair. "But you still have your talk with the gallery owner to look forward to. What was her name? Zoe?"

Libby nodded.

"Maybe Heath can drive you to Coos Bay on Monday? It's a lovely area. You can make a whole day of it."

Yeah, I don't think that's going to happen.

For an instant, Libby closed her eyes, wishing Heath's angry glare wasn't the first image popping into her mind.

"I would take you myself, but with the motel fully booked I really should stay here. You know, in case we run out of towels or there's a plumbing emergency. And speaking of towels, I can't believe how rude some guests are. There's a metal bin near the pool that's plainly marked for used towels, yet I found at least five of them just tossed to the pool deck this morning. What's wrong with people these days? Were they raised in barns?"

Heat rose up Libby's neck, flaming her cheeks.

If Gretta knew the truth behind how those towels had been strewn, she'd no doubt suffer from an apoplectic fit.

"Will you be all right if I go throw another load in the washer?"

"Of course. Is there anything around here you need me to do?"

"Not particularly. Thanks for the offer but I'd rather you rest. You've had enough excitement for one weekend."

Wasn't that the truth!

"Oh—and when Heath wakes up, ask him about the picnic. I really think it'll be fun."

If your idea of a good time includes chilling with a morose, brooding, foul-tempered, miserable wretch of a man.

Just as Gretta left out the back door, Fred wandered over. He sat. Scratched a bit at his tummy, then plopped back on his haunches to stare at her expectantly.

"You think food solves everything, don't you?"

He barked.

She fished a few dog biscuits from the canister Gretta kept on the counter, then tossed them to the begging dog.

"Where's Sam?" Since Fred wasn't answering, Libby made a sweep of the house, only to come up empty. Not only was Sam not home, but neither was Heath.

Her anger with Heath morphed to worry when she found that the bedding Gretta set out for him every night had been left untouched. Had he been gone all night? Should she launch a search?

In her room, she dressed in maternity shorts and a draping floral blouse, slipped her feet into sandals and ran a brush through her hair.

In the kitchen, she checked Fred's food and water bowl, only to find them both full.

"Hold down the fort," she said to the dog before creaking open the back door.

Outside, the day was far too pretty to suit her dark mood.

Why couldn't Heath just be a normal guy? Sleep with her, thank her for a good time, *then* leave? Why'd he have to storm off, making her worry about his emotional well-being?

Moreover, why couldn't she just let him be? Why did it matter how he felt, because it was obvious that after what they'd shared, he couldn't give two figs about her frame of mind.

But then why should he? For all practical purposes, as pleasurable as their union had been, it was essentially a one-night stand—not anything she'd ever imagined herself indulging in, but if she had to put a label on it, there was nothing else their impromptu hook-up could be called.

That said, she was deeply sorry for bringing up his obsession with Patricia. First and foremost of the issues she planned to discuss, that one topped her list.

When she'd shuffled her way around the motel's lot and found Heath's truck, but no sign of Heath, Libby decided to take her search further by borrowing his keys.

She'd made it to the house and back to the truck without being seen when Gretta emerged from one of the guest cabins with her arms laden with bed linens.

"Where are you off to?" Heath's mom asked. "And where's my son? I'd feel better about you leaving if you have someone to keep an eye on you."

"Actually—" Libby crossed her fingers behind her back for the fib she was about to tell "—Heath just called the house phone. He's with Sam, and they walked a little too far. He, um, asked me to pick them up."

"Why is he bothering you? He knows you're supposed to be resting."

"I'm feeling great." Libby hated lying again, but in this case it couldn't be helped. She not only needed to find Heath, but talk to him. And it wasn't a conversation Gretta needed to be a party to.

"If you're sure you're okay. But be back soon. Morris and I still want to try for an afternoon picnic. Oh, and when you grab Heath, tell him to invite Mason and Hattie and their kiddos. Just to be neighborly, I think I'll even call Hal and his boys."

"Sounds good."

Hattie had hauled herself behind the truck's steering wheel when Gretta shouted, "Libby, hon, wait up! You didn't even tell me where you were going!"

Vowing to ask forgiveness after she came home with Gretta's son, Libby pretended to not hear Heath's mom or see her chasing after the truck in the rearview mirror. Thankfully, the circle drive allowed her to make a clean getaway before Gretta could catch up.

Now the only question was, where did she even start looking for a man who obviously didn't want to be found?

CHAPTER ELEVEN

NOT ONLY WAS Heath hungry and tired, but Sam looked as though he was wearing down, too. Heath had believed he was alone when he left his mother's property, but apparently Sam was even smarter than Heath gave him credit for since the dog must have nosed open the screen door to follow.

"Right about now, I'm guessing you wish you'd stayed home, huh?" He rubbed behind the dog's silky ears.

Sam licked his hand.

It was one thing to run himself to his physical limits, but now he had the added guilt of worrying about his dog.

They'd walked quite a way down the shore, rounded a bend and had just made it back to the public parking lot when Heath groaned. "You've got to be kidding me...."

The lot was deserted save for one familiar truck. His.

Even worse, farther down the beach tottered Libby.

Lord...

He sharply exhaled, then swiped his fingers through his hair. He didn't know how to face her. He hadn't just botched their situation, but annihilated it.

Sam adored Libby. One look at her and the traitorous mutt found his second wind, bounding down the shore, barking the whole way.

While his dog and Libby shared a touching reunion, Heath regrettably knew what he had to do.

Facing her, bolstered by the rhythmic waves that had always brought solace, he blurted, "Sorry."

"No—I'm sorry." She wiped tears. "I never should've said anything about Patricia. It was heartless and cruel and mean-spirited."

He couldn't help but cast her a faint smile. "There you go again. All of those mean the same."

"Does it matter?"

"Nope."

"All right, then. Accept my apology, I'll accept yours and let's get on with our day."

Hands in his pockets, Heath kicked at the sand. "What if I feel like there's more to say?"

"Then say it. You're a grown man, Heath. You used to be a navy SEAL. Do you have any idea how amazing that is? You've seen and done things I can't even imagine—probably don't want to imagine—so I can't for the life of me understand what you're doing holed up in Bent Road, fishing or lounging around your mother's house when you could be off saving the free world."

Heath hung his head in shame.

Her words hurt, but he couldn't deny their truth.

"I know we hardly know each other," she said, "so maybe I don't have the right to say any of this, but on the other hand, your mother's so kind that I almost feel like she's doing you a disservice by not giving you an earful. Last night..." She flopped her hands at her sides. "It was hot. Beyond unexpected. And really, *really* great. The way you ran off, I got the feeling you're ashamed of what happened between us, but you don't have to be. You're a single, handsome man who acted on natural feelings. End of story. No, actually—"

"Okay, whoa." Hands to her shoulders, he held her at arm's distance so she'd be sure to face him while he took a turn at venting. "Everything you said is true. Me running away was the equivalent of slapping a Band-Aid on a gaping wound. I get that. My problem is figuring out what to do with this wad of emotions I can't seem to shed."

After releasing her, he took a step back, covering his face with his hands. "I loved Patricia like I didn't know it was possible to love. When I lost her…there were days I wished I'd died myself. When Sam was gone, I caught myself slipping back into that frame of mind."

"Heath…" She touched his forearm—barely—but it was enough to begin his unraveling.

"Please understand, I—I'm not suicidal or anything, but I don't know where to go, what to do. I'm lost."

"You're in luck, *lost* is my specialty. I've lived most of my life there." Her tone said her words were meant to be a joke, but the shine to her eyes told a different story. "I've been fortunate enough to have never lost a loved one the way you have, but my own dad kicked me to the curb like I was garbage. Liam, the father of my baby and man I thought I'd spend the rest of my life with pretty much did the same. So when it comes to loss, I consider myself a specialist."

"Yet you're always smiling. How do you do it?"

"Sheer will…" Her misty-eyed smile ignited a long frozen corner of his soul. "Because really, what's the alternative? Sure, I could curl up in a ball and cry night and day, but what would that prove? Especially, when I have so very much to be thankful for." Hugging the baby, she said, "I have a daughter on the way, and you and your mom and so many other great friends that up until a week ago, I never even knew existed. Then there was the craft show—making so many sales and meeting Zoe. As if all of that weren't enough, there was last night…with you. In my bed this morning, I pinched myself to make sure I hadn't dreamed it all."

"See? You have your baby to look forward to—your work. I have nothing."

Waving off his comments, she argued, "Okay, so you might

not have a child on the way but, Heath, do you have any idea how much your mother and uncle love you? As for work, you're a SEAL. I'm not an expert about navy stuff, but seems to me that someone with your kind of training would be in high demand."

"I'm out of shape."

Hands on her hips, she pursed her lips and cocked her head. "Really, Heath? That's the best you've got for me? How long would it take you to get back into *shape*? Especially since you're looking pretty good to me." Her cheeks flushed adorably.

"I don't know..."

"How about this? You dared me to skinny-dip last night, so I dare you to at least call your boss or major general, or whoever's in charge of letting you get back to what you do. If he tells you to take a hike, then resume your busy schedule. But, Heath, what if he says he needs you? How amazing would you feel to once again be giving to others instead of sitting around replaying a tragic situation day after day that you have no hope of ever making better?"

Libby's speech struck an anticipatory chord that stayed with Heath throughout the day. Could Libby be right? Did he have a shot at getting his life back on track?

He was grateful to her for keeping what had transpired between them confidential, meaning he could spend the sun-flooded afternoon picnic his mom had organized enjoying himself as opposed to standing around, feeling awkward—at least when his mom wasn't off flirting with Hal.

Stuffed from too many servings of his uncle's fried chicken, Heath sat in the sand beside Mason, who was building a sand castle with his girls. Like everything the man did, the structure was top-notch, featuring a moat, dragon and princess high atop a turret.

"You've got a great-looking family," Heath said.

"Thanks, man. Coming from you, that means a lot."

"Yeah?"

His friend gave him an odd, indecipherable look. "Yeah. I always looked up to you and Patricia. You two seemed to have it all figured out. When she…well, when she passed, none of us knew what to do for you."

"There's wasn't much anyone could do." He drew a pattern in the sand with a twig. "Which made it all the harder, considering we were in the business of solving any problem."

"My point exactly. We felt helpless. And for that, I'm sorry."

Heath shrugged. "I appreciate it, man, but what's done is done."

They sat a few more minutes in companionable silence, Mason helping the girls while Heath stared into the crashing surf where Sam frolicked.

Fred stared on disapprovingly from dry ground.

His mom, Hal, Libby, Hattie and the baby shared the picnic table, while Morris and Hal's boys chatted up a brunette down the shore. All in all, it'd been a surprisingly good day. Far different from how he'd expected it to develop in the dark before dawn.

Who did he have to thank for that fact? Libby. For a woman five years his junior, at times she seemed dozens of years wiser.

"Hey, Mason?"

"Uh-huh?" His friend was focused on flying buttress construction.

"Not saying I'm gonna do it, but what would you think the reception would be if I approached the CO about resuming my post?"

"Are you kidding me?" Mason rocked back onto his heels, brandishing a goofy grin. "He'd be thrilled. So would the rest of the guys. We miss you, man. But what're you going to do about Libby?"

"What do you mean?"

"Aren't you two an item?"

"No. Not at all." But if that were the case, why did his stomach knot at the prospect of his life moving on without her?

* * *

"Don't look now," Hattie teased, bouncing Charlie on her lap, "but a certain someone can't stop staring at you."

"He's just being friendly." Libby glanced up to find her gaze locking with Heath's. She smiled shyly before looking down, ignoring the flush of achy awareness flooding her system from the memory of their brief but hot encounter.

Thankfully, with Gretta and Hal in lawn chairs nearer the surf, immersed in their own conversation, Gretta wouldn't have overheard Hattie's comment.

Libby would be mortified if Heath's mom had so much as an inkling of what had transpired between Libby and her son.

Hattie snorted. "If that's the look of a *friendly* man, then I'm about to be crowned Miss America!"

"It could happen," Libby mused. "You have gorgeous hair."

"Thanks, and you're sidestepping the issue. Spill your guts. Is there something going on between you two?"

Dear Lord, yes. Fanning suddenly flaming cheeks with a paper plate, Libby shook her head. "No, nothing like what you're hinting at, anyway. If anything, we're like squabbling siblings."

"Uh-huh…" Hattie leaned to the table's opposite end to dredge her pinky finger through the frosting on the chocolate cake Morris made for the occasion. "Thank the good Lord I never had a brother who looked like Heath—because well—" she laughed "—he'd be my brother instead of my boyfriend."

"Hey," Libby teased, "you've already got one great guy. No fair hogging them all."

"Aha! So you are admitting you like Heath as *way* more than a brother?"

"I'm admitting nothing." She sipped pink lemonade. "And unless you want to get on Gretta's bad side, you might want to assess that situation…" She nodded toward the cake where one of the twins was helping herself by tiny, chubby fistfuls.

"Vivian!" Hattie shouted. "You know better."

"Yum!" The chocolate-smeared cherub grinned. "Good!"

"See what you have to look forward to?" Hattie asked.

Hugging her belly, Libby said, "I can't wait." And she meant it. But as much as she looked forward to finally meeting her baby girl, she was that afraid of raising her all on her own.

"I don't mean to pry," Hattie said while cleaning Vivian's fingers—Vanessa still worked on her castle with Mason, "but you mentioned when we first met that you don't have a birth plan in place. What're you planning to do?"

Libby sighed. "As soon as my car's fixed, my only real option is heading back to family in Seattle with my tail tucked between my legs."

"I take it you don't get along?"

"That'd be putting it mildly. Long story short, when I was eighteen, my dad and I had the mother of all fights. He made ultimatums I knew I couldn't live with, so I didn't even try. I left home and never looked back."

"How's your mom? Was she supportive?"

"She tried, but she's old-school—believing her husband should be *obeyed*. When Dad sent me packing, she agreed it was for the best. For a while, I had a hard time accepting what I took as her betrayal, but now that I'm older, I see she probably felt like she didn't have a choice."

"A parent always has a choice when it comes to supporting their kid." Libby hadn't realized Heath had stepped behind her. How much had he heard? "What both of your parents did is unforgivable."

"Thanks for the support," she said, "but it's not that black-and-white. Back then, I was a wild child, and they're about as straightlaced as they come. Mom was thinking debutante balls while I was plotting tattoos and piercings. Thankfully, I grew past that rebellious stage, but considering some of the things I'd done, all of the money in private school tuition I pretty much wasted, I guess I'd be upset, too."

"It shouldn't be just about the money." Heath sat beside her, forced by the cooler on her right side to be close enough for their shoulders, forearms and thighs to brush. She tried playing it as no big deal, but her pulse raced as fast as the twins chased barking Sam. "You're their daughter. No matter what, they should accept you for who you are."

Even after they'd all shared cake and laughter when Vivian and Fred slinked off with the leftover corn on the cob, Libby struggled to get Heath's words from her mind.

When she finally became a mother, she hoped to share his high ideals, but she also wasn't naive enough to believe all parenting situations would be easy.

On the ride home, Libby shared the truck's seat with Sam and Fred. Heath drove, and she couldn't help but admire the color the day spent in the sun had left on his stubbled complexion. So much had transpired between them in the past twenty-four hours. Their lovemaking felt like a dream. His running off, and their squabble that morning seemed a million years away.

Where they were concerned, time seemed to hold no meaning. Even though they'd only officially known each other a little over a week, she felt as if she'd always known him. Moreover, she inherently knew she'd always *want* to know him.

"Have plans for in the morning?" he asked.

"Nope—unless Hal announces my car's done."

He snorted. "Back at the beach, Darryl told me they were waiting for parts from literally all over the world, so I wouldn't hold your breath on that one."

"Okay, so since I apparently have my day wide-open, what did you have in mind?"

He rubbed Sam behind his ears. "Thought we might wind our way over to Coos Bay. See about getting you a meeting with that gallery owner."

"Sounds good." She was careful to not let her voice betray the amount of excitement she actually felt at the prospect of spending her day alone with him. "But if I do that, you've got to promise me to call whoever you need to, in order to see about getting back to your job."

"Yes, *Mom*." When he cast a wink and grin combo in her direction, it was all she could do to keep from swooning. Good thing the man seemed to have no idea how handsome he actually was, or she'd be in big trouble!

After a few more minutes' companionable silence, Heath cleared his throat and said, "Thanks again for this morning. I never talk about Patricia, and..." her heart ached to witness his eyes well "...it was time."

"You're welcome. Feels good to finally do something for you."

"While we're on serious topics, do me a favor and stop dwelling on any debt you think you owe me. I only did what any ordinary nice guy would."

That might be, but so far in her travels, Libby hadn't encountered anyone quite like Heath or his mom and uncle. They were lovely, remarkable people she one day aspired to resemble.

When the tires crunched on the gravel drive leading up to Gretta's home, happiness of the kind she'd experienced precious few times in her life flowed through her. It was probably hormones making her hypersensitive to the role her new friends played in her life, but that didn't detract from her overall sense of well-being.

And dread.

Because any day now, this illusion of having a true home and family would be shattered with one call from Hal announcing her car was done.

"Sit tight," Heath said upon parking his truck alongside the shed. "I'll help you down."

"Thanks." Ordinarily, she resented needing his help, but in her current mellow state, she not only appreciated his assistance, but welcomed—craved—his touch.

Sometime in the past twenty-four hours they'd turned a corner in their friendship. It hadn't just been the making love that had solidified their bond, but an intangible something more she couldn't have defined if her life depended upon it.

When Heath lifted her from her seat, had she imagined his hands lingering longer than necessary on her torso, or the pads of his thumbs brushing the tender sides of her breasts?

"No offense," he teased, "but I swear you've put on twenty pounds since the first time I hefted you from the middle of the road."

"Did you just call me fat?"

He laughed. "Absolutely. And you have no idea how happy it makes me to see you with meat on your bones. When you first showed up, you reminded me of a scrawny kitten. Now..." He hastily looked down. He still held her, his thumbs still singeing the tender sides of her breasts. Her breath hitched in anticipation and hope of him once again kissing her as if there was no tomorrow. Because for her—them—there wasn't.

As soon as her car was fixed, she'd march into the proverbial lion's den to make nice with her parents and give birth to her baby. If Heath had a lick of the sense she suspected him to possess, he'd do what it took to get back in his boss's good favor, then return to at least a portion of his former life.

"Now..." When he released her, a part of her wanted to cling to him still. "You look healthy and pretty and like the kind of woman any kid would be happy to call Mom."

His compliment shined a light on a long-buried place within her that had been dark for far too long. But it also made her crave more than just being a good mom. Would she ever have the chance to also be a good wife?

CHAPTER TWELVE

MONDAY AFTERNOON, while Libby met with Zoe, the gallery owner she'd met at the craft fair, Heath raised his jacket hood against the downpour. Zoe had suggested he return in about an hour, so he ducked into a nearby restaurant for a steaming bowl of chowder.

For a Monday, the place was surprisingly crowded, but he figured the rain had driven tourists from Shore Acres or Cape Arago State Parks into town for something to do.

The next table over held a family of three—parents fussing over a newborn girl who wanted nothing to do with her bottle.

While waiting for his food, Heath alternated his view between the baby and the rivulet-soaked view of the gallery that would hopefully soon house Libby's art.

He'd promised her that if she worked up the courage for this visit, he, in turn, would contact his CO, but as yet, he hadn't found the nerve. It hurt enough missing Patricia while a continent away from where they'd shared their lives. How much worse would it be, blasted by daily reminders like their house, the beach where they'd walked Sam, their friends, her favorite coffee shop or nail salon or the hospice where she'd died? He couldn't bear the vision of the cemetery where she'd been buried.

Once again eyeing the couple with their baby, he struggled with the knowledge that he'd soon be losing Libby, as well—most likely before she even had her baby.

The knowledge shouldn't have bothered him, but did. Just as she had with seemingly every other inhabitant of Bent Road, she'd unwittingly worked her charm on him, as well.

The waitress brought his soup.

The recipe's creamy warmth initially eased his chill, but the more he thought about Libby leaving, him leaving, the more antsy Heath grew. Maybe he wasn't ready to return to his job? There was the matter of Sam to consider. Sure, he could take the dog with him to Virginia Beach, but who would watch him when he was off on a mission? He supposed he could ask Hattie to watch him, or even Pandora—the wife of another one of his team members—but he wouldn't want to impose.

Maybe it was best he stayed put.

In Bent Road, every day was predictable. No highs or lows. Just status quo. At the moment, that suited him just fine.

What about the day you found Libby? What about the night you made love to her in the pool? Weren't those good times?

That hadn't been lovemaking, but sex. Satisfying an itch.

He instantly regretted even thinking such cruel words. She deserved better than a one-night stand.

What do I deserve?

Patricia had wanted him to start a new life without her. He just wasn't sure he could.

What would Patricia think of Libby? Would the two of them have been friends? Heath liked to think so.

The rain had finally let up, but the clouds were still ominous and low.

"Need anything else?" the waitress asked.

"No, thanks. Just the check."

After paying, Heath still had fifteen minutes to kill, so he rounded the block. Thinking, thinking, wondering what was the right thing for him to do.

He'd only burned off five minutes of time and zero nervous energy, so he pulled out his cell and took a deep breath.

His CO answered on the second ring.

"Commander Hewitt, it's Heath Stone. I know last time we spoke, I told you I wouldn't be coming back, but, sir, I've had a change of heart and—"

"Stop right there, son. Are you one hundred percent certain this is what you want? I pulled strings to get you this long of a leave, but I'll move heaven and earth to get you back—if you're sure."

Am I? If he screwed this up, there wouldn't be another chance. On the other hand, if he chose to spend the rest of his life on the course he was on now, he'd not only end up old and alone, but with nothing to show for it. At least if he re-upped, he could be helping people. That sense of once again having purpose was good.

"Stone?" his CO nudged. "Can I count on you to not flake out on me again?"

Heath took a deep breath, then sharply exhaled. "Yes, sir."

"Thank you, Zoe," Libby said. "I'll hopefully get at least fifteen or so pieces made before I leave for Seattle. After that, we'll talk."

"Sounds perfect." After a hug, Zoe added, "Let me know when you have your baby. I want to make sure my new favorite artist and her daughter are healthy and ready to get back to work."

Libby laughed. "Once my mom recovers from the shock of being a surprise grandmother, I'm sure she'll send formal announcements. I'll add you to her list."

She left the gallery, accompanied by the happy tingling of bells on the door.

Outside, the rain had stopped, although the clouds didn't look quite ready to make way for sun. Didn't matter. Libby felt sunny all on her own.

The baby kicked, and she rubbed the spot near her navel. "You're excited, too, huh?"

Libby glanced up to have her afternoon look that much brighter when she found Heath strolling her way. If possible, he seemed taller, his shoulders more broad. His smile took her breath away.

Acting on pure impulse, she ran to him as best she could, crushing him in a hug. "Zoe not only took all five of the pieces I brought her today, but she wants more! I promised her fifteen! Plus, she charges like double what I ever have. Do you have any idea how much money that is? If all of those sell, I'm rich!"

Not thinking, she kissed him with joy.

And then he kissed her back, at first tenderly, but then with an urgency that tempted her to draw him into a private alley to take things to the next level.

"I'm happy for you." He cupped her face with his hands, kissing her again. "You're the first real artist I've met."

"Oh, yeah?" She kissed him.

"Yeah…" As if only just now realizing they stood on the sidewalk of a busy street, making out like horny teens, he shook his head before releasing her and stepping back. "Looks like it's been a big day for both of us."

"What happened for you?" she asked while they walked to his truck.

"I worked up the courage to call my commanding officer."

"And?"

"And…he says he'll take me back." This was huge. Why didn't he look more pleased?

"Heath, that's wonderful! I'm proud of you for taking charge of your life. Why don't you seem more psyched?"

"I am," he said, opening her door, "but he wants me back sooner than I'd expected."

"How soon?"

"Two weeks." Before her baby was due. For some unfathomable reason, the thought sickened her. Odds were her car would be fixed way before then, and once she returned to Seattle, her time with Heath and his mom and uncle would be nothing more than a beautiful memory.

"At least that gives you time for proper goodbyes. What happens with Sam?" When he helped her into the truck there was the usual tangling of arms, but this time with the added pressure of a heady awareness she knew better than to act upon. If she had her way, she'd kiss him again and again, but especially now, she knew for her own emotional well-being she had to keep her hands to herself.

"I want to take him with me, but considering how often I'll be gone, he'll probably be happier with Mom and Fred."

A knot gripped her throat, threatening to close off her oxygen supply. *Don't cry. Don't cry.* "Sounds like a good plan, although I'm sure he'll miss you."

"Not as much as I'll miss him, but your speech back at the beach gave me a much-needed kick in the ass. You were right. About how I'll feel better helping others instead of sitting around my cabin day after day, moping about what might've been."

Don't cry.

"This may sound crazy," he said, bracing himself on her still-open door while rain pattered the windshield, "but the more I'm around you, the more I wonder if instead of me saving you, it was the other way around."

"So much excitement for one day," Gretta said with tears shining in her eyes after Libby and Heath had shared their news. She stepped out from behind the motel's reception desk to deliver double hugs. "I'm so proud of you both. But with you," she said to her son, pinching his cheeks, "I'm also a little miffed. Why didn't you warn me this was your plan?"

Libby felt as though she was intruding upon the intimate mother-and-son scene. A part of her also felt guilty. If it hadn't been for her prodding, would Heath be staying home? Safe and sound in his cabin?

He shrugged and turned away from her to stare out the window. "I wasn't entirely sure myself. After talking with Mason, it just sort of happened. But I'm glad it did. It'll be good for me. I'm restless. I've got to…" When he spun to face her, his eyes had welled. "I've got to move on, you know? Not forget. *Never* forget. But…"

"I understand," Gretta said as she hugged him again. "And I completely, wholeheartedly agree with your decision—at least if you'll let Sam stay with me. I can't bear to think of him being cooped up in a kennel whenever you're gone."

Heath laughed. "Agreed—especially since I was just about to ask if you'd watch him."

As Gretta was wont to do, she turned the night into an impromptu party, inviting not only Mason and Hattie, but Hal and his sons, Eloise and the other women from her poker club and a few of the single fishermen who happened to be staying at the motel.

By nine that night, the scent of steaks on the grill and classic country music filled the cool night air, and Darryl and Terryl played a rowdy game of football in the pool. What little peace the music didn't fill, their rowdy shouts did.

Chilled, seated alone on one of the deck chairs, Libby smiled when Hattie wandered up, offering one of Mason's U.S.Navy sweatshirts. She was happy to take it, but embarrassed that even the men's extra-large strained to cover her belly.

"Thank you," Libby said. "I didn't realize how cold I was."

"You're welcome." Hattie sat next to her. "I always carry layers wherever we go. Seems like ever since I had Charlie, I'm always either super hot or super cold. Never just right."

"Where is the baby?" Libby asked.

"In the rec room, napping in his carrier. Gretta offered to keep an eye on him."

The twins chased Sam, who had as much energy as the munchkins.

Fred, on the other hand, had fallen asleep by the grill.

Hattie said, "You've got to be thrilled about your big art deal, huh?"

Nodding, Libby said, "Zoe even mentioned the possibility that other galleries she's connected with all up and down the West Coast might eventually request to carry my work. It hasn't fully sunk in that I'll soon be able to support myself, but also that I no longer have to constantly travel to art shows to make my living."

"Has this changed where things stand with your folks? Do you think maybe now you might not even go to Seattle?"

Libby shook her head. "I owe it to my daughter to make things right with her grandparents. They're good people. The last thing I want is for her to grow up with no sense of family. I take full responsibility for my part in the events that came between us. I just hope that after all this time they'll accept some responsibility, as well."

"I hope so, too," Hattie said. "And since I'm already being nosy, where do things stand with you and Heath?"

"What do you mean?" Libby's heart lurched. Had he told Mason about their wild night in the pool? And had Mason in turn told his wife?

"How do you feel about him leaving?"

Awful. The more she thought about it, the more depressed she grew. Which made no sense. They barely knew each other. Why couldn't she be happy for him to be getting his life back in order? "I think it's great that he'll be rejoining his friends, doing whatever it is SEALs do."

"Sure—it's great for him, but, Libby, what about you? I've seen the way you two are around each other. Tonight, when you were eating, he hovered, catering to your every need. A guy doesn't do that unless he's trying to impress."

"You're imagining things." Only Libby had noticed, too. And liked the extra attention. In her heart of hearts, she'd even fantasized about a repeat pool performance, but obviously that wasn't meant to be.

"Uh-huh…" Hattie grinned. "How amazing would it be if before Heath leaves, he proposes?"

Libby coughed so hard that Heath jogged over to make sure she wasn't choking. "You all right?"

"Fine." She had been. Then he ran his hand up and down her back, releasing all manner of delicious havoc along her spine.

"Good," he said. "You gave me a scare. Need anything?"

"No, thank you."

"Okay, well, Mason and I are deep into shoptalk, but flag me down if you're thirsty or need a snack."

The second Heath was out of earshot, Hattie asked, "You don't think that was a bit much? I could sit here for a week and it wouldn't occur to Mason to ask me if I need a drink."

Libby thought about Hattie's reflections in regard to Heath for a long time after her new friend was gone. In fact, she couldn't stop thinking about the downright nutty ideas where she and Heath were concerned—especially that bit about him proposing.

Even though the very idea was ludicrous, the one thing Libby couldn't seem to shake was that from the moment the suggestion left Hattie's mouth, Libby realized her answer would be yes.

Not that it mattered, she mused, standing at the rec room's sink, washing serving platters. Even if she and Heath were an item—which they weren't—no way would he be in the market for a second wife. Not when he'd already had perfection.

But because she had nothing better to dwell on while scrubbing a deviled egg plate, what would it hurt to indulge in a daydream at this time of night?

Heath would be everything Liam hadn't been. Dependable. Loyal. Take-her-breath-away sexy. Judging from the times she'd watched him play with Vivian and Vanessa, he'd also be great with kids. She sighed.

"Give you a buck-fifty for your thoughts?" He'd snuck up beside her, causing her to jump.

"That's an awful lot of cash, big spender." She grinned in his direction, willing her pulse to slow when he grinned right back.

"What can I say? The way your forehead was so adorably scrunched in concentration, I figured I'd for sure get my money's worth."

No kidding! "Sad for you—" she crossed her fingers beneath the suds for the fib she was about to tell "—that the only thing on my mind is wondering how to best tackle the baked bean pan."

"How about you sit—like you're supposed to be doing—and let me scrub it?"

"That'll work." She wiped her hands on a dish towel, then backed into the nearest chair, content to let her gaze wander to his strong shoulders and biceps and the way he did an excellent job of filling out the backside of his faded jeans.

After cleaning the cast-iron skillet that had held the beans, he asked, "What're your plans for tomorrow?"

"I almost forgot. It's the Fourth, isn't it?"

"Yes, ma'am. There's a parade and the carnival we still haven't been to. The barbecue cook-off in the park, and then fireworks at the beach."

"I'm exhausted just hearing about all of it. Got anything more low-key? Assuming you were asking me to tag along with you to any of those events?"

"I was asking, and what do you think of fishing? I know of a nice, shady spot by the river that I can pull the truck right up to." He finished washing a baking sheet. "If we have any luck, I'll catch you a couple fat trout, then fry them for you for dinner. Sound good?"

Unable to speak past yet another knot of happiness in her throat, she nodded.

"You okay?" he asked while drying his hands on the same towel she'd used.

"I'm great."

"Then what's with the waterworks?"

"I'm not sure..." Only she was. Honestly, her latest round of tears were because never in her life had she shared a more intense chemistry with a man. Heath held the power to infuriate her one minute, then have her laughing the next. He was sexy-hot, but also tender and kind. If she hadn't been carrying another man's baby, and if he hadn't been headed to relaunch his career in Virginia Beach, who knew what the two of them might've shared?

CHAPTER THIRTEEN

"DON'T YELL AT ME!" Libby said above the river's gurgling rush when she'd fouled up his fly rod yet again. Heath had promised this stretch of river would be gentle, but he'd failed to account for the previous day's deluge.

"I'm not yelling. But, Lib, you're not even trying to do it right. Plus, we really should be out by that deeper pool, but in your condition, I'm not sure that's such a great idea."

"You think?" she snapped. Had it been only last night when she'd thought he'd make good relationship material?

"Okay, let's try this again." Making her all the more flustered, he stood behind her, easing his arms around her, covering her hands in what she assumed was an attempt to demonstrate the proper way to hold a rod. Alas, all it really achieved was making her entire backside tingle.

"What I need you to do is hold the pole parallel to the water."

What I need you to do is kiss the spot on my neck where your warm breath is making me all achy.

"Next, keeping your elbows by your sides, you'll need to draw the pole back to about the two o'clock position."

Or, we could just stop pretending I'll ever catch on to this technique and spend the rest of the afternoon making out on that picnic blanket you stashed in the truck bed.

"Once the line's straight, snap it back to ten o'clock."

Oh—she could snap something, all right. Maybe his boxers' elastic waistband?

"See how the line's straightening out? Now, you want to guide the fly, presenting it like a gift to our waiting fish...."

She licked her lips. Oh, my, what she'd love to gift him with...

"Make sense?"

"I'm sorry, what?" Was it possible to actually be dizzy from desire? Did he have any idea how good he smelled? Like a leathery, sweat-salty blend that encompassed her every male fantasy?

"Libby? Haven't you heard a word I've said?"

"Yes, but—" *my rich fantasy world is* way *more entertaining* "—maybe I'm not cut out to be a fisherwoman?"

"But we drove all the way out here to fish."

"What if I watch you fish?"

"Isn't that going to be boring for you?"

Have you looked in a mirror lately? "Probably, but I've got Sam and a good book to keep me company. Or maybe I'll take a nap?" She feigned a yawn.

"Want me to drive you back to Mom's?"

"Not at all." What she really wanted was a kiss, but since that wasn't likely to happen, she'd settle for watching him from afar. "Go ahead, catch me a big, fat fish. Then we'll talk."

He blanched. "Why does that sound ominous?"

"It shouldn't. Relax and enjoy yourself. Before too long, this will all be a memory."

Heath knew Libby had meant her words to be comforting, but she couldn't have done a better job of missing that mark. Her not-so-subtle reminder that in a short time he'd not only be leaving this wild place that he loved, with its sun rays slanting through fragrant pines and boulders strewn along the river's edge like a giant's game of marbles, but he'd also be leaving her.

How had she come to mean so much in so little time? He

hardly knew anything about her, yet he craved knowing everything.

Even worse than the guilt stemming from wanting his next taste of her was the curiosity he held for her unborn child. What would the baby look like? Would she have her mother's blue eyes and curls? Freckles? Cute giggle?

He found himself fighting an irrational longing to share those precious first days with mother and child, but then what? What would he even have to offer a woman so—literally and figuratively—full of life as Libby? Where his emotions were concerned, he'd long since established himself to be an empty shell.

Still… In between casts, he glanced in her direction. She sat on the blanket she'd spread beneath a towering fir. While she read a tattered paperback from his mother's library, Sam happily snoozed with his head on her thighs. Every so often, she stroked the soft fur behind his dog's ears. Heath knew the texture well, as it was his favorite place to give Sam affection.

Just looking at her produced a foreign tightening in his chest. A yearning for the kind of closeness he'd once shared with Patricia, but would never be his again.

Why?

The lone word resonated deep within him. It suddenly turned his carefully constructed emotional walls to dust.

His whole reason for keeping Libby at a safe distance was because of his promise to Patricia. But with her blessing for him to forge ahead with a new life, new meaning, what held him back?

His loyalty for her? Yes.

His rock solid belief in the sanctity of their marriage? Hell, yes.

But through no fault of their own, death had seen fit to part them far sooner than either had expected. So where did that leave him? Was he wrong to crave not only more of Libby's kisses, but the comfort and solace he found when he held her in his arms? In the pool, inside her, he'd felt alive and empowered and as if Libby had been the gatekeeper holding the key to this new dawn of his life.

All of a sudden Heath found himself jealous of his dog and the attention Libby lavished upon him.

Though he hadn't caught a single fish he'd promised Libby for dinner, he removed his hip waders, tossed the rest of his gear in the back of the truck, then joined her on the blanket.

"Already catch your limit?"

He laughed. "Try none."

"What're you planning to feed me? As usual, my back hurts and I'm starving, and your mother's spoiled me rotten when it comes to eating a lot—often."

"I know. Sorry. Some days they just aren't biting." Or, more likely in his case, he'd been so distracted by her beauty that he couldn't have caught a trout if it jumped in his back pocket.

"Uh-huh…" Her grin did funny things to his stomach. "Likely story. So what are you going to feed me? Besides another line about the fish not biting."

"How about we go to a little town south of here? We'll buy salmon from this guy who smokes them fresh from the boats. Then, we'll drive up to Calabash Point, and watch the firework shows all the way from Bent Road to Marble Falls?"

The light behind her eyes was all the answer he needed. But it didn't hurt his ego when she said, "Not only do I love smoked salmon, but when you smile at me like that, I'd go pretty much anywhere with you."

"Let me hold your hand. Sometimes, the dock can be slick."

"Sure," Libby said, easing her fingers between Heath's. Though his explanation for his actions was plausible, it lost credence considering the sun-faded wood planks were dry.

As they strolled past commercial fishing boats and mom-and-pop charters, Libby couldn't shake the sensation of fleeting perfection. Perfection in the sense that never had she felt more at ease or content. Fleeting with the knowledge that in two weeks—sooner if her car was repaired—this lovely dream of being with Heath would end.

The pale blue sky was streaked with early evening oranges, reds and violets, and the temperature by the water was cooler than it had been in the lot where they'd parked the truck.

When she shivered, Heath bought her an oversize Oregon hoodie from a tourist shop.

Outside of the shop, he paused to help tug it over her curls. When it got stuck, he pulled it the rest of the way down, landing him once again in perfect kissing range.

This time, instead of kissing him, Libby's pride forced her to wait for him to close the distance. Lucky for her, the wait wasn't long.

"You're beautiful," he whispered so softly she wasn't sure she'd heard it at all.

His kiss managed to all at once be sweet and tender and laced with the urgency stemming from knowing their time together would be brief. If this was indeed the start of a relationship, sadly, the end was already in sight.

"Get a room!" a passing teen hollered from his bike.

Laughing, Libby regrettably called a halt to the impromptu make-out session. "Do you always have dessert before dinner?"

"Hell, yeah…" Though his language was all man, Heath's expression came closer to one worn by a boy caught eating the ice cream straight from the carton. "Don't you think it's better that way?"

She kissed him again. "Yes. Definitely."

They resumed their gentle stroll to the smoked fish stand, sharing more laughs and kisses at the picnic table where they ate their meal.

From there, they took their time returning to the truck.

As much as Libby cherished their every moment together, the day's activities had worn her out to the extent that she napped all the way to the lookout point.

"Wake up, sleepyhead."

"Mmm…" She slowly stirred, pleased to find Heath's smiling face once again within kissing range. "Are we there?"

"Yes. But unfortunately, I'm not as original as I thought, because there are about a dozen families up here with the same bright idea."

"That's okay," she said, gazing over the glistening Pacific. The sun had set, but the moon was now rising, fat and happy as if enjoying the holiday as much as the rest of the crowd. "This will be even more fun. I love hearing everyone ooh and ahh for the really fancy ones."

He helped her from the truck, then took the picnic blanket from the back, spreading it on a grassy area amongst the rest of the parents and kids and grandparents and young lovers.

What had Heath been like before his heart had been shattered and his hopes disillusioned?

"Did you used to come here as a kid?" she asked once they got settled. She sat between his legs, leaning against his chest for support. Her hands rested atop the baby and Heath's hands were atop hers. His heat warmed her, protecting her from the chilly night air.

"Once in a while. Mostly—if my dad was lucky enough to be on leave for the holiday, and was stationed close enough that we could visit my grandparents—they took us to the beach in Bent Road. I'd set up a lounge chair in the sand, pretending I was a tough guy while drinking root beer and smoking candy cigarettes."

"My, my," she teased, "weren't you the rebel."

He laughed. "All right, Miss Jailbird, what are some of your favorite Independence Day memories?"

Libby turned introspective. She preferred not to think of her parents at all, but back when she'd been a kid and hadn't yet learned there was a way of life that didn't involve wearing heels and pearls for every occasion, she supposed she'd had at least a little fun. "First, I'm not proud of my time behind bars. I was in the wrong."

"Sorry. I was poking fun where I shouldn't have."

"You're forgiven."

"Whew…" He feigned relief by sweeping back her hair to kiss the bit of her neck he'd bared. His warm kiss in the cool night air brought on shivers so delicious she temporarily forgot her aching lower back.

"Cold?"

She shook her head, snuggling closer.

"Good. So back to your story?"

"Mom and I always wore matching custom dresses, of course, in red, white and blue. Or some variation thereof. Dad's tie matched, too. Some years we watched fireworks on yachts. Other years, from the house."

"And by 'house,' you mean freakishly ostentatious mansion?"

She cringed. "I suppose you could call it that. But I just called it home, at least until I hit my rebellious years. The cook, maids, gardeners and chauffeurs were as much—or more—parents to me as Mom and Dad. Looking back on it, I suppose they did the best they could in raising me, but my grandparents on both sides were just like them, so they were probably mimicking their own upbringings. Anyway, at my house, a picnic consisted of the servants setting up an elaborate outdoor sit-down meal. Children were rarely invited to sit with the adults, and when we were, we were expected to be seen and not heard."

"So were you friends with the other rich kids?"

"Some of them. But in high school I volunteered because my guidance counselor said it looked good on college applications. I don't think anyone expected me to actually enjoy it. I met all kinds of new people. Once I realized how different I was from the rest of the world, and just how much of a difference I could make to the local homeless shelter by donating my monthly clothing allowance, something inside me changed. Though lately I've been too busy eking out a living to do as much charity work as I used to, one of these days I'd like to get back to volunteering."

"That's cool. If this gallery thing with Zoe works out, you might have more time. You know, spend a few days a week on your art, then the rest of your time working at a shelter or some other place where you'd feel needed."

"I like that plan." Almost as much as she liked him.

The fireworks began.

Even though Heath explained they were ten miles from either town, from this high, on a night so clear, both displays could be seen in Technicolor glory—even faint booms could every so often be heard.

More than the actual show, Libby enjoyed the camaraderie that came along with sharing the occasion with so many appreciative folks. The oohs and ahs and hearty applause by far outshone any of the brightest displays.

Eyes closed against stinging tears, she swallowed hard, recalling a long-ago summer night....

Libertina, you mustn't jump or cry out during the fireworks display. Never forget that above all, you're a lady. Daddy and I expect you to behave as such.

Hugging her baby, Libby decided she'd encourage her daughter to behave with zero decorum. In fact, the very word would be shunned in her home.

When the shows from both towns had finished with spectacular grand finales, Libby was so tired she needed Heath's help to stand.

It was strange to think that only a short time ago, she'd been embarrassed about needing his assistance. Now she welcomed his every touch.

"Have fun?" he asked, setting a slow pace for the return to the truck.

"This was my best Fourth of July ever. Thank you so much."

"You're welcome. Judging by where we both are this time next year, maybe we could do it again—only next time with your daughter along for the ride."

THE SEAL'S BABY

"I'd like that," she said, even though the possibility of them ever meeting again once they went their separate ways was slim.

The notion made her unspeakably sad.

Heath woke to a renewed sense of purpose.

He and Sam did a ten-mile run. It felt strange wearing his boots again, but they'd slipped on like a pair of good friends. They'd seen a lot of action together and it was a rush to think they soon would again.

Mason and Hattie would be leaving today for a brief stay in Alaska to visit their respective parents. Mason's mom had died when he'd been a child, but as far as Heath knew, both of Hattie's parents were still alive, and eager to see their grandkids.

Up until the past couple days with Libby, Heath had been looking forward to getting back to the privacy of his cabin, but now that his time in Bent Road was limited, he'd have just as soon camped out on his mom's sofa. He wished he could tell himself it was her motherly love he craved, but he wouldn't have been fooling anyone.

Libby's blue eyes, easy smile and gorgeous hair had him hooked far more effectively than the trout he'd tried catching. Trouble was, he wasn't trying to catch her. If anything—given the fact that the clock was ticking on the time he had left in town—he should give her a wide berth.

On the deserted beach playground, he did eight pull-ups on the monkey bars before he was shaking from the exertion. Not acceptable, considering he'd need fifteen to twenty to be competitive. Ten was the minimum. Sit-ups and push-ups weren't his idea of a good time, but they were at least doable at a hundred each. As for how long it had taken him to complete the exercises? No comment.

Despite the morning fog and brisk temperature, he'd worked up a hellacious sweat. Knowing he also needed serious boning up on his swimming skills, he stripped down to his skivvies and dove into the surf. The water was cold—like dunking in a vat of ice—but now was hardly the time to wimp out. He only had a short while to get in some semblance of shape, and although he knew there was no way he'd be where he wanted by the time he reported for duty, for his own pride, he'd have to be a helluva lot further along than he was now.

Finished with what he gauged to be three-hundred yards—two-hundred shy of his minimum—Heath sloshed his way out of the water and collapsed on the sand.

Even Sam was exhausted, crashing alongside him, panting.

Heath rolled over to his gear to grab his water bottle, then poured some into his hand for the dog to lap. After repeating this drill three times, Sam fell back asleep and Heath drank some for himself.

He was mortified to have let himself go to this degree. Instead of fishing every day, why hadn't he at least had enough personal pride to maintain his physical strength?

The answer was a no-brainer. Grief did funny things to a man. It made him doubt everything he'd once cherished. Losing Patricia had been the equivalent of having his life's foundation ripped out from under him. Without her, he'd been lost.

Now he felt better, but ironically, it had taken another woman to get him there. As much as he'd grown to care for Libby, he didn't like the fact that he hadn't been able to reach inside himself for self-motivation. What had Libby given him that he hadn't been able to find on his own?

Another easy answer—even when he had believed himself incapable of anything more than the most rudimentary motions of getting through his days, she'd believed him capable of so much more. Her strength had become his. And he'd always be grateful. But what else would she expect from him? What else did she deserve? What was he even capable of giving?

Last night had been the best he'd had in years.

Death had been an insidious, cumbersome beast that had starved him and Patricia of happiness and dignity and quality time.

Watching those fireworks, holding Libby in his arms, he'd felt ridiculously high—and capable of anything. But this morning, faced with his lackluster physical performance, he knew the rest of his time in Bent Road needed to not be spent holding hands or making out, but working himself to the edge of his physical endurance, then pushing still harder.

As for where Libby fit in that picture?

As much as it pained him to admit, she didn't.

CHAPTER FOURTEEN

LIBBY WOKE TO hard rain pelting her bedroom window, but even a glum day couldn't dampen her mood.

Her night with Heath had been romantic beyond anything she'd ever imagined. Sure, there may not have been candles or roses or fine chocolate, but she was a low-maintenance gal, and smoked salmon and holding hands and fireworks had made for a perfect first date.

After a yawn and stretch, Libby gasped from sharper than usual lower back pain. She'd had Braxton Hicks contractions, but this was different—more of a sharp pain. She was so huge, she had to roll from the bed.

Once up, she stopped off at the bathroom. After taking care of necessities, she fluffed her hair, brushed her teeth and pressed a cool washcloth to her splotchy face. It'd been so long since she'd seen her real figure, she'd forgotten what she looked like.

Would Heath have been attracted to her back when she wore a size six, or was her baby part of what drew him to her? She knew he'd wanted to be a dad.... Could part of him wonder what it might be like to become part of a ready-made family? Was that why he was with her?

But then was he truly *with* her at all? Both of them would

soon go their separate ways, meaning this was little more than
a fling to him.

The notion made her sad. But realistically, it also forced her
to search her own motives. What did she hope to gain from
their last few days together? More making out? More skinny-
dipping? More of the simple, basic comfort that stemmed from
talking with a friend?

Sighing, she knew she'd never figure it all out in the next
few seconds, so she got on with her day, ignoring the especially
nagging ache in her lower back in favor of maybe nabbing a
secret, good-morning kiss.

Only she didn't find Heath on the couch, but Fred, gnawing on a slimy rawhide she knew he wasn't allowed to have on
the furniture.

He froze, as if in hopes that if he didn't move she wouldn't
see him, and as soon as she left he could carry on. When that
technique didn't work, he applied a guilty tilt to his head and
wide-eyed innocence.

"You're not fooling me," she said, pointing toward his perfectly comfy bed. "Down."

He begrudgingly obeyed.

She soon found that she and Fred were on their own. Hattie and Mason were heading to the airport, so was Heath at the
cabin? But that didn't make sense, because Hattie had promised
to stop by to say goodbye.

Though her aching back made every step agony, Libby waddled to the motel office in search of Gretta.

"Good morning, sleepyhead." Heath's mom looked up from
a stack of bills and her checkbook. "What time did you two get
in last night?"

Libby yawned. "I think it was around midnight. After dinner, Heath drove me to watch the fireworks from a point—I
can't remember the name."

"Calabash?"

"That's it. We had so much fun." Libby left out the part where she and Heath had lingered long after the rest of the crowd had left. They had shared kisses and conversation. He'd shared his thoughts and fears on returning to the navy and she, in turn, had voiced her concerns about single-parenthood and failing to reconnect with her family.

"I can tell. You're glowing."

Hands to her cheeks, Libby said, "I'm sure I'm just hot from the walk over."

"Nope." Gretta smiled. "Don't even try fooling me. I didn't just fall off the turnip truck. I know sparks of romance when I see them. My son's finally courting you, and I couldn't be more pleased." She rounded the desk to give Libby a hug. Only instead of returning her friend's embrace, Libby winced.

"What's wrong?" Gretta asked, her expression pinched with concern. "Something to do with the baby?"

"No…" Libby backed onto one of the lobby's comfy leather chairs. "I think I spent too much of yesterday sitting on the ground. Too little support left me using muscles my body apparently forgot I had."

Gretta didn't seem so sure. "Let me know if you feel worse. You could be in back labor."

"Thanks for worrying, but I'm fine."

An hour later, Libby wasn't so sure. If anything, her back pain was even more intense. Still, with Hattie and Mason at the house with the kids, she didn't want to waste a moment of their good-byes worrying about a minor ache.

"I'm going to miss you," Libby said to her new friend, rocking her in a hug.

"Likewise," Hattie said, along with a kiss to Libby's cheek. "I was selfishly hoping for a super sneaky surprise engagement so I could have you with me at home. We SEAL wives are always looking to recruit quality ladies for our single guys, as opposed to the female flotsam that sometimes washes up in my bar."

Libby laughed. "Sorry, but there's no chance of a proposal from Heath—or even a kiss—in my future."

"Uh-huh… Deny it all you want, but you can't fool me. I know you two have something going on."

Libby couldn't help but grin through her latest wince. "What's it going to take for you to believe me?"

"Hmm…" She tapped her upper lip with her index finger. "How about a marriage license to another guy?"

"Now you're talking crazy." Because Libby couldn't imagine herself with anyone other than Heath. A definite problem since this morning, after returning from his workout, he'd been uncharacteristically cold, reminding her of the way things had been between them when she'd first come to town. Which, in light of the good times they'd recently shared, made no sense. A fact she planned to drill him on the moment Hattie and Mason hit the road. "But in the unlikely event I do get married, you'll be the first to know."

"Thank you."

"Hat Trick." Mason tugged the back of his wife's lightweight jacket. "If we're going to make our flight, we've got to go."

"Okay, okay…" Libby's throat tightened when Hattie gave her one more hug. "Don't rush me."

"Babe, it's not me putting a time limit on you, but the airline."

Being overly emotional wasn't new territory for Libby, but she was surprised by just how much she hated seeing Hattie go. Sure, she could talk to Gretta, but having a woman her own age to talk to had been a lot of fun.

"Bye, Wibby!" Vivian and Vanessa ambushed Libby's legs with sweet hugs.

"Aw, goodbye, you two. It was so nice meeting you. Hope I see you again real soon."

"Uh-huh," Vivian said.

Vanessa busied herself kissing Sam.

"All right," Mason said, "Libby, it was a pleasure meeting you, but we've really got to go. Come on, crew..." As Mason herded his brood out the door and to their rented SUV, Libby felt a profound sense of loss.

She now knew the friends she thought she'd had on her craft show circuit hadn't been true. What kind of friend carried on business as usual while knowing the man Libby loved was engaging in multiple affairs?

As if sensing Libby's sadness, Gretta wrapped her arm around her shoulders. "It's okay. Now that you and Heath are an item, I'm sure you'll see all of them again soon."

"But we're not—"

"Hush. It's disrespectful to lie to your elders."

"What about you and Hal?" Libby asked, glad Heath was still talking to Mason. "I've seen you two together. When are you going to make an official declaration?"

Blushing furiously, Gretta waved off Libby's question. "Stop being fresh and get out of here. You should be resting."

Mmm...a nap did sound divine—if only she fell asleep cocooned by Heath's strong arms. Too bad that sort of pleasure would only be found in her dreams.

Heath had mixed feelings watching his friends go. He knew once he returned to Virginia Beach, once he rejoined the old crew, he'd be with them probably more than he'd like, so what bugged him about their leaving?

His answer was found when he looked Libby's way to find his mother consoling her.

What bugged him was the fact that today marked the first of many tough goodbyes. His mom and Uncle Morris traditionally visited often, but he wouldn't soon see his dog, and Libby... How did he even start letting her go? Especially when she wasn't even his?

Gretta cleared her throat. "Well, you two. I need to get back to washing towels. Libby, do you need anything before I go?"

"No, thank you."

On her own with Heath, Libby wasn't sure what to say, so she settled for chitchat. "How was your workout?"

"Good." He aimed for the house.

"What's wrong?" Following him, still holding her throbbing back, she said, "You seem like a different person from the guy I was with last night."

"You're imagining things." He held open the back door for her.

Sam romped past them both, knocking her into Heath. He easily supported her, saving her from toppling, but the moment he had her safely upright he let her go. There was none of the lingering contact she'd grown to expect—and enjoy. Instead, he'd become a study in cold efficiency.

"Am I? Last night you couldn't keep your hands off of me. Now you act as if I have cholera."

"Point of fact—" he took a bottled water from the fridge "—the odds of catching cholera from person to person isn't all that high, but you damn sure wanna watch where you get your water."

"Thanks, Mr. Walking Encyclopedia."

He finished half the bottle in one gulp. "Just sayin'…"

"W-what's wrong with you?" Her lower back screamed, but her questioning heart hurt worse. "Last night you were funny and romantic and considerate. Now?" She shook her head. "You're being an ass. I don't even know you."

"Ever think you shouldn't?"

"What's that mean?"

Ignoring her, he left for the living room and started cramming his clothes and books and Sam's toys into a duffel. From there, he headed for the bathroom, shoveling in his toiletries, as well.

"Answer me." She tried tugging him around by his shirt-sleeve, but he stood firm. The effort cost her dearly, as the stretch left her doubling over in pain. *"Ouch…"*

As if her need had flipped a hidden switch deep within him, tender, caring Heath was back, ushering her to a chair. "What's wrong? Is it your back?"

She nodded, but the pain had grown to such an extent that she lacked the focus to speak.

"Shit…" Tossing his duffel, he scooped her into his arms, stormed through the house to kick open the back door, then somehow got her into the truck. Without slowing to even tell his mom where they were going, he drove straight to the clinic, stopping in front of the stairs.

"Stay put," he barked. "I'm gonna get help."

She did as he asked, hugging her baby, crying and moaning for relief. What was wrong with her? Was her baby okay? This kind of pain couldn't be normal.

Moments later, Heath returned with Doc Meadows, Lacy and Eloise in tow.

After Heath hefted Libby from the truck to a wheelchair, the doctor took over, pushing her up the ramp and into an exam room. She wanted Heath with her, holding her hand, reassuring her everything would be all right, but he wasn't following and she was too consumed with pain to ask.

Heath had been in the clinic's waiting room listening to Libby's muted cries for fifteen minutes before he couldn't take a second more.

Ignoring a coughing kid and his mom, Heath stormed past Eloise to the closed door leading to the exam rooms.

"You can't go back there!" Eloise shouted, chasing after him while he searched room by room until finding poor Libby.

"Babe…" he said, surprised to find her on her hands and knees on a blanket stretched across the floor. "Why aren't you on the examination table?" To the doctor he barked, "What's up with her being down there? Can't you see she's in pain?"

Doc Meadows sat on a rolling stool, scribbling something on

Libby's chart before even looking up. "Relax, son. This might
look odd, but I can assure you I've delivered hundreds of healthy
kiddos and I've got this under control. The baby's heartbeat is
strong, but Libby's baby's in what's called an occiput posterior
position. In layman's terms, the hardest part of the baby's skull
is resting on Libby's spine. What we're going to do is try coaxing the baby into a more favorable position. In the meantime, I
want Libby like this to take the pressure off of her back."

"How long does she have to stay like that?"

"Unfortunately, as long as it takes. The good news is that
she's already at six centimeters, so she's well on her way to a
safe delivery, I just want to apply pressure to convince this little one to turn around."

Heath's head was spinning. In a situation like this, he wanted
to call on his training to get Libby safely through this crisis, but
how could he do that when he obviously knew nothing about
labor or delivery?

"What can I do to help?" he asked.

"Honestly," Doc Meadows said, "I'd feel a lot better with you
back out in the waiting room."

That might be what the doctor wanted, but what did Libby
want? "Lib?" he asked, sickened by the pain marring her beautiful features. Her lips formed a tight grimace and her eyes
were shut. Every few seconds, she moaned. Sweat dampened
her forehead, and the nurse had already pulled Libby's long
hair into a ponytail. "Do you want me to stay? I will—if you
need me."

As if she were in a trance, she didn't even look his way. Had
she heard him? Did he need to get on her level to make sure?

"Heath," Doc Meadows repeated, "you need to go. I know it
may not seem like it to you, but all of this is natural. Libby and
her baby will be fine. If I spot even the smallest sign of mother
or child being in distress, I can have her transported to a hospital in thirty minutes."

"Shouldn't she just go now?"

"It'll only increase her discomfort."
"Still…"
The doctor pointed him toward the door.

CHAPTER FIFTEEN

"HONEY, YOU NEED to relax," Heath's mother said three hours into Libby's ordeal. While he paced the clinic's waiting room, with Eloise glaring in his direction, she added, "She's in good hands. Doc Meadows has delivered ninety percent of the kids born in this county. I know that look on your face. You're thinking this is going to end badly, like Patricia, but sweetheart, having a baby hurts. That's just how it is. But in the end, when you hold that precious bundle in your arms, the pain magically vanishes and all that's left is love."

"Yeah, but why won't the doctor let me back there? Shouldn't someone she knows be with her? At least holding her hand? I've seen how this goes on TV and movies, and the dad's always in there with the mom. You know, like a family."

"But, sweetie, you're not a family. As much as she's come to mean to me—and I suspect, to you—when you get right to it, we hardly know her at all."

But that wasn't how he wanted it to be.

Why had he been such an ass this morning? Determined to push her away when all he really wanted was for them to be closer? But it wasn't right for him to welcome her into his life just as he was leaving—her, too, for that matter. He'd been about to explain that to her before bringing her here.

"Do you care for her?" Gretta asked under her breath, presumably so only he could hear.

"Of course," he snapped. "Why else would I be a nervous wreck?"

"No." She rose to rub his back. "I mean do you really care for her? As in have feelings beyond friendship?"

What could he say? Of course, he did. But he shouldn't. And the guilt was eating him alive. It was no longer about guilt over Patricia, but the fact that he was in no shape to emotionally support anyone. Hell, these past months he'd barely cared for Sam. Libby and her baby deserved way more than he had to offer.

"I know you do," his mom said, "so you can stop with the act of playing it cool."

He drew her into the area of the clinic that had once been the grand home's foyer. "Okay, so what if I do have feelings for her? That doesn't change anything. I'm leaving. She's leaving. It would never work between us."

"Why?" Her crossed arms and jutted chin told him she fully meant her question. "Come on, Heath, I dare you to give me one legitimate reason why two lovely young people who clearly need each other should spend even one day apart. And these days, distance doesn't count. It's not as if she'd have to take a covered wagon east to be with you."

"You're not funny." He pressed his fingertips to his stinging eyes.

"I'm not trying to be."

"Heath?" The nurse appeared. "The doctor has the baby turned, and Libby's ready to push. She asked for you."

"Th-thank you, for being here," Libby managed, out of her mind with pain and looking for any comfort. Right now, the only thing she could think of to bring her a moment's peace was Heath.

"Of course, angel. Where else would I be?" He stood at the head of the bed in one of the two hospital-type rooms the doctor used for any patients he needed to keep a closer eye on, but who weren't sick enough to be transported to Coos Bay.

"Enough chitchat," the doctor said. "Libby, girl, I'm gonna need you to push for all your worth."

Teeth clenched, Libby held tight to Heath, craving not only his comfort, but strength.

She had no idea how long she'd been pushing, but forever didn't seem too terribly out of line. Day had turned to night, and through it all he'd stood alongside her, pressing cool rags to her forehead and sweeping back her hair. Telling her she was beautiful, and he couldn't wait to meet her baby girl, who would no doubt be as pretty as her.

Over and over, she bore down. And every time, just when she thought she couldn't stand any more pain, Heath gave her hand a reassuring squeeze.

"She's crowning!" the doctor finally said. "Come on, Libby. You're almost there."

"Arrrrggghhh!" she cried. "I can't!"

"Yes, you can," Heath assured.

"Noooooo..." She thrashed her head back and forth, gritting her teeth through agonizing pain.

"Come on, angel," Heath coached. "Stay strong just a little longer and you'll be holding your gorgeous baby in your arms. One more push."

"E-easy for you to say..."

He laughed. "That's my girl. Get mad at me if it helps. I deserve it."

"Y-yes, you do..."

"What did I tell you two about the chatter," the doctor said. "Libby, I need you to focus like you never have before. One or two more pushes and you'll be done."

She nodded, bearing down, squeezing Heath's hand for all she was worth. *"Arrrggghh..."*

All at once came tremendous pressure, then bliss when pain was replaced by her baby's precious first cry.

And then, when the doctor placed her daughter on her chest, Libby was crying and laughing, as was Heath.

"She's amazing," he said, his voice an awestruck whisper. "I've never seen anything more perfect."

"Hello," Libby said to her daughter, skimming her hand over her tiny fingers and toes. "Boy, am I glad to see you."

Everyone present laughed.

After more bonding, the doctor asked Heath to step out.

Once the infant's cord was cut, the doctor volunteered to clean up the baby while the nurse helped Libby.

"By this time tomorrow," the nurse said, "you'll be surprised by how much better you'll feel."

"Hope so," Libby said with a faint smile.

Twenty minutes later, the efficient nurse had cleaned Libby, dressed her in a new patient gown and tidied the room. Anyone who hadn't been present during nearly the entire day of labor would have never guessed what had just happened.

"I'm sure Gretta and Eloise are itching to see you and the baby. Feel up to a short visit?"

Since Gretta was the only mother figure currently in her life, Libby nodded.

Heath hovered over Doc Meadows, who, in turn, hovered over Libby's baby girl.

He considered himself blessed to have witnessed quite a few things in his life, but watching this perfect, tiny creature enter the world had been better than watching the sunrise from atop Kilimanjaro.

"Good job," the doctor said upon filling out a sheet with Apgar Score Table in bold letters at the top.

"What's that?" Heath asked.

With a chuckle, Doc Meadows said, "This little lady's first standardized test. It scores her color, muscle tone, activity level and so on."

"How's she doing?"

"Solid eight out of ten. She's a smidge early, so at six pounds, she's smaller than I'd like, but other than that I see no cause for alarm."

Heath released the breath he'd been holding.

"You were great with Libby. I'm sure she appreciated your help."

"Thanks, but I didn't do much."

"Don't be so sure. Labor's one of the scariest things a woman can go through. The fact that you held strong for Libby I'm sure means the world to her. Gives the two of you a nice, solid foundation for your shared future."

"Whoa, whoa, whoa..." Heath held up his hands. "You know I'm not the father, right?"

"Sure, but what would it hurt if you were? Libby's going to need a lot of help in the coming days and months. I can't think of a better man to tackle the job."

Heath wasn't so sure, but it somehow meant a lot to him that the doctor who'd known him since he was a kid held him in such high regard. Heath wished he deserved the praise—especially after the way he'd treated Libby this morning. Just because he was messed up inside didn't mean he had to take her along for the ride.

After swaddling the sleeping infant in a thick cotton blanket, Doc Meadows handed her to Heath. "Want the honors of being the first to show her off to her mom and the woman who will hopefully soon be her grandmother?"

Of course, Heath took the baby, but again felt the doctor was getting way ahead of himself.

Then he looked down just as the still nameless baby girl opened blue eyes that reminded him so much of Libby's. Sure, he'd heard the old adage that all babies have blue eyes, but not like this. She was breathtaking all the way from her few pale blond whisps of curls to her tiny, perfect fingernails.

A knot formed at the back of his throat that refused to let go. He made it through the next thirty minutes in slow motion, almost as if he were underwater. While his mom and Eloise and the nurse cooed over the baby, he resumed his place at the head of the bed, beside Libby, stroking her hair, bringing her water, making sure the new mom was as comfortable as possible.

Once Gretta and the other women left, Heath watched as Libby first tried her hand at breastfeeding, his heart impossibly full. He had a feeling the image of her with her daughter at her breast would stay with him a long time—if not forever.

"What're you going to name her?" he asked.

"Gosh, I suppose with all the excitement around my car and meeting all of you in Bent Road, I haven't even thought about it. I figured I still had a couple weeks to figure it out, you know?"

He nodded. "Well, I suppose Heathette's out of the picture, but I think it has a nice ring."

"You're incorrigible," she said with a faint grin.

"I—I want—need—to apologize for the way I treated you this morning. After working out, and realizing just how out of shape I am…" He ran his fingers along the bed's cool metal rail. "Well, I figured if I just made a clean break from you then focused on my training, I'd be all right, you know?"

Eyes welling, she nodded.

"But after what we shared, I see it's not that simple. I'm not sure when it happened, but you've come to mean a lot to me. And I need you to know that I'm not pulling that freeze-out crap again, okay? You deserve better."

"Thank you."

Though he nodded, he didn't feel worthy of her thanks.

"What would you say if I called the baby Heather?"

His heart nearly burst. "I'd say you're probably nuts, but hey, who am I to complain?"

A week later, Libby had settled into somewhat of a routine with Baby Heather. She'd found that the only truly dependable part of motherhood was the fact that if she wasn't breastfeeding, she was changing diapers, or rocking, or singing lullabies. Oh—and just staring in wonder at the miracle of her baby girl.

"Ninety-nine, one hundred…"

From her cozy perch on Gretta's backyard swing, Libby paused the stopwatch Heath had given her to monitor his training.

Heather stirred from her slight movement, but didn't wake.

"How was it?" he asked, still breathing hard.

"You're under four minutes, but if you're serious about making it to two minutes, you've got a ways to go."

He groaned, collapsing onto the grass.

"You'll get there. And you shaved a whole minute off your run this morning." Libby loved that instead of excluding her from his workout routine, he let her help. The sensation of them working toward a common goal only made her feel that much closer to him.

"I know, but I want to be at the top of my game when I get back on base."

"Obviously, but even you said you can already notice a difference in how much better you're feeling."

"True…" On his feet, he cast his most handsome grin on first her, then the baby. "She's zonked. Must be nice, doing nothing with your days but sampling boobies then napping."

"Heath!" Libby couldn't help but laugh. "I'm glad your mom wasn't around to hear that."

"You'd think by now she'd realize I'm no saint."

"Whatever. Ready to start on your push-ups?" Because if his six-pack abs weren't enough of a sight to behold, his backside was even better!

"I probably should." He kissed the baby on her forehead, then Libby full on the lips. It was a foregone conclusion that with each passing day she was falling more for him, but to what end? With both of them going their separate ways, officially moving forward didn't make sense. But then neither did anything in regard to her feelings for him. For now, her only plan was to enjoy what little time they had left and sort out the rest once he was gone.

From inside, the phone rang, the sound carrying clearly through the open windows.

"I'll get it," Heath volunteered.

Libby was all too happy to let him. Though she felt a thousand times better than she had before giving birth, she still lacked her former energy and felt as if she catnapped almost as much as her baby!

A few minutes later Heath emerged from the house, wearing the kind of scowl he'd once been famous for, but she thankfully hadn't seen in a while.

"What's wrong?"

"That was Hal on the phone."

"And?" She steeled herself for the next bit of bad news concerning her disaster of a vehicle.

"The last part came in yesterday, and today you are the proud owner of a vehicle that actually runs. Plus, he grabbed the last few parts for less than expected, so he's giving you a break on labor and only charging five hundred bucks."

"That's all? I mean, that's a lot, but I already have that much saved from my art show profits. I can't believe it." She grinned. "After all this time, it's finally done." But then reality set in. She'd planned on at least six more days with Heath. Who would've thought she'd be the one leaving ahead of him? "Guess I need to ask Doc Meadows if it's safe for Heather and me to travel."

"No. I think you need at least a couple months—maybe even more—to fully heal."

"Who made you a doctor?" And why did he care, considering he wasn't even going to be here?

"Lib, think about it. You're all the time drifting off. What if you fall asleep behind the wheel? It just doesn't seem safe for you to drive all that way on your own. Besides which, your car isn't exactly baby friendly—especially once you cram all your pottery gear in the back. Poor Heather's going to be crushed."

Libby loved that he was concerned, but he didn't exactly have a say in the matter. "Let's agree to disagree."

"What's there to disagree with? I'm right. End of story. Don't you have a doctor's appointment tomorrow? I'll bet even Doc Meadows tells you there's no way you can travel that far for a *long* time. You're talking a good seven hours, babe—without traffic. No. I don't want you going."

"Do you have any idea how crazy you sound? As much as I love kissing you, that's really all we share."

"How can you say that? We share Heather. I was there when she was born. You even gave her my name. No matter what, we'll always have that bond."

"True, but a bond is a lot different than a commitment, Heath. You have no more say over my life than I do yours. How would you feel if I said, nope, you can't leave for the navy so soon after I had the baby? I need you to stay here and help with late-night feedings."

"Is that how you feel?"

Yes! She was terrified of being a single mom, but figured she would eventually have to get used to it. Why prolong the inevitable? She'd always been a rip-the-bandage-off-quick kind of girl.

"No. I would never ask you to stop doing something important to you, and I'd appreciate you doing the same for me."

He sighed before dropping to the ground for his push-ups. "We'll talk about it later. Mind timing me?"

"Yes, I mind timing you. Since you apparently control everything, do it yourself." Cradling Heather to her chest, Libby was off the swing and headed for the motel office to find Gretta. On her way, she dropped Heath's stupid stopwatch onto the soft grass near his stupid—albeit handsome—head.

* * *

"I don't mean to be nosy," Gretta said on the way to pick up Libby's car, "but were you and Heath arguing? I had all the windows open and could hear you from the front desk."

"I wouldn't call it arguing so much as having a difference of opinion." Since Heather's car-safety seat was installed in Gretta's SUV, it made sense to ask Heath's mom to drive her the five minutes to Hal's shop. As an added bonus, she was able to get away from Gretta's son for at least a little while. Libby needed to not only cool down, but have time to think. She hated that Heath had made valid points. What would she do with all of her pottery supplies? Ship it to her parents? Store it here in town, then drive back down for it later? One thing she couldn't do now that she had a baby was pile it all in her car. "He thinks it's not safe for me or the baby to travel so soon."

Gretta shocked her by telling her to ignore her worrywart son. "You know, if you were still in rough shape or Heather had complications, I would agree, but you and the baby seem stronger every day. Heath was born three weeks before his father was being shipped out to Japan. Well, he thought I should stay in San Diego, but the whole reason I married a navy man— besides the fact that he made my heart flutter every time he smiled—was because I craved the adventure of that lifestyle. No way was I staying behind."

She pulled into Hal's lot, parking her vehicle beside Libby's. "I'm not saying it was easy, but I did it and was glad. If you feel compelled to finish your journey home, I won't even lie about missing having you and the baby at the house, but I knew from the start that this was only a temporary layover for you."

Teary from Gretta's admissions, Libby unfastened her seat belt and leaned over to give her a hug. "You've been so amazing. Really. No matter what happens with my parents, I want to keep in touch."

"Absolutely." With a wince, she said, "I almost hate to ask, but what about Heath? Do you think you two will ever be more than friends with benefits?"

"Gretta!" Libby's cheeks superheated with mortification. Had she found out about their night in the pool?

"Oh, you know what I mean. I've seen you two kissing when you think no one's looking."

"It's complicated...." Libby would've liked nothing more than to tell Gretta that her long-term forecast with Heath looked sunny, but honestly? Nothing could be further from the truth.

CHAPTER SIXTEEN

THE NEXT MORNING, Heath still detected a chill from Libby, which was no doubt why he'd been relegated once again to being stuck in the clinic's waiting room.

Because of the whole car-seat issue, he'd driven Libby and the baby in his mom's SUV. Libby had wanted to transfer Heather's seat to her car, but to his way of thinking, the very idea was ludicrous. So much so that he'd called Hal to see about maybe making a few *arrangements*. Libby would be so excited when she found out what he'd done for her.

Hell, he was excited. He'd never pulled off this big of a surprise.

From behind her battle station, Eloise glared even more than usual. "Your mother told me you're leaving soon. Heading back to Virginia Beach?"

"Yes, ma'am."

"Good." Not even bothering to look his way, she carried on with her paperwork.

"Are you ever going to get over me picking your roses?"

She snorted. "Oh—I was over that a long time ago. Now I just don't like the way you're toying with Libby's affections."

There were about a half dozen verbal grenades Heath

would've loved to toss her way, but instead he focused more intently on the teenage heartthrob edition of *People*.

"Is this a new top secret SEAL skill you're working on?"

"What's that?"

"Reading magazines upside down?"

"As a matter of fact, yes. So would you mind leaving me to my work?"

She just shook her head.

Annoyed by pretending he couldn't care less what was going on back in Libby's exam area, Heath tossed the magazine to a side table in favor of pacing out front.

What was taking so long?

Could something be wrong with Libby or the baby?

Should he storm her exam room to check for himself? Just in case? He raked his hands through his hair that would need to be cut before heading back to base.

Libby made him feel perilously close to losing his sanity. And he never would have expected to fall so completely for a long-lashed, blue-eyed vixen who barely weighed over six pounds! He loved everything about Heather, from her tiny fingers and toes, to the adorable sucking sounds she made when she slept, to her impossibly sweet smell when she was fresh from her bath.

He didn't want to admit what the sight of Libby breastfeeding her did to him.

He hadn't meant to go all caveman on her the previous morning when they'd found out about her car, but this was uncharted territory for him. Sure, he'd heard his friends talk about how they felt when they had kids, but he hadn't really understood until he'd experienced it himself.

True. Only one problem, his conscience was all too kind to point out. *Heather's not your kid, any more than her mother's your girl.*

That sobering thought sent him jogging around the lot.

Fifteen minutes later, Libby finally exited the clinic with Heather's cumbersome carrier in her hands.

"Well?" He jogged to her, taking the baby. "You were in there forever. Everything okay?"

"Yes. Why wouldn't it be? In fact, the doctor said as long as I have plenty of rest before the drive, he didn't see any reason why I couldn't leave tomorrow."

That soon? No. No way was Heath ready to give either of them up just yet. Trouble was, her leaving wasn't his call.

"Are you sure you don't want to wait until Sunday to go?" Gretta asked. She held napping Heather to her chest as they sat out by the pool. They'd just eaten turkey sandwiches Morris had brought from the diner. "That way you can have a little extra time with Heath. See him off with me that morning at the airport. Lord knows I could use the moral support."

"I'm sorry...." Libby swallowed the lump in her throat with a sip of iced tea. After all Gretta had done for her, Libby felt awful making her say goodbye to her son on her own, or with just Morris. But she knew there was no way she could watch Heath leave for his flight's gate without losing it. No. She'd be better off leaving first. That way she wouldn't be tempted to beg him to take her and Heather with him. She'd already sold enough pieces in Zoe's gallery to prove to herself she could make it on her own. But did she want to? What was the point when sharing Heather with Heath would mean so much more? "I wish... I were strong enough, but I'm not...."

Gretta placed her free hand over Libby's. "I'm sorry, too. For all practical purposes, Heath's been lost to me since Patricia's been gone. But you changed everything—for all of us. You brought him back to life, and for that I'll forever be grateful. But I've spun this fantasy about you two becoming more to each other, and that wasn't fair to either of you. For that, I'm sorry."

Libby shrugged. "No need to apologize. Heath's a good man. Any woman would be lucky to have him."

"Just not you?"

* * *

Heath's mom had wanted to throw a party for Libby's last night in town, but Heath had nixed that idea. Selfishly, he wanted Libby all to himself when he presented his surprise.

He couldn't wait to see her smile. This was gonna be big. *Huge.* He'd blow her mind with how much he cared for not only her, but tiny Heather.

With Gretta safely off at her Friday night, all-girl poker game, and his uncle busy at the diner, the moment had finally come for Heath to make his presentation.

"Lib?" he called from the kitchen.

"Yeah?" she answered from the bedroom.

"Could you please come here for a minute?" Excitement had his heart racing.

"I'm busy. With Heather finally full and napping, I've got to pack all of my stuff to store in the shed. Your mom said she wouldn't mind me stashing it there until I get settled."

"Okay, well, I'll be happy to help you finish if you'd just help me for a sec."

Sighing, she left her room. One hand fisted on her hip, the other holding the baby monitor, her hair piled into a glorious mess of curls atop her head and her full lips pressed into a frown, she for sure didn't have a clue what was coming. "Okay, I'm here. Where's the fire?"

"Outside. But first, you're going to need to put this on." He took a red bandana from his back pocket, waving it like a flag.

"Put it where? And why?"

"Like a blindfold. Here, I'll put it on for you." She wasn't making this easy. In fact, since he'd told her he didn't want her leaving, nothing between them had felt easy or *right*. He hated her running off to Seattle with the gaping rift between them, but as soon as she saw her surprise, any awkwardness would be behind them. He was sure of it.

"Heath…" Her voice warned of a pending explosion. "You

and your mom didn't plan something nutty like a surprise party, did you? Because—"

"Relax. Mom wanted to, but I shut her down. This surprise is a simple gift from me to you."

Libby's heart galloped. "I don't know about this...."

"Trust me. Take my hand and just trust me that this will make you deliriously happy—at least I hope so."

Mind racing with the forbidden, slightly kinky thrill produced by the blindfold, Libby's mouth went dry while other parts of her grew damp.

Alone in her room, with Heather fast asleep in the antique oak cradle that had once been Heath's, she'd focused on packing to keep her mind from straying to how much she'd miss Gretta and Morris. Fred and Sam. Even Hal and his sons. But the one person she'd miss the most was Heath. His sexy smile and haunting pale green eyes. His laugh and especially his kisses.

She'd never seen him downright playful like this. Could he be on the verge of proposing? No. No way. But what if he was? What would she say? Would she and Heather go with him to his base right away, or wait until they were married? She put a stop to the thoughts rambling in her head, driving her mad. Most days, he seemed more enthralled with her baby than her.

"Just a little farther," he coaxed, when the screen door creaked behind them. "Watch out for the uneven brick...."

Having temporarily lost her sense of sight, his voice alone both carried and thrilled her. She tried not to get too excited by the hope in her heart and what she thought his gift might be.

"Ready?" He held her safe by bracing his hands on her shoulders.

She nodded. "I should take off my blindfold?"

"Yes, ma'am."

Excitement turned her knees to mush. Hands trembling, she inched the bandana back, wanting to prolong the delicious anticipation and thrill soon to follow.

"Aw, come on," he teased, taking the baby monitor. "You're killing me. You've gotta go faster than that."

She tugged it the rest of the way off, then brushed flyaway curls from her eyes before thrill turned to confusion.

Alongside his old truck, parked where her Bug used to be hulked a massive, candy apple–red SUV.

"Well?" Heath moved to the car, giving the rear side panel a Vanna White flourish. "Isn't she a beauty?"

"I don't understand...." Was her ring inside?

"It's yours. Well—like not officially, until you sign over the title for your Bug, but I got you a sweet trade-in deal, then paid cash for the rest, so you're all set. Plus, since you're artsy, I figured you'd like the bright color, right?"

"Wait, what?" So the surprise she'd stupidly, naively, insanely thought would be a proposal was this? "Without even asking, you sold my car? The first car I could afford with my very own money."

"Well, yeah." He opened the rear cargo door with additional flair. "Look at all this space. Not only will Heather's gear fit, but your pottery wheel and kiln. Plus, this has the highest safety rating in its class—airbags everywhere—but not the kind that could suffocate the baby. I checked."

With him beaming as if he'd just presented her with the crown jewels, Libby couldn't very well yell at him. *But he sold my car!*

Deep down, and infinitely more upsetting, her disappointment had nothing to do with her car. His grand surprise hadn't been an engagement ring. His gesture was generous, kind and thoughtful. By far the nicest thing anyone had ever in her wildest dreams done for her. But it wasn't a declaration of love.

"What's wrong? If the color's not right, the dealer said we can have another model down from Portland in a day."

Tears started and wouldn't stop. Turning away from him, she dashed for the back porch.

"Babe?" Jogging after her, he asked, "Talk to me. I expected you to be thrilled."

She flung herself onto the wicker love seat where Gretta sat in the mornings to do the newspaper's crossword.

"What's wrong?" He perched alongside her, tugging her into his arms, against his chest, overwhelming her with the special masculine scent that was uniquely his. A scent she was likely never going to enjoy again. But what had she expected? She'd set herself up for this catastrophe by always looking at her glass not just half-full, but bubbling over.

"Say something—anything. I'm dying here."

"G-good," she sniffled, "because I am, too. Thank you, but I can't accept your gift, Heath. It's too much." It was the kind of thing a guy presented to his wife. The mother of *his* child. Not a random stranger he'd plucked from the road.

"You're being ridiculous. Of course you're taking the car. It's a safety issue. I'm already going to miss you and the baby like crazy. But I'll seriously never be able to do my job if I'm constantly worrying about you and Heather rolling around in that sardine can on wheels."

"Thanks for that," she said with a half laugh, "but I'm still not taking it. You'll have to get my old car back."

"Is this a pride thing? Like when you first got to town and never wanted my help? If so, you need to get over it. Put Heather first. Just like you probably should've called your parents for help a long time ago. Pride can be a bitch. You're damn lucky you ended up with me and my mom instead of some psycho serial killer."

"Oh—if you want to take this conversation to the gutter, hon, let's go." Standing, because she couldn't bear a moment's more of her bare thigh touching his, she placed her hands on her hips. "You wanna know why I'm really so upset? It has nothing to do with the car. I'll concede to you that as a newborn's parent, it's probably time to give up my old ride. But what're you giving up, Heath? If you're so concerned about not only missing me, but worrying about my safety and Heather's, then why not take us with you? The real reason I don't want that shiny new car? It's because I'd set my every hope and dream on you presenting me with an engagement ring. It could've been a bread tie for all I cared, I just want to be with you. I want to raise Heather with you. Which is stupid, right? Considering we've only been on one official date, and even that wasn't so much a formal affair, but more of an excuse to get out the house."

There. She'd said it. Admitted just how much she'd come to care for him. And what did he do? Absolutely nothing other than lean forward, covering his face with his hands.

Classic Heath. Totally avoiding the issue.

His silence was crushing.

The ache in her chest was unbearable.

What had she done? She never should've set her cards out on the table, but instead, kept them close, where no one—especially him—would ever see.

Finally, he stood, rammed his hands in his cargo pants pockets. "Your car was already sold to a collector, so there's no getting it back. Mom's a notary, so when she gets done tonight, you'll need to sign off on the old title, which I found in your glove box—not a safe place for it, by the way—and the new one. The keys are in the ignition. There's also what I hope is enough cash for gas money and food and tags once you get to Seattle. I already paid the tax. Sorry I went behind your back, but it is for your own good—and the baby's. Despite what you think, I care about you both—deeply. But marriage?" He drove the rejection knife deeper with a short laugh and shake of his head. "That's something I just can't do."

CHAPTER SEVENTEEN

RATHER THAN FACE Libby in the morning, Heath grabbed Sam and spent the night at his cabin.

He woke to thick fog.

It reminded him of the day he'd encountered Libby on the highway, and of the myriad changes that had occurred in him ever since.

Memories of their brief time together accosted him, making the pain of letting her go all the more acute. He recalled chopping wood, glancing up to see her standing on his front porch, curls a tousled mess with his favorite blanket wrapped around her. It had smelled of her floral-fruity sweetness for days. There was her finding Sam, and then him acting like an ass for no better reason than she'd altered his status quo. He saw her sitting at her pottery wheel, looking sexy covered in slick clay. Laughing around the dinner table with his mom and uncle and Mason and Hattie. Spoiling his dog. That wild night in the pool he'd tried a hundred times to pretend hadn't mattered as much as it did. Her yelling at him to get back to work, to life, to never forget Patricia but to also never forget to live.

Memories hit faster and harder, culminating in those precious few moments after Heather's birth. How lucky and blessed had he been to bear witness to such an intimate moment. Inviting him in had been such a gift. Yet now, he was essentially throwing her away—Heather, too.

Why? What was he so afraid of?

Sitting on the wooden porch steps, listening to Sam's bark echo through woods, Heath realized he didn't have a clue what he was afraid of, just that he was. He wished he could offer Libby marriage. With everything in him, he wholly believed she deserved her happily ever after. But was he really the guy who could deliver?

Not even close.

"If you'll stay a few minutes longer," Gretta urged Libby at 6:00 a.m., "I'm sure Heath will be here for a proper goodbye."

"No, he won't." Libby had cried so much after he'd left the previous night that she had no tears left. It didn't matter if he showed up, because at this point, they had nothing to say.

"But I don't understand...." Gretta looked to the car, then back to Libby, no doubt noticing her tearstained cheeks and bloodshot eyes. "Are you sure you're even all right to drive?"

"I'm good." She crushed Gretta in a hug. "How do I begin to thank you? You literally saved my life."

"Since you saved my son's, consider us even. Although, this sure isn't ending the way I envisioned. When he told me about this car, I assumed he bought it with the express intention of you and Heather driving east to join him. It'd make a perfect family car. Plenty of room for even more gorgeous babies."

True. Which made how they'd left things all the more depressing.

The SUV was over-the-top sumptuous with heated leather seats, a sunroof, built-in DVD players in the seat backs and On-Star complete with a one-year service contract. Who did that? How could Heath claim to feel nothing for her, yet pay cash to buy her a vehicle that must've cost more than she'd made the whole previous year?

Heath had already installed Heather's safety seat, and Libby had to admit, even the new car smell made her feel good about slipping the baby inside.

"I guess now that Heather's settled, I'm good to go." True to Heath's word, all of her pottery equipment fit neatly inside, meaning she hadn't even needed to take Gretta up on her offer for storage. Another sobering thought, considering she'd looked forward to at least having an excuse to visit Heath's mom and uncle again.

Morris jogged over from the diner. "Good! Glad to see I'm not too late." He handed her a bulging white paper take-out bag. "Here's a little something for your trip. A couple of those turkey sandwiches you like, cookies, chips and a few bottles of water. Hopefully, that'll tide you over."

"You're such a sweetheart." Throat tight, she hugged him, as well. "Thanks so much—for everything."

"It's been my pleasure. Come back anytime."

Unable to speak, she nodded, ambushed them both with more hugs, then climbed behind the wheel of her new car, apprehensive of what the next chapter in her life would bring.

"If you weren't taller than me, I'd turn you over my knee."

"Mom, please give it a rest." Heath had checked his duffel and been given his boarding pass. Now all that remained was saying goodbye with a promise to at least try to be home for Thanksgiving. "I know you spun this fantasy of Libby and me ending up together, but it wasn't meant to be."

After a sarcastic snort, she crossed her arms. "Not meant to be, or you're just too scared to love again?"

Her words cut to his core. Of course, she was right, but he'd be damned if he'd admit it.

"Please, Mom, leave it alone. I gave Libby a pretty awesome parting gift, so—"

"Wait—" she laughed "—that car was your attempt to bribe her into forgiving you for not wanting to take things further?"

"Do we have to do this now?"

"Not at all." On her tiptoes, she kissed his cheek. "You'd just better make darned sure you come home safe, so when we have more time together, I can knock some sense into you."

"Yes, ma'am. And thanks again for watching Sam. I appreciate it."

"Since that dog is the only grandson I'm likely to have, did I really have a choice?"

"Ha-ha." He hugged her for all he was worth, kissed the crown of her head then launched his official fresh start, praying it was better than the possibility of a future with Libby and Heather that he'd just left behind.

"Miss Libertina! You're home—*with a baby.*" Olga, the housekeeper who had been with Libby's family since Libby had been a little girl, made the sign of the cross on her chest. "I'll go get your mother."

Just like that, Libby was left on her own in the white marble-floored entry hall. Though it had been five years since she'd been home, nothing had changed. The double staircase still looked imposing and the compass rose table still held a towering fresh floral arrangement that was no doubt still replaced every four days. The cloying rose scent did nothing to calm her upset tummy.

She hadn't been called by her given name of Libertina since she'd left. It was her great-grandmother's. Libby had always found it a comfort that her namesake had been a bit of a rebel—driving her own car, cavorting without a proper chaperone and even wearing makeup! The thought of these supposed horrors made Libby smile.

Cradling Heather closer, she drew strength from her baby's sweet scent. "How much easier would our lives had been if Heath had taken us with him?"

Easy, yes, but a solution to finally heal the rift in her own family? No. For her daughter's sake—for her own—she needed this reunion. Whatever the outcome may be.

"It's true. You're really here…." Her mother ran—something Rose Dewitt never did off of a treadmill or personal training session—to embrace her daughter. Her tears crushed Libby, making her all at once guilty and sorry and ashamed for causing her mother pain. "I was so afraid we'd never see you again. And who's this?" she asked, cupping her flawlessly manicured hand to Heather's cheek. "She's beautiful."

"This is my daughter—Heather."

"And her father?"

Libby raised her chin. "Is long gone."

"I see. May I?" She held out her arms to hold the baby.

Libby transferred her sleeping child to her mom, whose eyes shone with tears.

"Thank you," her mom said.

"For what?"

"Trusting in us enough to come home. This is where you belong, and now that you're here, Daddy and I will find you the perfect husband—I'm sure he has loads of eligible bachelors at his firm. You might be a single mother now, but trust me, you won't have to bear that stigma for long."

The longer Rose spoke, the more Libby's stomach roiled. Now wasn't the time, but before her mom got too carried away, she needed to know Libby had no interest in a marriage of convenience. She'd had nearly nine, long months to adjust to being a single mom, and though she knew it would be tough, she was no longer afraid.

Yes, her life would've been more fun with Heath, but just because he'd rejected her didn't mean she planned on shutting down.

Her mother fingered Libby's long, pale curls. "First thing in the morning, we'll take you to my stylist to tame your hair. From there, you'll need clothes and a facial and nails—but listen to me. I'm getting ahead of myself. Of course, first, we should find your father. I know he'll be just as pleased you're home as I am."

I wouldn't be so sure.

"It's about damn time you got home!" Heath's longtime friend and fellow SEAL team member, Deacon Murphy, slapped him a high five. "Man, am I glad to see you."

"Likewise." Heath accepted the longneck beer his friend offered.

The guys had all gotten together Sunday night for beers and a beach bonfire.

Right after he'd unloaded his gear in the three-bedroom apartment he'd share with the only two other single guys on the team, "Cowboy" Cooper Hansen and "Dodger" Clay Monroe, they'd loaded him into Cooper's truck to haul Heath to the beach that had once felt like his second home.

His mind had a tough time wrapping around the fact that he'd started his day on the Pacific and ended up on the Atlantic. Regardless, water was water and the crashing surf and briny tang both comforted and gave him strength.

It had been on this very beach that he'd proposed to Patricia, yet all he could think about was Libby. How she was doing with her folks and whether or not they were as accepting of her being a single mom as he and his family had been.

"Hello, Daddy." Libby's father, Winston, Seattle's former mayor who now ran his own law firm, sat at the head of the dining room table looking every bit as imposing as he had back when he'd ruled the city.

"Libertina…" Though he'd never been an overly demonstrative man, he rose, circling the table to hold her, lightly rocking her back and forth.

Relief and love for this man whom she'd alternately hated and adored flowed through her like a healing balm. The years and harsh words that had spanned between them faded, leaving only love.

"I'm sorry." He gripped the back of one of the ornately carved chairs. "I—I made a lot of mistakes. Namely, putting my need for reelection ahead of you—your feelings. Forgive me?"

"Of course." Could it truly be this easy? Erasing years of confusion and pain? She had a hard time believing it would. A long time ago, she'd stopped trusting her father. He'd turned on her at a time when she'd never needed his guidance more.

Now here she was again, needing his emotional support, which he oddly enough seemed willing to give. But at what cost?

By October, Heath and his team had performed a pair of in-and-out covert ops in Syria and a two-week stint in Afghanistan. His body was rock hard and once again accustomed to constant abuse. His mind was sharp and senses honed.

As for his heart—it ached.

Now he hurt almost as badly as he had when Patricia died. But he hadn't *lost* Libby. Instead he'd been too cowardly to even try for something deeper. He couldn't stop wondering what would happen to him if he did go all-in, and then something happened to her, too. Or, God forbid, something happened to Heather? He wasn't sure he was capable of surviving another loss on that scale.

A little past seven on Halloween, he pulled his truck up to the curb at Mason and Hattie's new place. The two-story brick colonial sat in a quiet Norfolk neighborhood that was all decked out for the holiday with orange lights strung on white picket fences and hay bales, scarecrows and mums decorating every front porch.

Ghosts, witches, vampires and fairies roamed the streets in all directions, making him wish he'd stayed back at the apartment, nursing a few beers and playing "Call of Duty."

He didn't have to ring the bell as he damn near got run down by a gang of Power Rangers on sugar highs.

"Glad you could make it," Mason said. "Especially since you're my excuse for turning this gig over to Hat Trick and Pandora."

"Good call." The last thing Heath needed was to be reminded of a holiday that was predominantly for kids. Had Libby bought Heather one of those little baby costumes he'd seen the infant crowd wearing? If so, she had to be the cutest kid in the history of the holiday. The fact that he was missing out on sharing it with Libby and her, taking dozens of pics he could brag about Monday morning made him sick inside. But that longing still wasn't enough to override the fear.

"Nice meeting you," Libby said in the entry hall on Halloween night to Drew Corbett—a junior partner at her father's firm. She'd wanted to get Heather one of the cute costumes she'd seen at the mall, but her mother had thought it would be déclassé. Instead, she'd opted for a taffeta dress in burnt orange with chocolate-toned tights and matching patent-leather Mary Janes. The only holiday concession her mother had sanctioned was a candy corn and silk flower headband. "My father's told me a lot about you."

"Likewise." He handed her a bouquet of yellow, orange and white mums. "Happy Halloween."

"Thank you." She repositioned the baby to her other arm. "Come on in. The party's this way...." Party being a relative term. This was hardly the kind of lively, the-more-the-merrier affair Gretta would've thrown. With aperitifs, champagne, a full bar and five-man jazz band, the night was by invitation only. Libby had quarreled with her mom about Heather even making an appearance, but surprisingly, her father served as her champion, explaining that Drew should see what he's getting into. The comment hadn't set well then, and still didn't now, but as was the case more and more, she swallowed her feelings to please her parents and keep the peace. "Hope you're hungry. Mom's caterer made enough to feed a small country."

"I'm always hungry," Drew said, following after her. "I run marathons."

"That's great."

"I think so. Running gives you quite a natural high. Do you? Run?"

She laughed. "I change diapers."

"Oh. Sure." The night only got worse from there.

By the time her "date" left, Libby had long since put Heather to bed and was headed that way herself when her parents called her into her father's mahogany-paneled office.

"You sure did shine tonight," her father said from behind his desk once she'd sat next to her mother in one of the leather chairs facing him. "I've never been more proud."

"I feel the same," her mother echoed.

Libby wished she found more joy in her parents' statements, but all she really felt was flat. A nanny had been hired for Heather, and Rose kept Libby so busy with hair and nail appointments, shopping and club lunches that she couldn't remember the last time she'd worked with her pottery wheel—not that it would've even been allowed in the house. She'd touched base with Zoe the previous week, and the gallery owner had all but begged her for more merchandise.

"You're probably wondering why I've got you in here so late." Winston sat taller in his leather desk chair.

"Yes." She hid a yawn behind a tight laugh.

Rose patted her knee. "Your father and I have wonderful news. You're going to be so pleased."

Had they refurbished the boathouse to serve as her art studio as she'd requested? For the first time since her arrival, they'd actually piqued her interest in what they had to say.

"You and Drew seemed to hit it off."

She shrugged. "He's okay."

"Well, since he's my sharpest junior partner, I'd hoped—of course in due time—you'd find him more than just *okay*."

While Libby sat shell-shocked, her mother prattled on.

"I've always had my heart set on a June garden wedding for you, but if that's too soon, maybe September? Or even Christmas. Your bouquet could be poinsettias mixed with white orchids."

Mortified didn't come close to describing the thick disappointment making her limbs and heart heavy. "You guys can't be serious?"

"Honey," her father said, "Drew's a wonderful man. Your mom and I have noticed how lonely you've seemed, and thought maybe a handsome new fella in your life might make you smile."

"Whoa." Libby stood and forced deep breaths to keep from saying something she'd later regret. For Heather's sake she wouldn't burn bridges, but enough was enough. "While I appreciate you both caring how I feel, please slow down. Ever since I came back, I've let you two dictate my every move. What I wear, eat. How I style my hair. Do you have any idea how long it took for me to grow it that long? It made me feel pretty.

"Now…" She touched her trembling hand to her shorn locks. She might have a sophisticated bob, but she didn't feel like herself. "I feel like a robot, constantly following your commands."

"Sweetheart…" When Rose reached for her hand, Libby stepped just out of reach.

"I love you two. I hoped coming back would change things, but everything's the same. You don't want me to grow into a self-sufficient adult, but keep me under a glass dome. Like a doll that's for looking, not touching. But that's not who I am. I hate these uptight clothes—" she tugged the jacket of her Chanel suit "—and I miss my work. Did you know my pottery now sells out of a gallery? No, you don't, because you never asked and I knew it'd only upset you if I told you. But how sick is that? That I knew you wouldn't be happy learning that I'm actually a working artist."

"Libertina, honey—" her mother went to her, tucking Libby's hair neatly behind her ears "—calm down. Of course we're proud of you. We just thought that with the baby, you'd be too tired to work. I was exhausted after having you. And if you don't care for Drew, your father has lots of other men whose company you might enjoy."

On the heels of a near-hysterical laugh, she said, "My name's *Libby.* And the last thing I want is another man. Especially when there's someone I already care deeply for."

"The baby's father?" Eyebrows raised, Rose cautiously smiled. "You haven't told us much about him. What's he like? By all means, invite him up for a weekend so we can get to know him. Please, *Libby,* all we want is to see you smile. We know we're not exactly part of the hip crowd, but maybe we could be—if you'd meet us halfway?"

"Mom…" Libby was touched by her mother's speech, but she wasn't sure what else to say. "This isn't about you being *hip,* but letting me be me." Sighing, she cradled her forehead in her hands. "Maybe it'd be best for everyone if Heather and I just leave."

"And go where?" her father asked. "I promise I mean no disrespect by this, but, Libertina—Libby…" He smiled through silent tears that made Libby's heart ache. "The time you were gone was easily the darkest of my life. I may sound melodramatic with this next admission, but I honestly don't think I could survive if you left again—especially not taking my granddaughter with you. In light of that fact—" Fresh tears shined in his eyes as he looked to Libby's mom and then her. "If you promise to stay, and give your mother and I pointers on the proper etiquette of proud parents of an artist, I promise to never play matchmaker again—unless you want me to."

Her mother added, "And not only will I promise not to meddle in your love life, but leave you alone when it comes to your choice in hair and clothes. I'm sorry." Now, her mom was crying, too. "I thought I could make things the way they used to be, but what I never stopped to consider was that when you left, we weren't exactly functioning as a family, but more like a campaign machine."

"Mom…" Libby swiped tears of her own.

"Your mother's right." Her dad passed around a silver-plated tissue box, then took two for himself. "The way I treated you was deplorable. I can never apologize enough—to both of you. I put pride before family. Having you back, holding Heather…" He blew his nose. "With the benefit of hindsight, I realize you three ladies are my world. I love you."

Her parents weren't the demonstrative type, so when her dad stepped around his desk to give Libby a hug, then kiss her mom full on her lips, she couldn't be entirely sure she wasn't dreaming.

Gazing back to her daughter, taking Libby's hands in hers, her mother said, "If you stay, assuming you're okay with it, how would you feel about all of us transforming the boathouse into your ideal workspace? Whatever you need, sweetheart. Name it, and it's yours—even a second nursery so Heather can be with you while you work."

Libby crushed her mother and father in hugs. "I'd love that. I love you both so much." Through more tears, she added, "Daddy, I really am sorry for harming your campaign all those years ago. All I ever wanted was for you to love me for who I am—not who you *want* me to be."

"Done. Only…" Once she released him, he reached for his archaic Rolodex. "I do have contacts in the art world. I'll make some calls and then—"

"Winston!" her mother admonished. "Before you do anything regarding Libby's art career, don't you think it would be wise to first ask her?"

He reddened, but in a soft, uncharacteristically lovable way that prompted Libby to dive in for another hug.

Without Heath, Libby feared her life may never feel totally complete, but with her parents' emotional support, she'd just taken a giant step closer to finding happiness and that elusive sense of belonging she'd been looking for.

"Thanks for having me," Heath said to Hattie the Wednesday before Thanksgiving. His team had just finished debriefing from another run to Syria and he badly craved home cooking instead of the jar of mayo and pickles that were pretty much all he had in his fridge.

Mason was in the playroom reacquainting himself with his kids.

"Of course," Hattie said. "You know you're welcome anytime." After giving him the first decent hug he'd had in a long time, she asked, "How are your mom and uncle?"

"Good. Mom's relieved I'll be home for the holiday." While Hattie sprinkled crushed Corn Flakes atop her famous chicken casserole, he sat on a kitchen bar stool. "Truthfully, I'm shocked the CO gave me the time off. As long as I was gone, I was sure he'd keep me on lockdown."

She waved off his concern. "That's what the baby SEALs are for. You've earned your break."

"I guess. Got any beer?"

On her way to the fridge, she said, "That's a dumb question. Here."

"Bless you." He downed half the bottle.

After grabbing one for herself, she said, "I know this is no doubt the last thing you want to hear, but I got an email from Libby. She's doing well."

"Good for her. Glad one of us is."

He hated Hattie's wide-eyed look of concern.

"Don't even start. I'm honestly glad to be back at work. It's great being busy. Libby and I…" He finished his beer. "Got another?"

"Not unless you admit you two were more than friends."

"Let me get this straight—you're blackmailing me for beer?"

"Yep." She retrieved another cold one, wagging it in his face. "What're you gonna do about it?"

Sighing, he said, "You win. Had I stayed in Bent Road, we'd probably still be together, but did you know she actually wanted to marry me?"

"Of course, I know." She grinned. "It was my idea."

"Are you kidding me? Why'd you go and tell her something like that? You know my history. I've already done the marriage routine, and there's no way I'm setting myself up for that kind of pain again should something go wrong."

"Yeah, but—" she popped the beer's twist-off cap and handed it to him "—what if you did marry her and the rest of your life went *really* right?"

CHAPTER EIGHTEEN

COME MORNING, Heath rose extra early.

He stopped off at a grocery store for flowers, then drove through light drizzle toward Patricia's grave.

He needed to talk to her.

At 6:00 a.m., the lot was deserted. The groundskeeper waved Heath in upon opening the gate.

"How've you been?" Arthur asked. The hunched-over old guy had to be pushing ninety, but he always wore a smile. He lived in a small caretaker's house with his wife and a yappy little poodle that sometimes dug out from under his backyard fence and ran around peeing on graves. "Haven't seen you in a while."

"Some good days, some bad," Heath said. "How about you?"

"Happy wife, happy life." He knelt to fish an empty beer can from under an azalea. "Though this damp weather's got my arthritis acting up."

"Sorry to hear it."

"I'll be all right. By the time my Gladys adds a little whiskey to my coffee, then gives my shoulders a nice rub, I'll be A-okay."

Heath laughed. "Sounds good. I'll leave you to it."

He envied Arthur's seventy-year marriage. That was the way it was supposed to be. That's the expectation he'd had when saying his vows.

With two hours to kill until he was due on base, Heath took his time winding through the graves. He liked looking at the really old ones, wondering about their lives. He was always surprised by how young people had been when they'd died in the 1800s. Patricia had also been stolen in her prime.

In front of her tombstone, he knelt, tearing out the few weeds before placing her flowers.

"Sorry it's been so long," he eventually said, "but you know how I never set much stock in these kinds of things. When you left me, I watched you go. Wherever you are, you're sure as hell not in this grave—at least not your spirit."

He sat back on his haunches, plucking more weeds and the too-long grass.

"Anyway, I've got a bit of a situation, and I don't know where else to turn. Everyone seems to think I should just jump right into another marriage, but…" He bent forward from the waist, pressing the heels of his hands against his stinging eyes. "It's not that easy, you know? I used to envy you for going first. I imagined you partying up there with angels, while I was stuck down here in hell. Only something happened this summer—I met someone. When we're together, she makes me feel like I could gladly go another fifty or so years.

"I'm pretty sure I really care about this woman, but not only do I feel guilty about leaving you behind, but what if she dies, too? It's scary—this whole relationship thing. I just wish you were here to tell me what to do."

Heath was so lost in his fear that he didn't notice the woman approaching until she was nearly on top of him.

"Good morning," she said. Her hair was blond—though not as pale as Libby's, and cut short. She pushed a stroller, and when he got a look inside, he saw an infant not much bigger than Heather was when she'd been born.

"Morning."

Just as soon as she'd appeared, she was gone, heading over a small hill.

But then a man appeared, chasing after the mother and child. Soon, he'd also vanished over the hill, leaving Heath once again alone.

All the times he'd visited Patricia's grave, he'd never seen anyone pushing a stroller.

"Was that supposed to be some kind of sign?" he asked. "Am I supposed to go after Libby, then bring her here? Home?"

He wasn't sure what he'd expected, but all he got was the familiar tightening in his chest from missing Libby and her baby. In that moment, he finally realized Patricia, his mom and Hattie had all been right—even Libby. They'd all told him, maybe not in the same words, that he couldn't spend the rest of his life with a grave.

Not only did he need Libby, but hopefully, she and her baby still needed him.

Over Thanksgiving weekend, Heath started what he considered to be the toughest mission of his life when he flew to Portland for a brief bit of dicey—and expensive—business. He'd gotten Libby's snail mail address from Hattie, then programmed Libby's Seattle location into the map application on his phone.

After an excruciating five-hour trek in what felt like a tuna can of a car, he pulled into the circle drive of the largest home he'd ever seen. The damn thing looked like a mini White House—complete with a chandelier hanging from the portico's sheltered ceiling.

Whoa. He'd known Libby came from money, but nothing like this. Why hadn't he stopped for flowers or chocolates? For that matter, he didn't even have a ring. His sole focus had been on finding Libby, then apologizing for not having figured out how much he cared for her sooner.

After that, his plans pretty much depended on her reception. He rang the bell.

It chimed with an elaborate, cathedral-like series of rings.

From inside, he heard footsteps, and then the sound of someone opening a dead bolt.

"Yes?" a uniformed maid asked. "May I help you?"

He cleared his throat and stood taller. "I'm, ah, here to see Libby."

"Miss Libertina's no longer in residence."

Seriously? Libertina? And if she wasn't there, then where was she? "Do you know where she is?"

"One moment, please." Instead of inviting him inside, she shut the door in his face.

He glanced down at his desert fatigues and boots, wishing he'd thought to dress for the occasion. Could he have mucked this up any worse?

A good five minutes later, the door opened and an imposing man stepped out. Without even a courtesy greeting, he asked, "How much do you want?"

"E-excuse me?"

He held a leather-bound checkbook in one hand and a pen in the other. "You are my granddaughter's father, I take it? The one who broke my daughter's heart?"

"No, sir. I'm Heath Stone. Libby stayed with my mother and I when her car broke down."

"But she's driving a reasonably new car."

"Yessir, because I bought it. If she'd had her way by driving her old car, she'd have no doubt broken down again." As soon as the condemning words left his mouth, Heath felt disloyal for even saying them. This was the man who hadn't believed in her. As such, he didn't deserve to hear how amazing his daughter really was—even if she had argued with Heath regarding car safety.

"Then you're wanting reimbursement for that?"

Eyes narrowed, Heath said, "I don't mean to be disrespectful, but the only thing I want is your daughter. Is she here?"

Her father stared him down, giving Heath the sensation he was being appraised. "Yes and no."

"Okay…" For all the home's grandeur, the occupants were about as warm and fuzzy as a chunk of dry ice. "Which is it? Is she here or not? I really need to see her—and Heather."

The man's eyes narrowed. "What business do you have with my daughter?"

"With—or, even without—your permission, I plan to marry her."

Late November days didn't get much more beautiful than this. With the temperature in the high seventies and the sky streaked with orange and violet, Libby cradled Heather more snugly in her blanket, breathing deeply of the water's briny-rich smell.

Sam chased down the shore after a seagull.

"Doggy's silly, but we're lucky girls, aren't we? Have you ever seen a more gorgeous view?" Seated on the boathouse's newly installed swing, staring out at near-glassy Puget Sound, Libby almost felt whole.

Her parents had been wonderful in their support—more than she ever could've hoped for. The boathouse's lower floor now served as her studio and the upper floor was a posh one-bedroom apartment with a sumptuous nursery alcove. True to his word, Winston had stopped matchmaking and her mother joined all the right committees for the Seattle art scene.

Over the weekend, Libby and her parents and the baby had driven down to meet Heath's mother and uncle and even Zoe. The days had been idyllic. Libby cherished the time spent with everyone she loved—all save for one stubborn man she feared she may never get over.

She'd returned to Seattle with not only Sam, who'd been miserable cooped up with lazy Fred, but two gorgeous container gardens that had prompted her to make more until the deck surrounding her new home now made her heart sing from the dizzying array of colors and scents. Sweet snapdragons and petunias, pungent marigolds. Delicate lobelia and even robust tomato and pepper plants Hal had dug up for her from his vegetable garden.

Five more galleries had requested her work, and she'd even been invited to speak about her process at an upcoming showing. So many aspects of her life were incredibly satisfying, yet she'd be lying if she didn't admit to constantly missing Heath.

The sun took its sweet time setting, but that was okay. After a long day of spinning new projects, she was officially pooped, and all too happy to sit.

Just as the sky darkened, the faint sound of an engine alerted her to the fact that she soon wouldn't be alone. A service road made her home accessible for supply deliveries, but she wouldn't get one at this late hour.

"That's odd," she said to the baby. "Were you expecting a package?"

Heather gurgled and clapped her hands.

"That's what I thought."

Libby rose, assuming whoever drove the car was a lost tourist, and set Heather in the playpen she kept on the porch on sunny days, then crossed the pebbled parking area.

"Lose your way?" she asked the driver, who was exiting a VW Bug similar to the one she used to own. The resemblance was remarkable. It could've easily been her car—only better, as this one had been restored to its former glory.

"Yeah, I am lost," a dear, familiar voice said, "but not in the way you mean."

"Heath?" She didn't dare hope what his presence meant.

"I'm sorry." In four confident strides, he walked to her, wrapping his arms around her waist to lift her into a hug. She was still furious with him, but God help her, he was still the first one on her mind every morning and the last thing every night. Burying his face in her now shoulder-length hair, he breathed her in. "I'm so, so sorry. I messed up everything. Not telling you how I really felt. Selling your car. I was so afraid of losing you, I couldn't even conceive of keeping you."

"Keeping me?" she teased once he'd set her to her feet. "I'm not livestock." Smile fading, she added, "In all seriousness, you hurt me. I love you, Heath. I offered myself to you, and just like every other man in my life, you didn't want me."

"The hell I didn't. I'm pretty sure I've loved you from the first day we met, but I couldn't give myself permission to be with you. On so many levels, it felt wrong. But then, the more we were together, I couldn't get enough of you."

"And so you bought me a car that looks like my old one? Heath…" As lovely as the gesture was, she didn't want a car, but *him!*

"It's not a clone, but the real deal. I know it doesn't make up for the way I treated you, but what we shared scared me. You scared me."

"How?" She'd taken his hand, tracing the deep lines on his work-roughened palm. Dare she hope his being here meant he was prepared to at least try opening himself to another chance at love?

"You forced me to take stock of my life. You woke me from a deep sleep. For the longest time I didn't know what to do, or even how to act. But now I get it. I understand that loving you doesn't make what I shared with Patricia any less valid."

"Didn't I tell you that back in July?"

"What can I say?" When he kissed her, liquid heat coursed all the way to her toes. "I'm slow on the uptake, but now that I'm here, will you marry me? Oh—and if it make a difference, your dad even gave his consent."

"You asked my dad?" Her eyes widened.

"Well," he said, sheepishly smiling, "I sort of just told him. At the time, it seemed like the right thing to do."

"What did he say?"

"That he loves you. And more than anything, he wants you to be content. Does that make you happy?"

For once swallowing a knot in her throat caused by joyful tears, she nodded. "But not as happy as this…" She kissed him and kissed him until the sky turned dark and stars twinkled overhead.

Together, they played with Heather and made plans.

Sam returned from his latest adventure and bayed with excitement for a full five minutes upon discovering his former best buddy.

After Heather was fed and tucked into her cradle for the night, and Sam had fallen asleep in front of the crackling fire Heath built to ward off the chilly evening air, Libby and Heath shared a simple meal of scrambled eggs and toast much as they had the first day they'd met.

And then, finally, finally after months of yearning and hoping and praying and longing, Libby's body hummed with pleasure when Heath carried her to the bed, vowing to always love her in the most intimate way a SEAL can.

EPILOGUE

"WAIT—YOU NEED something blue!" While Libby dashed off to find the racy blue garter she'd purchased for Gretta's wedding, Hattie and Pandora worked on the glowing bride's makeup and hair.

"I'm all of a sudden so nervous," Gretta said. "Libby, when you and Heath were married, did you feel this scared?"

Libby laughed. "Yes—but only because I was afraid the big lug might bolt. As tough as he was to catch, I wanted him officially mine as soon as possible. That's why we had a Christmas wedding."

"You were smart to not give him too much time to escape," Hattie said, with Pandora nodding in agreement.

"Gee, thanks guys." Hands on her hips, Libby shot her friends playful daggers.

"You know we're teasing."

The upstairs room had grown stuffy, so Libby opened the double doors leading to the veranda and the sweeping Puget Sound view. Since she and Heath were married, her parents had only grown more supportive. Libby and Heather often stayed with them when Heath was deployed. Not only had they purchased a Virginia Beach condo for east coast visits, but her mom had even gone so far as to offer their Seattle home for Gretta's

June wedding. Rose was ecstatic to finally have a special occasion that called for raising a tent on the lawn.

A knock sounded on the bedroom door.

"Who is it?" Libby asked.

"Me," said a muffled male voice. "I wanna kiss my bride."

Gretta swiveled on her makeup chair. "Hal Kramer, you get away from that door this second or the wedding's off!"

"Not even one kiss?"

"No! It's horrible luck! Now, get!"

Fortunately for Gretta—and everyone else who'd shared in the planning—the ceremony went off without a hitch. The hundreds of pink roses and lilies were fragrant, the cake was beautiful and the dinner delicious.

"There you are," Heath said when Libby finally sat long enough to rest her swollen feet. At three months pregnant, overall, she still felt great, but knew the day was soon coming when she'd be huge and perpetually tired all over again. But it would be worth it—especially if her Norfolk obstetrician's suspicions came true. "I've missed you. Mom's been hogging you all to herself."

"I know. I'm sorry. Wanna dance?"

"Absolutely." Easing into his arms and resting her cheek against the muscled wall of his chest, Libby couldn't remember having ever felt more content.

Even Heather was giggly while Grandpa Winston waltzed her around the tent.

Turning introspective, Libby looked up at her handsome husband. "Do you ever regret all of this—*us?*"

"Are you kidding me?" Right in the middle of the dance floor, he thoroughly kissed her. "Even though combined we have more family and friends than we know what to do with, I wouldn't have it any other way."

"Good. I feel the same. Only, Heath?"

"Yeah?" When he looked down at her with his gorgeous, white-toothed grin, her heart never failed to flutter.

"How would you feel if I told you that during my last ultra-sound—you know, the one when you were in Ghana—that the doctor told me he's pretty sure we're having triplets…?"

"How would I feel?" he asked, looking ecstatic but a bit dazed. "Like I might need a stiffer drink."

* * * * *

The Courage To Say Yes

Barbara Wallace

Award-winning author Barbara Wallace first sold to Harlequin® in 2009. Since then her books have appeared throughout the world. She's the winner of RWA's Golden Heart Award, a two-time RT Book Reviews finalist for Best Harlequin Romance, and a winner of the New England Beanpot Award.

She currently lives in Massachusetts with her family. Readers can visit her at www.barbarawallace.com and find her on Facebook. She'd love to hear from you.

Other books by Barbara Wallace

THE BILLIONAIRE'S FAIR LADY
MR. RIGHT, NEXT DOOR!
DARING TO DATE THE BOSS
THE HEART OF A HERO
BEAUTY AND THE BROODING BOSS
THE CINDERELLA BRIDE
MAGIC UNDER THE MISTLETOE

Other titles by Barbara Wallace available in ebook format at millsandboon.com.au.

Dear Reader,

I love all my characters. Every once in a while, however, a character pops into my head whom I feel very protective of. Abby Gray is one of those characters. It was very important to me that she get not just a happy ending but the *right* happy ending—with the right man. Believe it or not, several auditioned for the role before Hunter Smith came along.

When Abby first sprang to life, I found myself with a spunky but downtrodden young woman just out of a horrendous relationship. I wanted to show how even smart women can get sucked into a spiral of insecurity and abuse. Getting out of that spiral isn't easy.

Fortunately Abby has Hunter to help her. Unfortunately Hunter has a few issues of his own when it comes to connecting with people. He'd much rather keep them at a distance to prevent himself from getting hurt. But, as happens with true heroes, Abby forces him to embrace his inner white knight. Before he knows what's happening, this sideline guy is involved in Abby's world and losing his heart!

Underneath all the romance there is an important lesson. That it's not enough simply to find a man who treats you right, but you must find yourself, as well. It's the lesson Abby needs to learn to get her happy ending. I hope as you're reading about Abby and Hunter's journey the lesson resonates with you, as well.

Thanks, as always, for reading my stories. I love writing them, and hope to entertain you for many more stories to come.

Best,

Barbara

To my boys Peter and Andrew—you are the best.

Thank you for your patience, your support,
and your sacrifice.

CHAPTER ONE

"HEY, WHERE DO you think you're going?"

Pudgy fingers gripped Abby's wrist. She froze, hating herself for her reaction. "Let go of me, Warren," she said.

Her ex-boyfriend shook his head. "I'm not done talking to you."

Maybe not, but Abby was done listening. "There's nothing more to talk about." At least nothing she hadn't heard a dozen or three times before.

She tried to yank her arm free, but Warren held fast. "Since when do you tell me what to do?"

His fingers dug into the top of her wrist. He was going to leave a mark, dammit. "Warren, please." The plea slipped out from habit. "The customers…"

"Screw the customers." A couple heads turned in their direction. Abby didn't dare look to see if Guy, her boss, had heard, too.

"This is your fault, you know?" Warren told her. "I wouldn't have to come down to this—" he curled his upper lip "—this *diner* if you weren't being so childish."

As if his pouting and tantrums were the height of maturity. Abby knew better than to say anything. Hard to believe she'd once considered this man the answer to life's problems. Now he was the problem. One hundred ninety-five pounds of un-shakable anger. Why couldn't he let her go? It'd been six weeks.

When it comes to us, I make the decisions, babe. Not you. That's what he always said.

How on earth was she going to get loose this time?

"Hey, Abby."

The sound of her name cut through the breakfast din, and made her pulse kick up yet another notch. Abby knew the speaker immediately. The photographer. She'd been waiting on him for the past dozen days. Always sat at the back cor-ner table and read the paper, his expensive camera resting on the chair next to him. Quiet, hassle-free. Good tipper. Hunter something or other. Abby hadn't paid close attention. Whatever his last name, he was heading toward them, weaving his way through the tables with a graceful precision. Warren was not going to like the interruption.

"You want something?" he asked, before she could.

"I could use some more coffee." Hunter directed his answer to her as though her ex had never spoken. "That is, if you can pull yourself away from your conversation."

"Um…" She looked to Warren, gauging his reaction. After six years, she'd become an expert on reading his facial expres-sions. The telltale darkening of his eyes wasn't good. On the other hand, she knew he preferred discretion, choosing to do his bullying in private.

"You heard the man. He needs fresh coffee," Warren replied. "You don't want to keep your customers waiting."

Leaning forward, he placed a kiss on her cheek, a marking of territory, as much for her benefit as Hunter's. Abby had to fight the urge to wipe the feel of his mouth from her skin. "I'll see you later, babe."

His promise made her stomach churn.

"Nice guy," Hunter drawled from behind her shoulder.

"Yeah, he's a real peach."

She rubbed her aching wrist. What made her think she could

walk away, and Warren wouldn't try to track her down? Just because he told her repeatedly that she was a worthless piece of trash didn't mean he was ready to give her up. As far as he was concerned, she was his property.

Warren's car pulled away from the curb. He was gone, but not for good. He'd be back. Later today. Tomorrow. A week from tomorrow. Ready to beg, scream, and try to drag her back home.

Oh, God, what if she wasn't in a public place when he returned? Or if he decided to do more than beg and scream? There were all sorts of stories in the news....

Her breakfast started to rise in her throat. She grabbed the chair in front of her.

"You okay?" she heard Hunter ask.

"F-fine." For the millionth time in six weeks, she pushed her nerves aside. Worrying would only mean Warren still had control. "I'm fine," she repeated. "I'll go get your coffee."

"Don't worry about it," he replied. "I'm good."

"But you said..." She stopped as the meaning of what he'd done dawned on her. He'd interrupted on purpose.

"You're welcome." Hunter turned and headed for his usual table.

Abby didn't know what to say. She should be grateful. After all, he'd just bailed her out of what could have become a very difficult situation. In all her years with Warren, no one had ever stepped up to help her before. On the other hand, she hadn't asked for his help. He'd just assumed she needed it, as though she were a helpless little victim.

Aren't you?

No. Not anymore. Despite what the situation looked like.

Oh, but she could just imagine what someone like the photographer thought, too. Her hand still shaking with nerves, she ran it through her hair before looking over at the back table. There sat Hunter, sipping the coffee he didn't need refilling. With his faded field jacket and his aviator sunglasses perched atop his thick brown hair, he looked exactly the way you'd picture a photographer. If you were casting a movie, that is. One where the daredevil photojournalist dodged bullets to get the shot. To be honest, his whole outfit—worn jeans, worn henley—would seem silly on anyone who didn't look like a movie star.

It didn't look silly on the Hunter. He had the cheekbones and complexion to rival any actor in New York City. Might as well throw Los Angeles in there as well, Abby decided. The build, too. Whereas Warren was soft and doughy, Hunter was hard, his body defined by angles and contours. Small wonder Warren had backed off. Her ex might be a bully, but he wasn't stupid. He knew when he was outclassed.

Too bad she couldn't get Warren to back off so easily.

"Abby, order up!" Guy stuck his craggy head out of the order window and slapped the bell. "Get your butt in gear. You want to stand around, you can go find a street corner."

As if this job was much better. She moved behind the counter to pick up the two plates of scrambled eggs and bacon Guy had shoved onto the shelf. "What about the home fries?"

Guy slapped a bowl of fried potatoes in front of her. "Next time, write it on the slip. And while you're at it, tell your boyfriend if he wants to visit, he can order like everyone else. I'm not paying you to stand around talking."

"He's not my— Never mind." She grabbed the potatoes, wincing a little at the pressure the extra plate put on her sore wrist. No sense arguing a losing point.

"Ignore him." Ellen, one of her fellow waitresses, said as she walked by. "He's like a bear with a sore head this morning."

What about the other mornings? "No change there then." Abby went to serve her customers before Guy blew another gasket. Miserable as her boss might be, he was the only employer who'd been willing to hire an inexperienced waitress. Life with Warren hadn't left her with too many marketable skills, unless you counted walking on eggshells and knowing how to read bad moods. This job was the only thing keeping her from complete destitution. Without it, she might actually end up standing on a street corner.

Halfway through her rounds topping up customers' cups with fresh coffee, Abby felt the hair on the back of her neck began to rise. Someone was watching her. With more than the usual "trying to get the waitress's attention" stare. Automatically, her head whipped to the front door. Empty.

She didn't like being studied. In her experience, scrutiny led to one of three things: correction, punishment or a lecture. With a frown, she looked around the room until her eyes reached the back table where Hunter was sat. Sure enough, his attention was focused directly at her.

For the first time since she'd begun waiting on him, she took notice of his eyes. A weird hybrid of blue and gray, they looked almost like steel under the diner's fluorescent lighting. She'd never seen eyes that color. Nor had she been looked at with such... *Approval* wasn't the right word. It definitely wasn't the disapproval she was used to, either. She didn't know what to call it. Whatever the name, it caused a somersault sensation in the pit of her stomach.

Finally noticing he had her attention, Hunter nodded and held up his bill.

Abby's cheeks grew hot. Of course. Why else would he be looking for her other than to settle his bill? Warren's visit had her brain turned backward. After all, it wasn't as if she was the kind of woman who turned heads on a good day, let alone today. Her face was flushed and sweaty. And her hair? She'd given up trying with her hair hours ago.

She made a point of approaching his table on the fly, figuring she could grab his credit card and sweep on past, so as to avoid any awkward conversation. Considering his intervention earlier, she doubted there could be any other kind.

Unfortunately, as soon as she reached for the plastic, his grip on the card tightened.

"Is there a problem?" she asked when he wouldn't let go.

"You tell me." His eyes dropped to her wrist. To the bluish-red spots marked where Warren's fingers had been.

Dammit. She'd hoped there wouldn't be any evidence. Letting go of the credit card, Abby pulled the cuff of her sleeve down to her knuckles. "I don't know what you're talking about."

"Do all your knishes look like eggs over easy?"

"What?" His question made no sense.

"The bill says I ordered blueberry knishes and rye toast."

"Sorry. I gave you the bill from two tables over by mistake."

"Again."

"Again," Abby repeated. That's right; she'd made the same mistake with him yesterday. She wondered if she'd messed up any other tables. Guy would kill her if she did. Again.

"Happens when you're distracted."

"Or busy," Abby countered, refusing to take the bait. She was trying to put Warren out of her head, and while she wasn't having much luck, talking about him wouldn't help.

Taking her order pad from her pocket, she flipped the pages. "Here's yours," she said, tearing out a new page. "Eggs over easy, bacon and whole-wheat toast. Same as every day. You want me to ring you up?" The sooner he settled his bill, the sooner he'd leave. Maybe then she could pretend the morning hadn't happened.

"Please."

Hunter noticed that this time when she reached for the card, she snatched it with her right hand, keeping her left still tucked inside her sweater. How hard did you have to squeeze someone's wrist to leave a bruise, anyway? Pretty damn hard, he imagined. A man had to have some serious anger issues to grab a woman that tightly.

Sipping the last of his cold coffee, he watched Abby ring up his bill, the sleeve of her sweater stretched almost to her fingertips. A poor attempt at hiding the evidence.

He'd known the minute the guy walked in that he was a first-class jerk. The overly expensive leather jacket and hair plugs screamed needy self-importance. It took him by surprise, though, when the jerk approached Abby. If anyone could be considered jerkdom's polar opposite, it was his waitress. Since his return stateside, Hunter had spent his meals at Guy's trying to figure out what it was that had him sitting in the same section day after day. Certainly wasn't the service, since Abby messed up his order on a regular basis.

Her looks? With her overly lean frame and angular features she wasn't what you'd call conventionally pretty. She was, however, eye-catching. Her butterscotch-colored topknot had a mind of its own, always flopping in one direction or another, with more and more strands working their way loose as the day progressed. The color reminded him of Sicilian beaches, warm and golden. Luckily, Guy was lax about health-code regulations. Be a shame to cover such a gorgeous color with an ugly hairnet.

She had fascinating eyes, too. Big brown eyes the size of dinner plates.

The bell over the front door rang. Hunter watched as she stiffened and cast a nervous look toward the entrance. Worried the jerk would return? Or that he wouldn't? Could be either. For all Hunter knew, his butterscotch-haired waitress had a big old dark side and liked being manhandled. Nothing surprised him anymore.

Well, almost nothing. He'd managed to surprise himself this morning. Since when did he step into other people's business?

A soft cough broke his thoughts. Looking up, he saw Abby standing there, coffeepot in her grip. Her right hand again. "Wrist sore?" he couldn't help asking.

"No." The answer came fast and defensively. "Why would it be?"

How about because she'd had the daylights squeezed out of it? "No reason."

If she wasn't interested in sharing, so be it. Wasn't his business, anyway. "Can I have a pen? For the receipt."

Her cheeks pinked slightly as she handed him the one from

her pocket. Hunter scribbled his name and began gathering his belongings.

"Thank you." The words reached him as he was hanging his camera strap around his neck. Spoken softly and with her back turned, they could have been for the thirty percent tip. Or not. He saved them both the embarrassment of responding.

Distracted didn't begin to cover Abby's mental state for the rest of the day. She spent her entire shift expecting Warren to tap her on the shoulder. By the time she finished work, she'd managed to mess up four more orders. Not all the customers were as forgiving as Hunter, either. Guy was ready to run her out the door.

"Make sure your head's on straight tomorrow," he groused when she clocked out.

She wanted to tell him that if her head had ever been on straight, she wouldn't be working in a greasy spoon and dodging her ex. Common sense kept her mouth shut. No need to make a bad situation worse by adding unemployment to the mix.

To her great relief, she stepped out to an empty street to wait for her taxi. Thank goodness. How she hated being back to looking over her shoulder. After six weeks, she'd foolishly begun thinking her life might actually be her own again. Granted, it wasn't the best of lives, but it was hers. Or rather, she'd thought so until Warren tracked her down. You'd think he'd be glad to be rid of her. Wasn't he forever telling her how she made his life so difficult?

Letting out a breath, she leaned against the railing in front of Guy's storefront. She hated taking a taxicab, too. Spending money earmarked for savings. It wasn't that she was so afraid of Warren. Sure, he'd gotten physical a few times—more than a few times—but she could handle him.

Liar. Why are you taking a cab then? Just a few hours ago, she'd worried today might the day he'd go over the edge.

Breaking up with Warren was supposed to be her new beginning. The end of walking on eggshells. Now she was stuck either leaving the one lousy job she could find, or praying that Warren had lost interest now that he'd tracked her down.

Angry tears rimmed her eyes. She sniffed them back. Warren wasn't going to win. She wouldn't let him.

Just then, movement caught the corner of her eye and she stiffened, hating herself even as she gripped the iron railing. Slowly, she pulled her thoughts back to her surroundings.

It was the photographer, coming down the street, camera slung around his neck. His sunglasses had migrated to his eyes, hiding their unique color. Didn't matter. He was still looking in her direction, his attention causing her stomach to quiver with unwanted awareness.

"Everything okay?" he asked as her taxi pulled up.

For crying out loud, couldn't a woman buy a moment of privacy? As it was, he already knew more of her business than necessary.

She slid into the backseat without answering.

Hunter spent the next day shooting landmarks around the city, updating his portfolio of stock photos. By this point he had more than enough shots for his files, but the project kept him busy. Downtime and he weren't good friends. Too much time off the job and he got antsy, a trait he'd inherited from his father. Inherited, or learned from watching. Either way, he hated being between jobs same as his father did. Only difference was Hunter didn't have a teenage son in tow.

It was midafternoon when he returned to his apartment building. One of the things he liked about this particular piece of real estate was that his street was basically an alleyway, meaning it had less crowds and traffic than other parts of the city. This time of day, the traffic was particularly slow. Guy's had closed, and rush hour had yet to begin.

As he rounded the corner, a familiar flash of butterscotch caught his eye. It was Abby, her angular frame bundled by a woolen coat. She was leaning against the diner's stair rail, her face and attention a thousand miles away. Her topknot, he noticed, had transformed itself. What was left of the mass had fallen to the nape of her neck, while most of the strands had worked loose and were framing her face.

Hunter felt a stirring deep in his gut, the sensation he got whenever he found a special shot. In Abby's case, the special element came from her posture. While she looked as exhausted as you'd expect a woman who'd spent eight hours on her feet would do, her shoulders and spine were ramrod straight. Pushing back against the weight of the world. Before she could notice his presence, he raised his camera and clicked off a half dozen frames. He managed to snap the last one as she turned, zooming in until her face filled the entire frame. That's when he saw the unshed tears that turned her eyes into shining brown mirrors. Hunter wondered if later, when he uploaded the shot, he'd see himself reflected in them.

He clicked one last photo and lowered the camera. Perfect timing, because she suddenly gripped the railing. She was still on edge from this morning, he realized. The reaction bothered him. He wasn't used to women growing rigid in his presence.

"Everything all right?" he asked, just as a taxicab pulled up alongside her.

He didn't expect an answer, and he wasn't disappointed. She slipped into the backseat without a word.

There was a padded shipping envelope propped atop his mailbox when Hunter finally entered his building—an advanced copy of a travel guide he'd shot earlier in the year. New Zealand, New Guinea; one of those places. He tossed the envelope, unopened, on his sofa. It landed with a puff of air, sending stray papers and a Chinese take-out menu sailing. Place had gone to pot since his assistant, Christina, had left to make her mediocre mark on the photography world. Not that she'd kept the place in great shape to begin with. She'd been far more interested in taking her photos than assisting him—a less than stellar characteristic in a photographer's assistant. At some point, he supposed, he should hire someone new and put this mess back in order. Unfortunately, like his last assistant, he was more interested in taking photos than in finding her replacement.

He thought about the pictures of Abby he'd just shot. He was eager to see how they'd turn out. If those eyes of hers were as riveting on paper as he suspected. When it came to photography, his instincts were rarely wrong. Then again, he'd learned through the lens of a master.

"No amount of raw talent can replace the perfect image," his father used to tell him. Joseph Smith had spent his life chasing the perfect photograph. Hell, he gave his life for the perfect shot. The rest of the world had to fall in line behind his work. A philosophy his son had learned the hard way how to embrace.

Sometimes, though, great images fell into your lap. Moving a pile of research books, he fired up the computer that doubled as his digital darkroom—one difference between his father's brand of photography and his. Modern technology made the job faster and easier. No makeshift darkrooms set up in hotels. All Hunter needed was a laptop and a memory card.

Though he had to admit that, every once in a while, he missed the old way. There was a familiarity to the smell of chemicals. As a teenager, he'd come to think of the smells as the one constant amid continual change. There were nights when he still walked into hotel rooms expecting the aroma to greet him.

Maybe he should install a darkroom in the building. Might make the place feel less like a way station.

Then again, building a darkroom was a lot like hiring an assistant. Nice in theory, but not as important as the photos themselves. Besides, nothing would make this apartment feel less like a way station because that's what it was. A place to sleep between assignments. No better than a hotel room, in reality. Less so, seeing how he actually spent more time in hotel rooms than his apartment.

Thumbnail images lined his computer screen. He'd shot more than he realized, a luxury of digital photography. He scrolled down until he found the series he'd taken of Abby. Sure enough, her face loomed from the screen like a silent-movie actress. The emotions bearing down on her reached out beyond the flat surface. He could feel the weariness. The grit, too. Hunter could see the glint of steely resolve lurking in the depths of her big, sad eyes.

To his surprise, he felt the stirring of arousal. A testimony to the quality of the shot. Good photos should evoke physical responses.

Of course, he didn't usually respond to his own work. He knew better than to get emotionally involved anymore. Start caring about the subject, and you set yourself up for problems. Images were illusory. The world on the other side of the lens wasn't as welcoming as photos made it appear. On the other side of the camera was pain, disinterest, loneliness, death.

Better to stay at a distance, heart safely tucked away where the world couldn't cause any damage. Of all the photography lessons his father had taught him, distance was the most important. Of course, at the time, he'd been too young to appreciate it, but eventually life had helped him to not just understand, but embrace the philosophy.

Yet for some reason, Hunter found himself being drawn in by a simple photo of a waitress. Seduced by the emotion he saw lurking in her eyes. So much simmering beneath the surface...

Only for a moment, though. He blinked and the distance he prided himself on returned. He was once again the observer, and Abby's face merely another photograph. An intriguing, but ultimately meaningless, two-dimensional moment in time.

CHAPTER TWO

To most New York residents, McKenzie House was nothing
more than an inconspicuous brick row house with a faded green
door. To the women inside, however, the house represented far
more than an address. The run-down rooms meant a fresh start
without abuse or domination. Abby was well aware that her
story was mild in comparison to her roommates', but she was no
less grateful. The gratitude rose in her chest once more as she
fell back on the living area sofa. She was soon joined by Carmella, one of her fellow residents. "You look dead. Long day?"

"The longest. Warren showed up."

"What?" Carmella sat up like a shot. "He tracked you down?
How?"

"I don't…"

Wait. Yes, she did. Oh, all the stupid…

"What?" Carmella asked.

"My mother. I called and gave her the diner's phone number
in case of an emergency."

Abby grabbed her phone from her bag and punched the speed
dial. Two rings and a harried female voice answered.

"Hey, Mom."

"Abby, um, hi! What a surprise." Joanne Gray sounded like
she always did, as though looking over her shoulder. Which she

probably was. "I can't really talk right now. I'm getting ready to put dinner on the table."

Abby checked her watch. By her calculations there was still ten minutes before the assigned dinnertime. "I'll only take a second, I promise. I was wondering if anyone's called the house looking for me."

"No one except your boyfriend, that is. He lost your new work number, and figured I knew it."

Mystery solved. "Mom, I told you Warren and I broke up."

Same way she had when Abby told her about the breakup, her mother disregarded the comment. "Warren explained how that was all a big misunderstanding."

"No. It was a breakup. I moved out of the apartment. Remember, I explained to you?" Along with the rest of the sordid story.

"I know what you said, honey, but I figured you'd changed your mind. Warren was so polite on the phone. And he's doing so well. You're lucky to have a man like that interested in taking you back."

Because that's what mattered. In Joanne Gray's eyes, a lousy man was better than no man at all. Didn't matter how miserable or mistreating—

"Joanne!" Abby's stepfather's bellow came through so loud she had to jerk the receiver from her ear. "What are you doing, talking on the phone?"

"I'm sorry," she heard her mother reply. "It's Abby. She had a question."

"She should know better than to call when it's dinnertime. Hang up. I'm hungry!"

There was some shuffling and her mother's voice came back online, a little more ragged than before. "I have to go, honey."

"Sure, Mom. I'll call soon."

Whether her mother heard the promise or not, Abby didn't know. She'd hung up, leaving her daughter on the line, with a headache and a sense of defeat. Some things weren't ever going to change. Not her mother. Not the way her mom viewed life.

"I was right," Abby said, letting the phone drop in her lap. "Warren called her."

Talk about ironic. When they lived together, Warren had no use for her parents. Called them useless white trash. He'd spoken to her parents no more than three times at most.

But of course, her mother would cave with the phone number. Warren, salesman that he was, would hardly break a sweat sweet-talking her.

Abby rubbed her suddenly aching head. "I honestly thought that, after six weeks, he'd move on."

"Well, some guys just don't like to give up what they think is theirs."

Carmella should know. Her ex had torched their apartment during a fight. Thankfully, Warren never did more than twist Abby's arm or deliver a swift backhand.

The silver bracelets lining Carmella's arm shimmered against her dark skin as she pulled back the curtain covering the window. "Any chance he followed you?"

"No. He, um…left." Aided by a field jacket and aviator sunglasses. "Hopefully, he got the message and won't be back."

"Yeah, right. And I'm gonna be on the cover of *Vogue* next week. You're kidding yourself if you think he's giving up now that he's tracked you down."

That's what she was afraid of, Abby thought, rubbing her wrist. The marks had blossomed to full-blown bruises. Annoyance and shame rose in her throat. She was mad. Mad at Warren. Mad at her mother.

Most of all she was mad with herself for believing that living with him was the best she could ever do in life. For letting him take over her entire world, until she'd lost control and herself.

Well, no more. She'd rather be alone for the rest of her life than lose herself in a relationship again.

Why her mind drifted to Hunter at that moment, she didn't know. Correction. Hunter *Smith*. She'd read the name off his credit card. Now that she thought about it, she was mad with him, too.

A new emotion joined the others already warring inside her: embarrassment. She'd worked long and hard to escape Warren's clutches and start her new life. Last thing she needed was her action-hero customer thinking he knew her secrets. Or worse, sending her pitying looks with those steel-colored eyes of his.

It'd be too much to ask that he leave town by morning, wouldn't it?

Knowing her luck, he'd be back at his table tomorrow, with that field coat and those big broad shoulders. Checking the bruises on her wrist.

She'd rather face down her ex.

"Eggs over easy, wheat toast, side of bacon."

Abby held her order pad in front of her face like a shield. If she didn't look at Hunter's face, she wouldn't have to see his expression. Bad enough that the mere thought of facing him gave her stress dreams.

Given everything that had happened yesterday, she'd think Warren would be the one haunting her subconscious. But when she closed her eyes, it was Hunter who invaded her thoughts.

She knew why he was on her mind. It was because he knew her dirty little secret. For so long, keeping secrets was how she'd lived her life. Her mistakes—and man, did she make some whoppers—were hers to hide. To think that now someone else knew—saw—the evidence... Part of her wanted to crawl into a hole. Another part wanted to tell Hunter to take his sympathy and shove it. She settled for focusing on the two-by-three square in front of her face.

"You going to write the order down?" Hunter asked.

"Not necessary."

There was a long, drawn-out pause. "You sure?"

Against her better judgment, Abby lowered the pad to stare at him. "You don't think I can remember?"

"Did I say that?"

His silence said so for him. Granted, she'd forgotten a few orders in the beginning, but she'd improved a lot since then. "You've ordered the same thing for twelve days," she told him.

"Nice to know I'm so memorable."

More like predictable, she wanted to say. Though that wouldn't be quite true. She certainly hadn't predicted his behavior yesterday. "I'll go get your coffee."

"How's your wrist?"

Exactly the topic she hoped to avoid. "Fine," she replied in a stiff voice. Her fingers twitched with the urge to tug on her cardigan, to hide the gauze bandage peering out from beneath the cuff. The bruises were darker this morning. Dark enough that simply wearing long sleeves wouldn't be enough to hide them, so she'd covered them with a bandage. Her plan was to tell anyone who asked that she burned herself. Didn't it figure, the first person to say anything would be the one man she didn't want to hear from?

"I'll be back with your coffee," she said, turning on her heel.

Damned if she couldn't feel him watching her walk back to the counter. Awareness washed over her, making her insides quiver. She wasn't used to being looked at under any circumstances. In fact, Warren was the first man who'd ever paid her any kind of attention. Look how terrific that had turned out. Naturally, having a man as handsome as Hunter scrutinizing her set Abby's nerves on edge. Doubly so since she knew his scrutiny wasn't anything more than sympathetic curiosity. It made her feel like some wounded animal in the zoo. Out of the corner of her eye she caught her reflection in the stainless steel. Limp, uncooperative hair; pale skin. Yeah, like she'd attract attention. It scared her to think Warren was right. That he was the best she could do.

Good thing she didn't mind being alone.

Tugging her cuff down to her knuckles, she made her way back to Hunter's table.

"You're going to pull that sleeve out of shape," he remarked.

So what? It was her sweater. If she wanted to stretch it out, she would. "Do you need cream?"

"Don't tell me you forgot already?"

"Sorry. Guess you're not so memorable, after all." She reached into her apron pocket and removed the plastic creamer pods she'd grabbed when getting his coffee. The motion caused her sleeve to pull upward. Whether Hunter looked at the exposed bandage or not didn't matter; she felt he was and that was enough.

"I know what you're thinking," she said suddenly.

"You do?"

"Yeah." He thought he knew her story based on one short encounter. "You're wrong, though. I'm not."

"Not what?"

"Not..." She raised her bandaged arm. "Not anymore. I left Warren."

"Oh."

That was it? *Oh?* Abby watched him as he blew across the top of his cup, his lips pursing ever so slightly. It was the only change in his expression.

"Doesn't seem to be taking the breakup too well," he said finally.

"He'll adjust. Yesterday was..." No need getting into a long, drawn-out explanation. "Look, I'm only explaining because you—"

"Saw the bruises?"

"Say it a little louder, why don't you? They didn't hear you downtown." Swiping at her bangs, Abby looked around at the other tables. Fortunately, no one had heard, or if they did, had decided not to share.

"I wanted to make sure you understood the deal. Because of yesterday. Not that I don't appreciate what you did and all."

"You're welcome."

Abby pursed her lips. "Point is, your help wasn't necessary. I have the situation under control."

"I could tell."

"Seriously, I do." She didn't like how his response sounded mocking. It made her even more defensive. Maybe she hadn't had control at that exact moment, but she would have handled the situation. "So you won't need to repeat the performance."

"In other words, mind my own business."

Exactly. "I'm saying it's not necessary."

Hunter nodded into the rim of his cup. "Good to know. I'm not really into rescues to begin with."

"You're not?" Could have fooled her.

"Nah. Like you said, it's not my business."

"Then why...?"

"Did I step in yesterday?" He shrugged. "What can I say? My mother was a Southerner and raised me to be a gentleman."

So he was protecting her honor? Abby's stomach fluttered. "Well, you can tell your mother the lesson sank in."

"I would, but she's dead."

"Oh. I'm sorry."

He shrugged again. "Don't be. It was twenty years ago."

When he was a kid. The action hero had a sad past. A human side to balance the movie star exterior. Her edge toward him softened a little.

"Abby! Customers!" Guy's voice cut over the clanging of plates and silverware. "Stick and move, will ya?"

"Duty calls." Any more conversation would have to wait. "I'll be back with your eggs soon as they're ready."

Under control, huh? Hunter watched as she bustled off to wait on two businessmen seated two tables over, her knotted ponytail bouncing in cadence with her steps. The gauze on her wrist flashed white as she raised her order pad. Who was she trying to convince with that statement? Him or herself?

Not his business. The lady said she had the situation under control. He was off the hook.

Which suited him fine. Besides, he thought as he raised his coffee mug, maybe the lady did have the situation under control, and that air of vulnerability was all in his head. Wouldn't be the first time.

He reached into his messenger bag and pulled out a manila folder. Probably not the best way to keep the dark thoughts at bay, but he looked at the photo anyway. It was the picture he'd taken of Abby. After much deliberation, he'd decided to print the photo in black-and-white, finding the absence of color highlighted the shadows on her cheeks.

Hunter stared at her eyes. There it was. The sadness. They always said eyes were the windows of the soul and that photography captured a little slice of that spirit. In Abby's case, her spirit was wrapped in a kaleidoscope of emotions. Question was, what emotions were they? Photography, like all art, was open to interpretation. What looked soulful could really be distant, simmering resentment waiting to blow up in your face.

Another argument for focusing on simply taking the picture.

Finished with the businessmen, Abby had moved back to the order window, where she was now dancing back and forth with another waitress who was laden with plates. Hunter let his eyes skim Abby's figure. The misshapen cardigans she wore every day didn't do her silhouette any favors. She had great legs, though. They managed to look shapely despite the sensible shoes. He tried to imagine what they'd look like with her in a shorter skirt and high heels. Not bad, he bet.

He was still contemplating when Abby set a plate in front of him. "What's this?" she asked.

She'd spotted the photo. Since the subject was self-explanatory, he took a bite of his eggs before answering. "You."

"I know it's me. When did you take it?"

"Yesterday. Right here on the sidewalk."

Her brows drew together. "How? Were you following me?"

"Don't be ridiculous." Although given her ex, he could see how she might jump to that conclusion. "I live across the street. I took the photo on my way back to my building."

"Without saying anything?"

"Alerting you to my presence would have spoiled the shot."

"So instead, you creeped."

Hunter set down his fork. "I was discreet. It's what a good photographer does."

"Is it now?" Shooting him a dubious look, she wiped her hands on her apron and picked up the photo.

"Wow," she said after a minute.

Exactly his reaction when he'd finished the digital enhancement. Hunter didn't usually care about compliments; he had enough confidence in his skills that other opinions didn't affect him. But hearing Abby's whispered surprise, and seeing the look of genuine wonder that accompanied it, set off an eruption of heated satisfaction.

"I look..." As she paused to find the word, she worried her upper lip between her teeth. It was such an expressive gesture, Hunter had to fight the urge to grab his camera and snap away.

At last she set the photo down. "Tired," she said. "I look tired."

"Yeah, you do." No sense lying when there were such pronounced circles under her eyes. "But I think you're missing the point." The weariness was part of what made her—that is, her picture—so captivating. "The photo is telling the story."

"What? Woman works hard for the money? Donna Summer already covered it."

"Very funny."

"I'm here all week." Her mood sobered as she brushed her fingertips along the glossy paper. "Sadly, this might be the best picture I've ever had taken."

"Not surprising. It's probably the first time you were shot by a quality photographer."

She laughed. A short, sweet laugh that turned her features

bright. To Hunter's surprise, seeing her face light up sent the heat in his gut six inches lower. "Wish I'd known. Might have saved me from years of awful holiday photos. Warren said I looked like a deer about to be plowed into."

"Were you?" Hunter asked. "About to be run over?"

Brown eyes raised to look at him. "I thought you said the problem was the photographer."

"Photographers also capture reality."

"Doesn't that just support my argument about looking terrible?"

"Only if you're terrible-looking to begin with."

"Generally speaking, of course." Pink colored her cheeks and she looked at the floor. It made him wonder how often she heard compliments. Considering her d-bag of an ex-boyfriend, it likely wasn't often.

Hunter handed her the photograph. "Here."

"You're giving it to me?"

"Why not? It's a picture of you."

"Yeah, but..." Whatever she was going to say drifted off as her hand brushed against his. Hunter watched as her eyes widened at the contact. Fear of another man's touch? Her pupils were wide and dark, turning her irises into thin, brown frames.

For some reason, he found himself wanting to extend the contact, and so he dragged his index finger slowly across the back of her hand as he withdrew. Beneath his touch, he felt her skin quiver.

"Thank you," she whispered.

"You're welcome."

"So *this* is how you take care of your customers."

Warren. Abby yanked her hand away, sending the picture fluttering to the ground. Before either she or Hunter could move, her ex-boyfriend leaned over and picked it up. Abby tried to snatch it from his grip, but he held tight. "Nice picture. You look...good."

Abby couldn't answer. Her insides were too tense. Across

the way, she could see Guy watching them. *Please don't let there be trouble.* "I thought I told you yesterday that I didn't want to see you."

"That was yesterday. I figured now that you had time to sleep on things, you'd changed your mind. Course, that was before I realized why you didn't want me around."

Warren's eyes were hard and glittered like diamonds. Abby knew the look well. His calm demeanor was an act, a respite before the storm.

Hadn't she told Hunter she had the situation under control? She squared her shoulders. "Warren, you need to leave."

"Not until we talk. You changed your phone number."

"That should have been a clue that I don't want to talk with you."

"Come on, babe, stop being stubborn. I know I messed up, but that's no reason to run away. Let's get out of here and talk. You'll see how sorry I am, and you'll change your mind."

No way. "I'm not going anywhere with you," she told him.

"There you go, being stubborn again."

He moved to grab her hand. Abby jerked out of his grasp. "Oh, sure, I can't touch you, but you got no problem letting him paw you," he snarled.

"She said she didn't want to talk with you."

Great. Until then, Hunter had been quiet. What happened to staying on the sidelines? "I've got this, Hunter," she told him. Last thing she needed was for him to butt in and make a bad situation worse.

Warren's mottled face grew a shade redder. "'This'?" Too late, Abby realized her poor choice words. The switch flipped and the true Warren appeared. "You think I'm something you need to 'handle'?"

"That's not what I meant."

"I know what you meant, you ungrateful cow." This time when he reached for her, he was successful, latching on to her arm with an iron grip. "I'm done playing around. Let's go."

She stood her ground. "No."

Warren yanked her arm. Abby winced.

"The lady said no." Hunter had gotten up and moved between them, essentially blocking their exit.

"Get out of my way," Warren said.

"How about you let go of her arm?"

By now the other customers were watching. Guy had come out from the kitchen and was about two seconds away from throwing them all out. Abby's pulse began to race. She half considered going, if to only keep the scene from escalating any further.

"We can talk," she said, scrambling for a compromise. "But here. Sit down and I'll bring you some coffee."

It didn't work. "Since when do you tell me what I can and can't do? After everything I've done for you? You're lucky I'm taking you back after the way you humiliated me."

"I'm not going back!" For crying out loud, it was like a broken record. Abby yanked herself free, only to stumble backward into Hunter's table, knocking his coffee cup off balance. The cup fell on its side, hot liquid spilling over the edge, where it dripped on the camera below.

"Son of a—" Hunter grabbed for it just as the liquid began running down the outer casing. "This is a five-thousand-dollar camera."

"Serves you right for butting in where you don't belong." Warren sneered.

Hunter set the camera down on a clean table. "That so?" he asked. His voice was low and precise. Compared with Warren's bluster, the quiet deliberateness sounded like ice. The air in the diner chilled.

"Seems to me," Hunter said, stepping into the other man's space, "that the problem started when you walked in the door. Now if my camera has any damage at all, you're going to pay."

Her ex-boyfriend scoffed, not realizing he was out of his league. "I'm not paying you for anything."

Hunter took another step. "Oh, I think you will."

"Okay, you three…"

A standoff. Just great. It figured Warren would choose today to become macho and proud. It was the money. He would run into a burning building to protect five thousand dollars. Meanwhile, Guy was limping over to them. Abby almost groaned out loud. This could only end one way. Badly and with her getting fired. Quickly she stepped between the two men, hoping to regain control before Guy took action. "Look, guys, I'm sure if there's a problem we can—"

"Stay out of this!" Warren snapped. With that, he did what he did best—shoved her aside. Stuck between two tables, Abby found herself with little room to maneuver. Her feet tangled with a chair leg and she fell to the floor, but not before her back slammed into the edge of one of the tables. The table tipped, scraping her skin from bra strap to waist, and sending its contents spilling. Glass and silverware landed on the floor behind her.

So did Hunter's camera. It hit the floor with a crack. The diner went still.

After that, everything happened in a flash. A patron gasped, Guy started yelling, and Abby barely had time to catch her breath before Hunter's fist connected with Warren's jaw.

"Still think you have the situation under control?" Hunter asked.

The two of them sat on a marble bench in the corridor of the new courthouse. After Hunter threw his punch, and Guy threw the three of them out on the sidewalk, Warren had insisted on dragging a nearby traffic cop into the mess by claiming he'd been assaulted. All three of them had ended up in a police station, where Hunter, ever helpful, had suggested the police ask about the bruises on Abby's wrist. They did, and after a whole lot of questions, she found herself here, at the courthouse, waiting to speak to a judge about a nonharassment order against Warren.

"No," she said, answering Hunter's question. She felt anything but in control. Though she might have been if he'd minded his own business. "I could have sworn I told you to mind your own business."

"You'd rather I let him twist your arm off?"

What she'd rather was if the whole incident had never happened. "You didn't hit him for me," she pointed out.

"No, I hit him because he damn near destroyed my camera. And because he shoved you to the ground."

"Yeah, let's not forget that," Abby replied, arching her back. No sense pointing out she was the one, technically, who'd knocked over the camera. Nor the fact that the camera wouldn't have fallen in the first place had he minded his own business—as he claimed he preferred to do.

Letting out a frustrated sigh, she looked down at Hunter's hands. They were big, strong hands, she noted. Showing barely a mark where his fist had connected with Warren's face. "You get most of the ink off?" she asked.

His shoulder moved up and down. "Most of it."

That was another thing. Because Warren had cried assault, Hunter had found himself being charged. Good thing her knight in shining armor didn't have any outstanding warrants, or they might still be at the station house. Abby supposed she should feel bad about the fingerprinting and all, but again, it wouldn't have happened if he hadn't interfered. In fact, if he hadn't interfered the day before, none of today would have happened at all.

She let out another sigh. "Do me a favor. Next time I say I've got a situation handled, stay out of it. I don't care what your Southern mother taught you."

"Do I have to remind you that saying you could handle the situation caused part of the problem? Unless your idea of handling was to get dragged out into the street. 'Cause that's where your ex-boyfriend was taking you."

Recalling Warren's grip on her arm, Abby winced. Hunter

was right, unfortunately. She just couldn't bring herself to say thank-you. Not quite yet. "Well, after I meet with the judge, I won't have to worry about Warren bothering me again. Nothing says 'we're over' like a restraining order."

"I'm surprised you didn't get a court order before," Hunter remarked.

"I didn't think I'd need one." A stupid assumption now that she thought about it. She should have listened to the ladies at McKenzie House. They'd told her Warren wouldn't let her end things on her terms.

Why weren't courthouse benches made more comfortable? The narrow space forced Abby and Hunter close together. Well, that and the fact that his long frame took up so much space. His thigh was pressed against hers and she could feel his jacket brush against her sleeve every time he breathed. The increased body heat had her feeling off balance. She tried shifting her weight, but nothing changed. Everywhere she moved, Hunter was there, his hard, lean body pressed tightly against hers, the contact sending disconcerting tingles up and down her arm.

This was crazy. She was in a courthouse, for goodness' sake, filing a restraining order. Wrapping her cardigan tightly about her, she stood up, only to wince when her clothing rubbed her bruised skin.

"How is your back?" Hunter asked.

The truth? Her back stung like heck every time she moved, and a headache pounded her temples. "I've had worse."

"You always such a bad liar?"

Abby looked at him through narrowed eyes. "What can I say? I'm off my game."

And who could blame her? Too much had happened in a very short time. Her system needed recharging. She crossed the hallway to lean against the wall, grateful for the additional personal space.

Hunter stayed on the bench, forearms resting on his knees.

Abby had been too annoyed with him earlier to notice, but he looked as tired as she felt. "Why are you still here?" she asked, voicing a question that had been bothering her for a while. "The police said you could go a couple hours ago."

"I've stayed this long. Might as well see the process through."

Thus making a difficult situation all the much more awkward. Abby combed her fingers through the hair around her face. "I thought you weren't into rescues."

"I'm not. But I'm also not into leaving loose ends."

"That's how you see me? As a loose end?"

"Your goon of an ex-boyfriend is," he replied. "What on earth were you doing with him, anyway?"

Something she'd asked herself a million times, hating the answer. "He was different when we met. Bought me gifts. Took me places. I bought the act." She could feel Hunter's eyes on her, waiting for more. "You've got to understand. I wasn't used to nice.

"Or attention," she added, fiddling with a button. "I mean, he lost his temper once in a while, but he was always really sorry. Wasn't all that different from other families, right?"

Hunter raised a brow.

"I was nineteen years old. What did I know?" Obviously not a lot.

What bothered her the most about her story was how easily she'd made Warren the center of her world. Everything these past years had been about him. His moods, his wishes. Letting herself disappear. That was her biggest crime. All because he'd been nice.

"Sounds pretty stupid, huh?" she said to Hunter, although she could have easily been talking to herself.

Her companion hadn't changed his position other than to lower his gaze to the floor. She wished she could see his eyes, to know what he was thinking. How could someone like him ever truly understand? A man who looked like Hunter, who carried himself with as much confidence as Hunter—his world was probably filled with men and women begging for his company. What would he know about "falling for a kind word"?

"I try to make a point of not judging," he said as he studied the palm of his hand.

"Really? I think you might be the first."

Though his eyes remained focused on the ground, Abby saw his cheek tug in a smirk. "Let's say I've learned not to make assumptions about things. Or people."

"Bad experience?"

He looked up and it shocked her to see how closed off his face had become. As if a steel curtain had dropped over his eyes. "You could say that."

Abby knew the terse tone of voice. He didn't want to elaborate. Apparently, she was the only one who was required to share.

"Anyway," she said, "eventually I came to my senses, and one day while he was at work, I took off with three months' worth of grocery money." There was more to the story, of course. Much more. Situations like hers didn't blossom overnight. But she'd said enough to make her point. Hunter wasn't the only one who could refuse to elaborate. "Never thought I'd be sitting here, though."

All right, technically standing. She pulled her sweater tighter. The thing had been tugged at so much she was amazed it had any shape left. She was tired. The day's events were finally catching up with her, pressing down with an unbearable weight.

"Do you still love him?"

"Good Lord, no," she replied, surprised at how emphatic she sounded. "Those feelings died a long time ago." Sometimes she couldn't believe she'd once cared for the man. "Tell you one thing," she said, toeing the marble floor. "Six years ago I never would have believed I'd end up here."

"That, sweetheart, makes two of us."

The courtroom door opened, preventing Abby from commenting. "They're ready for you, Miss Gray," the uniformed woman said.

This was it. Abby looked to Hunter, hoping for what, she didn't know. "Time to get Warren out of my life once and for all," she said, forcing a determined note into her voice. It wasn't until she reached the courtroom door that she added under her breath, "I'm just sorry I have to be here."

Me, too, thought Hunter as he followed her into the courtroom. There were a thousand better ways he could be spending his day.

She was right; he didn't have to be here. So why was he? Why on earth had he spent two extra hours sitting on hard marble benches and watching some woman he barely knew fill out forms?

Maybe because you're the reason she's here in the first place. If he hadn't thrown the first punch—the only punch—Warren would never have gone wailing to the police. But that camera was Hunter's baby, dammit! What was he supposed to do? Just let the jerk damage it?

Yeah, because Hunter's outburst was all about photography equipment, and had nothing to do with seeing Abby fall backward. He could try to sell himself that excuse all day long. Truth was, he hadn't gone after Warren until she'd lost her balance. Then Hunter had seen red.

What the hell was wrong with him? His job was to capture action on film, not become the action. Yet here he was, playing hero two days in a row. Civilized society be damned.

After dragging all afternoon, the process in front of the judge moved quickly. Hunter had to give Abby credit. It couldn't be easy answering the same questions over and over. Although he could tell from her posture that she was wound tighter than tight, the only outward sign of stress were the fingers fidgeting with the hem of her sweater. He found himself wanting to snatch them up and hold them still.

It took less than ten minutes for the judge to approve her petition and grant a temporary order. A member of the sheriff's department would serve Warren that night. Hunter didn't miss the way Abby's shoulders relaxed at the announcement.

"Congratulations," he said when he met her at the door.

"You make it sound like I won the lottery."

"You got rid of the ex."

She seemed far from relieved. Surely she didn't regret the order?

"Don't be ridiculous," she snapped, giving him a dirty look when he asked. "It's just..." She swiped at her bangs. "I feel like an idiot for buying his act."

"Happens to the best of us."

She glanced at Hunter sideways. "Meaning it happened to you?"

"Meaning you're probably not the only one Warren fooled." The elevator doors opened and they stepped inside, Hunter immediately making his way to the rear. Truth was, he understood what had happened to Abby all too well.

Shoving bad memories back where they belonged, he continued. "If it's any consolation, I know his type. Faced with a real obstacle, he'll back off. Fifteen days from now, he'll have moved on to someone else."

"In other words, some other woman gets suckered and goes through what I went through. Lucky her."

Hunter didn't know how to reply.

They rode down the three floors in silence. It had been a long day. Stealing a look in Abby's direction, Hunter regretted packing his camera away. She wouldn't want to hear it, but her appearance at that moment told a real story. With the fluorescent light casting a gray pall on her skin, he could see the cracks in her stoicism. The pronounced circles under her eyes, the subtle slump of her shoulders. Her makeup had worn off hours earlier and her hair... Her hair was an all-out mess. The morning's haphazard ponytail was now an out-of-control bunch. Most of the strands had fallen loose, and those that hadn't weren't far behind. Made him wonder if her insides weren't in a similar state.

And, strangely enough, wonder if she could use a hug.

When they stepped outside, shadows were crawling up the sides of buildings, engulfing the lower halves of high-rises in shade. Sunset came early this time of year. In a few hours, the streets would be dark. So much for taking any pictures. His flash and lighting equipment were back at the loft.

"What are you going to do now?" he asked Abby. "Head home?"

Asking only reminded him that he knew very little about her life beyond the diner. Did she have a home? She'd said she'd left with only a few months of grocery money. What kind of apartment did that get a person? He was embarrassed to realize he didn't know.

"Actually, I thought I'd go back to the diner. I need to talk to Guy about my job. If I still have one," she added in a low voice.

"I'm sure once you explain the situation…"

From the look she shot him, Abby didn't believe that possibility any more than he did.

"Sure, he'll understand. Because Guy's such an understanding person. I bet when he yelled 'get out and stay out,' he was only kidding."

Unfortunately, she was probably right; her job was history. Hunter felt a little bad about that.

A cab pulled to the curb. He beat Abby to the rear door, opening it and motioning for her to climb into the backseat. "We're going in the same direction. No sense grabbing separate taxis."

"True." Despite sounding less than thrilled, she slid across the leather seat, only to stop halfway across. Holy Mother of—Had she been hiding those legs under that ugly skirt all this time? Her uniform had bunched up, revealing a pair of creamy white thighs. "One thing," she said. "On the off chance I convince Guy to let me keep my job, there's something I'd like you to do."

"Sure." Still blown away from the legs, Hunter was more than glad to let her talk. Especially if it kept the view from disappearing. "Just name it." He forced himself to look her in the eye.

The gaze that met his was hot and frosty at the same time. "Find somewhere else to eat."

CHAPTER THREE

"GET OUT."

Abby looked over her shoulder, hoping Guy was talking to Hunter and not to her. Apparently her request in the cab had fallen on deaf ears, because the photographer had insisted on following her inside after the cab ride home.

Her plan had been simple. Catch Guy before he locked up, apologize and assure him that Warren wouldn't be back. If necessary, beg and plead a little. Instead, she barely got through the door when he came around to the front of the counter. Dish towel slung over his shoulder, he jabbed the air with his gnarled finger. "Both of you," he said. "Out."

Abby almost went. After all, six years of being pliant didn't disappear overnight. Taking a deep breath, she held her ground. "Can't we talk about this?"

"There's nothing to talk about. I told you when I hired you to keep your drama outside, and I meant it. You can't do that, you're out of here. There are plenty of waitresses who can do your job and who won't cause fist fights during my breakfast rush."

"Abby didn't cause the fight."

"Stay out of this," she snapped to Hunter. His help had caused enough problems.

"Fine." He raised his hands in mock surrender. "You're on your own."

"Thank you." Too bad he hadn't backed off so readily this morning.

"Can't you give me another chance?" she asked, turning her attention back to her boss. Her ex-boss. Hopefully soon to be boss again. "I know this morning was bad."

Guy waggled his index finger again. "Not only did you cause a fight, you left us shorthanded."

"I know, and I'm really, really sorry. I promise to make it up to you."

"Who's gonna make it up to the customers I lost?"

It was a neighborhood restaurant with regular customers. He hadn't lost anybody. Telling him he was exaggerating wouldn't help her cause, though. If she'd learned anything from her years with Warren, it was when to keep her comments to herself. Instead, she moved to the second half of her plan. "Please, Guy. I'm begging you. I really need this job."

"You should have thought about that before bringing your little love triangle to work."

Love triangle? That's what he thought today was about? A love triangle?

"That is definitely not what happened," she said.

Guy dismissed her with a slap of his towel from one shoulder to another. "Don't care what it is," he said. "You're still gone." He turned his back.

Gone. As in fired. She couldn't be. "But Warren won't be back," she said, chasing after him. "I went to court. I got a restraining order."

The kitchen door swung shut in her face. "You still owe me a paycheck!" she hollered through the order window.

"What paycheck? I'm keeping it to cover the damages."

Damages, her foot. A couple broken dishes wouldn't take a whole paycheck, even with Guy's cheap wages.

Could this day get any worse?

"Come back tomorrow after he's calmed down," she heard Hunter say.

What good would that do? Guy wasn't going to change overnight. Why was Hunter still here, anyway? "Don't you have pictures to take or something?" she asked him. She would have thought he'd be on his way a long time ago.

"Lost all the good light," he replied.

"Oh, good. Then we've both lost something. I feel so much better." Rude? Yes, but she wasn't in the mood to be pleasant. Pushing her way past him, she headed to the front door. As if he had all day, Hunter accompanied her.

"You'll find another job, you know."

Easy for him to say. He had a job. "Do you have any idea how hard it was to get this one?" Of course he didn't. "News flash. Jobs don't grow on trees. Especially when you don't have skills. Or experience." Only thing she knew how to do was cook, clean and manage Warren's tantrums. Hardly stuff to build a résumé on.

"Thanks to today, I can't even use Guy as a reference."

Suddenly exhausted, she sank down on the steps of the building next door. Her body felt as if it'd been hit by a truck. Come to think of it, she might be better off if she had been hit by a truck. At least then she'd be in a hospital bed, and Guy might feel bad enough to let her keep her job.

She jammed her fingers through her hair, destroying what was left of her ponytail. "You know what really stinks?" she asked Hunter. "Warren's the bad guy in all of this and he's got everything. The apartment, a job, money—"

"A shiny new restraining order."

"Big whoop. So he can't come within a hundred yards. You said yourself, he'll move on before the hearing. Meanwhile, what do I have? No job and nine hundred lousy dollars in the bank. You tell me where that's fair."

"I can't."

Tears burned the back of her eyes. She blinked them away.

Very least she would do was keep her pride. "All I wanted was to get my life back. Is that so freaking wrong?"

"No."

"I was close, too." She was. She had a job. She was saving money. Until Mr. Action Hero decided to live up to his looks. Now everything was ruined. "Why'd you have to punch him?"

Hunter sat on the step next to her. "I already told you."

"I know, I know. He almost broke your fancy-schmancy camera."

"That fancy-schmancy camera, as you put it, happens to be my life."

"So was my job!" Abby flung the words back at him. "Bet you didn't think about that when you decided to get all tough with Warren, did you? Who cares about Abby, right? Not like she matters. She's just some useless piece of..."

The dam broke and all the frustration that had been building since the morning came roaring free. She was angry. At Hunter. At Warren. Mostly, though, at herself for letting herself be held down for six long years and ending up here in the first place. With hot tears threatening to blind her yet again, she lashed out at the first thing she could reach, which happened to be Hunter's chest. "Damn you," she said, slapping at his jacket. "Damn you, damn you, damn you."

A pair of arms reached around her body, reining in her blows. *Not on your life,* she thought. She wasn't going to let him trap her and force her to stop. No one was going to force her ever again. Blind slaps became shoves. "Let me go."

He didn't. Nor did his grip grow harsh, as she expected. He simply held her in a firm but gentle embrace while she shoved and slapped until she didn't have any struggle left. Worn-out, she collapsed against his chest. Sometime during her tirade, the tears had escaped; she could feel the cotton beneath her cheek growing damp.

Eventually her breathing slowed and Abby became aware of the heartbeat beneath her ear. Closing her eyes, she listened to its slow, steady thump, letting the cadence calm her own racing pulse. Hunter's clothes smelled faintly of detergent and fresh wood. As she inhaled, letting the scent fill her nostrils, it dawned on her that she'd never been held like this before. Without anger or ulterior motive. The experience was comforting and unsettling at the same time.

"Let me go," she muttered one more time into the folds of his jacket.

"Depends. Are you done?"

"I'm fine."

"I didn't ask if you were fine. I asked if you were done."

Abby let out a sigh. "I'm fine and I'm done. Better?"

Hunter's answer was to release her. Abby shivered at the abrupt departure, the way a person did when having the covers ripped from them while sleeping. The warmth she'd been feeling disappeared into the autumn night.

"I don't like being restrained," she told him, hugging her body.

"I don't like being slapped."

As if she could do damage to a body as firm as his. "Sorry. Been a long day."

She could feel his gaze on the top of her head. The sensation made her want to squirm, and she had to stare at the top button of his shirt to keep from doing so.

"Come on," he said finally.

That made her look up. "Come where?"

"I haven't eaten since breakfast and I'm starved," he said, as if that would explain everything. "Judging from your meltdown, I'm guessing you could use some food, too."

"I'm not hungry."

"Again, I didn't ask if you were hungry, I said you probably needed food."

"So?"

"So, there's an Indian restaurant around the corner."

"You're asking me out?" The hair on the back of her neck stood up.

"I'm offering to buy you something to eat. You coming?"

Everything she'd ever experienced in life told her to say no. Despite spending the day with her, Hunter Smith was a stranger, and by going anywhere alone with him, she'd only be buying trouble. After all, everything came with strings attached. Lord knew what kind of strings Hunter Smith wanted.

"Why?" she asked, swiping at her damp cheeks. "What's the catch?"

"No catch."

So he said. Last thing she needed was a man thinking he could take over her life. "Because if this is some kind of come-on, you can forget it. No matter what you think, I'm not an easy—"

"No catch," he repeated, a little more emphatically this time. "I want to eat. I'm offering you a chance to eat, too. You can come with me or you can stand out here until Guy tosses you off the sidewalk. Your choice."

Hunter stepped off the curb. "And by the way, as far as easy is concerned? You've got way too much baggage to ever be easy."

Damn straight she did. Abby considered the broad shoulders walking away from her, deliberately not thinking about how good it had felt when she'd rested her body against him. What she did think about was how her head felt as if it were about to explode. As much as she hated to admit it, having food in her stomach would help. Free food would help even more, given her return to unemployment.

"Fine. But you're paying." She stepped off the curb to join him.

For a dinner with no catch, Hunter certainly picked a fancy-enough restaurant. Abby looked around at the rust-colored walls and copper fixtures. Bathed in amber light, they glowed with a warmth that rivaled the candle table toppers. Even if the rest of the patrons weren't dressed in business attire, Abby would be underdressed. The setting was much too intimate and lush. Quickly, she checked the front of her uniform to make sure it was at least clean, then buttoned her cardigan tight.

A short ball of a man in a black suit greeted them with a smile. "Good evening, Mr. Smith. You picking up to go?"

"Not tonight, Vishay. We're going to eat here."

With a deferring nod, the man led them to a table near the back of the restaurant, next to a bronze statue of what Abby assumed was some kind of Indian god or goddess. It didn't escape her notice that Hunter, though as underdressed as she was, looked perfectly at home. Worse, he looked better than all the other men in the room. Any glances in his direction were admiring ones, and there'd been quite a few.

"First-name basis," Abby noted after Vishay departed. "You come here a lot?"

"Two, three nights a week when I'm in the city."

And breakfast every morning at Guy's. "Not much for home cooking, are you?"

"Never really had the chance to learn. Eating out is easier."

For him maybe; certainly not his wallet. Abby's eyes bugged when she saw the prices on the menu.

"Is something wrong? Don't you like Indian food?" Hunter asked.

"Wouldn't know. I've never eaten Indian food." What she did know was that Hunter had very expensive tastes when it came to take-out restaurants.

"Warren wasn't big on eating out," she explained when Hunter looked surprised. "Said he did enough of that at work and didn't see the need. Not when I could cook for him." She unfolded an amethyst napkin and covered her lap. "I used to think that was a compliment until I realized he simply didn't want to spend the money.

"On me, anyway," she added, smoothing the purple wrinkles. She felt Hunter studying her again. "What?" she asked, looking up. He wore a perplexed expression, one that made his eyes gray and unreadable. "Did I say something wrong?"

"I'm trying to figure out how someone like you got stuck spending six years with that idiot."

"I told you. He didn't start out a bully. He grew into the role over time."

"Still, you don't seem the type to be bullied."

Oh, how little he knew. "Guess I grew into the role, too." That's what happened when you believed you couldn't do better. "Warren was the only person I knew in the city."

"You didn't have friends?"

"No one close. There were a few women in the building, but no one I felt comfortable going to."

"What about your parents?"

She didn't mean for her laugh to come out so sharply, but it did nonetheless. "Let's say my mother and I have similar taste in men and leave it at that."

She saw him digesting the information. "So you stayed because you didn't have anywhere to go."

"Partly." If it was only that simple, she thought, playing with the edge of her napkin. "Warren was the first man who… He had me convinced I couldn't do any better." A weight settled on her shoulders.

"Hey." To her surprise, Hunter reached across the table and covered her hand. "You've already done better."

"I have?"

"Sure." His expression was deadly serious. "You dumped his sorry behind, didn't you?"

She was struck by how much the candlelight made his eyes sparkle. An optical illusion, no doubt, but mesmerizing all the same. She found herself falling into them. "Thank you."

He pulled his hand away, leaving her skin cool once more.

Scrambling for some sort of mental purchase, she changed the subject. "How about we talk about something else instead?"

"Like what?"

"How about you?" she asked.

Hunter lay down the menu. "Not much to talk about."

"There's got to be something." An entire day together and she knew very little about the man. He spoke little, revealed less.

Case in point, the way he shrugged off her request. "Not really."

"How long you been taking photographs?"

"My whole life. My father bought me my first 35 millimeter when I was eight. I blew a whole roll taking pictures of my mother's Pomeranian. Dad told me later I should have used better lighting."

"He was a photographer, too?"

"You ever see the photo of the schoolkids saluting the president?"

"Sure. It's famous." Her eyes widened again. "He took that?"

"Among others."

"Wow. I'm impressed."

"Yeah. It's a memorable shot." For a moment, he seemed to lose himself in the candle flame. "Anyway, I got started by studying him. I used to travel as part of his crew when I was on school break."

She noticed Hunter said *part of his crew,* not *with him.* Abby wondered if there was a story behind his choice of words. If she knew him better, she'd ask. "And what do you take pictures of?" she asked instead. "Besides unsuspecting waitresses."

"Anything and everything. Wherever the job sends me."

A waiter suddenly appeared. He wore a bright gold jacket and carried a bread basket that matched. Everything in the place seemed to glisten in jewel tones. Between the surroundings and the man across from her, she felt like a unkempt, drab mop. If the food was gorgeous-looking, too, she was out of there.

It didn't help that the host had placed them in what she swore was the most intimate corner of the restaurant. She and Hunter sat tucked behind a potted plant, in a nook illuminated by jeweled votive candles. Hunter's eyes changed color in the soft light, turning indigo to match their surroundings. She tried to shift her position, but her foot brushed his, making her doubly aware of the closed space.

The waiter placed the basket in front of her. "Naan," he explained.

Abby unfolded the napkin to reveal an aroma that made her mouth water. "Indian bread," Hunter told her. "Best I've had outside of New Delhi."

"You've been to India?" She wasn't surprised. Seeing how at ease he appeared in these surroundings, she could easily imagine him in exotic lands. *A real-life action hero.*

"Couple times on assignment," he said, tearing off a chunk of flat bread and handing it to her. "Once to northern India and once to New Delhi. Beautiful country."

He was right. The bread was delicious. She reached for another piece. "Must be nice. Traveling all over the world. Photographing exotic places."

"I'm not sure you'd call my last few assignments exotic. I've been doing a lot of work for *Newstime.* In fact, I leave in a few days for a swing through the Middle East."

"Sounds pretty exotic to me."

"Sure, if you like dodging potential violence."

"Yeah, I wouldn't know anything about that," she drawled.

Hunter cocked his head, eyes catching the candle flame. The shift brought out the blue even more. "Are you always this sarcastic?"

"Unfortunately." Warren called it her smart mouth. "I try to bite my tongue, but for some reason, with you the tone slips out."

"Should I be flattered or insulted?"

"I'll let you decide," she told him. Mainly because she didn't know the answer herself. She didn't know why she was so free with her thoughts today. Fatigue? Not having to fear a reprisal? With Warren she was always so careful about her words, never knowing when she'd say something to set him off. She was pretty certain all Hunter would do was snark back.

Or maybe it was the fact she didn't feel the need to impress. Rather, knowing she had no need to impress, she didn't have to worry about trying.

Perhaps she should try. A little. The man had spent the day at the courthouse with her. Then again, the day at the courthouse was largely his fault. Besides, he wasn't exactly putting his best foot forward for her, either. And after tonight, they'd probably never see each other again. He'd be off living his exotic adventurous life, and she'd be at McKenzie House, sitting in the common room circling Help Wanted ads. The agreeable mood she'd been nursing faded away.

Dinner was delicious, as always, although Hunter's companion didn't seem to enjoy the food as much as he hoped she would. Abby retreated into herself and never completely returned, and he…well, he apparently was battling his conscience. Why his chest knotted up every time Abby's face sobered, he couldn't explain. After all, it wasn't his fault Guy was a self-serving slug. Hunter hadn't asked the diner owner to fire Abby, any more than he'd asked her d-bag of an ex-boyfriend to track her down. She—they—were not Hunter's problem. So why did every crestfallen expression that crossed her features have him feeling like Attila the Hun? Worse, why did he feel the insane need to take her out to dinner? Here, where the candlelight turned her hair the color of warm caramel?

That reminded him: he needed to have a talk with Vishay. The man had sat them at the smallest, most candlelit table in the restaurant. Beneath the table, their knees touched. Above, every little movement caused their personal spaces to collide. Hunter spent the meal far more aware of her body than he should be. Every brush of her leg against his jeans reminded him of how it had felt when he was holding her earlier. He'd reacted with a lot more than compassion. At least his body had. How could he not? With her head tucked beneath his chin as if she was a perfect fit. Her hair…damn, the way her curls tickled his skin. Like baby-soft strands of silk. The mere memory made his fingers twitch. What he wouldn't give to smooth his hands through the untamed strands to learn for himself if the softness lived up to its potential.

How long had it been since he'd touched a woman, anyway? Five, six months? Longer.

Too long, apparently. Unfortunately, he wasn't kidding about the baggage. Abby had a freaking wardrobeful. He wasn't into taking on other people's burdens. It was enough shouldering his own.

Nope. If he wanted to scratch his itch, he would have to find somewhere else. Wasn't like he didn't have plenty of opportunity. There were always women—available women—drawn by either the excitement of his profession or his money, who were more than willing to visit his bed for a night or two.

"It's after seven," he said, looking at his watch. "Think the sheriff's paid your ex a visit?"

"Hope so. They didn't give a time." She poked at a piece of chicken with her fork. "Warren's going to be furious," she said in a low voice.

"Who cares how Warren feels? His feelings aren't your problem anymore."

"Old habits are hard to break. You're right, though. Warren brought his problems on himself. I've got far bigger ones to worry about."

The twisting sensation seized his chest again. "I can talk to Guy. Smooth things over. Explain."

"You'd do that?"

"I offered, didn't I?" No need to tell her he was as surprised by his offer as she was.

Abby shook her head. "Thanks, but I doubt he'll listen to you any more than he listened to me. Looks like I'll have to start from scratch. By the way, since I can't list Guy, I'm putting you down as a reference."

"Me? What am I supposed to say?"

"I don't know. Tell people what a great waitress you thought I was. How I'm efficient and invaluable."

"You kept forgetting people's orders."

"Only at the beginning," she replied, eyes narrowing. "And you owe me."

Hunter decided not to argue the point. "Fine. If a prospective employer tracks me down while I'm in Tripoli, I'll tell them you were the best waitress I ever had. How's that?"

"No need to exaggerate. Just be realistic." She leaned back in her seat, looking as if she was about to withdraw again. "I doubt you'll get many calls, anyway. The job market for un-skilled help is pretty competitive."

"I doubt you're that unskilled," he said. He didn't like that her expression was getting to him again.

"Weren't you listening? Guy's was the first job I ever held. Taking care of Warren doesn't count. Unless you know some-one who needs a glorified housekeeper, chief cook and bottle washer."

"Actually…" Hunter sat back without finishing his state-ment. He wasn't sure if she was hinting or if his mind came up with the thought on its own. Either way, he thought as he stud-ied her candlelit face, the idea was a bad one. A truly bad idea.

On the other hand—he considered the disorganization tak-ing over his loft—Christina did say he needed a housekeeper more than an assistant. It would be a temporary fix at most, a win-win for them both while she looked for a real job.

Besides, he was leaving the country. By the time he got back, he'd have scratched his itch and put an end to the twist-ing, unsettled feeling that gripped him every time he looked in Abby's direction. And she couldn't say he hadn't made amends for Guy firing her.

From across the table, her big brown eyes watched him with interest. Waiting on what he'd started to say.

"Actually…" Leaning forward, he started again. "I have a proposition for you."

CHAPTER FOUR

"YOU'RE EARLY."

Abby flashed a nervous grin. When Hunter suggested she work for him—temporarily—she'd accepted immediately. What could she say? Recent unemployment and the threat of poverty made her overeager. This morning, however, she wondered if she should have thought things through a little better.

Especially since her new employer answered the door half-dressed.

To be fair, she *was* early, although no more than twenty minutes or so. Again, she blamed unemployed eagerness.

"Just trying to impress the boss," she said.

Amazingly, she managed to answer without stuttering. Based on his damp hair, Hunter had been in the shower when she rang the front doorbell. Droplets of water clung to the brown hair dusting his chest, and she was pretty sure she saw one drip traveling downward, toward what she was sure was a very con-toured abdomen. Visions of last night's embrace popped into her head. She'd leaned against that torso. Spread her palms across those shoulders.

"You could have told me to wait outside," she told him.

"Next time I will. Is that coffee for me?" He gestured to the cardboard tray in her hand.

"Yes." Abby felt her cheeks grow warm, although that could be from the near nakedness as much as anything. "I was getting myself some, and figured you'd be looking for breakfast. Since Guy threw you out, too."

"My money would have put me back in Guy's good graces quickly enough."

True, but she needed breakfast and she wasn't in Guy's good graces. "Does that mean you don't want your fried egg sandwich?"

"You got me a sandwich?"

"With cheese on whole wheat. Not exactly your usual order, but it was the best I could do while commuting."

"That's…" There was an unreadable expression in his eyes as he looked in the bag. "Thank you," he said, turning those eyes back to hers. "That's very nice of you."

You'd think no one had ever been nice to him before. Or that she'd ever received a compliment, for that matter, seeing how her blush shot straight to her toes. Come to think of it, she couldn't remember the last time she *had* received a compliment.

"I thought you were broke."

She gave her best shrug. "I found temporary employment. And, like I said, I'm simply trying to get on the boss's good side."

"Food isn't necessary. Just do your job and clean my apartment."

Did he have any idea how liberating such a simple request sounded? To simply do anything without worrying about reprisal was all she ever wanted. "You got a deal," she said, smiling. Her eyes locked with his. Their color was definitely bluer today than last night. Bluer and darker.

The heat of the air in the hallway kicked up a notch.

"You, um…" Maybe it was the woodsy smell of his aftershave mingling with breakfast, but she suddenly remembered Hunter's state of dress. "Could you…?"

"Right." He blinked, as if realizing himself, and backed away. "Of course. Come inside while I put a shirt on."

Don't rush on my account, Abby almost said. Fortunately, she didn't.

While Hunter jogged upstairs, she wandered into the kitchen area, looking for a place to set the coffee down. She needed a good dose of caffeine to clear the topless-Hunter images from her head. Today was supposed to be fresh start number two. No way she was ruining the milestone by acting like a flustered schoolgirl. The squirrelly sensations in her stomach would simply have to go away.

She wasn't stupid. She knew exactly what was happening to her. Her libido, after years of being bullied into dormancy, had decided to wake up. Hardly surprising, when she thought about it. A woman would have to be literally dead not to feel some kind of physical awareness around a man who looked like Hunter. It was like being attracted to a movie star or a handsome model in a magazine advertisement. Enjoyable but unrealistic.

What shocked her, though, was the intensity with which she reacted. She didn't simply look at him with attraction; she felt it all the way to her bones. Her skin grew hot every time he glanced at her, and her insides seemed on a perpetual trampoline. She hadn't felt this much with Warren ever. Thank goodness Hunter was leaving town in a couple days. Her attraction was obviously making up for lost time by overreacting.

On the plus side, she could, with relief, say that her years with Warren hadn't deadened her completely. That was one piece of baggage she could unpack.

In the meantime, she needed to act professionally. She was here to clean and organize, not fantasize. Setting her packages on the black marble countertop, she looked around her temporary assignment. Hunter's apartment was not what she expected. In her imagination, she'd pictured him living in some rugged man-cave, a location that matched his action star exterior. She certainly didn't expect an airy, light-filled loft. It had one of those open floor plans where one large space was meant to be broken up by furniture into smaller living areas. Hunter hadn't broken up anything, however. He barely had furniture.

It was pretty obvious why he needed a housekeeper, though, because what he did have was clutter. A lot of clutter. There were piles stacked all over the place. In one corner sat a work-station piled high with miscellaneous items, half of which she didn't recognize but assumed were photo related. Probably equipment that spilled over from the collection of cameras and materials on the shelf above.

It was as though he'd decided to decorate with clutter instead of real furnishings. And yet, in spite of the mess, the apart-ment felt empty. Incomplete. As if it was missing something besides furniture.

She was in the kitchen studying the impressive array of un-used appliances when Hunter reappeared. He'd slipped into a faded T-shirt. The tight red cotton still obscenely emphasized his body, but at least he was dressed. "Getting the lay of the land?"

"I'm trying. This kitchen is a cook's dream."

"So the Realtor told me." He was busy digging into the sack for his egg sandwich.

"I take it that wasn't a big selling point for you." Wonder what was? Meanwhile, watching him devour his poorly pre-pared breakfast, she got an idea. "If you'd like, I could cook for you. I mean," she added when he looked up, "while you're in town. For a change of pace."

"I didn't hire you to cook."

"I know. I'm not a gourmet cook, either. But you've got to admit, a home-cooked meal before leaving for the desert might be nice, don't you think? Comfort food for the road?"

"I wouldn't know. I've never had a home-cooked meal."

"You're joking." He was, right? The look on his face said no. "Never?"

"Not really. They don't have personal chefs at boarding school."

"You went to boarding school?" How sad.

"When I wasn't on the road with my father. You needn't look so horrified," Hunter added. "They're not all Dickensian nightmares."

Abby wasn't quite sure what he meant by his comment, but she did know he wasn't as indifferent about the experience as he'd like to appear. The way he fiddled with his sandwich wrapper gave him away. Hard to picture the strong, aloof man she'd spent yesterday with being affected by anything. But then, as she'd already noted, she didn't know him, did she?

The apartment's incompleteness hit her again.

"How about I cook you your first one today?" she said, returning to the topic at hand. "Nothing fancy. Spaghetti and meatballs? A side salad. It's a shame to waste all these fancy appliances."

"Not to mention it would add another item to your job description for when I write you a reference."

Cheeks warming, she found it was her turn to study the counter. "I did call myself a chief cook and bottle washer. Kind of implies cooking."

"Suppose it does." Hunter gave a sigh, but his expression was one of amusement. The crooked smile brightened his face. If possible the look was even sexier than his bare torso. The squirrelly sensation returned, causing her knees to buckle a little. Dear Lord, but he was too gorgeous for words.

"So it's a deal?" she asked, clearing her throat.

"Sure," Hunter replied. "Spaghetti and meatballs it is."

"Great. I'll cook for you tonight."

As if on cue, the squirrels began dashing around even faster.

"I think I'm signing you up for that reality show about hoarders," Abby remarked an hour later.

Hunter didn't even look up from the spreadsheet he was working on. "You're exaggerating."

"Barely." All right, she was exaggerating, but seriously, did the man not know the meaning of the term *file cabinet?* Before she could do any kind of serious cleaning, she realized, she had to take care of the piles. What she'd discovered was that Hunter's apartment wasn't so much messy as it was simply chaotic. Needless to say, most of the equipment was job related. There were research books, photo proofs, magazine articles. Then there was the equipment, and equipment-related stuff—the unrecognizable junk on his workstation table. Who knew there were so many different kinds of camera lenses? And lens films. What the heck? Wasn't film for inside the camera?

"Did you know," she continued, picking up another travel magazine, "they invented this new machine a few years ago. Called a paper shredder."

"Very amusing. I told you. I'm only here between assignments. The apartment's nothing more than a place to stow my stuff."

"Pretty expensive storage space. Wouldn't one of those rental units work better?"

"The building's an investment." He looked up from the screen. "You never talked this much when you were a waitress."

Meaning she was talking too much now. Abby felt her cheeks grow hot. "Sorry," she murmured. Biting her lip, she went back to her cleaning.

Behind her, Hunter let out a breath. "You don't need to apologize," he said.

"Sorry. Force of habit."

"Let me guess. Warren didn't like you talking, either."

"Said he needed quiet after a hard day at work." Thinking of all the aspects of her life her ex-boyfriend had controlled, Abby cringed. Thank God he was out of her life for good.

"Hey." Hunter's voice, soft and low, sounded behind her. "You don't have to stop talking."

"But you said…"

He touched her shoulder. "I'm not Warren."

No, he definitely wasn't. Far from it. For starters, Warren's touch was never as gentle, nor had it sent warmth spiraling around her spine.

"I—I found a bunch of receipts," she said, edging away before she grew too used to the feeling. "Underneath a pile of photos. Are they important?"

"Probably. What are the photos of?"

"A demonstration."

"Right. Damascus, last month. I should submit those."

He said it casually. Abby handed him the paperwork, glancing again at the photos. The images were violent and rueful. It was jarring to think a person could be having breakfast at a streetside café one moment and photographing brutality the next.

One picture showed a man being dragged away, blood staining his torn jeans. "Do you ever get worried, taking photos at events like this?"

"No."

"I would."

"I worry about missing the shot."

"Would that be so bad?"

Hunter, who'd been settling back into his seat, stopped what he was doing to stare at her in disbelief. "Yes, it would. It's my job to get the shot."

"Even if it means putting your life at risk?" No photo seemed that important.

"Doesn't matter. They aren't paying me to run away. The only thing that counts is getting the shot. And since you never know when that perfect shot is going to happen, the only thing you can do is click till you run out of memory space."

How ironic. It sounded as if the action-hero costume fit, after all. He really was literally dodging bullets. "Did you learn that lesson from your father?" She'd borrowed a computer last night and done a little research, enough to know Joseph Smith's famous photograph was only one of many famous shots he was known for. Hunter, she'd discovered, was famous, too, a little fact he never mentioned. She found site after site celebrating his coverage of a school explosion in Somalia.

"My father was right. You can't do your job if you're worried about staying safe."

"I'm sure your mother disagreed."

A curtain came down over his features. "Seeing as how she was dead at the time, I doubt it."

"Oh. Right." *Idiot.* The internet didn't mention his mother, but Abby should have put two and two together based on his comment yesterday.

Somehow, though, she imagined that had his mother lived, she would have objected. Especially seeing as Hunter's father died while on assignment. That Hunter's life might end under similar circumstances…for what? A photograph? The idea bothered Abby. Seemed sad and rather senseless, if you asked her. "The way you talk, you make it sound like your life doesn't matter," she said.

"Photography is my life," he relied.

Now that truly didn't seem right. She refrained from saying so, though. The photos, she realized, were still in her hand. As she moved to set them down, she found herself turning over the top one. The image was too harsh to look at. "I don't think I could do it," she decided.

"Do what?"

"Stand there and take pictures without being afraid. Or affected. I mean, how do you look at what's going on around you without reacting?"

"You learn."

"How?" She wanted to know. Had his father taught him that lesson, too?

But Hunter had turned back to the computer screen. "You just do," he told her.

Once again a curtain had dropped over his features, clos-ing his expression to scrutiny. There was more to his story. His answer was too emphatic, too absolute. Had something happened to hammer home the lesson? She wondered if she'd ever find out.

They worked in silence for the next couple hours. Hunter wasn't sure if Abby's silence was in response to his comment about talking too much—he hoped not; the way she'd shrunk back in apology made his stomach hurt—or if she was thinking about their other conversation. It was clear she didn't approve of his answers, even if what he told her was the truth. What other an-swer did she expect? Might as well ask a soldier if he worried about being shot in battle.

How many times had he watched his father risk life and limb for the perfect picture? When Hunter was a kid, his father's risk-taking used to scare him. But oh, the shots he'd pulled off. *Makes all the risk worth it,* he'd overheard his dad tell a coworker once. Okay, so sometimes he did wonder if, had his mother lived, his father would be as daring. He'd certainly seemed more cautious when she was around. Ultimately, how-ever, the answer didn't matter. His mother had died, his father had lived for his job, and Hunter understood why he'd taken the risks. Abby would understand, too, if she were a photog-rapher. Maybe he should put a camera in her hands, train her to be one. He shook off the notion as quickly as it popped into his head. Why should he care whether she understood or not?

A flash of red caught the corner of his eye. Abby on her knees in front of his filing cabinet. She'd taken it upon herself to organize the film and stock images he'd neglected. Already proving herself a better hire than Christina.

And once she was finished, he would get a proper clean-ing service. Preferably one where the employees' rear ends didn't look so enticing. Today was the first time he'd seen Abby dressed in something other than that shapeless waitress uniform. He missed the blue-and-white sack. Today's turtleneck and narrow-legged jeans revealed way too much. What he'd assumed was angular and too skinny was really long and lean. The big glimpse of leg she'd flashed in the cab? Tip of the iceberg. One thing for sure, legs like that should not be encased in attention-getting red. He must have made a dozen inputting errors because the color distracted him.

"Hunter?"

Breaking off from his thoughts, he turned his attention to the file cabinet. With a photo clutched in her hand, Abby was staring at him as if he had two heads. Dammit. How long had she been talking?

"Should I label the back of the photos with yellow notes like the ones already in the file?" she asked.

Thank goodness it was a question where he didn't have to be listening in order to answer. "For now. The notes are reminders for labels." Another project Christina had failed to complete. With luck, karma had gifted his old assistant with an equally distracted and inept assistant of her own.

"Looks like I have another project to tackle while you're gone," Abby said, grabbing a pen and yellow notepad.

"Unless you find a job before then."

"I meant if I didn't find a permanent position." Her expression faltered again. Hunter wished she'd stop looking so forlorn. Made his gut hurt.

Why had he said anything in the first place? They both knew the job was temporary. He didn't need to remind her.

Maybe you were reminding yourself? As his gaze dropped to the brass grommets dotting her back pockets, he wondered if the reminder wasn't to keep him from doing something stupid.

"Where was this picture taken?"

Abby held up the photo in her hand.

"Let me see." Joining her, he took it from her and saw it was a black-and-white shot of an old man enjoying a cigarette while sitting on a stack of luggage.

He smiled, remembering. "Mirpur Khas," he said. "Waiting on the rail platform. We got to the station before sunrise and he was sitting there, patient as can be. When the sun got bright enough, I snapped his picture. He didn't even blink."

Reaching around her shoulder, Hunter pointed to the band on the man's wrist. "See? You can read the time on his watch? And how wizened his skin is? I remember seeing those wrinkles and thinking he looked like he'd been waiting forever."

"Maybe he had," Abby replied. She turned to Hunter, and he found himself nearly nose to nose. "Do you remember every picture you take?"

"The memorable ones stick in your head." *Like yours,* he thought. Looking at her now, he saw glimpses of the same wistfulness and steel. She still wasn't wearing much makeup. He liked that. Showed the imperfections and emphasized the character of her face. No wizened skin here. What would if feel like if he traced the back of his hand across her cheek? Would her skin feel as soft as he imagined?

To his disappointment, she turned away, back to the photographs.

"Now that one," he said, recognizing the shot of elephants marching in the mist, "was taken in the Congo rain forest. I waited two days in the rain for those blasted creatures. Caught a wicked case of paddy foot from standing in the mud and had to spend the next week changing my socks twice a day."

"Better paddy foot than getting shot."

Back to that, was she? "Better I came away with the photo," he reminded her. "I could have sat in the rain for nothing, which happens more than you know. A lot of this job is plain old luck. Being in the right place at the right time."

"And yet you stick with it. Guess the job can't be all bad."

Hunter slipped the photo from her fingers. "It has its moments, that's for certain." Good and bad.

He waited as she wrote "Africa: Wildlife" on a sticky note, then handed her back the picture.

"I'm curious," she said. "Under what category would you file my photo?"

"Why do you want to know?"

"Well, as far as filing goes, you've got old men, old women, street people, occupations."

"Standard stock categories."

"I was wondering what category you'd stick me in. Women at work, street scenes or—" she scanned the tabs "—New Yorkers."

"None of the above. You'd get your own special category."

"I would?" She blushed, making him wish he had a camera then and there instead of across the room. The soft pink suited her. People should compliment her more often, to draw out the shade.

"Uh-huh. I'd file you under strangely compelling waitresses."

Another blush, followed by a swipe of her bangs and a duck of her face. A trifecta of shyness. So sexy he felt his jeans tighten.

"You mean the photo, right?" she said in a low voice.

Catching her chin with his finger, he lifted her face back to his. "Sure." In reality, he found far more than the photo compelling. But saying so would only open a dangerous can of worms.

Perhaps she realized it as well, because her smile was tinged with gratitude. "I'll make sure to label it appropriately should I run across a copy."

"Actually, you'll find a few copies on the printer. From the other day when I was working."

The look she gave him, as she scampered over to check, said *really?* "I lost my copy during the fight."

"You can take one of those if you'd like," he told her. "Personally, I think the black-and-white version has more depth. Highlights the contrasts."

"You mean the bags under my eyes."

This dumping on her appearance was becoming a habit. "Are you always so negative about the way you look?"

"Generally. Another force of habit, I'm afraid. Along with jumping when called and blaming myself for mistakes.

"I'm working on it, though," she added over her shoulder.

"As for the photographs…" She left the page in the tray. "Thanks, but I'll pass. Not sure it's a memory I want to keep, if you know what I mean."

He did indeed. Photography had the power to instantly transport you to a place or time, even ones you wished you could forget. "I'll take another of you if you want," he offered. "One with a nicer memory."

"No sense pressing your luck. I can't guarantee I'll take a second good shot."

There she went, denigrating herself again. Warren and whoever else had put those thoughts in her head should be shot.

Moving back to his computer chair, Hunter told her, "I can."

"How confident of you," she said with a laugh.

"Simply stating a fact."

"Of course you are. I think I'll go back to filing."

"Suit yourself." He'd take a shot of her sometime when she wasn't paying attention. He preferred candid, unaffected ones, anyway.

He returned to his expense reports. Had to admit, the numbers weren't nearly as interesting.

"Uh-oh," Abby said a few minutes later. "One of your files is missing a tab."

"Must have fallen off."

"Either that or your former assistant never created one. Did you know she couldn't spell?"

"Doesn't—"

"Wow!" Abby's gasp of amazement cut him off. "These photos are…"

He wondered what he'd photographed that she found so impressive. "Are what?"

"The kids playing soccer. They look so happy."

Kids? Hunter's insides turned icy. Couldn't be. He'd ordered those photos thrown away.

Even as he dreaded seeing the images, some perverse need made him get up to look. Over Abby's shoulder he saw what she didn't. The hard black eyes hadn't changed a bit. Hatred hidden behind a broad smile. The memory came flooding back. *Mr. Hunter! Mr. Hunter!*

"Throw them out," he said.

"Why? They look perfectly good to me."

"I said throw them out!"

Abby sat back on her heels, eyes wide in confusion. Hunter immediately felt like a jerk. Wasn't her fault. She didn't know. "Sorry," he said, washing his hand over his features.

"Is something wrong? I don't understand."

"Nothing's wrong. Just— I don't want to keep the photos, okay?"

The walls started closing in. He needed fresh air. A break. "I'm going to go out for a bit," he told her. "Lock the door behind you when you leave for the day."

Grabbing the one anchor he could always count on, his camera, he headed for the door. As he closed it behind him, the last thing he saw was Abby, still kneeling on the floor, surrounded by photos and questions.

CHAPTER FIVE

ABBY MADE SPAGHETTI and meatballs, anyway. She'd promised, and she intended to keep her word. If Hunter returned in time for dinner, terrific. If not, at least his gourmet kitchen got one good use. Besides, it wouldn't be the first time she'd spent time and energy on a meal that was ignored.

Although in this case, the circumstances were a bit different. Hunter wasn't ignoring her, nor did he storm out in anger. On the contrary, he'd been upset for a different reason. The minute he saw those photographs, his entire demeanor had changed. He went from warm and open to closed off in the blink of an eye. Why? What about those pictures set him off?

Hunter had told her to throw the photos away, but curiosity wouldn't let her. Once she'd finished making the sauce, she turned to study the pictures across the countertop, looking for something that might explain Hunter's agitation. The shots were of kids playing soccer in what looked like Africa. What could possibly be so upsetting about kids playing a game?

She thought about the moments just before she'd found the file. It'd been a pleasure to work around him. While he spoke little, his presence was comfortable, friendly. Then, when he knelt behind her on the floor... She used to hate it when Warren approached her from behind. Mainly because if she couldn't see his face, she couldn't judge his mood. A hand gripping her shoulder could mean anger as easily as it meant anything else. But when Hunter knelt behind her, she didn't so much as tense. At least not with uncertainty. Instead, it brought her back to this morning in his doorway, when he'd greeted her damp and half-naked. Even now, in a kitchen smelling of tomatoes and garlic, she could, if she concentrated, recall his aftershave. How the scent had teased her nostrils when he reached around her to point out landmarks. Much like the way his breath had tickled her temple when he spoke.

Focus, Abby. Bad enough her libido caused problems when Hunter was in the room; she didn't need it flaring to life while thinking of the man, too.

She returned to the photos. There was a woman in several of the shots. Tall and voluptuous, she had auburn hair and a toothy grin that leaped off the page. Was she the bad memory? A broken heart would certainly explain his distant nature.

What kind of woman would Hunter fall for? Abby traced the image. That she'd be beautiful was a given. This woman's looks, however, went beyond surface pretty. One glance at her photos told you she had a special sort of vitality. Her eyes literally sparkled with life. A far cry from Abby's dead insides, that's for sure.

Keys sounded in the lock, causing her to drop the photo she was holding and jump back. Hunter walked in, camera around his neck. He looked tired, as if he'd walked a marathon. One he'd lost. Abby wasn't used to seeing his shoulders slumped with such weariness. She grabbed the counter edge to keep from wrapping him in a hug.

"Hey," she murmured softly.

"You're still here."

Not the most enthusiastic of greetings. "Promised you dinner, remember?"

"So I can smell. You didn't have to go the trouble."

"We're talking spaghetti sauce, not a gourmet meal. Besides,

I enjoyed being able to cook again." McKenzie House didn't have much of a setup beyond the basics. Anything that involved more than a microwave and a jar was a treat to make, as far as she was concerned. "Hopefully, you'll like how everything turned out, because I made a lot. And by a lot, I mean a lot. You'll be eating leftovers for a week." She was babbling, trying to fill the awkwardness with noise. The fact that Hunter hadn't moved since setting his camera down didn't help. He simply stood in the kitchen entrance, staring.

Shoot. Abby followed his gaze, and realized he'd spied the photographs. Quickly she moved to gather them. "Sorry, I didn't get to throw those away yet. Let me do it right now."

Hunter reached over and stopped her. "S'all right. I'll take care of them." Except he didn't, continuing instead to stare off into space. Abby wished she knew what he was thinking. He felt so far away.

"I shouldn't have walked out the way I did," he said after a few minutes.

"No big deal. You didn't swear or throw anything. Makes it a step up from most of my walkouts."

He arched a brow. The gesture almost—almost—breached the distance he'd retreated behind. "Just because I wasn't violent doesn't make it right. You shouldn't roll over so easily."

"You think I'm rolling over?"

"I was rude, and you made me spaghetti. What would you call it?"

What she'd call it was deflecting the focus away from himself. She "rolled over" and left the challenge unspoken. "Next time I'll skip the cooking. Would that be better?"

Hunter didn't answer, his attention having returned to the images spread across the counter. Coming around to join him on his side, Abby picked up the shot that seemed to be holding his attention. It was a close-up of the woman, with several young children gathered around her. A wave of envy washed over Abby as she was yet again struck by the woman's vitality.

"She's very beautiful," she said.

"Her name was Donna."

Was. No mistaking the finality in his voice. Abby turned the photo over, ashamed that she'd been envious of a dead woman.

"I shouldn't have said anything." No matter how curious she was, she had no business picking the scab of an old wound. Better to let him process the past in peace. "I'll go check on the sauce."

"I took these shots in Somalia," Hunter said, stopping her.

Somalia. Hearing the name gave her a déjà vu feeling. Nonetheless, Abby shook her head and told him, "You don't need to explain." Knowing what dragging up the past was like, she felt the need to let him off the hook.

"On the contrary, I think I should explain more. I *want* to explain more."

"Why?" No one had ever bothered explaining their behavior to her before. She leaned a hip against the countertop. "Is this because I shared my sad story with you? Because if that's your reason, there's no need to go tit for tat."

"I know, and you're rolling over again."

"No, I'm offering you an out."

He half smiled. "So you are. Thank you."

Abby felt a warmth settle over her. It was nice to have her consideration acknowledged, despite the sober circumstances. "You're welcome. And I'm sorry if the photos brought back bad memories."

"They did." She waited while he set the overturned photograph right side up again. "It was my first assignment after my father's accident. I thought I was prepared. I'd seen war and horrible conditions before, so I figured I knew what I was getting into. The people, though…" He blew out a long breath through his nose. "When I traveled with my father, the attention was on his work. Even if I was taking my own shots, it was second to what he needed to do. That's how being an assistant worked. Something Christina, my old assistant, never understood.

"Anyway, for the first time in my life I was the lead photographer. The one who did the talking, the interacting. I was
supposed to spend a couple weeks there, but I stretched it out."

"Sounds like the place made an impact on you."

"Not the place, the people," he replied. "They were so grateful, so eager to learn. The kids, especially. Like little sponges,
absorbing everything. Slightest little thing would make their
faces light up. Could be anything. A piece of chocolate, a book,
even something like a soccer game."

"And Donna?" Had she made as powerful an impact? He'd
yet to say, and Abby was surprised at how anxious she was to
find out.

"Donna taught at the school. Second or third grade, I can't
remember which. Maybe both. Didn't matter. The entire school
loved her. Camera loved her, too, in case you didn't notice."

"So that's why there are so many photos of her?"

"Did you think…?" He shook his head. "No, she wasn't. Not
the way you think. Yes, she and I—"

"I get the picture." They'd been lovers; she wasn't the love
of his life.

"Given my reaction, I could see why you might think otherwise."

"Why did you react so badly?" So far, he'd revealed nothing but a fondness for the school and the country. Sliding onto
a nearby stool, Abby eagerly waited for more.

"Like I said, the place was special. I didn't expect to get so
sucked in, but there was something addictive about the sense of
community. It was like being in the middle of this giant family."

Which, to a man who'd recently lost his father, must have
been incredibly appealing. Abby could relate. Loneliness was
an incredibly powerful weakness. Hadn't she grabbed hold of
the first person she'd found to fill the emptiness in her life?

"There was this kid named Naxar," Hunter said. "Not so
much a kid, actually. He was only a couple years younger than
me. Worked as a janitor at the school. Always following me

around, calling 'Mr. Hunter, Mr. Hunter!' I made him my pet project. He'd carry my equipment, help me set up."

"Your first assistant," Abby noted with a smile.

"The beginning of a very bad trend," Hunter said, giving another half smile. Like before, it failed to reach his eyes. "You'd think I'd learn."

The smile faded. "He blew himself up during a school assembly."

Dear God. Abby's stomach dropped. The explosion. The photos that had made Hunter's career.

"The evidence was there all along, but I was too involved to see it. Too busy focusing on the kids' smiles."

Hunter fished a photo out of the pile and slid it toward her. A crowd watching two boys racing after the soccer ball. Abby knew right away which young man was Naxar. While all the others were cheering, he stood on the edge of the action. Hunter's camera had caught him unaware, capturing a face icy with rage. It was that expression that had caught her attention when she first unearthed the pictures. Looking again, this time knowing the whole story, Abby shivered. To think one man could cause such death and destruction. Even Warren, for all his rages, wasn't capable of that level of violence.

And Hunter, seeing the community he cared about blown apart... She couldn't imagine how that felt.

Or the guilt he might be feeling.

"It's not your fault," she said. Wasn't that what the abuse counselors had told her? That the victim isn't responsible for the abuser's rage? "There's no way you could have known what he planned to do."

"Not my fault, but a mistake all the same."

"What was?" She figured he would say missing the signs.

"Letting him get close. Letting any of them get close."

"You mean the people at the school?"

He nodded. "There's a reason the camera stays between you

and the subject. It's your buffer. Keeps you focused on the job. I forgot."

"You make it sound like caring was a mistake."

"It was. The only thing I should have cared about was getting the shot. Everything else…"

He shrugged the rest of the thought away, but Abby got the point. He was saying nothing else mattered but the shot, same as he'd said before. Not his subject, not the people around him, not his own safety. With one raise of his shoulders, Abby suddenly understood why he wanted the photographs destroyed. He wasn't trying to bury the memory of a woman, or even his guilt. He was burying his feelings. How well she understood that desire. She, too, had wrapped her heart in a blanket of numbness, stuffed it in a hole of self-preservation, where pain couldn't find it. Life was simpler that way.

Only for some reason, when it came to Hunter, the desire felt wrong. Why, she couldn't say. In fact, she couldn't say anything at all. She settled for touching his shoulder.

Hunter covered her hand with his. The cool touch of his fingers wrapped around hers ran straight up her arm, reminding her that while her heart was numb, the rest of her was still alive.

"You're not wearing a bandage today," he said.

Changing the topic. "Didn't see the sense," she told him. "You know the bruises are there. Why bother hiding them?"

Turning her hand palm up, he gave a small nod. "Your skin shouldn't have bruises."

"He says, stating the obvious." She was being flip, but inside, she'd grown warm. Could he feel her pulse beneath his fingers? If so, he would know it was racing. Shouldn't be. He was simply making an observation. There was no compliment, no seductive overtone. Her body was reacting to the tenderness.

Maybe she was the one, then, who needed distance. Especially now, as Hunter ran his thumb across the pulse point. "You deserve good things, Abby Gray. Good things. Good people. A good life. You know that, right?"

Of course she knew that. This sudden switch in conversation didn't make sense. It was almost as though he was trying to tell her something else.

"So do you," she told him.

"Don't worry about me. I get exactly what I need." Dropping her hand, he gathered up the photographs. "I'm going to get rid of these before dinner."

A few minutes later, Abby heard the high-pitched squeal of a shredder—the very machine she teased him earlier about not owning. She listened, unconsciously stroking her wrist. Got what he needed, huh? She couldn't help wondering if that was enough.

"Explain to me again why, if you hired me to be your housekeeper, we're taking a walk in Central Park?" Abby stood on the top of the apartment building's steps, watching Hunter fiddle with his camera.

"I told you," he replied, "I get stir-crazy if I stay inside too long."

"I got the stir-crazy part. What I don't get is why I needed to come along. Shouldn't I be, I don't know, cleaning your house?" Which she'd been doing, until he'd insisted she join him.

"You have a problem with taking a break?"

"Suppose not."

He watched a squirrel drag a piece of pizza crust across the sidewalk.

"Are you planning a long walk?" They seemed to be walking at a very determined pace for just a simple stroll.

"Does it matter?"

"It does if you want me to get dinner started for you."

Hunter stopped in his tracks. For a second, Abby thought they might turn around. "I told you yesterday, you don't have to cook for me. That's not part of the job."

"And I told you, I don't mind cooking for you."

"Well, I mind. If I'd wanted a private chef, I would have hired one." He started walking again. Abby hurried to catch up.

"Most people would enjoy the opportunity," she pointed out.

"I'm not most people."

That, she thought, looking at him from the corner of her eye, was an understatement. He was back in action-hero mode again today. Fortunately, she'd been spared a shirtless greeting when she arrived this morning. Unfortunately, he chose to wear a painted-on henley with the buttons undone. Rather than hide his muscles, the thin cotton emphasized them by rippling every time he moved. She'd decided to scrub bathrooms so she wouldn't stare.

"Besides," he added as he draped the camera strap around his neck, "it's not like you stuck around to eat."

Did he really expect her to? The mood following Hunter's story had been intimate enough. No need compounding the atmosphere by sharing dinner. It was also another reason she'd barricaded herself in the shower this morning.

His story affected her in a way she didn't expect. Until then, Hunter had been this sort of larger-than-life figure. The reluctant—potentially tragic—knight in shining armor. Sexy but not quite real.

But then he'd told her about Naxar and she'd glimpsed a sliver of something more. Something real and familiar. She preferred sexy and illusory. She wasn't interested in feeling anything deeper than physical attraction. And so she took a page from Hunter's book and pulled back.

Until he insisted she join him for a walk. She'd caved and now was stuck strolling the park path, with him looking sexier than a man had a right to.

"I didn't realize my company was required," she replied. Or wanted, for that matter. He'd pretty much shut down himself.

The look he gave her was made unreadable by his sunglasses. "The situation reminded me too much of Reynaldo," he said.

"Who's Reynaldo?" Another assistant? He'd lost her with the reference.

"Reynaldo was the cook my mother hired the summer after fourth grade."

Abby's jaw dropped. "You had a private chef?" When he said he never had a home-cooked meal, she foolishly assumed he meant a meal not cooked at home.

"Not a chef. Reynaldo."

Sounded the same to her. "What's the difference?"

"Chefs are trained cooks. Reynaldo was…" He let out a long breath. "Reynaldo was Reynaldo."

"Meaning not trained."

"Not in the least.

And she reminded him of the man. "You're saying you don't like my cooking?"

"No, your cooking is fine."

"It's all right if you don't. Warren certainly complained enough about it." Oddly enough, Hunter's response disappointed her more.

"I said your cooking is fine. In fact, the spaghetti was delicious."

Abby couldn't help it. She smiled. "Really?"

"Yes. Trust me, your leftovers will not go to waste."

"Then I don't understand. How do I remind you of this Reynaldo?" She grabbed his arm. "Please don't say I look like him."

"Definitely not."

Again Abby smiled.

Hunter, meanwhile, had returned to fiddling with his camera settings. "My mother hired Reynaldo the year she got sick," he said in a low voice. "I ate most of my meals alone at the kitchen counter."

As he had last night.

"Oh." Abby swallowed hard. Damn, but when he dropped a comment like that into the conversation, how could she not get a lump in her throat? It was as though he was dealing out pieces of the Hunter Smith puzzle one by one. The picture she was building wasn't a cheerful one, either. "If I'd known…"

"What? You would have stayed? Kept me company?"

Abby blushed. Her answer would have been yes. He made the suggestion sound like pity, which wasn't the case. "I was going to say that I wouldn't have offered to cook in the first place," she said, scrambling to cover herself. "As far as company is concerned, I'm sure you could find some without my help."

"I'm sure I could, too."

Oh, she bet he could. She imagined he had a whole bevy of women interested in sharing a meal. Along with other things.

"Let me guess. A girl in every port, right?"

"Something like that."

Good for him, she thought, with an uncomfortable twist in her stomach. "If that's the case, then I'm off the hook, aren't I?"

"How so?"

"Well, if you were truly lonely last night, you would have whipped out your little black book."

Pleased with herself, she skipped ahead and turned to walk backward, only to stumble over a crack in the asphalt. Her foot twisted and she fell back, arms flailing. Hunter caught her just before she landed on her backside.

Abby gasped. His arms were wrapped around her waist, pressing her tight against him. So close she could feel every contour and ridge of his muscles. His face looked down upon her. Her mouth ran dry as she imagined his silver-blue eyes looking into hers.

"What makes you think I didn't?"

Abby swallowed hard and blamed her wobbly knees on falling, not his slow growl of a response. "If you did, you certainly shipped her out early."

"Maybe I don't like overnight guests."

"Certainly would fit the profile," she retorted. "You said you kept your subjects at a distance. Why not your lovers at a distance, too?"

Hunter flashed a crooked smile as he righted her. "You might want to try walking forward. Would make the trip easier. No pun intended."

Abby blushed. Fortunately, the tumble had knocked her hair loose from its clip, forcing her to fix the damage, and giving her an activity to hide behind. "I'll keep that in mind," she said, barrette stuck between her teeth.

At least her tumble had cooled the atmosphere. The sizzling whatever-you-want-to-call-it that rose up between their closely pressed bodies seemed to recede. If it ever existed in the first place.

For the next several yards, they walked in silence. In spite of her original reluctance, Abby had to admit the day was perfect for being outside. Overnight, Indian summer had decided to visit the city, blown in on a warm western wind. Above them, the sun hung high in a cloudless blue sky. She couldn't blame Hunter for feeling stir-crazy. It looked like half of New York had had the same idea. Central Park was full. Business people making phone calls while on park benches. Mothers pushing strollers. Couples relaxing in the sunshine. Everyone enjoying summer's last gasp.

Hunter appeared oblivious to this. Instead, far as she could tell, he appeared to be on some kind of mission. Pointing to the camera around his neck, she steered the conversation to safer topics. "You haven't snapped a single picture. Do you plan to, or do you carry it around till you see something worthy of having its picture taken?"

Again, Hunter gave her an indecipherable look. Even with his eyes mirrored, having his gaze focused so intently in her direction made her feel exposed. So much so, she almost looked away.

"Look up ahead," he told her, pointing. On the hill in front of them, a gray building rose above the tree line.

Abby felt a familiar rush. "Oh, wow, that's Belvedere Castle!"

"You know it?"

Of course she knew it. Although he didn't realize it, Hunter had guided them to one of her favorite escapes.

"I used to come here whenever things with Warren got too overwhelming." She craned her neck so she could see the main building through the trees. "Did you know the observation tower has one of the best views in the park?" When Hunter shook his head, she rolled her eyes. "Unbelievable. And you call yourself a world traveler."

Built on top of a large, craggy rock, the granite building had been part of Central Park for over a hundred years. Without giving it a second thought, Abby pulled Hunter off the path and across the grass. Leaves rustled beneath their feet as they made their way across the great lawn. "You can see practically the entire park," she told him.

Hunter could care less. He'd taken plenty of views of the park, the skyline and the castle. The only view he was interested in today involved the woman whose hand held his. She was, after all, the reason they were here. Although at the moment he was wondering if his idea was a good one.

He hadn't handled yesterday well at all. Seeing those photos from Somalia, Naxar's face, had kicked him hard. Especially since Hunter had been fighting hard all week to keep those memories from bubbling to the surface.

Interesting how they'd chosen to rise around the same time he'd met Abby. A reminder from the universe? Maybe.

Yet here he was, taking her to Belvedere Castle for a photo session. He guessed he thought the gesture might put an end to the agitation that had plagued him the past twenty hours or so. The churning, empty sensation that made him feel as if he was leaving business unfinished. In a way, he was. If she found a permanent job while he was out of the country, there was a good chance he'd never get to photograph Abby a second time, as he'd promised.

Like an artist who'd found a favorite model, he wanted another opportunity to capture her on film, in a different atmosphere, with a different emotion on her face. To see for himself if the elements would come together as seamlessly as they had before.

What he hadn't expected was for her to be so enthusiastic about the location. She practically dragged him across the grass in her rush.

Nor did he expect to be holding her hand. Her delicate fingers nestled in his felt strangely natural. Uncomfortably so. Relaxing his grip, he pulled away to regain his distance. Immediately, she blushed, then ducked his glance by brushing the hair from her face. Damn, why didn't he have his camera ready?

"I found this place totally by accident," she told him. "One day after an argument with Warren. When I saw the turret above the trees, it was like finding a little piece of magic."

"Magic?" He was surprised to hear her talk so whimsically.

"When I was a kid, I read a lot of fairy tales. Rapunzel, Sleeping Beauty, Cinderella. I wanted to believe Prince Charming existed. That he would come riding in and whisk me off to his castle in the sky."

They reached the stone stairs. "I ended up with Warren instead. Guess we know how well that turned out, don't we?"

Hunter could tell from her frown her thoughts had gone to that dark place she went whenever Warren's name came up. How bad had things gotten? he wondered. How bad were they before that, to make running off with an overweight loser look like a better option?

Didn't matter; whatever happened was worse than she deserved, just as he'd told her last night. No woman should have bruises on her skin. And Abby had such beautifully pale skin. To think anyone would ever want to mar its surface made him want to punch Warren all over again.

"Anyway—" hearing her voice jerked him from his thoughts "—seeing a castle in the middle of New York City gave me a little hope that fairy tales might still exist for some people. Stupid, I know. Chasing Prince Charming. I'd have better luck chasing Santa Claus. Maybe I wouldn't have stuck it out with Warren as long as I did."

"Or ever come to New York," Hunter replied, not realizing until after he spoke how the comment sounded. "I mean—"

"No, you're right. A healthy dose of realism might have saved me a lot of trouble from the start."

She was right. Still, he didn't like hearing her take such a defeatist attitude. Didn't like the shadows that killed the light in her eyes.

"You wouldn't want to be a princess, anyway. Sleeping in a castle isn't all it's cracked up to be."

As though a switch had been flipped, the darkness left her expression. You had to admire her resilience, Hunter thought. She refused to be kept down.

"Please don't tell me you lived in a castle?" she said.

"For ten days. It was drafty and cold."

"When?"

"All the time."

"I meant, when did you live in a castle?"

Hunter knew exactly what she meant. He just liked how her eyes flashed when she got exasperated. "A couple of years ago. On a job. And there were no princes. Or princesses, either. Just a very cranky caretaker."

"Another fantasy bites the dust."

"Fantasies are overrated."

"Not to mention completely unrealistic," Abby said. "Too bad there's not always someone around to help us cope when we realize the sad truth."

Sad indeed. "Who helped you?" He had a suspicion he already knew the answer. She'd told him how isolated Warren had kept her.

"You're looking at her," Abby said with a smile.

Making his suspicion correct. He was beginning to realize the resilient woman he'd captured on film the other day was the real Abby. Took a lot of inner strength to pull yourself from a bad situation. Clearly, her strength ran even deeper than he'd thought. Made his admiration for her that much deeper, too.

They reached the terrace on the rampart. Despite being early afternoon on a weekday, the pavilion was crowded. Tourists taking pictures, mothers herding young children. A violinist had set up shop by the top of the stairs, his case open for passersby to toss in money. Hunter dug into his wallet and dropped in a few bills to say thank-you for the live soundtrack.

When he turned around, Abby was by the wall, looking out at the pond below. "Gorgeous, isn't it?"

He had to agree, though in his case, he wasn't thinking about the landscape. He found the way Abby's skin glowed far more intriguing. She'd lit up in a way he hadn't seen before. Even her hair, which had yet again developed a mind of its own, seemed brighter. As she brushed the strands from her face, tawny highlights caught the sun.

"Drafty or not, you've got to admit having a view like this would be amazing," she said.

Amazing was the perfect word, he thought as he stood to the side and snapped away. "You'd still freeze your behind off. No window or heat."

That earned him both an eye roll and a look in his direction. "Buzzkill."

"Realist," he countered.

A second eye roll, and she returned her attention to the landscape. Hunter watched as she rose on tiptoes and leaned forward to get a better view. A move that caused her sweater to creep up her back, revealing an enticing strip of bare skin. Remembering how soft her skin felt, his body grew hard. He was beginning to see how Warren had grown so possessive. Did she have any idea how good she looked right now? Even the violinist was staring.

Hunter joined her at the wall, partly because he wanted to get closer, and partly to block the musician's view. The water below them was a smooth black mirror. Zooming in through his lens, he could make out the two of them peering over the edge. "How often did you come here?"

"More than I care to admit. Usually when Warren was at work. I'd sneak over while I was supposed to be running errands. That way if he called, I would have a reason to be out."

Hunter's dislike for the man grew with each slip of Abby's tongue. A pretty big feat, given he'd disliked the man intensely upon sight.

Abby turned around and leaned back against the rampart. Faced with a perfect shot, Hunter did what he did best. Let life play out on the other side of his lens.

"Did you just take my picture?" she asked when the shutter clicked.

"I've taken a lot of pictures."

"Well, stop." She averted her face, killing his view. "You know I don't like it."

"But I told you I'd photograph you again."

"And you pick another day when I don't have makeup on and I'm pale as a ghost."

"I don't want you made up. I prefer you the way you are." To prove his point, he pressed the shutter, despite her turned head.

"Now you're just being obnoxious," she murmured.

"No. I'm taking pictures. Not my fault you're a good model." He could practically hear her silent scoff. "You don't believe me?"

"Oh, I believe you," she replied, glancing over her shoulder. "The term *model* might be an exaggeration."

"Why are you so hard on the way you look?"

"Because I'm female," she replied with a smirk.

He didn't buy the answer, not for a second, and so he waited to speak again.

"I hate when you stare like that," she said.

"Stare how?"

"I don't like how you turn my comments into questions, either. You know what I'm talking about. The way you stare like you're looking through me."

"Not through you," he replied, shaking his head. "At you. I wish you could see yourself the way my camera does."

Abby curled the hair around her ear. "Unfortunately, your camera doesn't speak, and it hasn't spent twenty-five years telling me how average and unappealing I am."

God, but he really hated Warren now. Her parents, too, if they'd helped fill her head with such ragtime. "You're wrong," he said. "My camera does speak. I make it speak with what I see through my lens." Ignoring the doubt in her eyes, he moved a little closer. Perhaps if he showed her in the viewfinder the scenes he'd been photographing... "And what my camera says is that you are a woman of strength and character who has really amazing hair."

She smiled a little at the last part. "Amazing hair, huh?"

"Fantastic hair. Like a lion's mane," Hunter said, smiling back.

He meant to show her. He meant to hold out the camera so she could see for herself. Instead, their eyes caught and his intentions fell away. Everything fell away. The pavilion, the crowd, the violinist. All he could see was Abby. Her pale, unmade-up face, her shining eyes. A piece of hair blew across her cheek, the end clinging to her lower lip. Lucky strand.

He reached out and brushed the hair free, letting his fingers linger at the corner of her mouth.

"Your skin's cold," he said.

"Sun's going down. Guess Indian summer's all over. Time to return to reality." As she said the last part, she ducked her head, breaking contact with his touch. Not, however, before he caught the note of regret she was trying to hide.

"Not yet," he told her. "Come with me."

CHAPTER SIX

SHE MAY HAVE given up princess fantasies, but Abby had to admit she was starting to feel a little royal today. And her mood had nothing to do with visiting Belvedere Castle. Not at all. It was the look she saw on Hunter's face. He'd told her last night that he kept his subjects at an emotional distance, but standing there, stroking the hair from her cheek, the way his eyes held hers made her feel…special. Beautiful.

Must be what photographers did to charm models.

Even so, her lips continued to tingle from his touch as he led her back through the park and across the street. As she stepped inside the tavern, she felt she'd traded one castle for another, only this one was far more intimate. The narrow space was a honeycomb of velvet sofas and candlelit nooks warmed by a giant fireplace. Because it was only midafternoon, the establishment was empty except for a few couples tucked in dark corners. The emptiness only added to the romance, making it feel as though Hunter had brought her to his own private hideaway.

Abby brushed the hair from her face. Lion's mane or not, between the wind and her tumble, her hair had to look more of a tangled mess than usual. Way too messy for a place like this.

The hostess led them to a seat in front of the main fireplace. "This is amazing," Abby said as they settled on velvet cushions. Even though the fireplace was off on such a warm day, she could imagine the warmth.

"I come here to unwind sometimes," Hunter replied, sliding into the seat next to her. "Reminds me of a place in London."

"I can imagine. The unwinding, that is." She decided curling into the sofa would be uncouth, and settled for crossing her legs and sitting back against the pillows. "I walked by this place a few times when heading to the park, and always thought it was some kind of private club." Or maybe the upscale atmosphere just felt off-limits to her. "Not that I would have gone in, anyway," she added.

"Why not?"

"Stopping off somewhere for a drink? Oh, yeah, that would have gone over real well. Coming home with liquor on my breath."

Hunter turned so he could face her. Abby noticed he didn't have a problem tucking a leg beneath his body. "Let me guess, Warren had a double standard when it came to drinking."

"Warren had a double standard when it came to lots of things. Drinking, outside friends. Money. Took me almost a year of overstocking the pantry so he wouldn't notice when I began skimming off the grocery money."

It wasn't until she said it that she realized how much her simple comment revealed.

Hunter looked astonished. "I had no idea," he said.

"Hey, we do what we have to do." She waved a hand dismissively. To think about all she'd had to do to escape only reinforced how bad she'd let the situation become.

"But to plan for a year for walking away…"

"I wanted to be prepared. Coming to New York with Warren was a hasty decision, and look how good that turned out. Figured this time I'd 'repent in leisure,' as they say." Plus, if she were to be completely honest, it had taken her a while to work up the nerve, as well.

"Somehow I don't think leaving an abusive boyfriend is quite what the phrase means," Hunter noted.

She shrugged. "Repent, regret—same thing."

The quirk of his brow said otherwise. Fortunately, the waitress arrived then, cutting short any comment, and he turned his attention to ordering.

"Do you mind?" he asked, indicating the menu.

"Be my guest." It was, she realized, the second time he'd taken charge like this. Part of her considered balking at the high-handedness. She was, after all, perfectly capable of reading a wine list. However, as in the Indian restaurant, Hunter clearly knew more about the contents than she. Besides, he asked, whereas Warren would have taken over without a word.

"Impressive," she remarked once the waitress departed with their order. Although not surprising, considering his background. A family who could afford a private chef no doubt held food—and drink—in high esteem. "Did you learn about wine from your father or the infamous Reynaldo?"

"Neither. I learned from a bed-and-breakfast owner in Napa Valley. I was photographing a wine festival, and she offered to help me with my research."

"She. So, we're back to the little black book then."

"What makes you think she's in my book?"

"Is she?"

His smile said yes; Abby decided she didn't like the woman.

"Reynaldo was a lousy cook," Hunter said a beat later. He'd gone back to fiddling with his camera, twisting and popping off the lens cap, then putting it back on again. "Used to burn the macaroni and cheese."

"Doesn't sound like much of a private chef."

"That's because he wasn't a chef. I'm not even sure he had proper training. But then—" he gave Abby a strange smile "—my mother didn't hire him for his cooking."

"I don't understand…" Abby dragged out the sentence. Surely

Hunter wasn't suggesting what she thought he was suggesting? Didn't he say his mother had been sick?

"He made her laugh," Hunter replied, and Abby gave a silent sigh of relief. For whatever reason, she didn't like the idea of Hunter's mother having an affair with the help while her son ate alone. "He'd flirt and say these outrageous things to her, like calling her 'Senora Seximama.' Stupid, I know, but she giggled every time."

His eye roll had a wistful affection to it. "I think that's what I remember most. Her laugh.

"Anyway," he continued, "I think she hired Reynaldo more for comic relief than the food."

"Your father didn't mind?"

"My father laughed with her. The two of them laughed together a lot before..."

Suddenly interested in the lens cap again, he let the sentence trail off. Finishing wasn't necessary. Abby heard enough sadness in the words Hunter did say. It was a different despair than when he'd told her about Somalia. It was a deeper sadness. A lonely sadness. Coupled with a resignation that came from carrying the burden around for a long time.

Abby hated to think she understood, but she did. Not losing a parent—the parent would have to stick around for you to lose them. But the deep-seated feeling of loss in general—that she understood too well.

She wanted to reach out and squeeze his hand, but the moment shifted before she had the chance. Their server arrived, discreetly setting their drinks on the table.

Hunter handed Abby a glass. "You know, you never said where you lived before moving to New York."

Changing the subject. Abby could understand that, as well. "Schenectady," she answered.

"Ever think of going back?"

"What for? My parents?" She shook her head. "Maybe, if

it was only my mother, but as long as my stepfather is around, no way. I'd rather live on the streets." Nearly damn near did.

"A bad guy, is he?"

"Remember when I told you my mother and I both had bad taste in men?"

Hunter nodded.

"Mine's the better of the two. At least I can blame being too young to know better. Mom? I don't know what her reason, other than she didn't learn her lesson the first time." Abby plucked at the piping on the sofa arm. Who knew what drove her mother to cling to the jerk? Fear of being alone? "He was the reason I ran off with Warren after graduation."

"Did he—"

"Oh, no!" She shook her head. Aaron was a bully, but he wasn't a monster, thank goodness. "You know that phrase 'spare the rod'? He was a big believer. Particularly when I messed up, or mouthed off." Or caught his eye on a bad day. "Lucky for me, I got used to his moods. A good skill to have. Came in pretty handy during the Warren years."

"Not every man requires you to spend your time walking on eggshells, Abby."

She knew he'd say something like that. "So the counselors tell me."

"They're right."

"Maybe." Whether they were or not didn't matter; she didn't plan to test their theory by becoming emotionally involved again.

She sipped her wine. The dark red liquid was rich and dry. "Listen to us, will you? Last night I said we didn't have to go tit for tat, but here we are, swapping sad stories. First Reynaldo, then my stepfather."

It took only a swallow for the wine to seep into her veins, melting away a chill she didn't know she had. "I don't know about you, but I'm tired of being depressing. It's too beautiful a day. I'd much rather exchange happy stories."

"Such as?"

"Such as is there anywhere in the world you'd like to visit but haven't yet?"

"Schenectady."

She nudged his ankle with her toe. "Seriously. Where would you go?"

"Good question." Abby took another sip while he appeared to give the question real thought—a first for any man in her life. "I've never been to Antarctica," he said.

Not the answer she would have guessed. "You want to go to the South Pole?"

"Why not? In one of my father's photography books I remember seeing photos of Shackleton's ship, the *Endurance*. He ran aground there in the early twentieth century. The contrast of the white icebergs against the gray sky was so bleak, yet powerful. I'd love to do a modern black-and-white study."

"I have to admit, taking photographs of icebergs would not be my idea of a dream trip." Although she'd gladly listen to him talk about the project if it meant watching his face brighten. Whenever he spoke about his craft, he grew animated. The enthusiasm brought out the blue in his eyes, reminding Abby of dark water. She liked the color on him. She liked the brightness.

Maybe it was the wine, but she suddenly felt warm in a whole bunch of places deep inside her.

Hunter, meanwhile, had shifted in his seat so he was leaning closer. "All right, smarty-pants, where would you go?"

"Europe," she replied. She didn't need to think twice.

"Anywhere in particular? Or just Europe as a whole?"

"I've always wanted to go to Paris."

"Maybe someday you will."

Sure. She was still earning the down payment for an apartment. "Today I'll settle for having seen a little more of New York. Six years here, and I feel like I haven't seen anything." Hadn't lived much, either.

Someone had turned on the sound system, adding soft jazz

music to the atmosphere. Abby drained her glass and sighed. The heat was beginning to spread through her limbs. She was relaxed and melty-feeling. "Today has been really nice," she told him. "Thank you."

"You're welcome." He was looking at her in that way again. Zeroing in on her as if there was nothing else to focus on. In her new relaxed state, she found herself noticing new details about her employer. Like the way the hair curled about the tops of his ears, and the regal slope of his nose. Long and graceful. Like the way he moved.

She noticed his hands, too. How they were large and capable, yet cradled the base of his goblet with gentleness. She'd watched how those hands treated his camera the same way. The touch never too hard or too soft, but always—always— with assuredness.

Heat changed to an ache. Desire, Abby realized. The feeling curled long and low inside her. With one look he made her feel like more of a woman than Warren had in six years. No way that little black book of Hunter's was anything short of a mile thick. Not with that skill.

He believed in keeping the world at arm's length. No commitment; no false promises. No strings, demands or control.

Last night she'd questioned his rules, thought they were wrong for him, but now the idea of emotional distance sounded just about right.

Just about right indeed.

His lips were dark and shining from the wine. "Something on your mind?" he asked.

"I was thinking about dinner," she replied. "Be a shame for you to fly to the Middle East tomorrow without one last home-cooked meal."

She shifted in her seat, closing the distance to less than a foot. If Hunter noticed her new proximity, he didn't seem to mind. In fact, he set his goblet down and moved in a hair closer.

"We've been through this," he said. "You don't have to cook me dinner."

He brushed his knuckles along her cheek, causing a thrill to run through her. "I don't expect you to wait on me hand and foot."

If she had any doubts about what she wanted, those magic words blew them away. They, along with his gentle touch, turned her bold. Tomorrow, he would be overseas. Why not give herself tonight?

"Then I won't cook," she said in a soft voice. She couldn't help it; her eyes had to look at his mouth again. "How about I just keep you company instead?"

She kissed him.

At first he did what any man would do. He kissed her back. Hunter opened his mouth and drank her in, savoring her taste and texture. He heard her sigh, and he kissed her even deeper as her fingers twisted in his jacket, pulling their bodies closer together, oblivious to their surroundings. That is, until his foot nudged the table leg.

What the hell was he doing?

This wasn't some woman. This was Abby, who'd spent the afternoon telling him about shattered fairy tales, and who was laden down with baggage. Gripping her shoulders, he reluctantly pulled himself back from the embrace. "I can't…"

"Ohmygod!"

There was no need to finish. Slapping a hand to her mouth, she shot to her feet, embarrassment and confusion turning her eyes black. "How about we pretend that never happened, okay? Turn back the clock, act like we never left the apartment. I mean, never… Never mind. I'm going to leave now."

"Hold on." This was not how he wanted to leave town. With the picture of her looking so wounded stuck in his head. He tossed a few bills on the table and caught up with her by the front entrance.

"It's not that I'm not flattered. It's just that—"

"Don't." She silenced him with both hands. "Please spare me the 'it's not you, it's me' speech. I've had a crappy enough week as it is."

A lousy week because of him. He could kick himself for not stopping her when he'd seen her leaning toward him. He knew exactly what she was thinking, and he hadn't done a thing.

Because you were thinking the exact same thing. You wanted to kiss her. God, but did he want to kiss her.

Least he could do was apologize. He moved to lay a hand on her shoulder, but she shrugged off his touch. Arms folded, she stood staring at the street outside, the barriers firmly in place. "We should be heading back to your apartment. I left my pocketbook there.

"Besides," she added in a stiff voice, "I'm sure you have a lot to do before you leave town. Packing. Getting takeout."

Abby shoved open the door. Too bad it didn't have a proper hinge so she could slam it behind her. Block Hunter and the memory of what happened. She knew she'd screwed up the second Hunter's hands had gripped her shoulders. What an idiot. Thinking Hunter, who could have any woman he wanted, would add her to his list.

So much for being amazing. Oh wait, it was her hair Hunter called amazing. What was she, again? Regrettable, apparently. Oh, and baggage laden. She couldn't forget the baggage. After all, Hunter clearly hadn't.

She wished she'd never agreed to take the stupid walk with him. Now she was stuck walking back, too. A couple miles of awkward silence. The only reason she was returning to his apartment was because she needed her pocketbook. Otherwise she'd jump on the nearest subway. Disappearing into a hole sounded awfully good about now.

"I should explain," he said about a half mile in.

Oh no, he was going to apologize again. She'd rather the silence. "You don't have to."

"I want to. You're an attractive woman, Abby, but kissing you…kissing you was a mistake."

"Really? Never would have guessed."

Hunter winced. *Good,* thought Abby. He deserved to feel a little more stupid.

"What I'm trying to say is that I'm… That is, I…" He took a deep breath, presumably to start again. "You deserve better."

"Better than what?"

"Than a guy taking off for the West Bank in a few hours."

"Oh." So that was it. He'd heard her talking about fairy tales and princes this afternoon, and he'd assumed that's what she was looking for. She grabbed his arm.

"No offense, but what makes you think you know what I deserve?" Rejecting her was one thing, but who was he to make assumptions? She was going to set him straight right now. "You better than anyone know that I just got out of the relationship from hell. Did you ever stop to think I might not want more than a few hours?"

"That's not who you are."

Says who? Him? "Excuse me, but you don't know who I am," she snapped. "And you sure as hell don't get to decide whether I'm looking for a fling. Six years having my life dictated is enough, thank you very much."

"Fine. Next time we make out, I'll ask before I stop kissing you. Okay?"

"Thank you." She tried to keep the flutter that erupted at the words *next time* under control.

CHAPTER SEVEN

"GOT YOUR COFFEE, I see."

It was two weeks later, and Abby and Hunter were having their regular video chat. Originally, when they'd said their uncomfortable goodbyes, Hunter said he would check in "once or twice" to see if she needed anything. Once or twice, it turned out, meant daily. In a way, talking regularly was a good thing. It helped them get over the awkward hump left behind after their kiss.

You mean after you threw yourself at him.

It probably also helped that they'd come to some silent, mutual decision to pretend the kiss had never happened. If Abby every once in a while felt a flash of heat when cleaning Hunter's bedroom, or experienced a passing, random memory of how good his lips felt...well, she quickly shoved the thoughts aside. No point dwelling on the embarrassing. Even if it was the best kiss she'd ever experienced.

Despite her resolve, however, there was one nagging thought she couldn't shake: for a brief moment, Hunter had kissed her back. More than kissed. *Kissed.*

Originally, after the disaster in the wine bar, she'd briefly considered quitting. In fact, she'd rehearsed her speech on the trip back from the bar. Nothing else to do, since neither of them were talking to each other. Before she could say a word, however, Hunter had surprised her by shoving his door key in her hand.

"You still want me?" Abby had immediately asked. "I mean, as a housekeeper?"

"I promised you temporary work until you got back on your feet. I see no reason why I shouldn't keep that promise. Do you?"

Actually, Abby could have given several, but in the end, he was leaving town and she needed money, so she stayed quiet.

Which was why she now sat in front of a computer monitor with a coffee mug cradled between her hands, while across the ocean Hunter did the same with a glass of beer.

"Don't know why you're so surprised," she said, when they were finishing up their morning chat. "These calls of yours are the perfect excuse for a coffee break." To illustrate her point, she took a large swallow, while in the back of her mind she wondered if the reason they both brought drinks was to keep their hands occupied while they talked. Empty hands led to fidgeting, and fidgeting would reveal the awkwardness they were both trying to hide.

"Did you get the package I sent you?" she asked, raising the cup to her lips again.

"Waiting downstairs when I checked out."

"Good. I was afraid the protests would delay delivery."

"You needn't have been concerned," Hunter said over his beer. Today's selection was a dark-looking ale. "Protests are several miles away from the hotel."

Maybe so, but Hunter had been in the middle of them. Abby hadn't forgotten his cavalier attitude toward his personal safety. He might not care what happened to himself, but someone should. For now, the task fell to her. She owed him. After all, he did step in to help her. She'd spent the week scanning the internet and news reports to keep abreast of the action.

Which reminded her. "I saw one of your photos online yesterday."

"How'd it look?"

Thinking of it, she shivered. "Violent. Bloody."

On his side of the computer screen, Hunter nodded, and she knew he was remembering which shot. "How's everything else?"

"Good. I bought you a plant to green up your windowsill. For a photographer, you have surprisingly bland walls."

"I meant the job hunt."

"Oh, right, that." She set down her cup, the coffee having turned sour-tasting. "Going."

"Didn't you have an interview this week?"

He would remember. "I did. They hired someone with more experience."

"Happens."

A lot. In fact, it had become a pattern. Every morning she circled want ads and filled out applications, only to hear she either didn't have enough experience or the job had been filled before she got there. The other day, she'd lost out to the woman who showed up fifteen minutes before her.

What bothered Abby most, however, wasn't losing out on the job. It was the fact that none of them appealed to her. Surely her fresh start meant more than waiting tables or answering phones? For crying out loud, she'd gotten more satisfaction from buying Hunter his plant.

That fact might bother her most of all.

"Abby?"

She blinked. "I'm sorry."

"I said my flight gets in at seven-thirty. Could you call the car company and confirm the reservation?"

"Sure. Of course." She scribbled a reminder note, and told herself the flurry of emotions in her chest was embarrassment. "Bet you're looking forward to coming home."

"It's only a quick stopover. I take off again at the end of the week."

"Well, with luck I'll be out of your hair before you leave. I mean—" she glanced up "—luck can change, right?"

There must have been a flicker in the connection, because as she was looking up from her notepad, it appeared as if his expression slipped. However, on second look, his face was the same as always, handsome and impassive. "With luck," he repeated.

His words sounded flat.

They spoke for a few more minutes, mostly about travel arrangements, before Hunter told her he had to sign off. "I won't have a chance to check in tomorrow morning," he told her.

"You'll see me tomorrow night."

"You don't have to stick around. I have no idea how long it will take getting back from the airport."

"That's all right, I don't mind waiting for you." Realizing how her comment might come across, especially after their kiss, she scrambled to add, "You forget, tomorrow's payday. Even temporary employees get paid."

"Yes, they do," he said with, unless she was mistaken, a little bit of relief in his voice. "I'll see you tomorrow night, Abby."

"Hunter?" She caught him as he was reaching to sign off. "Be safe."

He gave a quick nod, and the screen went blank.

Hunter jogged up the stairs to his apartment. He must have slept better on the plane than he thought. Normally international flights left him drained.

Could also be that the drive from the airport took less time than usual. He'd have to thank Abby for double-checking the reservation.

Abby. As he rounded the second floor landing, the smile her name brought to his face faded. He'd been thinking about her, or rather their arrangement, a lot this trip. Wondering if he hadn't made a mistake offering her a temporary job. Granted, she appeared to be doing well, but the whole reason he'd made the offer was to ease his guilty conscience, and thus far he wasn't feeling less guilty at all. If anything, he felt worse.

That's what happens when you slip up and kiss someone you shouldn't. Problem was he didn't know if he felt guilty for kissing her or because he didn't have nearly the amount of regret he should have over the incident. If he concentrated, he could still taste her when he licked his lips. Her uniquely Abbyish taste.

Damn, he never had scratched that itch. God knew he'd tried to, but with every woman who crossed his path, he found himself comparing her mouth to Abby's or her dark hair to Abby's butterscotch curls. In the end, it was easier to sleep alone.

The apartment was dark and empty when he let himself in. "Abby?" He got a sinking sensation when he realized the apartment was empty. She'd said she'd be waiting for him.

Guess she got a better offer. *Did you ever stop to think I might not want more than a few hours?*

Unacceptable, he thought as he looked around the empty space. Completely unacceptable. Temporary hire or not, if she was going to change plans, she needed to let him know. A call, a note. Something. Grabbing his cell phone, he punched out the phone number she'd given him. *There'd better be a good explanation.* What if he'd counted on her being here for business or...or some housekeeping emergency?

Abby answered on the fourth ring. "Hunter! You're back in New York!"

He ignored the rush he felt at her enthusiastic greeting. "Funny thing," he said in return. "My apartment's empty."

"Yeah, I know. I meant to be there when you got in, but something came up."

Something or someone? His jaw remained as stiff as his spine. "An emergency?"

"Sort of. I'm..." There was a pause, followed by the sound of muffled voices. Wherever she was, she wasn't alone.

"Abby? Where are you?" Hunter squeezed the phone as he waited for a response.

"I'm at the police station."

Hunter found Abby sitting on a bench in the precinct corridor. As soon as he saw her, the nausea that had been churning in his stomach since her phone call eased.

He called her name and she looked up with big brown eyes.

He rushed over to her. "What happened? Are you—" He looked her up and down for signs she'd been roughed up. Her hair hung in her face. He reached out to brush the strands aside.

"I'm fine," she said, backing away. It was a lie. There was a palm-size red mark on her cheek. His blood began to boil.

"Warren showed up where I live," she told him.

"I thought you made sure he didn't know where you lived?" Hunter didn't even know.

"I did. Apparently he went to the diner looking for me, and Guy suggested he check across the street."

The miserable old— Hunter was going to wring his scrawny neck.

"Anyway..." She sat back down. He noticed she'd gone back to wearing her baggy cardigan, which she now pulled tight. "Anyway, he must have seen me coming out of your building, and followed me home. He cornered me by the subway stop this morning and wanted me to get in his car and go somewhere to talk. I managed to get away and head back to the house. We've been tied up with police stuff ever since."

"We?"

"My friend Carmella. She came with me. She's in the ladies' room freshening up. Been a long day, to say the least." Heaving a sigh, Abby swiped the hair from her face, the very hair Hunter had reached for earlier. When she looked at him again, he saw that her eyes were overly bright and shining. "I'm sorry I wasn't at the apartment like I promised," she said.

"Not a big deal. Obviously you had a reason." Looking back,

he felt like a heel for overreacting the way he had. Especially now that he had a clear view of the mark marring her cheek.

"Does it hurt?" He tried to look closer, but she quickly shook her head, bringing the hair back into her face. "I meant to leave a message letting you know what happened, but then we got tied up with statements and filling out forms."

"It's all right."

"I said I'd cook dinner, too. You're probably starved. As soon as we're done—"

"Abby, I said it's all right." The words came out sharper than he meant them to.

She pulled her sweater even tighter. "It won't happen again."

"I'm sure it won't." Although he appreciated the promise, her comeback sounded wrong. It lacked her usual sharpness.

The flight was catching up with him. Stifling a yawn, he sat down on the bench next to her, only to have her scoot a foot in the opposite direction. About ten inches more than she needed to. That's when he finally caught the fearful look in her eyes.

"Hey." Making sure his voice was as soft and gentle as possible, he shifted so he could look her in the eye. "You know I'm not Warren, right?"

"Of course," she replied. There was too much defensiveness in her voice, however, to sound very convincing.

Dammit, now he really hated himself for sounding so harsh on the phone. Must have scared the daylights out her. Worse, he had absolutely no good explanation for why he'd gotten so upset.

None of that mattered at the moment, however. He needed to reassure Abby.

Poor thing looked worn-out. With the exception of Warren's ugly reminder, her skin had turned pale as powder. The mouth that he'd found amazingly kissable only two weeks before was a colorless line. He wished he could run his thumb across the surface and bring the color back.

"Are you sure?" He wanted to be absolutely certain she understood that he was nothing like her ex-boyfriend. It had sud-

denly become very important she know that. "Are you really
sure? Because while I might lose my temper, I would never hurt
you. You know that, right?"

Giving in to the impulse to touch her, he covered her hand
with his, relaxing when she didn't flinch and pull away. "I believe you," she said with a sad smile.

Relief spread through Hunter's chest.

He coughed to clear the sudden tightness. "So is Warren
under arrest?"

"They're going to talk to the prosecutor."

"Which is a total joke," a strange voice boomed. A short
African-American woman, whose build definitely didn't fit her
voice, walked toward them. Carmella, he presumed.

"It's up to the lawyers to decide if there's enough evidence
to do anything."

"Problem is I don't have any evidence or witnesses," Abby
said.

"What do they call that mark on your cheek? Chopped liver?"

Hunter agreed. "Don't forget, you had a restraining order.
You told me he skipped the hearing last week. Doesn't that mean
the order is still in effect?"

Both Abby and Carmella looked at him with jaded expres-
sions. "Again," Carmella said, "no witnesses. He can lie through
his teeth."

"Probably will, too. God, I feel so stupid." Abby buried her
face in her hands. "I actually thought that once I left, he'd forget about me."

"It's not your fault the guy's a jerk," Carmella said.

"So people keep telling me. I'm just tired of the whole thing."

It killed Hunter to hear the defeat in Abby's voice. This wasn't
the woman whose photo he'd taken outside the diner.

"Problem is," Carmella said, "you're exhausted. A good
night's sleep and everything will seem brighter."

"Hope your right," Abby said with a sigh. "Lord knows, I am
beat." She looked to him. "We may be stuck here for a while."

In other words, she was offering him an out to go back to the apartment. His reluctance to leave her outweighed any exhaustion he was feeling. "I already came across town to get here. Might as well wait till you're finished."

A hint of a smile curled her lips, the first positive sign he'd seen since arriving. Though only a small thing, seeing it made him happy. "You said that last time, when we spent the day at the courthouse."

"What can I say? I like hanging in municipal buildings with you," he told her. "Why don't you and your friend find out what's happening? I'll call a car and catch up with you."

"Seriously, Hunter, there's no need for you to—"

He held up a finger to stop the protest. "I need a ride home, anyway. Might as well travel in style. Now go."

"That's the photographer, huh?" Carmella asked as they walked back to the squad room.

"That's him."

"I can see why you took the job. Guy looks like a movie star."

"I took the job because I need the money," Abby replied. "Besides, the job's only temporary. He threw me a bone because he felt guilty over getting me fired from the diner."

"And did his guilt or the bone make him come all the way over here?"

"I'm not in the mood." Abby wasn't really upset. Her friend was only trying to lighten the mood.

She still couldn't believe Warren showing up the way he had. He'd been as unreasonable as ever, spewing angry comments about her and Hunter. *You really think a guy like that is going to let you stick around? You're just a bed warmer.* Had she not been focused on getting away, she might have told Warren his rantings were not just irrational, but completely impossible.

"You didn't answer my question," Carmella pointed out.

Abby wasn't sure she had an answer. Why had Hunter ridden all the way across town? To check on her? There were men who did things like that simply because they were decent people. Hadn't Hunter said his Southerner mother had taught him manners?

"I assume he came because he was worried. He knows what Warren's capable of, so when I told him I was at the police station, he got concerned."

"Uh-huh. My boss wouldn't drive across town to check up on me."

Her implication was obvious. In spite of everything that had happened, Abby had to roll her eyes in amusement. "For crying out loud, I'm at the station house filing charges against my ex-boyfriend. What on earth made you think I'm even interested in Hunter Smith?"

"I don't know. Maybe because he's hot and rich?"

And off-limits, Abby added silently. Which was a good thing. Not that she was interested in men at the moment—one look at her surroundings was confirmation enough of that point—but if she were to someday return to the dating scene, it wouldn't be with a man as overwhelming as Hunter. In retrospect, it was a good thing that he turned her down. If the way her insides leapt at the sight of him was any indication, a fling would have been a bad idea.

"Unfortunately, since it's your word against his, there's not a lot we can do," the officer told her.

"In other words, her ex can just do anything he wants." Carmella shook her head.

"He can't do anything," the officer replied. "If we catch him breaking the order, we can arrest him. But without firm evidence…"

"There's nothing you can do," Abby finished for him. This was great. When was she going to catch a break?

"Isn't there anything more you can do?"

Abby started at the sound of Hunter's voice. She hadn't heard him join them. Turning around, she saw him hovering over her like a big protective bird. Too bad he wasn't really an action hero.

"We're doing everything we can," the officer replied. He seemed to sit up straighter before addressing Hunter's concern. "We've reminded Mr. Pelligini what will happen if he steps out of line. And we'll have a patrol car keep an eye on McKenzie House. That way, if he shows up again, we can act immediately."

Abby nodded. Wasn't much, but it was something. "Thanks."

"Wish we could do more, ma'am."

Yeah, she did, too.

"I can't believe this," Carmella said when they left the squad room. "We spend all day here and the best they can do is to keep an eye on the house?"

No sense pointing out the fact that both she and Carmella had predicted the outcome. "There's only so much they can do, without proof. Maybe we'll get lucky and Warren will do something stupid."

Carmella scoffed. "What are you supposed to do in the meantime? Lock yourself in the house?"

"I could always stay at a hotel." So much for her apartment nest egg. Still, she'd certainly sleep better in a new location. "Maybe the desk officer can recommend a place that's not too expensive."

"You're not staying at a hotel."

Again, Hunter's voice startled her. Up to that moment, he'd been unusually quiet. Regretting ever meeting her, Abby assumed. Lord knew, she would. "Where would I stay, then? Because I truly don't want to sleep at home tonight."

His expression was as unreadable as ever when he looked over at her. Didn't matter, because his words caused her heart to skitter. "My place," he said. "You'll come stay with me."

CHAPTER EIGHT

"No way." Abby shook her head.

"Why not?" Hunter looked at her as if she had two heads. "It's the perfect solution. I have a second bedroom. State-of-the-art security. You would be going back and forth to my place for work, anyway. This way you won't have to worry about running into Warren while you're commuting."

"Makes a lot a sense to me," Carmella said.

Perfect sense. But Abby's gut said it was a horrible idea. "The whole reason Warren flipped out was because he saw me at your place," she told Hunter. "What's he going to do if he finds out I'm sleeping there? He'll go even crazier."

"I hate to break it to you, sweetheart, but Warren's going to think what he thinks no matter what you do."

True enough. When they were going out, Warren had constantly accused her of conspiracies, from shrinking his clothes to purposely forgetting his favorite foods to "hurt" him. If he thought she was involved with Hunter, nothing would change his mind. But to sleep in the same apartment as Hunter? His essence was all over that place. Surely that wouldn't help ease her rest. It definitely wouldn't help her attraction. Just thinking about the arrangement sent her pulse into overdrive.

"I'll be fine at McKenzie House," she told them both. "There are plenty of people around. The police will be patrolling—"

Hunter cut her off. "This isn't up for debate, Abby."

What? Of course it was up for debate. She was the victim, for crying out loud. Who did he think he was? She looked to Carmella for support. Her friend merely shrugged. "Sorry, I think he's right."

Unbelievable. She was being bullied into where she should hide from a bully.

An hour later, still angry at being forced into the arrangement, Abby headed downstairs. Her plan was to make one last argument. Instead, she got to the third step from the bottom and found Hunter sprawled across his living room sofa, his long frame illuminated by the computer screen. While she'd been upstairs fuming, he'd changed into a pair of track pants and an unzipped sweatshirt. She paused, struck by how different he looked in the moment. Stripped of his action-hero uniform, with his hair mussed and his attention stolen, the vulnerability he normally kept barricaded seeped out. This was a softer, gentler Hunter. His lips were parted in concentration.

Noticing how his eyes picked up the gleam of the computer screen, she wondered, if she were closer, would she see the computer image reflected in their blue-gray depths? This was a different Hunter. The one he showed only glimpses of. Her heart jumped to her throat, killing her irritation. This was why she'd argued against staying. How could she fight an attraction when she saw Hunter unguarded? Given what she'd been through today, she shouldn't be feeling any attraction at all toward anyone. Yet here she was, mesmerized by the man. Clearly, her self-destructive tendencies were alive and well.

She must have sighed or made some other noise because he looked up. "You're awake."

"So are you," she countered.

"Couldn't sleep, so I decided to answer a few emails. Thought you'd collapse the minute you went upstairs. It's not every day you get attacked by an ex-boyfriend."

"Just every three or four."

Surprisingly, the sarcasm earned a smile. "Nice to know you're back on form. Have you settled in?"

"Pretty much. It's not like I had a lot to unpack."

"You could have brought more."

"Didn't have much to begin with." She came down the rest of the stairs, joining him in the living space. He'd sat up while speaking, his sweatshirt falling open to reveal his bare chest. "There's coffee if you want some."

Abby had to smile. "Someone finally used his coffeemaker."

"What can I say? Someone stocked my pantry with coffee."

Padding to the kitchen area, she poured herself a cup, while Hunter sat up and cleared room for her to sit. It felt strange being in his house this late at night. She wondered how he felt about his space being invaded, he who spent so much of his time alone.

"Thank you letting me stay."

"Wasn't about to let you go home and risk getting beat up," he replied.

"A hotel would have worked just as well."

"Right. I would have felt real good about dropping you off somewhere in your price range."

Abby joined him on the sofa. "I wouldn't have minded."

"I know. Sadly." He picked up his coffee cup, started to drink, then set it back down again. "This isn't a punishment, Abby. Even your friend thought staying here was a good idea."

Because her *friend* was as bad as Warren when it came to thinking something was going on between the two of them. Hunter was right, though. Most people would be thrilled by his generosity. "I'm sorry. I don't mean to sound ungrateful. I was being a brat."

"I wish you'd stop apologizing."

"Sorry for that, too." Before he could open his mouth to lecture, she grinned to let him know she was joking. He mock-glared back.

"Why did you argue the point?" he asked.

"I think you know."

"My kissing you."

Hearing him say the words aloud brought the memory shooting to the surface. Remembering brought a sigh to her lips, and she had to bite down to keep the sound from escaping. "I kissed you, if I recall."

"We kissed each other, and I also recall us settling things."

Oh yes, they'd settled things. To a point. "I was afraid it might be…awkward."

Hunter studied the contents of his coffee cup. "We've been talking over the internet for the past two weeks. Are you saying you're still thinking about what happened?"

"No," she quickly assured him. "What I meant was we haven't seen each other in person since that happened. It's one thing to communicate by computer, but when you're in the same room…"

"My personality hasn't changed, Abby, if that's what you're wondering."

"Never would have guessed."

Setting deeper into the corner, Abby sipped her coffee and thought about how intertwined hers and Hunter's lives had become the past few weeks. The level to which he had ended up involved. A lot for a guy who preferred to be on the sidelines capturing the action. She could only imagine his regret. "I bet you're sorry you ever sat in my section of the diner, aren't you?"

"Why do you say that?"

Wasn't it obvious? "I've been nothing but trouble from the start. Since meeting me you've been kicked out of your favorite breakfast place, hired a housekeeper you didn't want, been arrested for assault—"

"My lawyer assures me the charges will go away," he interrupted.

Still, he faced the hassle of fighting the charges in the first place. "And now you're stuck with a roommate on your first night back from overseas."

For a moment, Hunter didn't reply. Then he slid a little closer. "My apartment needed cleaning," he said. The simple response made her vision blur.

"I'm sorry for messing up your life," she said, blinking.

"You don't have to apologize."

"Maybe I want to." Over the years, she'd given so many apologies simply to avoid conflict. It felt good to give one on her terms.

To her relief, he understood. At least that's how she chose to interpret his nod. "Apology accepted then."

She suddenly had to blink again.

Silence settled between them. Tucking herself in the corner of the sofa, Abby sipped her coffee and tried not to think about how intimate the setting felt. The computer screen cast no more light than a candle, and with Hunter only a foot away, she became acutely aware of his presence. Every breath, every rasp of cotton against his skin, every gap in his open sweatshirt. Especially every gap in his sweatshirt. Despite the shadows, she could see every contour of his sculpted torso. He must have taken a shower, for with each breath, his skin gave off the faintest aroma of soap. The scent mingled with Italian roast to create a unique aftershave that instantly reminded her of how it felt to be wrapped in his arms.

Interestingly, it wasn't the kiss that popped to her mind, but the other embrace. When he'd held her during her meltdown, surrounding her with calm and security.

Next to her, she felt Hunter shift his weight. He was facing her. "I was thinking. About you being my housekeeper. There's no need for you to keep looking for work."

Abby had to pause to make sure she'd heard right. "I thought you said the arrangement could only be temporary."

"Those were the terms you offered me. You're a lousy negotiator."

He was offering her a full-time job. "Why?"

"I just told you why. I need my house clean."

He'd needed his house clean before he'd gone away, and had seemed in no hurry to have a full-time employee. She could think of only one reason for this new offer. "Your change of heart wouldn't have anything to do with Warren's reappearance today, would it?"

"What if it did?"

"At least you're honest."

"Look…" He slid across the leather until they were knee to knee. "Does it matter why I'm offering? You're not having luck finding another job, anyway, so why not? It'll help you get back on your feet that much faster."

True on all counts. Problem was, it did matter. She didn't want Hunter to see her as some charity case who needed help; he'd seen her that way enough. She wanted him to see her as…

As what? A woman? The notion stirred awareness deep inside her.

And if he looked at her that way? What then? She hung her head. Stress and exhaustion had her thinking in circles. Hunter was right about one thing: she wasn't having any luck finding other work. Only a stubborn fool would reject his offer.

"A job and a night in a luxury apartment. A girl could do a lot worse."

"You're welcome. Glad to see you've stopped being stubborn."

Stubborn. That's what Warren called her when she didn't do what he wanted.

At the thought of Warren, Abby felt the day finally catch up with her, and exhaustion pressed hard on her shoulders. She needed to turn in before she did or said something foolish.

"Good night, Abby," Hunter said when she stood up.

She offered him a smile. "Thanks again. For everything."

"You're welcome. Again. Oh, and, Abby?" His fingers caught hers. "Just so you know, the room is yours for as long as you need."

Her heart leaped to her throat again, killing her ability to speak. Too bad she couldn't say the same for the voice in her head telling her she'd just made a very bad decision.

Hunter watched until Abby's stocking feet disappeared up the stairs. What was he thinking? He barely stayed in the apartment. He didn't need a housekeeper, certainly not one full-time. And living here to boot. Granted, the living arrangement was temporary. But then again, that was how the job had started.

He ran a hand over his face. What the hell had happened?

His coffee was long cold. No matter. He drank the liquid anyway. By all rights he should be dead to the world in a bed, like Abby, but he couldn't shake the image of her sitting on the police bench, her color drained away, and worrying he was mad at her. *You're probably sorry you ever met me.* He hated hearing her say things like that. He hated that ex-boyfriend of hers for dredging up her insecurities. Couldn't stand the idea Abby thought so little of herself. She was better than that.

Would you listen to him? Hunter slammed down his coffee cup. He sounded so protective. Hell, he was *acting* protective. The woman was sleeping in his spare bedroom, for crying out loud! When had Abby gone from being some waitress he saw being hassled, to sleeping upstairs, with him downstairs worrying about her? So much so he'd offered her a job and told her she could stay as long as she liked? When did he start *caring?* He wasn't supposed to care.

The only thing compassion did was cause you to get burned. He turned off his laptop, plunging the area into darkness. Sitting back, he closed his eyes and waited for his emotional wall to rebuild itself. The wall that since childhood had kept him whole, shielding him from loneliness, betrayal, desertion. Brick by brick, he would build an invisible fortress until the outside world stopped affecting him.

Only this time, the walls refused to rise. At some point between landing at the airport and now, his insides had shifted. There was a breach in the protection buffeting his soul. Because when he closed his eyes, the only thing his mind could see was Abby.

Abby tiptoed down the stairs, trying to be as quiet as possible in case Hunter was still asleep. He wasn't. Just her luck, she found him awake and propped against the kitchen counter eating a toasted frozen waffle slathered with peanut butter. He smiled when he saw her, an unusually shy smile that he managed to make look sexy, and raked his free hand through his curls. "Morning, Sleeping Beauty."

Talk about your misnomers. It was her turn to rake a hand through the mess on top of her head. Most women were cursed with either limp bangs or unruly curls. She'd gotten both, meaning bed head was not her friend. "I didn't mean to sleep so late." Unfortunately, her thoughts had kept her awake long after she should have slipped unconscious. "If you give me five minutes, I'll make you breakfast."

"Already made." He licked a dab of peanut butter from his lower lip. Abby tried not to focus on the sheen his tongue left behind. She'd thought the one good thing to come out of her tossing and turning was that she'd woken up determined to keep her fantasies in check. Instead, rather than improve, the awkwardness felt as if it increased tenfold. Seeing Hunter in his sweatshirt only reminded her of last night's eerily intimate conversation in the dark.

"See you're becoming a regular barista, too," she said, noting the full pot of coffee.

"Had no choice. My housekeeper slept in.

"Relax," he added when she began to protest. "It was a joke. Should I bother asking if the bed was comfortable?"

"A lot better than the thing the shelter calls a bed, that's for sure." Realizing what she'd said, Abby winced. Up to now, Hunter hadn't commented on her living arrangements. A fact she had hoped meant he didn't know.

He was in the middle of pouring her coffee. "Did you say 'shelter'?"

So much for hoping. Abby nodded. "McKenzie House. It's part of a network of houses around the city for battered women." She waited for the inevitable reaction.

"Damn!" Hunter swore with disbelief. "Why didn't you say anything?"

For what? So he could look at her with greater pity in his eyes? "Do you drop where you live into everyday conversation?"

"No."

"Neither do I."

"But a shelter?"

"McKenzie House isn't a homeless shelter. Not really. It's more like a halfway house where women can stay while getting back on their feet.

"Look," she said, leaning against the counter. "I'm not ashamed of where I live." Her only shame was in letting her life become such a mess in the first place.

Hunter held out her coffee. "Fair enough. Although I'd like to point out you no longer live at McKenzie House, either."

"This arrangement is temporary. Soon as Warren backs off, I'll go back."

"We'll see."

What was that supposed to mean? She'd opened her mouth to ask when Hunter turned on his heel. "Before I forget."

His messenger bag lay on the dining room table. Striding over to it, he reached in and retrieved what looked like a yellow plastic shopping bag. "Here." He thrust the sack in his direction.

"For me?"

She pulled out a gold-and-coral-colored scarf. *He'd bought her a present?* "It's beautiful."

"I was shooting near the marketplace, and one of the vendors had a bunch of them. I figured I should buy something."

Tiny embroidered flowers danced across the linen material. Abby ran her fingers over the raised metallic thread. She couldn't remember a gift that didn't come with an apology.

Or an expectation. Her stomach twisted. Hunter's kindness. Would there be a price tag attached to that, as well? Did she want one?

Her thoughts must have played out on her face, because suddenly there was Hunter, closer than he should be, catching her chin with his fingers. Forcing her face upward, he met her gaze with a gentle seriousness. "It's only a scarf."

He was halfway upstairs before Abby found her ability to speak—too late for him to hear her whispered thank-you. She could kick herself for jumping to such a wrong conclusion. Then again, she was still seeing the world through her Warren-skewed lens. Goes to show, old habits die hard.

And old baggage never quite went away.

"I can't believe you don't have a single picture."

Hunter looked up from the shot he was editing. "I beg your pardon?"

"On your walls," Abby replied. "I can't believe they're bare. You're a photographer, for goodness' sake."

"Which means I'm required to hang photographs?" He was teasing her. She'd been muttering about photos and artwork for the past twenty minutes. so he knew exactly what she meant. He just enjoyed seeing her gear up for a discussion.

They'd been living together for three days. That is, Abby had been his live-in housekeeper for three days. With each tick of the calendar, she seemed to get more comfortable.

Personally, Hunter wasn't sure how he felt. Having spent the better part of his life alone, he was used to silence and solitude. Abby brought chatter and activity to his otherwise quiet workday, knocking him from his rhythm and interrupting his concentration.

On the other hand, she brought chatter and activity to his otherwise quiet workday. Suddenly he had noises in his kitchen, and conversation over dinner and...

And midday debates about whether his walls were too bare.

"You are planning to stay here while I'm in Libya, aren't you?" he asked. It was a question that had been bothering him since their arrangement began. There'd been no sign of Warren since she moved in, a fact that he knew hadn't escaped her notice.

"I was thinking about it, and decided I should go back to McKenzie House." A ridiculously small plant sat on the windowsill. She picked up the pot and carried it to the kitchen sink. "Why? Does that bother you?"

Did it? "Yes."

"Why? You won't be here. Besides, if I don't go back, they'll give away my spot."

"And would that be such a bad idea?" he asked her. "Is staying here so awful?"

"No. Of course not." A shadow crossed her face. She was holding part of her answer back. He wondered what. "Why do you care so much?"

Truthfully? He didn't know why he found her insistence on keeping one foot at the shelter bothersome. It shouldn't matter to him at all, or so his brain would tell him. It was his insides—his gut, his chest—that seemed to cramp up at the idea. All he knew was that when she talked of leaving, his nonthinking parts told him it was a bad idea.

"I think you should stay. You've got a bedroom. Going back only takes a bed away from someone else."

"I..." Clearly, she hadn't thought of that point. Mentioning it might have been underhanded if it weren't also true. If there was one thing Hunter had learned about Abby this week, it was that she believed strongly in McKenzie House's mission, and the people it helped.

He could tell the moment she acquiesced by the nervous darkness underscoring her expression. "Cheer up," he told her, trying not to be annoyed. "I'll be gone. You'll have a whole week to hang photos."

Surprise replaced the darkness. Her eyes grew wide. "While you're out of town?"

"Sure," he replied with a wave of his hand. "Hang away." If it would make her face light up like that, he'd let her knock down walls. "What's wrong?"

Only one reason could dim her enthusiasm. Warren.

"He had to approve everything," she said when Hunter joined her by the counter. "The food we ate, the shows we watched. I never would have been able to decorate."

"Abby—"

"You're not Warren. Don't worry, that lesson's been hammered home."

Soft fingers touched his cheek. Hunter felt their contact all the way to his toes. It was like velvet against sandpaper.

"Thank you," she said.

"For what?" He was distracted by the hand warming his skin. "Letting you hang pictures?"

"For trusting me. For not assuming I'll mess it up."

Never had someone's words hit him so hard. They gave birth to a sensation like nothing Hunter had ever felt before. A primal sensation that rose from somewhere deep inside him, filling his chest and fueling his protectiveness.

Just like that afternoon at the castle, everything disappeared from view but Abby's face. He felt as if he was falling, and grabbed the edge of the counter to stay balanced. His eyes dropped to her mouth. He wanted to kiss her again. But having pushed her away, he couldn't. Kissing her now would only confuse them both, and make him no better than her miserable, selfish ex.

"If you want to hang pictures, come with me," he told her. "And bring a sweater. You're going to need it."

"Where are we going?"

"I'm going to show you something no other person has ever seen." With a small smile, he presented his offering. "My archives."

CHAPTER NINE

PULLING HER CARDIGAN tightly around her middle, Abby unlocked the door to Hunter's archives. He'd built the climate-controlled room in the basement of the building. The smell of cool, dead air drifted out the darkened doorway. As she flicked on the overhead light, bathing the space in fluorescent white light, Abby yet again marveled at the row of boxes organized by date and location. Alberta, Arcadia, Athens. People and events from around the world.

"You did this?" she'd asked the first time she saw the meticulous organization. "Impossible."

"What makes you say that?"

"You forget I clean your living room. This is way too orderly."

Hunter had pretended to be hurt. "I happened to have spent days creating this room." When she'd responded with a sidelong look, he'd shrugged. "Supervisorally speaking."

He'd given her a tour, pointing out certain countries and projects he remembered fondly. "If you can't find a photograph or two in here to hang on my walls, you're in trouble. We're talking a lifetime of pictures."

"A lifetime, huh?" She'd pulled a box off a shelf at random. "Did you always know?" she asked. "What you wanted to be?"

He'd shrugged again, a more serious gesture than the first one. "I'm not sure. I think part of me did. God knows, I drove the Pomeranian crazy." Abby had smiled at the image.

"Mostly, though, I wanted to be like my dad. Then, what kid doesn't?"

"Me. My stepfather was a landscaper. I can safely say I never wanted to mow lawns."

"Point taken. *I* wanted to be my father, though. I guess I thought…"

Hunter had drifted off before finishing, both his voice and his presence. It had taken Abby touching his arm to bring him back. "You guessed what?"

"It would give us something in common. After my mom died, photography was the one thing we could talk about. Then, when I got older, he started taking me on his expeditions during the summer." There'd been a wistful note to Hunter's words when he said them.

"Father-son photo trips," she'd remarked.

"More like father-photo-son-set-up-lights trips. I worked on the crew, remember?"

"Must have been fun."

"I definitely learned a lot from watching him, that's for sure."

Twice he'd said he learned from watching his father. What about being with him? She had yet to hear Hunter say anything about sharing their passion. "He didn't teach you directly?"

She recalled Hunter fiddling with the metal label holder on one of the boxes, running his index finger around the corners. "My father," he'd told her in a voice quieter than she'd ever heard him use before, "taught me that in order to take great photos, you couldn't have distractions. That the best photos froze time at the exact right moment. He was famous for waiting for days to find that right moment."

"It's all about the shot," Abby had murmured, parroting the words he'd said to her.

Hunter's eyes became gray mist. "He did take some amazing shots."

But what about his son? Abby wondered. What did he do while his father focused on the all-important picture?

"You were lucky." Sensing a sadness about to descend on his shoulders, she'd decided to change the subject. "You had a passion. Only passion I had was wishing I lived somewhere else."

"Like Cinderella's castle?"

He'd remembered. "You saw how well that worked out," she'd pointed out. Looking back, the memory seemed childish and foolish. "Maybe if I'd had someone to warn me, life might have turned out differently."

"But then you might not have ended up here," Hunter had replied.

Somehow the matter-of-fact words still managed to make her breath catch. "No," she'd replied. "I wouldn't have."

They'd smiled at each other like a pair of shy children.

Back in the present, Abby ran her fingers across the perfectly aligned boxes. It had been a compliment, Hunter showing her this room. She didn't want to think about the significance of his compliment. Staying with him the past week already had her on edge. Adding speculation would drive her mad.

Funny, she'd thought the days of feeling on eggshells were over the day she'd left Warren, but no. Here she was, still unsteady and living on constant alert. At least this time it wasn't fear of an outburst keeping her on edge. Rather it was a fear of her own weaknesses. She worried she might misread a smile or a gesture, and tumble deeper into attraction than she already was.

Take the other day. Right before Hunter mentioned his archive room, he had been staring at her with an intensity that made her heart race. The pupils in his eyes had darkened until only a thin sliver of silver showed around the black. Coupled with the way his expression intensified, she'd been certain he was about to kiss her. Instead, he'd invited her down here.

Leaving her back on edge.

She found the box by accident. It had been pushed to the back of the uppermost shelf. If she hadn't been moving a pair of photo containers, she might have missed it.

Standing on tiptoes, she pulled the brown cardboard closer. While the other boxes were organized, this one had clearly been thrown together. A range of dates had been hastily scrawled across one side in faded red marker. Abby smiled. Hunter's early years. Realizing the treasure she held, she couldn't resist her curiosity. Who knew, maybe she'd find the Pomeranian.

She pulled off the lid to the smell of chemicals and age. Whereas the photos in other boxes were organized in crisp plastic sleeves, the ones in this box were tossed in haphazardly, without regard to size or subject. Abby smiled again. This was the Hunter she knew and loved. No, not loved, she quickly corrected. She was nowhere near love.

Flipping through, she discovered a time line of his photography career. There were pictures of the infamous Pomeranian, one of which she set aside. A photo of a handsome man in linen pants and a white cotton shirt unbuttoned to his navel. He was beating the contents of a stainless steel bowl. Abby smiled. *Reynaldo.* A woman lying on a chaise longue, head covered by a floral scarf. Abby's smile faded. *His mother.* From there the photos moved outward. Views from his window. Kids playing ball. A girl petting a dog.

And of course, more photos of his father. On location, in his office and behind the camera. So many photos of the man behind his camera. Photo after photo of a world without Hunter.

She almost missed the envelope at the bottom of the box. Manila and faded from time. As she undid the clasp, she felt the hairs rising on the back of her neck. The fact the contents were separate from the rest of the box suggested she was treading into extremely private territory. But Hunter had told her she had permission to look, hadn't he?

A collection of photographs spilled onto her lap, both color and black-and-white. A laugh burst out when she saw the top one. It was of a pudgy-cheeked little boy offering an ice cream cone to a dog. Hunter at his most giving. Hunter's mother must have found the idea funny as well, because she was in the background, a huge grin on her face. Lord, but she'd been beautiful, Abby realized.

Another shot showed Hunter and his father rolling on the grass in a park. Both of them were laughing, their heads thrown back, mouths wide-open with glee. And a third was a professional portrait of the whole family. Hunter the impatient toddler, with the proud parents looking on with love.

No, check that. Hunter's mother looked on with love. Joseph Smith's smile was for his wife. One of complete adoration.

With a sudden, sickening heaviness, the final piece of the Hunter Smith puzzle slid into place. These photos were *before*. Before Hunter's mother had passed, before Joseph Smith turned to his career. It all made sense now. Joseph's lesson to his son: keep your distance. Losing his wife had been Joseph's Somalia. The moment he'd decided to bury his heart behind the lens of a camera.

Hunter had told Abby a good picture told a story. These did that and more. They showed a time before life had given way to solitude and separation. His father hadn't just focused on his career. He'd pulled away from his son, leaving him to be another observer in a crowd of observers.

No wonder Somalia had hit Hunter so hard. He'd found a community, a place—people—he'd cared about, and a terrorist had selfishly destroyed them all.

Her poor Hunter. Abby looked at a photograph by her knee. It was of his father, behind the lens as always. The window behind him showed the reflection of a child. A small boy, with a brown mop of curls, hiding behind his own camera. Abby suddenly found herself picturing a young Hunter following his father around the world, doing his best to emulate the man in order to spark a conversation.

A good photographer fades into the background. No wonder Hunter was so good at what he did. If she was right—and her gut told her she was—he'd been practicing fading into the background for most of his life. Staying on the sidelines. This room held thousands of photos, all taken from the sidelines.

Her heart wept. She felt a tear slipping down her cheek. They had something else common, she and Hunter. Loneliness really was a great equalizer. He chased the emotion away by hiding behind a camera; she ran away from it by heading toward Warren. They were two peas in a pod.

With newfound understanding, she placed the cover back on the box. If Hunter were present, she'd wrap him in her arms and tell him he didn't need to be lonely anymore. That she was here.

Thankfully, he was thousands of miles away, and she was safe from making a fool of herself.

"Is this centered?"

It was three days later, and Abby stood on a too-small step stool, trying to hang a framed shot of Belgian soccer players over Hunter's sofa. She lifted a corner before looking over her shoulder. "Is it?"

"Close enough," Carmella replied.

"I don't want 'close enough.' It needs to be exact."

"I'm going to go with yes, seeing as how you measured three times."

"I'll measure again." With a sigh, Abby set the frame on the sofa. "I thought you came over to help me?" she remarked, heading in search of her tape measure.

Her friend swiveled her stool back and forth. "I came over to say hey. You're the one who tried to put me to work."

"Key word *tried*. So far all you've done is drink our coffee."

Hunter's coffee. Abby corrected the slip in her head.

"That's all I'm going to do, too," her friend replied. "Why are you going so crazy, anyway? Will he really notice if the picture is half an inch to the left?"

You never know, thought Abby. "Doesn't matter. I'll know.

Now come here and hold the tape level so I can mark the spot again."

"Man, you're being nitpicky." Despite the grumbling, Carmella did as she was asked.

"I just want everything to be perfect." Hunter trusted her, and it was important he see his trust was well placed. This could be her one opportunity to say thank-you for all he'd done for her.

There was another reason she was taking her task so seriously. Her visit to Hunter's archives had opened her eyes. She finally realized why his apartment had felt incomplete. The emptiness wasn't caused by lack of artwork or the echo of footsteps, but by the lack of personality. A home reflected the people who lived there. Hunter had created a residential limbo, because that was how he lived. That wasn't who he was, however. As she'd seen over the past few weeks, Hunter Smith was far more complex than a man who merely snapped pictures on the sideline, or a gorgeous action hero. He was funny, smart, heroic, charming. It was important for Abby to create an apartment that showed the world all of Hunter's many sides. Why it was important, she wasn't sure. A niggling, nagging voice in the back of her head kept trying to speak up. Warn her about something. She pushed it aside.

Carmella was giving her a dirty look. "Are you going to mark the wall or aren't you?" she asked.

"Why? You in a hurry to get somewhere?"

"Actually, yes. I'm going apartment hunting." Abby almost dropped her end of the tape. Looking left, she saw Carmella grinning. "Finally pulled some money together. I'm out of there by next month."

This time, Abby did let go, to free up her arms for hugging. There was a crackling noise as the metal tape hit the ground. "I'm so glad for you! You must be so happy."

"You don't know the half of it," Carmella said, giving her a squeeze and a grin. "Then again, maybe you do. I never thought

I'd scrape enough up. I thought I'd be stuck paying for being with Eddie the rest of my life."

"I know that feeling," Abby muttered, though, thank heaven, things had never escalated to the terrifying heights of Carmella and her husband's fights.

"Warren given you a hard time lately?"

"Not in the past week, though I'm not relaxing yet." He could be biding his time. "Warren is like a bad penny. Just when you think he's gone, he pops back up."

"Let's hope when he does, he'll pop up when your big bad bodyguard is around."

"Hunter is not my bodyguard, Mella, and you know it. He's my boss."

"A pretty darn protective boss, then," the woman muttered over her mug. The comment made Abby shiver. *Protective* reminded her too much of *possessive,* which she'd done, thank you very much. In her experience, no good ever came from either one.

"His mother raised him to be chivalrous. He's only doing what he's been taught," she told her friend.

"Whatever. I hope he and Warren meet up again. I'd like to see the big fat weenie get pounded."

Abby would prefer Warren never came by again. "What makes you think I can't protect myself?"

"If you could, you wouldn't have wound up in McKenzie." It was a point that, sadly, Abby couldn't argue.

"How is your boss, anyway?" Carmella asked.

"Don't know. I haven't talked with him in a couple days." Three, actually, but who was counting?

"I thought you guys did that daily video thing."

"We usually do, but he's in an area with very poor connections." She reached for the hammer while doing her best to sound nonchalant. "We probably won't get a chance to talk until he gets near a city."

"That's a bummer."

Yes. "I'll survive. We're talking a week tops." She refused to acknowledge aloud how long the past three days had felt. Without Hunter's lanky frame, the apartment was too empty and quiet. Surrounded by his belongings, she felt his absence keenly.

Worst part was the not knowing how he was doing. Every morning she scoured the headlines to make sure nothing had happened in that part of the world overnight. So far, she'd read about demonstrations, but nothing major. Thank goodness.

Her tense nerves were Hunter's fault. Every time she did talk with him, she made a point of reminding him to be safe. The warnings fell on deaf ears. He would wave them off with a obligatory "I will," then go off and do his thing, without concern for who might be home worrying.

"Ouch!" She hadn't been paying attention, and the hammer slammed down on her thumb.

"You okay?"

"Fine." Served her right for thinking like she was more than a housekeeper. As if he had a responsibility to her. Hunter didn't consider himself responsible to anyone. *Which is how you wanted things, remember?*

In fact, she should be glad circumstances hadn't switched. Maybe she should ask Hunter for some pointers on how to keep the world at arm's length. She seemed to be having a problem in that area....

Her cell phone rang. "Would you grab that? I want to run my finger under cold water."

"Speak of the devil," Carmella replied. "It's Hunter."

"What's he calling for?"

"Maybe he misses you."

More likely he'd forgotten a piece of equipment. An important piece, no doubt, for him to make the drive to where he could get service. Abandoning care for her swollen thumb, she scooped the phone from Carmella's fingers.

"What's up?"

"Abby Gray?" The voice on the other line was definitely not Hunter. "My name is Miles Bean. I'm a colleague of Hunter's."

Colleague. Hunter's. Abby's stomach clenched. She gripped the countertop to keep her knees from shaking. A few feet away, Carmella held herself rigid, studying her. Abby had the feeling it was because she'd grown pale.

"Yes, Mr. Bean," she asked. "What can I do for you?"

"I'm afraid there's been an accident."

CHAPTER TEN

TWENTY-SEVEN STEPS to the rental car counter, fifty-four steps round-trip. Abby had pacing down to a science. It felt as if that's all she'd done since getting Miles's phone call.

As she made the turn for another lap, her eyes shot to the Customs exit. Nothing. The plane had landed twenty minutes ago. What was taking so long?

Hunter was hurt. Miles's news replayed itself in her head. There was a protest that turned ugly. Hunter was taking photos. Somehow he'd ended up crossing paths with the wrong people, and they'd attacked him.

"Brutal" was how Miles described it. "Though Hunter was more bent up about his camera being damaged."

Of course he was. That camera was his life, wasn't that what he'd said? She looked around for something to kick, settling for the air in front of her. Hadn't she warned him before he left to stay safe? But no, he had to get his perfect shot. Like father, like son.

She spotted him. Ducking through the exit door, sling hugging his right arm to his body. Abby let out her breath. She'd never been so happy to see someone in her life. For the first time since Miles had called, her chest didn't feel as if it had a giant weight sitting on it.

"Before you say anything, the doctor said both breaks will heal perfectly," he said. "I'll only be laid up a couple months. Eight weeks tops."

"Only eight weeks? How lucky." Upon closer look, she could see why Miles had said his injuries looked "nasty." Along with a cut above his left brow, Hunter had a vicious black eye that spread close to his cheekbone.

There was a second bruise on his chin, less noticeable thanks to his stubble. Lightly, she ran her fingertips along his jaw, surveying the damage. "You're lucky to be alive, from what Miles said."

"Miles can be overdramatic. You should read his wire pieces." Hunter caught her hand and gently squeezed her fingers. "You were worried." It sounded more like a question than a statement, and Abby realized he was unsure. Keeping the world at arm's length had its consequences.

"Couldn't help myself," she replied. "I tend to freak out when I get emergency phone calls from strangers. I was afraid I'd be unemployed again." Not to mention scared to death he might be lying battered and bruised in a street somewhere.

Her attempt at sounding unaffected failed, and, smile fading, he leaned forward until their foreheads rested against one another.

"I'm sorry I scared you, sweetheart."

She closed her eyes and exhaled as much of the stress and fear as she could. "I didn't know what to think. Not after talking to Miles."

"I told you, Miles is dramatic."

Dramatic or not, he'd painted a pretty horrible picture. Listening to him describe the scene, she'd felt physically ill. "What happened?"

"Wrong place at the wrong time is all." That wasn't all. He'd been attacked, for crying out loud. Abby knew there had to be more to the story. She wouldn't press, though. At least not now.

They stood nuzzled together as the crowds filed past, until

Abby felt the trembling. It was coming from her. Her body was shaking. Hunter must have noticed, because he wrapped his good arm around her shoulders and drew her closer.

"Shouldn't this be the other way around?" she asked. "Me comforting you?" Though even as she spoke she was burying her face against his jacket.

Hunter's hand rubbed up and down her spine. "You are comforting me," he told her. "You have no idea how much."

He buried his nose in her hair. She could have sworn she felt him press a kiss to the top of her head. "Absolutely no idea."

Hunter took a pain pill before they left the airport, and dozed in the backseat while the driver weaved in and out of New York traffic. A few feet away, safely strapped in her seat belt, Abby used the respite to study Hunter's bruised face. The tiniest of muscles twitched beneath his eye, betraying the tension otherwise hidden by his relaxed posture. Every so often his mouth would draw into a frown as well, the lines in his face growing more pronounced. Below the neck, his ever-present field jacket had a stain on the collar. Blood. The discovery made her own run cold. How close had she come to losing him?

All because of a stupid photograph. Brushing a hand through his curls, she silently cursed his father for making him believe nothing else mattered.

"Mmmm. That feels nice."

She smiled at the drowsiness in his voice. "Someone's feeling no pain," she teased.

"Feel great. It's good to be home."

"We're not home yet."

"S'I am." He nudged her hand with his head, like a cat seeking petting. Abby obliged him with another stroke. "Mmm," he purred. "Missed you."

That was the painkillers talking. However, having a mind of their own, her insides decided to flutter anyway.

Hunter's eyes blinked open. "You were really worried about me?" His voice might have been low and husky, but Abby heard the lonely little boy with a camera. The one whose photos touched her so deeply.

She stroked his cheek. "Someone has to," she told him.

"I'm glad it's you." He searched her face, his eyes so dark Abby felt like she might drown in the grayness. He was touching her, she realized. His fingers tracing a path up and down her arm, each stroke leaving a trail of warm goose bumps.

"You're so beautiful," he murmured.

She could feel the flush working its way across her skin. He didn't mean it. If anything, he was reacting to his own stress by looking for a connection.

"I think your painkillers are making you loopy."

"Not so loopy," he replied in a voice so low she could feel the reverberations. His hand moved up to cup the back of her head, pulling her closer. "Not so loopy at all."

Then he kissed her. A slow, deep, lingering kiss that turned her inside out. Sighing into his mouth, Abby melted closer. She'd been thinking of his kiss ever since she kissed him in the wine bar, and while somewhere in the back of her mind she knew warning bells had to be going off, she chose not to listen. Yes, kissing Hunter in return was a bad idea. No doubt he would back off once he came to his senses. She didn't care. In fact, she was glad he had his emotional walls. It meant she could keep hers.

Hunter woke up on the sofa alone. He had a vague memory of climbing the stairs to his apartment with his arm wrapped around Abby's waist, and refusing to go any farther. Before that, they'd been in the Town Car and he'd been...

Kissing Abby. No way he could forget *that*. He'd only thought about kissing her the entire flight. Amazing how getting jumped in the middle of the street could knock some sense into a man. Had he really told her he'd missed her? His skin grew damp as he thought of the chance he'd taken. He'd come back from Libya determined to stop pussyfooting around, and take what he wanted. It was the only way to deal with all these strange feelings haunting him.

Granted, the seduction wasn't quite how he'd envisioned it going. For one thing, in his fantasy, he wasn't doped up on painkillers, and was able to take the kiss a lot further… But he wasn't complaining. He'd simply have to kiss her again properly later on.

She'd been worried about him. That still boggled his mind. No one had worried about him since his mother died. He'd always soldiered on by himself. If bad things happened, he grabbed his camera and took photos, while his inner walls kept the emotion out. So he didn't know quite how to handle the idea that another person cared about him. But when he'd looked into Abby's eyes and seen the concern reflected there, a window had opened and light poured inside. For the first time, he'd felt what it was like to have a connection with someone. A real connection, far deeper than simple desire. Frightened the hell out him. But if getting the snot kicked out of him had taught him anything, it was that he needed to do something. Otherwise, Abby would continue rattling around in his thoughts, distracting him from his work and causing him trouble. So he'd kissed her, and miracle of miracles, she'd kissed him back twice as hard. If only the stupid painkillers hadn't kicked in.

A noise in the kitchen caught his attention. Abby was washing dishes in the sink. Seeing her with her hair hanging limp and curly in her face, and her sweater sleeves rolled to her elbows, he felt a new rush of desire. She was wearing the scarf he'd bought in Israel. The dark gold thread wasn't as warm a color as Abby's hair, but the shade was close, and in the right light, they almost matched. Had he bought the scarf for that reason? Wouldn't surprise him. Even that first week, Abby had occupied his thoughts.

She definitely dominated his thoughts this week, so much so that here he was, lying on a sofa with a broken arm. He fingered the cast through his T-shirt. *Wonder what she'd say if she knew the entire story?*

"I thought you were sleeping."

Returning his attention to the kitchen, he discovered her wiping her hands with a towel. "Much more fun watching you work."

"Because housework is such a spectator sport."

"It is when done by the right person."

A magnificent flush colored her cheeks. The way she blushed so easily was one of the qualities he found so attractive. Her skin turned such a pure color. Made him want to kiss every inch to see what other shades he could bring to the surface.

Unfortunately, she insisted on staying across the living area. He couldn't very well kiss anything if she was thirty feet away.

Wincing as stiffness in his shoulder made its presence known, he sat upright and patted the sofa cushion. "Come here."

A nervous shadow passed over her. Regret over the kiss? God, he hoped not. "I can't. I have to work. This apartment doesn't clean itself, you know."

"It's all right. Your boss won't mind. I have an in with him." Hunter patted the sofa. "Come sit."

"Thought you said you liked watching me work?"

"I'd much rather look at you close up."

Though Abby rolled her eyes, she put down her dish towel and came to sit on the nearby chair, posture perfect.

"You can sit closer." He motioned to the sofa next to him.

She shook her head. "This is good." Good if you were into sitting ten feet apart. "I don't want to hurt your arm."

"Unless you step on me, the bone should be fine."

"Just in case, I'll sit over here."

"Suit yourself." Ignoring the twinge of disappointment her answer caused, he moved on. "You decorated."

Instantly, her face brightened. "You noticed."

Of course he'd noticed. Although it took him a moment for the changes to register in his medicine-soaked brain. During his short absence she'd taken his "barren beige walls," as she'd described them, and turned his living room into a photo gallery. Reprints of various location shots hung on the walls, filling the room with color and action. She'd added a few other touches, as well. Curtains and a few vases. For the first time since he'd bought the place, the apartment looked like home.

Home. A word he thought he'd never use. Must be the day for new experiences and feelings. Tripoli was.a far bigger eye-opener than he'd thought.

Abby was waiting for his verdict, he realized, as though he was delivering the most important statement in the world. To think his opinion yielded such power for her made the hair on the back of his neck start to rise. That was a warning signal, he decided. But for what, he wasn't sure.

"I like your photo choices," he told her. He looked over his shoulder at the Belgian footballers. Wasn't the perfect selection for the space, but it wasn't bad, either. "You have a decent eye."

He might have told her she was Da Vinci from her beaming smile. "Thanks. I was nervous hanging the darn thing."

So was it nerves regarding his reaction to the apartment that had her sitting miles away? "You needn't be. I told you I trusted your judgment."

"So you said, but..." Abby swiped the bangs from her face. How to explain something she wasn't sure about herself?

"Please don't compare me to Warren," Hunter told her.

"Okay, I won't." Pushing herself to her feet, she walked to the sink and poured a glass of water. "Nor will I mention this was the first apartment I ever decorated on my own." And he'd barely noticed until now.

She set the water in front of him, along with a plastic bottle of pills. "Here. Should be close to your next scheduled dose."

Probably. He couldn't tell the time, because his watch face had been smashed in the fight. No matter; he'd rather deal with the pain than fall asleep again. "I don't need them."

"But your arm?"

"Isn't as bad as people are acting."

While he was talking, Abby had been busying herself with wiping a water ring from the coffee table. Every time she bent over it, the proximity brought him a hint of her presence—a glimpse of skin between her scarf and sweater; her scent. The sweet smell of her skin was enough to ignite his need to touch her.

"Stay," he said to her. A simple request, but at the same time, one that carried so much weight. "Don't go back to your chair."

To his great relief, she understood his message and sat down. On the edge of the sofa, but at least closer than she had been.

"What changed?" she asked him. "You were very clear the afternoon we were at the castle."

She meant why had he kissed her? Hunter decided to answer her honestly. "I did. Actually, to be more accurate, I didn't change."

"I don't understand."

Neither did he, completely. "I couldn't stop thinking about you. Nothing I did to shake my attraction to you worked. When I saw you in the airport, I realized it was a waste of time, fighting what I really wanted. So I kissed you.

"And—" deciding it was time to take matters into his own hands, he slid over, closing the space between them "—based on your reaction, I'm guessing you want me, too."

Her blush was enough of an answer.

She was staring at her lap, thoughts unreadable. "Abby, look at me." He cupped her jaw, bringing her face in line with his. What he found was a pair of lips, and eyes that shone bright as stars. "You're so beautiful," he whispered.

"Don't..." She shook her head. "It's not necessary. I don't need a lot of compliments."

Maybe not need, but she deserved to hear she was special. The emotions that had taken up residence inside his walls grew stronger still. If she wouldn't take words, he'd find another way.

With that, he lowered his mouth to hers and poured every compliment he wanted to say to her into his kiss.

"I knew you'd get restless. How on earth are you going to survive two months of inactivity?" He hadn't made it two full days.

Hunter had dragged Abby out for a walk along the Greenway. "I can't help it if I like fresh air," he said. The night was unseasonably warm, more like midspring than midfall. Stars dotted the cloudless sky like a big, sequined blanket. Occasionally a cyclist or jogger would pass them, but mostly they had the road to themselves as they walked the Hudson's edge.

It was the perfect setting for lovers.

Lovers. Was that what she and Hunter were? They'd never quite defined what it was they were doing. Unable to say why, she found the term sat uneasily with her.

It certainly wasn't Hunter. As a lover, he was everything she'd expected him to be. Passionate, skillful, generous. Set the bar high for his partner. Maybe that was the problem. She wasn't sure she could match the standard set by the other women who'd visited his bed.

Or maybe it was the word *love* that upset her. Lord knew, that particular word was a land mine for her.

Plus, they weren't lovers. *Lovers* implied permanency, commitment. They shared neither. They were simply two people enjoying each other's company.

"You are a million miles away," Hunter said as he pressed a kiss to her temple. "Where'd you go?"

"Just enjoying the view." The lie left her uncomfortable, but she didn't want to rock the boat on such a beautiful night. Funny how easily a person could slip into old patterns. "I love how black the water is."

The only patterns on the water were the columned reflection of streetlights.

"Mmm."

She wondered if he was wishing he'd brought the camera.

It was weird, not seeing him with the strap around his neck.

"Do you feel naked?" she asked him. "Without your third eye?"

"Interestingly, no. Would have been too much hassle with my arm in the cast, anyway."

"Really? You have no trouble doing other activities."

"That's because I'm more motivated in those 'other activities,'" he replied. "Speaking of the word *naked...*"

"We weren't."

"Weren't we?"

He leaned down and kissed her. As always, the moment went from sweet to heady with a speed that left her breathless.

"I could kiss you forever," he whispered, before pressing another small, hard kiss on her lips.

All Abby could do was nod as his comment stilled her insides. Something about Hunter had changed over the past twenty-four hours. Maybe it was her imagination, but he seemed different. He was definitely more tactile, using every opportunity to kiss or touch. She chalked up that change to a sexual haze; she had the need to stay in physical contact with him, too.

If it was only the touching, she wouldn't think twice. But his whole manner had shifted. She could feel the change in Hunter's kisses, and in comments like this one. Romantic, tender gestures that left her off balance. Could it be, after years of Warren dysfunction, she simply didn't understand how real couples behaved?

But we aren't a couple! The protest screamed loudly in her brain. She clung to the fact like a life preserver. Knowing this... thing between them was temporary kept her grounded. It would be too easy to fall otherwise.

They'd resumed walking. After a few moments of silence, Hunter cleared his throat. "Our visit to Belvedere Castle the other week got me thinking."

"About what?"

"Besides our first kiss?"

BARBARA WALLACE   671

There he went again, saying things that made her heart skip
a beat. Abby shivered. Without saying a word, Hunter pulled
her closer. "I was thinking it might be interesting to shoot some
of Europe's castles."

"What about your other work? For *Newstime?*"

"I was thinking of cutting back on the hard-core news stuff
for a little while."

"Because of what happened in Libya?" He never had told
her what happened during the riot. "Do you feel like talking
about it?"

"Nothing much to say. I doubt my version is nearly as interesting as Miles's."

No, but it would be *his* version, and Abby was willing to
listen. After all the listening he'd done for her, she owed him.

"Anyway," he continued, completely dodging the conversation, "the pictorial I had in mind would be Europe's forgotten
castles. The smaller ones that had gone to ruin."

"Crumpled fairy tales," Abby quipped.

Hunter looked in her direction. Since they were between
streetlights, his expression was marred by shadows, although
she suspected he was shooting her a disapproving look. "We
need to work on your fairy tales," he said.

"I already have." Or wasn't he listening at Belvedere when
she'd said she was over her princess fantasy? "Prince Charming turns out to be a jerk, Cinderella moves out and learns self-
defense." Apparently she could add the castle falling into ruin,
too. "A much more realistic version, if you ask me."

"What about the sequel?"

"What sequel?"

"The one where she meets a new prince and he whisks her
off for a two month European vacation to check out castles?"

"I don't think..." She paused as Hunter's words caught up
with her. "Wait a minute. Are you inviting me to go along with
you? To Europe?"

"Why not?"

"I—" Abby was floored. "You're talking weeks."

"Couple of months, more likely."

Months? "I don't know what to say."

"Yes would be a good start."

"Y-yes."

He gave her shoulder a squeeze. "I can't wait to show you Europe, sweetheart. There are so many beautiful things and places."

He began listing the various cities he wanted to show her.

Any other woman would be thrilled to receive such an offer. Especially if offered by a man like Hunter.

All Abby could feel at the moment was fear.

It was starting. Listening to him tell her what they'd be doing, where they'd be going, she felt her control slipping away little by little. He was making plans for a future she hadn't agreed to. She'd never said she wanted Europe. "I don't have a passport."

Even the shadows couldn't mask his frown as he stepped back. No doubt he expected her to be bursting with excitement. "We can have one expedited. We can have one done practically overnight."

"Great." She forced a smile.

"There's this hotel in the French Alps with a view you won't believe." He paused to study her face before running a hand along her cheek. She couldn't help her tremor. "I'm thinking I might have to trap you in there and not let you out of the bed for days."

"Let?" Abby whispered.

"For days."

He meant the comment as playful; she knew as much. "You make it sound like I'm your personal property."

Eyes never leaving hers, he planted a kiss on the inside of her wrist. "Would belonging to me be that bad?" he breathed across her skin.

That's when she saw it. The desire glowing in his eyes. Brilliantly lit by the streetlamp, a possessive gleam in his gray-blue eyes that said *you're mine*.

It had been there all along, hadn't it? That's why she'd felt so unsettled. The light had been there all along. Damn him.

Worst of all, a thrill actually passed through her when she saw the gleam.

It was happening again, wasn't it? She was on the cusp of being swallowed up. The signs were all there. Her obsessive need to avoid mistakes in decorating his apartment, her fibbing to keep from rocking the boat. He now he wanted to whisk her off to Europe, and she, like an idiot, had almost agreed. Before long, she'd be completely under Hunter's spell, and then what? The bottom would fall out. He'd leave or she'd fail him like she did Warren and...

Dammit! Hunter had promised. She'd believed him when he said he had nothing to offer emotionally. That he couldn't give her a relationship. Then he went and looked at her like a man staring at his prized possession. As if he cared.

"I have to get out of here." She broke from his grasp, hoping to flag a cab before Hunter could stop her.

"What the hell is going on?" Naturally, he ran after her. "Why are you leaving?"

She fought against the tug on her heart his confusion caused. "I just have to get out of here. I have to go...."

Go where? She couldn't stay at his apartment anymore. She'd have to pack her things and head back to McKenzie House. So much for fresh start number two.

And where were all the taxis? This was New York, for goodness' sake. Weren't there supposed to be taxicabs everywhere? A flash of yellow appeared. She waved her arm, only to have the car speed by her, backseat occupied.

Hunter gripped her shoulder, forcing her to turn around. "Whatever's got you worked up, you need to tell me. I'm not going to let you run off without an explanation."

He was right. She owed him more, but couldn't find the right words to explain.

"It's going to Europe, isn't it? You don't want to go. Fine."

"It's more than Europe."

"More how?"

She sniffed back the moisture threatening her eyes. He looked so confused and worried, and maybe just a little bit hurt. In a flash, she was back in the archives and remembering the boy on the sidelines. Regret tore her in half.

The tears she'd sniffed away a moment early burned her eyes. "I made a terrible mistake," she whispered.

"A mistake?"

She saw the second he understood. The shutters closed over his eyes and he pulled inward. Gone was the tender man she'd made love to. "I see."

"I'm so sorry." She hated that she'd hurt him. Like his father, like Naxar. He'd let her in, and she was going to have to betray that gift. If only she could explain. "I never— That is, I can't…" She stopped while a pair of joggers ran by. "I told myself I wouldn't make the same mistakes I made with Warren."

"Warren. For crying out loud." Hunter jabbed his hand through his hair. "How many times do I have to remind you I'm not your ex?"

"I know." He was, though, in some ways far more danger-ous. "Which is why it would be so easy to make you the cen-ter of my world."

"I don't understand."

"I lost myself with Warren. I became this weak-kneed woman I didn't recognize, all because I decided he was my Prince Charming. Except he wasn't, and when I got free I promised myself I wouldn't lose myself for anyone ever again. I would rather be alone."

"I see." He stared at the ground for a long minute before turning his eyes back on her. Just before they hardened, she caught a glimpse of the lonely little boy in their depths. "Just one question."

"What?"

"When are you going to stop letting Warren run your life?"

"Warren isn't running anything." Hunter should know. He'd gone to the courthouse with her.

"Could have fooled me. Everything you do goes back to him."

How dare he? "Did you not listen to what I was saying? This is about not making the same mistakes. Excuse me for being cautious."

"Cautious or afraid?" he asked.

Silence filled the widening gap between them. Afraid? Who did he think he was? What did he expect her to do? Ignore the lessons of her past?

If he didn't understand that, then there was nothing more for them to say. Abby folded her arms across her chest. "Goodbye, Hunter."

Rather than say anything, he raised his arm. Within seconds, a yellow cab pulled to the sidewalk. As he opened the door, the scent of his aftershave drifted past, stabbing her in the heart. She hoped she never smelled the wonderful woodsy scent again.

"I'll be out within the hour," she told him.

"Suit yourself." With a shrug, he shut the door, leaving her to drive away without him.

CHAPTER ELEVEN

"I THINK I'VE LOOKED at every low-wage job in the five boroughs." Abby flopped down in the faded Queen Anne chair. "Nothing. Not even a fast-food job." She either lacked qualifications or arrived after the job had been filled.

"Cheer up," Carmella told her. "It's only been three days."

Three whole days since she'd left Hunter standing on the sidewalk. Three days back living in McKenzie House, looking for work. She had a running bet with herself which would take longer: finding a job or getting rid of the ache in her chest that had been constant since she'd closed that cab door. Odds were in the job search's favor, and so far, she hadn't gotten a single nibble.

"Wait, there is one," she told Carmella. "Overnight shift cleaning crew in an animal testing lab."

"Sounds fun. I've got to go answer the bell. It's my day for door duty."

"Maybe I'll be able to bring us home a pet," Abby called after her friend. She was secretly rooting for the job; working nights might keep her from tossing and turning in her bed.

The restlessness came from her perverse habit of replaying their parting argument in her head every night. Correction: her parting argument. In her replay, she was laying out her reasons for ending their affair, while Hunter said hardly a word. Except, of course, for his parting ones. *Cautious or afraid?*

Why was it when she listened to her arguments, they didn't stick the way those three words did?

Carmella came back into the room. "You have a visitor."

He was the last person Abby expected to see. But there Hunter was, handsome as ever in his faded field jacket and sunglasses. Seeing him, she leaped to her feet. Her first instinct was to run up to him, but she caught herself in time.

"Hi."

He didn't return the greeting. Last time they saw each other, he'd worn a cool, shuttered expression. He wore the same expression today. It was obvious he found seeing her uncomfortable.

What did he want then?

"How's your arm?"

Ignoring her question, he pulled a manila envelope from his bag. "I came by to give you this. It's from our day at Belvedere Castle."

The day of their first kiss. How could she forget?

In the envelope she found an 8 x 10 photograph. He must have snapped it when she was rambling on about castles and fairy tales. In this shot, she had her face tilted as she gazed beyond the camera, her hair blowing about her face.

"You said you lost the other one."

This photo was nothing like the one she had lost. In the photos he'd taken outside the diner, she looked tired and put-upon. In this picture, her face was animated. She was *smiling*. And her eyes sparkled with a vitality she didn't realize she was capable of. She looked alive. Happy.

"Thank you." She had trouble getting the words out; her throat had a lump stuck inside. "This is—"

"I missed the shot."

Abby looked up. "What shot?"

"In Libya. The protest. I didn't get the picture. My entire

career…" Whatever he was going to say faded off as he paced away from her. "It's all about the shot. That's what I was always taught. That nothing is as important."

"I remember." Like father, like son.

"The day of the protest, I moved to the far end of the square. That's where I was when I got jumped."

"I'm sorry. I didn't know." She'd known there was more to the story than he would admit. Although why he was telling her now, she wasn't sure.

"You don't understand." Pivoting, he paced back to her. "I moved because I wanted to get out of the way of the crowd."

"What?" Was he saying he chose to move on purpose? Why would he do that?

"Because getting the picture wasn't as important to me as coming back in one piece."

Hunter stopped and looked her in the face. "Apparently my housekeeper wanted me to stay safe."

He'd done it for her. The man who put his photos first, who believed in staying uninvolved and on the sidelines, had taken her advice. She didn't know what to say. Her heart was racing too fast for her to form coherent thoughts. If she'd heard right, he was saying that he…

She hated the skip in her pulse. The way her heart leaped to life. Why did he have to go and make things worse by unlocking feelings she so desperately needed to keep under control?

She knew he'd come back different from his last trip, but she'd attributed the change to his being attacked. She had no idea that the attack was actually a result of his change. A price he'd paid for putting someone else's desires first.

What a huge risk he took, this man who'd been taught by life to hold the world at arm's length. Allowing himself to care about another person again. To care about *her*…

And what did she do with this precious gift he risked giving her? Turned it away. In her lowest of lows, she'd never felt as despicable as she did right now.

Tears burned the back of her throat. "I'm so sorry," she whispered. There had never been a more inadequate set of words in all the English language.

Fingers caught her chin, forcing her to look him in the eye. Into blue-gray depths whose shutters couldn't block the pain and hurt in their depths. "Me, too."

Hunter brushed her jaw with his thumb. Abby shut her eyes at the feeling. So good. So tender. She felt his body close to hers. His breath on her skin.

Then it was gone. As if she'd never felt it at all. When she opened her eyes, Hunter had left, the only trace of his visit the photograph in her hands.

Long after she heard the front door close, Abby stayed and stared at the picture. His admission—or rather, what he was implying—turned everything upside down. He'd chosen safety and her over his career. Chosen her. How could he care for someone like her? A baggage-laden mess too scared to accept his gift.

Thing was, all her previous arguments still held. She was still weighed down with baggage, with the same concerns. Hunter was too good for her. Too good to her. It would be so easy to make him the center of her universe.

Moisture began to pool at the corners of her eyes. A tear slipped out and trailed down her cheek. She wiped it away, remembering how Hunter had once done the same. He was right. She was afraid. Afraid to take the same risk he'd taken.

Ironic, really. That day at Belvedere Castle, Hunter had told her he couldn't have a relationship. How wrong he'd been. Turned out it was Abby who couldn't.

Hunter had been the one to risk his heart. Too bad she didn't deserve it.

Abby didn't think her week could get any worse. She was wrong, of course. Seemed as if she was wrong a lot lately.

It happened as she was walking home from another fruitless day of looking for work. Turned out the lab cleaning job was a no-go. She'd lost the position to a much more attractive woman who'd interviewed before her. It figured. Abby couldn't even get a job cleaning animal droppings. Maybe it was karma, punishing her for hurting Hunter.

She was so busy kicking herself, she didn't see him until it was too late.

Warren's bulky figure blocked her path. "I was hoping I'd run into you." His voice had that false conciliatory tone he liked to use.

"Hoping or waiting for me to show up?"

"You're always so dramatic." He sneered down at her. "I just want to talk."

Yeah, well, she remembered the last "talk" he wanted to have. It had ended with her almost being dragged into his car by her hair. "There's still a restraining order out. I had the temporary one renewed."

"There you go again. Why do you always have to turn everything into an issue?"

"I turn...?" Abby shook her head. Engaging him was only going to make matters worse. "It's been months since we broke up, Warren. I'm not making an issue out of anything. In fact, the only thing I'm doing is leaving."

She started back down the sidewalk. Fortunately, they were on a busy street. There were enough passersby that she could hopefully walk away without incident. When she got to the house, she'd call the police. They might not be able to do much, but they would at least pay Warren a visit and remind him to lay off.

"Where you going?" He grabbed her upper arm. Damn.

"Let go of me, Warren."

"I treated you good, and you know it." Like that, the mask slipped. He squeezed her arm a little tighter. "The problem is you never appreciated all the things I did for you. You were always ungrateful."

Just the opposite. She'd been too grateful, Abby realized.

Convinced she didn't deserve better, and that was why she'd stayed as long as she had. But now she had experienced better. No way was she going back.

She looked long and hard at the man she'd once pinned her hopes and dreams on. Her "Prince Charming." The second biggest regret of her life.

Huh. All this time, all this power she'd assigned him, and he'd dropped to *second.* A distant second at that. Losing Hunter, a man so above Warren in every conceivable way, was far, far worse. The realization made her laugh aloud.

"What's so funny?"

"You," she said. "I just realized how truly unimportant you are in my life. God, I wasted so much time."

Warren stepped closer, his eyes narrowing into an angry glare. "What's that supposed to mean?"

"It means..." Giving a hard yank, she broke free of his grasp. "It means I don't have to put up with you anymore. I put up with your abuse for way too long, but no more. Not ever. We're through. We've been through for a long, long time. I don't ever want to see you again."

He reached for her a second time, but expecting the movement, she stepped backward.

"Do. Not. Touch. Me. Again." She said the words with deliberate precision. Inside, her heart was racing a mile a minute; this standoff could end up backfiring. "We are over. If you come near me again, I will have the police on your behind so fast you won't be able to sit down for a month. Got it?"

"You're not serious."

"Try me." When he didn't move, she turned and walked up to the nearest pedestrian. "Excuse me, sir," she said in a voice loud enough for everyone on the sidewalk to hear. "Could you do me a favor? That man by the maroon sports car is my ex-boyfriend and he's violating the restraining order I took out on him. Would you mind being my witness while I call the police and have him reported? I'm afraid to stay alone for my personal safety."

The stranger, who happened to be a very large, very intimidating-looking man himself, glanced at Warren, then back to her. "Sure," he said, folding his arms across his expansive chest. "Be glad to." Abby gave a silent thank-you that her luck had finally started to turn.

"No need to call the cops," Warren said. "I'm leaving."

As Abby had known he would. Two things she could count on when it came to Warren: his mean streak and his sense of self-preservation.

"But when that fancy new boyfriend of yours dumps you, don't come crawling back. I don't do sloppy seconds."

Add a third thing. His need for the last word. "Too late," she said as she watched his car drive away. "Hunter's already gone, and I'm still not coming back."

After making sure Warren had driven around the corner and out of her life for good, she finally let out the breath she'd been holding and thanked her Good Samaritan.

"Not a problem. I got a sister around the same age as you who had a boyfriend like that. Till she decided she deserved better."

"We all deserve better," Abby told him. For the first time in she didn't know how long, she truly believed those words. She *did* deserve better.

This, she realized, must be what empowerment felt like. She suddenly felt as if she could do anything, be anyone she wanted to be. Her mind flashed to the picture Hunter had taken at Belvedere Castle, and she smiled. She knew now who she wanted to be. And who she wanted to be with. First, though, she had some planning to do. Serious planning. She still didn't deserve Hunter. Not as the woman she was today. But maybe, with some hard work, she could become a woman who did.

Hopefully, when the transformation was complete, she could convince Hunter to let her have another chance. After all, when it came to second chances, third time had to be the charm.

* * *

Hunter hated waffles, but he ordered them anyway. Truth was he hated all the breakfast foods he'd eaten in the past three months. But he didn't want eggs. He'd lost his appetite for them.

He was sitting in Guy's Diner. As he'd told Abby, the scrawny little man wanted money more than he wanted to banish Hunter from his restaurant. New table, though. He didn't like sitting in the back anymore. And he didn't like the new waitress. She was too short and too brunette. He missed the color of butterscotch hair.

Abby. He breathed her name over the rim of his coffee. Beautiful, screwed-up Abby. But he'd finally learned his lesson. Photos were meant to be taken, not participated in. Next time he found himself drawn by his subject matter, he'd follow her example and run the other way.

It was getting increasingly hard to rebuild the walls around his heart, however. Three months and he was still struggling to feel numb again.

At least he'd had the cast taken off his arm. He'd already accepted an assignment.

A plate suddenly slid in front of him. He rolled his eyes. Just his luck, the new waitress not only got his order wrong, but had delivered eggs. Over easy, with a side of bacon and whole wheat.

Slowly he raised his eyes.

"So the thing with fairy tales... No one ever tells the princess that in order to get the castle and Prince Charming, she has to believe she deserves to live happily ever after."

Abby stood before him.

"Mind if I sit down?" she asked.

Before he could respond, she pulled out a chair. "You got your cast off," she said. "Good to see."

He couldn't do this. Whatever numbness he had managed to achieve threatened to crumble. To mask his pain he turned harsh. "What do you want, Abby? Or have you torn a page from your ex's book and taken up harassment?"

"No harassment, I promise. If you want me to leave, I will. Guy would have a fit if I caused another scene. Do you want me to go?"

Yes. It hurt too much for her to stay. "Up to you."

"I missed that shrug," she said. The waitress came by and Abby turned her cup over, signaling she wanted a coffee. Whatever the reason for her reappearance, she wasn't planning for it to be quick.

Hunter wasn't sure if her lingering was a good idea or not. Part of him wanted to hold her in the seat and keep her there forever. The other part wanted to tell her to go to hell.

Why was she here, anyway? His pulse picked up with hope. Damn, but he hated that he had hope.

She looked different. Hunter wasn't quite sure how. Her hair was still stubbornly independent. Today's topknot had already slid to the right and was half undone. Beneath her winter coat, she wore some kind of uniform, pink and institutional. It'd be boring except for… Was that…? Beneath the table, he squeezed his knee to remind himself this wasn't a dream. She was wearing the scarf he'd bought her in Libya.

She must have noticed what he was looking at, because she offered a shy smile. "I got a new job. At the Landmark. I'm a housekeeper. Who knew cleaning your place for a couple weeks would pay off?"

Even without his reference. "Good. I hoped you'd find work." It was true. He regretted what had happened between them, but he never wished that she'd do anything but land on her feet. "That's not what I was looking at, though."

"I know." Her cheeks turned pink to match the uniform. "I wear it every day."

"That's nice." He didn't dare think it meant anything more than a fashion accessory.

"You know why?"

"Because it matches your uniform."

She looked down, and smiled. "So it does. Honestly, I never paid attention. See, I don't wear it to be fashionable."

"Then why do you?"

While speaking, she'd picked up a sugar packet. Now she fidgeted with the little white square, flattening one end against the table, then the other. "As a reminder," she replied softly.

A reminder of what? Another set of mistakes to avoid?

Abby's palms were sweating. This was harder than she'd thought it would be. Then again, three months was a long time. What if he'd decided during that time that he'd been wrong? That he didn't care about her? What if she'd been wrong and his feelings weren't as deep as she thought? It was quite possible everything in her heart was one-sided.

She wished she'd thought to lay her new cell phone on the table so she could look at the lock screen. The photo of her at the castle was on it. As she did with the scarf around her neck, she used the picture to remind her of the woman she wanted to be. And the man she hoped to become worthy of.

As if seeing Hunter wasn't reminder enough of that goal. Time off hadn't been good to him. The ruddiness was gone from his skin; he was pale from spending too much time indoors.

He'd shed the field jacket, too, in favor of a battered leather bomber that had seen better days.

"Are you planning to answer?" he asked. "Or stare into space?"

Same old Hunter. "I didn't expect to see you here," she said, ignoring his question. "I came in for coffee and saw you sitting here."

"You happened to come into Guy's?"

"I was on my way to your apartment."

"Oh." He was doing his best to sound disinterested, but the crack in his voice betrayed him.

"I have to admit, I was afraid you might have left on assignment already."

"I leave in a couple of days."

At the news, her heart started to sink, but she gave herself a mental kick. *What did you think he'd do? Stop working?* She would consider herself lucky she'd caught him when she did. "Where to?" she asked.

"Seychelles. Photographing the cinnamon harvest."

"Still laying off the protests?"

"Decided to start slow. What do you want, Abby? I thought we said everything we had to say three months ago."

Her answer was interrupted by the waitress, who set an order of waffles on the table. Abby looked at the plate.

"I'm taking a break from my usual," Hunter replied, shoving the plate Abby brought to the side.

"That why you aren't sitting in the corner?"

"I thought I'd try something different."

Both answers, for no logical reason, fueled her resolve. If he was avoiding his routine, perhaps it was because he was looking to forget?

"I made a few changes myself," she said, taking advantage of the opening. "I moved out of McKenzie House. Carmella and I got an apartment."

"Glad to hear you're back on your feet."

"Well, that is the point of a temporary shelter. Though I didn't completely leave. I'm volunteering there."

"You are."

"Three days a week. Leading a discussion group for women who were in the same place I was."

"You are?"

He was trying to hide the surprise in his voice. "It's okay. If I were in your shoes, I'd be skeptical, too. Like I told you, I've made a lot of changes."

Following her encounter with Warren, she'd done a lot of thinking about the paths she'd taken in life. Most of her decisions were because she'd been looking for someone to come save her, she realized. That's why she'd lost herself to Warren, why she'd been afraid she'd lose herself to Hunter—because she believed those men were her only hope at grasping the fairy tale. Once she'd figured out that responsibility, and success, lay with her, she'd started looking at her decisions in a new way.

"These women help me as much as I help them. We're learning we need to earn our happy ever after."

Hunter leaned forward. "You always said there needed to be a new version of the fairy tale."

She had his attention. "I did, didn't I? By the way, when I say earn, I don't mean doing everything perfect. That's where I went wrong. Prince Charming doesn't expect you to make him the center of your universe, like Warren did.

"I know," she added, holding up a hand. "Most of the men in the world aren't Warren. I get that now. He's gone, by the way. Haven't heard a peep from him in three months."

"You must be relieved."

"I'm glad not to have to look over my shoulder." Otherwise, Warren was nothing but a bad-tasting memory. There was only one man that mattered, as far as she was concerned, and he was sitting at this table. While they were talking, the coolness in his eyes had changed. They'd grown bluer, more receptive.

Abby waited while he sipped his coffee and absorbed all she'd told him. She'd done a lot of work in the past three months. While it only the tip of the iceberg as far as the changes she wanted to make, she hoped she'd made enough headway that he might let her past the walls again.

Finally he set down his cup. "Congratulations. You're finally getting a second chance."

"Again. By all counts, this is my third second chance this year."

"Well, you know what they say, third time's the charm." He offered a smile. A small one, but more gorgeous than any Abby had seen in months.

Seizing the smile in her heart, she decided it was time to take the biggest leap of faith she'd ever attempted.

"There's something else I wanted to tell you." Sliding the

breakfast plates aside, she laid her hand on the table, a breath away from touching him. It felt as if her heart was trying to beat its way out of her chest, her pulse was going so fast.

No one said laying yourself bare would be easy. "I love you."

Silence. Abby fought against the sinking sensation by reminding herself that saying those three words wouldn't fix everything. Hunter had been hurt, truly hurt. He needed time to accept that she meant what she said.

"You were right," she told him. "I was afraid of my feelings. Running from relationships was no different than running away from my parents' house with Warren. Only without the bruises. Bruises might have been easier. They didn't hurt nearly as badly as being apart from you did. Does."

Hunter stared at the Formica beneath their hands. When had he laid his hand on the table? Abby wondered. They were side-by-side, close enough that she could feel the heat.

"I don't know what to say. It's been three months."

So little time, but such a long time, too. "How about that you still have feelings for me?"

"I leave for the South Pacific in three days."

She'd waited too long. He wasn't able to let her past the walls anymore. Now she knew how Hunter had felt that night on the Greenway. Her chest seemed to have been stomped into a million pieces.

"Good thing I tracked you down when I did." No sense staying and making the awkwardness worse. She pushed away from the table and turned her head away. "I just wanted to make sure you know that when faced with a choice between security and you, I chose you."

"They tell me Seychelles is gorgeous this time of year."

Slowly she looked back at him. The vulnerability on Hunter's face took her breath away. Gone were the walls he'd hidden behind for so long. There was nothing but pure, open emotion.

"I've never been there before," he was saying. "Nothing I'd like better than to discover it with the woman I love."

He still loved her. Moreover, he was showing her by putting himself and his heart out there for the taking. To Abby, it was the bravest gesture she'd ever witnessed.

"There's nothing I'd like better than to go with you. But that's what I've been working on all these months. I don't want to make you the center of my world. I want to be the kind of woman who walks with you, by your side."

He cupped her cheek. Abby wondered if the shine she saw in his eyes was from tears. Hard to tell, since her own eyes were filled to the brim. "You always were that woman," he whispered. "You just needed to meet her for yourself."

"I have."

"I'm glad." He pulled her to his lap so fast she squealed. "This mean I should order a second plane ticket?"

Exploring a tropical island with the man she loved. Abby couldn't think of a more perfect ending to a fairy tale.

Which was why it killed her to give him her answer. "I'm sorry, Hunter, but no."

CHAPTER TWELVE

SEEING HUNTER'S FACE FALL, Abby rushed to explain. He'd taken such a chance himself; the words she said now would affect them both forever.

"It's not that I don't want to," she said. "I want nothing more than to run away with you." Doing so, however, would ruin all the work she'd done these past few months.

Plus there was another reason. "Please understand, I can't go. Not yet."

"Why not?"

"I have class. I started school," she added, seeing his confusion. "Remember when you asked me what I wanted to do with my life? I want to help women like me. Help other women get the power they need to rewrite their own life stories."

To her relief, she felt Hunter relax. "You found your passion."

"Oh, I found my passion, all right. Unfortunately, he's heading to the Seychelles to photograph cinnamon farms. Helping other women…that's what I want to do with my life, though.

"So," she said, lowering her forehead to his, "as much as I want to go with you—and believe me, I *so* want to go with you—I need to stay here. Do you understand?"

She held her breath. Changes and choices were all well and good, but the freefall moment where you learned the consequences were hell. Finally Hunter nodded. "After the way I lectured you, it'd be a little hypocritical if I didn't."

"No," Abby said with a watery smile, "it wouldn't. And I never said I wouldn't come for a visit. That is…"

Suddenly she felt shy and exposed. "That is, if you'd like," she finished, biting her lip.

"Oh, I'd like," Hunter replied. "I'd like very much."

His face was close to hers, warm and welcome. So welcome, Abby could barely breathe from the longing. And when his hand tangled in her curls, it felt as though she'd finally become whole.

"Very, very much," he whispered above her lips.

She kissed him with all the love in her heart, telling him with her body what she'd already said with words. That she loved him. That she chose to be loved by him.

The abandon with which Hunter returned the kiss told her the same.

They broke apart, breathless and clinging, foreheads pressed together, neither ready to break the connection. "What happens when I get back?" Hunter asked.

The love she saw in his gaze almost made her want to change her mind about her plans and go to the Seychelles with him.

Almost.

"I'll have my apartment, you'll get a new assistant—preferably male, by the way—and we'll work on sharing each other's lives."

"I'd like that."

Abby's heart gave a happy jump. They'd both come a long way since that day he'd interrupted Warren. Somewhere along the way, Hunter had set down his camera and opened his arms to her, to include her in his world. And she…well, she'd found herself.

Happiness threatened to overwhelm her. Before the tears could come, she buried herself against Hunter's chest. Those strong arms that had once held her at her worst moment were here for the best.

His fingers combed her hair, making a bigger mess. She didn't care. She could stay like this forever.

"I've got one condition," she heard Hunter say.

Condition? Suddenly, her good feelings paused. "What condition?"

"That someday in the future I can ask for a merger. Your life, my life, one life."

"Oh, is that all?" She let out a breath. "I thought you were going to ask for something impossible."

"Does that mean you're amenable to my proposal?"

His proposal to propose? Absolutely. What's more, she knew that when that day came, and Hunter made that proposal a reality, she'd be ready, and she'd have the courage to say yes.

"Very amenable," she said, wrapping her arms around his neck. "Now, unless I misunderstood, we still have three days before you leave, and I have the afternoon off from work. Do you really want to spend our free time in Guy's Diner?"

"Sweetheart, Guy's Diner is the last place I want to be." After setting her on her feet, Hunter threw a wad of bills on the table and held out his hand. "How about I take you across the street so I can show you how much I missed you?"

"Now it's my turn to name a condition." She slipped her hand in his. "You have to let me show you back."

He grinned. "It's a deal."

Side by side, they walked out the door to whatever future life had in store. Abby didn't know where they were going or what they'd see, but so long as she had Hunter walking along next to her, she knew their ending would be a happy one.

* * * * *

MILLS & BOON
Swoon ♥ Club

Why not try a Mills & Boon subscription? Get your favourite series delivered to your door every month!

Use code **3MONTHSFREE** to get 50% off the first three months of your chosen subscription plus free delivery.

Visit **millsandboon.com.au/subscriptions**

or give customer service a call on
AUS 1300 659 500 or **NZ 0800 265 546**

No lock-in Contracts

Free Postage

Exclusive Offers

*For full terms and conditions go to *swoonclub.millsandboon.com.au*.
Offer expires 30 June 2020

Wild as the western wind!
These Montana cowboys
are sure to please.

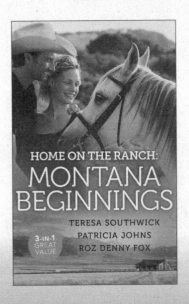

Available now in-store and online.